Rulers by Blood
True Legends of
Frost

Steam Age Volume 5
by Miss C.C. Auclaere

FOR THOSE WHO BELIEVE
IN OTHERS, IN PEACE, AND IN FAITH

ACKNOWLEDGMENTS

Three lovely ladies worked on this novel and our identities are secret. Anyone claiming to be us is not. May we be your three wise women and guide you toward your path for peace, truth, and valor.

Special Note: No AI technology was used to create any part of this story in any way, aside from some autocorrect; this creation process first began in the early 2000s, including the drafts of the first four volumes of Frost's Steam Age.

PROLOGUE

The flag of the Coltari trade organization was yellow behind the infamous trade symbol, known across the frost, sewn intricately into the fabric in a series of blue and black squares that represented two interlocking orchids.

It was long thought to be yellow so that it could easily be seen at night by other Coltari ships in the waters of the great ocean, Argal, which covered half the planet from the eastern coasts of East Ahria to the opposite western half, one of six separate continents of Frost. This great ocean, one of two major oceans splitting the land of the frost, bordered the four other continents that either floated within it, in shattered islands like Titanus, or wove around it until reaching the southern glaciers like Olympus.

Captain Klive Kisin, with the black hair and dark eyes of his Gakayon islands descent--which in many ways was similar to any of the East Ahrian of the Far West--had taken the helm as their trade frigate drifted through well-traveled waters on the dark Bacine sea. He stayed alert by drinking coffee; this brew grown in the Miranda rainforests of North Olympus.

Coffee was an invention of the 1200s that made it possible for less desperate sailors to take to the seas for longer stretches at a time. The old longboats of the Normen used to brave the waters over long distances to escape the never-ending march southward of the ever-present glaciers, but the trade of men had long been from port to nearest port.

Even in modern times, most fishermen wouldn't dare leave the safety of the shallow water. There was always the risk of leviathan, sea serpent, kraken, or pirate on the open ocean--each with its own deadliness--but a frigate like his was large enough to take them on easily if the guns were called to the ready before the hull was breached.

There were still other vessels in the Coltari network to watch for and sometimes protect. Despite the increasing use of Orichalc, 'red gold'--a light and hot burning chalky stone--the smaller oiler schooners, half his frigate's size, still chased after whales, serpents, and leviathans for their fat. Sometimes being locked in battles they could not win without aid. Often the two, similarly sized, were locked in a deadly fight for the oilers to earn their annual millions in bounties and to light the old fires in the ancient capitals of industry like Akre and Rorik, and powering the lamps of the world. An oiler schooner waving a yellow flag may have needed saving on a dark night like this night.

"Quiet night below deck, Captain," said Dist, his first mate, who looked over the wooden rail along stern of the ship to see if he could make out any extra ripples in the waves. The captain nodded to Dist and squinted his eyes to watch the low sails ripple in the wind.

The two men could barely see each other. A few sea oil lamps burned as softly as they could allow on the deck, covered partially by metal cages that shown the light downward onto the wood. The moon should have been in its waxing phase and almost full, but the sky had been darkened. A storm was likely very near, but there was no sound of rain or thunder. Just the same, pirates could take advantage of seeing the lantern light from afar in the near darkness.

Despite the many concerns to ocean travel, the Coltari trade organization had enjoyed a firm grip on trade and travel over the Argal for centuries by this point. The risks were many, but the occurrences were low.

"Captain, we have a bird on our tail."

"What?"

"An airship, a big one, is gaining on us quickly."

Kisin pulled the looped rope over the wheel to hold it in place and turned to look at where Dist was pointing. He pulled out his spyglass and peered through into the night, optimistically wandering over the shapeless void of clouds barely different from the rhythmic waves of the ocean behind them.

"How are you seeing this?"

"My night sight was always better than yours. It's there, clearer than what waits beneath the waves."

"Alert the men, Dist."

Dist, a man from the coast of East Ahria, who shared many similar physical traits with Kisin without some of the ruggedness of Kisin's battle-worn facial features, nodded and sprang into action while Kisin considered the options. The Coltari shipmen couldn't fight against an airship with their cannons. Depending on their hunter's size, it could be carrying far more crew members than they had on their trade frigate, which left them with additional limitations--how to fight and how to run were two equally bad options.

They could fight with the few muskets they had on board, courtesy of the few Coltari's organized military regulars who though often from Albion were nevertheless loyal to no crown; or they could jump into the longboats and hope for rescue in the morning before something of the deep swallowed them or the tempest echoing forth from the distance caught them.

He sensed the rain coming. You couldn't smell it on the open water like you could on land. It could be fast or slow moving but it was cutting across the ocean on its way to the northeast and the coast of Albion, where they too had been headed until now. An airship could only mean privateers, pirates under contract.

Kisin would have to put it to a vote. There weren't enough longboats, named after the old Normen ships that they looked nothing like, for everyone anyway, but all of those risks to the open ocean were magnified in the helpless miniature escape ships that were so rarely used and so often useless that the Coltari had considered abolishing them completely. There was seldom a survivor tale from a longboat escapee that could not have simply swam to shore.

The men were rallied, and Kisin told them the plan. Some could stay and fight. Their enemy was likely to take no prisoners, or they could try their luck with the brutal ocean, launching in the escape boats.

Everyone was made to understand that the chances of survival were likely none on either end. It was a matter of how you'd rather die. In the stomach of an ocean beast or fighting against whatever boarded them from the fast-approaching ship.

The votes were made. Almost everyone planned to stay. Kisin ordered Dist onto a longboat, and they were launched away. Dist accepted the assignment grimly. He understood that Kisin wanted someone with authority from the ship to have the slim chance of escape, but if a kraken began pulling them over the low ship side, he wouldn't fight a hopeless fight. He would welcome death on his own terms.

Dist and twenty men watched from one of the longboats as the Orichalc lights split the night and the modern airship descended on their captain and the men who stayed to fight. Shots rang out, but cannon fire answered and then the boarding party was launched from above as percussion pistols and muskets traded fire from both sides in sharp blasts of light that were soon blackened out by the black clouds of gunpowder. Only the sounds traveled slowly across the ocean. Dist imagined he could still see the flashes of fire, even as the rain began to fall. The other longboat near them suddenly disappeared beneath the waves, swallowed by something terrible and unseen.

Lightning crackling through the clouds made the distant airship visible for a moment, and Dist made out the flag of the States of Imeria as clear as if it were day. As the rain began to fall, he and the men he was with could no longer hope to see any ripples in the waves of beasts to come as the water began to rise with the storm.

As they crested a wave, he caught another glimpse of his former home on the water; through the flattening gunpowder smoke and the early rain of the dark storm, the cargo of the Coltari ship was lifted into the air under the bright Orichalc lights of the Imerian airship. The small longboat fell to the bottom of the wave, and then crested again to see their ship behind them go up in flames.

Dist watched for as long as he could to see what little else there was to see, but the rain intensified, and their distance became too great to see anything but the fading flames. He lay down at the bottom of the small ship, motioning for the other men to do the same. Some followed his suggestion, but many gripped the sides for dear life, trying to row the ship through the waves, which took their tiny craft where the current pleased. He only hoped that it was in a similar path to the storm and toward Coltari's home ports in Albion.

* * *

The Secondwind caught sight of the shredded longboat bobbing in the quiet water from the air and circled around to investigate the miniature wreck.

Lying alone on board was a small East Ahrian man with a thin cut across his chest from whatever sea beast had grown tired and left the small ship barely floating after taking who knew how many souls into the deep for feed.

"Admiral Ferrara! There's a survivor!"

"I can see that, Prince Eduard! I have eyes, and a spyglass," she said and waved the instrument at the young man. Admiral Jacquelina Catalina Ferrara was a veteran of the open ocean as well as of flying airships, having circumnavigated the globe as what some might have called a pirate.

Now, she worked as essentially an admiral among the Coltari trade organization with an upgraded version of the old beauty she had run through ports and temples from here to any lost city you could name. To the skies, into the jungles, to the farthest depths of the ocean. She had seen it all but Ramelon, the lost city of the desert.

"Clayton and Li, don't just stand there. Cheval secured the ropes. Bring him up before whatever did that to that boat brings him down."

They didn't waste time with excuses. The two men rappelled onto the small boat carefully tied to their mothership and hoisted the injured man aboard the battleship-class airship, pulled to the main deck by their compatriots.

Ferrara, and in some ways by extension the prince, who had both tagged along and helped come up with the idea, weren't just being nice. Frigate-class trade ships, the largest generally used specifically for trade by the Coltari organization, had been going missing at an increasingly alarming rate as of late, and the two wanted answers.

The prince, on behalf of Albion, and the Admiral Ferrara had an integral economic stake in discovering the truth behind the disappearances, and the de facto head of Albion's state, Prince Eduard's father had seemed to shrink from his responsibility to aid one of his nation's greatest allies.

While the king of the coastal nation tight-walked a complex political landscape where almost every nation in this small corner of the world served the senate in Akre, the adventurous duo guiding the airship above the perilous Argal believed that the only way these frigates could be raided at such a high rate in their home ocean was if Imerian airships had been ordered to harass their northern neighbors across the Bacine sea.

The narrow Bacine was one of the many seas narrowly separating North Olympus, dominated at this end by the Imerian states, and West Ahria, where Albion lay along the western-most coast. Each on its own in years past pledge fealty to the same senate, but this had left Albion in control of almost all of the western trade and the growing power of a united Imeria could not be denied.

Coltari informants had heard rumors of a new class of airship out of the states, named after the largest decked ships of the sea, a Brig. If the conventions of the sea to air were continued, the ship would theoretically be of similar size to a Coltari Battleship, but with an extra deck and as many as sixty more cannons, to a side.

One impressive airship like that or even many such impressive airships wouldn't be as concerned with the Coltari's own fleet of battleships that patrolled the airs above the ocean, to deter this type of occurrence.

Eduard believed they were entering quickly into a 'trade' war, but Eduard's father, Lord Stone, had failed to see the merit in the idea that the Imerians would brazenly attack them unless they were to openly support the East Cardane's mission to extend into the

Coltari-controlled region of the Argal.

The ships survivor coughed up ocean water and kneeled on the steady deck of the airship, surrounded by Ferrara's long-time crew of international sailors.

Eduard saw many scars across the tiny, thin man's arms from whiplashes and tangles with the deep. He could only think that perhaps with a survivor's help they could chase down the truth, and as he thought this the sun disappeared momentarily behind a column of wispy clouds, casting a shadow on the Secondwind.

The Akrin peace as it had been known in Ahria had been broken many years ago, but the new peace that had returned to the empire of Akre's core states was being threatened.

While Eduard thought of the possible futures, Ferrara considered an engagement with a larger vessel of Imerian make. She as sure that her longer-range Albion guns and higher top speed would make quick work of any adversary, no matter the size.

PART ONE: DRAGONS AND THE STEAM TRAIN
1513 - Chapter 1

In the year 1513 of our planet, Frost--in the old tongue known as Vatna--and nearing twenty years after the end of the golden peace of the Akrin Empire, war between the nations of West Ahria drew ever closer while few worked to divert it. Many even yearned for it. If we look back on our history closely, it is surprising how often a vote of men and women yields war.

One after another, vote after vote, until all the men are dead, and we seem to forget that men, too, are a part of this world. Even if our nation claims to love them. A nation, a city, crumbles slowly during a prolonged period of war, almost unnoticeably, and if it doesn't return to peace soon enough, it risks losing everything.

It's a privilege of our modern-day world to think about war, in the scale that it can be, as a foreign concept. It, too, was a privilege of those people then who lived across the Akrin Empire, before the golden era ended with the rebellion in the north and Valgaard's return as a kingdom, spelled the end of a century of peace. Some say there must have been a good reason for the peace to end.

Think about it, over one hundred full years of peace brought unequaled prosperity to this quarter of the continent. We haven't lived through one hundred years of peace, yet, and not imagined what might happen soon if the nations of the world once again choose to engage in yet another brutal war unchecked by anything save the imagination of those willing to spread fire.

With its many beasts, like werewolves, minotaurs, angels, demons, and dragons, it isn't those creatures of the night that harbor as much death and destruction on our humble planet as the men who seem to always find or make new reasons to raise up arms and go to war.

Can you imagine what the people of the time were thinking?

* * *

"You know it was a night like this, about twenty-five years ago, give or take, that I set out on my adventures around the world."

Lord Stone pushed his friend Theodore Everett through the hallways of the Everett mansion. It was hard to believe that his friend, Theo, confined to a wheelchair for almost as long as Lord Stone had known him, had ever sailed on a sea ship, or flown in an airship, or done much of anything outside of the walls of his idyllic mansion in the low hills of the Ash Vale.

"You're not listening? Have I bored you again?"

"Theo, you're not much older than me, and as long as I've known you, you've been stuck in this chair. And despite, how often you refer to it, you've barely told me a single story with any real detail."

"Ah, well, sworn to secrecy--in a way. Personal secrecy, and I guess fear, of..."

"Of?"

"Of what might be out there, or who."

"Who?" Lord Stone laughed. If there was anyone who should be afraid of anyone here, his friend Theo should be afraid of him, the Lord Stone. His father and his father before him had controlled this edge of the continent, Albion, for centuries, but unlike any of the other Lords of Stone that ruled from the Castle Rorik before him, Stone had suffered a terrible curse that had left him questioning whether he could live up to those heroes of men before him.

He wheeled Theodore through the doors into his inner library sanctum and looked out the window, darkened by rain splashing against the glass in waves. Just across the Ash Vale from Theodore's private mansion and nearer to the south coast, through those windows, you could see his family's tower, rising above the rolling hills on a sunny day.

"Oh, good, they're not here yet."

"Who? Ani?"

"Our guests, my friend."

Theodore took the shawl off his lap, revealing a small wooden box.

"You thought I was going to invite you out here to my mansion to talk about shipping lanes again?"

"Isn't that what it's always about?"

"Not this time." Theo looked down at the little box, almost too small to be relevant.

Lord Stone sighed and adjusted his collar, wondering if his regal attire, might have been a little too ostentatious for the moment. His topcoat was bright red separated into four squares by two bright bars of gold fabric, running across his chest one vertically and the other horizontally, with dark blue shoulder pads, tassels, and trousers, which matched the sash he wore across his chest. "Who would come out all this way, well after the middle of the night, besides me of course? I mean, I was here earlier in the evening, well, you know what I mean."

"Your son, Jack, is he well?"

"Eduard?"

"Did you have another one? Yes, Eduard."

"He's off with that old Captain friend of yours, Ferrara, who I'm amazed is still flying a ship at her age."

"Oh, when did he leave? She didn't tell me anything of it."

"I'm not sure she realized it was the same Eduard."

"I'm almost sure she did." Theo laughed privately, in on his own joke.

"Where's Ani lately anyway--testing out some new contraption of yours?" Lord Stone looked at Theodore's box and at his gloves, remembering the old days when Theo liked to show off new ways of exploding fruit.

"Dealing with some shipping lane business."

"Ah, forget I asked."

"You never did like the minutiae of managing the intricacies of the economics and logistics of your kingdom." Theodore stated, though he had a hunch it was an act his friend put on, "Yet, you're good at it. What's the purse at these days?"

"My father and father's father didn't give me a fortune to squander it."

"And, that's exactly why you're at this meeting."

"What exactly is this meeting?"

There was a knock at the open door.

"Ah, Mr. William," Theodore smiled at his long-time butler, and as far as Lord Stone knew, the only staff member, save the groundskeeper that Theo had hired on.

"Have our guests arrived?"

"They indeed have. They are sneaking in through the back now as you requested, and little, Erold, I am told, has agreed to be confined to guest chambers on the second floor, as per your request, for the duration of the meeting. Was there anything else you needed, after I've shown Erolin into the library?"

"Good, and yes, actually, see to it that you've swept the house again. I seem to have a feeling that there may be one or two bugs that need zapping."

"Will do, sir."

That was certainly a bombshell moment for Lord Stone as his collar suddenly felt that much tighter and better suited despite the dim lighting and roaring rain, because the honorable Erolin, was technically in line for the Akrin throne if the senate wouldn't stop blocking a vote on the matter of his ascension. They'd only put it off for twenty years while the palace and inner city were rebuilt. No one was getting any younger as the time flew--

Mr. William rapped again at the door, and announced the royal highness, Erolin, and his chief aide, Elara Moon.

"King Erolin, Chief Inspector Moon, it's a pleasure to see you both again," said Theodore. Lord Stone, mentally forgiving Theo for his brevity of manners, bowed deeply. Moon closed the door behind them and stood at attention as rigid and emotionlessly cold as the day he had first met her.

"Theodore, Lord Stone," Erolin nodded his head to relieve Lord Stone's formal bow, though for some reason the king-in-waiting was dressed in civilian clothes.

"Mr. Everett, I'm glad to see you. It amazes me again how uncannily like Redbridge this old, new house of yours is. Even your gardens we came through in the back are the exact same as I remember."

"Thank you, Mrs. Moon. Down to the very stone." Theodore peaked at Jack, slyly, before continuing, "I ended up becoming rather fond of that place, and I regretted that I spent so little time there as a young man. Our house now shares many of the same exact pieces that made up the old one, save furniture or books." Theodore looked up at the wooden arches that enclosed the library. Their dark wooden color and brassy sheen made that much darker by the stormy night and dim oil lamps. "What wasn't burned in the fire, I had shipped here in various ways from Akre over the years, but that's enough of the pleasantries for now, I think. Down to business, Erolin, you seem keen to open our discussion?"

"Lord Stone, I'm happy that you have accepted this meeting, and I shan't waste your time." If it wasn't as dark as it was in the dim lamp light, maybe the three other people in the room would see Stone color as red as his jacket.

"My old friend, I'm unaware as to the circumstances of how we meet this evening. Please enlighten me your excellency."

"Ah, my friend, Jack, we all have agendas tonight, to get to, but first, Erolin, I didn't tell Jack why you wanted to speak with him. In fact, I didn't inform him that it was you, who would be here."

"Right, wise," Erolin remarked with a dash of chagrin. "Well, then please allow me to begin with my agenda items first. Lord Stone, it has come to my attention, that the national autonomy that we, my son and I, have enjoyed in Normany and you, here in Albion, since time immemorial, is nearing an end. The Senate knows you're practically sitting on the entire world's silver. Not to mention the Orichalc, and they plan to simply write you off of the top of the heap with the flick of a pen."

"I thought you'd be giving me another one of the conspiracy theories I've often heard in brief from old Theodore here, but, I must admit you have my attention, but why would they do this, especially to you?"

There was a silence that hung uneasily for a moment as Theodore caught Moon's stare, and Erolin, glanced uneasily from one to the other.

He brushed it off with a brief cough, continuing, "Normany, even more so than Ithlin and its Azuri hills, or Elessia, or any other nation, is the core of the Empire. Of old Galdir! It is one of the most populous and largest nations under the banner, the breadbasket of our modern--"

"Spare me the continued lecture on economics, my King, please. That's not what I meant. I understand that Valgaard has the salt mines, as do other colder nations in the Eight Lakes region." Lord Stone feigned disinterest, but the king knew he was speaking in the details Stone liked as he ran his fingers through his hair along the gray streaks. The old Stone couldn't help but become intrigued by a conversation about moving boxes from one nation to another, for a fee of course.

"I'm getting there. That is only to mention--or highlight, if you will--that Akre sits within my territory of Normany, and while I have never exercised that power, it is my ancestral territory. When my uncle, lost his head, God rest his soul and following the quick and tragic death of his only son, he left only three people in this world who claimed a direct right to the law of the land by lineage of Arandil, who claimed lineage to the old Galdir kings. My claim and now my son's claim rest higher than the third's, who you know is Aurelia, and with one stroke of the pen, they plan to erase over fifteen hundred years of unbroken rule over that land."

"So, I stand to keep my kingdom, and you, a right to the city of Gold, if we what? What's the point that you are getting to, old friend?"

"My dear Lord Stone, isn't it obvious? We need an alliance to stand against the Empire."

"An alliance against the Republic?" Stone corrected. He shrugged, not altogether thrown by the logic, but wondering how this brought Theo into the mix.

"Yes, if the Senate dissolves our provincial rule, sure, each nation will be governed exclusively by its elected officials. As you say, it is a republic, but my uncle died to prevent war. That was his, and I feel, somewhat ironically, what my grandfather's sole missions were in life. The only thing preventing the senate from having conscripted soldiers out of my territory, has been me putting pen to paper, to notify provincial officials that they are not by any means to contribute soldiers to the legions, which they've begun calling corps now anyway under that brash commander, Polesar."

Stone pushed fingers into his skull. Theo motioned for him to take a chair.

"There are a number of things I'm not following here. The first of which is why you've been so quiet Theo. It seems the only one that has had anything on his mind tonight is me, and usually you're the only one speaking, thinking, or absorbing the attention, especially mine...Now, tell me, what does any of this have to do with you Theo?" Stone asked as he took a seat in a comfy chair near the fire behind the darkened oak desk. "I'm sure Ani won't mind if I sit in her chair, will she?"

"Yes, well, there is simultaneously a lot on my mind and nothing. You see, while you are delicate to dance around my past, as you think it really doesn't concern you, it still exists, and well, anyway, before I get ahead of myself, which question of yours, would you like me to answer first?" Theo smiled, "On a serious note, I cannot claim to be preventing war, or to be saving lives. My business is getting shipments delivered from point A to point B. I married into this family business, and my once future wife warned me that a trade war is coming. What I didn't realize is how much it would feel like every day for the last eighteen years, that I've been fighting a real war. And, it all comes down to the shipping lanes, my friend."

Theo held up his hand to silence Lord Stone, and continued, "The Imerian navy has gotten more aggressive. They are clearly getting intel on my wife's ships, and merchant vessel after merchant vessel, whether ours, or from either the Menetorian islands in the north, or the Fire Islands of the south, they are being harried and harassed across Argal, the entirety of this great west ocean by privateers. A larger war is coming. A war of expansion, clearly, and the trade wing of the Empire's east, which also happens not to be, my wife's company, is lining whatever pockets it can fill to give it better odds. We don't play that game. Never have had to. You're rich enough as it is, I'm rich enough as it is, and my wife's family has spent the better part of its history here in the Ash Vale."

"Spare me any further," Lord Stone almost groaned, "your wife's Coltari shipping company owns practically all the trade across the islands, and the contracts here were in place, as you describe, long before I entered the picture."

"It does own the west, but it didn't always. And the question, is will it continue to? It's as if the Imerian navy is launching new airships each day, and that their reach is getting longer, further and deeper into the ocean than ever before. If a merchant ship is sunk by a privateer in the employ of the Imerians, it isn't an international catastrophe, but how long before running out of apples or beer in Menetoris becomes a weekly occurrence and despite the countless naval confrontations my fleets have won on behalf of my wife against the East Cardane Shipping Company, the northern island King, Mitas of Menetoris, then chooses to go with them instead of us?"

"What do you propose?" Stone felt annoyed that Theo, too, spoke of Imerian privateers. His son had become relentless about it as the summer went along.

"It's partially Ani's idea. I'm upset she's not here to cement this proposal, and, I should take a step back, pardon my inability to physically do so. It wasn't a proposal that I, or Erolin, expected, nor one that I'm sure you've entertained, though I'm sure you have had a visit from one of her ambassadors in recent days, or across the years. It seems her intelligence is good, for she has realized that I have a closer relationship to you than would have been judged by your rare public hours and nocturnal inclinations."

"Spit it out," Lord Stone growled. He knew where this was going now, and while it gave him no happiness to say no, it made it hard to say yes.

"Valgaard's lady Valessa--"

"I'll stop you right there." Lord Stone hated the Valgaardians even if he had never known them as his enemy. They had been the ones to break the century of peace and sack Akre, burning Theodore's centuries-old family home and the golden Chelsea Palace; he had heard described as a wonder of the world.

"Let him finish," Erolin spoke.

"Why don't you take over from here," Theo swallowed, and looked up at Moon who opened the door to ring in the hallway for some water to be brought up. In a moment, she came back in and closed the door.

"Jack, it's simple, I have goods like wheat, you have more than just your money, but just those two things are enough to keep the senate, salivating, sitting atop their little hill in Akre, filled with want and anxious to profit in secret, acting as if it fulfills the wishes of the common man. In our nations, we, both, have people who frankly haven't been getting enough of what they deserve, but especially across Galdir, and no more so than in Normany. Neither of us can stand alone, and we don't stand much chance, just us two together. Sure, the senate won't write you out of the tale in one swoop. It will be a gradual choking of your resources until you're written off completely, but Valgaard is there. It's a nation of nearly the same number of people as Albion and Normany. Any war that the senate begins, if I'm not there to stop it, would certainly be to take back those territories they feel they lost wrongly, which for the same reasons, that you don't want to hear, is why Valgaard needs us as much as we need them. Together, I'm not sure of the numbers, but let's say we're over sixty million. The senate would have to somehow mobilize its entirety, all of its underlying nations, most of which still cling to an identity apart from the Empire to strike at a piece of us, risking everything in a war they couldn't possibly win."

Mr. William knocked on the door, breaking a silence that had fallen over the quartet, listening to the rain quiet down against the glass and the night breeze begin to whistle along with the patter of rain now barely audible.

"Thank you, Mr. William, set it on the table there. How was your sweep?"

"Uneventful, though I will remain vigilant. Do you require anything else?"

"No, Moon can take care of us for the remainder of the evening, you may retire without worrying that we may need anything."

"You've been an excellent driver, just as you always have been Mr. William, I thank you for the smoothness of your ride. I haven't seen Erold that quiet in a carriage in some time. It's not quite the same as riding in one of those new trains or an airship, the bouncing can agitate him."

"Thank you sire."

Elara closed the door after him and stood again at attention, then nodded to Theodore who took a sip of the water that Mr. Williams had brought in, mulling over his words carefully.

"Yes, well, that's not to say even what my part in this is, but it doesn't go without saying, if you split from the Empire, the senate will launch an embargo, which will end East Cardane shipments that right now, as far as I'm aware, make up a substantial amount of traffic at two southern ports across from the Imerian coast, and in GoldArrow. Coltari would become your exclusive partner, and for probably the first time since King Karles III passed." Theodore, this time, looked over at Moon whose face did not move a muscle, "you would need us, possibly more, or as much as the Coltari, we, need you."

"I'll have to think about it."

"Yes, well, Mr. Everett. As always, your family's service to the royal family is as gracious as it has ever been. We've tired our mutual friend here, and we cannot delay much longer, my son and I must get back to our quarters quickly or we risk an enemy of this potential alliance being made aware that I'm not where I'm supposed to be. Well away from the two of you, in Seylil. You said that you have something for me."

"Yes, I do, and it is imperative that knowledge of this object, its whereabouts, or its current owner, does not leave this room. With the prospect of war on the horizon, there is increasing risk that Albion is no longer safe. And as my friend, here, reminded me earlier tonight, I am not the man I once was." Theodore tapped lightly on his knees, looked off into the distance, and closed his eyes, "This is not an obsession or a dark power, it will not control your waking thought, in fact, you may forget that it is even there. You won't feel it, and it won't touch you, not even if you have a magical gift. I've never been touched by the innate ability to throw fireballs or manipulate minds. I can't stop time or conjure arcane shields. I have these gloves." Theodore put a glove on as he spoke and snapped his fingers on that word, shooting a lightning spark barely an atomic yard into the air, as if for good measure to prove that he could.

"--that I built myself. My point is, what I've created, I've done so with my mind, not with any natural talent, and certainly not with any help from anyone else. I learned the ways of space-time, bent electro-magnetism to my will, and in the end, only conjure up imitations of what others can, especially those with elven blood." Here, Theodore paused again, to nod at Erolin, "are naturally inclined to achieve with the flick of a wrist or the nod of a head. Sure, it comes with many risks that I am not at risk for, but I am not immune, as you can see, to the dangers of failure and hubris. And now if I've kept your attention for this long, I show you the object which much of my adult life has revolved around."

He lifted up the box, and with the flick of his wrist, flipped open the lid, revealing a little, white orb, that looked like glass folded in on itself over and over. It glowed faintly, in the style of a cave creature, not used to the sunlight or that of the oil lamps hung along the library. It paled in comparison even to their dim yellow glow, flickering along the walls like fire.

"This, my friends, is a rare object, known as an Orb of Domiscus. Six were made and placed in pillars around the world, from which Domiscus launched her clockwork armies to end the blights that threatened every continent at one point or another and would have continued to do so. Only her intentions were not as they seemed, and it's for this reason, that this, a seventh and secret orb, not fall into the wrong hands."

"How did you get it, if you don't mind me asking, and how do you know it's real?" Lord Stone asked.

"It's a longer story than we have time for today, but suffice to say, I could walk at one point, and I made one of these myself, only it is not quite that simple, and it involved five of the six continents of this world. I guess potentially six, but I didn't go to that one. But, that's not how I lost my ability to walk, it's how I gained an ability to see. You know metaphorically. I wasn't blind, I was naïve."

"Which one of us are you giving it to, and could you remind me again why you are revealing this now?"

"Erolin, I am giving it to you. I feel the reason is clear, but I'll say it in sharper words. I believe spies from Imeria have infiltrated Albion. Certainly, spies from Valgaard have, so it's only natural to suspect. As Imeria is still a territory, controlled by Akrin, and I would bet my life on the same forces behind the Akrin senate being the ones behind the rigamarole I went through to get this object, it can't stay here. I'm already suspect number one as far as I'm concerned, and it's in many ways my lack of any natural, unbridled, hidden magical talent, that made me the perfect carrier for this little orb."

"Why is that?"

"If you're wondering if you could have a demonstration the answer is no. Mostly, because I can't use it. It's not like any direct use of this orb would alert the darker forces of this world to its presence, though mind you, it could. As far as I know, I don't know. It's not a beacon, it is a beacon. Who knows? The wisdom in me about these types of all, powerful objects, that other people shouldn't know about, is this, if you don't use it, whose to know you have it at all?"

"Of course, as winded-ly eloquent as ever. Why give it to me?"

"I feel it's a move those searching for this object would never suspect, and if you end up staying in Valgaard for an extended period of time, it may be safer there in your hands than if, or when, they come for me."

There was a chill in the air that hung between them as they each thought of this man, who had played by the rules of the senate for so long, might prolong his stay in the company of a former enemy after arriving to discuss an unlikely alliance that relied on forgiving the past.

"At your wish. Moon, we must be going." Erolin grabbed the box with the orb inside expressly from Theodore's held out hands, and then the king, that he truly was, appeared, as he raised his posture and nodded curtly to his old friends, Theodore Everett and Lord Jack Stone.

"How will you be getting where you're going, didn't Mr. William drive you?" Lord Stone asked.

"It's been arranged ahead of time that Moon would drive us to the hotel after Mr. William collected Erold and I. An overlap of sorts to help not raise suspicion. We can't exactly take a taxi out here and remain conspicuous. Moon, let's wake Erold."

Moon went to open the door, and found it ajar, as she flipped it open in a moment of panic, there stood the fifteen-year-old boy, still becoming a man.

"You startled me."

"How much of that did you hear?"

"I couldn't really hear anything."

"Let's hope your son, Erolin, is a better man than he is liar, but no matter. Don't let us keep you any longer."

"My lord, Erolin, and Theodore, there is something that I would like to speak with Lord Stone with in private if you don't mind." Erolin nodded and pulled Erold into the room, nodding for Moon to use the hallway and Stone to join her.

Lord Stone followed her into the hallway quickly, where she unwrapped her shawl to pull out a hidden package, wrapped in brown paper and twine, shaped like a miniature spear.

"One thing you should know Lord Stone, is that everyone is being watched and listened to. There are ears everywhere. None, hopefully here. Theodore, always had an eye out for bugs. And he, isn't the only one with a past. A younger version of myself, stole this scepter, for essentially the same reasons, Theodore stole the orb, and I never had a purpose for keeping it. At least not until now. I've heard a secret of yours that you might not be able to keep hidden for much longer. I always knew there was a reason that they called Albion, the 'Silver Coast,' and it wasn't because of any silver mines."

"Your point, Moon, make it."

"This object, the Scepter of Lyse, was stolen from the Akre museum many moons ago, and it's been modified to have an unnatural connection to the phenomena you call a curse. With it, you can activate, theoretically mind you, activate, not control, your curse, on any day of the month, and any of those citizens who may be most afflicted with the same such curse, such as in the cliffs or islands in the north."

The door opened and Erolin stepped out, dragging Erold behind him, "We best get going. Jack, walk with me." They walked at a brisk pace to the back door, dragging the blonde-haired man-child, who appeared to be half-asleep again as Erolin spoke under his breath in a harsh voice, "please think about this proposition quickly. We are on the precipice of war whether we like it or not, and what we decide will depend only on where the battle lines are drawn and how many people are caught up in the war. If we do not form an alliance. If we do nothing to protect ourselves, and more than ourselves, countless many millions will die. Valgaard is only the tip of the iceberg."

"God speed to you my friend," Lord Stone said.

"And to you."

With that, Erolin was out the door and into the rain. Before a dash of water had gotten on his lordship's shoulders, Moon, somehow unfolded an umbrella over the rightful king of Akre and his only son of a beautiful wife, long gone. That loss was something that he and Erolin had shared.

It was such a shame Erold was not sharper like his own son, Eduard, who was almost too sharp, but then again, brilliance could draw the wrong sort of attention like Theodore's orb, though there was nothing particularly brilliant about it.

Lord Stone closed the door slowly as heavy rain splashed mud across the woodwork and onto his boots. He was caught between believing in the idea of the senate and a return to that normalcy once taken for granted, where his king led the people in times of peace. They had once coexisted, the senate and the king for centuries of shared rule, but he was naïve to when it changed and what forces or events had changed it.

He looked down at the scepter still wrapped in now wet packaging, dripping onto the floor. It was the only sound he could hear in the house. He easily tore open the package, pressing his finger into the soggy paper, and found the harsh silver color of the scepter too bright at first. He blinked rapidly and held his other hand over his eyes, until the color began to pale, and the scepter didn't appear to him to be the color silver at all. It appeared to be nothing more than a jeweled stick with a grayish shadow, maybe half an atomic yard in length with a closed flower in place of the spearhead at the tip.

It was unclear how it could have been 'modified' as it looked as if anything on it had been a part of its construction from the start. He returned to the study to find his old friend, Theo, sleeping in his wheelchair. He propped up Theo's head and wheeled him out of the study.

If things weren't complicated enough already, running an autonomous provincial nation that had grown right before his eyes, with the help of the mountain of gold his grandfather had left him, now he had military matters to sort through, and the only things he had ever cared for were administrative or economic, beside his late wife of course. God rest her soul, and praise be to him who kept the world from knowing her wrath if Albion was to be dragged into a war across nations.

A moment of clarity struck Lord Stone. It was not just a question of nations, but of nations of nations. Each like a nesting doll, filled with other nations. Valgaard and Imeria were each collections of over ten nations held together by necessity, Albion was two, and Normany was just one nation that had once formed part of Old Galdir, of which four other nations, that had once become independent nation-states, were now core to Akrin's Empire, or 'Republic,' which controlled or affiliated with even a few more still, to the east, south, and further west.

Lord Stone shook his head. Yes, he wanted to believe in a republic, but the senate also stood to profit from acting in their own interests, which Stone couldn't bring himself to define.

All he knew was that he understood the crux of Erolin's argument now. Before being consumed by the old Akrin war machine, there were the seven or eight nations of the gulf and the nations that were once independent in Imeria. Each of those nations were conquered by the armies of the golden city on the river, Akre, which were in turn, largely, built from the provinces of Old Galdir.

It didn't matter whether the conquered nations had banded or not, their armies fell.

How many more nations could Akre consume if it were to re-assemble its core under the senate?

1513 - Chapter 2

Erolin opened the door at the knock of the chief of his royal guard, Volstad, who looked at him with an eye of suspicion, noticing the signs of fatigue on his king's face, despite Erolin's attempt at disguising the dark lines and weary features.

"Out late last night?"

"Quite the contrary. I couldn't keep asleep." It wasn't a lie, and for a moment the two men stood gazing each other. Erolin tilted his head for a moment to one side, wondering if this was some other test.

Erolin had once heard that Volstad had dealt with shapeshifters. It had been one of the reasons he had first hired him when he started to suspect he would never return to his home city of Akre. He had once imagined he would be going back one day to the city where he was born and its many diversions of high society, such as theater. Instead, he waited in halls carved out of the side of a mountain in an impregnable fortress, waiting for something and nothing. Every day it felt as if war came ever nearer, and when the royal guard dwindled in number and devotion, he turned to mercenaries like Volstad with experience.

Volstad relented, "we best be getting to the airship. It doesn't set flight for another few hours, but your insistence on flying a public vessel has made things difficult."

"I understand your concerns, and I trust that you've handled any additional security concerns that there may be."

"Yes, we have booked out the flight in a random pattern as civilians, using false identities. You will be in one of the private boxes with me."

"And what about Brigham and Moon?"

"Moon will be in the adjacent compartment toward the rear of the vessel. Brigham will be at the furthest compartment forward among your block of the wing. We've taken the other adjacent compartment to yours on the right wing, but there will be civilians in the others."

Erolin checked his desire to explain everything to such a loyal man, but it went without saying that no one was supposed to know that he had made this trip, nor were they supposed to know that Erold had ever left Seylil, a mountain fortress and city just northwest of Akre, to spend time near one of the academies in Albion. Magecraft, also known as wizardcraft or witchcraft, among nobility was in a polite way of saying it 'not typically encouraged' historically, and if the senate heard of Erold's particular strength, Erolin could only imagine what their reaction would be.

The history of mages across the distinct histories of many nations was a frightening convolution of confusion, hate, and perhaps envy. Of course, except in Normany, and he refused to believe his son would devolve into a demon, succumb to an emptying of his mind, or find other evils waiting in the dark spaces that exist around the edge of consciousness.

However, these were also just partial explanations of why the nobility of the world seldom lived openly with their magical proclivities. He, himself, could conjure a few spells naturally without a word, but his son had a dangerous potential that even the best seers he could find, at an outrageous price to be kept secret, could not read. No one could tell Erolin of what destiny his son might hold.

On his own judgment then, Erolin relied, and given that even as people began to follow the words of the Lord and to trust the guidance of the men of science and magic, Erolin remained hesitant to put full faith in people.

"My lord? Are you ready to leave?"

"Have you woken Erold?"

"Yes, he's waiting in the carriage with Moon."

"Was he hidden?"

"Yes, they are both disguised, and we best be putting on our disguises now too. We'll put them on at the same time."

"Right you are, Captain." Erolin pulled on a false face, and Volstad did the same, marking an indicator on his side to make sure Erolin still knew who he was.

Volstad checked the room once more and picked up the king's two bags, "We'll take the disguises off while on the ship to Seylil. There's no reason to keep them on at that point, but we can use them in transit once we've arrived if it would ease your worries."

"Yes, yes it would."

The two men walked down the hallway, through to the stairs, which they began down as quickly as possible. Volstad put the bags down at the final floor and checked the door to the lobby. Satisfied to see whatever it was that he was looking for, he nodded to the King who followed closely behind him out the door. The two of them walked briskly enough and out through the doors, into the horse-drawn carriage and then toward the air-docks.

The city they were in was not overly large. It might have been 5 to 10,000 people, but the Everetts had installed one of the larger airship stations here to be close to the ore in the hills that powered the massive airships. Times were changing and Erolin could always count on the Everetts and the Coltari network at large to invest in the future. They had already installed airship stations throughout the south of Albion, when the first commercial or passenger airship had only been completed and made its maiden voyage some nine atomic miles in 1503.

Erolin looked from the window to the other three in the car, recognizing Erold as the young boy, even though his features were obscured by the shifting of the false face mask. With times as uncertain as they were now, Erolin wondered if any of his forefathers had felt certainty; or if they had felt that they were leaving behind a good world for their children.

As the carriage crested over another hill between the two and three story houses of the city, he could see the airship. It had the shape of one of the first oval designs from decades ago with the balloon inside rather than above, but it was cruiser, where those were merely discovering flight. Decks ran around the outside of the core of the vessel, enclosing the steam engines and machinery inside that powered the rear propellers. It appeared like something never to touch the water, leaving the sea completely behind, and he wondered how something so large could even get into the air.

Erolin marveled at it, and the miracle of the Orichalc ore. Orichalc burned red smoke unlike wood, and at such a power that it could boil water with an ounce, producing enough residual energy to lift ships into the air, achieving lift through a combination of forward force and the offsetting weight of the internal hot air of the ship's balloon.

The ore had long been known, but now it was being put to use; just like how the old Dwarven metals that were once mined 1500 years ago for armors were being boiled down and re-shaped into glittering, glorious monstrosities like this one, clipped together with mass produced iron fittings. The white and bronze of the two metals contrasted against each other made the whole of the ship look like it gathered the dazzling sunlight on its exterior as diamonds.

As they neared the bottom of the hill, the ship disappeared momentarily from view behind the hills and houses, and they followed a winding path through the town. Volstad was watching Erolin carefully between checking outside. Moon appeared to be asleep.

Erolin realized that he was holding his breath and let out a sigh in sharp exhales to hide his nervous excitement. He saw Volstad twitch out of the corner of his eye, and then check the windows. Moon snapped alert. The silence continued as Erolin looked between the two of them.

"Something wrong?"

"We're here."

Erolin leaned over the seat to get a look up close, and it did not disappoint. The Vagalla Airship. The largest passenger airship, if not airship in the world had been built to be two hundred atomic yards long, and just over forty atomic yards tall. Even before 'take off', it floated against the station that held it securely in place. It looked as if it would just hover in place forever, covered in windows.

"Quickly now," Volstad reminded him, taking the King's bags and the remaining luggage. Moon helped. Volstad sent the car away and jogged to catch up with Erolin.

They found their way up the ramp as one of the first sets of passengers, gave their ticket to the constable at the top of the ramp, and entered into a decorative entrance near the front of the vessel that appeared to have a counterpart archway on the opposite end and was little more than a semi-circle hallway that widened from the opening to facilitate passengers entering to find either the staircase or their way to the decks that wrapped around the outside of the central oval balloon.

"Essentially an over land wharf ferry," said Volstad.

Erolin nodded, but he saw a bigger picture. If trains were set to revolutionize the transport of goods, airships would change the transport of people like the telegram had made it almost possible to communicate with anyone at any moment as long as they were near a tower.

Yes, the world was changing. Erolin put his hand on Erold's shoulder as they disappeared into the leviathan of a ship and made their way to their compartment down a hallway to the other side, and up the staircases to the center deck where the cabins were largest.

They fell into a plush set of couches, with bunks above their heads, and Erolin couldn't help but smile at the simplicity of travel as a non-royal, if you for a moment, ignored the masks and the secret codes. The knocks and the overlapping guards, the night watches, and the sneaking through the night to visit an old friend after you've picked up your son. If you ignored those things, you could almost imagine that you were living a normal life, and that this was what normal was like.

"Your majesty, I'll relieve Moon to your compartment on your command."

"Yes, please, Moon, move to your compartment."

Brigham appeared, his disguise gone or never in use. Volstad gave him a strange tap on the shoulder, which Brigham responded to with a whispered code.

"Major, please report."

"Yes, we've checked all the compartments, and we've begun an orderly embarkment of the vessel by the royal guard. There are as many as 4-500 passengers on the vessel. Of which, we will be nearly half or more. After the rest of the crew have boarded, I will make another sweep of the vessel, using the teams we discussed to divert any suspicion. Then, we'll run a third official inspection once the remainder of the passengers have arrived."

"Will this be completed before we depart?" Volstad asked.

"Most certainly, Captain. The ship only looks big from the outside, but I assure you that we have had no trouble with the team assignments as specified."

"Thank you, Brigham, you may continue with your duties."

"Your majesty," Brigham bowed curtly, and then departed for the forward compartments. Volstad relaxed his posture, closed the door, and then sat on the couch opposite Erolin, beside Erold, who finally removed the mask from his face, revealing his bright blue eyes and characteristically blonde hair.

It was the hair and eye color of Erold's mother. Erolin, himself, whose lineage traced back to Normany from long before the tribes of fair hair, to which Erold's mother had belonged, descended from the north as ice covered old lands, had dark hair and darker eyes, though not all men of Arandil had. While it may not have been clear on the surface of their respective features--his black and hazel, his son's fair and blue--it was from him that his son had inherited the elven trait to be bound to life as a secret mage, though not exclusive to elven blood.

As Erolin continued to think, Volstad and Brigham continued to communicate off and on, and suddenly they were taking off. For a moment, Erolin was surprised. It was so strange to be taking off with so little fanfare, it took him a second to remind himself as well that this was by design. Erolin had assumed they were under constant threat of assassination after 1495, and he turned out right, which had helped him make it to almost twenty years later but not his wife.

Erolin turned to the window to watch as the countryside disappeared below and noticed that Erold was looking out the large square window as well. It gave a wide view of the shrinking countryside with its many copses of trees and rows of fields, tucked between hedges.

"Do you know these places?" asked Erolin.

"Yes, father."

"Father, hah. Are you trying to be polite? What's the name of that river below us?"

"That's the Kalopha."

"And, what province is it in?"

"We're flying over Normendin."

"Precisely, and where does it lead?"

"It runs along the hills here in the north, toward the capital of Albion, Rorik, beside Angel Bay in the West. If you know all of these things, why are you asking me?"

"You should get to know your kingdom, more than just where it sits on a map. What about all of these other tributaries, running south from the hills? Do you know any of their names?"

"Some of them are larger than others. To be honest, there are too many to try to remember. Most of them are not as large or deep as they might appear from the glint of blue that cuts between the color of the hills."

"And suddenly an artist with words. I feel like this is the most I've heard you speak--"

"Well, it is, since we haven't seen each other for a couple years. It seems strange to be going back to Seylil."

"Did you enjoy your time at school? Did you learn anything interesting in Albion?"

"Many things, but there's only more to learn. It doesn't feel right to leave it half-finished."

"That's what I like to hear, though unfortunately, we can't keep you away from court duties much longer, especially now that you are close to sixteen. At the rate of things, I may be asking you to marry a princess to keep us--"

"Yes, my cousin, probably," Erold rested his forehead against the window.

"I didn't mean it like that."

"It's the reality. We're both living it. It doesn't feel like much choice. Though, one of my teachers always said that choice is an illusion in the hope of free will."

"We can't always listen to our teachers."

"No, we can't."

"What about this river coming up here?"

"Not sure."

"You didn't look."

"I'm tired."

Erold closed his eyes and leaned his head against the back of the plush couch. Erolin looked at Volstad who was watching patiently from near the door. It wasn't clear if it was a moment of empathy, but Volstad closed his eyes and nodded at his majesty.

"I'll order us some refreshments."

Erolin thought that Volstad might be giving him and Erold some privacy, but it was a little more of an adventure than he expected. Volstad pulled down one of the bags, an odd-shaped case, that he had placed in the car when they had first climbed up from the carriage. It was square shaped, and box like, about a third of an atomic yard deep and double that wide.

"What's this?"

Volstad rummaged through whatever was in the case and pulled out an odd syringe and vial of purple liquid. He placed the syringe into the top of the liquid and pulled out the purple liquid.

Erolin tensed. His heartbeat quickened and he watched Volstad's movements carefully, as his chest began to tighten. He was unarmed and smaller than Volstad, but his son was sitting there with eyes closed. If he rammed Volstad against the wall he could alert Moon, who had saved him once before, and had pledged to him to defend his family's life.

"I can't trust that anything we get on the ship is safe, so this is to test it for poison."

Volstad placed the syringe within an inner pocket his jacket, and then he stepped out into the hallway and made his way to the refreshment station.

Volstad made his way down the hallway and checked in on Brigham who appeared to be sleeping. He knocked on the window of the door, and the man didn't move. Volstad went through the wing's forward door, and then to the left to the bridge between the right and left wings, where the refreshments station unfolded in a wide semi-circle bar around the forward compartments, reserved for some of the engines and operations. Four shelves of liquors and assorted foods, but no staff.

Volstad leaned over the bar. There they were passed out. Three fully grown women passed out as if they had just drunk a sleeping draught.

Volstad lifted a half full glass of water, slipped the syringe out of his pocket, and splashed a dash into the glass. First, it was a lilac color as the deep purple of the liquid filtered through the innocent-looking water.

A breath of a second and then as if a switch flipped, it turned a glowing orange. Not a deadly poison. Indeed, a sleeping draught. Not dead but knocked out. Whoever it was, thieves or assassins--that remained to be seen--they must have distributed the draught with the water service, and he had told Brigham to check it multiple times. Volstad was thankful he had asked not to be disturbed.

Volstad spun and took off running the way he had come. He burst through the door into the King's compartment and grabbed a small vial from his case.

"What's wrong?" Erolin stood up. Erold still asleep.

Volstad turned and left the compartment. He went first to Brigham and injected the vial straight into the man's shoulder. He instantly stiffened and woke up.

"Volstad?"

"We don't have much time. Sleeping draught. Here," Volstad handed the vial and a second syringe to Brigham. "Wake as many as you can and head toward the forward bridge. We have to make sure it's our men flying this thing to Seylil."

"Aye."

Volstad turned to go back to the King, listening to hear if anything was going wrong. He looked out Brigham's window as the man rushed out to administer to sound the alarm among their passengers throughout the ship.

He could see nothing but the calm blue skies of the countryside off to the south and west as they flew along the mountain line that lay to the north.

On the other side of the ship, for those passengers still awake, as if out of some pirate novel on the high seas, an iron balloon, painted white like a cloud, lifted a small schooner-sized ship, suspended by chains out of the mountains.

Out in the hallway, Volstad ran to the King. Just as he reached the door, the two ships collided, throwing Volstad to the ground. Instinctively, he pulled out his pistol as he got up.

"Your majesty," Volstad opened the door, finding Erold bolt

upright and for a moment he feared the worst. His majesty looked up at him, having braced himself against the couch.

"We have a situation Volstad. Report?"

"Sleeping draught. It's unclear what the aim is."

The king looked at his son and then at Volstad. They began to hear the footsteps of people running above.

"How many do you think there are?"

"Depends on the size of the ship."

"Give me a guess."

"No more than two hundred, making it about even with the guard."

"I'll rally the guard," the king said. "You take Erold and go with Moon."

Moon had appeared over Volstad's shoulder.

"We can't leave you sir."

"Says everyone, you can and you will. Where's Brigham?"

"He's checking the men down in general passengers."

"I'll go with you to the aft, then we'll have to fight our way to the bridge."

"Is this the best plan?"

"The gliders are in the rear, but we're going to have to assume that they are here for me. That they don't know my son is aboard, and that they can't find out."

The door slid open at the end of the hall. It was Brigham with five men. He ran to meet Volstad.

"What's the plan?"

"Send someone forward to set defensive positions. We will rally in the rear, protecting the escape gliders, and then you and the king will draw the enemy forward, take the bridge and guide the ship to Seylil. Signal to us if it's safe."

"Right, James, you and Áeric go forward, gather at least ten from the lower compartments and hold the staircases. Make sure no one reaches the lower decks. Send anyone else to the rear and then we will clear the top deck from the rear and reinforce your position."

"Aye."

The two groups split up with Moon, Volstad, the King and Erold heading to the rear ahead of Brigham and the others. They reached the back staircase that was little more than a single file iron ladder between compartments.

The King turned to Volstad. "There is a direct line of communication between the ship's bridge, the lower engines, and the gliders. If we take the bridge, we will communicate with you in the rear. Brigham, you go below and make sure we control the lower decks before we enact this plan. Be careful, rendezvous here in five minutes and we'll make a play for the top deck."

As the door to the bottom deck opened and codes were given, a door at the top opened. Volstad looked up, cocked his pistol and blew a hole into the light canvas encasing their position. A rifle clanked down onto the black iron of the stairs as blood followed. Men, fought through the door as Moon and Volstad opened fire. The King in waiting, Erolin, pulled a pistol from within his tunic and began firing, holding the men from opening the door above them.

Brigham returned.

"We control the lower deck."

"Too late to take the top deck from here."

"Quickly, below while I cover you!" yelled Erolin and Moon fired off a few more rounds, while Volstad grabbed the kid and pushed Erold through to the lower deck and the gliders.

Brigham pulled up his rifle and covered for Moon between the railings as she followed Volstad. They slammed the door shut.

"New plan," said Volstad, "We hold this door. You and Brigham work up to the bridge through the forward staircase; and if you make it to the bridge, give us the 'all clear,' or we will use the gliders and escape into the countryside."

"They could follow you."

"We'll have to take that chance."

"Okay, Brigham leave as many as we can spare here with Volstad and Moon." Brigham went off and began directing traffic. The full of the lower deck wrapped in a wide oval-shaped floor around the central balloon of the airship. It gave the impression of walking on the bottom of an old, curved sea ship.

Erolin waited until it was only Volstad and Moon near the rear door, hearing the clank coming from the staircases beyond the thick iron that they had slammed shut and barred.

"Erold, I have something to give you."

"Yes."

Erold, pulled something bound in cloth out of his pocket and shoved it into Erold's hand and closed it. Volstad barely noticed the motion, and only saw it as if they were holding hands. He tried to hear what was being said, but the noise of the steam engines and hurtling wind made it almost impossible to hear the King's whispering.

"Erold, protect this orb. If you are to land in Normany, seek out your uncle Sven. He has many loyal to him across the Solgra and in the hills, he will pro--."

Something slammed against the door behind Volstad, but the humming sound of the lower deck began to grow louder and louder. Erolin yelled something to Volstad, but he couldn't hear. Ten of Erolin's men came and Erolin went forward. Volstad followed and pushed Moon and Erold into the glider bay ahead of him.

Volstad and Moon helped Erold into one of the gliders, then Erold helped Moon get in alongside him, while Volstad went to the comm system. The glider escape ships were awkwardly shaped, but about large enough for four to be seated uncomfortably.

Erold watched Volstad as he went to the comm system, wondering if he'd hop in or they would wait for his father. Instead, in a moment of foreboding clarity, Volstad and Moon nodded to each other. It was just the three of them in the glider bay. Moon hit the release and launched away.

Erold watched as Volstad shrunk, while Volstad returned Erold's glare, seeing the dull bronze of the glider fall away from him until Moon and Erold had disappeared from the sight of the naked eye.

Volstad listened at the comm for a moment, before stepping out into the hallway, ordering for the royal guardsmen to start evacuating the ship. He motioned them into the gliders and confirmed that it was time to go on his orders.

There were a few gliders left when he sent another group out into the early evening sky. He planned to reserve at least one for himself and the king, while simultaneously acknowledging quietly in the depths of his mind, that whatever the situation was above, they had to begin the retreat.

Then, he held his breath, straining to hear through the comm if anyone was on the other side. Ambient noise gradually increased as if his hearing receded with each passing second. He could barely make out the sound of gunfire in the distance, but it appeared to be gradually moving forward and up through the ship. Perhaps, that was wishful thinking.

There was something about the noise that was familiar and awe-inspiring to Erolin as he and Brigham fought their way through the forward stairs. They had given up the high ground, but they had much larger numbers.

The fallen men appeared poorly armed, and he was starting to question this as an assassination attempt rather than an act of piracy gone wrong, when he saw it. A flash of wing and a golden eye. A talon about six atomic yards long smashed through a window above him. The whole ship shuddered.

Dragon.

"Dragon!"

Erolin heard the yell cry out throughout the ship as everyone realized what was going on.

"Brigham, they must have baited the dragon here."

"They drove the ship toward the mountains!"

"My son needs to launch off of this vessel now!"

They began to hear splintering metal, shattering glass and the roar of dragon flame.

The ship shuddered again and Erolin broke for the bridge. Men were holding onto railings for dear life as Erolin miraculously found his footing as the ship began to melt or fall apart. He could feel the heat emanating off of whatever had begun to melt.

He aimed his pistol ahead of him and took out whoever was standing at the top of the stairs, friend or foe. He pushed a hunched over body out of his way.

The ship shook. He braced himself.

He fought as if fighting against a greater force of gravity to not fall as the floor behind him began to give way. The door to the bridge was open. A civilian lying asleep, or dead, blocked it from closing.

One of the false pirates was standing over the wheel in the bridge, alone. He recognized Erolin and lifted his gun, but Erolin shot first, putting a red hole between the eyes.

There was only one thing certain now and that was that he wasn't making it off of the ship alive, and that must have been the plan. Through the forward windows he could see another dragon snaking out of the mountains to collect the ball of flaming iron and melt or cook them from outside in or inside out.

He went to the iron comm and yelled.

"Volstad launch the gliders now, get out of here! Dragon!"

Volstad couldn't hear exactly what was going on, but the shriek of metal and the increase in residual heat had led him to launch the remaining gliders. He, alone, waited there in the glider bay, with one last glider, still waiting to see if his king would be there to join him.

But, he wouldn't be coming.

Volstad leapt into the glider and shot the rope tethering it to the airship. He jettisoned away, watching the glider bay, never seeing a single face of an attacker appear through the iron doorway. The

Royal guard had done the job it could. Erold was away safe, somewhere in the hills north of the Solgra.

For a brief moment, the force of the ship pulled him along after it, but as his glider hit colder air, it slowed, and the momentum of the enormous airship carried the two objects in different directions. The doomed ship, slipping ever more left, guided by a hand anxious to lead the dragons away from the falling gliders.

Volstad turned the rutter, transferring the momentum in a circular arch until he was aimed at the hills, looking for the outlines of his men in gliders as darkness began to truly fall.

He could barely make out the outline of the hills, navigating from the air by the glitter of the river in the moonlight, desperate not to look back and see the burning carcass of the passenger ship crashing into the mountain, wary that the bright bronze of his little glider could attract a dragon that had lost interest in crushing the machinery of man.

* * *

Erold watched the gliders of the royal guard slip out from beneath the airship one by one. Just a shadow and a reflection of light in the setting sun, like a pod of clouds being left behind, some of them eaten mid-air by molten fire.

He watched as the dragon, about one hundred fifty atomic yards long, nearly the size of the airship, plunged its claws into the metal and windows of the doomed airship, aiming fire, with precision, to melt and burn everything inside. Like a comet, the fire and melted metal began to leave a trail of yellow and molten red behind it in the darkening night. He could see the glow like a halo as the airship began to crumble.

Then a second dragon followed, ripping the smaller ship that had boarded the passenger cruiser in half with one burst of fire and then the smashing of its tail through the molten iron. It was only the white dwarven metal that had prevented his father's ship from yet succumbing to the dragon fire.

He could see that there was no hope that his father would survive as few escape gliders escaped the fury, and he knew his father had gone to the bridge. He could see that clearly, and still, he was glued to watching the ship dive toward the mountains engulfed in flame. The melting metal and passenger compartments had been replaced by shadow and fire as the molten ball, slowly curved further to the left and into the mountains.

The dragons tore through the iron with their claws, roaring and blasting fire into the inner compartments. Erold could see bright displays of ash, lit by fire fall from the bottom of the ship.

A third dragon arrived as the first two still dug their claws into the hull of the ship, still trying to rip the dwarven metal in half.

Finally, as the ship edged closer to ramming into the side of the mountain, the flame leaked through a hole made in the inner cocoon of the ships bubble, bursting through the middle of the ship.

As if cracking like a twig, the glittering ball of white and orange sparkling light split in half, the forward half, still floated ever onward as if guided on the wind, while the rear half began a sudden plummet to the ground, trailing red light into the sky.

The dragons released their crushing talons from the crashing ship and traded roars as they lifted higher into the air with long thrusts of their dark, glistening wings that caught the dueling light of the embers, sparking off of the doomed metal, and that of the setting sun that cast beams of red and pink from behind Erold and still lit the tips of the mountain range. The forward half of the once majestic passenger cruiser, no longer discernible from a blazing meteor, slammed into the edge of the mountain, exploding into a cacophony of fiery bursts that Erold could hear from the hills, louder than the roar of the mighty beasts.

Erold looked down at his fist clenched around the white orb, but suddenly, he could see was the reflection of the exploding ship in the black of the Evorul river at night. The fire of the rear half lit the hills and looked in the water as if the entire countryside was ablaze.

His sudden hatred of dragons began to seize violently through him. He could feel a power pulsating through the little ball, and he began to feel very alive, very aware. He began to believe that he could--

Moon grabbed his shoulder.

"Erold?"

"Yes?"

"Let's get you to safety."

They climbed down away from the glider, toward the river. As they descended, the distant light of the wreck faded with the cooling of the flame, and only a dim glow lit up the edges of the hills to the north and east.

Soon, they were picking their way through the rocks to find a place where they could discuss what would happen next and if they could link up with the rest of the remaining guard.

1513 - Chapter 3

The telegraph operator manning the desk in Rorik listened to the dots and dashes as they came in. The machine used to scribe them for her to be read, but now she could listen to the playback and transcribe it in letters. If she missed one, she had to translate or rework it on the page as if she was playing a game to find missing or wrong letters until it replayed. The guy who usually did the job had been out sick, so she had gotten an opportunity to do it. For many reasons, she was glad.

When she had finally transcribed the message, she had a piece of news, the newspapers would pay a gold piece for or more. There was no doubt this message being sent from Umfell, by urgent communication, would have been sent all over the empire, where telegraph stations were going up over the last twenty years. Comparatively, it took as many as four weeks or more for a standard letter to arrive from Akre.

The news read that the Vagalla, the largest passenger airship of all time, made from dwarven metal reserves to be uncrashable, and had recently originated the Ash Vale to Seylil connection which would someday be extended into a Rorik to Akre line, just a little bit too far out of range still, had been attacked by dragons over Umfell.

After she flattened her dress and walked calmly to the door, she negotiated with the man from the paper to get the gold piece, sight unseen. He was skeptical about such a big price. The newspaper didn't generally authorize more than a couple silvers, but this woman had never steered him wrong before.

His eyes almost burst out of his head when he saw it, and he rushed off. She pocketed the gold piece and then went back inside the station.

"What'd you sell today?" asked the super attendant, knowing full well everyone hustled what they could out of the paper. "A bit of gossip on the archmage's court in Akre? We get a lot of those."

Now that she'd sold the information, she swallowed and choked out the words with surprising difficulty, "The Vagalla crashed into the Evoruls last night, taken down by dragon!"

For a moment, the older man continued to circle words he didn't know in the previous day's paper, then the news hit, "A dragon attack on the airship!"

"Yes."

"Do you still have a copy script of the message?"

"Of course, it's in the telegraph room. Why?"

"That message should go to the lord of the duchy, Lord Stone."

"Should I take it?"

"No, no," he said, getting up and getting on his coat, while slicking back his hair, "There's a procedure for this. I'll deliver it to the adjutant at the castle. You man the desk."

The man was wishing he had worn his good pants. He was annoyed that he didn't have a half-silver piece for a cab. It had rained, so he dodged puddles filled with horse shit as he navigated the city streets from the station on the city's central hill toward the palace, which was nestled away from the bay, though it rose high in one central tower.

He gave the copy of the transcript, addressed to the Lord Stone to the adjutant at the door by the gate. The adjutant stood there, in his large black boots and red suit with blue and yellow detailing. One shoe in a puddle while he adjusted himself and began to read over the transcript.

"Is this true?"

Some people were skeptical about news that didn't travel by letter.

"Every word, most certainly. It's from the official line from Umfell."

"I'll have it delivered to the Lord Stone."

That man at the door took it to an adjutant to the palace staff, who delivered to a member of the direct staff adjacent to the personal adjutant of the lord. Instead of delivering it to the hands of Lord Stone's adjutant, this staff member rushed it through the gray stone palace, along enameled stucco floors to take it to the Lord Stone himself.

He passed over red carpets with gold lining, banners that were bright red with the golden eagles of Akre, encircled in dark blue. The only local image was the wolf, with light blue crystal eyes, of old Rorik that adorned some of the doorways carved into the old stone, watching out with barred teeth, dulled just slightly by time.

The same process played out all over the world in palaces and in newspapers. The messenger found Lord Stone looking over maps of the islands spread out across the Argal, the largest ocean in the world, mapping out shipping routes from Albion to the far west kingdoms of Yin. An activity that Stone often did after speaking to his friend, Theo.

"Lord Stone, you've received a telegram."

"I'm busy." Lord Stone continued looking over his maps, using a ruler and a pencil.

"It's urgent."

"It can wait."

"It's a matter of the Vagalla, your lordship."

Lord Stone put down the pencil and his drawing instrument. He folded the map under his arm and went to the door of his study, looking the messenger in the eye, then letting out a sharp exhale before snatching the sheet of paper.

He read the first sentence aloud.

"Vagalla Airship crashed. Stop."

Then, he finished the rest under his breath, knowing after the meeting just the night before that the king-to-be of Akre, lord of Normany, had been on the Vagalla after he, Lord Stone, had asked Theo about that very ship over dinner.

Foul play not suspected. Stop. Evidence of multi dragon attack. Stop. Ship got too close to the mountains. Stop. No survivors yet found after crash. Stop. All presumed dead. Full stop.

"Thank you," he nodded to the messenger and closed the door as the man went back to his post. It took Lord Stone a second to breathe, before he sat down at the desk. The animal inside him wanted to tear the desk in half, and it may have if he let it. He went to the other side of the study, pulled a small, brass key out from underneath his jacket and inserted it into a lock in the cabinet.

There were vials and vials of liquid silver. He pulled one out and drank from the bottle rather than inject it. It would help him to forget his emotions better than a bottle of whiskey could, but it killed his insides bit by bit until it warped them and devolved his mind into a catatonic state, hopefully one thought stacking on itself rather than onto another.

It hit him hard and sudden. He collapsed suddenly, catching himself on the ash desk. He stumbled forward and against the wall, knocking maps and a pile of books onto the floor. He forced himself around the desk, and into the chair, where he slouched and looked up at the ceiling.

No one knew the king and prince were on board, or hopefully they didn't. How could he not suspect foul play? Everything about Erolin's trip to the 'silver coast' had been secretive, when even a few years before, he had arrived in and left Albion with ten thousand spectators at least.

If Erolin had lived, he would have made a great king and

hopefully would have ascended soon, but how long had he been thinking that and what about his son, Erold? Uggh, how could he think such terrible things about his friend's son? If the boy prince had lived, Stone would certainly have supported him in the same way that he had supported his father, which had that even been enough?

He couldn't even play the political game well enough for his own son, who having grown tired of his father's inaction was off on some kind of adventure with Captain Jacquelina Catalina Ferrara, who Stone did not believe was a great influence despite Theo's complete faith.

This wasn't about himself, and yet, Stone couldn't think of anyone else to blame. Was his friend's last wish for an alliance a concern for a potential future where someone made a move on his life? Erolin had always been wary of the senate where his cousin, King Karles III, had been concerned.

Stone stared at the mural of the constellations he had had painted on his study ceiling, but it was the imperfections in the paint that his attention gravitated toward. He could have spent a few hours, listlessly, in his melancholic state, watching the immobile flecks of paint. Each place where the paint had begun to drip, where it was not perfectly flat.

A knock rang out harshly from the thick wooden door. It may have been a few minutes, or a few hours, since the messenger had arrived with the news of Erolin's death. Stone didn't know, but he sat slightly taller and rolled his eyes over the door. He knew what it was like to take silver when he wasn't changing into the form of the beast within, but he hadn't taken precautions. He was glad he didn't use the needle and syringe. If he had used them, he might not have woken up.

"Come in."

It was another messenger sent from the telegram office.

"Is it urgent?"

"No."

"Leave it on the table."

The messenger looked away at the sight of Lord Stone, likely with his eyes unfocused and his skin visibly clammy. Stone sat up, or tried to, and then ushered the boy away.

Stone looked at the note, sitting there, unable to bring himself to clear his mind long enough to read it with coherent thoughts. He was upset, and anticipating how angry he could have gotten, he had rushed to self-medicate the pain away.

He blinked, trying to force some recognition back to his brain, and looked at his 'special medicine' cabinet, momentarily flushed, worried that it was open, but he had shut it. He grabbed at the key wrapped around his neck. It was there. He didn't want anyone to know his secret, even if somehow Moon knew. Even if it felt like the staff it took to run the castle was a revolving door, there remained very few people, who Stone let in that close like Erolin.

Erolin was one of those very few, very few men that Stone had ever called a friend. Erolin had needed him, Lord Stone, to step up before it was too late. Now, Lord Stone, told himself, it was too late. Who could lead Normany? How could he ensure that Albion remain an autonomously governed region? How much time did he have before it wasn't?

There was Erolin's supposed cousin, Sven. There were doubts about his lineage, but he was popular. It was a risky move, but the man had political support in the Sun grass plains, or the Solgra as the Normen called it. Either way, it would go against Lord Stone's decision to support the royal family. With Erold now dead as well, the princess Aurelia, Erold's cousin, would now be in line to be queen. That is if the senate would have followed the old laws.

Even if Erold had lived, it would have been hard to know what the senate would have tried to do. It was likely that he would have been in the same position as Erolin. The boy would have legally been the next in line for the throne of Akre, being Erold's son, but the senate could have manipulated anything they wanted to prevent it being confirmed by a vote of the people, leaving him only to control the direct hereditary throne of Normany. If Erolin hadn't been able to force the senate into a vote on ascension, how could his younger son? This tragedy had the senate's fingerprints all over it, and at this point, there could be no hiding it like the implications of the spring of 1495.

Stone swallowed the drool that had pooled in his mouth and tilted his head to look at his reflection in the sunlight drenched window to the outside world. He'd gotten so used to self-medicating the transformations away, that he had begun to take the silver whenever he needed to ease his mind, which was a lot lately. Only not during the day.

Lord Stone's mind began to clear as the rush of the silver began to clear from his system. It left him groggy, and he felt as if his insides needed to be cleaned out with a brush. They probably did.

As his mind cleared further, he saw the scepter from Moon and wondered why anyone would want to activate an affliction like his at any time, or even how it would work. His episodes were a manic rage filled with desperation and destruction.

His eyes found the map of the world on the ground, where he had been tracing shipping lines. Clearly marked were the boundaries of the republic--or 'empire,' depending on how you viewed it. He decided that he couldn't capitulate to the empire.

Lord Stone couldn't give the senate what they wanted. His family's money. The earnings, that if anyone, the people of his kingdom deserved to continue to reap the rewards of.

He would wait to see what Sven would do in Normany. Yes, this time waiting made sense, because this time, waiting meant trying to live up to his lost friend's last wish. Besides, capitulating to Akre possibly meant abandoning Theo and the Coltari as well, which would go against his sense of loyalty.

He shook himself and went to the desk to look at the communication. It was an official message from the senate on Lord Erolin of Normany having gone missing.

Lord Stone picked it up. Skimming the telegram, he had only to read, if the king is found dead immediate vote for the appointment of a new Emperor of Akrin to feel doubly sick to his stomach.

This all but confirmed his increasing suspicion, but it also confirmed Erolin's. The senate would elect an emperor for only one reason: war.

If Erolin had known they were planning a campaign, he would have told Lord Stone. They must not have told Erolin, which makes sense, especially if they knew that he would try to block it, and yet, even without them telling him directly, he was standing in their way by blocking conscriptions in Normany.

Hmm, by waiting to make a decision in this case, Lord Stone could delay a fight, but what would a fight look like? Was Theo right about the nations of Imeria, positioning to help Akrin consolidate control in the west?

Lord Stone had not been blind to the troop movement, but he had thought, rightly in his prior opinion, that it was related to the defense of Imeria's coast against the invasion from the island nation of Ispiarda. Perhaps, that was a convenient excuse to put even more troops on the west side of GoldArrow, which did not enjoy the natural defenses of an ocean being between it and the states of Imeria.

The ultimate reality was simple. He needed to decide whether he would secede from Akrin in advance of them trying to absolve his autonomy. A reality he couldn't quite imagine happening, or he could wait for them to make a move. Right now, none of their actions seemed to immediately affect him, but he was sure that Erolin would have already contacted him if he had somehow survived the dragon attack.

Somehow was wishful thinking.

1513 - Chapter 4

"Yes! I'm the king! It's a beautiful day, ha ha! Am I right, lads? And, what's more? Once again, the beautiful people of Valgaard have come to say hello." King Hughgar skipped into the Peth palace's inner court, greeting the guardsman, standing against each white-stone pillar with a nod.

Inner arches separated the main room, with its lofty ceiling from two separate side hallways, lit by stained glass windows as tall as two men, casting colored spindles of light in front of the king as he danced through to the golden throne, placed at the other end of the room.

The king mocked a frown though, because the room remained dark, and he thought he caught the partial yawn of one of his favorite guards. The oil lamps, built into the inner room of his modern castle remained unlit, and so were the two brilliant crystal chandeliers, carved from a crystal so clear that they looked like ice sculptures suspended from the ceiling.

"I love what my daughter has done with the place, yes, but where is the fire?" King Hughgar snapped his finger and launched pale blue beams of fire from his fingers at a set of candles he had placed along the far end of the room.

One beam, snaking like lightning and as fast as it too screamed through the air before hitting the middle candle. The candle snapped in half, toppling in on itself and dissolving more than melting back into wax in an iron metal dish below. The other twisting beam of blue hot fire perfectly glanced across the wick, leaving the candle burning.

Each snaking beam slammed into the white-stone wall behind the throne, leaving an ashy stain.

"Yes! You saw that?"

"I did sir."

"What is this, thirty atomic yards?"

"We put the marks on the floor sir, so you can see. Your front foot is on the thirty-two-yard mark. We placed them this morning ahead of your arrival."

"I still got it!"

A pair of men ran out from the wings of the room, wiped as much of the ash as they could while the king walked to the end of the room, and then hung the King's banners along the rear wall to cover the marks the king had left along the rear wall from this daily ritual.

"Bouvedere?"

"Yes, my lord."

"Could you see about the lights, and let the guests in early," he paused for a moment and then despite being king, he added, "please?"

"Yes, my lord," said Bouvedere.

The King relaxed into the throne and looked at the large hall from the pedestal of pure gold, with its green pillows, decorated with gold thread. The banners, hung crisply between each arch, the oil lamps being lit between them.

As the lights came on, he admired the tapestry work, hand-woven into each of the eight enormous banners hanging on either side of him. The hand-made details all looked identical, at least from here. The symbol of the golden sun, woven in golden thread against the bright leaf and forest green made his heart swell with pride. They shined in the light of the oil lamps, also fixtures of solid gold, and the dancing light of crystal chandeliers above, that reflected the oil lamp light.

"Thank you Bouvedere. I feel particularly generous today. We are nearing the beginning of autumn. The sun is shining. I believe we reached a high of seventy-five on the Odin scale! I could go out among the people on a day like this. And without the beast skin! Make sure to give each of the men, and yourself an extra ten. No make that twenty gold coins today."

"Are you sure, sir? Your daughter--"

"Is not the king. I am, so--"

"Sir, the last time you did this, you remember the incident with your favorite daily ritual when she iced the floor."

Hughgar nodded lightly, but his face remained as unphased. He leaned over to Bouvedere and whispered.

"Take it out of the 'salary' she gives me. I could do with one less trophy this month."

He could have gotten a unicorn head mounted this year to place on the wall of his trophy room. That would have been an interesting one, or he could have tried to get a Pegasus shipped north from Elessia to fly around the city upon. His mind had begun to drift as he contemplated more changes that he could make.

His daughter had really begun to run the show and she wasn't even seventeen. She had all the rage that he had, but none of the flare, quite literally. She breathed ice. He had burned every Akrin outpost north of the border with his own magic.

But, he had promoted her, because she was a keen administrator, which he had no interest in being. She liked to play politics and make court dates with the nobility of his land and others. She enjoyed the pomp and aura. He just wanted people to sing "Good King Hughgar," which they had written for him because he was their good king--who had cut taxes--and to listen to his stories about melting giant's faces and riding mastodons north of the mountains.

His other changes were mainly superficial. He had long been debating adding a unicorn to the center of the sun in the insignia on the Valgaardian coat of arms, since they were almost completely unique to Valgaard.

In contrast, upon promoting his daughter just three years before, she had instituted a program for building two lane, paved roads between towns of at least ten thousand people, so that during the winter months it would be easier for people to travel between villages, and paid staff could, miraculously, clean them after the weekly blizzards.

In the history of all the realms of dragons and beasts, had there ever been a queen, or king for that matter, so dedicated to modernization or the advancement of her people? No. He could barely remember a history book describing clear roads before the 800s, and in the 1200s, he assumed they were at best, dirt. It was almost chilling, but the world was changing quickly. The telegram, automatons, the modern airship, what next? He had even heard that steam trains were somehow revolutionizing the movement of goods in the southern Empire. He was sure his daughter was on it.

Then the great oak doors opened, snapping his wandering mind back to reality, and the first city dweller or villager who had traveled to see him was ushered within the court. The old man was clearly awed by the magnificence of the decorations. First, the gold and then the way the different lights of the room exhibited the king's choice decor.

"Your majesty," the man bowed deeply and was about to begin his plea, when Hughgar realized something odd.

"Hang on! I know you!"

"You couldn't possibly your majesty."

"Haven't I seen you here before?"

The man seemed to be lost for words, possibly debating whether to lie. He was probably worried about what could get him in trouble or lose him his head.

"Or maybe it was in the old court down the road, but you're

Olgaf, the barber from Lendolin. Tell me, I'm right?"

"Hamberlin, sir, but yes, I'm Olgaf, the barber. I can't believe you remembered."

"Aye, I never forget a face, especially one I've dismembered," he winked at everyone, but Olgaf was the least amused as he began to shake. "Remind me, your neighbor tried to fake the land grant for your?"

"Father's farm. My father almost lost his family farm. I came to you, because we were desperate."

"And, I am glad you did. I am happy to help. What can I do for you today?" Hughgar leaned in, enraptured by another tale of the seedy manipulations of the people that lived within his kingdom. Falsifying documents, mysterious potions, illegal sorcery, you name it, it had happened.

He had even had a case of impersonation by shapeshifter, brought to him by the shapeshifter, himself, who thought he could trick old Hughgar, but a de-shrouding spell with the snap of the fingers and a beam of fire through the chest before an attempt to steal another face could be made, solved problems quicker than trying to turn things into a game of he said, she said. For him, it was always easier to melt faces than steal them, and if he had to behead them, he had.

As one visitor left and another was about to be led in, the sun brightened and glinted off the guardsmen's sabers. Their polished wood rifles glistened, and Hughgar noticed that the new model of pistols had been issued to his specifications with the green and gold insignia of Valgaard imprinted on the side.

At Valessa's direction the royal guard had now been upgraded from percussion pistols along with the officers, though the general soldiers would still use muskets and percussion pistols. The lack of mass production of rifles that used .54 caliber bullets and the expense of .54s over musket balls made it impossible as of yet to upgrade the full standing army.

Considering that she had added the decals, he had to think that maybe his daughter did listen to his droning on. The princess had seemed particularly obsessed with something lately, so it was hard to tell when or if she listened.

A tall, blonde woman, impeccably dressed in a flowing green dress, let the doors, adjacent to the court be opened ahead of her as she left the long, green carpet of the hallway behind. The sharp staccato of high heels rapped on the lacquered stone floor as she entered the court, brazenly, a slight frown on her face.

"Father, did you hear the news?"

"Speak of a dragon by its name and it appears," said Hughgar, turning to smile at her. "And, no I didn't."

"My Lord, father, you say that every time I see you lately," she smiled back, "Could you come with me for a moment to speak in private?"

He nodded to her and got down from the throne and remarked to Bouvedere to hold for his return. He was glad that there wasn't a visitor at the moment that would have to wait in the court. He followed Valessa back to the hallway from where she had come, and the doors closed behind them.

She turned to him, "why are you holding open court again? You do know that we have a mage court system that I've been working to implement throughout the nation. It's been very hard to get established, despite the fact that the 1200s were three hundred years ago!"

"Yes, as you remind me, but if you think about it, I'm a wizard too, so it's like I'm holding high mage court."

"This doesn't help."

"As I've said in the past, I like to hear the people's appeals. What's the point of being the king if you can't be the king for the people?"

"Father, we are a country of almost twenty million people. We have to work within the framework of a modern monarchy. There's a constitution for it and everything that you helped to draft."

"And that is true, as you have said, many times before, and as you pointed out, I helped to draft it. I did read it too. I know what it's about. Generally."

Princess Valessa stopped walking for a moment to stare at her father, trying to determine how much of what he said was true. He stared back for a moment and then began to admire the detail of the hallways. All the windows were lined with gold around the sill and panes.

"Is the news serious?" he asked.

"It's best we discuss in private, if that's what you mean by your question," she said.

He nodded and they started walking again. They rounded a bend in the hallway. Hughgar nodded to the guardsmen that they should give them privacy. They walked tentatively through the hallway, making sure no one was around and quickly past the guardsmen rooms in silence.

Hughgar motioned for her to come with him toward the inner chambers, where the king's advisors were likely waiting for Valessa to make her morning appearance. They walked silently together for a moment, before he knew Valessa couldn't help herself but to say something.

When he felt they were out of ear shot of any of the palace staff, he turned and asked, "So, what is this secret news that I should have heard?"

"If you had been reading my daily briefings, you would know," she quipped. "The king-in-waiting of Akre, and acting sovereign of Normany, is presumed dead in a fiery accident, killed by a dragon!"

"I'm supposed to be moved to tears?" Hughgar played with the rings on his fingers, nonchalantly, with little interest for whatever happened outside of his borders.

"That's your reaction."

"Presumed dead. Besides, we ride dragons here in Valgaard like the--

"Norlander king of the southern isle, yes. I've heard you talk of him, since I've had ears. As far as I'm concerned that's a distant fairy tale."

"It wasn't that long ago," Hughgar said defensively, considering he was named after the foreign king, "Am I to assume that you believe he is dead, dead?"

"Yes. As dead as dead. No coming back. Dead! One does not just somehow survive!"

They neared the inner door that would open to the meeting chamber where the advisors waited. Hughgar stopped, turning to look at his daughter, confident that she would be able to handle the evolving landscape, and absolutely certain that she was fretting for fretting's sake. She worried enough for the two of them, but he wanted to choose his words more carefully.

"I just want to remind you that we can handle ourselves."

"Erolin was more important to the real-life version of Valgaard than the fairy tale in your mind."

"Once again, he didn't do a very good job of whatever he was doing anyway."

"He was one of our chief allies."

"Was, or could have been?"

"He had agreed."

"Pending a formal announcement, he couldn't make."

"I said, he had agreed. He meant to secede Normany from the empire."

"I'm not sure I believe it. He could have been using your allegiance as a bargaining chip elsewhere. He wasn't a Normen, in my opinion. And, we have other options too."

"Our options are running thin. My plan was simple if I could get Erolin and Normany, the whole of the north, not just us, would be secure."

"As always, the plans you have been hatching my daughter will come to fruition. Perhaps, not in the way that you expect. I give you free rein to reign over my kingdom, and you act like it's a queendom." She winced, even though she had already heard him use that word. Perhaps, Hughgar thought to himself, he was sticking his foot deeper in the dragon poop here. He waited for her to speak.

"Father, the armies in Akrin will not sit idle for long. They will attack if we don't do something about it."

"Let them come. See if I care. I defeated them once. I will defeat them again."

"Are you being obstinate or stupid? Look around. It is just me here. You don't have to put on an act. I know as well as you do, that you are, or maybe were, a powerful man, but the terms of war have changed. When you fought, you fielded a force of eighty thousand men. Respectable, I'll admit, but we have plans to have a standing army of eight hundred thousand conscripted by 1522, and it still won't be enough. Ispiarda just attacked the Imerian coast with a fleet commanded by one hundred thousand men. Akre commands the largest empire, and they do want to strike back at us. They've professionalized their mages and spread them throughout their divisions. No doubt to counteract talented mages like you.'

'Have we made the same modifications? No. Despite my attempts to reopen and fund all of the old academies, as well as to establish new ones, there is still general resistance to magic, innate to many of our people, for events that happened centuries ago. And what do you think that means?"

Hughgar once again kept quiet, waiting for her to tell him, as he was accustomed to his daughter explaining everything to him, and he was well aware that he did not think as deeply on matters such as this as her. This was exactly why he let her run the show behind the banners.

"It means we are losing the arms race, father. Mage schools are not, by the leading philosophers of our nation now, 'corporate greed machines' or even as others in the newspapers, which I do read, call, 'my personal agenda for placating the masses.' They are tools to protect us in the ever-changing landscape of world economics and power. If we don't keep up, the enemy will do it for us, and the kingdom you built through sheer force of will, will be broken the same way, in a lightning-fast war, where we roll over and die."

"I will personally open the academies in the northeast that you so long to open, my darling daughter, but focus on the positives. We have had a lovely summer here for another year in a row. It appears our atmospheric mages, scientists as you sometimes prefer to call them, are right, the risk of the glaciers covering the mountains or affecting the coastlines is minimal. We are living at the peak of a mostly partial ice age. You have a kingdom to sweat over, and that should be appreciated."

"Don't mock me."

"I do not. I did not hear about Erolin, and I did not know that he was a chief target among the many allegiances you have tried to and are likely still attempting to create. As I've said, your plans are in motion. Be patient. Don't forget that these are not games that you play, and that the people of the nation, however few or many there are, are the key to everything, which is why I like to take open court."

He opened the door to where a cluster of advisors were waiting, no doubt aware from the muffled sound of their voices through the thick wood that the king and his daughter were arguing in the hallway. Her passion could worry some, but her temper catered fear, tempted silence, and courted fealty.

Hughgar nodded politely to the many members of the 'inner chamber' before he ushered her ahead of him. Valessa stepped inside.

The king slammed the door shut, quickly. Then, as quickly as he had thrown the door against the stone with the flick of his finger, he spun and at a brisk pace walked back the way he had come, through the white-stone hallway to the safety of the public eye, where he could avoid his daughter's attempts to interest him in her affairs, and he could instead take in the less global yet equally intricate, daily concerns of his people where murder and theft did not alter urban engineering plans or the number of highways built in a given month, usually.

The palace was split into two halves. There was a north wing in the almost directly east-facing, white-stone palace. This is where the princess resided, once with her much older brother, who had passed away a number of years before. On the south side, the king and queen lived.

Valessa had dedicated an inner room to "inner chamber" meetings, as well as claimed one of the two 'inner sanctums' for matters of national attention. Her father had turned the other sanctum into a trophy chest for his collection of legendary weapons of kings long dead.

The "inner chamber" room was a simple concept, where there was a small podium at the front and a series of concentric semi-circles rising to the wall at the rear of the room. Each of these had its own table wrapping around most of the room, except for a central walkway and two walkways along the sides. The king's hired staff had a designated space at one of the tables, where Valessa had begun to meet with them instead, when her father had hired her as the chief advisor to the throne.

Behind the podium, she couldn't escape her father's decorations of the Valgaardian flag. From the ceiling two of his green and gold banners hung, but for the most part the golden detailing for fixtures and extra bits of metal was saved for more public facing places.

Her podium was much more modest in comparison to his golden throne. It was simple, polished elm, as the southern part of their nation resided along the great Lake of the Elms.

As usual, he leaves me to run things, Valessa thought to herself as she looked at the gathered aides and advisors, waiting to speak to the princess about the events of the day before. After years ago, the allegiance with Cardane had fallen through, and Cardane had recommitted to their status as subservient to the Akrin Empire, Valgaard had long been looking for a new alliance to stave off the threat of invasion from Akre. The contact with Erolin had taken years, and he had agreed to be on his way to Peth, the capital of Valgaard, after spending some of the Frostmas holiday season in Seylil.

Valessa stood up in front of the room to begin the discussion of the day on the most significant topic, "We received a report that Erolin Ardrada has passed away in a dragon attack on his way to Seylil. This, to state the obvious, likely ends the possibility of alliance with Normany and unfortunately Albion unless we can find new angles. Any ideas are welcome."

"Is there any other way we can get Lord Stone to bite on an allegiance?"

"Erolin was the key in that regard."

"It will be difficult to reach him anyway. Now that we've lost our point of contact."

"It would seem the obvious choice to try to find a new way to reach Lord Stone. I'll think of something," said Valessa. "Just our two nations aren't going to be enough."

"The Fire Islands would never commit forces."

"The Kingdoms of Yin?"

"It seems they are perpetually at war internally, and they would likely never close off trade to the East Cardane."

"That likely leaves out Roon Kalada too."

"Why?"

"It would be almost impossible to reach them through Central Ahria. That territory is still covered in giant monsters and the wrecks of Domiscus."

"Right, we'd have to sail into East Cardane controlled ocean territory."

"We can't risk that right now."

"We would need the Coltari fully on board."

"Right, which leads us back to Albion and Lord Stone."

"I agree, they will follow suit with what Albion does."

"For the sake of Roon Kalada?"

"They have more people."

"They are also trade partners with East Cardane already."

"Historically, yes, but I have been able to confirm that there has been a split and there is a civil war."

"When were you going to share this information?"

"It didn't seem relevant to previous discussions."

"Anything and everything could be relevant."

Valessa blamed herself for the fallout with Cardane almost ten years before, and now, it was making allegiances across the globe difficult. The Great Southern Island didn't have a large enough population, but she was trying to reach the dragon riders. Olympus was largely low contact due to language barriers and their tendency to distrust foreigners, still millennia after repelling the Otum Elves. They were also hard to reach, because of the Land of the Fae.

"If we can't get Lord Stone on board directly, what are the other options?"

"Have we had any luck contacting the States of Imeria?"

"No," said Valessa, disappointed.

"Even if we did, I don't think there is any way they break off from the Akrin Empire for us. Akre has promised them almost anything they could want and just defended them from the Ispiardan invasion."

"That means we only have Menetoris--"

"Who won't speak with us due to their position of neutrality in global affairs and distrusts Albion."

"--and to support the right to rule of Sven in Normany."

"If he even claims the throne. He wouldn't have a higher direct claim than the Princess Aurelia, who we know is back in Akre."

"I am still working on Menetoris," said Valessa. "It was always our best option. And for that reason, Aurelia. Even if Sven claims the throne, he could be attacked by Akre in response. It's best to wait on that and react rather than be too proactive. In summary, we are still focusing on Albion, but need a new way to contact Lord Stone and find some way that he might be interested in joining into an alliance. Any other comments before we break session?"

There were none.

"We will go over the logistics of the school openings that my father has promised at a future session. You are dismissed if you could please give me the room."

She thought more about it to herself as her father's advisors and aides departed. She had been working to install spies within different kingdoms, and through this had hoped that she had found a route to connecting Menetoris to the outside world. They were the largest of the island kingdoms and also the nearest collection of islands in the Argal Ocean to the coast of Albion and therefore the inland nations, organized under the rule of Valgaard.

If Sven, who was possibly a pretender, could solidify control of Normany through his influence in its most populous provinces, those of the Solgra, then he would need allies. He would connect with her, then from that, she could convince Lord Stone, and then with Lord Stone would come the Coltari, who could likely bring Menetoris into the fold later.

However, it seemed she would instead have to work backward and find a way to connect with Menetoris first. Then, from there leverage that for an audience with Albion, who had no other reason to speak with her, except for the Coltari network, who was based in Albion and had been shrinking for decades as the East Cardane grew in power. If she had Albion and Menetoris on her side, she wouldn't need Normany. At least not yet.

She was frustrated beyond belief, even if there was just a slim glimmer of hope. It was complicated. She felt like she was juggling it all by herself. And she was relying on her influence being extended by spies to foreign nations when ambassadors had failed.

Meanwhile, she internally had to make nice with all of the separate nations of Valgaard by hosting their ambassadors regularly, their many appointed courtiers constantly, and organize regular state dinners to force local lords to visit Peth, which were becoming poorly attended affairs.

Some good news was that the mage academies might open. The country would hopefully be able to surpass Imeria in mage strength, quickly, if that were the case. They had a fraught history with mages as internally they didn't agree on the sanctity of God's gift of magic within different sects of the same religion. They, like Valgaard, had at one point, had witch hunts.

All of the aides and advisors had left, except for her main confidantes. Eleanor and Onya. They had, both in separate ways, helped to establish a spy network that Valessa had gradually gained firm, singular control over, no longer needing their help.

"Ladies, you have stood by me through everything these last eight years or so. I just wanted to let you know how much I appreciate it as war draws closer."

"Thank you, my lady," said Onya.

"We are a sisterhood, my lady," said Eleanor.

"I'd like to speak to the two of you alone, in my inner sanctum," said Valessa, taking them into where she regularly swept for clockwork bugs and they had spent many a conversation or day together, learning about geopolitics.

"It's tragic what happened to Erolin," said Eleanor.

"Yes, very tragic," said Valessa. Valessa unlocked the inner sanctum door and opened it.

"What do we do now?" asked Onya.

The two ladies stepped inside, and Valessa closed the door behind them, locking it.

"Do you have more of a plan than what you said in front of the chamber?" asked Onya, relaxing on one of the two green chairs that had been brought into the room and placed up against the wall looking at Valessa's long table, a map of part of the world. "Is there any way that I--or we--can help?"

She didn't answer Onya right away. She first swept the room for bugs again. She was more paranoid than ever. When a foreign official you are attempting to work with suddenly dies in a freak dragon attack accident, you begin to question loyalties, she thought to herself.

There were no bugs, so Valessa put down the little zapping device, and turned around to where Eleanor stood beside the table and Onya reclined in the chair.

"Eleanor," said Valessa, pausing and waiting until her once most trusted confidante turned to look at her, "Who did you tell that Erolin was meeting with Lord Stone on our behalf?"

"No one."

"How do you explain his death then? How did someone find that out?"

"I can't explain," said Eleanor, "Onya?"

"Onya couldn't have known, because I hadn't spoken to her about it."

"What are you saying?"

"You were the only one I told. I trusted you." Valessa studied Eleanor's eyes. Eleanor charged an energy spike below the table, just where Onya couldn't see it from behind her, and where Valessa couldn't see it from in front of her.

Valessa advanced closer. She knew that Eleanor was the enemy spy, but she didn't know what Eleanor would do. Eleanor had seen Valessa's power in action. There was a reason why they called her the Ice Queen, and she didn't play nice. There had been a few dead bodies over the years of the traitors to the nation.

Valessa walked in closer, "Who did you tell Eleanor?" Onya perked up in her seat.

"Long live the emperor!" yelled Eleanor, as she swung her body around.

Valessa froze Eleanor's throat in place. The woman clutched at it, as her body fought for air, drowning and choking at the same time from the loss of ability to fully use her neck. She collapsed to the floor, unable to hold up her head as she convulsed on the ground.

The spear spell, a spike of ethereal particles, was the most important spell in a mage's arsenal because it could almost always be cast and was lethal with the right amount of force. But, one couldn't cast it if their brain had been disconnected from the rest of their body.

"Well, that was quick," said Valessa, looking down at the body, without the slightest bit of remorse, and then up at Onya, who for the moment, held her tongue. "He hasn't even been confirmed yet. It's a pity that I gave her the wrong dates, but they must have figured it out from multiple sources."

"Who hasn't?" asked Onya, confused but having clearly seen Eleanor try to kill Valessa, she was processing as quickly as she could.

"Polesar. The former southern army general. A talented mage, who rose the ranks quickly. I believe that he is about to be made the emperor, and it seems Eleanor, here, has confirmed that."

"You suspected her?" asked Onya, thinking about what Valessa had said about wrong dates. She couldn't help but think about whether she was being fed false information, or if it was just Eleanor. "For how long?"

Valessa didn't answer.

"Do you suspect me?"

Valessa definitely didn't plan to answer that in a complete truth. Onya stood up from the chair and took a step toward the table that stood in the center of the room. She would have paced, but instead she recentered herself and glanced at Valessa.

"Onya, I trust you, and because of that, I have a mission for you. Dangerous may be a bit of an overstatement, but I want to make sure it's something you want to do. In case I need to find someone else."

"What is it?" Onya stood up straight and looked squarely at the princess.

"If you accept, you must not fail me, because Valgaard's future is at stake."

Onya simply nodded.

"Not only is time of the essence, but there likely won't be another opportunity should you fail."

"What is the mission?" Onya repeated.

"I need you to go to Rorik in Albion. I have already mocked up work papers for you to take a job on Lord Stone's staff and find some way--I don't care how--to convince Lord Stone to join us in an alliance. If I can convince him, perhaps I can get the Menetorian islands on board as well, or possibly through you we can communicate to him about Menetoris being on board. With that alliance, we could buy ourselves more time, and hopefully figure out an alternative option for Normany if that doesn't come through."

Onya thought through it for a moment, "yes, my lady."

"So, you accept?"

"I've heard the Ash Vale is nice this time of year. Very pretty, with the leaves changing colors over a longer period of time."

"Wonderful. Will you let me know once you get there if that's true with your first report?"

"Certainly. How will I communicate back to Valgaard? Do we have any contacts through the telegram?"

"No, on second thought, any communication to me must be strictly of only the most urgent matters. It cannot be sent by telegram as these could be read in transit. Any letter will have to be coded."

"How will I deliver it back? There aren't any direct mail services between our nations."

"Correct, but there is still some trade that we promote through smugglers from Albion. Any merchant that is smuggling through the northern pass near Imor Valsen with a small army, or one that is running over the mountains with airship. Otherwise, I'll have to remain in the dark."

"So, I have to figure this out on my own once I am in Albion?" asked Onya.

"For the most part, yes," answered Valessa and tried to hide a glance at the dead body, still at their feet, "I have the utmost faith in you."

Onya could see that Valessa was thinking of the implications of her lost faith in Eleanor, but she would soon be far enough from the palace to no longer worry about Valessa's temper, "yes, thank you my lady. If I may ask, what have you heard about Lord Stone, that may help me?"

"He's a loner, very secretive. Once widowed, over ten years ago. He's in his mid-forties. He has one son and hasn't had any relationships since. Appears to have some sort of substance abuse problem, according to what recent intelligence we could gather-- though we haven't been able to get anyone too close to him, and we've been informed that he's taken the loss of Erolin especially hard, though the general public still believes that it was an accident."

Onya nodded, "Thank you."

When Onya didn't request to depart, Valessa, now looking over the central table, her map board, asked, "Was there something else that you wanted to mention?"

"Yes, when you were speaking in the other room, you mentioned Sven, but what about Erolin's son? What is, or was his name? Is it true that he has disappeared?"

"Erold. He wasn't a public figure yet, but yes, he hasn't been seen in Seylil for some time. Erolin had some kind of antiquated concern about his son's identity. One of those superstitions, I suspect, about people knowing one's secret, or sacred, name."

"Erold's a common enough name though like Abrim or Ivan,"

said Onya.

"Yes, that's what happens when it's an old king's name."

"Do you know what he was like, or wait, do you think he might have been on the ship that crashed too?"

"My suspicion is that yes, he was on the ship with his father, and that was the original reason that Erolin had gone to the Ash Vale. His meeting with Lord Stone was by chance as he had recently reached out to us after years of trying to connect."

"I hope the boy wasn't on the ship for his sake."

"Yes, I agree, though not even my network of spies would be able to confirm that for me. Erolin was tight lipped about Erold, so I'm sure few people knew much about his whereabouts besides those closest to the un-ascended king."

"It's just terrible if he was," Onya looked at the princess and wondered if she could just take a moment to look at the humanity of the boy, rather than think of the political positioning or the probability he was on the ship.

As if Valessa read her mind, she paused and said, "Yes, terrible." She trailed off and then switched back to her calculating self, "but fortunately, for our purposes, I think he was more of an after-thought at this point in the grand scheme of things. By law, he may have even been superseded to the throne by his uncle, given his age, and if Akre could reach Erolin, Erold was just as much at risk. We are in desperate need of something that can permanently stave off an attack."

"Hence, why I am going to Lord Stone for help."

"Ultimately, he may be our best and only hope, but even with his help, in the long run, it may not make a difference. I'm sure that's weighing on his mind as well."

"I'll get to work. I've been in the field before, and I've been training for the moment that you would put me back on an active mission."

"Onya, do be careful. One of the reasons I'm sending you is that you're the best. The other is that the last intelligence officer stationed near Stone has disappeared."

1513 - Chapter 5

Polesar rode in a horse-drawn carriage from the river docks where his ship had come in--on the bank opposite to the shipping district that extended along the east side of the Evorul to the Pides districts--toward the man-made hill near the modern center of the city: 'Lion's Den Hill.'

As the carriage rode smoothly along on modern roads, he looked out of the windows at the city. To the left was the "old city"--now just one district of many--running along the far south and nearby north banks of the Atlan River, which snaked through the city before meeting the Evorul in a confluence to the south of the sprawling metropolis of stone, brick, and wood.

To the north and right of the carriage's ride from the docks and through victory square were the modern parks built over the last century and a few other monuments installed at the centers of other new squares that connected roads, extending from the old city through the central districts, up to the district of Kingston, where, for example, the enormous Brandon Gates were built at the center of a spindle of roads to the west of what was once the new Chelsea Palace.

The elite of the nation used to live on the sloping small, grassy hill, Everett's Hill, north of the palace, looking down on it and the city in the far distance, separated from the palace and city by the small White River from the north that cut through the countryside after being fed through the natural dam at the southern tip of the great Lake of the Elms, which bordered most of south Valgaard.

The north borough of Kingston had been built in anticipation of future growth by Karles III while his father was giving him more authority ahead of him officially taking over the kingdom in the 1490s. When the Visgollan invasion sacked the city, they had forced most of the poor that had moved into shacks north of the city to move instead to the south end, had burned and pillaged the houses of the rich, and set the Chelsea Palace building, once considered the newest of the marvels of the world, on fire to its foundations. Out of all of the buildings erected in what was supposed to one day be a walled-off 'central city' for the elite, only the Lucherene cathedral had remained intact.

Kingston was just beginning to fill with new low to the ground developments built by merchants and the nation's new, growing 'middle-class,' but the inner city had been gradually converted into mainly modern parks as the Lucherene and Chelsea Palace gardens were gradually connected. Everett's Hill remained empty rather than have new buildings built.

Conversely, Lion's Den Hill, where the carriage entered a large city circle by taking a right to follow a curved road leading between the buildings, had gone from three buildings to six as the three giant monuments to Akrin power were mirrored on the other side of the hill by three identical buildings. The centerpieces of these were the two largest of the six marble buildings, each with large central columns at their twin entrances that were thirty atomic yards high and four people wide.

The hill had gotten its name, because one of these two main buildings was the high mage's court, where Polesar had once dreamed of hearing his name called as a future member of Akrin's high mage court of Chief Justicars. The other large building, opposite of that, on the west and facing east, was the new senate building. The high court and senate had once shared the same stone roof, and as these two authorities were affectionately termed the lions of Akre, their hill was therefore their 'den.'

As the carriage stopped in the center of the circle, Polesar stepped out. Directly to his south, he saw the old Abrim Plaza with the city's first, ancient cathedral, Saint Drosef's. Across the river was the old castle and its five fantastic turrets made of gray and white stone, decorated with brass and topped with cerulean conical peaks. It stood silent now, having once protected the river from invading ships.

Beyond the castle to the south one could see the new airship docks with hundreds of bronze and iron-colored merchant ships with white and gray of various other metals such as the once rare compound, steel, loading goods to take to surrounding towns from the train depot.

There were two train tracks running through the city. One was a quiet, envisioned passenger track or connection to the north that ran from west of the Brandon Gates in Kingston to the south village station in the district known as West Bluffs. It would help create more traffic between where people lived and where new buildings of commerce were being constructed out of the necessity of space. It was hypothetically set to run faster than carriages and on less Orichalc than airships, which still saved time and therefore money on trips to the surrounding towns.

Its only issue was safety, as braking and communication issues had shown to result in the telescoping of passenger cars by oncoming iron engines. Thankfully no one had died in testing, but testing was limited by the calculated possibility of explosions of overheating steam engines due to weight strain.

The other track, running along the east side of the city, connected the airdocks to the sea docks across the Atlan River, to Polesar's left. A planned expansion of the passenger line was meant to meet the south goods line south of the city, but sufficient iron had yet to be put towards a dormant line. At the depot south of the city, the steam train lines of Akre could connect as far as Newkassel in the south, to Ithlin in the east and even to much of the Solgra to the west.

Tracks were being laid in each direction with a mind to connect all of the Solgra and Ithlin to each other and to Akre as well as to extend the Newkassel line all the way through Ingra along the southwest coast of the empire's core. These lines would eventually go to Trungla, Verdas, Altonia, and Elessia, before extending to other parts of the empire like Albion on the far west coast or possibly through to even further east.

Technology naysayers, who had said more complex flight would never be possible and had laughed at the telegram--despite being some of the pioneers of their own generation in things like magical engineering--were saying the same thing about the steam trains. They would crash and burn like the telescoped cars in Akre, but Polesar had a vision of transporting soldiers from one end of the empire to the other in the hundreds of thousands.

Polesar looked up and around at his immediate vicinity, flanked by an escort of his armed men. The six government buildings, including the city's library were built of pure marble to recall the ancient capitals of man that once stood in Elessia before the wars with the Otum. The circle under his feet was a large lake of various colors of white-stone in small bricks that created the appearance of rippling waves between the tall buildings.

As he walked toward the Senate building, he stared up in awe, as he always did, at the enormity of the columns. There were nine columns, one for each of the core nations of the Akrin Empire. He passed between them and into the building through the large, oak doors.

As he entered, he was met with the red and gold banners and carpets, the colors of the old Akrin legions. These legions were established following the unification of the east and west of Old Galdir as an era of expansionism hit.

In some places, there were hints of the ancient dark blue, recalling the precursor nation whose reunification had spurred on the wars that had birthed the Akrin Empire. Alongside many of these banners were trophies and memorabilia from these unification wars, which had spanned across much of Akre's history between the early 1100s and late 1300s.

Polesar had switched the Akrin Empire's uniforms to dark blue, partially in homage to Old Galdir, but also to make them more visible to friendly units on the battlefield as black powder clouds made it increasingly impossible to see. Blue was also a cheaper fabric dye than red.

As he neared the large, central door between two armed guardsmen, the last and most important of these relics stood in a prominent display just before them. It was the Kalsvebir sword that gleamed in the light. The red blade mimicked fire as the white shine of the Orichalc lamps traveled up the surface like a tongue of flame trapped in a cage of metal. Only half the blade and the hilt were visible.

This legend of Old Galdir, a ceremonial sword, used to be delivered annually by the king to this simple stone, where it was placed now, once a year to commemorate the resistance of Akre against the clockwork hordes of Domiscus. During the great era of peace, the ceremony became known as the 'Closing of the Gates of Evorul' and was meant to signify that the country had set aside its warlike ambitions. The ancient kings had once taken the same red sword with them during times of war.

It had not left the stone for ceremony or otherwise in almost twenty years. Despite the wars that had engulfed many of the corners of the Arkin Empire, the blade had remained in its ceremonial stone sheath. Polesar had been dreaming of the day that he as once the southern and recently the western general could convince the senate to allow him to pull it from its prison and lead the legions against Valgaard in the north delivering vengeance for the sacking of Akre and death of the king's son, who would have replaced King Karles III on the throne.

Polesar entered into a hallway adjacent to the large senate room, alone. His men waited in the long entrance behind him. He then turned left through smaller oak doors into the senate's large meeting hall.

He found himself at the floor of the senate hall, looking up at the senators, bathed in Orichalc light. Rows of dark, polished oak benches, without desks or other adornment, ran up to the ceiling in semi-circles viewing a central, marble wall fixture where the flag of Akre in its bright red with the golden eagle hung at the center, flanked by two golden eagle busts, staring at each other from separate placements in the stone.

This marble fixture acted as a centerpiece in the room of mainly oak. Ahead of it was a series of three benches with marble desks where speakers would sit and address the assembly. Polesar was introduced by the speaker at the middle platform of these three benches, which at the center had a podium overlooking the rest of the delegation.

Polesar nodded and then waited as the senate discussed the recent tragedy of the Vagalla. They had not confirmed whether the king-regent of Normany had been on the ship for certain, but his disappearance from Seylil was believed to be linked. There were search parties being sent to the crash site now that were also looking for civilian survivors.

Erolin's son had also disappeared. He had not been seen in Seylil for at least two years, and he had not resurfaced following the crash. They would continue to search for the son, but Erolin was the only one who could ascend to the throne directly under the by-laws of the constitutional document, the Storr Ríta, extended for the Akrin Empire after being used for founding documents of Normany and later all of Galdir under the central authority of Akre.

A direct male heir needed to be at least twenty years of age to claim the throne. A direct female heir needed to be appointed prior to the death of the king and not be superseded by any male heir. Otherwise, the senate ruled directly over the land. Just as they did historically in times of war. Under the strict terms of the law, Erolin's son would not have been able to attempt to take direct control of Normany as his father once had.

There was certainly a risk that the boy could rally populist support like Erolin's cousin, Sven--who would be foolish to attempt to claim rule with Princess Aurelia still alive--but due largely to his father's stubborn refusal to live in Akre, the boy was a complete unknown outside of Seylil.

The boy therefore did not threaten the senate's plan to go through with formally absolving Normany's independence under a constitutional amendment to confirm that all matters of 'state' control be decided by the senate in accordance with the traditions of the Akrin Empire rather than by hereditary line as they had been exempted for in Normany, especially.

While other nation states that fell under Akre's various constitutional documents had also been exempted for, in the case of Albion and Ingra, Normany had special veto rights on policies to be implemented in Normany and through the same hereditary link held certain historical authorities over portions of Galdir and Akre itself.

What went unsaid was that the senate had combatted Erolin on these matters for most of the last twenty years while slowly wrestling any legacy control within the core territories from major landowners or landowner groups who had conditionally joined as 'vassal' or 'allied' territories under Akre while maintaining general, local rule--to avoid or join in various wars. Some referred to them as states or reserved regions. The senate considered them Akrin first whether they were on the east coast, west coast, or in between. Where they couldn't absolve these via the wave of a pen, they just ignored their existence and historical alignment on any key matter, referring to conquered nations as wholly enemies rather than partial allies.

This special assembly was called to vote expressly on one such matter of great importance. It was the matter of officially electing an emperor for military rule. In the case that the king, though he didn't refer to himself as such because he had never been coronated, was confirmed to be dead, they would announce it formally to the public as the senate's formal response, positioning the death of Erolin as an accident that they would not appear weak or leaderless in the wake of.

Polesar found it a little strange that the senators appeared unequivocally happy in the wake of Erolin's death. He kept hearing them speak of a fortunate result of the tragedy. They appeared not to concern themselves with the fact that up to one thousand people might have died in the crash.

It was then that they called the western army general, Polesar Rolard, to the podium in the place of the lead speaker. The proud man with his long, straight nose, hazel, almost-yellow eyes and graying, brown hair walked to the front of the room and looked out across the senators from their various districts, mainly east of the Atlan River, and key advisors, whom he recognized and would speak to after, Tanneran and Alger.

They admired his formal military attire. The navy-blue tailcoat with red and yellow bars across the full front of his chest. His white pants and large blue and white hat that hid most of his hair. On his left chest were pinned a number of golden and silver commendations and other various medallions, representing his high military honors earned through successive successful campaigns.

"Polesar Rolard, General of the First Rank. We, as the high senate, authority of the land, once intended, years ago in the 1490s, to vote you as an archmage to the high court of Akre at the suggestion of many of the senators here, that came to admire you for your early reforms within the army. We are glad, in the end, that this didn't come to pass, as we all have come to admire you over the course of your illustrious military career in defense of the Akrin Empire's borders.'

'We are glad that instead you have further advanced the additional posting of Western Army general after your recent appointment and have performed exemplarily in your additional reforms of the legions into corps. The successful defense of the Imerian coast against Ispiarda is a great example. You completely routed the enemy with almost no casualties, once again proving your merit as a leader. We now wish to vote you emperor!"

Everyone cheered. There was a series of additional formal announcements of how the votes were to be cast. Everyone voted in favor of Polesar being elected the emperor. He bowed upon hearing the unanimous result.

"Long live the emperor!" they cheered, drowning the sound of his voice.

"Thank you, thank you" he said, continuing to bow. He held up his hands to quiet them, and they rose up to cheer again even louder.

Slowly, they stopped the chanting.

"I'll keep my speech short, and God willing I will succeed in the efforts for which you have appointed me. Thank you for the command of the Akrin South and West Armies. I will guarantee that the West Army will now be in the capable hands of my second-in-command, Danta, who will take over the task of subduing the elven rebellions across both the northern and southern Westernlands. We have already transported an additional portion of the forward army across the coast southwest of Imeria, and we intend to push back tenfold against the raids that have continued to occur against the peaceful settlements there. These settlements moved into lands that were unoccupied, and after years of peace, many of the elven kingdoms in the heart of the Westernlands have grown violent and the nature of their crimes against the settlers is indescribably brutal. We will crush this barbarity. Furthermore--"

They cheered too loudly for him to speak over their combined voices. He raised his hands to quiet them once more, smiling as he looked from face to face.

"Furthermore, on all fronts we will advance the safety of our merchants and nation. We will support the development of the navy in the west, and we will continue to build and professionalize the military. We will support the development of modern technologies and increase the funding for more advanced schools. We are set to being graduating more than one hundred mages a year from our academies this spring. That number will continue to grow."

They cheered. He smiled and repeated his gestures.

"A good portion of which--"

They cheered still louder. He waited calmly. His hands held in the air as if he were an orchestra conductor.

"A good portion of will be distributed throughout the military to bolster our divisions, making them the finest fighting force in the modern world."

Some cheered vehemently at this, but most remained subdued, waiting for the next pause.

"Underlying this effort, as many of you know, is a cause near and dear to all of our hearts. It is my goal to once again, unite the borders of the Akrin Empire across their historical length, returning the empire to its recent glory, that was so hatefully taken by evil forces in the north."

Some booed and hissed, throwing hand gestures in the air at the mere mention of the northern nation. Others began to tense and cheer in excitement for what Polesar might say next. He held the pause with just his right hand raised as if swearing an oath of high allegiance.

"It is my pleasure first to announce that the princess Aurelia, who thankfully escaped the unfortunate events surrounding the attack of the Visgol hordes from the north--"

More excitement, more boos.

"--and I are officially to be married. She shares my singular vision to subdue the world of the Normen menace, and to retake the territories of Valgaard!"

The cheering at this point, with the layout of the room, sounded more like a stampede combined with the yells of one thousand men rather than the over three hundred that stood, jumped, stamped, and yelled madly around him.

After a few more statements by Polesar and the gathered

senators, he left the stage and returned the small hallway adjacent to the floor. The meeting continued, but he was not surprised to be greeted in the hallway by the senior advisors Tanneran and Alger.

Slightly surprising was that the Senators Hammel II and Karlson had followed him out, missing the follow up and closing comments within the senate chambers.

Tanneran was a long-term 'senator' appointed rather than elected by special consul among senate committees. He was often referred to as the "Duke of Dawson" as he was originally a commoner from the small city in Ithlin. He had been with the senate since even before 1495, while Alger was another such appointed official, who was attached to the high court of the mages as an archmage representative from among them to the senate.

"Senators, to what do I owe the pleasure?" asked Polesar, after they had re-introduced themselves.

"We both wanted to just say, that we were affected personally by the events surrounding the invasion by Valgaard, and we are excited that you will soon be doling out justice."

"Yes, both of our fathers died during that time, and the suspects were mainly Valgaard--"

"--despite the assurances of the chief inspector among the detectives at the Pound at the time if I might add. We disagreed with her strongly based on the circumstances."

"It may take some time for us to build up the military to sufficient strength," said Polesar, worried he might have over-promised.

"Yes, as the emperor says, we would appreciate your support on any military matters brought to the floor," said Tanneran.

"I speak for both of us when I say that you have our support," said Karlson.

"Yes, unequivocally. I don't care what 'evidence' is, my father's soul cannot rest until he is avenged," said Hammel.

Polesar nodded in complete agreement, assuming that he only meant that there was evidence in support of the murder being at Valgaard's hand as well as not, though the senator did not state that specifically.

"If you could now excuse us, senators," said Alger, "we have other matters to direct to the emperor on behalf of the high court and senate." He nodded to Tanneran when referencing the senate and the two senators took their leave and returned to the grand hall with bows.

"Wonderful job promoting Danta," said Tanneran.

"He deserves it," said Polesar, not having spoken about it with anyone directly even Danta before his own announcement had been confirmed. They had fought together for years, and Danta had always been at his side, even when he was a young general in the army before ever having gotten the attention of the senate for the appointment of archmage.

"And wonderful news about your plans to marry the astonishing, the beautiful, the Princess Aurelia of Akre!" said Alger, raising his hand in the air and dancing as if he was a bard.

"Yes, I agree. Very smart tactical move," said the older Tanneran, who frowned at the black-haired, Alger.

Polesar almost blushed. He had, in reality, fallen madly for her ever since he had met her the second time. He had met her once, following his success in driving back the Visgol hordes from the city gates. They had been far too young then. Only sixteen or less than that. He couldn't remember exactly, but shortly after, he had been wedded to a commoner.

It became an unfortunate first marriage when he had met Aurelia again, years later when on an assignment in Elessia, where she had been spending her days, listlessly. There had been an instant connection between the two, and despite her fair features, she was taken in with his sharp, yellowish eyes. For the first time, making him feel a beauty in them.

"Any word on the developments of the crash?" asked Polesar. "Is it certain that the king is suspected to have been on the ship?"

"Yes," said Tanneran.

"And what about the boy?"

"Are you concerned for his sake?" asked Tanneran.

Polesar shook his head, but he wasn't sure whether lies had become truths or truths lies. He had courted power too long to let a boy stand in his way of ascension.

"There's been no word on the boy as they said inside for two years or more," Tanneran began.

"We hadn't heard that he was a particularly bright boy," Alger added.

Tanneran nodded in agreement, "hopefully, with his father's death, poverty or fear will help to eliminate him from our list of concerns."

"So, if it has been confirmed, what is the status of this crash?" asked Polesar.

"Survivors, if there will be any, are being round up in secret to confirm whether the king is dead. It was stated by staff at Seylil that they were expecting the king for pre-Frostmas planning today. We believe that we've already come into contact with a witness who states that some escape vessels that departed from the ship were not eaten by flames," said Alger.

"And onto other business. What about the houses of Akre? Will they be behind the new emperor?"

"There seems to be no trouble from the Marcinis or the Roths, both prominent in banking. Though the Roths have officially finished a move to Albion, they are helping to finance trains in the Solgra. The Vidulcci's mining is behind you, and after finding new gold, are set to double the nation's treasury."

"What about the Everetts? Theodore and his wife, the Coltari heiress? Have they completely abandoned the city?"

"It appears so. They still technically own the land of both Chelsea Palace and Everett's Hill, but we are expecting to put paperwork through to absolve their rights to it. They have collected lease payments long enough."

Polesar nodded in affirmation. The Coltari network was just over half the size of the East Cardane, but they had a similar military might and held the rich western trade routes that also catered to the Westernland colonies. It was suspicious that a married couple of two of the nation's most powerful families, would abandon the capital with their financial power intact.

"You of course, already heard from Karlson, whose family controls many of the local factories."

"Yes, of course, how could I forget," said Polesar, "Anyone else? Any new names in trade? Orichalc? Trains?" Polesar knew that the trades of energy and movement were far more important than most others did. Orichalc powered the trains of the future and the airships of both today and tomorrow, which could get even larger.

"There are a few names that are circling," said Tanneran, who wasn't sure the fledgling industries mattered that much, especially trains.

"Find me whoever rises to the forefront of the trade on that," said Polesar, issuing perhaps his first official command as emperor.

"Yes, sir," said Tanneran.

1513 - Chapter 6

An exhausted Captain Volstad caught up with Erold and Moon, waiting on the side of the road that ran along the southern bank of the Evorul River. He waved when he noticed them, and for a moment, both Erold and Moon sat, transfixed, weary and watching him together as he approached in languid strides. He stepped cautiously among the many rocks and pebbles that dotted the dirt road like someone had scattered them purposefully and smiled at Moon, who looked away.

To Erold, Volstad looked the same as ever. Perhaps too big a smile on his face, but it seemed he was happy to see the two of them. There was nothing out of place, except for his long graying hair that, for once, did not stay tightly back behind his ears. He pulled it away from his eyes a few times as a cold wind rushed through the river valley, cutting between the rocky hills and down toward the plains in the south.

Erold and Moon caught their breath and enjoyed the sunshine of a late summer day. They had collected about twenty or so of the royal guard, who wandered the valley. There was no way of knowing how many had simply left, or how many were contemplating leaving and disbursing among the hills, heading for home or wherever better fortunes might take them.

Moon had made the decision on behalf of Erold to fall in as if they were just another pair of the guard. Erold was about the height of a grown man, and just looked like a young man. The perfect fit for a new face to the guard that no one but the senior personnel who hired him might have met before.

Since the entire guard had been traveling incognito when the ship went down, their civilian clothes made them look just the same as everyone else. In fact, it was impossible to know for certain if the men and women congregating on the riverbank were fully the royal guard. Only Brigham would know for certain, and he had followed the king to the bridge.

No one really knew who Erold was by his father's design, and while it seemed strange at the time, here they were among people who were suddenly little more than strangers. Only Moon and Erold had been in the glider bay when Volstad had hit the release, and only they had known Erold while few others knew that he had even been on the ship bound for Seylil.

Any of the royal guard could walk away, and no one would have known that they had been in the presence of Erold, heir to the thrones of Normany, Old Galdir, and Akre, through ascension by claimed birthright through the family line of old Galdir kings, modern birthright through the dynasty of the unified Normany, and by conquest through the many centuries of war as the kingdom of Akrin.

It was his family and his people that had united Normany, and then Galdir, after building and defending Akre against the many blights that followed the fall of the Otum and the clockwork hordes that came after the blights, and now, by the will of the senate, the legacy of kings would be unwritten or rewritten by the stroke of pen and the decree of the high justicars of the archmages' high court.

Volstad reached the two of them and wiped sweat from his bushy, gray brow, "Good to see the two of you made it. I see there are a few more stragglers like us, spread out along the river there."

"Where are we Abrim, do you know?" Moon asked Volstad, as he studied Erold for how he was feeling.

"We're in the hills north of the Solgra."

"Well, that's obvious. I mean to get anywhere else, where do we go from here?"

"You mean, do I have a plan?"

Moon nodded.

"Do you?"

She shook her head.

"We could link up with Sven in the Solgra," Erold said quietly. "He's always been kind, and he has a lot of supporters. I'm not oblivious to the fact that the senate will be putting the matter of Normany's autonomy to vote."

Volstad nodded, surprised, "Right, Sven would be doing his best to keep the autonomy by advocating with local councils. Sven does have a lot of supporters in the Solgra and across Normany, and he's your--."

Moon cut him off, "Best chance at a paycheck, now." She looked around, making sure the rest of the crew were out of earshot, and then made a face at Volstad to make sure he understood that some topics were off-limits, perhaps permanently.

"Right, that's the plan, then. We contact Sven and link up with him in the Solgra."

"Where do we go from here to get there?"

"I think whatever we do we have to contact Sven. The closest telegram office is probably in Umfell almost due east, following the river to the southeast and cutting north across the bridge before reaching the Erstber, but on second thought, I'd rather keep our distance from Akre for now."

"I think we both would as well," said Moon, looking at Erold who rested on a rock, letting the sun cover his closed eyes.

Erold spoke, "We're in Dalvalles. Sven is in the Solgra. The Solgra is close to Akre. Though, there are a lot of towns on the plains, I think we could avoid going by Umfell on the way. That plan seems good. I've never seen much of the countryside. I would like to."

"So, stick to the hills, but move south through the hills, keeping a distance from Akre?"

Erold nodded. Moon sighed.

"Okay," said Volstad.

Moon held in another sigh and took a long blink. The river was on the south side of the mountains, the mountains were across from the river from them, and she was facing the river. If she turned to her right, that was the direction of Akre and of Umfell, where she assumed search parties were looking for survivors.

If she looked behind her that would be south, and she could theoretically trace a straight line to the coast. She had gotten turned around when she hit her head during a rough landing, but her senses felt like they were coming back to her now, though her fingers still tingled a little bit every now and then.

Volstad watched her. They had worked with each other for a long time, but nothing had ever gone wrong. Volstad was used to things going wrong in his previous line of work, but he had no idea what Moon had done. She didn't run in the personal security or mercenary crowd. He had never heard of her, but she was always at Erold's side since long before Erolin had brought him on, years back.

"So, we go west for now. What's west?"

"I may have grown up in the countryside, Elara, but I'm not a walking map. I think we have to just start walking. I only know of Umfell, because it's large enough to make it on a globe. There's only a handful of cities in these hills, and I don't know where they are."

"Shouldn't we be able to find a city soon? There are houses dotted all over the hills across the river. Shouldn't the first city we find have a telegram?"

"Most of those are just local farmers. That's the farming side of the river. See those fields. I never took you for a city girl, but the towns out here aren't that big. We should run into one soon."

"Okay, we'll find a town then. How many towns could there

actually be?"

"I'm not the expert on this. That would have been a question to put to Erolin."

Erold winced at the hearing the name of his father, and the two senior members of the royal guard stopped talking. Volstad felt badly. He had never heard of a dragon attack before, outside of story books, or world history texts, generally through the almost unrelated topic of dragon slayers who actively sought the danger. The dragons that made the mountains their home, and especially these ones, generally left men alone. But, for the one night that they didn't, his father had paid the price.

Volstad looked to the northwest, along the river that snaked along the mountain, meandering around the hills that were dotted with pines and lush green maple trees. It was so calm that it was hard to completely reconcile with the fiery assassination the night before.

"Are you ready to go?" Volstad asked.

"Yes," replied Erold. He stood up and stretched with a quiet release of air, "We go west, deeper into Dalvalles."

Erold did a sideways nod to motion to Moon to follow him, and they began their trek along the dirt road. Moon had never really spent any time in the 'countryside' as Volstad put it, and if she hadn't, Erold most certainly hadn't.

Her feet had grown sore almost immediately the night before when they were looking for a place to spend the night and get out of sight of the dragons. He hadn't once mentioned anything or complained, which was new for him.

Erold spent the morning as they walked along the river, trying to block out the anger and frustration that he was feeling, while reminding himself that his father was really gone. It had happened so quickly, and he felt like an event like that should have changed him naturally, without conscious effort. But, the reality was that his mind kept telling him of the circumstances as if he wasn't aware.

He was hungry. He hadn't slept the night before while they had curled up on a patch of grass that grew in the shadow of one of the steep hills. He ended up focusing on putting one foot in front of the other, while trying to remain as visibly emotionless as possible.

He wanted his father back. He wanted to let the inner emotions bleed out. But, he didn't want to die. And, it didn't take an archmage to figure out that whoever killed his father would want him dead too.

It was convenient for them that he was on the ship, but Moon and Volstad were taking the same leap of faith that he was and banking on any number of circumstances that didn't coincidentally line up.

For one, that their unknown enemy didn't know he was on the ship, wouldn't be able to track him if they were looking for him, and most of all, that it wasn't Sven, the saint, who had killed off his father.

Erold walked out ahead of the crowd, flanked by Moon, taking in the scenery, and investigating the shacks and fishing huts as they passed anything with four posts dug into the ground. When they started seeing well-trodden horse poop in the middle of the road, he decided they would be closing in on a town soon.

Moon fell a little bit behind Erold, far enough that he might be out of clear earshot, and scanned their group for secrecy's sake before turned to Volstad to whisper, "What are you thinking about?"

"Why?"

"Curiosity."

"You're wondering if we're thinking the same thing."

"Who did it, and how?"

"Yeah."

"The dragons were lured by the smaller ship, but it was a suicide mission."

"I'm not sure anyone knew the full plan."

"Right, how could they? Survival instinct would have kicked in."

"The hijacking, the sleeping potion. They could have just crashed the ship."

"We don't know who was asleep and who wasn't. Anyone could have been replaced."

"Are you suggesting, we can't vouch for any of our men here?"

"We do have to make sure that they weren't after the kid as well. Somebody leaked something, somewhere, and in some ways, it's as if whoever planned this wanted it to look like a freak anomaly rather than a calculated act."

"We don't know anything for certain, but that's probably enough talking about this. We can't overthink it. We just need to keep moving."

They walked in a long, broken line along the flat river road that followed the meandering of the great, old, river, avoiding the need to fjord as most of the river's tributaries came down the mountain and through the hills on the other side of the river and fed the lush green of the river's north side in comparison to the craggy south of the rocky foothills of the south. The one or two southern tributaries to the Evorul River, they came across had rough wooden bridges barely the width of the carriages or wagons that appeared to still the use the road. They were in want of repairs, with cracked and rotting boards, but at least the water had been bridged.

After walking for about an hour they came across a similarly rough, wooden sign that pointed away from the river to Kaarmekello, or 'Snake Bell' in the common tongue.

"Volstad?"

"Yes?"

"Have you heard of this town? Kaarmekello?"

"No, but I'm sure they'll have water, bread, and salt. Since, it's this close to the Evorul river, maybe they saw the crash and will help survivors."

"You mean in case we lost everything in the crash?"

Volstad grimaced at Erold's choice of phrasing.

"For now, I'll have you covered, but it won't last."

"Good to know, kid."

"Then, Kaarmekello it is. We'll go get a room for the night, and, then we'll decide where to go from there."

They left the sign behind, following the fork in the road to the left, rising from the riverbed up the hill, where they found a small town wrapped in on itself within the valley between four craggy hills.

The central road cut through the middle of the town in a backwards 'S' shape with a single second road, jutting off into a town circle where any buildings not on the main road were built in a tight line together, resembling the steep hills around them with the high slope and curve of their connected rooves. There might have been forty to fifty buildings in all, and from their new vantage point, they could see that some houses dotted the other hills around the town.

Erold led the way down the other side of the hill and into Kaarmekello with Volstad and Moon jogging down the slope of the hill to keep up.

The first buildings in the town appeared to be houses, but then they passed a general store and what appeared to be a constable's office. Erold noticed that here too, repairs were needed, and the street was still dirt, but someone had taken the time to clean it of excrement. He couldn't see anything that resembled the plumbing of Seylil or Albion, so he imagined that someone must be hired to shovel shit, which maybe they used in fields across the river as fertilizer.

"Where are all of the people?"

"Even though it's sunny, it's cold outside today. I'm sure most of them are inside."

Finally, a tavern appeared on the left at the corner of the town's lone intersection. Erold went in first, and Moon and Volstad followed him in. The group of travelers began crowding in behind him, but it was slow as the tavern was small, and the seats along the wall were taken.

Wooden planks had been sanded and polished and set over a pair of logs that looked fresh cut from the tree. One of the men at the tables stood up and went behind the makeshift bar.

"Are you folks from the crash last night?"

"Yes, most of us are looking for a place to stay the night and some food and drink."

"Well, if you'd like to stay here it will cost ya, but the townsfolk have been talking about whether anyone might show up. We've set aside some rooms in houses for you. We can offer you some beer, but water and bread will cost ya."

"What will the bread cost?"

"It kind of sounded wrong when I said it after all to charge ya's for the bread, but we can be hard up in the hills to get wheat from further south. No one comes through the forest west of here, so maybe we can cut a deal. If you can pay at least half price for the bread, I can do that. One Akrin dollar a loaf or two loaves for a sovereign silver coin if you have it. Mind you this is only for tonight. You will have to figure something else out by tomorrow."

"We'll manage something. What about salt or water?"

"Right now, salt's not for sale until we get our next shipment from Mondelvania."

"That is a far way to go for salt."

"It don't come down from Valgaard, since the war."

"Thank you, you wouldn't also happen to have any advice on how to get through the hills to the Solgra?"

"There's a pass through the hills just a little further west of here and a little to the south. You'll get there fastest by taking the road through the city away from the river."

"How far will that take us?"

"That pass cuts through the hills to the Erstber River, which you'll have to cross and then follow back to the east until you reach the pass through to Solgra. Can't miss it."

"Why do you say that? Have you walked it?"

"I haven't walked it, no. I took a carriage down to Leidyn when I was younger. It is a wide pass and would be an easy walk to make. You could ride twenty horses or a little more across without hitting a pebble."

"Is it a long walk?"

"Depends on how fast you want to go. If you're not in a hurry, maybe a few days. It's a good distance. I'm not maybe the best one to ask."

"Okay, thank you, for all the help."

"A dragon helps his own kin."

Erold bought bread for him, Volstad, and Moon with a piece of silver. Some of the other passengers had money and they pooled it as well in groups to purchase bread. Everyone got at least an atomic pint of beer and they distributed among what was left of the tables or stood until they were offered seats.

Erold, Moon, and Volstad split a loaf of warm bread evenly and saved a loaf for the next day, expecting that it might not be easy to get another one as fresh and perfectly made in the morning if the town was waiting on a shipment of salt.

They ate in silence for a moment until Moon suppressed a laugh, "We're getting the geography lesson we so sorely needed on the countryside."

"Yes," said Erold as he finished his chunk of bread and began to drink the beer tentatively. Moon apologized for her outburst, a momentary lapse as the events of the past two days dented her self-control.

Volstad looked Erold over. If Erold was as weary as he, himself, was, then he didn't show it. At some point, though, this energy would fail him.

"We'll set out for Leidyn tomorrow. That would be a good spot to spend some considerable time, if we have to. It's just south of hills and nearer to the coast than it is to Seylil and the mountains," said Volstad. What he left unsaid was that it meant it was the closest city in the Solgra to Sven that would also be as far as they could be from Akre.

"Can we contact Sven easily from there?" asked Erold.

"It'll have telegram service, yes, though it might make sense to mail him a letter from there. He's famous throughout Normany, so someone will be able to deliver it to him."

"The Akrin postal definitely could," said a stranger, who sat down. He might have been one of the passengers from the crashed cruiser, but neither Moon nor Volstad recognized him as one of the royal guard. They each shot each other glances across the table, but neither could read the other's expression clearly. Given the size of their new friend, it was hard to believe that they could have missed him among the walk from the river. He must have been over two atomic yards tall and was a bit round in both his stomach and his red cheeks.

"We might be looking to get it to him faster than the postal can deliver," Erold said.

"I didn't want to interrupt you. I just meant to help."

Erold eyed the stranger over his beer. "I'm Erold, this is Elara, and this is Abrim."

"Nice to meet you. I'm Deronson. I like that we have very similar names. I heard you talking about going to Leidyn, and I'm headed that way too."

"Were you on the crashed cruiser?"

"No, I live in this town. My family volunteered to take people in for the night. I figured it would be a good opportunity to make new friends."

"Speaking of places to spend the night, the sun will be going low soon, right, and it will start to get colder. Could you show us where we will be staying?"

"I can only take one person in tonight, but if you got to the lady near the door, she can help you find a home for the night out of the cold, unless you're staying at the tavern. I'd recommend the hospitality. We're glad to be doing something to help people, especially in times like this when you don't know who you can trust, and it feels like people in far off cities are deciding whether you get to eat the food on your lawn."

"Well, Deronson, I'll take you up on your offer," Volstad said, and he stood up, "I'm exhausted, so if we could be on our way, I'd be much obliged."

Deronson stood up as well, easily dwarfing Volstad, and turned to smile at Erold and Moon, "It's nice to meet you."

"Nice to meet you too," replied Erold and finished his beer.

Moon turned to whisper in Erold's ear, "Remember to be careful who you trust."

Erold took another gulp of beer, feeling relaxed. Maybe, it was good to get away from the paranoia of the city. Moon never relaxed. There was just something about her that felt as if she was watching shadows for snakes.

Erold looked up at the lady at the door and saw that there was a pretty woman next to her, smiling and distributing extra blankets. She was so friendly and kind looking too. How could he tell Moon that that was the house where he wanted to spend the night?

Moon noticed Erold looking over at the door and couldn't help but roll her eyes. She had been feeling just a little bit more than sorry for the kid, but before half of his beer was gone, the teenage boy was eyeing a young woman from a random town in the hills.

Thirsty, herself, and along for the ride, she took a deep gulp of her beer and looked around the pub. Almost all of the royal guard had dispersed without awaiting orders. It looks like they were just happy to survive, and for them the mission was over, the king that never was, Erolin, wasn't rising from the dead. For her, Erold was the new mission, but she could wonder about a career mercenary like Volstad. Standing by an exiled king would not be easy, especially one who may find himself guided by desire toward a wrong situation or saying something in an intimate situation that could reveal his true identity. Then again, maybe this was part of his way of coping. Moving on, or at least letting himself focus on the moment rather than past or future.

Erold stood up and went to the door, "Excuse me, we're still looking for a place tonight. One of the townsfolk said that there were some homes arranged for the survivors. Do you have any place we could stay the night?"

"Ours is the only house that isn't hosting anyone yet," said the older woman. The young girl smiled at Erold. "You could stay with us, but I'll bet my husband won't be happy. Are you able to afford the room at the inn?"

"I'm sure he could stay with us, mother. He looks like he'd be eager to help around the house. Father hasn't chopped firewood for the week yet, and this young man, certainly looks like he has the muscle for it. Besides, we have enough space for him in the main hall to sleep on the floor."

"It'll be getting dark soon, Lynna," the older woman eyed her daughter suspiciously, and then relented. "I guess we don't have much time. If you've finished your bread and beer, come along with us when we leave."

Moon watched Erold dote at the young woman's side, while he waited to follow the two ladies out the door. She slowly drank her beer, and when he motioned for her to follow him, she finished it, making sure to keep hydrated, despite the fact that the best choice was alcohol and followed out into the early evening that cast familiar shadows over the hills like the night before.

The two women went into one of the nearest houses, but Erold didn't go in after them. Instead, he told Moon to go inside and informed her that he would be inside to sleep after he chopped some wood for the fire.

Erold went around the back of the house and found the communal outhouse. He had been embarrassed to ask where it was, but now he needed to relieve himself. As he wandered behind the village's houses to the outhouse, he shook his head at the way things were for his people.

He had assumed that all the people of his kingdom enjoyed the common things that he enjoyed in the city, but that clearly wasn't the case. If he was king, could he change that?

He opened the door and instantly regretted it. He had never smelled a smell like that in his life. But, he couldn't piss on the hill. He kept the door propped open with his leg and pissed into the trough from as far a distance as he could, arching his pee over the dirt floor of the shack.

He got a little pee on his hand, and without any towels or running water, he had to find a patch of grass after all to wipe his hand.

The grass was cold to the touch, and he found himself with a good view of the river, sparkling in the twilight. He sat for a second and let out a deep breath. He lamented that he couldn't tell that pretty girl Lynna who he was. He wasn't sure that he ever could tell anyone. And, he couldn't go around telling people that his father had just died. Someone could spread a rumor, and he hated it but how could he trust his own people?

Then again, there was no one around. He was the king of nothing. He had already given up on the idea of being king a long time ago, but Moon and Volstad still followed him around. He sat down on the cool grass and simply watched the smoke from fires start to spit out of chimneys. No matter what happened, he vowed to himself, he would use this opportunity to see what his country needed and not what he needed.

As the sun faded, he could see a new church being built on the opposite hill, facing the rising sun. He thought of his father, and how they hadn't spoken much in the past few years. There was always the risk that something could happen, but he just wanted to forget that it had happened. He had no other place to be, and he had no one else to be.

Before the sun faded completely, he found his way back to the house. A small wood axe was propped up against the back of the house and there was a large stack of woods.

The sun was nearly gone, and surprisingly, there wasn't a single oil lamp on the outside of the house, or even lighting the town road for the night.

He put a log on the chopping block and felt the rush of the cold, night air around him start to fall away as he started slamming the axe through wood block after wood block. Moon watched him until the light had gone completely, and then she took the axe from him and let him fall onto her shoulder. He just stood there. He didn't cry, but she felt like he needed to know she would be there.

They took the chopped logs into the house, where Lynna and her father sat beside the fire, and her little kid brothers ran around mimicking griffins, eagles, dragons, and more. Lynna's father stood and took the logs from both Erold and Moon and set them close to the fireplace where Lynna's mother, sweating in the direct heat of the fire, hung iron cookware while guarding meat and potatoes.

"Thanks for chopping so much wood," Lynna said, and she smiled at Erold. Suddenly taken with guilt at his frustration with the riches his father had lavished upon him, Erold lied and said his head hurt a little from the cold outside, despite it still being the second full month of summer, Midur.

He lay down on one of the blankets that they had left in the corner for him and Moon, from where he watched as the family went about their daily routine.

When the food was ready, he declined. Instead, he listened to Lynna's father telling stories of the angels of the savior. Erold watched the rapture in the eyes of the young boys, who imagined glorious battles of orcs, ogres, and trolls, pitted against the men of Galdir.

Moon, too, shared stories of the golden city of Akre with Lynna and her mother. She described its shape, sights, and sounds with its different districts, its museums, theaters, and monuments to Akre's past. They asked many questions about the food, the people, and about how easy it was to buy clothes there rather than to make and mend them.

Everyone helped clean up, even the little kids, who kept trading looks at him, laying half-asleep against the wall. He suddenly felt very tired.

In the middle of the night, Lynna crawled into the blankets with him and pressed her warm body against his. They lay there barely moving, while she tightened her grip around him, pushing her body closer against his, and placing her lips into his lips, smothering him in warmth and soft skin. When he tried to take a breath, her hot breath filled his nostrils and he breathed deeper in to avoid coughing, her mouth glued to his, dripping wet as they passed the night in the shy embrace.

* * *

Moon woke Erold late the next morning, letting him sleep well into the long daylight hours of summer's approaching end. She had packed what little they had left after the crash and set things in order for their walk through the Erstber River pass. His eyes flashed open, alert and alive.

She gave him the sack with the bread to carry, and he pulled his same clothes on over his night shirt, while hidden by the blankets.

When they were ready to leave, Lynna and her parents hugged the two of them goodbye and gave them cookies and suggested buying a canteen and filling it with clean water for the road.

The duo took the advice and headed over to the general store near the northern entrance to town. Erold caught Moon spying into every window from the corner of her eyes. She looked for any remaining members of the royal guard, confirming that it was just the two of them alone from here on out.

They were buying a canteen from the general store and getting it filled, instead with beer. It was easier to purify from the river and just as hydrating to a desperate man. It was also cheaper. As the shopkeeper gave them the canteen back, filled, they were caught up with by Deronson and Volstad, who had been looking for them for most of the morning.

Volstad confirmed that they were the last of the royal guard in the town.

"You don't mind if I tag along with you to Leidyn, do you?" asked Deronson. "It's a long walk on your own."

"It's fine," said Erold.

"Just how long a walk is it?" Moon asked.

"It could take a week or so. It depends on if you're in a hurry. Are you in a hurry?"

"I'd rather it doesn't take a week."

"Then let's get moving."

They walked through and out of the town to the south and then up the hills and down them again until they reached the pass, a wide gap between the hills that had been paved naturally by centuries of traffic, beast, elf, and man. It sloped gently downward, following the gradual descent of the hills toward the coastline in the west.

"How far is it to Erstber?" Volstad asked Deronson, suddenly glad that they had someone coming along who might be able to show them the way.

"It's about a day's hike just through here. We'll get to Graabern by sun's fall, if we're lucky."

"If we're unlucky?"

"I'd say we could get there well after night falls, if we don't walk fast enough. How much walking have you done?"

"Plenty," Erold lied on behalf of himself and the trio, before he took off, leading them through the ancient pass.

After a few hours hike, they settled beside some trees, and discussed Deronson's trip to Leidyn, where he would be picking up spices shipped in from the spice islands through either the East Cardane Shipping Company or the Coltari Company traders, whichever had the goods for cheaper. They both came in from the same spice islands in the end, but the Coltari ships went west and the ECSC ships went east, circumnavigating the globe to bring flavored leaves, grown from trees. Deronson made his money by making the trip down on behalf of the town and some of the surrounding villages and charging a markup on the goods when he got back to the river valley.

Lately, it hadn't been as profitable, because the Coltari ships hadn't been coming in as often--so he would have to make a few more trips between now and the winter solstice in the month of Vetfal. It helped to get to the shops ahead of the Merchant's Day and the holiday rush of Frostmas, which were both coming up in the next month of Ivanssun.

Volstad and Moon did most of the questioning, while Erold sat in silence, eating bread and cookies, drinking beer, and most of all thinking. He had taken for granted the holidays at home with his father, and he wondered what the plans would have been this year had they been able to make it home.

Maybe the rest of the party sensed his brooding, but they let him be and soon they walked on in silence. For most of the rest of the trip to Graabern, the day was fading fast, and Moon felt they were fortunate that even though the path wasn't lit, that the sun cut between the hills and lit their path. The walk was at times gravel, at times pocked with grass, and at times the path was filled with mud. She found herself maneuvering around days old horse poop that had melded with the dirt to make a fine powder that stuck to the shoes. Erold also stepped lightly, though Moon assumed he had other reasons to watch the ground as he walked instead of up at the road ahead.

They reached Graabern only just as the sun disappeared beneath the horizon after a long summer day. Moon was aching and tired, but as usual, the rest of the troop could not tell. It appeared that they were all silently suffering the same ordeal and would not share their pain.

The city was much larger than Kaarmekello and nestled into the Erstber river valley where the hills still rose up from the river and had flattened out, giving it a view over the riverbed and the approach from the pass. From the pass, you could see into the center of the city, where numerous stone bridges crossed the river. A traveler had to first go down into the riverbed on the pass and then follow it up either side of the river to enter Graabern from within the city walls, which didn't provide much defensive cover and appeared more to line the edges of the city to prevent someone from falling off the outward facing walkways that wrapped around the town, allowing townsfolk to view the valley where they lived.

They followed the path on the north side of the river and entered the town through the short pathway that rose up to the wall. There was no gate, and most of the roads had been paved with stone.

Erold pointed at a welcome sign that listed a population estimate as they entered, which seemed far too large compared to what Moon would have imagined from up on the hill. They went into the first tavern they could see from where they entered, nestled just off the river, which felt perilously far below the stone bridges, on the south bank. It had a single oil lamp lit above the window.

The tavern was nearly empty. Erold once again did the talking and ordering for Volstad and Moon. Deronson got himself something separately.

Erold sat down with the table's beers, and then went back to grab the bread, cheese, and olives that he felt he had splurged for.

"If we keep going like this, we better be getting to Leidyn soon," Erold said.

"Why, how much do you have left?"

Erold shook his head as Deronson sat down next to him with his own beer and some of the same kinds of food, except with some slices of spiced goat's meat as well.

Volstad, for a half second, felt like he might have underestimated Erold, because he hadn't anticipated needing handouts from the prince. He had forgotten his coin purse in the Vagalla cabin. And despite the fact that he technically provided protection, there likely wouldn't be any highwaymen within Empire limits, especially this close to the capital.

"Do you want to split the room fee tonight?" Deronson asked as he began to eat greedily. "Uggh, I haven't had goat in a few weeks." He paused to chew. "We need two rooms, and the fee is pretty steep for a hill town."

"Yes, I'll share a room with you again," said Volstad, still unsure of their over-friendly companion. One of the other patrons stood up and walked over to them.

"May I sit?" he asked.

"Excuse me. Maybe start with why?" Moon postured defensively.

"Pardon me, I'm but a humble merchant. I heard you say something about rooms and Leidyn." Erold winced, having momentarily forgot that someone else could be listening in on what he was saying.

The merchant continued, "If you don't mind me asking if that's the way you're going, we might be able to come to a mutually beneficial arrangement."

"And what is that?" asked Moon.

"I could give you a ride to Leidyn if you like in my merchant's wagon."

"What makes you think we're looking for a ride?"

"As heavily armed as you are," nodding to Volstad's holstered pistol and sheathed sword, "and to be coming here after night fall, I'm not expecting you to be a simple merchant like me."

"Let's say that maybe you're right, then what's in it for you?" asked Volstad, having just wondered at the unlikeliness of highwaymen, he doubted the merchant would be paying them. And, he had a lot of confidence in the decrees of the Empire to be walking up to a stranger he noticed armed.

"A small fee, of course. This is no act of charity. I could use some extra money with the holidays coming, and it's a long way to Leidyn."

Erold started drinking some beer, watching the merchant,

waiting for him to speak.

"I'll charge half of what rooms would cost you along the way, seeing as you would have to spend that money if you had to stop along the way."

"Deronson, is that a fair price?" asked Erold.

"Why are you asking me?"

"You've walked this way before, right?" pressed Volstad. Moon bristled, wondering again about the amiable stranger.

"Seeing as we would probably have to stop." Deronson thought for a moment and then as if to double check his mental math, started slowly counting on his fingers, "one, two, three, more times, at least, if we walked the whole way, then I'm not sure, since we also wouldn't make it there in one day riding."

"How long do you think it would take us to get there, merchant?" Erold arched his back as he started to feel the effects of the alcohol soften the edges of his concentration.

"I could get you there in two days."

"Bully, that," said Deronson, and he forced a laugh.

"How would you know how long it takes to get there by wagon or carriage? I don't see you with any horses."

"I know it's not that fast."

"Now, hear me. It's only two legs of forty atomic miles or a little more. My team of horses could cover that in a day easy, if you're willing to wake up for the morning."

"Or a little more." Deronson swung his arm in exaggeration and drank.

"The most I've heard of someone covering in a horse-drawn carriage regularly is only fifty atomic miles a day, but that could be riding your horses hard." Volstad said.

"It's an easy enough ride. Very flat."

"So, if we do take this deal, we only save on half a night at a tavern if you make it in two days and otherwise, lose out?" Erold asked aloud.

"Well, when you put it like that, it don't sound near as nice a deal."

"Fair's, fair. You're the one with the horses," said Erold.

"Couldn't have said it better meself," cried out the merchant and took off his cap to put it over his heart.

"Where's the next stop?" asked Erold, looking over at Deronson.

"By foot, we'd be in Elklin."

"And what about by wagon?"

"We'd be at the inn at the foot of the pass, in Godrland," said the merchant.

"How about we pay you one night of two rooms at the next inn and also cover yours in Godrland?"

"Downright thievery that could be half the rate. As you said, I'm the one with the horses."

"And, we're the ones with the gold."

"Yes, of course. What about we go halfway in price, and you cover me room at the inn?"

"If we make it in two days?"

"I can agree to that."

"And, only if we make it in two days?"

"Yes."

"I can make that deal."

There was a moment of silence as it appeared the terms of relief from a four day walk were near for the group. Volstad and Moon thought Erold's haggling could have gone lower, and yet was maybe a little brazen for a fifteen-year-old, who didn't seem to have ever ventured far out from under the protective wings of his father.

"Will you?" the merchant broke the silence.

"Only if we pay when we arrive."

"Half up front."

"Half at the Inn in Godrland."

"Okay. Do we have a deal?"

"Yes."

"Great," cried the merchant and Moon privately let out a sigh of relief. She assumed that Volstad and Erold did too, otherwise he wouldn't have been so keen on bargaining.

"We'll meet tomorrow morning as soon as the sun rises," said Erold, "Deronson, is that all right with you?"

"Am I to be included in this?"

"You're part of this adventure, now, aren't you?"

"I'm not paying anything."

"That's fine."

"Then, yes, I guess I am."

Erold finished his atomic liter of beer and told Moon that he would be in their shared room for the evening. He didn't say it, but he desperately wanted to sleep, after not having got much unbroken sleep the night before. The walking, too, had felt a little surreal, considering how groggy he felt.

The next morning as the sun crested over the hills, the merchant and the small band of travelers met on the road on the south side of the Erstber River. The trio of Moon, Volstad, and Deronson rode in the back, while Erold asked to ride up front with the merchant.

As they went, Erold asked about different places and towns that they passed along the way. The merchant described these and more, explaining how the river was rather young and ran straighter than the Evorul, for example, or the Áelin River in the south, where he'd go after Leidyn. That made it an easy ride, even if the road was mainly dirt, because as a result, they had built the road high on the bank, it didn't get muddy, and it stayed flat and straight along the side of the river.

Erold asked him what he was doing in Leidyn, and he pointed to his cargo in the back. "Eggplants." The merchant said, "They grow throughout Dalvalles, but he thought the best ones came from the villages dotted along the Erstber river valley. They liked the rocky ground, and the farmers seemed to conglomerate in Graabern to coordinate pricing together.

He'd try to make it a few times a year and wait for a crop before heading south and then cycling goods on the way at each stop.

Erold asked if he ever made it north, and the merchant, pointed out the pass to the Hoenheim valley, which ran to the southwest before cutting back to the north and into the valley, which was the fastest route from the Erstber to region of Normany, north of Dalvalles, Gardnor.

If he didn't take the route along the coast, he'd go through there, but typically, the only time he traded in the valley was on his way south from Gardnor. He'd try to buy enough Orichalc from the merchants who went north to Albion to feed the steam tech in the homes and businesses throughout Dalvalles, and he was far from the only merchant making runs like this across the countryside.

They didn't need to pass through Elklin, so Erold wouldn't get to see what another city of Normany looked like before they would reach Leidyn. The Erstber curled around to the north and Elklin lay directly on the riverbank, on the river's east side, cut into the hill.

The pass opened up with a view almost directly into the route of the river, so much so that it looked like it could have once been the path of the river until it had run into a stronger wall of rock that crumbled slower under the pressure of the river than the alternative path the river took to the north.

They took the pass and pretty soon, the hills to their left and right gave way to a view of endless rolling plains of yellow-green grass, only cut by intermittent fields of wheat, making the countryside look as golden as the sun. As they followed the pass, the sun fell, marking the hours that went by, and slowly changing the way the seemingly endless fields of southern Normany shined back at the wagon.

Erold could see a few towns from the hill, but there was only one little tavern at the end of the pass. There they stayed for much cheaper than it had been for a night in Graabern, and the next morning they were on the way to Leidyn.

The merchant rode his horses harder on the second day, intent to make it there on time, and perhaps, he was annoyed that the price at the inn had been so low. The path was much better maintained than the Dalvalles roads had been and followed the hills just south of the rockier Dalvalles hills. These flowed in long, smooth ups and downs, obscuring and then presenting the rest of the golden countryside as the packed wagon took them slowly up and quickly down.

It was almost hard to believe that it was the same countryside given the lack of trees, or rocky outcroppings, as they drifted just slightly far enough away from the Dalvalles hills to start hiding their details from the naked eye. It was also a very different forty atomic miles. The previous day had been a long relatively flat descent while today, they were getting a bit of a bumpy ride up and down hills.

The sun was just starting to near the hills on the horizon when they came across Leidyn, unmistakable among the towns that dotted the landscape, because of its size compared to the rest of the little collections of houses and huts that scattered across the fields of wheat and tall grass. They could see it coming from about a fourth of the distance to travel give or take. Erold merely guessed, but it rose out of the rather monotonous view as a mixture of red brick, white paint, and green marble in stark contrast to the gold fields and blue sky.

He could see church towers and bell towers rise above the city among many two and three story buildings that stretched out and up two of the larger hills within the surrounding plains. You could see the rows of houses on either hill were built to face in at the center city in rows of neat concentric rings, giving it an appearance of one large stadium-like bowl. Many of the houses' doors were painted matching colors, and at the center of the vast distribution of houses was one large lake with an island in the center connected to the town by a series of bridges. You could see some of the bridges from far away when you had a view of the city from a hill, looking over the distance of the lake, but then at other times, the center of the city was hidden.

The city wrapped around the lake and the lake looped around the city like one large 'e' shape, where the 'e' was warped in such a way that the island at its center made up only a slim portion of the rest of the lake, making it so that the houses on one end of the lake were much closer to the center of the city, surrounding its island than the ones on the hill that bordered the lake, along the far side from their approach.

"Leidyn of Godrland. Is this the biggest city you've ever seen?" the merchant asked him puzzled. "You look awe-struck."

"No," replied Erold and he bit his tongue from revealing anything more. He had never known of Leidyn, but he found it beautiful now that he was this close. His father had always told him about the provinces and their regions and the capitals of those regions. His father had one day envisioned cutting the provinces further into self-governing municipalities, complete with their own mage courts and schools for science and magic.

His father was a dreamer though and didn't seem to recognize that the people were doing a lot on their own already, and the wars of conquest that those same people had fed their lives and livelihoods into for centuries had failed to bring them riches or glory enough.

It had enriched and emboldened the biggest cities, but he had seen more of the countryside in four nights on the cold ground than he had from the sky in fourteen years.

The merchant pulled up in front of a tavern, and Erold gave him a gold piece, which covered the rest of the trip. He hid the rest of his money close, knowing that a quick cut purse would leave him and his two companions, for lack of a better word, stranded in Leidyn.

"This is where I take my leave," Deronson said, straightening up and giving a polite half bow.

"You're not staying at the tavern with us?" Erold asked.

"I have family in Leidyn."

"Shouldn't you go in the morning rather than calling on them at night?"

"No, they knew I'd be back in town even if they're not expecting me for a few days. Thank you for allowing me to accompany you on the ride from Graabern, and I hope you have a happy Frostmas."

"Happy Frostmas," Erold said automatically, while Moon and Volstad were each a mixture of pleased that Deronson had quitted the company.

Moon and Volstad followed Erold into the tavern, where they were finally able to get a drink of water for close to the price of beer. They relaxed at one of the tables, eating simple food and each mulling over the next stage of their own plan and how it might fit into the group as a whole.

They had made it out of the hills. They had gotten close enough to Sven that they could cable or write to him, and he'd be able to round up his nephew in a matter of days if not hours. For Volstad, he had spent the better part of the last three days wondering if this is something he could keep doing. Everyone else in the royal guard, men and women, had left, except for Moon, who had some kind of life debt or something to make her cling to first Erolin and then this kid.

If Volstad had thought about it rationally, maybe this was the best path to take, since he didn't have any money. But, he could have just taken the kid's gold like old times and walked away.

As it stood, maybe the reason he stuck around had less to do with what he needed, and more to do with a lingering sense of duty for the kid's father. He and Moon were the only ones who knew Erold was on the flight. They were likely the only ones who could pick Erold out of a crowd. Maybe that's why everyone else left, because they didn't know there was a job still to do. Unfortunately, it wasn't a job he could guarantee paid, unless...

Volstad looked up to see that Moon was staring at him as if she was reading his mind. Maybe, she could. If so, he'd find out if some of the stories were really true.

"What's the plan and how do we contact our mutual friend?" asked Moon.

"Do we still have to talk around topics, or can we start moving this along? I just want this figured out, and it feels like I'm..." Erold stopped himself from complaining any more. He took a second to breathe and then asked, "Do either of you know who to telegram, or who can send us a letter?"

"I do," said Volstad. "A telegram costs--"

Erold pushed a silver across the table, "I know what a telegram costs."

Moon was in a tough position. Volstad was getting up to leave, and she was wondering if she could trust him. Should she have them all go with him? She couldn't go with him and stay beside Erold at the same time.

Volstad pushed the piece of silver back across the table and said,

"We'll go together in the morning. The telegram office won't be open this time of night."

Moon spent most of the night awake thinking, while Erold slept in the room's only, large bed. Surprisingly, the half-beds that had been in the last two taverns had been more comfortable to her, but this was the first one Erold's feet didn't dangle over the side of overnight.

On the other hand, for the first time in a few nights, she was able to rinse herself in a bath. Leidyn had indoor plumbing, which Erold had seemed pleased with as well.

Moon was starting to think through things with a little more sense for the bigger picture. She was going to stick by Erold's side, and that meant there were some things she would have to figure out. She wasn't going to follow along as closely again if she saw him with some fresh-faced girl, but an assassin could hide in a lot of ways.

At this stage of his life, though, Moon needed to be more realistic about whether there were going to be any assassins. She started debating how she would figure that out. A good step would be to buy a newspaper to see if anyone was even looking for the kid publicly. The next step, and maybe the most direct at this point, was seeing how things played out with Erold's 'uncle,' Sven. There was no doubt in her mind that Sven would try to claim the right to rule Normany with his cousin, Erolin, dead, but having a newspaper handy would really help clear up what Akre's possible response to that might be.

In Akre's back pocket was the 'lost' princess, who Moon believed the senate would very likely never vote to take the throne, but had the second-highest claim to it, behind Erold, now that Erolin was dead. The senate controlled her and wouldn't risk giving her any real power. If they did, she could ultimately turn on them and attempt to usurp them. Moon was well aware of the motivational power of self-preservation.

If the senate had planned the assassination of Erolin, then Moon was sure that they had a plan to work around any potential attempt by Sven to claim the territory of Normany. Moon needed to figure it out soon, because joining Sven could prove to be more dangerous a route than finding an alternative option.

Though, sitting on the wooden floor of a tavern room, after having washed up in a communal washroom, the fourth night after surviving an airship crash in the mountains, she felt like the only reason that she was thinking this much about it was that she wasn't likely to sleep.

"What are we going to do about money?" Erold asked. When Elara didn't answer he sat up. She was asleep. He had sworn she was awake just a moment ago, playing with the splinters in the old wooden floor.

Erold went to the window and peaked through the curtains. The street had lit up with the morning sun. He felt guilty about waking her, but he felt like he had to. The time limit approached quickly on the amount of time they could spend waiting for answers while he watched their money dwindle.

Erold shook Moon awake, and she snapped alert.

"We've got to get moving. It's already bright outside. If we need to figure something else out, we need to know now."

Elara had slipped back into the same clothes after bathing yesterday, so she was really not feeling up for walking around a city, smelling like sweat and eggplants. She didn't seem to have many options though.

The duo came down the tavern stairs to find Volstad waiting at the door, drinking a beer.

"I thought you were out of money," said Moon.

"I decided to start pulling my own weight."

"Resourceful or under the table?" Moon asked under her breath.

"A bit of both," Volstad replied and then whispering into her ear. "What's the matter? You look a little spooked to see me this morning."

"After the last few days, I wasn't sure you'd still be here in the morning."

"For now, I'm just looking to see how this plays out."

"You and me both."

Waiting by the door, Erold finally pushed it open, "I don't know what you two are talking about, and I'm pretty sure I don't want to know. If 'we're' going to send a telegram, we better do it before I leave you two behind."

They walked through the city, conspicuously failing to blend in as anything more than rugged out of town folk on some misbegotten adventure like a fable of old heroes. Even if their business couldn't be anything more legitimate than paying a half-silver to send a five-word telegram to Áelin City.

They passed by some local girls, dressed in expensive looking lace dresses that glided just above the road, who laughed when Erold smiled at them, which Moon couldn't help but smirk at. Erold didn't seem to mind though. He seemed at home in the summer sun with the temperature likely ticking up close to as high as seventy degrees on the Mercury scale and a breeze running in between the buildings from the lake, bringing the smell of baking bread up through the street.

Volstad sent a coded wire to Sven's chief of staff, knowing that among the trio, he would have been the only one to know this aspect of Erolin's staff procedures. This option was much easier and faster than sending a letter. For now, that had been the only reason he had stuck around for one more day. He would need to be the one to read the code back too, and they soon received a message back that 'uncle' Sven, whose legitimacy as a potential royal in a quickly thinning pool of possible heirs, which had always been questionable at best, was only outweighed by the size of his overwhelming likeability and waist, would be arriving in a week or less.

Moon saw a newspaper headline from a kid peddler, reading 'King Confirmed Passenger on Doomed Vagalla!' and beneath that an ode to the senate response, 'Senate to name first official Emperor-elect in coming days.'

1513 - Chapter 7

"On final approach into Rorik," said the smuggler air-ship captain, Drake Peak, after they had snuck over the Evoruls in the north of Valgaard toward Albion; a trip that apparently took much, much longer to do in the late fall and winter, because an airship required hot air to rise. The severe cold on the Valgaard side of the mountains shut down air travel for part of each winter.

It was late summer, and even before they descended from the cold heights of the sky, the warm air from ocean currents that wrapped around the frost from the Fire Islands--called this because of their flame-like shape when viewed on a map, and the equatorial heat, resulting in dense rainforests covering the islands--to Albion had altered the weather dramatically from that of the sky over Peth, which was still warm this time of the year.

As they descended, the stifling over eighty-degree weather gradually surrounded them. An intense rush of humidity enveloped Onya and persisted, making her cold-weather skin crawl with the prickling feeling of sweat that began to bead on her neck and slowly tickle her back.

Onya wondered if any of the clothes--dresses, corsets, and garters--she packed, which had been meant to be of Albion-make, would not still be too thick for the weather.

She was surprised by how warm it was. She had known about the air currents, but the weather was as warm or warmer than the Solgra, which was five hundred atomic miles to the south. Peth, which was on almost the same latitude as Rorik would be lucky to get a high much over seventy on a summer day. The difference of over ten degrees was almost unbearable.

She hoped for her sake that she would get used to it and quickly. The ship descended quickly from high over the Ash Vale, where the densely packed Valley Ash trees grew to enormous heights of over one hundred fifteen atomic yards, almost to the heights of the Coastal Reds southwest of Rorik that extended from the Salgar cape to the southern coast. The moist air from those same coastal currents that was forced to settle and fall by the mountains to Albion's east in dense rain and almost daily fog helped the giant trees to grow.

Onya had been worried about the flight over the mountains, because of the recent dragon attack. The smuggler captain had been confident, having made the run before in as little as seventeen hours--a seemingly impossible feat.

Their ship was much smaller too, which the captain said was a good thing. It didn't make Onya feel any better or safer. What made the biggest difference was that Valessa, who Onya still trusted despite Eleanor's death, had also told her that the attack on the Vagalla was definitely an assassination, though when the stone peaks of the mountains appeared beneath the ship, she did not forget to pray.

Until she was actually flying over the mountains, she wasn't sure how much anxiety she would have to quell, but her trip essentially had to go over the mountains by air. The pass through the south of the Evoruls was blocked by Akrin as a military border and went into the Solgra so far to the south. It would take her weeks to get across Normany rather than just less than a day of flight, split by one overnight stop.

The main overland route called Pili's Pass, which connected central Valgaard to northern Normany, was currently blocked by a massive dragon often referred to as simply the Loch Monster--not many that had traveled the pass in recent years had lived to tell the tale--plus there was a tall wall on the Akrin side, though she had been assured that it was easy to go around.

Finally, the northern pass, which was the one most often used by large, merchant caravans that couldn't ship by air was the longest and coldest, having to cross near to the southern-most portion of the glaciers. It also had additional dangers like sabretooth tigers once north of the mountains, and outside the boundaries northern Valgaard or Albion. Caravans often had to deal with magical pests and cursed beasts, which mercenaries ran around the north killing on behalf of Valgaard's large northern population.

To send a letter back to Peth, and Princess Valessa, would not be easy, because Onya would need to rely on the same smugglers going by land or air. Due to the nature of their business, they didn't maintain any formal schedule but at least didn't keep a formal log of all correspondence transferred. The smuggler captain said he would notify her if he was making a run to Peth, but he often stayed away from it during the fall and winter.

"We should be touching into the airdocks in twenty minutes and then I'll have to handle customs before anyone gets to leave the ship," the captain informed her, just as she had thought of him. His eyes lingered on the beautiful, slender Onya, but she was too enraptured by the view to notice.

As they had neared the city, the giant stone citadel of Rorik emerged from the haze of the distance and rose above even the impressive height of the trees. It stood at over one hundred fifty atomic yards tall, overlooking Rorik, its twin harbors, and the surrounding edge of the valley.

The large Angel Bay wound around to the south, where the distant mouth to the bay was only visible on the edge of the horizon as a narrow gap between the dark green bluffs of either peninsula, each covered in the Coastal Reds where the fog and mist of the ocean spray collected the densest.

Rorik was on the northeast side of Angel Bay and had a second harbor on its north end that touched the Burlgate Bay and a second harbor, formerly Piruma township. The second bay was a long cut out from the bluffs to the west of the city, that almost looked like a dragon's head from the sky, where the teeth of the mouth were the sea ships of the bay.

Burlgate was the further of the two bays, but the closest to the Orichalc mines in central Albion and thus the busier of the two harbors. Because of this there was a long, walled off road that could be seen from the sky that ran from the Piruma Harbor beside Burlgate Bay to the north end of the large city of Rorik that stretched away from Angel Bay along the gradual incline of the large bluff of the Salgar cape. Along Rorik's water's edge were a series of calm beaches, protected by the high, green western bluffs.

The city itself was of about one million people at the time, nestled within a series of stone walls that encircled the port and the tall castle. These had been reinforced with iron just as the palace tower was built around an iron and wood framework. Only the outer facades were essentially a multitude of large granite obelisks that gradually thinned toward the top. Each of the four façades and windows were carved into the wood behind the stone obelisks at intervals, and on these vertical lines, faux stone was placed on the external wall to give the appearance of congruity.

The tower was pulled to the northeast of the city, at its lowest level and where it connected with the hypothetical limits of the Ash Vale. The bluffs that rose to the south of the tower were dotted with many houses that either faced toward the bay or overlooked the city itself, which mainly lay between the palace tower and the bluffs to the southwest. The houses were mainly white with dark brown stained wooden supports in large, crossed bars between vertical support beams--a diagonal pairing for each floor.

The smaller harbor on Angel Bay, Haley's Harbor, looked more like it was meant for smaller, leisure ships, though the airdocks had also been placed west of the beaches on the northern end of the bay along a series of green bluffs. The smugglers' ship rounded far to the north of the palace, giving a wide view of the city, and then curved back to the south to reach the airdocks, showcasing the stone palace with the backdrop of the thousands of leafy green giants. Thankfully, had the land been a Jotunheim, giants' territory, once like the far northern mountains beyond the eight lakes were rumored to still be, the maneaters had long been rendered extinct to Albion.

The city was lit up by the sun when they arrived and sea eagles, birds as white as the sails of the ships, sea and air, swept across the sky, cawing at fish in the sea and circling over those that the fishermen unloaded in barrels at the Haley's Harbor port. As the ship neared, Onya could see the men working from the sky and fending off the swarming birds, who scattered at the sound of a percussion pistol firing powder into the air.

There were many also smaller, colorful birds that appeared on the trees at the edges of the city walls as the airship neared the docks. Yellow, blue, and red ones. Often called finches, jays, and cardinals. She had never seen so many of any bird in one place, let alone four species.

The airship docked against a tall, vertical iron beam, meant to hold it in place while regulating air to the ship's balloons. Onya checked that she had her paperwork in order. After docking, she would still have to wait while the smugglers worked with the customs officials, likely bribing them to say that there was nothing contraband on board, while they made a faux inspection of some of the boxes and stamped the large wooden crates and their paperwork.

Onya would then have to hope that her falsified documents weren't out of date, and that if they were, she would be allowed into the city anyway, un-accosted. She doubted she would have any trouble, but proof of travel authorization was generally required to move between nations. If anything failed, she would show her employment expectation form, which was also meant to get her into the palace, starting in a matter of days.

She waited for hours as the night fell before the smugglers were finally let off the ship. They stayed behind to work the contraband out of its hidden compartments, while Onya dodged the captain, who looked to make another advance, and after a brief glance by the customs officials, she disappeared into the city.

She gave up trying to find her intended lodging as the light died and the city switched to oil lamps. Instead, she took a nearby inn's room near the bay, and would find the house where a room was intended to be let for her in the morning by a Mr. Elliot and his wife, Mrs. Robin Bunting. They had apparently recently put an ad into the newspaper that Valessa had been able to secure through her network ahead of Onya's arrival in Rorik. Until she was given a titled position on the staff at the palace, she would have to rent rooms rather than live in the staff quarters.

The trip was largely no hassle. Onya had been given enough gold and silver coins to get started. As a trained spy, she could handle herself in most fisticuffs and being honest with herself, she saw this as an easy opportunity when compared to working long hours with Valessa, overseeing the management of Valgaard's border safety.

This was also much less stressful than working with the 'Ice Queen of the North' who had aptly earned her nickname for her high standards and despite her youth, her ruthlessness toward traitorous behavior over the years. It would be nice to not have to worry about any of that for a while, though Onya knew she would eventually go back.

* * *

She found the Buntings' house the next morning. The couple appeared to have been hard up due to an injury to the elder Mr. Bunting's leg making it difficult for him to take one of the dock jobs or renew his services as a butler. The young renter, Onya, had spared them from yet another week of simply bread and water on the meager cleaning wages that Mrs. Bunting, a former maid like Onya was to be at the palace, had gotten. After Onya had paid for the first three weeks with a gold piece, the Buntings had begun to attend to their affairs.

After unpacking her things, carefully defensive about the bag that held her clockwork devices, and getting situated in the house, Onya let herself relax by the window in the drawing room with the paper at a small table for two; a couch and a lounge chair looked at a fireplace, which surprisingly had been used during the warm summer, likely for light. At night, they lit the oil lamps for the first time in months, and Mr. Bunting mentioned that there were long-term plans for the city to switch to Orichalc power.

The next day Onya went to the palace where she was shown around by Miss Logan, the head housekeeper. There were essentially thirty-five floors to the building, which were largely empty or related to trade management and exports. The floors were serviced by four staircases, made of iron and wood at each of the corners.

It would be Onya's job to help to clean the fireplaces and stock the pantries that were on almost every floor. It was essential that she did this as there was no real fire suppression system, though the floors themselves were separated by solid bricks of granite. If a floor started on fire, it would take a long time and money to repair. Any messes made on her assigned floors would also be her responsibility. There were other maids on hand that would clear other floors.

For now, she mainly had to attend to the pantries on her assigned floors, during the afternoon. Once winter arrived, she would be working late at night in the palace as the fires would burn during the day. She would have an oil lamp for heat and light as she worked, and if it was too cold to leave the palace afterwards, she could stay in the staff quarters, bunks mainly for titled personnel, such as Miss Logan and the butlers, that made up some of the middle floors. These staff members attended to the Lord Stone from morning to night and kept various other aspects of the palace in working order.

Also among the middle floors was the palace kitchen that served the lord and much of the attendant staff such as herself and the other maids. After Miss Logan had showed her how to do the job, where the storage room was adjacent to the kitchen and where to deliver tea leaves, biscuits, and hot water to on her assigned floors by walking up the stairs and doing each floor one at a time, and then repeating the process, she was left to her devices at the kitchen level.

Onya, like most staff, was forbidden to go into any of the staff offices, especially Lord Stone's. She didn't expect to be sneaking into small rooms, though. She only needed to make Stone's acquaintance and learn more about the rest of the staff to protect herself. Only after that could she figure out a way to promote an alliance with Valgaard.

For a moment, Onya just stood there. It had been a lot to take in and a lot had suddenly changed, but she needed to start doing her real job soon, espionage. She wasn't sure how careful the last spy had been to be spirited away, so she didn't want to make any rash movements.

There were many secret organizations in the world of which she only knew of in theory. In reality, it could be as simple as someone from Akre on assignment by the senate having a permanent position among Stone's staff to maintain order, noticing someone out of place.

Before she went about her tasks, she just listened. She was just outside of the staff mess hall that was adjacent to the kitchens and the storeroom. If she was to place one of the clockwork devices, somewhere around here would be perfect. She was alone, and people would not linger for a prolonged amount of time in this nook.

On second thought, she realized that she couldn't hear anything, so she walked around. She also needed to find an alcove to hide the clockwork bug from prying eyes. It was not a small device. The clockwork creature itself fit easily in her palm, but it carried a large, blue wax cylinder on its back that was carved into by tiny arms whenever the creature picked up sudden noise.

Both the carved wax dust and the bug itself needed to be hidden. Someone who recognized the device only had to melt or smash the wax to render the information lost forever.

Onya strained to hear anything at all as she walked along the hallway from one end to the other, quietly. At a vent between the room and the hallway, she could hear the muffled conversation coming from within the mess. As she strained further, she realized she could make out just a bit of a conversation, especially an agitated exclamation.

"He doesn't care for the people!"

"Yes, I agree!"

Onya strained still further to hear.

"In response to the tragedy of the Vagalla that killed so many civilians, all he did was get high."

"Yes, that's what my friend said."

"Who is this friend of yours and why should we believe him?"

"He was one of the telegram messengers on the day of the crash."

"Why didn't the butler take the message to the lord?"

"My friend thought it was urgent."

"Like we all should!"

"So, he skipped the appropriate channels?"

"Yes, but he found Lord Stone all right. He was just getting high in his office alone! Could barely speak. It was as if he had too much gin or whiskey is what he said. Only he was lifeless awake."

"That's all he does lately I heard. All he does is hide away in the castle and get high."

"True, he rarely ever leaves the castle walls, and if he does, it's only to meet with the rich and elite of Albion!"

"What are you doing?" came a stern voice from behind her rather than from behind the iron grate.

Onya turned from where she had been frozen in place, just at the edge of where she could hear through the grate. Miss Logan was watching her curiously.

"I wasn't sure where to go first," said Onya, smiling.

"You should likely start with getting the hot water from the kitchen and taking it up to floor thirty-five then, shouldn't you?" asked Miss Logan, pointing to the other side of the hall and ushering Onya along.

Onya rushed to get the hot water and the other items to stock the simple pantries, so the gentlemen who worked in the palace could make themselves afternoon tea. She couldn't have placed the bug now anyway. Not only had she not brought one along, but she would have to find a time to make sure the space behind the grate was large enough--and to remove it without anyone hearing her unscrew the metal.

She carried the hot water up twenty flights of painted iron stairs and then brought the pot back down to repeat the procedure for the thirty fourth floor. She wasn't sure if she was being punished to walk up so high, but out of convenience these were the floors that the Lord Stone was supposed to be on. She planned as she was carrying the next pot of hot water up the stairs to take a look around.

Onya regretted wearing one of her dresses to her first day, despite the outfit requirements, as it was hard to see the dark stairs beneath each step. The light of the sun lit the stairs of the tower from windows, made to look like cutouts from the faux stone at the landings and in the middles of each set of stairs, though because of this lack of artificial lighting, there were many dark corners, where it was hard to judge her footing and made carrying the heavy, pot of boiled water ahead of her up the stairs exceedingly difficult.

She had to watch her step over the heavy iron, still searing hot to the touch, as she did little more than waddle up the long staircase. She was thankful that there were no gaps in the wood, because had there been, she would have seen how the iron skeleton of the staircase, jutting out from four central pillars looked almost as if they left the stairs encircling them suspended in air.

Finally, she reached the nineteenth platform, having lost count of the flights and only knew her way from the numbers on the inward doors back into the building. She turned the handle of the door with her elbow and then began backing into the hallway, nudging the door along with her back.

As she turned around to exit through the doorway, she bumped into something solid, stiff, and warm. She jumped, looking with a touch of fear at who she ran into. Realizing only too late that she had let go of the pot.

Lord Stone dipped down to catch the falling iron pot out of the air with one hand. As he rose to hand the pot back to her, it looked as if he had bowed to meet her.

When he lifted his eyes to hers, her gaze bored into him. Her piercing brown eyes and slender form struck him instantly. It was as if he had grown hungry. Her small figure, not much taller than an atomic yard and a half, cut sharply in her tight-fitting dress, with her small chest hidden by the shape of the corset beneath it. She had pulled her brown hair back into a tight, circular bun. Her red, painted lips looked inviting, forcing his mouth to water.

Onya rested her hands on the iron pot in his hands, surprised at how easily he held it in the air. When he didn't let go, she found herself staring back into his light blue-gray eyes, almost the color of ice over a shallow lake. His thick arms, broad shoulders and sharp jaw sparked up a drumming heartbeat in her chest. His light brown hair had been swept to the side in a short haircut, and his facial hair was neatly trimmed in a thin beard, touched with gray.

"I'll take this," she said and lowered her gaze, almost attempting to wrestle it from his grip.

"Nonsense, how many flights did you already carry this?" he asked, transfixed. "I'll take it the rest of the way."

She curtsied to him, and he followed her to the pantry where he poured the hot water into a tea jug and returned the iron pot to her, for her to take back down to the kitchen.

"What is your name?" he asked.

"Miss Onya Wilde, sir."

"Did you start recently?"

"Today, sir. And your name is?"

"My apologies, I am Lord Stone," he bowed, formally. "Pleased to make your acquaintance."

She nodded, masking her partial surprise mixed with self-satisfaction, and disappeared back to the staircase. Her heart raced. She had hoped to meet him but had not expected that she would be so taken by him. A painting would not have done him adequate justice.

* * *

In the coming days, she was glad that she had run into him at all. She unfortunately had few opportunities to see him, even working on his floor.

One night she stayed later than usual, hiding in the need to clean a mess on an upper floor that she had, 'inadvertently,' caused herself. After coming down the iron stairs, she checked every room before leaving a first bug in the vent between the hallway and the mess. Its small horn for collecting sound was luckily able to fit in the tiny space, though barely.

She had to hope the clockwork contraption wouldn't move the legs that it used to climb into place on walls and ceilings. In this tiny nook, it could run into the metal grates and draw attention to itself and alert those who found it to the presence of a spy. Onya would have to come back regularly to replace the cylinder and clean the shavings, while checking to see if the bug had been tampered with.

The whole process would be much easier in the winter if she was able to stay overnight. By then, she hoped that she would be able to get more cylinders made, discretely, to replenish her stock. She had gone through the first recording much faster than expected, because it had picked up so much more noise in the mess than just talking.

She had a few more bugs to place, along with other devices at her disposal. She only didn't know many other places to put them that would be both hidden and near enough to people.

Late at night at the Bunting's to not disturb their sleep below her, she worked on prepping these additional, clockwork contraptions. She listened to the first recording as quietly as she could with the side of her face and ear pressed into the horn, both to magnify the sound for her while muffling it for any other potential listeners.

During the mornings, she journaled and reviewed the timeline of events since she had arrived. There could have been someone in counterintelligence agitating the people in the castle, but there were many staff, and it was hard to add any weight to that theory with respect to any one staff member in particular.

This is likely why the previous spy didn't make it, she thought to herself. There was no way to know there was a threat until it was too late, and thankfully no one seemed to suspect her yet, likely because she was a woman.

She would have been worried that the bug could have been swept for and destroyed by shockwave, but it did not seem like any one on the staff locally paid any attention to the possibility of agent infiltration. No one appeared outwardly paranoid. Stone seemed to have some process in place to filter poison, but it was unclear how.

He took meals alone in his office rather than in one of the dining halls, fit for a variety of numbers of guests. During her short time at the palace, he hadn't even yet entertained any of the Albion dignitaries, who oversaw the land as lesser lords and ladies. Albion had once been largely a collection of city-states that had eventually submitted to one lord rule when they joined Normany during the reunification of Galdir.

The morning after one of these late sessions tweaking clockwork parts, listening to a recording, and burning the sea serpent oil well after midnight, Mrs. Bunting confronted Onya.

"What are you doing up late every night?" asked Mrs. Bunting. "It's not proper for a woman of your age to be working too hard. You should be settling down."

"Yes, of course, Mrs. Bunting."

"Don't try to placate me, Miss Wilde. You've been working late hours the entire time you've been at the palace. It's the second weekend you've been here. You should be enjoying the shops like a proper lady rather than doing whatever it is you're doing upstairs at night."

"Yes, of course. Perhaps, you're right."

"Of course, I'm right."

"Would you kindly direct my attention to the shops then, please? I could use a change of wardrobe for the next season. It's much warmer here than in the north of Albion."

"Oh, is that where you're from?"

"Yes."

"The shops all around Kenshunt Park are what you'll be needing. Some are more sophisticated than your budget may allow, but you should be able to find any, more suitable replacements."

"Thank you."

"I should be warning you as well that you may have to get used to the heat, but your clothes 'as is' don't seem much like the proper fashion for the palace."

"Quite right. Thank you again Mrs. Bunting. Where is Kenshunt Park if you don't mind me asking?"

"Just east of the bay and as the hill rises. You can't miss it." Mrs. Bunting eyed her suspiciously, and Onya took her leave then departed.

Onya relaxed when she was out of the house. The last thing she needed to do was draw attention to herself from the Buntings while she was focused on navigating the palace. She needed to still behave like an Albion woman. She had been more than a bit suspicious thus far while in their home.

Onya had belongings that she kept under lock and key. She was always burning notes and other articles of clothing in the upstairs stove. She had kept late hours at night and had come home at inconsistent times from the palace.

She followed a long road that ran northwest from the Buntings home in the east, along the underside of the south hill, until the road reached the main city avenue, which cut from east to west through a hypothetical center of the city. The palace itself, and both harbors, were on the north side of this road, while most of the shopping and houses were on the hill.

When Onya took the left off the road and walked up the hill, she came quickly to the large, green Kenshunt Park, surrounded by shops and covered in people, enjoying the sun. She was glad for the breeze off of the ocean, because she could already feel the sweat all over her. Any time one of her articles of clothing left and then re-touched her skin it felt cold and damp.

She went from shop to shop, admiring summer dresses that went above the ankle on custom wooden stands that rested in small lines near the front of the shops like artists' easels.

While shopping, Onya could not help but notice that each shop had flags for Albion rather than flags of Akre adorning their spaces. They either had the blue and silver wolf or the two gold bars on red and blue. She saw no gold eagles.

When listening to other customers make purchases, she often heard the shop keeper and customer exchange the words 'long live the lord.' Whatever upset the people in the palace staff, clearly did not extend to the rest of the city.

There were many beautiful options, though much like Valessa's latest wardrobe, they were a touch tighter to the skin than Onya expected someone like Mrs. Bunting, or Miss Logan for that matter, to appreciate. While Onya was no lady in need of a cage to puff out the bottom of her dress, she had to look respectable.

Every one of the tailors from the most expensive to the cheapest options in the market district all had the name Elmore Quinn of Akrin make on their lips to describe the cut and style of their dress, no matter how different.

Onya would have found it more amusing, but regardless of what options she looked at, she realized that she could not afford any of them. Whether they were too large or too small, and whatever the color, they were all too expensive. She was paid monthly and without her first check, even a few dresses of the cheapest tailors' were too much.

At the beginning of the day, she might have planned to hold out until the next month and then hope that as the fall and winter started in full force that she could manage with the clothes that she had brought from Valgaard. After walking in the afternoon sun for a few hours in seventy or eighty-degree weather by Odin's degree, she felt as if the entire planet was actually in a heat age rather than an ice age. Only her memory of the cold, north of the Evoruls, could have proved otherwise.

* * *

On the following Maniday morning, Onya went into the palace early. She had decided to ask Miss Logan for an advance on her first month, so that she could buy the new clothes. It seemed like a reasonable request, and as it was the equivalent of two gold pieces in dollars, she felt like it couldn't be hard for the palace to afford.

Princess Valessa threw that money around and had Onya not been traveling lightly, she would have had far more money on her than a few gold pieces and about ten silvers. With another payment of rent coming up and wanting to buy the cylinders, she would need that money for a purchase like dresses, which with every day felt more necessary. Rather than getting used to the weather, it felt like the opposite was happening.

She climbed the stairs to the kitchen level where the staff offices also were, and after ignoring the grate, not even casting it a sideways glance, she knocked on Miss Logan's door.

"Yes, who is it?"

"It is Onya, 'mam. May I come in please?"

"Yes, and please shut the door."

Onya entered and stood before the stern woman silently as Miss Logan adjusted the paper that she had been writing on. She moved her quill and ink to the side and looked up at Onya.

"Well, what is it?"

"Firstly, I'm very grateful for the job. I've come to ask for an advance on my first month salary if I may please," Onya smiled demurely.

"That charm may work on the head butler, Mr. Carter, but it won't work on me. I'll hear nothing of the sort again."

"Excuse me, Miss Logan. If you please, the weather here in the south is much warmer than I expected. I feel a little overdressed being a girl from upcountry."

"Listen here, Miss Wilde, I don't know how you got your reference or what you expect from me, but I believe you are closer to being let go than being given an advance! You never seem to finish on time. I had been meaning to talk to give you a warning. You are always working later than expected, you've caused multiple messes on the highest floors, and now you ask me for an advance!"

Onya froze. She had thought she was careful that no one had seen her depart late--and most of all Miss Logan--as Onya often had, but she could not deny any of what Miss Logan said. Even if she had a good, albeit secret reason for it.

Miss Logan might have continued to yell, but almost as soon as she had started, she had stopped. Onya could sense the large presence behind her. She assumed that Mr. Carter, whose office was next to Miss Logan's must have heard the row and come to weigh in and help to settle the dispute.

When Onya turned around, it was Lord Stone.

She was suddenly equal parts mortified and relieved. She flushed completely red, blushing out of enjoying being in the Lord Stone's dominant presence while also being equally embarrassed that he would see her for the second time when she just happened to be threatened with termination of her duties. A failure as both a spy and a maid. And yet, she was also relieved as if he might be there to help save her from the sudden predicament, given he and he alone had absolute authority over the stone tower.

Lord Stone eyed Onya, giving no indication of his inward feelings as he stared. She felt undressed by his gaze. Each woman settled their outward angst and waited for his response. Mr. Carter approached from behind him, visibly concerned.

Stone looked from one woman to the other, "I'm sorry, I overheard the discussion from the other room. I had just been speaking to Mr. Carter about the current stock of wine."

"I'm sorry my lord," Miss Logan began, "I was just saying--"

"If you could please spare me a repeat of the details, Miss Logan. I heard them just fine." Lord Stone appeared to soften in his sharp features, visibly relaxing, but his chest and shoulders remained tense and upright. "I believe we can allow Miss Wilde to be here for a full month before we worry about the quality of her work. Clearly, she still has to adjust to life on the bay."

Onya's heart skipped a beat. She had hoped he would remember her name, but it still felt strangely meaningful that he did.

"But--"

"Miss Logan," said Mr. Carter, partially under his breath as Lord Stone continued to speak.

"As for the matter of the advance, I heard that the lady needs some adjustment of wardrobe to account for the warmth of the season." Lord Stone looked at her. His eyes piercing into hers. "I would be happy to accommodate you, Miss Wilde, if you would accompany me on a short adventure to the market district at Kenshunt Park." He pronounced the word differently than Mrs. Bunting had.

Mr. Carter and Miss Logan were stunned. The Lord Stone had not gone to the market district in years. They didn't even realize that he knew there was a Kenshunt Park, or especially that the shopping district had been built up around it.

"Miss Wilde?" Lord Stone continued to look at her, almost unblinking. She felt as if she was catching her breath after running up the iron stairs with a pot of water.

"Yes?"

"Would you like that? If *I* accompanied you to the park to shop for dresses?"

"Yes, very much," she heard herself say.

"Then, Miss Logan, Mr. Carter. We will take our leave now. As usual, I will not need a guard for this jaunt. I'm perfectly capable of handling myself."

Lord Stone took her by the arm and guided her toward the iron staircase. Until that moment, she hadn't realized that he used the same stairs to get up and down the tower that she did. She could feel his deep voice through her muscles as he spoke this close to her.

"I tend to get picked up and dropped off by airship at the top of the tower, so I don't have to walk all the flights of stairs but today we can make an exception." Then realizing that she walked them multiple times each day, he added, "That doesn't mean I don't ever use them though."

When they exited the palace, they took an almost mirrored route from the path she had taken over the weekend to get to the park. By following a southwest facing road at almost the exact same angle as the northwest road from the Bunting's, they arrived at the same, main east-west road, which they then took to Kenshunt.

As they went, it felt as if the entire city had come to life and every person that could was shouting and lining the streets, watching and cheering, for the Lord Stone. Onya had never seen so much adoration for one person before in her life, not even the good King Hughgar.

Even Stone seemed surprised by the reaction, and he simply waved as they had to walk down the middle of the road. All of traffic had stopped in place while the lord and the beautiful maid, who everyone must have suddenly assumed was a potential future lady of their deeply religious leader, so sadly widowed, went to the market.

Once there, Lord Stone refused to be given anything for free, and instead bought almost every dress at one of the shops in the middle of the market. It was also middle in quality and middle in price, and Onya couldn't be happier.

After Lord Stone had the dresses shipped back via the merchant to the lady's accommodations, the pair, enchanted with each other as they were, looked for any excuse to prolong the day. Stone pointed out that they were such a short walk from the water, he could show her a particularly special place--if it was still around.

Onya said yes quickly, so Stone took her the long way back toward the north end of the city and Haley's Harbor, which nestled within the nook in Angel Bay of the peninsula that separated it from Burlgate Bay to the north.

He longed to find a restaurant he had not been to in years that he had went to often as a young man, before he took over for this father as the lord protector of Albion. His mother had first taken him there back when it had overlooked both bays, giving its patrons a sweeping view of the natural beauty and all sea ships that came in for Rorik.

In days long ago Burlgate's Piruma Harbor had been an entirely separate town, north of Rorik, but over the last forty years as the Orichalc trade intensified, Rorik had grown along the idealistic beach to the south of Albion's industrial heart, and Burlgate quickly became part of the larger metropolitan area's footprint.

They reached a long, paved stone walkway that stretched out above the bluffs that ran down from the city to the sandy beach that stretched out from the far west of the bay toward the harbor that lay quietly below the watchful castle tower to the east. A soft, cool wind whispered along the coast to the northeast barely disturbing the water washing against the shore in listless lines of shallow white.

Many people sat along the beach, dipping their feet into the icy water. Tents and umbrellas had been stuck into the golden sand. There were men and women and families stretching out as the sun shone, hot and heavy, in a cold world.

Stone looked from end to end, along the long walk, that he had so rarely visited, looking at the buildings and the sand; the water, and the bluffs; the harbor and its ships, swaying in the gentle wind.

Eyes turned toward him, and he realized that the procession following the two of them had only grown. He blushed a deep crimson, realizing that he had known full well that the city papers would assume the two of them were a couple.

Onya watched the stoic face of the strong man change color, and she smiled, wondering what he was thinking and hoping it was about her. He towered over her, but he walked slow and easy at her pace. He spoke only briefly while listening to her share snippets of what she liked about the city and the view that stretched out before them.

As they walked along the cobblestone, the procession began to chant to him, "the true king of Albion! All hail the true king of Albion!"

Onya's eyes glanced back at Stone, who waved and smiled, blinking quietly at the crowd, simultaneously accepting their praise with quiet deference and waving it off as if it was just something to say.

In reality, the color had drained from his face as he thought of the peacefulness of the beachgoers, who turned to join the cheering that grew louder still. There were very real dangers facing his rich, little nation on the coast if he were to claim it as king.

He thought of his lone son, Eduard's, adamant claims that Imeria had been overstepping in the south. East Cardane ships had been used by Akre to move Akrin troops to the western colonies.

They were not surrounded, but their envious wealth had grown while the strength of their natural geographical defenses had weakened in importance and nations further to the south continued to gain power. Albion may have been rich, but they were a small nation by size and population who had enjoyed general obscurity amongst the many nations of the empire, until now.

If Eduard was right about Imeria's encroachment and his late friend, Erolin, had been right about the need to expand their allies, the silver coast was indeed a target, only protected for so long by the sheer size and mountainous nature of Normany, which separated the sun-filled western coast from the city of Gold, Akre, in the east.

Stone wondered if his day with Onya had been merely an excuse for a distraction from the concerns thrust upon him by the death of his old friend.

Even if it was, the temporary respite was welcome. He knew that Sven still lived, and it remained to be seen what Sven would do in the wake of his cousin's death. Even if waiting was all Stone felt he could do, he felt shackled to waiting as if he were in a walking prison that followed him beyond the castle walls, making him impotent and incapable of action. As he thought about any move that he could make, he inevitably felt that it would only invite open hostility toward Albion, which he knew could not stand long without allies or Normany.

Despite the breeze kicking up small drifts of leaves, falling from the trees along the shore, the sun beat down on Onya's neck, and sweat began to bead along her shoulders. She had worn too many layers for this section of the city, which seemed an entirely different climate from the tower by the trees and between the buildings, now laying to their east.

Stone noticed and his tension seemed to break as he chuckled gently and said, "if you think Rorik is warm, you won't last very long in Piruma."

"Why's that?" she asked and smiled as he purchased an umbrella from a vendor walking along the cobblestone coastal walk, resting on filled in and smoothed, rocky bluffs that ran along the majority of the coast.

"The temperatures feel at least five degrees warmer. At least," and he looked at her as he opened the umbrella to block the sunlight. His eyes caught the light of the sun just above the shadow, and she could see some slight dampness at the edges of his hairline. "It's lucky that it's due to its dry heat. Despite being further north and also on the water, the southern bay has always trapped the cool breeze off the ocean and kept Rorik just that much cooler."

Onya nodded, and those were almost the last words Stone spoke as they walked onward, toward the ships in the north, side by side joined by the hushed crash of the waves on the shore and the voices of those who watched them.

As they walked on, the silence between them grew heavy, and she slowly became increasingly aware that she, herself, had been sent here on a mission, and that she had become wrapped up, in some unknown way, with a man she knew very little about and who promised nothing. He had been impulsive, and she had reacted to it with a similar lack of inhibition.

When they arrived, the restaurant was just as he remembered it, except for the view, and he was given a corner table at the front, overlooking Haley's Harbor and the many buildings that ran on the peninsula between them and Piruma. Everywhere they went they were watched by the people.

Though the chanting had stopped, some people got bored or stayed busy and went on with their lives, most eyes darted to and became transfixed by the imposing image of Lord Stone. The people watched the way that the lord and his potential lady ate their midday meal and talked to each other. The kids mimicked them openly in the street while the others, mainly young men and women, made mental notes as to how they would next hold a fork or wipe their mouth with a towelette.

1513 - Chapter 8

The sound of the number of people walking was louder than the blare of one hundred trumpets. They followed just one, simple man. The people flowed toward him like a river, handing him seeds.

Saint Sven Greenski, the ever-popular, hero of the people returned them as fully grown flowers. He turned away dead pets, cats and dogs, he could not create life where none existed, but a sick man, an injured man, he would reach out and touch him as if he was touched by Fros himself.

The gentle giant, some murmured had more giants blood than that of the House Arandil was nevertheless much like his healer ancestor, who claimed to trace his own lineage back to the forgotten lords of Old Galdir, from the times before the blights and who were among those who stood with the prophet during the wars against the Otum elves.

Sven towered over everyone, and it felt like everything about him was larger than life. He stood taller, even than Deronson; he would have dwarfed him by a head or more. And he was as round as a wheel as if he had eaten one too many hams every day for five years, and yet, when someone tripped among his adoring people, as nimbly as an elf in a secluded glen, he got her right back on her feet and sent her ahead of him.

People held out their hands just to touch him, and the people of Leidyn welcomed him with celebration and awe. The only ones who didn't seem taken in were Erold and his two companions.

As Sven passed, he noticed Erold out of the corner of his eye, and briefly acted as if he hadn't seen him. He made a small motion with his shoulder as if to follow, but Erold, feeling spurned, didn't notice. Moon, did, though, so she pushed Erold into the stream of townspeople heading for wherever it was that Sven was leading them.

Sven looped around the city once, people cheering from their windows as he went, while he used a series of powerful conjuration spells to throw up decorations that were strewn from oil lamp to oil lamp or hung in midair above the street. After each time he cast another spell, the crowd let out another hurrah, louder than the one before it. It amazed even Erold that after all Sven's feats of magic, he could still have the stamina to throw up entertainments with the flick of a wrist that filled the world with color.

Sven led the entire company over the bridge onto the island

center, and then he did the loop again, this time letting the decorations fizzle as he walked past as if he were collecting trinkets back into a box. Finally, once the crowd had finally thinned, and he found himself near one of the lines of houses overlooking the lake on the far hill, he stopped.

Sven turned around to address the crowd. Erold didn't want to listen. Part of him was jealous of Sven, who distributed affection and received it in what seemed an ever-increasing amount. Moon and Volstad, however, did listen.

They heard Sven say that he and his men, who were among the crowd or arriving would be staying in these two houses behind him. He had arranged it ahead of time to rent them for his officers and men. He was, personally, happy to answer any questions as the rightful king had before him. Only he was here and not north in the mountain fortress at Seylil. He was a man among the people, who had come to show his love to all of the Solgra, including Leidyn, during the Frostmas season, and then he emphasized "as we all mourn the loss of our dearly beloved father and king, Erolin, who never stopped fighting for the rights of Normany."

Sven looked at Erold when he said these last words and felt a moment of shame and emptiness upon seeing how dejected his nephew looked, sulking beside his new companions, who Sven recognized as two of the most senior members of his deceased cousin's royal guard.

When he caught the eyes of one of them, he motioned to the house on the right, where he had said his men would be staying, then he disappeared into the house on his left, along with the officers of his own guard.

He would be along after night fall, or before then if the crowd thinned out to talk specifics. However, he had decided with the news of the Akrin senate moving to elect an Emperor, he wanted Erold's existence to remain a secret.

* * *

Moon and Volstad pushed and pulled Erold into the soldiers' quarters, curious to see how many men would arrive. The houses were large and long but appeared to have only about ten bedrooms apiece.

Perhaps, he'd have a bigger force arriving at some later date, but if he couldn't collect more than fifty men at five to a bedroom, or eighty to ninety total if all the rooms were converted, there would still be a rather large discrepancy in the field between the Greenski men and Akre.

Moon, Volstad, and Erold took a set of chairs and waited alone in the house, watching the darkening lake until Sven appeared, dressed in a new set of clothes, and having recently showered. He handed Volstad and Moon a set of fresh clothes and apologized to Erold for not having had anything his size.

"Let's eat."

A pair of officers came in shortly after him with cooked duck and lamb chops. Then another pair of officers came in with roasted potatoes and yams. After twenty or so men entered with trays of cooked food, they settled in around the table and began to eat as one large group. The officers did most of the talking, most meeting officially for the first time, so though no one was sure who the trio of new recruits were, they didn't pry.

Volstad and Moon had only ever met Sven, who had more recently been establishing a formal following, and had only begun to assemble the structure of a people's army of Normany by coordinating with the local militias, following the unfortunate and fiery downfall of his beloved cousin.

When the eating was done, Sven commanded the men to distribute their things to their rooms or to play cards while he had a private chat with the new recruits.

After the room had cleared out, Sven stood up to check outside the windows before turning to Erold and smiling that same, old smile that he gave to everyone freely and fully, with his fat rosy cheeks and aura of warmth, "Erold, my boy, I see you've shrunk since the last time I've seen you."

"I wasn't sure you had seen me out there in the street," Erold's frustration filtered through his voice.

"Easy there. There's been a lot of news, and I've decided it's best that for now, we keep your identity secret. My staff is mostly new, and I haven't determined I can trust any of them yet. But, you."

"What about me?"

"You're flanked by the Abrim Volstad and the Elara Moon. I have heard their praises many a time."

"You flatter us, Sven, but are you implying that you have any sort of plan with any of this? It's all seemed a bit haphazard, and are you staying in Leidyn through Frostmas?"

"This may be a difficult conversation to have in front of Erold, given the events of the last week or so."

"Let's have it," said Erold, determined to have a say in the matter rather than waiting to be directed from place to place like he was still his father's child.

"I'm sure you may have seen the recent headlines in the papers?"

"Yes, I have," said Moon, though not speaking for Volstad or Erold, she had assumed it was more relevant to her anyway, considering she was the one who still watched Erold's back. Her suspicions of Volstad's motives for staying by his side still hadn't become clear.

"There's been a lot of movement in the senate behind the scenes, and to try to put a long story short. There could be a fight for Normany independence shortly."

"What's the long version of that?" asked Volstad, "because I'm not following."

"An Emperor has been elected even if they haven't fully announced it yet. His name is Polesar, and he's led the modernization of the army ever since having led the recapture effort of Akre, after its sacking in 1495. He's instituted reforms throughout the armies, but none more poignant to now than the establishment of a coordinated central army. There have already been troop movements from Verdas and Ithlin to staging grounds near the city. It is my understanding that there are to be more announcements, but they intend to absolve Normany's autonomy to establish central rule over Old Galdir."

"So, this would effect Normany and Albion?"

"Yes, for the most part the other Old Galdir nations, having been conquests of Normany during the unification wars, haven't had independent monarchies since, except for Ingra."

"What does this have to do with me?" asked Erold.

"They'll label anyone who tries to claim the Normany throne an usurper, an offense punishable by death. Now, I believe in a free Normany, and my men do too. But, there is a point where idealism fades, and against the legions of Akrin, we're badly outmatched." Sven paused, "Akre doesn't know you live, and you supersede any claim to the throne that Akre may try to leverage, in effect, your cousin Aurelia. Rather than risk you gaining political support, they would kill you."

"So, Erold, we're keeping up the ruse that you're dead, so you may have a chance to challenge for the throne of Normany, in the future," Moon looked at Sven across the table, "if things go badly for Sven."

"Unfortunately, that is precisely right. The election of an emperor can mean only one thing. They intend to go to war. In my opinion first against Valgaard unless something stops them, and then who knows. The world is a big place, but once they've re-established control over Valgaard, they would be able to move their full legions with more freedom, without having to worry about an opportunistic counterattack on the capital."

"Like 1495," said Moon, thinking briefly on that spring long ago when King Hughgar had attacked, and she had met Erolin in the chaos. She had been following the thread of a case as chief inspector across a number of years, but when she had discovered the truth of it, she had been too late to save anyone else in Chelsea Palace as Valgaard simultaneously closed in.

"Yes," said Sven, watching Moon think. "Even if they wanted to attack somewhere else, they would be putting themselves at risk. And, even if Valgaard means to be peaceful, neither side can trust the other."

"So, if you got in the way of that potential attack on Valgaard?"

"Due to the movement of troops, they've already made, I am sensing that they anticipated my claim, and will move to meet me in battle."

"Then, I will fight too."

"I appreciate the spirit, but that's too risky. If I die, you will be the last and best hope of a free Normany."

Erold looked like he was about to say something, but Moon spoke, "Before you disagree with your uncle Sven here. He has a point. There is a lot more to the Empire than meets the eye, and my own experience with what the senate does in the shadows has led me here."

"What do they do in the shadows?"

"Perhaps that is a story for another time," said Sven, and he turned to Volstad who appeared to be mulling over what Moon had said carefully, "Abrim, you haven't said anything this evening. Do you have anything to add?"

"You seem to have everything very figured out here, and I appreciate the detail. I am struggling to see how Moon, or I fit into this dragon's shit."

"I would like you to be immediately retained as Erold's 'secret keepers.' I'll give you an officer's salary."

"We won't be obliged to fight on behalf of the army, right?" asked Volstad.

"No, I would have the two of you continue on as you have been with a bit of support," Sven looked across the table at the three of them, and then realizing the time was getting away from him, he turned to get up. "Are we agreed?"

"Yes, of course."

"Abrim?"

"Yes."

Erold was a little miffed that he didn't have any say in it, but Moon and Volstad had been decent companions thus far. Even if it felt like they would be chaperoning him out of trouble, they had done the same for his father.

"If you'll excuse me, it appears to have gotten dark, and I don't have a jacket. In addition, I have to run before anyone suspects anything strange among the officers. Regards."

Sven closed the yellow front door behind him, leaving the trio alone again in the house.

"What do they do in the shadows?" asked Erold again.

"I could never quite figure it out," lied Moon, annoyed, but not sure at what. The last thing she wanted to dig into was her past as the chief inspector in Akre with Erold. When you're the lead detective in a city of four and a half million people, there are more than that many secrets; some she wouldn't ever forget.

"You can tell me."

Moon left the room. She hadn't let the kid out of her sight for over a week, but at the moment, she needed some space to decompress. She had gone through yet another near-death experience and dead king, living the same past few days as he had. She needed a rest.

"Best to let it drop Erold," said Volstad.

"But--"

"The way she walked away...I'm guessing it's something that is still eating away at the edges of her mind." Volstad watched after Moon until she disappeared into one of the bedrooms. He saw that she had left her fresh change of clothes behind but thought it better than to give them to her right away.

"Erold, why don't you get some sleep? I'll figure out a way to get you a better change of clothes tomorrow, and we'll be safe with Sven. The holiday season is about to start with Frostmas, and it will be good to focus on something other than traveling the countryside for a change."

Erold nodded and headed off to bed, leaving Volstad alone at the table near the front of the house.

Volstad had said that Sven was the safe option, but he was beginning to not be so sure. Akre wasn't that far away, and troop movements were not a good sign. The first step would be to save up whatever money he could get, and maybe the next would be cashing in a favor with an old employer he had recently been in touch with, regarding other matters.

* * *

They weren't living lavishly, but they had regained some sense of normalcy in the days after Sven, the saint, had arrived in Leidyn. Moon had always been skeptical from afar, but the man's magnanimity up close had shaken her in a way. He seemed too good to be true, and yet continued to be convincing.

After a week or so, Moon had turned part of her salary in silvers and half-silver pieces into a timeline of events as told from the front page of the Akrin Ledger, which she had never liked much compared to the Leader, but the Leader didn't deliver any copies as far as Leidyn.

The first news coming out of Akre was of the public tragedy of so many innocent civilians perishing on board the passenger cruiser, the Vagalla, when it crashed into the mountains after being attacked by dragons. After a few days of search parties-- no doubt put together by the senate who she blamed for the incident-- investigating the incident, there had been few escape crafts discovered, which was seen as positive news.

The dire turn of events occurred when a confirmed survivor reported that the king who was acting governor-general of the independent duchy of Normandy had been not only confirmed on-board but to have passed when trying to rescue the ship from a boarding party there to steal valuables. The wreckage of two ships was confirmed by search parties. The paper went on to read that no doubt the commotion is what drew the dragons near, and that the heroic actions of the king, who would be ascended in death out of respect by the senate, should be regarded as superior to the circumstances despite the outcome.

In other news, it was reported that the king's son may have been on board, as he had been missing as well. Though little was publicly known about him, he had not appeared in Seylil and would be sorely missed.

Meanwhile, the senate was confirming the vote on the election of Emperor Polesar in response to the tragedy, He would in effect, lead Akrin's legions in Erolin's place. Commentary by the paper pointed out that Polesar would be a more than fit choice to lead. He had formally been the head of both the western and southern armies and already launched numerous reforms in the military to professionalize squadron mages and create units that could act independent of a delayed chain in command. His election would convince Akrin's many enemies that the Republic remains strong in the wake of this tragedy.

In a later issue, it was noted that Emperor Polesar would give an introductory speech, where he would commemorate the late king Erolin for his valor and the senate would further push the church to grant Erolin sainthood.

She had read all the papers and felt re-assured for the moment that they had time. Across all of the editions of the Ledger, there amounted to the equivalent of a footnote mentioning the potential disappearance of Erold, and they didn't even include his name, which in her opinion, likely meant that they were trying to appease the hard-nosed, secret royalists, who held out for a return to stronger joint rule. The senate itself had little reason to give up general autonomy on governing the empire, and while the paper didn't point it out, the election of an Emperor was a clear move to consolidating Old Galdir under their power.

Sven was right that the Empire's ultimate goal was most likely expansionism, and Valgaard was a first step. The conversation that Moon had recently been privy to with Lord Stone suggested that the election was to act as an indirect threat against Sven and Stone, who now had to consider the possibility of war against Akre if either was to attempt secession. Neither could stand alone, but combined they would still need a nation with the size and power of Valgaard to stave off Akre.

Moon had gathered at least that much, but she was also aware that Normany wasn't the only country in the world, and that Valgaard's princess was also aggressively attempting to counterbalance the potential offensive power of Akrin as the Empire consolidated its armies and resources.

Moon may have felt re-assured for the moment, but the danger to Sven was very real. If the new emperor, Polesar, made good on his promise to bring war on anyone who threatened Akrin dominance, then Sven would soon be first on the list.

In that case, it would be imperative that she and Volstad, or just her, figured out how to get Erold out of the country and into exile before the senate figured out that he was still alive and came looking to tie up a loose end.

Of the places they could go, there was really only one option, which meant having to cross one of the largest and highest mountain ranges in the world without the help of an airship and no chance of finding one.

To the south was the independent island of Pavol, but it was under constant threat from Imeria and surrounded by East Cardane shipping, which had fully allied to Akrin in recent decades. To the west was Albion, but Moon couldn't be certain that Lord Stone would survive the coming year either. East was of course the core of Akrin's power, which held a central position on the West Ahrian subcontinent.

This meant the only option was north to Valgaard, and to get there, going over the Evorul mountains, where dragons reigned supreme. Moon didn't want to be the one to convince Erold that it was their best and perhaps only option. The subject of dragons potentially being a sensitive topic.

* * *

Sven found unique ways to spend time with Erold under the guise of normal acts of service to the community of Leidyn, where he decided he would spend the month leading up to Frostmas before most likely moving further south back to the Áelin River as autumn began in full and winter neared.

It would give him time to collect a troop and keep him far enough away from Akre to see any armies coming. He could not conceive of the enemy marching during the month of Ivanssun, and after the autumnal equinox and celebration of Fros, the frost would fall.

An army would be foolish to begin a march in the autumn, with the risk of being caught deployed during the winter months and the numerous holiday celebrations of the late fall and early winter to mark the changing of the sun, would certainly devastate morale if they had to remain in makeshift positions during the long months of ice and snow.

One of these events that Sven conscripted Erold for was a special tradition that he had kept for himself once he had begun to earn a modest living in the Solgra. On the second Zenday of Ivanssun, a day when merchants traditionally slashed the price of their goods by half in advance of the holiday seasons of gift giving, Sven would help those who were in the most need by giving out gifts, food, and aid to those who could not afford even half-priced goods.

The desperate, needy, and poor had a special place in Sven's heart every holiday season, because of his own unfortunate circumstances as a young man. Sven would always have a soft spot for especially the children stuck in unfortunate circumstances, as he had spent the majority of his teenage years during the transitionary period in Akrin's history that followed the spring of 1495. It was a time period, which had marked generational upheaval in the history of the nation.

His family had been forgotten by the senate and the country, and they didn't have the resources or connections of his cousin, Erolin. For a time, they were left to beg and to start anew, wandering the nation for anything, whether work, food, or a decent place to sleep. Sven's father and then his poor widowed mother did not have the stamina to survive in the way that Sven had. He had watched them succumb to the desperation, surprised at the lack of good will that came their way despite their abilities.

Sven could have used that experience to make himself bitter and mean, especially at Erolin who eventually found him. He could have given up on the nation and its people, like they had given up on him and his parents.

But, that was not who he was. He may have been a mountain of a man, among mountainous men. Each of his legs were often measured against tree trunks from town to town, wherever he went.

Instead, he turned it into his fuel to bring back the Normany of old. The Normany that existed before the plush pillows of the throne of Akre, once only Normany's capital, decided to reunite Old Galdir, whether it was attacked or attacking, it altered the fate of the nation as Akre began using Normany's people to wage war across continents.

He longed to return to the time before the countryside had turned, led astray by the greed that seeped from beneath the metaphorical walls of the ever-expanding 'city of gold' that had long left the walls that once defended humanity from blight and Domiscus behind. The city was now protected instead by the desire of men and women across the globe to make a gold coin, and it was often said that 'few find its peace eternal.'

From house to house among the houses that could not be seen from the town square or the lake, Sven went and Erold followed, carrying the sack of toys while Sven carried trays of food. He could have also carried the toys, but the stubborn Erold insisted, trying desperately to keep the overflowing bag from dragging on the ground.

Some houses were little more than ramshackle walls to the point that calling them houses was a kindness. They were mere shanties, made of scraps of wood and metal that had not been made into bronze or had been discarded during the production of some other house in town. The floors were lined with old newspapers, and the fires were lit with them too, glowing strange colors as the ink caught fire with the pages.

When they were just out of sight or ear shot between a collection of shanties at one end of a hill to another collection at the next hill, Erold whispered a question to Sven, careful to make sure no one else was around to hear, "Who are these people, and why do they live like this?"

"Do you mean to assume that they choose this life?"

"I didn't mean it that way."

"No one chooses to be poor. Not in emptiness, only out of desperation or spite. Out of a loss of faith, out of a need for anything."

"Why are they here?"

"They are here on behalf of the senate to build train tracks for the empire to ship goods across the Solgra, and maybe one day passengers."

"Goods, like what?"

"Wheat mainly, but I've heard talk that there may be Orichalc in the hills."

"Orichalc," Erold repeated in a whisper, a significant upgrade over leviathan and sea serpent oil and much easier to get, sometimes mixed with coal but not if you wanted to fly an airship. Oil could light lamps, but it couldn't lift a ship into the sky like Orichalc could.

"It's what the airships that the nation is building rely on to fly, and who knows what else might one day soon be powered by the stuff. I've heard talk that they may one day soon have airships that can fly from Cardane to Rorik in Albion. Possibly, in as little as a day's time. I've been suspicious that there might already be some secret ones that can, and maybe they go even further than that." Sven explained before sneaking a peak back at his nephew, who he caught looking off into the distance in wonder.

"Further than that?" Erold repeated under his breath, imagining what it would be like. He had rarely even seen a map that showed a distance further than Cardane, even though the Empire's borders extended further. It was often the last place to the east that anyone used as a point of reference in casual conversation. Many maps of regions just cut off at the edges, and they didn't even allude to what lay beyond, though the empire controlled fractional parts of the massive nations, Mondelvania and Emira.

Erold had only ever seen one globe in the personal office of one of his professors in Albion. The professor had said that the globe wasn't nearly accurate or to scale, but it had been prepared based on the notes from the first circumnavigators, Normen and Imerians, who had begun attempts to be the first ones to sail the whole globe in the 1200s.

Few of those first explorers ever made it back between the sea serpents, dragons, and other monsters of the ocean and seas, those that were both deep and shallow. It wouldn't be until the modern ships, of mainly the 1400s, became better equipped to wage war and change distance faster that ocean trade could connect the world from end to end.

Airships, Erold understood immediately, could alter travel forever. Imagine crossing continents in a few days, and only having to avoid the few mountain ranges with dragons, completely avoiding the leviathans that might try to sink your ship when you accidentally approach their feeding ground.

The flight from Albion to Seylil had been advertised as the furthest a passenger ship could travel in a day, connecting passengers from the silver coast to Seylil, which was as little as a three-day trip to Akre by carriage.

Sven caught Erold looking glum and wondered correctly if the boy's train of thought had him thinking about his father. Sven knew all too well what it was like to lose his parents, but for Erold it was fresh, and he didn't need someone to purport to know everything that he was going through.

Instead, Sven refocused them on the task at hand, bringing joy to the children of Normany, and he would wait for his opportunity to share some wisdom on the topic, hoping that if Erold brought it up, that he would remain open to Sven. It had been Moon long ago that had spoken to him on it by mainly listening. She had been an immigrant orphan from the Far West in Newkassel and had given herself the name Moon when she had begun working to become an inspector after watching her parents die in front of her.

They continued on through the next makeshift row of houses and in each shanty, a little boy or girl, held in screams of delight, as they received gifts. Their hands and feet were dirty, but their faces clean. Everywhere they went, there was order among the houses, and they were all gracious to Sven and Erold, giving thanks to the Lord above for the help they received. Sven often stayed to pray with the families, bowing to God.

As they exited the town, there was yet another shantyville on the horizon, and something broke inside of Erold in a way that he would never explain even if he could articulate it. That other people could turn their back on their fellow men, using others suffering as an excuse of their own gain.

"You said the senate brings them here?"

"Yes."

"Why doesn't the senate provide for them?"

"Some are not full citizens. Some have already lost everything, and this is their only hope."

"But they came to work? They're not being paid enough to live a decent life?"

"The senate doesn't tend to help those that they believe have the means to help themselves, and people who come here to work are always the least of their concern."

"Does this look like they can help themselves?"

"It's hard to decide what anyone needs, but I have my own gripes with the senate." The key factor being that the senate seemed intent to line their pockets first rather than to lead the Empire with dignity.

"You seem to know what people need," said Erold, hoisting up the bag a little higher and nodding toward the trays of food that Sven carried.

Lived experience is a grave teacher, Sven thought but didn't say. One thing he didn't want was for Erold to go through the same experience, but the certain risks of the potential futures remained.

"I want to be the one to help them," said Erold. "But, I'm worried that I won't be able to. That's my greatest fear right now." He paused, waiting to see if Sven would say anything, but Sven did not. Erold continued, "I worry that I won't be able to live up to what I know I can do for other people. That I'll never get my chance."

"You're trying really hard to carry on as if things haven't been changing around you that are out of your control, but they are. Your country may need you someday. Not may. Will. And the only way to be there for all those people of this country that you want to help, is to survive."

"That's why we're doing everything in secret," said Erold, still refusing to let the feelings come in fully, preferring to deal with them in single waves as they happen.

"Until Akre's emperor business can be fully navigated, we have to play it safe. I'm just glad that you are alive and that we can enjoy the holiday together."

"Polesar," Erold said the name aloud with a touch of disdain, wondering if he was the man behind his father's death. "It's nice to spend time with you Uncle Sven."

The words warmed Sven, who had nothing but genuine love for Erold, and was touched that he would have a younger version of himself to look out for.

"That's it! It's settled," Sven began to grow almost jubilant, and Erold couldn't help but ask why.

"We're going to throw a ball."

Erold groaned. His father had thrown enough balls, and they always were attended by the same aristocrats every time. Erold hadn't been allowed to go, but he wasn't interested in meeting landed nobility.

"It's the holiday season. Where's your holiday spirit!"

"I'm not feeling up for parties at the moment, or celebrations for that matter."

"Nonsense. There will be women and wine," Sven's words began to sound a little bit better at that, "Not only am I going to order you to be there, but I order you to be happy. We will throw a massive ball, here in Leidyn to celebrate Frostmas and the days of the savior. We'll host it a few days before Frostmas, so the whole region can come. Then, you and I, and your two companions, we can feast on Spirit Day. I'll be giving out meals on Frostmas Day, but we can honor your father along with all the other fallen soldiers whose spirits rest in Heaven."

Erold and Sven finished donating things for the day, shortly after that, and despite Erold's frustration and increasing feeling of powerlessness, he did look forward to seeing girls in pretty dresses while he wasn't wearing dirty clothes.

* * *

Erold lay in the small bed and looked at the trinkets whatever family had lived in the house had left behind when they had rented to Sven. He had been feeling frustrated about his sleeping arrangement, but at least he had a soft place to sleep.

And, to top it off, he finally was alone. Alone, alone. Without having to worry about whether Moon or Volstad would pop in to check that he was still alive like they had the first couple nights after they had move into the house.

No doubt the uncertainty of what could happen with the emperor had spooked them, and they had gone through just as many changes as he had in recent weeks.

Erold felt into his pocket and pulled out the small, dark blue velvet bag that his father had given him. He undid the strap and tipped the contents of the bag into his open palm: a small, white orb that didn't shine particularly bright or feel particularly special.

It was the first time he had taken it out of the bag that his father had stashed it in, because it was the first time since the ship went down, he felt he was completely safe from any eyes. Erold wasn't sure what the orb was theoretically worth as it wasn't a diamond and it didn't sparkle, but his father had, in a way, died to protect it and keep it secret.

From a first glance, though, Erold could have imagined it was a replica of something that was supposed to be more meaningful. He had heard what Theodore, Mr. Everett, had said about it, though, at his mansion back in the Ash Vale. It was a dangerous power, basically, in the hands of a mage--like Erold.

He hoped the old man Theodore somehow knew that his orb was safe, but Erold wouldn't be the one to tell him. The real question, though, was what the orb did exactly, because from looking at it and touching it, he couldn't figure out. He would've tried a spell, but he didn't want to cause a scene by overpowering something and starting a fire or worse. In the end, he held it in his palm and stared at it, knowing that his father had entrusted him to protect it and not to use it.

He threw it up into the air. It came back down and landed in his palm. Just like any ball.

1513 - Chapter 9

"The proposal has been put forth," said the senator Hammel from the podium. "We are to give the new Emperor Polesar the authority to attack the usurper, Sven Greenski, who has attempted to establish authority over Normany as an independent nation rather than allow it to lose its duchy independence. Any concerns please share them now."

"Yes, please stand and speak your question," Senator Karlson pointed to one of the many senators, who sat on the benches below the podium.

"We would be attacking during the Frostmas holiday season if we issue the order now. Is that wise?"

"As the emperor explained, if we wait, there is the possibility that Sven could recruit a more substantial force over the fall and winter. We need to strike now," said Hammel in response, while Polesar waited at one of the benches below the podium, looking up at the many hundreds of senators. He had command of the military's strategic and tactical actions, but they held the joint right to deploy in force.

"Any other comments?"

"Yes, you, senator," Karlson pointed.

"I address to the senators, not a question, but instead as a call to all of us to act. If we strike now, we test our newest regiments and the latest command structure changes. By attacking now, we will be able to see how our force does against a well-respected foe who has yet to dig in a significantly fortified position while removing the last true threat to our senate's right to rule across the empire. It is not the men of Normany that we fight, but a tyrant who sees himself as above the men of this great frost."

There were a few murmurs in the crowd, but Polesar could sense that the general mood leaned toward having already decided. He watched their eyes.

"Our men have trained for this moment. Regardless of the time of the year, they will do as they are ordered to do to destroy the usurper now." Polesar's voice rang out across the great hall as if shaking the very walls even deep in the back.

There were no more questions. Hammel put it to vote. Ballots were taken and counted by section and announced by the leaders of the separate groups.

By many hundreds, the vote was for war.

Polesar looked up at them all. The hair raising along his neck as a shiver ran through him. For the first time in over a century, the Kalsvebir sword would be pulled from its ceremonial position and taken ahead of the new corps rather than the old legions.

He glanced at Tanneran and Alger, who didn't hold votes. They smiled at him. Both pleased.

The three of them met after Polesar was dismissed from the senator's hall. Rather than discuss the next matter of affairs in the hallway, Tanneran guided the three of them to a small breakout room where a wooden table with ten chairs, wrapped around it, sat for small committee discussions apart from the grand hall, where all larger debates took place.

The two men sat down, while Polesar remained standing. He touched the hilt of his modern saber, thinking how strange it would be to hold two swords. One ceremonial and the other meant for battle.

He addressed the two men, who had already congratulated him on his speech, advocating war, in front of the senate, "Now for the next order of business. What is the true disposition in Albion, and will there indeed be a coup to unseat the Lord Stone?" He would have been surprised, given the legacy of the nation, but he was happy to hear if it was indeed true.

"We have heard that a coup is planned."

Polesar looked at Tanneran, trying to hide his skepticism, "Do we know of how many men?"

"A considerable number," said Alger.

"And the potential responses by Albion's military?"

"Are you wondering if this coup will be successful?" asked Alger.

Polesar nodded, looking at both men, "If it fails, we can almost guarantee that Albion will break from the empire, and in that case, while we could reach Albion likely just before Vetfal, we would not be able to risk being stuck off the coast and at the mercy of winter in far Normendin or Dragnor."

"We have experienced intelligence units in Albion," said Tanneran, "As we do in all of our regional capitals. They assure me of success."

"And what do they say of Albion's ability to respond?"

"The army is not mobilized in Albion, and the locals can be stoked due to Lord Stone's tendencies. His lack of response to the Vagalla has rubbed many the wrong way."

"Stoked?" Polesar asked, wondering with how comfortably Tanneran said the word, whether it had been done before. When he had found Aurelia, rescued from the attack by Valgaard on Akre, he listened to her, and others, tell the story of her mother and brother's death by gunshot, but the whole of the palace had been burned to the ground when he arrived.

"Now is the time to strike," said Alger.

"Yes, I agree," said Polesar, but only with respect to Normany, he thought.

"Then, it is settled," said Tanneran, who chose his words carefully, "Our intelligence units in Rorik will be notified that they should join the planned coup and attack Lord Stone."

Polesar nodded. He was beginning to understand more of what Tanneran and Alger did. It wasn't merely reporting between the two major 'houses'--Senators and Justicars, elected men and appointed archmages--but also ensuring that information between the nations under the wings of the Akrin eagle flew back to the center. There was more to learn before he would speak further out of turn. He smiled.

* * *

Polesar found her, Princess Aurelia, on the balcony of the estate that had been set aside for two of them in west Ithlin, the Azuri hills, before he had been appointed emperor. It was a large, sprawling manor, made of alabaster, that looked over the gradual slope of the hills, dotted sparsely with trees, as they descended into the Atlan River's bed, reaching to the Akre sprawl.

If she looked closely, she could see the buildings atop Lion's Den Hill in the distance, where her future husband worked. She had seen his airship, among the many airships, coming and going from Akre, slowly drift nearer and nearer like a sea ship lifted into the sky and pulled forward with the speed of one hundred horses or more.

Aurelia turned to him before he spoke and looked into his yellow-brown eyes. His pupils were sharp. She couldn't read through the way he smiled at her, and she longed to know how deep her grip had ensnared him. He had been married, and yet, when she needed him the most, he had found her, Aurelia.

It was as if she had been locked in a tower and asleep, caged by the men who she had made a deal with--and yet never directly met--to spare her life in exchange for her brother's and consequently her mother's, who having married Aurelia's father, King Karles III, had no direct claim to the throne.

When he was executed for denying the senate the ability to rule after being convicted during a trial, her younger brother was to ascend.

If she had married Vincent Everett, she might have been in line to be queen and thus been their secret target instead. After Vincent's disappearance and presumed death, she had no real authority in the Akrin Empire. Something she had longed for, and now, she was soon to have more than a little power as empress to Polesar Rolard, of all people. The very mage whose appointment to the high council of Justicars her father had blocked in 1495 when he was just the southern general and spawned or finished the sequence of events that led to him losing his head.

When Aurelia had first met Polesar, years ago, she had been nearly twenty, but the stress of life had not altered her features until she had lived under lock and key, worried for years of her future. She did not know how much Polesar knew of the plot, or of how closely she, herself, believed his appointment to be tied to her father's death. She had met him in normal circumstances after that when he had been married. Later, when she had grown to know him anew, he had chased after her, but she was still in doubt.

"My beautiful love," Polesar spoke and embraced her, kissing her passionately. "I have had one thousand flowers delivered. One hundred each of ten different colors. They await you throughout the ground floor."

She had returned the kiss, but she still felt strange. Her very survival depended completely on his loving her. It was as if her worth in life had been stripped when she had left Akre and had yet to ever return. The two of them were due to be married, but he had never advanced further than a tender kiss.

"Are you all right my love?" he asked, holding her in his strong, sculpted arms. His yellow eyes searching her face as the wind pulled his dark brown hair to the side. "If you're not feeling like flowers, I will send them back."

"No, I'm sure they are lovely. Thank you, my Violet," she said, speaking the nickname she had given him after they had summered together in a town, known for its fields of violets, near the eastern coast of Ithlin.

"What's the matter, my love?" His eyes searched hers.

"Nothing, I love you very much," she said, seeing his face soften and pupils widen at her words. She caressed his arms, running her fingers to dig gently into his shoulders, beneath the soft suit. "I just can't wait to be married." She smiled at him, leaning in to kiss him again.

"Yes, I know how much you want that," he smiled as he pulled away from her and clasped his hands behind his back, looking over the hills.

"It's only a few weeks away," she went to grasp his hand.

"It will have to wait just that little bit longer," he said, as his eyes darkened and his smile dissipated.

"Why?"

"There has been news of a rebellion in the Solgra, perpetrated by Sven Greenski. We must act at once to put it down or lose Normany."

"But, you must not have to go?" said Aurelia. Her blonde hair caught the wind on the balcony. Her blue eyes, searched back into his. "I couldn't live with myself if you were hurt."

"I assure you, my loving angel. There is no risk to me. This is your ancestral kingdom. I cannot allow it to be taken from you by anyone."

He kissed the back of her hand, and the two of them looked at each other with soft eyes while he held her hand. Hers pleaded with him to be true to her. His saw what looked like an endless well of love, returned to him.

"Fear not, my love. We will be married soon." He kissed her hand again and departed. She watched him go. He said many nice things to her, but she couldn't help but wonder what was for show and what was true with him.

1513 - Chapter 10

Ti-Enna lit the candle in her room by pressing the wick with her two fingers and igniting a red spark that roared upwards as she took her finger away from the flame. Ouch, she thought as the magic of her fingers wore off and the heat of the blaze began to burn for real.

She took out a book and began reading from where she had left off, on the 'Principles of Classical and Magical Physics.' She longed to someday study how to make real fire--something that could melt iron--in an academy, but it took a lot of work to study for an entrance exam in Akre or even in Albion, especially if she wanted to get the scholarship she would need to attend. Her father had left her and her sisters some money but not enough to afford something on that scale.

Her and her two older sisters, Aurelia and Isabella, had each been given an inheritance of four thousand Akrin dollars along with shares of the house, meaning invested on an interest of the regular four percent, they each had annual income of one hundred sixty dollars. That was roughly equivalent to twenty-seven gold pieces, but the bank would round down on the exchange, so twenty six gold pieces a year. Tuition at an academy was likely to be a thousand or more, dollars that is, a semester. Meaning in two years out of four, she'd be with nothing, if she didn't get that elusive scholarship.

After about an hour of reading, the morning sun rose as well, and she put the book away to join her sisters at breakfast. They would mostly spend their days reading and playing music. Ti-Enna's father had bought a piano when her stepmother had moved in. The first formal schools were being opened up throughout the Solgra and the Republic. Since 1501 it felt like formal schools for children were being opened every day, but she and her sisters were too old to start in the first one to open in Leidyn. They didn't have the capacity for anyone over ten.

It had been her father's job to informally teach her and her sisters basic skills like reading, writing, and arithmetic, but once he passed away, her stepmother had decided to forego the cost of private tutoring, a service for kings and queens she said, for each of them, and instead, she required that any expenses for education be made personally, though she rightly expected, except for Ti-Enna, her stepdaughters didn't care much for books. Having already come of age, Ti-Enna's two older sisters were looking to marry as quickly as possible, or risk having to survive on sharing the respectable, though trivial for three or four, amount that was left to their stepmother,

Lady Dashaine, twice a widow.

A loud knock came on the door, and the sisters jumped at the sound. No one came around this early in the morning. Ti-Enna's stepmother opened the door.

A messenger, a horse and a mounted and armored guard behind him, stood, well-dressed, in the blue and yellow of Normany's local flags with a trimmed, pointy beard, puffy pants and pointed shoes. He cleared his throat, lifted a parchment and read aloud.

"Notice to all members of the town of Leidyn, the king-regent, Sven of the line of Arandil is inviting all members of the city and its constituency towns to a formal ball, celebrating this Frostmas. All ladies and gentlemen are invited to attend. Please wear your best attire and expect refreshments to be provided to all in attendance. Please arrive beginning no later than five in the afternoon hours on the twentieth of Ivanssun at the festival grounds near Leidyn proper. Good day ladies."

"Good day to you too sir," Ti-Enna's stepmother bowed and thanked him for the notice.

"That's only five days away! Can we go mother?" cried Aurelia, the oldest of Ti-Enna's two sisters.

"Of course, of course. You and Isabella will go, and I'll go with you. You've been to every occasion this summer. This will be a great opportunity to meet an officer with a pension."

"Can I go too, please? I've never been to a ball," Ti-Enna asked.

"And there's good reason you haven't. You are only fourteen, child!"

"Oh! Please, just this once? Aurelia and Isabella always get to go. I always have to stay home and clean."

"That's because they are over seventeen. They are looking for husbands of the local merchants and lords of the land. You're not yet concerned with that, my dear," said her stepmother.

"I'm sure there will plenty of young men there, mother. She can dance with one of them," said Aurelia.

"And it's not like royals are throwing balls in Leidyn regularly. Has there ever been one?" asked Isabella.

"Fine, you can go, but only if you buy your own dress," Lady Dashaine relented. "I'm sure if you do get into an academy, balls like this happen all the time in the bigger cities. Since, the king-regent will be there, I'll make an exception. But, I'll keep my eye on you."

"What difference does it make if he's a king-regent?" asked Isabella, "He's a royal. As far as I'm concerned, a king is a king."

"You'll see what difference it makes quick enough. If you didn't read the papers like I told you too, the last king-that-never-was died in that airship crash in the mountains, traveling like a commoner. That's the difference."

"You don't have to worry about a dress," said Aurelia, "I have a light blue one that you can wear. It's slightly damaged, so you'll have to fix it, and it may be a bit too long still. You're almost as tall as me, but not quite. But, you should be able to manage with a pair of heels. Otherwise, it will drag along the ground and in the well, you know. If you can't find a pair to buy, you can try an old pair of mine. If they are too difficult to walk in, you could tie a bow around them."

"Thanks Aurelia, I don't mind. That sounds lovely."

"It's settled then. I'll let your aunt know that you plan to go, and she can help you fix the dress," said Lady Dashaine, looking at her daughters with excitement. Their little house on the hill, southwest of Leidyn was just on the furthest edge of the city's limits. They might have been the last invite.

Ti-Enna went shopping with her aunt, and godmother, at every store in Leidyn, looking for the right fabric and thread to match with the dress, so that she could stitch it properly. At one store, they found one that matched, but it was too expensive, especially if she wanted to buy her own heels. After finding no other options, Ti-Enna lay in her bed staring at the ceiling, wondering why it was so difficult for simple things to work out the way you needed them to.

She had been cleaning the ash from the fireplace all last winter while her sisters went out looking for men to marry. And all summer, she had stayed behind to sweep the kitchens, clean the clothes, and tidy the rooms, so they didn't have to pay for domestic help--a frivolous expense, according to her stepmother, without her father's income and only his meager savings to split among four women. If she didn't go to the ball yet again, she'd be home sweeping and mopping.

The next day she asked her aunt and godmother if they could try the nearby sister cities of Dardin or Daldin, but her aunt chided her, reminding her that if what they were looking for wasn't in Leidyn, a city almost twice their size, it wouldn't be in either of them.

A tailor had what fabrics they had, and the largest tailors within a reasonable distance were in Leidyn. They would never make it back in time from somewhere as far as Áelin City.

Each day that the ball drew closer, she became more despondent over it. She longed to dance. She didn't just want to move, she wanted to break the monotony. Each and every day was the same. She liked what she did. Piano, reading, studying, but it quickly became repetitive.

One of the reasons that Ti-Enna wanted to go to a bigger city to study, on the east coast in Ithlin or the west coast in Albion, is that she wanted things to happen to her. She wanted to have new experiences.

Here in Leidyn, one of the largest, if not the largest, city in Godrland it just didn't compare. Besides, they didn't have a university yet in Leidyn anyway, but even if they did, nothing ever happened here of note. Besides this singular ball. Some of the cities nearby that did have new universities were generally smaller. One had just opened up that let girls in about six years before.

She didn't do any reading for those next four days as the ball closed in. Aurelia had given her the dress and a pair of matching shoes, crystalline blue. She had practiced walking in them the first day and used the bow trick that Aurelia had suggested with dark blue wraps tied in fancy, little Frostmas bows, but now she couldn't look at them. She had even found a silvery, blue sash to hold the dress in to make it not look so over-sized for her slender body.

None of that work had mattered. Her dress had a tear down the back she couldn't hide without fixing up. Now, her sisters were getting ready with their earrings, dresses, and their crystal encrusted slippers. There wouldn't be another opportunity like this, and she would have to wait almost three more years to be seventeen to go to a local ball in Leidyn!

They felt bad for her, but they couldn't wait up for her. Her two beautiful sisters got into their stepmother's carriage and rode to the festival grounds to celebrate Frostmas with the king regent and his men, while she had to stay home again, tending to the fireplace, which was covered in soot after a recent cold spell.

Ti-Enna tightened her apron and filled a pail of water, grabbed a brush and got ready to work, when she heard a knock at the door. It was her aunt, carrying the roll of fabric, glistening in the setting sun.

"You're like a fairy!" Ti-Enna cried out, "Thank you."

"Hush, now, if we get to work right away, we can have you out the door shortly after night fall."

"How will we make it?"

"I hired a carriage myself!"

"Isn't this expensive?"

"Oh posh, I knew how much it meant to you to go to this ball," she said.

"But, you can't have spent this much on me?"

"Your godmother has a bit of money squirrelled away just for a time like this. Now, are we going to going to fix up this dress together and get you out of that apron before you get soot all over you or not?"

The two worked quickly to patch up the dress, and when she tried it on in the mirror, she felt like a lady. Her aunt drove with her to the ball, where she was able to meet with her stepmother and sisters just inside.

Her stepmother was happy that she was able to make it, and her sisters had high expectations for her. Though, none of the boys spoke to her, and she felt terribly embarrassed. She had gone through all this trouble and cost all this time and money, and not one of the men there looked her way.

* * *

The day for the ball came, less than a week after Merchant's Day, when Sven had determined to hold it and well enough before Frostmas, which was on the twenty second, that it felt like people from every village from Leidyn to Áelin had come.

Erold had not expected the town to come to life in the waning days of summer, on a colder than normal evening to dance in a hastily constructed tent that looked like something the old Olympus Circus had used on its short run in Seylil when Erold was as young as he could remember.

He, Elara, and Volstad had dressed in well-fitted plain-clothes from a local tailor, inspired by a tailor in Akre that Erold had forgotten the name of as soon as it was spoken. As they entered, they weren't sure it was a wise choice. Almost all of the officers had come in full military dress, looking as sharp as ever, complete with tassels on their shoulders and even most of the enlisted men that had filtered into town over the weeks had dressed in crisp, clean uniforms.

Erold was surprised to see that few, if any, enhancements had been made to the decorations by Sven. It was a modest venue. There were no gold fixtures, or bouquets of flowers. The floor was little better than flattened dirt with a makeshift set of wood boards set across the center for dancing.

There were few places to sit, and at first, it felt as if there was almost no room to stand, until the crowd filled in the back and space opened in the center for people to dance.

There were small tables in the corners of the tent with candelabras lit with candles and a few oil lamps strung from the rafters of the enormous tent where they could vent heat into the open center and out into the cool night air.

When Erold and his companions had followed the crowd in and around toward the rear of the tent, he saw that there was even a band. He couldn't make out the number, but it appeared to be a quintet of string instruments.

They began to play a short, repeated melody, warning that they were about to start. The crowd tentatively began to collect, pair up and distribute in an orchestrated array that appeared choreographed. An officer would approach a girl, and sometimes it appeared her mother, to ask for the young girl's hand in the dance. First, the officers, then some of the enlisted men repeated the procedure.

At first, before the instruments began in full, you could feel the tension in the hush of the crowd, as some women stood dejected, while some were just so happy to have been selected albeit first. In a world that had been full of dire news, especially in Normany, as of late, it felt almost wrong to celebrate, and yet the glint and gleam of the lights began to catch the eyes of the pairs, waiting to dance.

The strings began their tune, and Erold watched as the dancing began. No one seemed to pay much attention to him, and it felt like every girl there had dressed well and looked happy. They were all sweet and pretty, so he instead found his way to the back where through a slight opening in the tent, he could see where Sven had set up old wooden tables with scuffed legs adorned with simple drinks and refreshments like lemon-flavored ice, for guests to drink if they became thirsty or the warmth of the tent became too much.

Erold wanted to dance, but no one looked his way. Volstad bowed to the division officers when they neared, and Moon surveyed the crowd in her usual way, like an eagle stalking mice in a distant field.

Erold stood a bit further away from them, and still a little bit further until he had found his way outside the tent toward the lemon ice. He was eating at it went Moon approached him from behind.

"What are you doing?" she scorned.

"Just taking advantage of the refreshments while they're still here," replied Erold.

"You're not nervous to ask someone to dance, are you?" asked Moon.

"It's like I'm not even here, so I just took a moment to myself, out in the cold, to get some fresh air."

Moon looked at him skeptically.

"What's going on out here?" asked Volstad. "We best be getting back inside. Sven will want you to be here when he arrives."

Erold took a last gulp of his lemon ice, and the trio went back inside, just as the crowd stopped at the arrival of saint Sven, who at the moment looked very grave. There were a few of his men, decorated as officers flanking him left and right. There were very few of the entourage of soldiers that had begun to accompany him around the city as of late.

"I have an announcement to make. I have gotten word from Valgaard and Albion that they will be allies of Normany in the days to come. We are hopeful that war can be avoided, so that Normany can remain as it was under the stewardship of the late governor-general, my cousin and friend, whom we lost so tragically, Erolin, of the line of Arandil. And, we mourn also for the disappearance of his son, my last counterpart in the line of Galdir kings. We hope he may be found."

Sven looked across the crowd, seeing Erold, he acted as much as possible that he wasn't looking at him, but he tried his best as well, to see his distant nephew's face. There was a bit of a subdued silence and a few murmurs in support of the late king. Few cared for Erolin's son. No one had heard his name.

"But, we gather here today to celebrate the coming holiday season, over which we will make many happy memories. We do not gather here to focus on the darker ones of the recent past. With us today are many of the fine young men, many who have done work in the Varanorian guard of Cardane in the gulf, meaning they have faced all manner of foe, and have now joined in the cause to support a peaceful Normany. As I can see you have already begun to give my staff a good time, let's continue the festival!"

Sven clapped his hands and an array of lights split from them and up into the rafters of the tent igniting an exclamation from the crowd, dazzled by yet another of his displays, copying a floating chandelier lit by candles. In the bright light, Erold could see the beautiful dresses of the girls in many colors, dark blue and bright pink. But, also some girls dressed in yellow and light blue.

Sven then walked as he did always, amongst the people, who gravitated toward him like a moth to unnatural light. He clearly enjoyed the attention and was happy with the size of the ball. He left no hand un-shook or person not listened to. The music picked back up and the dancing had begun.

Moon whispered something to Volstad who separated further from them into the crowd.

"I'm sure that young woman over there would love to dance with you, if you'd ask her. I'm sure she would be more than pleased, and at a ball, it is customary for one to dance."

Erold nodded and turned to see a beautiful fair-haired girl, also entranced by the dancers. Her hair was tucked up in a neat style above her head. She was tall, just a touch shorter than he was, and her bright, blue eyes looked as if they were filled with the same desire to dance, and the thought had just flashed through her mind that perhaps no one would want to dance with her.

As he approached, their eyes locked. She looked for a moment grateful and then equally entranced. She only had eyes for him in that moment and instantly, thought that she could hold him tight in the moonlight and run away.

Her light blue dress was slightly too long, barely lifted from the dirt by a pair of light blue heels that looked like they might get stuck if the frost didn't stay hardened by the cold, and she wore a shimmering blue sash around her waist. She also looked a similar fresh-faced fifteen to Erold.

"My lady what is your name?" Erold asked her.

"Ti-Enna. Enna for short." she smiled at his princely manners, despite dressing like a commoner like her. Though she was in her sister's old dress, and his tunic appeared new. Then, with a rush of blood to her cheeks, she remembered to ask his name back, "and what is yours?"

"Erold," he looked into her eyes and bowed, "Miss Enna, may I have the pleasure of this dance?"

"Well, sir Erold. Yes, you may. I'd love to dance with you," she replied, holding out her hand as if imitating a duchess. Erold held it for a moment and kissed it so lightly that he almost only kissed the air above her hand, sending chills up the young girl's spine.

"Excuse me," the older woman next to her said as she waved a fan at herself to beat the heat of the gathering crowd. Erold looked down at the shrewd older woman, "You have not asked me if you could ask my youngest daughter to dance. Where are your manners, young gentleman."

"My apologies madame. May I have the honor of asking your daughter for a dance?"

"Do you have money?"

Erold winced.

"No, then. But of course. It's more than fine. She's only my stepdaughter." The older woman with gray sneaking in among her jet-black hair then said to Enna loud enough that Erold could hear, "Enna, if you happen to change your mind, you may not get a second chance to dance with anyone half as good looking. But, no money, hmmph, your sisters are dancing with real gentlemen." She turned back to Erold and looked him up and down before saying, "See those officers over there, and why haven't you enlisted, young man. Where is your uniform?"

"Yes, quite well-tailored," said Erold with a hint of envy at the men outfitted for battle.

The young duo left the harsh mistress behind, and Enna turned to him, "Please don't pay my stepmother any attention."

Erold smiled and led her to the dance floor where they began to dance. He had taken many lessons, growing up around the court whereas she seemed out of practice. He showed her a few steps of a dance, and they fell in stride.

"She's been so bitter, since my father passed away." Enna explained.

Erold said nothing but listened to the sound of her voice and noticed the smell of her dash of perfume among the crowd.

"Well, aren't you going to ask me why?"

"What if you don't want to tell me?"

"That's a silly reason not to ask."

"Then, tell me," he said, matching her stare as she held him by both shoulders firmly and looked him in the eye. Then, he pulled her back into the rhythm of the dance, despite her resistance and she had no choice but to fall back into step due to his easy strength.

"He left me some of his money, you see, and she's never forgiven me that it was more than her. That's why." They danced a moment more, and she said, "Anyway, that's my story. I'm sure you're not interested in hearing anymore. Besides, you haven't told me anything about you, and I think it's only fair that you do."

He ignored her for a moment, but she insisted.

"There's nothing about me that would be as interesting as what you've told me about yourself. I can't say I've come into any money, only that I might."

"You might, that's something."

"As Sven announced, there could be peace in Normany," said

Erold.

"Wouldn't that be something? With the conscriptions all over the Republic, I had been worried my father would go to war." She stopped speaking for a moment, and the pair continued to dance into the next song, and after passing a song in silence, as two silhouettes against the crowd of dancers.

All of the men and women were older than the young pair, but they were tall like the rest and fleet of foot. The crowd had stayed strong and jubilant for most of the night, and the music continued as loud as ever. Sven met with more of his men and officers to laugh with them while Volstad asked a few young women to dance.

"What does that have to do with you though? Peace in Normany," Enna asked. "You aren't in uniform. You look like a merchant's son. It wouldn't make a difference to you."

"Never you mind the reasons," Erold said off-hand, "War is bad for everybody."

"For some more than others."

"That is certainly true."

They danced in silence. Erold could think of nothing but the joy it was to dance with her in his arms, how she fit between them easily like cradling a dove, helping him to forget about the coming of the cold, fall and winter months.

As the silence went on, she thought to herself as well about how it felt to dance with him. She regretted being so forceful on the subject, because she very much liked dancing with him. He was an easy partner with firm hands, who guided her through the motions as if he was a seasoned dancer with many years of experience.

"Where did you learn to dance?"

"Lessons."

"What kind of lessons?"

"All kinds."

"Do you always answer questions so vaguely."

"Only if I can."

"Well, what if I was to like you. How would I know that I could like you?"

"How would I know if I liked you?"

"Well, you would ask me to dance. And. Then, maybe we would keep dancing. If you liked me, you would know how to show me somehow." The tempo of the song picked up, and Erold guided her along.

"And if you liked me, I'm sure you'd find a way to show me you did."

"There's something I must tell you."

"Yes?"

"I'm not like the good girls that you see running around here, asking their mothers if they can dance with someone they like. If you expect someone like that, then I can't oblige."

"I don't."

"You don't," she repeated, skeptically. "I'm getting a little warm, would you like to see the moonlight?"

"There's lemon ice and other refreshments behind the tent; let's go out that way," Erold told her. She nodded in agreement and followed him toward the back of the tent.

They exited the tent, and Erold watched her as she took something to drink and began to wander away from the entrance to the tent.

Moon followed in the shadows, worried for a moment that she may have gotten Erold into a trap but hoping that he was just infatuated with the young woman.

Enna looked back at Erold while she took a sip, and he jogged a bit to catch up to her.

"If you're not one of the good girls, then what type of girl are you?" asked Erold when he caught up to her and grabbed her around the waist beneath the moonlight. She spit out what she was drinking in an abrupt laugh, intoxicated by the moment.

"It's a secret, only for boys I like."

"Is there more than one."

"No."

"Is there one?"

She nodded.

"Is it me?"

She nodded again.

"Then what type of girl are you?"

"I'm the passionate kind. The kind who likes to hold you tight and never let go. And." She paused as she turned to look at him, biting her lip.

"Like behind a tent at a party?"

She nodded, and the two of them embraced for a moment, kissing passionately beneath the stars.

"And what else? You said and?"

"And, the ambitious kind. You'll have to prove to me that you're worth it." She pulled away from him and then smiled devilishly.

Just then, she noticed that some of the other guests were leaving the party.

"My gosh, what is the time?"

Erold looked at the watch his father had given him.

"Just past eleven."

"I can't keep my stepmother waiting. She'd leave without me," Enna turned to go.

Erold went to grab her arm, but she had already gained two steps ahead of him.

"Enna, could you please give me a token of your affection to remember you by? A lock of hair perhaps."

"It may be a little too early for that," she smiled, "but, I will give you this sash."

Her dress danced in the wind as she unrolled the sash, no longer tight to her body. She handed it to him, and he wrapped it around his hand. A light blue sash.

"Oh, look. There they are now," she said, and turned to run to catch up with her sisters, who waved, and stepmother, who gave a slight frown.

Like something out of a storybook, he watched her go as she fought to keep her footing on the uneven ground. She waved at her family and joined them as they waited for a carriage to pull up at the front of the tent and take them to wherever it was that they were going.

Erold thought to himself, if she looks back my way, then I will make her my wife.

Then, she turned to look back his way and wave, blowing a kiss when her stepmother couldn't see as she hopped into the carriage after the others.

Erold clenched the sash tightly woven around his wrist, while Ti-Enna thought to herself that they had seen so little of each other and yet she would remember every moment so vividly. It was then that she realized that she had not given him her family name, and neither had Erold given his.

She was certain that it wouldn't matter. She was certain that if he was truly meant for her, that he would be able to find her, no matter the circumstances, like some kind of fairy tale.

Her sisters joked with her about being in love and being caught alone with a stranger while Erold stood transfixed, entranced by this girl from Normany, who would certainly haunt his thoughts for days to come.

The matter of finding her would be an issue, as he only had her first name. People had come from cities, villages, and towns all over the north Solgra province of Godrland. He became determined to start the search to find her the next day. That's when he noticed Moon come up behind him with a sly grin on her face.

1513 - Chapter 11

Onya had only been in Albion for a few weeks, but it had felt like a lifetime. So much had happened and yet, so much had yet to happen.

The impotent King Erolin's ship crash in Midur seemed so long ago. She had arrived shortly after, and now she had spent the past week in bliss in the palace, thinking not of war or trying to investigate the other staff but of Jack, the Lord Stone.

For whatever reason and quite by chance, they had run into each other at the most opportune of moments. Her first day and when she might have had her employment terminated, failing when she had barely started.

They had spent a little more time together during the week while he had been pulled away by various duties, and she had grown far more confident when she had realized over that first lunch just how interested he was in her. With all of these different things on her mind, she could have let it affect her work, as a spy.

Luckily, dragging hot water up flights of stairs was only physically taxing, not mentally. She had found a second place to put a clockwork bug and now as the middle of the morning on Solday gave her time alone in the Bunting's house while they left for church, she planned to listen to the two latest recordings, unsure of which was which, but both blue cylinders were full of shallow markings from the carving of the bug.

She put one of the blue wax cylinders that she had retrieved just before the weekend into the cylinder player, snapping it in, and held the horn to her ear as she hit play.

The hum of conversation and background activity quickly lulled her to sleep. She could even hear the sound of a lyre or some other type of instrument. It sounded like light conversation, growing louder and dimmer, as if people were talking to each other while walking through a hallway. She was beginning to wonder if there was any reason to suspect the other staff at the palace when she recognized a voice.

"This Solday, the twenty first, we launch the attack." Then static, quiet noise.

She brought the needle back to listen to the conversation at a higher volume. In broken pieces, she was able to figure out a general idea of what they were speaking. She couldn't believe she had missed it on a first pass.

"We are gathered here...Every Solday, Lord Stone attends a private church service within the palace. We will ambush him when he lets down his guard in prayer. We know what he really is. He's one of those beasts, a werewolf, and we know what he does with all that silver. We'll force him to drink more than he can handle of it on a day when the moon won't save him."

"Shouldn't we try get him to admit he's a werewolf first, before killing him over it?"

"If you can get him to talk, but we need to kill him before he tries anything. He's run this country long enough. It's the people's turn. This Solday, the twenty first, we launch the attack."

Onya grabbed a clockwork incendiary device, a clockwork shield, and a shell-firing officer's pistol. She wished that she could use anything else that she had brought, but it all seemed useless. She had her doubts about the firebomb too. The small shield was for the risk that there was a mage among the enemy, but it would do little against pistols, muskets, or even rifles. And some spells would be far too powerful. If that was the case, her only defense was to run.

Onya hid the weapons in the folds of her flowing dress, which unlike those fluffier versions that were worn by nobility or even the similar ones that she had worn when she first arrived, had far more give around the hips, chest, and legs, allowing her to sneak a belt beneath the skirt and had pockets. She'd have to hike it back up to pull out the pistol, but if she had to use a weapon, there was no reason to assume that showing a little bit of leg wouldn't be worth grabbing a gun.

As soon as she was out of the Bunting's house, she was on the move, walking and running in spurts when she hoped no one was watching. The last thing she wanted to be was stopped by a member of the roving police force and issued a citation for disturbing the peaceful Solday.

Instead of taking the northwest road toward the coast, she followed the road down the hill to the north, and then cut northeast on another road. The palace, disappeared and reappeared as she went, hidden only momentarily by two-story buildings, always growing larger.

When Onya arrived, she found the front door unlocked. She snuck in, quietly, and looked around. She put the bar over the door behind her. There was no one in the front hallway, which was a two-story atrium-like room. The guards had all disappeared. She saw an abandoned tea set near a guard station and all of the oil lamps were eerily dark within the typically bright room. The clock chimed that it was noon.

She breathed an exhale and checked that her dress looked flat in a mirror and then tied her hair into a loose bun behind her head. She knew that the chapel was on the third floor, but she didn't know the layout.

If she ran into anyone, she would simply say that she was coming into work to find something that she had forgot. She played out the scenarios in her head.

She came out onto the floor, and it was one long hallway, presenting a multi-story chapel, within the walls of the vertical tower. She passed carved stone decorations and realized now why there was stained glass along the third through sixth floors of the palace. As she neared the chapel, the stone cutaway from the outer wall, revealing two story oak doors that blocked a tall, relatively narrow arch.

Rather than knock, she pushed the door gently open. It creaked loudly, and she almost reached below her dress for the gun. When she craned her neck around the door, in the room there were only the priest and Stone, kneeling and looking back at her.

"What are you doing here?" asked the priest.

Onya looked at Stone, whose eyes appeared to be asking the same question. Though unlike the priest, he seemed far less bothered by the intrusion.

"You interrupted my sermon," said the priest.

"Lord Stone, can we speak a moment?"

"Anything that you may say to me, you can say with the good pastor present," said Stone, shifting to stand. The pastor placed a hand on his shoulder.

"I was minding my own business today when I overheard-- something! Something that I can only share with your grace," said Onya.

"You overheard something?"

Onya neared, watching the pastor, and said in Stone's ear, though not quietly enough for the man of faith to hear, "I overheard that there is a coup planned. They may be marching on their way here right now."

"A coup?" shouted the priest. "Preposterous as it sounds, we must do something to confirm this."

Stone pushed the man's hand away and stood up, "We could go to the sixth-floor balcony. It runs along the full outside of the building, or the third floor, it looks over the entrance."

"You're right. We could go now. To the third floor. Let's see them."

"What about the sermon?" asked Stone and then he looked at her. "Where did you hear this, Onya?"

"In the square."

"From who?"

"I couldn't quite tell. It was very hushed."

The pastor was walking quietly to the door. Stone shrugged and followed the old man. Onya followed Stone. Her hand pressed on the gun beneath her dress, which pressed against her inner thigh.

"I already locked the door on the first floor," said Onya as the pastor began going to one of the iron staircases.

"I was just going to check--uh--something else."

Onya approached him from behind.

"We shouldn't be splitting up."

"You shouldn't be here. We thought you were just the latest love interest."

"Excuse me?" Onya stopped and thought about going for her gun. She also wondered about whether Valessa was right that Stone was a loner.

He turned and in a sharp movement, pulled a gun from beneath his robe. She tried to spin away from him. The bullet fired and caught her in the side. She tried to get at the gun beneath her dress, but her legs had fallen awkwardly.

Another shot fired. The priest coughed up blood as one of his lungs was punctured through by a pistol fired by Jack. Onya saw a red mark symbol on the priest's chest through the hole in his garments as he fought to stand. When he noticed what she was looking at, he fought to the window and threw himself out, sending shards of glass everywhere.

Stone checked where the body had fallen, only to see that Onya had been right. Of the city of one million, there might have been three thousand slowly crowding around the palace. He wondered where his guards were, and he was dismayed at not being able to call upon the militias. Most of the standing army was under Akrin control, and he was sure, if they weren't behind this, they wouldn't stop it.

When the men saw the priest fall, they began to yell at Stone, calling him a pagan murderer. Bullets were fired upon him, and he ducked away. As more stained glass shattered, he covered Onya.

The shards fell around them. He shook his coat, sending shards of glass everywhere and looked down at her. She was bleeding heavily from her side, but her eyes fought to remain sharp. She held out a small device.

"Throw this at the front door."

"What is it?"

"It will buy us even more time."

He didn't risk getting too close to the window and threw the device in an arc past the smaller balcony that stood away from the front of the building. The device hit the ground and erupted into a fiery blaze. The men cried out and fired again. Stone picked up Onya and went to the iron staircase.

He cradled her while also avoiding looking directly at her wound. She whimpered in his arms. Stone knew just from one glance that it was an extremely painful wound that would most certainly prove fatal. It was the worst place to be hit, and feeling her soft back, the bullet had not gone through. She would be in agony for hours with no hope. Even if they had a doctor.

Stone carried her up another floor and then another. The only place that he knew that he could take her. He felt something around her waist press into his arms. It felt mechanical like the device he had thrown, pressing into his arm from between her legs and making it difficult to carry her from the pain it caused.

Onya couldn't think through the pain about anything other than how stupid she felt. One for letting herself get shot and two for being just the latest love interest. She felt that she had let herself be deceived in more ways than one.

Stone was getting desperate and tired, trying to get the woman, whom he felt he might love, to the top of the tower. She was the only thing that he could think of since he had run into her the other week. On top of that, she had saved his life, and now, he had to try to save hers.

He growled and grunted, straining from the long walk, carrying the tiny woman of average height, with flowing dark brown hair and beautiful mahogany eyes to his office up more than thirty flights of iron stairs. Why would he need to be able to become a werewolf at any time? To save the new love of his life would be a good reason. While a werewolf's regeneration abilities were limited, just one bullet wound even of silver, no matter where it was, would not be lethal. It would take well more than a few to take a wolf down.

Stone made it to the thirty fourth floor and kicked the door open, shattering the handle. He didn't know how hard it would be to replace, but for the moment he didn't care. He knocked open his office door and opened his silver cabinet. He would need it for afterwards.

Stone grabbed the scepter and wondered how it might work as he thought about transforming. It didn't start right away, but he began to feel the surge rush through his body. Breaking and re-forming bones into a half wolf form. Only his legs spared from the trauma as he felt his mind collapsing, his hand stuck grasping the small rod.

Stone had been a self-medicating werewolf, injecting silver to prevent his transformations for a long time, but now he needed to control the beast within to save someone he loved. It fought against him as if it wanted to take him to stalk the night beyond the walls. He fought toward her.

One paw pressing onto the floor, bit by bit toward her thin body. He leaned over her whimpering form as she looked up at him with her brown eyes, glaring in fear but unable to move. Her body failed her as the blood pooled. It must have dripped across the whole of the staircase, leading whoever was below right to them.

Stone leaned his powerful jaws to her shoulder and bit down, cursing her as he was cursed, fighting against the beast form, preventing it from taking him over completely.

She unleashed a primal scream of agony as his teeth dug into her shoulder. Her blood pooled there now too and then began sucking back into her veins.

She looked into his light blue, almost gray eyes. The only thing that remained of his human form within her sight. The silver-white hair of his massive beast form glinted in the oil lamps as she lost consciousness.

Stone wanted to tell her that it would be okay, but only a growl came out. He was losing control. He could barely grasp onto reality, but he forced himself to drop the scepter. He had not seen his full beastly claws in a long time. He went to the cabinet, now open. He tried to get a vial into the syringe. He plunged it into his veins, feeling his body remake itself around the tool as well as the pain. He had missed the vein completely and had just slammed it in.

As he felt the mind of a beast receding and his flesh start to return to normal, he formulated a new plan. He needed to block all four staircases with whatever he could before the men were able to break through the doors below. Something he assumed must have happened by now. He was only protected by the sheer number of flights that they had to climb to reach them.

He picked up desks, chairs, boxes and tables and piled them in the way of the staircases on the iron, blocking the doors from opening.

When he finally returned to his office after emptying every other room as well, she was awake, though still weak, leaning against the wall.

"Did you make me into a monster?"

"Yes."

"Hopefully it's better than death," she said.

"I think so," said Stone.

She nodded over at the cabinet with the vials of silver, now almost empty, "Doesn't look like it."

"That's complicated," he said.

"Sure, it is," she said. "The men who are coming up here said they thought you were that kind of monster. I guess they were right."

"Yes, the werewolves have long given the 'silver coast' its name, but my family wasn't always cursed. I have been a werewolf since I was a small boy. My father found a way for me to control the impulse, but my wife couldn't survive the birth of my son."

"I'm sorry," she said reflexively.

"Clearly, I didn't plan on turning you into a werewolf, but you would have suffered a long and painful death if I hadn't. We can rest and hide out here in the castle, hoping that the city police come to our rescue, but..."

"But, what?"

"It's about to be Frostmas. I'm not sure how many people will be on duty. A crowd of three thousand could keep us here for as many as eight days." He looked down and began growing thoughtful as to whether he should fight the men off or just let them take the country from him. It would take the question of establishing Albion's independence out of his hands.

"You want to know what I think about the people coming for you?" she asked. Her head was spinning, but she could still see the look of defeat in his eyes.

"Sure, what do you think?"

It wasn't so much what she thought as much as what she knew, but she wouldn't let him know that, "these people don't reflect the whole nation. Your people are out there, completely unaware of what's going on here. The people coming up here probably think that you should be in everyone's affairs. The people out there are just happy you stay out of it."

He looked doubtful.

"Everywhere we went in the city, people were happy to see you. Except for a few that are in the palace that might not even be your people."

She insinuated the same thing that he thought as well. It could have been Akrin from the start. Stone wished that if that was even true that it meant that his decision on secession was simpler. He didn't want to fight, and his people would be the ones to suffer either choice he made. There was also no true proof that this even had been a move by Akre.

The sound of banging and attempts to move the stacked furniture could be heard from the hallway. He wasn't sure how long it would take them to fight through the barricades, but he was thankful that the building was mostly made of stone like his namesake. The risk of the attackers starting them on fire within the stone central interior was nil without superpowers that didn't exist. Only powerful magic could reach them now, and they were immune to most spells as werewolves.

If the enemy believed he was a beast, it was unlikely that a powerful sorcerer would risk revealing themselves to Stone or to the civilians they worked with.

"I guess we may be spending the holidays together," said Onya smiling and reaching her foot out to touch Stone's leg as he sat beside her.

"Yes, if we are lucky, or perhaps unlucky," he said. "The next full moon is in a few days. Even if we did have enough silver to prevent the transformation for us both, trying it on you might kill you."

"So, you'll get to see the new me," she laughed.

"I guess that is one way that you could put it," he looked at her, and then couldn't help but smile.

"You shouldn't be doing that anyway," she nodded toward the broken syringe on the floor.

"You haven't seen the full me," he smirked.

"If it's not a full moon, how did you do that just now?"

"A recent and fortunate gift."

"And shouldn't you think of this power as a gift then," she looked at him as his eyes darkened in thought. "Can't you just use your monster form to bust us out of this barricade."

He was silent for a moment.

"I don't want the whole city to see me. Besides, I haven't used the form in a long time."

They could hear sawing coming from the hallway.

"You might have to. If we even get that chance."

1513 - Chapter 12

Sven felt pressure on his chest forcing him awake. The face of one of his generals, nearly pressed against his, looked frantic and wide-eyed; his emotions about to explode in a combination of fear and desperation.

"What is it general?"

"The emperor sir," the man could barely contain his fear. His brazen bravado from the days before was gone. His calls of valor, demanding his Normen troops to recall the old country, long left behind with the coming of the ice, and the modern history of their recent ancestors whose passionate valor and endless victories built the Empire, they were empty words.

"What about the emperor?"

"He's here."

"Here! Here?" Sven bolted up right, "Arm the troops, ready the cannons."

"No, not here, here. About eight hours ride. With a troop of one hundred twenty-five thousand!"

"One hundred twenty-five..." Sven, for a brief moment looked down at his hands, wondering what next move to make. He had mustered much less than that to say the least. He had intended to recruit to fifty thousand by the end of the year, given the success of his initial efforts, and his successful recruitment of senior officers who had fought in the Varanorian guard.

"That's impossible," Sven couldn't help himself but to say, but the look on his general's face told him otherwise. "Who confirmed the number?"

"Scouts sir. As you requested, we distributed in and around Leidyn. Our southern positions discovered them this morning as the sun rose. They were lucky to not be routed. They counted divisions set in fifty lines of fifty, supported by limited cavalry detachments and few artillery. They've, the scouts have, retreated to the position at Elksits hill."

"Elksits, right. We had planned--" Sven cut himself off. No use in considering old plans now. "He must have marched through the Ivanssun holidays, betting that we would never have expected it, and we didn't."

"No, we didn't," repeated his general.

"How did we not hear of this before now?"

"The enemy launched the force in secret across a number of

reserve encampments, surrounding Akre. We know they must have left in the night, because we have sentries posted. We would have received a telegram. Once they were in the Solgra, the emperor effectively disguised their movements with cavalry screens, which because of the Ivanssun celebrations were not investigated fully, and by utilizing the limited run of the train tracks, the Akrin force was able to ship a large number of supplies ahead. Their men may have been marched through the night, and not held back by the weight of cannons or significant munitions. They could be exhausted."

"Rally the men. We'll--" Sven had trouble thinking. With less than eight hours to plan, and numerous incomplete divisions of his own, meant to be organized into twenty groups of three thousand riflemen, supported for now by only artillery. He was far short of that, and desperately lacking in supplies.

He had requisitioned limited numbers of shells, hardly enough bullets to sustain an extended engagement over a number of days, and while they had fortified Elksits partially, they had planned additional distribution of redoubts to be built in the spring as their main fall back, pending an engagement with as many as eighty thousand.

"We'll rendezvous at Elksits, digging into the positions that we've already fortified. Can you confirm that the munitions and artillery are in place?"

"Yes."

Sven stood up. He needed to ensure that Erold was as far away from Leidyn as possible before the battle took place. Elksits was about an hour ride south, but a cavalry detachment of the enemy vanguard could catch any reserved troops in an engagement if too close to the battle.

"Where are you going?"

"I have to see to some of the troops myself. Disperse the orders. If I'm not back here in under an hour, send a detachment to find me."

The general felt for a second that the potential king of Normany was running from battle, but he checked himself from saying anything. There was a reason, the Varanorians had been the strongest of the three major northern tribes, they were the fiercest in battle, striking fear throughout the world for their ability to break concentrated groupings of heavily armored ground troops such as the Elessian phalanxes, whose spears and collected shields made range attacks and direct engagement near impossible for even the heaviest armed opponents of the world after the fall of the Otum.

The legendary berserk charges of the Varanorians closed the phalanxes in on themselves until the enemy were suffocated or crushed under their own weight, often defeating groups much larger their number. Today, would be no different, and the old land would be honored again.

While the general dispersed orders, Sven quickly dressed himself. He had a personal valet like any king or emperor, but he needed quickness, not accuracy. He could not wait for another man to be called up, and he would meet the foe on the battlefield in a night shirt if he must.

He felt that must have been betrayed, because someone should have alerted him. He couldn't say this out loud, but he felt that more was at work than using the convenience of the preparations for and celebrations of Frostmas and the following day, today, Spirit Day to be the only factors in contributing to the surprise of the engagement.

He couldn't say that out loud, but how could they have coordinated movements across the Solgra without someone noticing or pressing the enemy's cavalry. If the cavalry was running down his scouts, they must have known more about his positioning than he supposed, and it was almost guaranteed that they would have a plan of attack for Elksits.

It was no matter. Spirit Day like Frostmas was a special day across most of the nations of the Akrin Empire, which had blended traditions of the old Normen with those of Old Galdir and the men of the gulf. It was a day to commemorate the valiant heroes of war who had died in battle, and it was almost fitting that it would be a day of battle.

The enemy would be upon them in early evening, and Sven was only thankful that he had the foresight to refrain from drinking himself over the celebration weekend, in the case of an emergency, though he did not expect something of this scale.

He was into the next house, the men were on the move, and they made way for him, standing at attention as he passed. He nodded to them to get on with it. There was not time for formalities when there was to be a fight by the end of the day. Sven ducked through the doorways to find Erold--not in his bedroom, which was just like him lately.

This is exactly what Sven had feared when he had informed the general that he may take longer than an hour to return. He needed to warn Erold about the coming danger, but the boy had been so infatuated with a storybook romance that he had left every day before the sunrise, which had occurred at the very most an hour before, to find a girl he had kissed for a moment at the party on Zenday, only three days before.

Sven ran out of the house the way that he had come, pulling and pushing his hands through his long, dark brown hair. He would have little time to tie it into a Varanorian braid before the battle. He needed to get Erold himself before his officers thought to search for him, because Erold, more than ever, must remain a secret now.

Sven, who preferred not to ride, held up one of his messengers and informed him to tell the general that he was riding to a reserve position and would be back in less than an hour.

Sven then took the horse and rode in a loop through the city before cutting south toward Elksits and then west to the coast, where he believed Erold would be after having seen him come back from the surrounding villages to the north and east in the prior days. If he was lucky, he would not have left even thirty minutes before Sven had set out to catch him.

* * *

Erold had determined after the night of the ball, that he would go door to door until he found Ti-Enna. It was the ultimate mission of his life. He may not ever be king, but he had found a beautiful queen, whose fiery personality had resonated with him, deeply.

She was the type of woman Normany needed.

Moon and Volstad had tired of this endless game after the first day, and yet they followed along after the young prince, who every morning, ran out on foot to go door to door in the towns around Leidyn, carrying the sash in his arms and asking if a young woman by the name of Ti-Enna lived there.

After three days of this, and even doing so yesterday, on the quiet morning of Frostmas, with no one in the streets and everyone at home enjoying their family time on a brisk morning, it had gotten more than old. Both Moon and Volstad had been thankful that Erold had finally relented, stopping only to celebrate Frostmas with Sven in mid-afternoon instead of, as usual, by the latest possible moment in the evening when the sun had almost fallen beneath the hills to the north and west.

They were able to enjoy the day a little themselves then, even drinking a little bit of beer with the officers. The trio had eaten well too, feasting better than the first night that Sven had come and Volstad swapped stories well into the night with Sven and his officers, who had also spent time around the gulf fighting on behalf of Cardane's dedicated mercenary force of Normen, the Varanorian guard.

Each story had tried to one up the other, but it became clear from each tale that either the details were becoming fabricated, exaggerated, or the danger in the gulf was becoming greater and greater every year. Moon had no doubt that Volstad's words were true, but his stories could almost be dated by the relatively tame tales of fighting off rebellions or territory encroachments by distant kingdoms.

This time, Moon and Volstad had insisted on taking a pair of horses, so Moon had ridden with Erold. And, Volstad had ridden alone.

After yet another door being slammed in the prince's face, he continued on, unphased. There were a series of houses up on the next hill, and as they crested it, they could see off into the distance for many atomic miles and still not quite see the coastline, which they had at times been able to see from the airship to Seylil.

Just as Erold neared the first door among the small collection, they heard the neigh of a struggling horse and turned to see Sven riding up the hill alone. None of his usual entourage was anywhere in sight.

Moon got chills.

As soon as they made eye contact, Sven hopped off the horse to let it rest, and guided it to a water trough that had a little water, while beckoning the three of them to him.

Volstad understood before anything was said that they were back on the road. He was glad that he had brought his money with him. He had insisted that the other two do the same. Now, he could only hope that they had heeded his advice.

"There is no time to fully explain. To summarize. There will be a battle shortly. This evening at the latest. I see you took horses this time. I'm glad I caught you so quickly. You can take this horse too and go to the next town. Get whatever supplies you need and make for the coast and then up to Gardnor. Here's a few gold coins." He looked calm, but thoughtful and the lines in his face, not many years over thirty, began to tighten and wrinkle as the thoughts swirled in his head.

He continued, still speaking calmly, "I may not be needing them for long. The nearer you are to Albion, the safer, though I haven't heard from Lord Stone in a few days. I had assumed it was the holidays, but now I don't know what to think. Elara, Abrim, if you could give me a moment alone to speak to my nephew."

Sven guided Moon and Volstad with his eyes, until they were on the other side of one of the houses further up the hill. Then, he looked at Erold sternly, visibly upset.

"Erold, I haven't said anything, but how could you not take your personal safety more seriously?"

"I was trying to find--"

"The girl from the ball, I know. I admire you for chasing after what you want. For your passion. Whatever this girl's name is, I'm sure she's sweet."

"Her name's Ti-Enna," Erold informed him.

"Erold, that's not the point. Life is not a fairy tale. You can't be taking unnecessary risks."

"I didn't think--"

"Exactly, my point, Erold."

Erold looked put out, a little upset, and it wasn't the way Sven had wanted things to go. He pulled the boy to him, hugging him tightly and almost lifting him off the ground before he slipped what was left of the coins he had on hand, a couple silvers, into the boy's pocket.

Sven put his hands on the boy's shoulders, looked him in the eyes, and then embraced him again. He had known the boy for most of Erold's life, and much had changed since then in a world, not accustomed to war.

"I love you Erold, remember that. You owe it to all the men and women of Normany. Not just Ti-Enna, not just me, but also to your father."

Erold could feel the warmth from his uncle, whose embrace surrounded him, and whose musky smell of sweat had not been wiped off since the night before. It was like being hugged by a wet bear, and yet, he didn't want to be let go.

His mind slipped from its singular focus on Ti-Enna, and he thought of his father. An involuntary tear slipped from his eye, and he wiped it away.

"I love you too Uncle Sven."

"Now, I must go. Ride to the coast. Because these are trained horses, you can ride them hard. Though this one may be a little tired after hauling me after you this morning. If you rest every five atomic miles or a little more, you'll be able to cover the distance to the coast and a little up it by night fall. Don't stop long for anything. The enemy may be looping around to find deserters or a rear guard during the battle, trying to prevent escape."

Erold looked at him questioningly.

"We are badly outnumbered, Erold. It's likely to be four to one this evening against us."

"But, we are men of Normany. Four to one, we should still have an advantage."

"In the days of swords and steel, I would have rushed against one million with one thousand, but on the modern battlefield, the pistol kills the mage."

They embraced one last time, and this time, Sven picked Erold up, put him on the horse, and nudged him along to ride up the hill, toward Moon and Volstad, away from the battle.

"Remember, Erold. Fros walks with you always. Keep the Lord in your heart for we all follow the one true God."

Sven turned back toward Leidyn and began to walk. He'd most certainly be back before an hour had passed. He checked the timepiece in his waistcoat and breathed. It was nearing a quarter to ten.

He would do what he could to sue for peace and to buy time for Erold to escape. He could only hope that he'd be out of the country by this time next month, but no route, south, north, or west seemed safe.

The troops had been mobilized. Maybe he would see his ancestors soon in a warrior's death, his spirit returning home at last among them. A fitting celebration of Spirit Day indeed.

* * *

The morning sun rose ever higher, lighting up the hills and the yellow tall grass of the plains just that little more with each passing hour, taking away the shadows beneath the houses and warming them despite the chill in the air. They made it to the next town quickly, bought some food for the horses, filled canteens with water, and bought some additional supplies.

Erold bought a spyglass while Moon bought a compass and a map. Volstad bought more ammunition for his pistol. He was armed well as he had been for the last few weeks. His sheathed sword had been little better than decoration. The other two had confirmed that they had left nothing behind, save changes of clothes, while he had left the same and a few packs of bullets that he wished he hadn't.

Erold didn't say it out loud, but he touched the orb a few times to make sure he wasn't leaving it behind in Leidyn. For his father to die over a trinket he left behind on the eve of battle in a rented house in a small city in the Solgra--they would have gone back, but it would have been a stupid waste of time. There might have been a few pieces of silver stuffed somewhere that he had forgotten about, in the pocket of a coat or near the bed on the floor, but he had kept his money close ever since they had fallen out of the sky.

Few people, if any, were out and about, as they would have been on any typical second day of the week, like this Marasday might have been. Instead, it was a holiday, and only the general stores and taverns were open as the trio continued their ride along the dirt road out of town.

They tried to maintain a straight trajectory, but as they went toward the coast, they had to stay south of the hills, which forced them to head almost directly southwest, which kept them in the Godrland province that much longer.

The morning sun had gone completely away now, and Erold checked his watch to see it was the hour of the noon sun. They were gradually easing closer to the hills and drifting higher in elevation. The riding was easy, and the horses were strong.

They stopped at streams every five atomic miles like Sven had suggested. They ran down the hills and cut through the fields, toward the Áelin, which sliced through the middle of the Solgra, running almost dead west, separating the provinces of West Goodlin and Godrland.

At once such stop, Moon remarked that they were making good time, having already covered about half of the distance, give or take, that they had hoped to cover that day. They would be at the coast shortly and then could ride up to a town on the shore before dusk.

Erold checked his watch. It was about three. Looking up at the sun, he couldn't tell but they had about five hours left of daylight. He was disappointed that he had not found Ti-Enna, or anyone who had known her.

She could have gone any direction from Leidyn, which is almost directly in the middle of the nation. He had checked all over, in Godrland and Dalvalles, within a day's walk. She could have been in that last row of houses, or the next. He was sure he would have found her today. Now, he was hoping that he wouldn't damage her sash, as he rode to wherever they might be going. They hadn't discussed anything further than the day's ride yet, but he had a feeling that he would not return soon.

History was filled with kings in exile, and Erold understood, from talk of Albion, that his days were either numbered in Normany or in life. If only she wouldn't have relied on fate to force their paths to cross again, and yet, he would have had to leave anyway.

Erold rode up the foot of the hill as they were up against the rocky hills of Dalvalles and took the spyglass out of his pocket. Nothing more than a novelty for an amateur astronomer in the Solgra, or perhaps a gift for a child. He aimed it back toward Leidyn, aiming to see if he could make out the battlefield from maybe eighty atomic miles away.

Unfortunately, it was only a view of about one hundred atomic yards, less than a tenth of one atomic mile, and he could only look back at the beautiful countryside of sun-dyed, yellow grass, wheat fields, and streams while the horses grazed and drank, enjoying the rest.

* * *

Sven and his men had formed defensive positions across the hill, but they were clearly over matched. He might have had them train better and harder if he had expected an engagement this fall. Frostmas was the prophet's day, just after the autumnal equinox, and kicked off the gatherings of friends and family that ran through to the end of year, and the celebration of the Lord on the twenty fifth of Vetfal.

Few armies had ever waged war in the fall or winter, especially since the coming of the ice. The new emperor, Polesar, wanted to surprise his enemy and get it over with and so they would.

Sven had his men in two lines of two deep, angled slightly outward from a straight center, with staggered artillery support, but he had already sent a messenger across the battlefield to sue for peace. He was sure the enemy would want unconditional surrender, but the least he could do was to save his men. Their pride kept them here, as men of the north and as men who believed in a free Normany.

Sven spoke a bit to his generals and took up a battlehammer like the greatest of the Normen generals had wielded in the distant past. Hughgar, who had brought Akre to heel, had used the ancient Hammer of Nole, taller than the average man, to strike fear into his enemies. Sven hoped to do the same now. His men were similarly outmatched. They would fire rounds as the opponent rushed the hill and then the second lines would fire, until they would counter-charge and engage the opponent in fierce one on one combat, where the Normen would outclass their enemies.

Sven looked through a spyglass, murmuring to his generals

about trying to scare the enemy with the long history of Normany's defeats of unequal odds. The enemy did not look afraid in their dark blue coats and bright white pants, red and gold decals throughout their waist coats, however; they looked as if they were ready to slake a thirst for blood and dole out a return for all those centuries of defeats handed out by the Normen.

To add additional frustration on what might possibly turn the tide for Sven's force, who had yet to have matching uniforms, was that despite the Akrin horde having marched for days with no end, in the rapidly decreasing temperature of late summer, they did not look tired, and even this day's weather had turned out nice. The air was warm, and the sun shone brightly.

Sven watched his messenger requesting to sue for peace and have the leaders meet for terms of surrender. The man was dressed smartly in the blue and yellow of Normany, looking more than confident that he was being sent to the right place by the adjutant's staff, and now he was walking up to the commanders forward posting. Perhaps that was the emperor there.

Bang.

He couldn't really hear the sound, just see the puff of smoke and make the sound in his head, before there was a light echo, when the sound finally crossed over the battlefield. An elegant, if not ugly answer. There would be no peace.

The battle lines of the opponent stretched over the shorter southern hills and there were clear divisions. It was hard for him to not count them and yet he knew what the total would be. The enemy appeared to be using the classic tactic of hemming in both sides and gradually closing in on the sides, outflanking his men with numbers. A strategy Sven could admire.

They would have to hold the flanks strong, but the bulk of the attack would come in the middle and the flanking maneuver would help to prevent the enemy from disengaging to regroup. They were aiming to rout them here.

Sven took another deep breath. He had made his decision to fight on this battlefield. The battle would open up, and then he would go in as a good mage would. His defensive magic was powerful, and they were dug in. Perhaps they could force a stalemate for the next day if the positions held firm.

The enemy charged. His generals counter-ordered, unleashing the artillery. Some of the shells landed, sending shrapnel everywhere. The Akrin troops were cut down, and yet, on they came in neat lines marching forward. Round after round of shell, and still more than one hundred thousand men charged on until they began to break into a steady run, with bayonets held carefully forward ahead, not to kill themselves, or their own.

The Akrin forward runners were soon in firing range of the Normany lines as they charged through whatever fire that Sven's troops rained down on them. Then, the mages would engage, from force to force, and then, the infantry would follow the mages and Sven forward, in the countercharge.

The first line of his troop fired, and then the second. The first started reloading, and then the second. Sven stepped forward, and he could see the white in the eyes of the opposing battlemages that had somehow survived shellfire and bullets. Some using shield magic, others lucky.

Sven threw down an aura of protection over his men to limit the threat of the opposing mages, and the mage duels began. Like javelins, mage's spears and beams of fire and lightning crossed the field. Some were ricocheted or blocked, while others found their mark, splitting men, mages or otherwise, in half, leaving the battlefield drenched in as much blood as the raining artillery that continued to fire blasts into ever more oncoming troops.

The infantry units, reinforced with mage squadrons, led the Akrin forces onward and despite all losses, it appeared as if none had gone down. It was a diabolically elegant system that merged protective measures with the offensive efficiency of the muskets in the hands of the common soldier.

Sven led the countercharge, "For Normany!" And ran into the oncoming fray as his men unleashed another salvo and met the enemy on the field of Elksits hill.

He was badly outnumbered. He knew he could not win. But, he was glad that he had sent Erold up the coast. It was the smartest thing he could have done for the good of Normany.

A bullet fired from the gun of one of his generals found Sven's back and then another, and the powerful protection aura blinked out. The clash continued. Rifles, swords, and magic fired and flew as Normany men were massacred, and Sven, a saint and giant among men, was turned face down. The battlehammer had not been swung.

* * *

A glint of a different kind of blue caught his eye. He couldn't mistake it for anything but it what it was. The uniform of an Akrin soldier.

"Volstad, Moon!" Erold yelled and pointed off to the distance to where they couldn't see, "We're being tailed."

"How many?" yelled Volstad, then he hopped up on his horse and galloped to where Erold was on the hill. He took the spyglass and looked back. He cursed.

"What is it?" asked Moon, who had mounted her horse and positioned her horse to ride across the cut of the hill toward the coast, where they needed to go.

"It's a unit of the vanguard! Twenty or so. They must have made us when we were cutting across the hills."

Moon couldn't make out the second bit of what he said, but Erold could, and he followed Moon, who started off in the direction of the coast. They couldn't cut through the hills, because the enemy could catch them around the coast. They'd have to outrun them and hope that they gave up the pursuit forward of their divisions.

The trio were dressing in plain clothes, but that was probably why it was a cursory twenty or so, sent forward to investigate the rogues or deserters. Volstad followed after as they pushed their horses into a dead sprint into the setting sun.

They rode hard forward, and periodically had to stop to feed the horses and let them drink. Volstad would look back through the spyglass, and forgetting to grab a notepad for making battlefield remarks, he turned the bullets in his ammo pack to indicate whether they were being gained on.

Thus far, they had outpaced the pursuit. The trio continued on. The hills continued to break toward the south and flatten gradually as they neared the coast. The streams stopped heading south and began to turn in sharp curves to the west.

They rode up a hill, probably named by the locals, and there it was a coastline that stretched for miles, north and south, along the green seas between Normany and Imeria, dotted with numerous islands.

The beaches stretched from here as far as the eye could see in either direction. It was cut only by the occasional isthmus or the mouth of a stream, but neither could be seen from the hill. They took a right along the beach, staying above the sand, keeping the horses on the old dirt road, known to connect Akre to Rorik, in Albion.

The sun gradually fell faster and faster, as the trio continued to ride hard, knowing that their horses would need another break soon. They had gone over one hundred twenty atomic miles in a day already, almost three times the number the wagon they rode to

Leidyn could make traveling quickly.

These horses had lighter loads and were trained for the distances, but now that they were being run hard, the companions would no doubt have to exchange horses at the next available opportunity. If they were forced to run a third set of horses, though, they ran the risk of running out of gold again, between the costs of taverns and food and water between here and their next destination.

They stopped at a stream, letting the horses drink and eat, as the horses began to complain and try to force them to rest. The trio ate too. Volstad munched on his bread, peering through the spyglass, making markings in his bullets.

Their pursuers had gotten hungry and had pushed their horses harder. They had gained two bullets, which was counting intervals of distance that Volstad could clock with the landmarks on the road.

"We have to move." Volstad said, and he mounted his horse and helped Moon onto hers. Erold's horse wouldn't come, so they grabbed what things they could, helped Erold onto Moon's horse and left the animal behind. As if she was sad to be left behind, the tired mare began trotting after them, and as they pushed faster, it did too.

On, the trio pushed, galloping along the empty beaches as the sunlight continued to fall along the shoreline, and the cold began to creep from the water up to the hills like an invisible shadow that spread out before the shadow of night fell.

Volstad had expected a city by now, but there had been none yet. They were following the line of the hills, and the forest filled them, hiding anything deeper within, and left them alone against the coast, save for a shanty or forgotten ruin of a wooden abode lining the coastline.

The old captain Volstad, intent on finding them shelter before the night caught up to them and hoping to outrun the enemy by using the freezing night, spied forward through the glass, until finally he caught the tall belltower of a coastline town, make that two. Two twin bell towers of a port town beckoned them from a distance, alabaster white and rising up from the sand between the forested hills and the crashing waves of the sea, with bronze fittings rising still higher that caught the last of the sunlight. And behind, them a lonely citadel sat atop a cliff, overlooking the city and the coastline below it and to the south.

The sun now dipped fully below the horizon, coloring the curved edge of the world with a thin line of its last light. The horses, clearly tired, as they had run further and faster than they were expected to, breathed heavily. The night beckoned and still, they pressed on, closing the last leg as the color of night drowned the detail of the hills away and soon left them guided by the lonely torch of oil lamps hung out at the edge of town.

When they entered the town, the street widened to double the size and dirt was replaced by paved stone. Volstad led them forward, investigating each sign hung beneath oil lamps that ran along the length of the road. They had to move quickly if the pursuers had continued to follow them into the night, or they'd be caught in the street.

He caught the sign for a tavern off the main path, down a side street, and guided the trio of horses, including Erold's, into the stable. He motioned for Moon and Erold, mouthing at her to get a room in the tavern upstairs. He switched the horses in the stable, so that theirs were further in as if they had been there longer. Then, he followed the two of them inside.

The pub was filled with deserters from Sven's force, or troops that had been requisitioned and hadn't made the trip yet. A quick count, there were probably about twenty, though likely many more than that. Most armed with at least a pistol. None had muskets. Their sleeves were up, and they were a few rounds of beer in. They must not have had any news of the battle, because they didn't seem jumpy at Volstad walking through the pub and up the back stairs to the rooms.

Moon motioned for him to join them in one of the middle rooms, and she shut the door behind him as he entered. He pressed his ear to the floor trying to hear anything that might happen. He couldn't quite make it out. Erold was up against the corner of the wall, unarmed, and trying to remain silent.

Two against twenty weren't great odds. They had better hope if the pursuers came in looking for them that the lot below wouldn't let the cavalry soldiers know that they were just up the stairs.

Below, the drinks continued to flow, and songs were sung as the merry men, helped themselves to plenty.

Volstad relaxed from the floor, then guessed how many minutes it had been, and looked at his watch. He turned around bullets, until he had turned them all over. They must have escaped the pursuit for the night. If they could leave before sunrise in the morning, they could be deep into Gardnor and out of the Dalvalles before the end of the next day.

Their adversary would never follow them that far north, when the only substantial fortress north of the Áelin, at Gulldalr, would still be loyal to the line of Arandil.

Volstad could hear the front door of the tavern slam against the wall. Something was said about the horses, which had been brought around to be visible through the doorway. They were some of the men's inside, and they didn't like the vanguard's tone or their uniforms.

First, the muffled sound of punches thrown, and then shots fired. Neither Moon nor Volstad wanted to speculate on what was happening below, but then there were a few voices, and someone running up the stairs.

There were voices in the hall, while bullets still ricocheted below. Someone was kicking open the doors, when they went to kick theirs, Moon flung it open and dashed with a speed so fast that Volstad blinked and missed before she had slipped a stiletto knife hidden beneath her wrist up beneath the soldier's rib cage and into his heart.

She used his body as a shield as bullets flew from the end of the hall before she pulled a pistol out of his pocket and returned fire. The hammer of the pistol snapped down, snapping the flint, igniting the black powder loaded ahead of a round ball and sent a bullet between the eyes of a man in a dark blue coat at the staircase, who slunk back against the wall.

More bullets flew below, and Moon eased her way back inside the room, now covered by Volstad at the door, not letting the body down until they had closed the door again and blocked the door from the inside with the lifeless man.

Moon cleaned her stiletto on the soldier's white pants, and then unclipped the dead man's holster and put it around her waist, before loading and holstering the percussion pistol. Volstad watched her work, knowing now for sure that she was indeed armed, even without the weapon.

"I don't suppose those are .58 caliber balls?" asked Moon, looking from her gun to the bullets that Volstad had been playing with.

He shook his head. They were .54 shells, designed and recently put into mass production for long rifles, typically used for hunting elk. His long-barrel, flintlock pistol had been modified to fire them, one at a time as usual, so he would never be in short supply of ammo or run into the high risk of misfire inherent in the standard percussion pistols.

"I used to have a custom pistol like that. Only, it didn't shoot that type of bullet either."

"Speaking of bullets, it seems like the shootout has quieted down," Volstad said.

"I don't want to be the one to sneak a peek."

"I don't want to be answering to the constable tomorrow either."

"What are you implying? Ride out in the morning, or get an early start tonight?"

"The horses were pushed pretty hard, and it's too cold tonight. On the other hand--"

"We have a body in here, and it's pretty easy to call it self-defense."

"Nice shot, by the way, in the hallway. I saw him hit the ground."

Moon nodded, "I say if it stays quiet, we wait out most of the night here, sleeping in shifts." She looked over at Erold, "between the two of us." She motioned between her and Volstad. "I don't want you to be carrying around a weapon until you absolutely have to."

After some time had passed, and no constable showed up to investigate, Volstad covered the door, while Moon and Erold pushed the body into the hall.

Volstad checked the hall, and then they closed the door, leaving it shut for the night. He hoped that the problem had sorted itself out the night before, but they were going to need to put distance between them and this town quickly and quietly.

"I was thinking," Volstad began.

"About where we need to go to next?" asked Moon.

Volstad nodded, "Yeah, how did you know?"

"Pretty obvious." Moon said, and she adjusted, laying against the wall, exhausted and making sure that she still had all of her weaponry, including those that the others hadn't seen. "I'm thinking the same thing myself."

"Where were you going to say?"

"North, over the mountains," Moon said, "You?"

"The same."

"For once, we agree."

"I never remember arguing."

Erold shifted and opened his mouth to speak, then thought better of it. He felt that he had to leave the sash behind.

"What is it?" asked Moon.

"Over the Evorul mountains, right? Like, with the dragons we just saw rip an airship into pieces," Erold asked.

"The very same," Moon nodded. Her exhausted mind could not handle any disagreement, right now.

"Is there any other option?"

"If we both agree on it," Moon pointed to the two of them, "then no. I think we are out of options, Erold."

Erold thought for a minute, and then recognized that she was right. They were the only two people he had now and therefore, his only advisors. He needed to hide from Akrin, and the Empire had few other enemies near Normany. Theodore had even said that the orb hadn't been safe, entrusting it to his father, likely to hold it in the vaults of the mountain fortress in Seylil or try to send it further north somehow. Only, fate had caught up to him first.

"I'm assuming there's some logic or plan to this. What is it, and who wants to explain?" Erold asked.

Moon began, "We have to go to Valgaard, and ask the Ice Queen, Princess Valessa for help."

Erold nodded.

Moon continued, "I've been thinking of alternatives since we were first in Leidyn. This is the only one I can think of as being realistic. Valgaard initiated the peace talks with your father, they would have negotiated with your uncle, Sven. They stand by far the most to gain, besides Normany itself, from you winning your kingdom back from Akre."

"Couldn't have said it better myself," said Volstad, "I used to be a member of the Varanorian guard as well, so--"

"We know," said Moon.

"We need money in a bad way," said Volstad.

"It's not the safest option," replied Moon.

"We're not going to be getting any help for free."

"How would you know that?"

"Now, that Erold is in exile. With few allies, and the risk of war coming to Valgaard at any moment, high, I think we'd be lucky to get any help."

"Just to cut in here," said Erold. "Exile is a lonely place, and an option is an option. Let's not waste time arguing about it when we don't even know if we'll get there. If you see no other choice, I see no other choice."

Moon and Volstad both communicated their assent.

"I also see that I have nothing to offer anyone, but seeing how the people of Normany have fought countless wars and been left with nothing but scraps, I think for the people's sake, we do whatever it takes, whether it's the Varanorian Guard or something else," said Erold. "Now, just one more thing, how do we get there?"

"From where we are now, the only path we can take is north through Dragnor. It's called Pili's Pass, and it takes you directly to the old fort at Helmun Loch," said Volstad.

"It's not the best choice in an ideal world, but yes, it's the best option from where we're sitting now," Moon agreed, looking around the tavern's room.

"Why? What's wrong with the pass to Helmun Loch?"

"Rumor has been that not everyone makes it, because a particularly large and angry dragon has moved into the area near lake at the end of the pass. Not just because the pass itself is dangerous to navigate," said Volstad.

"Is there another way?"

"To the south, everything is guarded closely by Akre, and to the far north, the pass is filled with more sabretooth tigers than its worth," replied Moon.

"I feel like I'd rather have the sabretooths."

"We could sneak by the dragon while it's asleep, or we could talk our way past it. Or, we could not run into it all," Volstad explained, all ways that he had dealt with dragons before, having grown up in Valgaard, a country normally friendly to them.

"And it could just be a rumor," Moon pointed out.

As if reading Erold's mind, Volstad said, "You shouldn't hate dragons despite the circumstances. They are misunderstood creatures, and especially in Valgaard, very kind. They are not mindless killing machines and are rarely aggressive, except when provoked. Humanity has at various times tried to wipe them out where they've crossed paths, such as in Imeria to the south and Valgaard to the North, but Normany has rarely had any other bad history with dragons. Moon and I were discussing this earlier," Volstad said to Erold, "the attack on your father's ship must have been planned, because dragons wouldn't have attacked the ship otherwise. Those dragons were lured there with the intent to make it look like an accident."

"What about the pirates?"

"Imposters, who didn't know they were collateral damage."

"Okay, we go north, then," said Erold, and he turned to get some sleep against the wall. Too tired to crawl up to the bed that was left untouched by any of the three.

In the morning before dawn, they started their ride north along the coast. When the sun finally rose, Erold admired the rolling hills and lush green trees, that had been hard to admire in the dark the night before. His horse had seemed happy to see him. After he had almost abandoned it the night before, it was as if it appreciated that he was still there. According to Moon, they were only three days of decent riding from the province of Dragnor.

1513 - Chapter 13

They were still stuck in the palace tower with no escape options and their limited supplies dwindling. The pantry on Stone's floor had more food than most, and luckily pitchers of water had been left behind for Stone himself. But, after four days, they were running out. Stone had snuck up to the thirty fifth floor and raided that for supplies, but they would need to be more aggressive and fight to the kitchen floor if they were going to be stuck for much longer. Even then, the palace kitchen could have already been emptied.

Frostmas had come and gone. When Stone had missed the city's celebration, on the first day of the siege, the city had instantly been made aware of the battle of the palace. While Stone and Onya were forced to use more than a few bullets to warn off the men still trying to clear the barricade, they had also been aided by the city police, who, after coming to Stone's aid, had been locked in a second siege around the rebels, fighting at first for just the outer walls of the palace grounds.

They were locked in an even clash as there were few police in the city, and they were not as well armed as Stone had always allowed the militia to be. He had always prided himself on the marksmanship of the militia, despite having little to do with their organization. As small as they were, they were mainly riflemen, and if he had to organize a full force, they would have to switch to the less accurate muskets out of cost.

The sound of fighting had been loudest today, on the twenty fourth, as the city police had made a concerted push to breach the gates after fighting off the men that remained outside the tower on its high surrounding walls. After breaching the outer wall, the rebels had rained fire on them from the third and sixth floor balconies of the tower until the city police pulled back.

They now contemplated trying to take a small airship up to the top of the tower. The police didn't know if Lord Stone was still alive, but they assumed that he was while the rebels continued to fight. At night, one of the few lights in the palace came from Stone's window. But, if they landed a ship on the tower, there was no way they could be certain they'd be able to send in enough men to safely secure the top few floors or get Lord Stone, safely out.

Stone and Onya could hear the men redouble their efforts at the barricade by the doors, and Onya couldn't help but read the concern on Stone's face. He fidgeted in place when he sat; he paced when he stood; and he couldn't help checking the clock before a minute had passed.

The past two nights, Frostmas and Spirit Day, he had grown increasingly agitated, but he had not spoken much more than a few apologies for the lack of decorations among his personal quarters and office. He appreciated the season, but generally left his celebrations to attending city gatherings. Tonight, whatever was eating away at him was becoming full force, and Onya could no longer consider it a difference in their training, between a spy and essentially a civilian leader.

"What is wrong Jack? If they get through the barricade, we have the pistols, we'll fight it out as we've planned, holding out here as long as we can rather than try to defend four staircases at once."

"It's not that," Stone looked at the various maps. Some of which were strangely not of the planet but of the stars. He had numerous navigational instruments throughout the room, including a large, decorative globe with numerous notes taped to it, indicating the commodities and trading protocols of foreign marketplaces as well as distance in days of frigate travel. She had plenty of time to study it over the last few days and hadn't looked much further, other than a cursory glance before the shooting had started.

"What is it then?"

"We are going to change soon, or at least you are." He paced, "I'm not sure I should."

"How would you survive if I changed?"

"Werewolves don't attack each other if they are of the same pack."

"How do you know we're the same pack?"

"The same reason I assume that the whole of Albion's werewolves are my pack."

"Haughty words coming from someone who doesn't want to change into the beast to begin with." Onya crossed her arms and looked at him, doubtfully.

"Just trust me. There will be a big difference between the two of us if I change. I'm what they call a White Wervelrine. A term given historically to describe the werewolves of the coast. When one grows white fur, it grows larger too, and more violent than the gray fur."

"Have you always been a white--whatever it is that you said?" she asked.

Stone nodded, "I was cursed by a witch for my father's refusal to part with me or his gold. My parents were powerful mages, themselves, and they were able to subdue me when I first turned but not until after...let's say significant damage had been caused."

There was a loud bang as one of the barricades collapsed suddenly, avalanching through the staircase. Some of the men may have been injured, but it was clear to the two of them now, that the enemy was breaking through.

"We need to form a transformation plan while it is still barricaded. We don't have much time either way." Stone looked outside as the full moon already hung in the dying light as the sun sunk below the horizon.

"Even if we didn't need your power, I wouldn't let you take the silver," Onya said. "I've seen your arms. There are needle marks even where there aren't veins. You've been doing unnatural harm to yourself."

"What I am is unnatural!"

"No, it's not," she said, and reached out to touch him. "We are in this together now. I'm a werewolf for life."

"We need a plan."

"Normally, I would agree with you, but the only way I see us getting out of this alive is if you let the beast take control," she said. She would not admit that she was afraid of what the changes might mean, but after finding a man she felt matched her alpha mindset and surviving a bullet to the gut, she didn't plan to simply let the rebels win.

"It's not like that. I don't just grow big and run away. I attack, devour and decimate. It's all I've ever done. Friend or foe."

Onya still held onto him, "I'm here. I will stop you. We're the same pack. I don't want to be the type of werewolf you were, and I don't want you to be either."

"Even if you somehow maintain control of your beast form, there is no way that you could--"

Her leg snapped as the sounds from the hallway became more frenzied and intense. Stone reached out to her as she fell, but the enemy was approaching quickly. He went to go to the door pistol in hand. It dropped as his bones began to shatter and reform too.

Stone shook it off and went to the cabinet. He grabbed the needle from a hiding place and thumbed the key, shaking and convulsing with each broken bone.

The sounds in the hallway became louder. The rebels were through the barricade. He would have to trust his mild regeneration in human form to save him now. He keyed the lock and pulled the cabinet open.

Onya slammed into him, knocking him out of the way. Her snout snarling into his face. Her body still breaking and reforming in place. How she was able to handle the pain he could not know, but she crushed all of the silver vials in one swoop of her half-wolf claws.

"How could you do that?" Stone asked despite knowing that she was likely well beyond the reach of words. Even beyond the pain of her first transformation, he wasn't sure how she had any control left. She had just waited for him to reveal the vials beyond the cabinet to ensure she could crush them all.

The sounds in the hallway grew louder as the rebels neared the blocked office door. They readied to burst inside, knowing that they had to outrun the moon. They were certain that Lord Stone would either medicate as he always did or choose to fight them in his beast form. They knew it was the full moon tonight as well as Stone did. They needed to stop him from changing and pour the silver down his throat themselves.

Stone felt his body contort in the normal way of change. Far more quick and simultaneous than with the scepter. It felt as if his whole body was ripped apart at once and he fell to the floor, instantly losing consciousness.

Onya had not expected to be so alert and so aware in her werewolf form. Rather than lose total control of herself as he had described, it was as if all of her senses were heightened ten-fold. She could smell blood in the air, as if it was coming through the walls from the staircase. She had also hoped for something more dramatically awe-inspiring than a lump on the floor as Stone's body morphed quickly into a hairy white beast.

The doors burst open.

Onya threw the desk over and hid behind it as the rebels peppered the room, crashing the window out and destroying the maps and papers, with musket, rifle, and pistol.

They must have thought that she was Lord Stone, she thought, as the bullets lodged into the thick desk and split the wood. A shard of metal caught her in the arm and splinters dug into her leg as she shielded her face from the furious volley. After firing, the men began to reload and planned to wait to fire again for the beast to show itself.

The man on the right's upper torso splashed across the floor in front of the men, still reloading. Then the next's head splattered into the ceiling as his body was fileted with silver claws thicker than meat hooks.

A beast more than twice the size of man, as white as snow, with mouth dripping dark red with blood, stood, snarling and staring at the men in the room. They propped their partially reloaded guns at their elbows and readied to fire as the beast advanced swinging its claws like axes. Some launched misfires and others scattered bullets at full and partial speeds into the beast's flesh, drawing blood in splatters. The wounds closed slowly after they'd been opened.

With each swing of its merciless fingers, the beast tore limb from man and separated heads. With each chomp of its thunderous jaws, it sliced through flesh and tore bone from bone and threw raw flesh against the walls and floor.

Onya hid for a moment longer as the smoke continued to billow from the discharge of arms. Each blast made her involuntarily jump holding her arms around her head in fear. When the sounds subsided, she looked up and over the toppled desk. Her claws, digging into the wood, took a moment of getting used to. She blinked at them, but as she did, her mind refocused on the room around her.

Many of the lights were shattered. The oil fires flickered, casting the room in a dull yellow light beneath the haze of the black powder cloud. Bodies were strewn around the room drenched in blood, pooling beneath torn limbs. These were only recognizable as human by their shape. They lacked steel and their clothes had been shredded and colored red.

Onya could hear the sounds of screaming and gunfire from the hallway and then from the staircase. She had doubted that his transformation would be dangerous, but now she understood why he was scared to do it again. It could have even been the case that his self-treatments had made him stronger once he'd finally been set free from his own muzzle.

She looked at the broken face of the clock. If Stone, as a beast, was allowed to leave the palace, she wondered at how much destruction he could cause in one night. Without the army there, there would be no guarantee of anyone being on the other side of the wall that could stop his rampage, leaving it up to her to both stop him and prevent him revealing his "beast within" to the entire city.

She tentatively explored how it felt to stand on paws, no longer reacting but rather consciously exploring her new life. She couldn't grab onto anything small. She tried a quill but it didn't work.

She passed through the room into the hallway, where the carnage continued with the black smoke of gunfire rising to the ceiling. She walked slowly on two and on four paws, looking around the hallway that wrapped around the building, looking for any sign of men Stone hadn't torn to shreds. She may have had that strength now too, but it made her vomit in her mouth to think about tearing limb from limb with her teeth.

Onya found her way through the torn apart barricade, climbing like a dog on all fours over the desks and chairs. She could hear the fighting below her in the iron staircase as smoke rose from below.

The berserk werewolf was only held back by the shape of the stairs as the men below tried everything to hold the beast back, throwing the same materials they had sawed and removed into its way. It threw them back, snapped them into dust, and climbed through living bodies to snap apart men behind the front line with its jaws.

Onya cut across one of the lower floors to another staircase, making sure it was empty before descending. She couldn't hold the thin handle of a pistol or pull a trigger with her paws, so she needed to be careful if she didn't want to add to the death toll with her own sharp claws.

With each step, those same claws rattled on the iron as if they were made of the same material. She tried to go slowly down the stairs, but it made no difference. Stealth was no longer her greatest skill, and she realized that she also needed to beat Stone to the ground floor.

She began to run down the stairs, mortified by the piercing clank that came from each bound down the stairs as she fell painfully onto her front paws, winding her way through the empty iron stairs.

Stone had almost made it to the ground floor, leaving a trail of death and destruction in his wake. Those who had lived had been the ones who ran, cowering in rooms throughout the palace, clutching their weapons and waiting for the beast to crash through into their hiding place as if he smelled them out. Onya had not yet made it to the kitchen floor and had no way of knowing how far behind she was.

When Stone appeared in the grand entry hall, he was confronted by two men, who stood confidently before him without iron weapons, guns or sword. The brutish wolf walked on all fours, sniffing the air, smelling its prey and watching the adversarial creatures who readied to cast spells against the terrific beast. In some circles, it is considered that werewolves are completely immune to magic, but it is rather that their natural strength and mild regeneration make most magic too weak turn into paltry pains.

Before the wolf could lunge, they cast spells together to attempt to encase the beast within a cage of the spirit-like energy of magical aura. He batted the spell away, but it caught his hand and pulled him back as he raced toward them. The two men redoubled their efforts, sending more cages at the creature who split many of the spells in the air with teeth and claw, but was hampered by still more that caught his legs and began to pin him down. The beast collapsed under the weight. His head and neck were pinned to the ground.

The mages neared him, readying spells to spear the pinned creature through the head, knowing that despite the death toll, all that mattered was they chopped off the head of both the animal before them and the 'silver' coast.

Onya rammed herself into the mage nearest Stone, sending him along the ground and into the wall. She tried to slash at the other, but he was as other-worldly quick as her, dodging her strike and sending his spear spell through her arm. She collapsed to her knees in pain as her furry gray arm, specked with brown like freckles, slowly healed itself before her eyes.

The first mage stood back up after shaking off the blow and the second mage readied a spell to pierce through Onya, wary that she might retaliate before he could get the spell off. Stone was snarling but was pinned.

Or so they had thought. When he had seen Onya hurt, the angry beast lifted himself off the ground despite the balls of energy pulling him to the ground, willing himself to stand and before the mage could cast his spell, the alpha wolf had crushed the man's skull with one paw.

The second mage took off and ran for the door, fighting with the bar to open it. Onya tried to turn Stone away, chasing him on all fours biting at his neck, as he barreled toward the desperate mage still laden by the sticky magic weighing him down, but he shook her off of him and caught the mage by the leg with his teeth and then pulled him apart with two claws.

He to his knees under the weight of the spells, but he looked at the door, readying for another push to fight his way out of the palace.

Onya caught up to Stone again, kneeling before the door, and nuzzled at him with her head, pushing against his sides and back in gentle attacks. She dodged his attempts to push her away, as she continued to push at him with her forehead, knocking him off balance. He grew angry again, but when he rose to strike at her, she had gotten her way.

Stone fell back and the energy balls that pinned his limbs, now pulled at him from the back and at his wrists and legs, as if he had been cuffed directly to the stone floor of the palace. The energy would dissipate but not for many hours.

Onya pawed at Stone now, looking into his eyes as the fury slowly began to subside. She opened her mouth, but no words came from her wolfish lips. She grinned at him, hungrily, and pressed her snout against his in a werewolves' kiss. At first the beast below her was surprised, but he reciprocated. His primal fury suddenly replaced by primal lust.

She wondered to herself as she kissed him if the change in his eyes had signaled the human mind behind them to regain control of the beast. But, for now she simply kissed him, knowing that at least with this, she could keep him occupied even if he were to break his binds.

* * *

When the morning came and after Onya and Stone had helped each other to clean up the mess, the city patrol burst through the unguarded main gates. The city police quickly blamed the fables of the survivors on the dark wizards that they had found dead in the grand entrance.

Stone was proclaimed the hero of the day for stopping their monstrous slaughter by burning them as if it was one of the ancient witch hunts of the states of Imeria or the old nations of greater Valgaard.

Stone and Onya, together for the whole of the morning, were in the office together, after speaking with the police, when a pair of telegram messengers, a young woman and old man from the telegram office came up to deliver a grim message while also communicating that they wanted to meet the great lord himself who had somehow survived the siege by the enemy.

Lord Stone took the message and translated it into plain tongue as he read, "A battle, between Sven and Polesar, the new emperor. Numerous casualties on each side. The honorable Sven is dead."

He let out a sigh and sat down on the surface of the ruined desk. There was nothing he could have done, and now, as he has had begun to think more positively about the alliance with Valgaard, they'd lost a key piece of that possibility. As far as he knew, the line of Arandil had ended.

"Jack, what are you thinking?" asked Onya.

"Please everyone out," said Stone. "Not you, Onya." Stone got up and closed the doors.

"Are you okay?"

"This is strictly between us," he hesitated. He felt it was almost assumed that if he were to ask her for her hand in marriage that she would accept, but he felt it was an improper time. "I've been thinking of announcing a secession from the empire. The events of the last few days seem to have swayed me to a line of thinking that would have felt only right."

"What would be stopping you?"

"My family helped to build this nation and we've stockpiled quite a healthy sum. It didn't feel right to make people fight on my behalf to keep it when I could merely abdicate and abandon the throne."

"Wouldn't you also be abandoning your people?" Onya held his gaze, "They love you."

"It would seem that I partially misjudged the circumstances, though I have not ultimately decided anything. It seems clear and losing Sven, who I had promised to support, so soon raises it into question again. There is no way that we could stand on our own or even in a multi-nation alliance without Normany or a nation of its size."

"Why do you bring this up to me?"

"As a close person in my life, I trust your judgment as a second mind on which to consider matters. You've noticed much in a few weeks that has me reconsidering many of my opinions. One of which is the matter of secession and an alliance with--as I've said, strictly between us--Valgaard. Though without Sven it seems an impossibility."

The hair on Onya's neck bristled, "And what would you need to make this happen?"

"Even with Valgaard, there is risk, which at the moment means we must somehow turn to Menetoris. They don't like to get mixed up in international affairs, but they would be the key to making this work."

"Why is that?" she asked, innocently.

"No other nation is large enough, close enough, or strong enough."

"And what are you concerned about? Can't you just contact them and offer terms?"

"They only speak to us on the coast through the Coltari, however, and it may be some time, possibly too long a time, before we could organize any meeting in a clandestine way."

Despite feigning ignorance Onya already knew that Valessa had thought the same thing about the roads of an alliance possibly running to Menetoris, and she made a mental plan to check whether her smuggler contact could make a direct trip to Valgaard for pay on arrival, taking with him a coded letter before the winter.

"I believe it is still worth it," said Onya.

"You're not just saying what I want to hear? You think standing as our own nation, separate from the republic we once formed is a good idea?"

"I think it's a good idea," Onya replied, making a mental note that Stone still sometimes referred to the empire as a republic.

"Good."

"Now, about our relationship," Onya began, and he perked up like a retriever. "Should I be moving into the palace with you? I believe we are officially a pair, and you won't get rid of me that easily."

Stone reddened, embarrassed by the state of the office, whose window had been smashed. The wind curled inside and blood still splattered the walls, "Yes. Please move in."

"Then, I will start collecting my things."

They looked at each other, unsure whether to kiss, when they had only kissed the night before as beasts together. Now that daylight had come, the lust had been replaced by the mutual admiration, still carnal and primal in nature, just as they had instantly felt upon meeting.

Rather than let him speak, Onya leaned up to kiss him and then departed. She would speak more with him about the changing dynamic of the relationship when she returned but going back to the Bunting's to collect her things was a convenient excuse for her to write her letter to Valessa and track down the smuggler captain, Drake Peak, or another--if he was still in the city. She also needed a moment to herself with the way everything had unfolded in the modern stone castle. She had been in men's clothes for many days on end.

After she departed, Lord Stone looked at the scepter of Lyse, thankfully undamaged by the events of the night before. He was suddenly far more appreciative of the gift. Perhaps, he could use it in event of another attack on the palace. Knowing that he had her, Onya, made him more confident as well. She had somehow mellowed him out and given him control of his mind in his beast form.

If he could control himself, he could lead others.

* * *

Mrs. Bunting had been suspicious of her tenant's absence during the whole of the trouble at the palace, and now that she returned after the event had supposedly wrapped up, she kept a careful eye and ear on her actions.

Mr. Bunting had not believed there was anything to be concerned about until their tenant returned in men's garments, carrying her old clothes under her arm. Rather than question her though, they merely watched from afar.

The woman entered as if nothing had happened. She quickly changed into one of her dresses. The two of them heard the fire go up in the upstairs room, and then she left without even uttering a word.

The two silently communicated at the fire, wondering why their tenant had been gone, and if she had been a part of the dreadful affair as a rebel. After a moment, long enough that Mrs. Bunting felt like Onya would not return, she ventured into their guest's rooms, reasoning with herself that it was a matter of security and peace of mind.

Quickly, she ascended the stairs, leaving Mr. Bunting complaining for her to wait a little while longer in their drawing room together. Mrs. Bunting threw open the door and indeed found the fire still burning.

There were few belongings. Nothing was left out. There was a locked cabinet that must have held some secretive things as all of the woman's clothes were neatly hung in the closet. Mrs. Bunting could not go into the cabinet without her tenant recognizing that she had been there, so she continued to investigate. There were writing instruments out on the desk, and it looked like they had just been used. The ink was wet and there were spots on the wood where it had dripped.

Mrs. Bunting had suspected that the fire was being used to burn things rather than for warmth for weeks and now she felt she had a reason to dig around at the smoldering ash. The stranger from the upcountry had struggled with the heat and yet, had lit fires almost every day. It hadn't made sense.

Mrs. Bunting grabbed the iron fire poker and dug around through the embers. She immediately found a still smoking piece of paper that she dug out.

It looked as if it was a draft of something. Though she couldn't make out anything intelligent from the words on the draft letter, she could tell that it was likely addressed to someone in Valgaard.

Mrs. Bunting immediately turned around and ran down the stairs and out the door. Mr. Bunting called after her, but she paid him no mind, she had to take this information to the palace as quickly as her feet would carry her.

Once there, she had trouble finding anyone to talk to discuss her information. The palace was swarming with people as if they were ants, cleaning up, organizing, and fixing. No one had the time to speak with her even if she knew who to trust.

Finally, a young woman, in her late thirties or early forties, stopped to speak with her, "Hello, is there something I can help you with?"

Mrs. Bunting thought for a moment and then looking at the kindly eyes of the woman and said, "I have a bit of information for the Lord Stone if you may."

"Whatever you would say to him, you can say to me. I'm the head housekeeper," said Miss Logan.

"For the moment, I think it's better that I give it directly to the lord of the palace himself. With everything that has been going on."

"For the same reason, I feel it would be best if you passed any information you would like to go to him, through me."

"What's this?" asked Mr. Carter. "I thought you were busy Miss Logan."

"Our guest here believes she has something important for the Lord Stone."

"And so, if she does, you plan to take it to him instead?"

"Aye, that was my thinking."

Mr. Carter looked around, "Take her up the stairs to see him. It will take you just as long either way. I will attend to matters here for the time being."

"If you say so."

Miss Logan led Mrs. Bunting up the many flights of stairs, while the old woman wondered how anyone could walk this many flights every day. Her legs burned after eight flights, and she had more than twenty to go.

At the top, they navigated a disgusting mess to a new temporary office which Lord Stone would occupy while his old office was refurbished, and the window replaced.

"My lord, this woman would like to speak with you about

something urgent. Is it okay if I let her in."

"Yes, please," said Stone, "take a seat." Stone motioned to an undamaged chair that had been brought from a lower floor. Mrs. Bunting remained standing.

"What is your name?"

"Mrs. Bunting."

"Mrs. Bunting, would you care to share what you believe I need to know?"

Mrs. Bunting shook her head, "I believe it should be seen or heard by you private my lord."

Stone nodded, "Miss Logan, if you could please give us a moment."

Miss Logan nodded, and though she was dismayed, she left the room and kept her ear close to the door.

"Now, what is it?"

"I have a copy of a letter that I believe you should see, written by my houseguest."

Stone took the letter from the woman's hands, read it, and looked up from his desk to meet the woman's eyes, "And who is your houseguest?"

"The lady Onya Wilde, who has been recently working in the palace, sir."

Stone thought for a moment. He could see that, if this was a genuine article and it likely was--he had no reason to doubt Mrs. Bunting's words as true--Onya had plainly written a letter to the Ice Queen of Valgaard, princess Valessa.

Someone who hadn't heard of her wouldn't recognize the nickname in old tongue 'Ís' near the top of the page but combined with a passing reference to Valgaard in what appeared to be a point of address, it was clear to Stone, who had heard the nickname as more of a reference to her character rather than a name she might use in coded letters. This must have been a staging copy for translation of a letter into code.

Stone began thinking quickly. He felt betrayed. He had opened up to her just this morning, believing that he could trust her implicitly, but even then, he was not sure he blamed her. In her mind, she had done something right. He had spoken about allying with Valgaard and it seemed to him now, that she must have recently arrived from Valgaard to facilitate what in his mind, he was beginning to see as his only real option, moving forward too.

"Does anyone beside the two of us know about this?" he asked.

Mrs. Bunting shook her head.

Lord Stone lit an oil lamp and burnt the letter, "Make certain it stays that way. I will determine how to proceed, and do not say a word to anyone about this."

"What about Onya, sir?" asked Mrs. Bunting.

"Do not alter your actions toward Onya either. As I stated, I will determine how to proceed as there are many things with which you are not privy to."

The only thing that truly changed was whether he could trust her opinion on the matter of secession to be unbiased, but even now he could see that this woman here had believed that he as a ruler of the city and wider country was capable of acting on this information. Seceding could even possibly ignite a civil war, and even if it didn't, it could cost a lot of lives. Imerian ships and their navy would suddenly be at war with the Coltari in the west. His son, Eduard, had already left to combat the growth in piracy.

"You are dismissed, Mrs. Bunting. Thank you for this information."

"Thank you, should I send Miss Logan back in?"

"No, thank you," Stone nodded and smiled. He needed time to be alone to think. He was mad at Onya, but it could have been that this action of hers only helped him. It took the weight of what should have been a straightforward decision off his shoulders. Perhaps, she had acted on his desire to speak with Menetoris. If she was indeed a spy as this suggested, she was useful in more ways than purely primal instinct.

1513 - Chapter 14

At times, the day before, after leaving the sunny coastline city of Hafhamarr, the coast had cut away from the road, as long peninsulas curled out into the sea in odd, long shapes that separated them from the water. For a stretch of about forty atomic miles, they didn't even smell the sea in the air, yet the road remained straight, and the beach soon returned to them as the land of the large peninsula swept around.

They stopped at streams more frequently than they had when they rode hard away from Leidyn, so the horses could drink and rest, and they bought additional food and the water they needed for themselves at towns of different sizes that dotted the coastline.

As the sun rose in the air, they shared the coastline road with many travelers, going both ways, dressed in all manners of elegance, seated in carriages or on horseback, and in some cases walking in single file with dour expressions. Moon or Volstad would make some comment to those that pulled aside for the trio to pass, or they led the horses around a slow carriage.

They still had kept up a hard pace, but when the day warmed unexpectedly, Volstad had them pull off the road, tying the horses against trees that lined the edge of white sand, well away from the height of the tide.

Moon watched the horses as Volstad took off his shoes, throwing them off onto the grass and beckoning Erold to do the same. Then, he took off running toward the water, where he let his feet sink into the cold sand as the sun beamed down his face and the wind whipped across the beach.

Tentatively, Erold put his feet in the icy water that felt, at first, as if sharp knives were being dug into his skin. No lake could match the sea for its frigid temperature. Erold expected to see a chunk of ice floating in it now, but soon, he grew used to it and Volstad splashed at him, dipping his hand into the water and throwing it into the air, before taking off, leaving a trail of footprints, quickly disappearing in the sand as another wave rushed over the shore and pulled back out to the sea.

They stayed there on the beach for a while, eating careful rations of bread and drinking water from their canteens. They had sat on the edge of the road and watched the waves crash along the shore from far away. The barest of spray sometimes had caught the wind and swirled droplets thinner than a fog over them.

That had been yesterday, though. After stopping in Ohrinsros, the largest city that Erold had so far seen in Normany, which sat on the coast, at the mouth of the Ohrin River and the border into Gardnor, they left the beaches and the busy, main road to Albion, behind to cut straight across the Rovkha plains, trading varied scenery for the near complete monotony of green grass in waves of low hills that stretched out as far as the eye could see.

Dalvalles and its many coastal cities and rocky hills were well behind them. In Gardnor, they felt lucky that every so often, there would be an inn, sitting lonely on the side of the road, until they might stop in for a beer or food or to chat. Sometimes a few wagons or a solitary carriage waited out front.

About halfway across the desolate, empty plains, they reached a town that rose out of the distance like a solitary mountain, giving the contrary feeling of getting smaller instead of larger as they neared the city limits.

There they stopped. This town had a stable and inn just outside the edge of town, where Volstad left the horses while the other two found a table in the corner. A bard was singing about the exploits of various heroes of old. Stories that were never fully explained and yet some names were elusive, so he called them after flowers and said their tales were immortal, defeating tyrants like Domiscus.

"We should exchange horses here. We've been riding these for three days, and the stable boy was telling me the price of fresh horses. They're cheap here."

"What about Sven's horse?" asked Erold. "It seems to like me."

"It doesn't have a name, kid. Leave her behind. The next leg of the journey is a long one, and we should have exchanged horses in Ohrinsros."

"Abrim's right, Erold."

"Why didn't we talk about this then?"

"Why do you think?" Volstad tried to strongly imply something without snapping or being indiscreet, but Erold wasn't sure if it was staying hidden or lack of money.

Erold opened his mouth to talk about it, but Volstad gave him a hard look to keep shut, which he obeyed. No one had mentioned how much money anyone had, but water, food, and each night they spent at a tavern was adding up quickly.

Moon contemplated discussing getting bedding at a general store, and bringing it with them toward the mountain, but she thought better of it. It may have been just the start of autumn, but the nights were already sinking toward freezing. If they ended up splurging for gear they didn't use and couldn't easily carry without a horse, then they would be furthering a difficult position.

At the same time, they needed options that they weren't sinking money into. If they did keep the kid's pet horse, they could carry the baggage, and focus on making fires rather than finding a warm inn.

This one wasn't as warm as she wished it would be, and they were only going to be getting further north and further inland, where the coastal currents that affected the west coast, wouldn't reach them to offset the climb in latitude. Afterwards, they still needed to cross Valgaard.

"Abrim," Moon began and her former captain looked at her, looking more tired and older than he ever had before. "We can discuss it tomorrow, but let the kid keep the horse. Besides," she leaned over and whispered to him, "it's the kid's birthday today, and there's not much else we can do for him."

He looked at her skeptically but thought better of arguing about it in a crowded pub or questioning her on birthdays. Moon, on the other hand, thought it was a convenient coincidence, which she would briefly mention to Erold that evening. They could use the horse for their gear across the mountain, and it would definitely be a long way to Peth, the capital of Valgaard, on the other side of the mountains.

She didn't want to bring it up, but she had looked at her map closely. It was almost the exact length of the trip that they had just taken northwest, but instead almost due east. If they couldn't afford renting or exchanging horses now, they would be slowed down considerably on the other side of the mountains either way, and from the route they had been on so far, it might be an eighteen day walk at absolute best from Helmun Loch at the other end of Pili's Pass to Peth.

Moon whispered to Erold and gave him a hug for his birthday, while he acted like he was asleep. It had never occurred to him that all this would happen at once. He had forgotten the days and hadn't realized it was his birthday until Moon had mentioned it.

The next day they exchanged horses, except for Erold's, and left the city of Magimills, with its many churches behind. Volstad trusted Moon to explain what had gone through her mind in silence the night before, and once they were out on the road on the other side of the city, she did.

"We'll sell any gear that we don't need like the saddles, and we'll load up on new gear, packed onto Sven's horse, before walking north from Gulldalr instead of riding. The road's not as clear there from the map anyway, but the ruins at Helmun Loch are due north from the old fort near Gulldalr, meaning if we follow the road to the fort and then the compass heading north, adjusted for any magnetic interference, we should end up reasonably close to the south end of the pass."

"By reasonably close, what do you mean?"

"Should be able to see it."

"It's the wall, right, that's up there? Put up for the blights or something?"

Moon nodded, "can't miss it."

"Yeah, an eyesore." Volstad stretched and patted his new horse on the back, "It's a good plan. One exchange of horses was already more than I wanted to spend, and we'll get a night at a tavern, only if it's cold enough to snow."

Erold kept silent, not wanting either of them to change their mind, but also his mind drifted toward the pass and whatever infamous dragon the rumors referred to waiting there.

His horse seemed to tire much quicker than the two days before, and they ended up stopping at any stream, pond, or puddle big enough for the horses to drink from. It was still a good distance from Gulldalr, but the day went by quickly. Soon, though they could hear the rushing water of the Práezwa River, and they knew they were close to Gulldalr. Once they had crossed the Práezwa and left Gardnor and the Rovkha plains behind, there were many more lakes and streams to rest at as well as some marsh land, in between hills that rose up to the north and south, almost like gates into Dragnor.

They came to the city well after night fall, having made the trip much slower than the days before, and stayed at an inn and stable outside the city like the night before at Magimills. Erold found himself looking out the second-floor window at Gulldalr from a distance, where it shined all evening with what looked like one hundred oil lamps lighting the main street and some of the side streets as well in a yellow glow.

The next morning, they had to wait for it to be light again to exchange their gear before following the road towards the old fort, near Nik's basin. They walked into the city along the main street, which sunk slightly as they went further in as if the entire town, almost completely constructed of wooden buildings painted brown, yellow or blue, was built into an ever so slightly bowl-shaped valley.

The largest general store and the first one open was in the direct middle of the road, so they went in there. It was very rectangular and had windows that almost covered the entire front wall of the shop, making it easy to see everything for sale from outside. They got a fair price for the two saddles that they wouldn't be needing anymore and combined the horse feed and some more food, mainly sausages and elk venison, into two packs that they slung over the back of Erold's horse.

Erold was skeptical that the food would last until they made it over the mountains, if they didn't find a town on their off-road trek past the old fort, but Volstad was confident. He described how they might forage on the trip, finding apple trees or by buying from farmers off their farms, just like an army would have to in the field to supplement rations for both horses and men.

On their way out of town, Moon slipped a paper boy a copper to get a copy of the Rorik Tribune. She didn't want Erold to see the headline, so she tried to curl it a little as she read through the articles for anything that might catch her eye. Unfortunately, he had already read it over her shoulder: 'Sven the Good, Massacred at Elksits Hill.'

Erold was quiet. Moon noticed he had seen, but she also knew that it was inevitable that he, like Sven probably did, would realize that Elksits was the end. The battle was described in detail as if they had historians on hand, and there: what she was looking for.

'the fighting extended to a pub in the coastal city of Hafhamarr, where newly requisitioned troops rushing to join Sven the Good met an Akrin cavalry vanguard where thirty ended up dead, including the whole of the vanguard. The authorities have gotten no leads on those who fought in the pub and have turned the investigation over to Akrin authorities. The army has already moved back toward Akre, and military officials have not commented on the event to the press.'

Volstad watched Moon read the paper, and part of him breathed a sigh of relief. Being launched out the underside of an airship and being left for dead had started him thinking again about his life as a mercenary, and if Sven had survived then he would have missed out on a paycheck he intended to cash. He might have made good on it if Sven had survived, but this had made moving Erold north of the border much easier. Besides, he didn't know about Moon, but he had lost his passbook coming off the flight and had gone through a hard time in Leidyn to clear out his account before they left town. He hadn't want to draw attention to himself being alive, but he felt that the chances he needed the money soon were higher than his chances of regretting it later.

"What are you thinking about?" Moon eyed Volstad and he shook his head and smiled, before nodding them onward as they left the city, almost straight Northwest, following the road that ran into Normendin and eventually across the southern province of the north toward the Kalopha River before linking up with the coastline route to Albion that they had left at Ohrinsros.

The horse followed behind them as they walked as far as they could in a day before making camp in the hills. Even if they had gotten an early start, they wouldn't have made it to the old fort Ämelin, but it was hard to find a warm place as night folded in upon them. Moon ended up stoking the fire and keeping watch for most of the night, only waking up Volstad when she knew she couldn't stay awake any longer.

The trip had taken its toll so far, and they had been on horseback for most of it. At the same time, four days of riding had not been easy on her, and she assumed the other two were happy to use a different set of muscles too.

For his part, Erold could think about little other than money when he wasn't mourning the death of his uncle. He was thankful that his uncle had given him this horse. Except when they had spent what little time they had together, he had felt far away from the magnanimous, Sven the Good. He was a hero, and Erold wished that his uncle could have been the one to lead Normany.

Now, with him gone, Erold was almost out of the money that had been in his purse, when he had jettisoned off the doomed airship and what little his uncle had handed him when they departed, had been used for beer when it was cheaper than water.

He hoped for his sake that this journey over the mountains would be worth the time. He needed something to change money-wise soon. He was glad that there weren't tolls on the Empire's roads, but who knew what it would look like in Valgaard or wherever they had to go after that.

Despite his attempts at scrimping and Volstad's attempts at foraging, there was a day coming soon when the money would run out and he wasn't sure how long Moon or Volstad would stick around if he couldn't fend for himself or provide a reason for them to believe things would change.

Then, he let his eyes rest, and he woke up just before the sunlight split the horizon. As the sunlight lit the hills, Moon cooked some of the venison, while Volstad tried to show Erold how to find supplies, but there wasn't even a mushroom in the close vicinity of the camp. Disappointed, they headed back, but were happy to eat something and warm their fingers.

Erold thought to himself that he was glad the hills at least had trees, because without the fire, the cold of the early fall night would have likely frozen them to death.

They began the walk again, and the road remained almost empty except for the trio, leading the horse. Erold was surprised that there were so few people on the road the past couple days, but then he realized it was the Lord's Day today, Solday. On any normal week, they would be in church right now.

It was easy to lose track of the days when there weren't regular events to attend to. It had only been two weeks and a day before that he had been handing out food and gifts at shanty towns near Leidyn. He blushed to himself, realizing that he hadn't checked them to see if Ti-Enna had lived there.

They stopped to rest a few times but pushed on quickly and at about three according to Erold's watch, the fortress rose from the hills in the distance, looking simple and unadorned, with white walls almost at a shorter height than the hills around it.

Here, they would turn north, but Moon stopped them and led the horse down to a creek that headed back toward the Práezwa while Volstad began making something to eat.

"We have to save our dry food now that we'll be leaving the road behind," he explained while Erold sat on a small stone, looking off at the old fortress.

It had the same, unique alabaster, white-stone, walls that the coastal town had in Dalvalles, where they had escaped the vanguard. They could have been built around the same time. Perhaps each was older than Normany and dated back to the days of Old Galdir before the blights threatened each nation, separately, and, in a way, together.

The old country of Galdir had been made up of many of the same nations that Akrin's core comprised of today, but during the Domiscan wars, its territory and people had slowly retreated further toward Akre, while few other nations held out against the hordes, instead having fallen victim to her deceit. She promised an endless end to the blights that had plagued their lands for centuries, following the fall of the Otum Elves, but the price was freedom. It's possible the blights were a curse left behind, or a punishment by God for crimes against the free elves, who did not join the singular mind of the Otum and chose instead to fight alongside men throughout the world.

There were many theories. Each nation had their own. None had solved the riddle. Only Domiscus had, apparently, for the blights had indeed ended during her reign, and she was long dead, leaving behind her own legacy. Not just in the form of the pinnacles that had been built in nations that succumbed to her promises, that Erold had never seen and couldn't know if he ever would, but in the form of the little, white orb that the boy could feel in its little pouch, safe inside a jacket pocket.

"It's a defensive fortress that predates the empire," said Volstad, seeing Erold staring at the white walls, casting no shadows, in the bright sun.

"Who built it?"

"It was an ancient order of soldiers that banded together to fight against the blights, across nations, and often in secret. In Normany, they were called the Taivaan Vartijat."

"What does that mean?"

"Loosely. Guardians of the Sky. They ended up doing more dragon fighting than blight stopping. The blights never came to Normany. No one knows why."

"I thought you said dragons were friendly."

"Over the last one thousand years, there have been many battles between dragons and men. Men have usually won, so the dragons have retreated into the mountains. I could tell you the tales of many such stories, but the Normen of all the tribes have long had to live alongside the dragons in some way as both are from the north before the coming of the ice. That is why in Valgaard, over time, the people changed, and then the dragons did too."

"Why's that?"

"It's because dragons are smart. They have about the same sized brain as a human. That's why."

"Are there more outposts like this?"

"Not in Normany," Moon answered as she came back up the hill from the creek bed to join them for food, "The Taivaan, and whatever their kind were called in other nations only built one fortification in Normany, but they built others throughout the world. Though I don't know the name of the keep, I know the ruins at Helmun Loch are older than this one. Some say that the Taivaan originated there."

"Is it unmanned?" asked Erold, unable to see any activity within the fort.

"There are no Taivaan anymore if that's what you're asking, and yes, it's one of the only forts that were manned on behalf of Normany by the Akrin military. I can't speak on whether there is a force inside now. There are few outposts in Normany, because it is considered a core territory of the Empire."

"I see."

"Elara," Volstad waited for her to look at him. "How long will it take for us to get to Pili's Pass, do you think?"

"Another four days if we run, at least, but most likely more than that. Why?"

"Just asking."

They ate in silence after thanking Volstad for cooking, and then packed up and spent the next three hours following the compass, heading north.

As they left the main road and began to crest the hills that had surrounded it, they began to see small villages and houses, sometimes alone and sometimes in collections of two or three, dotting the hills in all directions.

Before the night had fallen, they found an overhang in the hills and slept for the night beside the fire. Erold looked one last time at the fortress of the Taivaan, now barely visible in the setting sun, before descending the hill to join his friends and help to build a fire before the dark.

The next day, they set off at dawn, putting out the fire with water from a nearby stream, and began the remaining leg of the trek to the mountain pass.

Now a quartet, the companions with Erold's horse, followed the lines of the hills, rising ever steadier toward the mountain range that began to grow ever larger ahead of them. Around them for miles, the towns began to become more sparse, and instead, there were solitary abbeys, churches, and taverns, between the hills and trees.

Sometimes, when they would reach a road, they would see feces of all kinds, discarded food, or other waste, decorating it on either side. Often, there would be a villager, who waved at them, between shoveling the scraps of waste into a wagon to be carted away.

It may have been as hilly as the Dalvalles province on a map, but they were completely different up close rather than from an airship, or in the dragon's eye view of a map. The southern hills of Normany, north of the Solgra, that made up the Dalvalles province were rocky and split out of the ground like spikes. These, in the north looked as if they had been rolled over and flattened in comparison, rising like piled rolls, crossing over one another in an endless mound, leading to the steep mountains that rose into the clouds ahead of the travelers.

1513 - Chapter 15

Valessa stood still as the cold wind whispered above the city over the glistening white of the picturesque buildings, glinting after a light dusting of early autumn that lifted into the air and sun like glittering white dust. The snow marked the beginning of what was essentially Valgaard's second season: six months of snow after six months of green.

Early every morning, since she was a young girl, she climbed to the palace rooftop to watch the bright yellow sun rise across the wide lake with strong waves crashing in long streaks of dark blue just against the shore.

As it grew colder, the waves would freeze in place with the spray jetting out above the water in a wall of ice, reaching for the land in thousands upon thousands of miniature needles. The ships that left the harbor quietly each morning on their journeys to many places would sit still when the coming of winter finally halted much of her large nation's trade.

She enjoyed this particular moment of solitude, away from the specific tasks of the day to reflect while watching the city gradually awaken in the dawn's early light. Often, she thought simply of how she would protect it.

This solitude was comfortable and by choice, whereas within the palace walls, she felt increasingly isolated. Unfortunately, this 'ice princess,' as they increasingly called her openly, was alone almost wherever she went within the palace walls, and it was beginning to wear on her. No matter how many people, soldiers or attendants, accompanied or surrounded her, she felt more and more of the princess and less of their friend.

Even some of her closest advisors clung to her for their position rather than for mere friendship or a sense of duty to the people. For years, the princess had lived and worked alongside Eleanor, after growing up together, and the whole time, the woman must have been a spy or even more frightening the enemy had reached out through discrete channels integrated into the remaining palace staff. The two had shared so many close moments, nearly intimate ones, talking about more than mere politics.

Now, the loneliness of Valessa's life began to consume her as she walked the halls and reviewed her map of West Ahria. She often began to find herself sulking over it instead of planning as fluidly as she used to. The minutiae of daily life distracted her, sapping her focus from her tasks. Alone, she watched, disheartened anew, as the Akrin armies grew with each month and were distributed, defeating every foe no matter the number or location.

Internally in Valgaard, the mood grew correspondingly tense, especially among the morning inner chamber meetings as invasion seemed ever nearer. Despite the fact their army and economic reforms were successfully being put into action throughout the empire, the optimism and joy had been sucked out of it for her father's staff as well as for her. The death of Erolin had quickly brought a new reality to the forefront of each discussion.

Fear overtook them all. All except her father, whose optimism seemed to buoy them all just that little bit. The constant sense that the survival of their way of life hung in the balance, weighed heavily still. Everything had always been on the line, not just their lives, and that had given their missions' purpose, but it had always felt that their actions could prevent the greatest of crises, war.

They had been infiltrated and a world leader was dead. Each move that Akre made increased the pressure. No matter how hard Peth tried, they all knew, they would only fall further behind. Every reform, every movement, every increase in troops; at some point no action they could take internally could delay the inevitable.

It was not a matter of if, but when Akre attacked. Each side was modernizing their military to combat the other, and at some point soon, Akre's military would not only be more efficient like it was now but would vastly outnumber Valgaard unless Valessa could successfully form one of the alliances she had spent so many years on.

She looked below at the palace courtyard as the unicorn guard completed their daily ritual, marching the white horse-like creatures in diagonal dances across the lawn. She imagined the circular gait of the ceremonial welcome march, the head of the guard had adapted from Imerian horse dances, the leaders of Peth had used to welcome foreign leaders to the city before Valgaard had formed as the nation it was today. Had things gone differently, they might have welcomed Erolin and his son in a secret meeting of world leaders this past holiday season.

She sighed at the many places her mind could travel to as she blinked, and her eyes glazed one again over the view of the city and its rivers. There were three rivers, which she had once thought of as her and her two friends.

The three of them, Onya, Eleanor, and her, had spent almost

every hour together. Now, it was just her, and as she walked through the halls, she returned the constant smiling of the staff, feeling empty. She had to believe in them, but she had been fooled by Eleanor for so long.

It would be hard to open up her heart when she now knew the consequences. Luckily, no one else that she knew about had known of Erolin's movements across Normany.

Despite the many comforts of the palace, chaises and views, lounging around, alone and lethargic, she tired. Still, Valessa had yet to even begin replacing the positions that these two women had occupied. Her mind flipped to yet another waiting game she was stuck within. One that had likely been one of the most significant reasons that the meetings among the inner chamber had become especially foreboding.

Sven had died almost as soon as he had attempted to claim the crown. No one was surprised at the results of the battles in the Solgra, except for the tragedy of losing the saintly Sven. He was just the latest king of Normany to eat the ice. In the last twenty years alone, that made five kings or princes of the line of Arandil dead. Six rulers, if you included the Queen Edriana, wife of Karles III, who died with her young son, Matthias. It was almost as certain as the weather that if there was a son of Arandil, his death would come.

This dire forecast dampened the one bit of good news to come on that front. An informant, long embedded beside Erolin and who had once long ago left devoted service the crown of Valgaard to become a mercenary, had given her a much-needed update. It would have been six kings of Arandil dead, but Erold still lived. At least for now. Her informant would be bringing the boy, king-in-exile, and last of a line that stretched to the founding of Old Galdir to Valgaard, or at least would try to; there were significant obstacles.

If they were indeed able to escape the Akrin military like the message suggested and were not run down after the battle during the escape, they would still have to go through Pili's Pass in the north of Normany.

This is where success seemed impossible, especially for these suddenly cursed men of Normany. This pass had for many years been guarded by the 'Thief of Life,' a dragon of such immense size and darkness of color, that it had been scientifically classified by the mage community in Valgaard as Grimr Njol. Valessa had personally placed a bounty on the beast's head, but there were many 'knights' who had promised swift delivery and failed to return.

Due to the danger, she had returned her informant's secret message with an offer of significant payment if Erold, the last male heir to the combined thrones of his fathers, was to make it to Peth, capital of Valgaard, alive. While she had not heard back, she had always been able to trust this person in the past. If there was one man who knew the art to dealing with dragons, she expected it to be him, one of the famed hunters, mercenaries of the ancient order of warlocks in Imor Valsen, like her father, who boasted of riding dragons above the glaciers.

Much worked against Erold's success and survival, but there was a chance. The positive thought flashed a momentary bit of warmth across Valessa's forehead despite the chill of the wind, but her mood soured at the thought that it likely didn't matter in the slightest anyway.

Even if Erold did arrive, he didn't have an army or the money to buy one. No one in Normany even knew who he was as he was born years after the events of 1495 in secret. And, on top of that as the young king-in-exile made his way to Valgaard, the paper rights of Normany and the other states of the Empire that once made up Old Galdir were being stripped in the senate, as they made moves also affecting Albion, who she only hoped Onya could somehow successfully infiltrate before the small, rich nation lost what remained of its autonomy.

Once again, every move that Valessa was making or even could make was being matched or thwarted in Akre, and even if it wasn't, invasion fast approached. Akre wasn't far away from having more than enough troops stationed near their northern border to virtually guarantee a victory if they were to attack the north in the coming spring, 1514.

At the same time, Valessa could see it clearly that it would be possible for Akrin troops to push into Albion and invade the north from across the mountains in a coordinated attack with Imeria as Akre didn't have to move their troops back to Akre from the Westernlands to force Valgaard to retreat to the hills and mountains in its northern states. These western troops had been auspiciously moved to protect new colonies from local aggression by small, unallied elven tribes, that never recovered from the blights that also hit Imeria fairly hard over the last millennia before Domiscus.

With the election of the emperor, Polesar, the machine had gone into full steam. One could only assume that reclaiming one of the largest land territories the empire had ever held or lost, with a significant population too, was the driving force behind stoking the Orichalc coals.

She blinked and realized she had left the rooftop as if her mind had guided her on its own. She passed through the decorated green and gold hallways. There were more false smiles from the maids. The stoic guardsmen barely shifted.

She knew they weren't thinking it, but she did: defeat felt like an eventuality. They would never outgrow the south. It wasn't warm enough to grow the food needed to support a vastly larger population, and yet, they still did grow. Almost too quickly to be able to meet the demands of the people.

It felt like monthly that one of the nation-states within the greater Valgaardian umbrella was beginning to foresee an issue, and rather than pull from reserves, she knew they needed support from imports. She couldn't continue to promise things if she couldn't re-open southern, year-round trade, and even if she was able to get Albion and the Coltari on her side, like she desired, the breadbasket of Normany's Solgra region was what she really needed, even more than the troop support.

Valessa looked up at the intricate paintings that stretched across the ceiling, depicting ancient, legendary horsemen rides against the Otum from warmer days of the frost. She wondered what she could do to receive some good fortune like that of the ride to save Seylil.

"Princess Valessa," said a voice from behind her. She turned to find one of the telegram messengers, Arla. She had a kind smile, dark reddish-brown eyes, and bright, red hair.

"Yes? A telegram?"

"A message, but not a telegram. A ship captain arrived today with this letter. He had difficulty finding his way to someone who believed him about being a friend of the princess's. He comes off as a little bit rough around the edges." As Valessa took the message, Arla whispered, "You might want to change the codes more often. I was able to break this one quickly."

Valessa reddened and looked around. They were the only two in this part of the hallway, but she motioned for Arla to join her in the small alcove of a marble bust.

"Yes, if that's the case, I'll certainly have to take your advice. Did you transcribe it here?"

"I did."

"And did you burn the original?"

"Of course."

Valessa nodded and began to read. She frowned when she read the first line. Coup in Albion. That's just what she needed at the moment.

"It's good news," Arla said. Valessa's frown deepened. "Keep reading. I should have probably rearranged it, but I didn't want to waste any time."

Valessa read on and had to shake her head at Onya, thinking to herself, 'why wouldn't Onya lead with the fact that the coup was 'attempted' and therefore 'thwarted.''

"She states that Albion would very likely be interested in working with us and has indicated a willingness to speak with Menetoris, burying ancient and recent grudges, but they would have difficulty making a clandestine trip."

"Yes, she says that she heard it directly from Stone. I don't care how she did it, but she gets results." Valessa caught herself from saying more, but Arla looked at her, imploringly, proudly, and innocently happy. Valessa had to wonder if she could trust Arla, but there was an obvious need to trust someone.

"Do you agree with her that we should send someone to Menetoris?" asked Arla.

"Yes," Valessa said. She began to think. She had a little bit of difficulty phrasing her next question. She had just sent another loyal staff member off on a mission of espionage.

Valessa knew that Arla had been successful in mage school, whereas Onya did not have that skill. Arla, though not slender and slim like Onya, may have been even more qualified than Onya, who Valessa had hoped could find some way into the lonely Stone's heart. King Mitas of Menetoris was different. He could not be finessed in that way. He was a beacon of purity, moderation, and firm justice, leading the large nation of islands firmly but fairly.

"I could go," said Arla. "I heard it's warm in the fall, and I've never cared much for the winter."

Valessa decided to take a leap of faith and trust Arla on this, "We'll have to write up an appeal for you to say to King Mitas, and we'll also have to figure out how you're getting to the island."

"The smuggler, who brought the message, was told that he'd be paid on arrival. He could be put to further use?"

"Smart, and it would get him out of Peth sooner without prying eyes, learning anything they shouldn't. Did you authorize any payment to him?"

"I don't have that authority, and I didn't know who to trust with this information but you."

"Good, I'll personally pay him now and offer to double it again if he takes you to Menetoris and back. We'll have to move quickly."

"And for appeals, I can begin working on it now and then we can meet at the smuggler's vessel together?"

Valessa nodded, "Yes, I'll allow that, though keep in mind that we aren't writing an appeal for King Mitas directly."

Arla looked at her blankly, waiting.

"I guess I should probably brief you on what we know. We have people on the inside that have informed me that it is his youngest daughter who is the keenest on opening foreign diplomacy. We'll have to find a way not just to tug at her heart strings, but to get a message to her aid to stoke the flame."

"Do we know what she's like?"

"She longs to be a part of the wider world and doesn't care for the Mitas family riches. She wants to be brave like her mother, but the king has maintained peace for years across the northern islands."

Arla nodded, "All we need to do is convince her that this is her opportunity to be brave."

Valessa nodded, and though she thought it was much more complicated than that she said, "I like the way you think. It's settled then, you will go to Menetoris alone--with the smuggler--and be the one to deliver an appeal to the king."

"Can we guarantee that the princess will be there to hear it?"

"You can relay a message through the Menetorian channels, but from my understanding, all of the king's children will eavesdrop on his foreign guests as it's a bit of excitement for them. Make an entrance. Show some passion."

"You want me to act passionate?" Arla had never expected that the skill of a traveling troupe, that would never asked for her--a very normal looking person--to join, was how she would have to make her next foray into Valessa's espionage group, where she had only served in a communication's role, until today.

"Fanciful, full of bravado. Storm the gate, but in a desperate plea."

"And this will make a difference?"

"We need them more than they need us. They think they are safe forever. We need them to think, safe for now."

"Noted."

"If we get their promise of mutual military alliance, showing them that Albion too would join, then we will have more than doubled our potential military might and will stave off an invasion for many years to come."

Arla nodded.

Valessa nodded back. She looked around. They were still alone in the hallway. She dismissed Arla with instructions on where they would meet to discuss a draft of the appeal to Menetoris. As the red-haired woman left, Valessa celebrated privately before she navigated the halls back to her sanctum with her map, where she would find a diamond or two for the smuggler to fence in the islands.

She was glad, in the end, that she didn't try to appeal to the hard heart of King Mitas first even though it would have seemed logical. Soon, Arla would arrive at its capital city of Saint Egrivan with much better odds of success. With Albion on their side and Menetoris's centuries-long working relationship with the Coltari, who were now based on the 'silver coast' after years of operating out of Akre, and had even integrated into the Albion military, Valgaard had a real chance of thwarting war by forcing a temporary stalemate before Akre could launch an attack in the spring.

Now if Erold arrived by then, it had the potential of ultimately being the difference to prevent war from reaching the lands of Valgaard for even longer.

1513 - Chapter 16

Erold, Moon, and Volstad, arrived in Moosewatch, a small town of no more than fifty people just south of Pili's Pass, on the second of Narsi-eld, the first full month of autumn. It had taken them ten days to reach this point after leaving Leidyn, and they were still not quite at the pass, though they'd be on the mountains by the end of the following morning.

It was much too cold to be sleeping outside, so the trio followed the distant lights of oil lamps, as the dusk settled in, to the lone inn in this small town.

As usual, Volstad took the horse, now only one, around to the inn's stables. This time, instead of the usual company, there were rock rams, surrounding the stable on either side. Volstad counted them. They were chewing on bundles of hay rather than just a bit of grass and stood as tall as a horse and a half and about as long as one too.

Notoriously short-tempered, the namesake ramming horns on either side of their head were almost the size of a man's torso each. They watched Volstad's movements carefully as he opened the stable door and guided Erold's horse, which he had finally named, Seaspirit, into a pen, gave her some food, and went back carefully and with as little sudden movement as possible to the inn, where he was sure to find the--

Ramriders.

Moon and Erold were among the company of the rams' ten accompanying riders, who yelled a cheery hello and forced him around the table with them, pushed an atomic pint in his face and waited until he began to drink to introduce themselves too musically for his taste. Volstad would have groaned but the beer slaking his thirst was the perfect temperature to risk spilling it over his clothes.

We're a merry band of scallywags
But, we ain't gonna be giving ya' scurvy
We've come to make a dragon run
And we'll be doing it in a hurry

"Captain Dale, Angela Reese, Atara, Kahron, Jim Li, 'Sultan' Jan, Happy 'Rick,' Leif and Lathin, not brothers, and Dillavin, a Vishgra from the Fire Islands."

Volstad, could have been sick. They sang another song, and he eyed them a little closer. While Moon and Erold seemed to be mildly enjoying themselves, watching the crew drink and sing, Volstad had run into ramriders before, and while they were mean fighters, they must have come for the dragon. If they thought it would be easy money, Volstad wouldn't argue but any dragon with a rumor attached, had been around long enough to attract this kind before.

Dillavin, the Vishgra, he might live. With their bladed tails and natural immunity to fire, they could be hard for a dragon to kill.

Jim Li, looked like he had seen a war, given the left side of his face had been burned and his nose had been cut off, Volstad wasn't about to ask to swap battle stories.

Leif and Lathin looked too old. Leif might have had Normen blood, but he didn't look like the type to throw the type of spells you'd need to sling in a dragon fight. He'd be better off being an elven mage, but he didn't look that either. Lathin had reddish skin as if the sun had tanned him and then continued to give him further bronzing. Southern Island, Roon Kalada, or Emira?

The rest looked even more out of place, like they were trying out for a part in a theater tour. Too young. Not fit enough. They were better fit to be running across the country than riding a rock ram over the mountains.

Even if they had trained hard, in the shape they were in, battles with dragons were not short distance sprints unless you were unlucky. If you were lucky, they were that long distance run...He took a sip of his beer.

Maybe they'd survive on stamina, then. It'd be tough to put odds on any of them. Volstad glanced again over at Erold. The real concern was keeping Erold out of whatever mess this group would be getting themselves into.

He needed him alive.

One of them turned to Volstad and said, "You'll be coming over the mountains with us, yeah? Do you have anything more than that puny gun and sword with you?"

Volstad shook his head.

"Then, I guess leave the fighting to us."

The last place he wanted to be was here or there, waking a dragon, but he'd step in if he had to.

He drank more of his beer. There were crossbows and pikes, axes, and throwing knives. Blunderbusses, and mages' staffs. They were outfitted to kill almost anything.

"Erold," said one of the riders, "take this. This sword was blessed by the ancient elves that lived in Emira. It's called Gleam-cleaver."

"And this," said another, and handed Erold a rifle, "It shoots .54s, so you know it will do some damage."

Erold admired the weaponry, mentally making note that this was the first time that he had been armed outside of sword fighting lessons or an archery range, in his life. Well, also other than magic of course, but he only knew a few spells. He knew nothing dangerous or exceptional and could rarely cast anything on a whim. It wasn't as easy as saying a thing and it would happen.

* * *

As dawn broke, lifting its light onto the mountains, presenting them before the assembled party like sheer cliffs of shimmering black steel, the ramriders led the way up the hills further, climbing ever higher toward the peaks.

As they crested a hill, Captain Dale pointed out the wall that guarded the mountain pass. It could have been as many as twenty men high and one hundred atomic yards across.

"That's the old wall. They still have a garrison up there, but we're going to go around it," he explained.

"Why's that?" asked Erold.

"They'd never let us through," said Jim Li, "They'd just think we're tourists. We could gut them all if we wanted to."

"But, they're paying the bills," said Angela.

As the rock rams preceded ahead, Erold watched them go, bringing the horse behind him. Volstad tucked his own gun into one of the packs, hidden from sight, and then casually threw Erold's new rifle into the bushes. A few paces later, he did the same with the 'Gleam-cleaver.'

He was inching along behind Moon, nearing the pistol in view on her waist with his hand, when she snapped around and grabbed him, gently, by the neck as to not make a scene, "What are you doing?"

Volstad whispered, "Hiding the weapons."

He nodded at his holster not being around his waist anymore and his sword being completely gone.

"Why would we do that?"

"That's the only way we're making it out alive."

She looked at him skeptically, and then slipped the holster off and added it to one of the packs.

"I hope you know as much as you think you do about what you're doing."

The rams jumped and skipped more than climbed the pass at points, but there was a clear way up the mountain that was about the width of a person.

Seaspirit had some trouble, but Volstad didn't mind anything that allowed the trio to be as far in the rear of the party as possible. When the crew ahead waited for them to catch up, he began to worry that they were going to be used as dragon bait.

Erold looked down behind him for a moment to check his footing and was in awe. It looked as if he could slip and tumble all the way to the foot of the mountain. There were some cliff façades off to the left and right that would be a short end, but the pass wound its way around where it was easy to walk.

The young prince, headed for exile, stole a quick look back at Normany, and then waited to look again until they were at the top of the thin pass, which turned back toward the main road blocked by the wall. Erold soaked in one last look back at Normany, his home country. He could tell that he'd get a rare sight backward on the rest of the route.

He could see very far into the distance, but not quite to the coast. Rolling gray of clouds and fog in the distance covered the place where the ocean would be, and green and swaths of darker green, split by the occasional hill, descended out from the gray and black of the mountain's stone. He could sort of make out the edges of the cities and towns that they had passed, but he couldn't be sure.

The wall, too, had already been left behind, and from the new vantage point, it looked small. They'd come around in the middle of the pass, which he could see narrowed from where the wall had been built, but he guessed could fit ten horses with riders along its width.

"Are you afraid?" asked Captain Dale from ahead.

Erold shook his head, not of the height, no. Not from this angle.

"Don't be, these are rock rams, who fight and escape dragons for their lives. They are natural enemies. Prey and predator. These beasts are larger than most dragons you'll see, and they'll make them pay." Captain Dale stroked the head of his ram, which appeared to enjoy it and then the rider tapped the horn as if to give a guarantee it was made of something stronger than metal or stone.

"And if the rock rams don't kill the dragon we will," Angela said from near Erold, "now, hurry up, you don't want to fall behind."

Pili's Pass across the mountain was as Erold had envisioned from above where they had snuck around, like they had been guided by a local, who knew their way around. It was wide and could fit condensed battle lines easily on an extended march. It was a highway for people and creatures. The forced detour of the wall was impossible to take a carriage up, but more than just men could find their way around the ancient garrison. Whether the wall remained lightly defended or not, this would be the place to re-enter Normany if he ever returned.

"Don't think too hard, you might lose your mind," Jan told him. "I've seen it before."

Angela chuckled from ahead of the pack as the ramriders had formed into a single line, going slow for the trio on foot to follow, some of them walking alongside their mounts. Everyone had an eye to the air.

"How'd you get this job?" asked Erold.

"As one of the only passes through the mountains, jobs like these often are left open by trade guilds, the big networks, or the odd investor, who wants the route open."

Erold nodded.

"That's why they've promised ten thousand gold coins," Kahron said.

"A high price," said Dillavin. "There was a bidding war."

Volstad grimaced from the back, wondering how many had to die for the price to get that high.

"Let's rest here," Angela commanded.

As they sat around in a loose circle of their rock rams, eating dry foods like bread and drinking from canteens, they talked about how they had joined the riders, calling themselves the Immortals.

Angela spoke about her daughter, who was apprenticing as a blacksmith in Normany. She had grown up here, but now that the group had formed and taken jobs internationally, there was no place that any of them called home.

Atara spoke of some jobs that they had taken in the gulf that the Varanorian Guard had failed to do. That's how they had gotten started.

Volstad didn't believe it, but he didn't speak up. He just listened to the group chat about their armaments, collected from missions across the world.

Though rock rams were also native to the Evorul mountains, these were from the Lisrakulian shifting hills of Emira. They had taken the trip with them by sea ship--they were definitely too heavy for an airship--around the peninsula of Harupht and up through the green seas until they had landed near Marolno, a city of Ithlin, just north of Ingra on the Atlan River delta.

Moon recognized the name of one of the major port towns south of Gulldalr as she watched Volstad's growing discomfort with increasing concern. It felt like there was something urgent that he wouldn't share until they had rid themselves of "the Immortals" crew.

Erold listened intently as the group talked about anything and everything, which seemed to bother Volstad even more. Atara, Jan, and Dale grew up around the gulf. Atara was one of the Kederan, who called themselves the wandering people after losing their ancestral home in the Domiscan Wars. With diaspora spread throughout much of the continents, including the islands and the Empire, she was sure Erold would meet another Kederan soon.

Similarly, Kahron was one of the Black Menetorians, who had worked for Cardane adjacent but separate to the Normen mercenaries. They had called the city home for centuries. He didn't talk much about those days though or if it was where he was from, but Volstad knew that many of the Menetorians had left the northern islands during the ancient floods when the ice had briefly melted. Few stayed in the north near Menetoris. Most went south to Olympus. Those who stayed near hoped to return to Menetoris, but when the ice returned, not enough of the lost land did, leaving many stranded like the stories of Arandil's ancestors, who had made West Ahria their new home.

And, while Jim Li kept shut about what had brought him to Normany, once Dillavin started he kept talking about the endless cold. The lizard man remarked on how he missed the gulf, where Cardane rested beside the sea. He didn't like the cold. It had been a long time since any of the Vishgra had lived out of the sun of the giant islands that were scattered throughout Argal, the great ocean.

Dillavin greatly preferred the warmth of the islands. Cardane was far north, but the gulf was kept warm by the same warm air currents that swept around the Fire Islands, where he was from, while other Vishgra might be from the great South Island, like the other three of their group, or live in or around the rain forests of North and South Olympus.

Rick, Leif, and Lathin were career sailors from the great South Island, who had fought sea serpents and other monsters of the deep, so that whalers could hunt leviathans and various kinds of whales. When their most recent captain retired after a successful run, they had joined Dale and the crew, where they had spent most of the last year.

The route through the mountains may have been long, but not as dangerous as Erold had expected. There were no dragons circling above, waiting to dive at them like an eagle or scavenge their remains like a vulture--both ways he had heard dragons had eaten their prey--and they were still far below the icy peaks that rose ahead and above them. He felt more than a little tired, after walking so many days in a row, but if they were through the worst of the climb, and starting their descent, the trip had been easier than expected.

As they crossed the middle of the pass, obscured from a view of Normany, Erold looked for his weapons, but Volstad touched his hand and whispered, "let's let them do the fighting. Best not to provoke the dragon remember."

They came down the other side of the mountain, with no sign of the dragon. The route was even easier here, and they explored a bit. With the sun setting faster now that they were in the shadow of the mountains, they made their way north to the nearby ruins of the fort, with the deep lake, Helmun Loch, on the other side of a rocky outcropping. That was where the dragon was said to be patrolling.

They made their way into the ruined castle and found a spot amongst the stone with overhead cover that would be a good place to camp as darkness faded fast.

Leif and Lathin made a fire, while Moon and Volstad discussed something in the corner of a half-ruined room in the keep. He was clearly trying to get them to move away from the camp. The rest of the group gathered more firewood and unpacked their gear, getting ready to sleep for the evening while doling out sentry duty.

A few of the members of the crew came and went. They were on guard and focused as the fire only lit so much of the immediate vicinity. Some quietly debated going further into the castle to see if there was a cave or some type of inner sanctum.

Guards rotated. The rock rams had been moved in close to help create a defensive perimeter. Some slept. They counted and re-counted the crew.

"This better be worth the ten thousand coins we were promised," someone whispered.

"They better pay up."

"We could get even more for just the carcass too if it's as big as they say."

"I'm getting a bad feeling about this. Maybe we should back out now."

Kahron's eyes caught yellow fire as if he was seething magic from within, "Shh. It's here. It's watching us."

The crew immediately closed in.

Someone was missing.

Dillavin. The Vishgra. He must have climbed away to find a different vantage point.

Two of the rock rams began to bleat. Someone counted. One of them had gone missing. Angela tried to shush them.

She dodged a talon just in time as the dragons claw fully encircled its prey, gleaming in the light of the fire. The helmet and torso of Dillavin crashed down from above at the same time, covered in what was left of him.

The riders sprang into action, gathering the rams that hadn't panicked and run, and formed into lines of two lines of three. The other trio formed defensive positions, readying whatever they had on hand. Pikes, rifles, and crossbows.

You could hear the dragon laugh in the night like the sound of thunder, and its face began to light up as it curled flame along its tongue. Its head alone was twice the size of a ram as it threw the enormous sheep into its mouth and crunched, armor and all, spitting the armor back out at the riders, decapitating someone in the nearest corner of the wide castle keep and shattering a stone support that had stood for centuries with no floor or ceiling above it to hold.

"I do love it when my prey comes to me. Rock rams are my favorite."

The taunting dragon blew a thin blast of fire at the riders, who cast a combined spell that impressed Volstad. A white light spread out in front of them like a cloud, steadily growing into a sphere, and then crossbows and rifles began to fire free. Beams of light began to fly from the shadows of the keep as the fire splashed against the stone and spread over the hills. The decapitated body, hanging over the rock wall of the ruined keep, melted and burned in the fire that was turned away, leaving nothing but molten steel and bone.

In the bright light, all could see that the bullets had no effect on the dragon's old, toughened skin, bouncing and ricocheting off like flies on a fire. The mages' sun beams left no wounds. And, then the dragon widened its wings, displaying its size to intimidate its prey. Its wingspan made the rocky mountain hills look small, as even the outcropping that the dragon had climbed over, looked half the size of a single wing. The dragon easily dwarfed the largest ship that any of them had seen on air or sea, even larger than the Vagalla.

Volstad pulled Moon away further, deeper toward the inside of the castle, hoping that if the dragon's attention fell on them, it would leave them alone because they were unarmed.

Erold was stunned, pinned near the doorway to safety, beside his horse, that he held by the neck trying to prevent it from getting up.

The tail of the dragon snapped around, carving a line through the defensive sphere that bent beneath the blow, flattening one rider and ram, and beginning to split the other in half with the whip of its barb. Volstad threw up his own defensive aura blasting the whip away from Erold, preventing the strike from caving in the very ground beneath him but leaving a body half mutilated struggling to understand existence in its piecewise form.

Erold, alive, turned around and looked at Volstad. There was something in his eyes. Fear, or anger. Volstad couldn't tell in the dimming darkness.

"Erold, you have to get out of there now!"

Volstad held onto Moon who shivered in his arms, as he contemplated abandoning the safety and ability to protect Moon from an attack to the left, as the rams and their riders scattered, avoiding the mouth of the dragon snapping down and clasping onto a rider and his mount.

It happened right in front of Erold, half of the sheep's limbs lay on the ground. The dragon said, "Uggh, the taste of human flesh. So disappointing, every time."

And there was Captain Dale's head looking right at him, cleaved from bone, eyes wide open as if he could still think and was trying to speak to Erold.

Erold thought he could hear Dale's voice, telling him to run, but he couldn't. He couldn't be the one to escape by cowering in fear.

Who was left? Erold thought to himself. He had watched them all die in front of him and done nothing. He reflexively touched the orb in his jacket pocket, wondering if he would fail his father too, unable to protect the object.

The claws of the dragon ripped through the wall of the castle separating stone from stone and limb from bone as the last of the riders remaining in the keep became shreds and their splattered blood marked the stone walls, Erold, and his horse. That last rider was left screaming looking for his lower half, apologizing to the dead.

Erold's horse wrestled free and stood, searching frantically for an escape route, failing to avoid blood in every direction it stepped.

Spooking at a severed arm, it rose on its hind legs and cried out. Volstad threw a calming spell, hoping to avoid getting the dragons attention, while remaining in view of being able to send a protective aura at Erold if he could.

He had only so many moves he could make. As a Warlock, he was made to be able to use magic from a man of no abilities. He was warped and changed by years of training to be able to copy a mage, and often be stronger than one. He was an elite field unit sent in as a shock trooper to decimate lines of shielded men and to turn mages who thought they owned the battlefield into pools of blood like what was before him now.

What was left of the rams fled up the mountain, leaving what was left of the riders behind. Volstad knew that they had walked right into a trap. One by one the rams were being gathered as the dragon followed them up the hill, eating them in single, greedy mouthfuls, armor and all.

A defensive shield?

One of the riders, still alive, fought back the hand of the dragon and then its fire by turning it away and against the mountain side. A crash of claws on stone, sent him flying down, and his or her ram, scurrying even for further heights to escape the carnage.

Volstad could go get Erold now as the dragon was focused on the hill!

The dragon sent a blade of fire through the air in an elegant arc at the fleeing animal.

White lightning split through the night, separating the space between spaces, shifting atoms angrily out of the way, charging furiously, and breathing a streak of angel's fire through the air in a thick strand. The light and then the afterglow, hanging over the hills, lit the mountains like by moonlight, but it was just the bolt from the hand of a wizard with a death wish. The blast split the fire ball in two, leaving just ash in the air, and the ram escaped into the night.

Then, the thunder came, an involuntary reaction of the movement of atoms, the sound of fire tearing space-time asunder, and it whipped across the mountain side and echoed beyond the lake and over the land. Peasants all over Valgaard turned to their wives and children to let them know a storm was coming.

But, it was no storm.

It was only Erold.

And, the dragon laughed at the little boy with his pet horse, looking at him cowering on his knees like so many others had and would when they saw a dragon. Had he not seen the enormous size or felt the fire.

Well, the little boy would soon.

Rain began to fall and in the dying light of the embers burning even the metal and blood, scattered over the floor and the walls of the castle ruins, the boy and his horse, frozen in fear, looked up at the dragon, which flew above them.

"Did you think little one that a little lightning or rain would scare me? I'm a dragon."

Erold could see just the silhouette of the dragon, only black in the night, and its face and teeth, outlined in a red glow of coming fire, as the heat from its flaring nostrils turned rain to steam up into the dark sky above.

"I'll forgive you this once if you run away now," the dragon said from the darkness as it landed too far away to see.

"Stop," said Erold as the dragon's head neared the castle keep, leaning in to get a closer look.

"Are you going to stop me child, from eating this horse. From melting that man, dying on the hill? No. Stand aside little one if you don't want me to melt you. First. Unarmed and human, I may let you live with a warning."

The dragon went in for the morsel of horse flesh, its teeth slicing the air toward Seaspirit.

"No," said Erold, and he lifted up his hand sending a rush of spirit fire, in a cloud of purple and blue, into the side of the dragon's head and turning the beast's face against the rock wall of the mountain, causing stone to crash off of the mountain's wall and cascade into the courtyard of the old castle.

The dragon ripped its head back, roared, and let out a blast of fire, larger than any before, whistling as it went through the air, growing into a ball, ever bigger with each passing second, tearing the oxygen from the wind, robbing the near world of all that could feed the fire.

The rushing blast headed for Erold, his horse, and Volstad and Moon behind him. No amount of money was worth this, thought Volstad.

Volstad used a push spell to jump himself and Moon out of the way, but the blast never came down the stone hallway. He had left the kid for dead, but something had happened on the other side of the wall, in the crushed castle keep.

Erold had stood rushing forward in front of his horse to take on the fire. He had no sword or rifle to protect them. He had only the power of magic, one fist clenching the orb.

At first nothing came as he tried desperately to kindle another bolt of lightning or even a breath of counter magic that could deflect the fire away.

A shrouded figure of white and yellow burst forth and split the fire curling it around into two halves and sending it back toward the dragon. It was a great power, the vision, a shadow of an Angel, but it began to fade.

Erold knew it hadn't been his magic that had stayed the fire, but he could feel himself begin to regain stamina. The rush of the power from the air, the world, amplified tenfold, then one hundred-fold by the orb. It swirled around him as the fire broke the angel spell from his unknown savior.

The fire rushed toward him, and Erold began to absorb it, sucking in the power. The rush as he levitated into the air, and sent the dragons fire back into the mouth of the beast as it poured forth.

In a sword of white light, the fire of the beast that Erold had gathered with his own lightning separated the middle of the dragon's oncoming blast, streaking through the air and widening like a scimitar of fire and lightning, shattering the fabric of space-time and the teeth of the dragon. The flaming bolt of fury snapped like the crack of a whip as it exploded when it hit the back of the dragon's skull, leaving only a million shattered pieces of bone and the inside of the dragon's skull splattered against the rock's face.

The flaming breath of the dragon still snuck from its lips, cooking the oozing liquid of its insides as it leaked out of its now empty eye sockets. Where its eyes had gone, no one could know, as the carcass collapsed in place, falling between the rocky outcropping it had crawled over and the courtyard of the castle ruins.

Erold stepped to the edge of the ruined room and looked down at the dragon, crumpled in a heap, below his feet. As the darkness returned and the fires smoked into clouds of black around him, he looked down at the simple orb in his hand. He could no longer feel the rush of its power, but he knew like never before that it remained there, waiting to be tapped into. When he looked back at Seaspirit, he noticed Ti-Enna's sash smoldering into ash on the floor of the keep.

PART TWO: ONE SHADE OF GOLD
1513 - Chapter 17

The ker-plonk slap of leather-bottomed boots on the polished wood faded as they met plush carpet within the captain's quarters. The middle-aged cartographer, Vintillo, with long dark brown hair, streaked with grays found the young master helmsman at work under a single dull oil lamp, preferring to conserve Orichalc on long journeys and drain as little as possible of the oil, made from serpent and leviathan alike, in a single hand-held lamp rather than light the room. Often reserved for its dual purpose as food and light, the thick, foul-smelling blubber oil failed to match the brightness of the Orichalc lights that waited along the walls, yet it was brighter than the candles the captain often kept lit. His latest wax evening companion had been burned through the wick, and while many half-used others sat on the mantle of an unused, mechanical fireplace, devoid of wood, humming lightly with the general vibration of the ship, he worked beneath the oil lamp.

The evening light faded slowly lighting graying clouds that filled the sky beyond the thick metal walls of the Santisma, an airship that could travel for more than a month in the air and pride of the Imerian navy. The large windows of the captain's quarters looked out behind them at the rolling waves of an ocean, as devoid of life on the surface as it was filled with life beneath the endless brim.

"Ah you're here," stated Captain Pierico Graneuva. His voice was easy and trailed off. He was lost in thought, staring every second he could at charts of sky and sea. He poured over each, every night and day, expending any bit of effort he could muster to understand the distances that separated Imeria from the many powerful island kingdoms that lay to its west.

For just a brief fraction, Vintillo, the half elf cartographer from the heart of Imeria thought he saw something of the brethren in the younger man. Perhaps it was merely that his ears seemed pointier when separating his long brown hair. The captain stroked his stubbled chin, which he had recently shaved, a rarity on the journey, and ran his fingers over his eyes. The faded shimmer of the gold ring on his left hand caught the gasping light that illuminated the table below him. Graneuva absent-mindedly turned the ring over with two fingers, thinking, longingly, of his elvish wife and children waiting, patiently, back home in the states.

The enormous multi-story ship with its unmatched batteries of one hundred thirty-eight cannons on each side, shook gently in a strong wind, setting a pencil that the young man had been using to roll lazily toward the edge of the dark wood table. Just as it was about to fall, the captain's hand shot out to grab it, then just as swiftly as he had saved it, he impulsively snapped it with a twitch of his thumb, pressing the wood against his palm.

"We're being tailed, and I think I know by who." He said it as if he had to excuse the brief show of emotion that broke his train of thought and Vintillo sighed stiffly.

"Is that why you called me here?"

"No, I wanted to go over how we can fill in more of the map when so much we've covered is just open ocean."

"You've said from the start you want to avoid Menetoris, captain. I think that's wise."

"There's almost nothing between Imeria's west coast and the eastern-most island of Menetoris, which happens also to be the seat of the king and capital, Saint Egrivan. Even with the entire navy, we'd never take and keep the capital alive."

The cartographer watched the captain think out loud, simultaneously questioning him mentally and marveling at the confidence with which he spoke as if the outcomes of battles were certain.

"It's just the nature of the world that there would be so much open ocean between Imeria and the islands," Vintillo voiced and looked at the circular shaped map that they had been slowly filling in at the edges with Imeria's west coast and Madeira making up the center of the east. The small ink marks for Saint Egrivan and Menetoris rested just north of a line going directly west from Madeira at the opposite end of the map.

When they had set out from port in Madeira, it had been an expedition mission to chart as much of the neutral Umbare islands to Imeria's southwest as well as find anything they could easily capture to the islands' north. In the end, there was barely an island between the shores that could act as a foothold for ships, air or sea, that would allow the eastern might of Akre, Cardane, and Imeria to not only launch attacks but divert the ships of the long entrenched Coltari and their many island trading partners from Albion to Gakayon.

St. Egrivan of Menetoris was the nearest city on a coast larger than a spray of spit and its massive coalition of ships and centuries of mechanic mastery made it impossible to challenge head on. Of course, directly to their south, now, as their grand airship, the Santisma navigated above the treacherous ocean, were the new colonies, the Westernlands. South of Umbare and east of the dangerous Land of the Fae, a world of shadowy moors, hypnotic glens, and rivers best known for tears and death, lay the vast uncharted, sparsely populated realms that had long suffered in the same blights that had threatened and impoverished Imeria before the rise, salvation, and betrayal of Domiscus.

Akre and Imeria jointly stretched their dominions boldly into those terrific landscapes where barely a native tribe lived. Even the Fae who controlled what some had once believed to be the wall of the world had left those mountains and valleys alone for half a millennium while protecting them from the island kingdoms of Titanus. It was that wall of the Fae and the violent, independent Ispiardans to their north that had also kept the Imerians from venturing too far south or southwest around the edge of Menetorian territory to any of the six great kingdoms of the Fire Islands that Graneuva had only ever heard about in children's books.

Graneuva glanced up at the great books that he had left half-read along the mantle. He was heavily invested in a raunchy, scandalous, and also daring and brave, first-hand account of a young sailor's voyages to Sinma and the Spice Islands, translated long ago into Imerian. It was said to be one of the greatest books of the time, but he didn't read much into that. It was at least better than the tales of the Vishgran maid that he often found in the possession of his thirsting sailors.

The captain rolled the ring over his finger again and looked over at Vintillo who shrugged. There were no quick ways to finding a pathway to new worlds on the Argal. The captain ran his hand over his stubble again, recalling the touch of his wife for a moment. Her soft hands against his cheek. Her deep, black eyes and pointy ears, her petite frame. He wished he could smell her like he had smelled her while she breathed softly and squirmed readily in his arms.

"Care for a drink, Vintillo?" the captain's eyes regained their liveliness and had the older half elf been staring at anything other than the map, he might have seen the bit of drool that had begun to pool at the edge of the Graneuva's lip.

"Why yes of course, my captain." At the thought of joining a captain of the great navy for a drink, Vintillo grinned. He imagined his choice of Solrean wines or any of the many assorted fruit liquors of the old castle monks of Aldarfarn. Instead, the captain pulled out two warm Maragden beers from among a massive supply in the simple wooden cupboard.

After a sip of room temperature beer, the captain looked over at Vintillo and grinned, lifting his glass into the air, "A life of simple pleasures is the only life we need. I drink to thee and to peace."

"Ah a man of the chants. I place praise the on the creator and to the true prophet."

"May her name not be spoken."

"Bless."

* * *

"Maybe I should be on permanent payroll," laughed the Captain, Drake Peak, before he swept his hair aside and casually turned the ship into a forward nosedive, falling through the sky like an acorn from a tree. The classic, unassuming merchant airship, with its main cargo hold and living quarters hanging perilously from thick metal chains that stretched in a sharp angle backward to an oversized metal-encased balloon, fought back against the captain's maneuver. The open-air bridge where Peak and Arla stood among a few others of the small crew rested for a moment in a suspended lack of gravity as if they had quickly crested a snowy peak on a sled before falling off a cliff on the other side.

Then, he turned the ship upward and the crew slammed into the deck. Arla, who had jerked her head back to bite back at the witty captain, caught whiplash as her head flung forward. She cursed herself for falling for his latest annoyance. She held the polished wooden railing tight while looking over the ocean.

Peak laughed and spoke in jabs, promising to save them from certain death while she waited for whatever came next. He turned the ship downward more slowly this time. The ocean's shade of blue in the distance was so dark, and the late sun so red, that the water had the color of red wine until it quite suddenly mixed into shades of blue with the red light of the sun merely dancing across the surface in shimmering rays. Wisps of thin clouds materialized, drifting close to the waves, changing color in the fading light.

"Look up Arla! Or you'll miss it," laughed the daring smuggler, who had cured boredom on the four day voyage with similar acts and jabs at her. The three overnight stops had been excruciating. He had never grown tired of speaking, and while the captain had often been charming, Arla had never felt he particularly warmed to her.

The flight from Peth had started out more exhilarating than it had been long, but she had only overcome her rational fear of a dragon attack by becoming ever more annoyed at the incessant prodding of Captain Peak.

After fighting the fear that had nested in her chest at the sight of the fast-approaching waves, she looked up. Growing quicker across the horizon directly forward from the direction of the airship was the nearest shore and upon it their destination and her mission manifested.

Dominating the forest green and light brown of trees above steep bluffs as white as marble were the white, blue, and dark gray stone buildings of Saint Egrivan, the capital of the enormous island nation of Menetoris, whose central island stretched toward mountains with peaks hiding in the clouds.

Captain Peak, let emergency flaps out that slowed the balloon above them first. As the ship began to curve gently underneath, the large chains swung forward like great pendulums of painted metal.

In her mind's eye, Arla could see the front end of the ship sticking deep into the underside of the balloon. In the next moment, the captain dropped the ballasts on the starboard side, forcing the ship to shudder and drift awkwardly to the right, with the bow pulled down by the concentrated force of increased density.

The smuggler's ship ran parallel to the shore, revealing enormous fountains and great stone arches, along with numerous layers of castle walls and eerie white-stone statues like mini colossuses standing sentinel and staring out at the sea from various vantage points throughout the stone city.

Arla heard the men pointing as a pair of gnat shapes flew toward them from the bustling port hub below. As they neared it was clear from the gold, white, and blue of the crest and the purple uniforms, these were as official a welcoming party as they were going to get.

Her face, though naturally a touch red, blushed a deep crimson as she grew embarrassed by the actions of the captain, no matter how friendly he had been. This was her first mission, and while it may have been his ship, they were inevitably here on behalf of the crown of Valgaard.

"Run up the colors of Valgaard, Captain. Less they think any less of us than they may already."

"I'm the captain of this ship--"

When the captain looked at Arla, who had lost the green air sickness from her eyes, and instead saw that the red of her cheeks made the red of her hair look pale, he felt an unwelcome wave of guilt wash through his skin.

"You heard her, raise the green flag of Valgaard."

As the green and gold ascended above the deck of the ship toward the balloon, hovering there, a golden sun danced in a light breeze on the green.

* * *

Arla had never felt as if all of the eyes were on her. No one had ever given her much attention. Now, she felt as if the weight of the entire world hung on her shoulders as she entered the towering hall of King Mitas's throne room.

He sat at the other end on a golden throne, even larger than King Hughgar's, that appeared to be carved into the very stone of the rear wall. Two columns of gold stretched above him from the back of the chair and up to the cavernous ceiling, which was so high, a bird could possibly hide by merely flying near to the rafters.

When she had first set out on this mission, she had felt important and ready for anything, but now, with King Mitas's long white hair, draping down over his shoulders and blending into the thick white of an enormous cape that fell easily about him, while one calloused, scarred old hand stroked at hi long beard that sat gently against a portion of his chest revealed by a thin cloak of linen thrown slightly open in a v-shape, she felt small.

His strong hand with thick knuckles, marbled by time, gripped a golden trident that lay against his thick shoulder, shimmering in the daylight from the sky-high windows and the bright lamplight from throughout the chamber. Even at a slight tilt, the woman could see that the majestic wand of power in the western islands may have been as tall as twice her height.

Captain Drake Peak and the smugglers stood quietly outside the evenly balanced wooden doors, that while towering above, were closed easily by one guard for each door behind her. Alone, the quiet woman who had spoken so few words throughout her life in the white palace of Valgaard walked across the emptiness of the vast hall, along a royal blue carpet lined with thread made of pure gold.

The ancient king, known to be many times the average age of a man of the continent, watched the humble woman as her mind raced, walking the long distance between him and the door at barely the speed of an injured mouse. She simultaneously stood tall and shrunk further before him. She had none of the air of self-importance that the men and women of the wider world had come to have.

The Menetorians, a proud and ancient people, though much

smaller in number now, had always outlived even their modern continental brethren, who had fled the island long ago when the great flood came. They had fled to the south and east and had never returned. Even if the ice had brought the flooded land back, unbeknownst to many, the islands had fallen into a centuries long civil war.

In modern times, the islands were a beacon of unity, largely because of their slow aging. In some cases, Mitas's rule had spanned the rulers' continental lands many times over, and yet, it was always the kings of those kingdoms who came to him, and to his forefathers, with lofty demands to make of his sprawling kingdom of icy islands.

This visitor was no king or queen. King Mitas would have been surprised to learn that she had no royal blood. She was little more than a tourist, walking there gaping at the purity of the ancient wealth that gleamed under the glow of the sun and a thousand lights cast by sparkling crystals in their own unique shade of white, like dancing pearls of white on the gray stone of the castle.

She was dressed modestly but well for the cold. To the king, it appeared that she was no stranger to the north, and she bore upon her chest, the great golden sun, a symbol seldom witnessed in the islands over the many centuries. It was the flag of the riders of the great way, called by many names, and now known as Valgaard.

Before she could get any closer, he raised a hand, "From far you must have traveled to visit me. From your own icy throne in the east? Although modern conveniences make a month's journey at sea but a few days trip by air? Tell me why you have come but know first that even a messenger will be held accountable for the words of their king."

"I've come with an offer from my princess," Arla said weakly, but just loud enough.

"I am too old for a hand in marriage young child," laughed the king, alone on his throne, but with a shy eye at the corners for the shadows of his three children.

Arla blushed a deep crimson, almost as red as her hair, "I did not come all this way from Valgaard to propose a marriage. We wish to form an alliance."

"What makes your princess think that she can speak on behalf of her kingdom, and to send you to do her bidding? An untold number of atomic miles lie between her and us, why should we even entertain the thought."

"If you value your lives of your countrymen and that of your children, you will look at the future of the world. Akre amasses an ever-greater army in the east. Five hundred years ago, we free people of the world that remained banded together against Domiscus, and now we can do so again before war descends upon — "

"Valgaard. We would only be protecting you. We are quite safe out here at peace as we have always been."

"We do not ask that you give up your peace or come to our aid."

"What do you ask for? Submission to the mountain king, is that still what they call him?"

"No, not submission. A trade agreement."

"We have had enough of those. We enjoy the Coltari very much, and even if allowing them to roam our waters means that we now have to work with Albion so be it."

"I have it under most recent knowledge that Albion would be willing to set aside the past and join an alliance with you, renegotiating any terms of their trade agreements for the sake of mutual defense amidst the rise of the Akrin legions."

"That may be no more than a rumor. It would take more than a mere promise of something substantial to come from those money loving barons."

The woman, though tall and rising in her confidence, seemed to shrink into her mind, choosing her next words carefully, "the way of the world and its future may not look like its past now, and neither will the past to tomorrow. This is a time to act as each new airship forever changes the possibilities. If you do not act soon, there may not be a friend left in the world when the Coltari disappear and the only ships that come are of the East Cardane Trading Company."

"Pretty words that I'm sure you don't even understand what they mean in full."

"It is madness to not consider the threats of the future that may come to Menetoris."

"You are not only, not the leader of your land. You are not even a messenger on behalf of your king. You come with no gifts, no gold or jewels! You speak of my people as if you know better for them than me! I've made no promises to the outside world, and my people will not promise their lives to protect others from death or even from slavery. Perhaps you should have known that appeals like yours would mean nothing to me."

"It is a dangerous world. I came with only what I could carry, because the world has become ever more dangerous. I do not plead to you. I appeal to Menetoris and its people."

"My people will not aid those who do not aid us."

"Albion wishes to negoti—"

"Albion wishes nothing. They have long gotten what they need from us in trade, even before the Coltari moved to Rorik from Akre, and given our history, they should be satisfied with that."

"And what if war engulfs them and you too?"

"I would not believe Albion would break away from the Republic even if the lord of Albion would raise the crown on his own head and come here himself. Fear not, you would long be gone before such events."

"They are closer than you think."

"No one would dare to attack Menetoris! Now leave. You may spend the night in the guest quarters with your ship's crew, but you may not return to the throne room. If you disobey or talk out of turn again, I will send your tongue back with you to Valgaard in a box, and please, tell that child of a king to come himself next time."

The king dismissed the messenger who kept her head held downward on her way out of the throne room. The golden-emblazoned doors swung open as easily as they had closed behind her when she had arrived, each pushed by one man and there stood Captain Peak with his cheeky grin.

Apparently, he didn't sense the defeat that Arla felt. What had been a quick trip to Menetoris might suddenly feel like a long flight back. She had seen no one but the king and had been dismissed quicker than she had anticipated. If war came to Valgaard as a result of a failure to make allies, she would blame herself and this moment. It had been her opportunity to change the fate of the world.

* * *

Muriel and Jasen appeared out of the shadow of one of the stone columns supporting the distant ceiling. The strawberry blonde twins, almost as tall as their father, glided from opposite sides of the room towards the throne like two ends of a string being pulled to a single point.

Slowly after Muriel had already closed half the distance to their father, the young, short Ivette appeared from the same hiding spot. Her dark red hair looked like a ball of fire with its curls dangling and protruding in every direction. Ivette tried to hide the concern from her expression, but she had long complained about their lack of cooperation with the outside world. For a woman to have come alone on a secret mission aboard a smuggler's airship, she wondered how dire Valgaard's situation might be. After all, they had heard through the Coltari of the death of the king, Erolin Ardrada.

"She was a lively one," remarked Muriel. Jasen concurred, smiling at his sister, and turning away quickly, to look at his father instead. Muriel had grown bolder in her dress, and it made him uncomfortable with the king's men positioned about the palace. Her long, thin body, dressed in golden bands and a long, white sash that drifted close to her slender curve and displayed every hint of the delicate figure beneath.

"Before you say anything Ivette —"

"Father."

"I said before —"

"Father, you know it's wrong. We must do something. One king is already dead."

"Two, didn't you hear?" Muriel chuckled.

"No, Saint Sven?"

King Mitas guffawed at his youngest daughter calling that common garden mage a saint, "Perhaps you're too young to remember, but they've gone through their fair share of kings. Besides, what would that have to do with Valgaard coming here begging for us to aid them and Albion against the Republic?" For a moment, he stopped to let the facts settle upon him, but the shrill sound of Ivette's complaining voice interrupted his train of thought.

"It doesn't matter father. There is something wrong with the outside world, and they've asked for our help and we can."

"Enough. I've already warned you not to argue with me in the throne room."

"But father. If all you need is proof that Albion is on our side, we can send someone. I am twenty-six now. I could go."

"I said enough! You will not be seen near those werewolves and vampire feeders of the mainland!"

She quieted. His booming voice echoed throughout the massive stone chamber, bouncing off the corners and returning to them multiple times, before he turned his weary, angry eyes onto her and softened.

"Tonight, is the National Orchestra's tribute to the royal family, and I will not have any more talk of politics. You will all three of you get dressed in attire befitting the royal family, and I shall see you in the balcony."

He stood and left the room in large, heavy steps, crashing his golden trident against the ground in a sound so thunderous, it reverberated through the marbled floor, sending shivers up his children's spines.

* * *

"Sandra, I know I can get through to him. It's only a matter of time."

Sandra, Ivette's favorite personal hand maiden, helped the princess to comb her hair. She had long black hair of her own, and a soft spot for the young woman but Sandra had been sent by the ice queen too. To help feed the young girl's obsession with the outside world, giving her trinkets and tastes of the technologies being created in far off lands like Roon Kalada that could only be acquired by special request and a certain amount of money through the Coltari. The days of Menetoris's technological supremacy had ended.

"I'm not sure you will," Sandra sighed, trying to overcome the curls of the childish young adult's long, red hair. "He seems certain that there is nothing he can gain from the outside world, and everything you have tried does not work."

"He is un-swayed so far, but he is just posturing. I just know it. He loved my mother. She was from one of the foreign islands near Albion."

"But it was not Albion, and all that transpired with your mother is one of the main reasons that your father still holds some grudge."

"I don't understand how. They are one of our main trade partners now, and he acts like they treat us unkindly, but they hardly take much profit. It is their soldiers who work on the ships, so that the Coltari can traverse the seas with ease."

There was a loud set of steps in the distance echoing off the stone staircase. The two stared at each other briefly, knowing what it likely meant.

"Quickly, hide. I don't want him to know that we haven't been getting ready for the concert!"

Sandra quickly fell prone to the floor and rolled beneath the bed. Ivette watched her body carefully, tracing the hair pinned by her torso rolling over her sallow cheek, and finding briefly what she was looking for. The familiar red edges of something hidden on her shoulder blade. Two prongs of it appeared, as if the twin tops of a letter tattooed on her neck.

Then, the thin form was hidden beneath the bed, and her mind went blank in the moment after as her father, angrily shouted orders, muffled by the large wooden door, and then burst into the room. The wooden door crashed against the wall, and Ivette thought she heard it break beneath his might. The faded light of the oil lamps cast a yellow hue across the sharp edges of his face and deepened the shadows in the crevices of his wrinkles. He looked so angry that any attempt at words was caught in her throat. They stared at each other, stewing in his anger until the broken door creaked closed behind him with a soft thud.

"Ivette! You lecture me in front of my men, and now I come here to find that you're not even ready! For a concert that you planned this year!"

"I didn't lecture you."

"You're not in a position to argue with me. Get that smug, self-satisfied look off your face. My own daughter embarrasses me in the throne room, and she can't even act respectfully here under the roof that I provide for her!" He remarked to no one in particular as he scoured the room, investigating it for any sign that they were not alone.

"You can't be certain that we won't be attacked father. You heard the messenger from Valgaard. War could come to the islands, and your own admirals say Valgaard is preparing to defend themselves from imminent invasion from the Republic."

"They would be getting what was coming to them."

"How can you say that?"

"Ivette. You think you know everything, because you hear something off-hand? We have it under the strictest confidence that the Ice Queen put money behind the Ispiardans attack on the Imerian coast! It is hard to trust someone who is dealing behind backs."

Her mind calculated while he continued to talk. She hadn't expected him to reveal something that she didn't' already know, and now she thought through how to respond.

"Father. We are not as strong as they are, nor do we have the resources or manpower to fight the war alone if they were to fail against what you still insist calling the republic. I call them an empire, and so should you now that they've elected one. The only difference between them and us is that they are asking for help before they desperately need it."

With each word, he seemed to only grow angrier and more distraught as if her making a strong argument only increased his frustration.

"Don't let your interest in the outside world cloud your vision of what matters most to the ten thousand islands of Menetoris! I don't know what we're going to do with you. Your argumentative behavior has gone too far this time Ivette. I have warned you about arguing with me in front of my men, and this is the last time."

"But father. I've heard more than rumors. Privateers have been attacking our ships!"

"Privateers? Where'd you hear that? Did you go to the docks again? How many times must we go through this. You could be kidnapped or killed!"

"I am twenty-six years old and have magic on my side!"

"You're a healer Ivette."

"The best in the nation."

"Still hardly dangerous for a trained assassin, and a child as far as a Menetorian is concerned."

"I had the royal guard there to protect me!"

"They're not soldiers with battlefield experience, and neither are you. You can't romanticize the outside world. You don't know the dangers that lurk beyond our shores."

"The docks are on our shores."

"Don't trivialize this Ivette. We let almost anyone dock in our kingdom, and that is why it's off limits. I am taking away your access outside of the palace until further notice. I will not expect you at the concert this evening!"

"But, you can't do this to me! If you would just hear me out, father. The outside world needs us. This isn't the first time they've asked for help."

"No it is not!" He bellowed, "They've asked for help many times over during my rule, and the last time I helped was the last time. And as long as you live in my palace, you will best to obey me too!"

"Father!"

"Not another word!" He raised his trident into the air until she trembled before his might. "And I'm never to hear of aiding the continents again. Is that clear?"

She broke down in tears, and he turned away, afraid of his own anger. The king left his sobbing daughter, wondering if he had been too harsh and spoke to the royal guardsman to return to their posts and not let her out of their sight. He might reconsider the punishment later, but for now she would be confined to her quarters until he could decide a more fitting punishment that would help her to see the risks that lie away from the ten thousand icy islands that made up the full kingdom of Menetoris. Privateers or pirates, Imeria or Akre, no one dared to disrupt the peace of his kingdom.

After he had gone, Sandra shimmied out from beneath the bed

and touched Ivette's shoulder. The young woman turned to her with blazing eyes, full of rage. The brief tears were gone. She had wiped them away with the back of her hand, leaving only a strange resolve behind.

"What am I to do, Sandra? I want so badly to see the outside world before it's too late. He almost hit me. He's never been like that before."

"He only wants to protect you."

"He wants to hide away from the world until it's too late."

"Now, now," Sandra rubbed the young girl's shoulder. "You know you've already thought about what you could do if you really wanted to leave. Now that you don't have to go to the concert, why don't you get some sleep and think about it? You've been plenty forceful. You've tried to sway him, like you said you would."

Ivette looked pained as she glanced up into Sandra's dark pupils, devoid of any emotion save for concern, "You're right I have made plans. I could take matters into my own hands and go to Albion and find proof that they are willing to separate from the republic to form an alliance. That's all my father needs, isn't it? Real, undeniable proof that harm could come to the islands if their trade partner is being backed into a corner. I could go to Albion and draft a treaty myself."

"That would surely only piss him off, Ivette. You said he almost struck you this time. I think it's best that you rethink this plan. Wait until the morning."

"If I wait until the morning, I will lose my best chance. I could find this ambassador from Valgaard, and we could fly out tonight!"

"You can't."

"And why can't I?"

"I heard that they had already left as soon as she was dismissed from the throne room."

"And how did you come to know that?"

"We maids talk."

"Well, if it's by sea, then it's by sea. Either way, I will get to Albion." By whatever means necessary, she thought to herself, but she kept a side eye on the impassive face of the sickly, thin Sandra, wondering again if she should trust her with any further secrets.

When she reached Albion, she would be determined to let bygones be bygones with respect to whatever had happened between her father, her mother, and the silver coast. He had outlived many of the men of the continent who had warred over it across the past two centuries, but he let that cloud his vision to the fact that even the Coltari were threatened this time. Life as they knew it was threatened, and she could do something about it.

Ivette scrawled a quick note and hid it. She packed her things, and quietly cast a spell on the guard, Fastian, at the door. A loyal man, who had followed her everywhere, would not even see her as she snuck out of her room, right beneath his unblinking but unseeing eyes. While Ivette tiptoed through the hallways, casting silent charms and dodging the eyes of the staff going about their way, Sandra had found the princess's hidden note and smiled unregretfully while she slipped the thin roll of parchment into the open end of an oil lamp where it burst into flames.

The concert was just beginning its first overtures with a lone violin taking center stage in a stunning display of acrobatics and musical achievement when the young princess with red hair having abandoned the diamonds and gold of her palace attire, slipped in a blue cloak out a side gate in a burst of disarming spells that hypnotized the guards until she had disappeared out of sight.

Night had fallen and the orchestra had joined the violinist when the princess appeared at the docks. One of her contacts directed her to a merchant captain by the name of Ricaldi who would be shipping out to Rorik in a matter of minutes. Sandra had secretly signaled to Arla that her plan to invoke the rebelliousness in the princess had worked, but she had failed to mention that she'd be shipping out to Albion on her own. The night was warm, and the crescent moon shone brightly, casting a yellow hue over the inland bay.

As the concert began in full with her father flanked by Ivette's two older, appreciative siblings, the princess Ivette boarded Captain Ricaldi's ship as his good luck charm, before casting one last look on the angelic city, sitting above the white bluffs to the south and north of the slowly quieting merchant bay. The large Coltari galleon broke away from the shore and cast a slim shadow in the soft moonlight on the rippling dark blue ocean below, with the barely audible promises of Captain Ricaldi ringing in Ivette's eardrums, which filled with the blood of her pounding heart.

The watchful eyes of the constant three-ram airship patrols buzzed overhead as justicars and taxmen patrolled as well as they could. Their powerful arcane light cast beaming rays of eerie green across the ships and ocean below, strafing the bow of their ship, looking for contraband but missing what her father would wish they had found in the morning.

The powerful wizards of the protectors' guild could only find what they knew to look for, and the kind Ricaldi didn't know the princess from any other paying passenger. They hit the open ocean, and the warm wind of the East Argal, coming softly and quietly from the southwest, caught the sails, billowing them out in one strong, noisy puff as if a man made of cloud had blown one hard wafting blow.

The night went on, and the concert entered the second act, while Captain Ricaldi told her about South Ithlin in the Akrin Republic, now Empire. He had always liked the warmth on the coast there, but left to make his fortune, preferring the life as an independent merchant, taking odd jobs for the Coltari, then working as a company man in the Otum Ocean for the East Cardane Trading Company. He preferred the warmth of the East Argal and the fire islands. The coldest it would ever get were his infrequent trips to Albion, and this was his last of the year. He would never go further north than St. Egrivan in Menetoris. He left that for other merchants of the network.

They stood beside the forward bow, carved with the outstretched arms of a beautiful mermaid. Ivette turned to Ricaldi and asked about privateers. He laughed coyly, remarking that even though times had been hard for many of the smaller ships that could no longer risk the long, profitable trips to Albion, not even the largest of the sea creatures this side of the green seas would dare to attack a ship of his size. For some reason, that did little to reassure her, and when she looked back toward St. Egrivan, she found it was gone.

Only the crescent moon hung in the sky, and the faintest outline of dark land shook on the faded horizon like a fading spell. Ivette realized with a pang of remorse that she did not know which exact way was home, and anything in the dark was no better than a mirage in the fractured light of the midnight sky.

* * *

Captain Graneuva knelt on one knee, bleary eyed in the slimmest light of the morning sun to cry the morning chants in the name of the prophet, who must not be named. Sometimes, he could see the faintest image of her, and he would think of the great builder's temples, the one God.

He prayed now, in the soft chants, to that faceless immortal, asking for forgiveness and to help him to understand whether his path was true. He meant only to protect the sanctity of the Imerian homeland, which for the first time since the days of Domiscus held sway over almost the entire peninsula. It was a reconquering of thought and an internal political consolidation as Imeria became a singular identity above what had once been its fractured kingdoms.

The men north of the green seas in the core of Old Galdir and to the west had their own prophet, Fros, and while Graneuva played nice with the men of Akre, he was well aware they were using each other to tame over the long, unruly west. The success of which would allow him and his internal allies to slowly build the independent strength of Imeria.

All he wished for now with these chants was a bit of guidance to help him find his way. His many ways. He wanted to be back safely to his wife and children. He wanted to find success on the great ocean of Argal without having to pay more privateers. He wanted to see the day when Imeria was proud, stronger than ever, and raised its flag as a nation no longer a vassal state to Akre, the morally corrupt, "City of Gold."

He finished the chants and added quietly under his breath in a voice too hushed for anyone but himself to hear, "Please great builder, let us either catch our prey, or be back to home to Imeria soon. Let us refuel and recharge successfully to take the fight to the evil Coltari if it be your will."

He was on one knee when he heard the alert go out. They had found a massive galleon, with a mermaid bow on the horizon, aimed for Albion. It must have, unluckily for its crew, crossed into the Santisma's path overnight just as it had turned around, bound for its own home coast.

"Men to arms! Remember take no prisoners!"

"Take everything you can carry. Any gold and goods will grow the great motherland of Imeria!"

Cannon fire and musket fire rang out in separate bursts from the ship below, as the yellow flag of the Coltari blew in the soft morning breeze. Of iron, steel, and dwarven metal, the Santisma, which easily dwarfed the miniature wooden vessel below, closed in as the harmless musket balls hit the metal sides. The cannon balls melted into the waves, unable to turn far enough toward the sky, unprepared for an airship to be this far out on the open sea. When they had seen the flag of Imeria in the morning, they had fired on first sight.

Survivors of other attacks had spoken. The large ship tailed downward, and the grappling hooks and ropes descended toward the deck below. Musket fire was traded.

Graneuva walked behind the long line of men jumping or firing from the outward deck. The airship turned slightly to starboard, and grapeshot rang out from one hundred guns, careening across the deck and shredding the musket men who dared to stand against the attacking boarding party, which landed on the deck almost unchallenged in the wake of the deadly salvo.

Men fought from below deck. Groans and cries came from the remains of the men who took swords and bullets into chests ungracefully. The fighting was a scrap and grapple. A sound of clanging metal, gurgling, and snapping bone.

There were beams of green light from a mage below deck that edged out the shadows cast by the Santisma over its prey below in the slowly rising light of the early morning sun.

An unfamiliar sound pierced his eardrum as a rare cannonball shattered the air beside Graneuva's head. A volley from an enemy airship bounced across the deck, shredding men and steel alike. He turned and ordered full steam, abandoning the battle below to get them out of the way of the surprising attack. Their enemy would not be able to withstand their broadside, nor catch them at full steam.

When Graneuva had regained the sense to do something other than react, he surveyed the damage and looked out over the horizon with his spyglass. The airship he knew had been tailing them for at least a month had somehow caught them. It had abandoned its duel with the Santisma, likely after seeing the size of its adversary and gone straight for the galleon standing dead in the water.

Graneuva stroked his heavily stubbled chin and ran his fingers through his hair. He would order his men to form a boarding party and they would catch and take the airship instead.

* * *

Eduard and Jacquelina, along with the crew of the Secondwind acted fast. Sharply and in a matter of minutes they had swept behind the Santisma and surprised it with a broadside from its rear, forcing the massive ship to take off and regain a holding pattern with which it could fight back.

This gave the crew of the Secondwind an opportunity to rescue what they could from the galleon below. The odd musket fire rang out, but the fighting had dwindled as the Secondwind neared the sad wreckage of the proud ship. Its forward bow had turned forward and begun a slow angle into the depths.

Prince Eduard could hear the words of Jacquelina clearly despite the noise of the steam engines, the propellers, and the gunfire cracking off from everywhere. The enemy ship was making its turn in the distance, and there was no way they could win in a firefight.

That thing whatever it was in the distance was an absolute monstrosity. Their ship was little more than a fast air frigate with seventy-two guns, thirty six to a side. They had two decks, and their opponent clearly had four. They were one hundred fifty atomic yards long, and it appeared to be over two hundred. The Secondwind was outclassed, and they could only hope that they could outrun it in a straight race downwind.

The fight below died down as the men on the Secondwind watched the scrum, unable to discern what they could do or for who. They were caught in between watching allies die a solemn death in battle, and potentially others being swallowed by the sea.

A glint of green light shone forth from the painted hands beneath a dark blue shawl and red hair appeared from below deck just as the Secondwind had closed the gap and for just the briefest moment began to cross above the sinking ship.

A woman, as clear as the sunlight that split the morning sky in bright pink and red, tried to heal dying men, holding them in her arms, trying to pull them up from nothing, crying out curses at their ship above, clearly unaware that the Secondwind had been their unable savior.

In a swift movement, Eduard, tethered already to the ship, ready to lead the boarding party that would never leap to the fight below, jettisoned himself off the edge of the ship. As the Secondwind crossed over the deck, the woman looked up just as the black hair and wolfish blue eyes of the daring prince, caught her beneath the arms.

As if they were flying the pendulum swung forth, but slowed and just as they were cresting, ready to plummet back to the ship below, far from high enough to make it to back to the deck of the Secondwind, a swift yank of the rope thrust them upward.

The frightened woman clung to the prince as their feet intertwined, their arms grasped each other and the only the ocean hung below them. The wreck of the merchant ship was behind them, and then it disappeared, replaced by the deck of the airship. She was the only survivor.

They landed on the deck, hoisted up by ten crewmen. The air had gone out of Ivette's lungs. She gasped, sprawled out on the wooden deck of the metal ship, and fought to her knees. It felt as if the whole world wobbled beneath her. She had never ridden merchant airship in the islands, or even a three-ram.

She coughed. The pain of her lungs losing air made it impossible for her to talk, but she tried. Her mind had caught up to the circumstances, and she had realized that she had alone been rescued by a passing airship that must have scared off that first cruiser.

"We have to go back. There are men aboard."

"There's no going back, honey," said the female captain, who directed the men to get the most out of the engines and turned the wheel over to her second in command, who she called Thomas Clayton before she pulled Ivette's young rescuer to his feet.

"Didn't you hear me?" Ivette fully caught her breath at last, and it felt like the longest, most satisfying breath she had ever had, "There are men still alive on that ship."

"I don't know who you think you're talking to," Jacquelina laughed, "But, we're not going back there. Did you see the ship that attacked you?"

Ivette turned now to where the woman was pointing far behind them. An enormous enemy ship was making a slow turn in the air toward them from southward. It was growing smaller quickly, and with sudden clarity, she realized that she was lucky to be alive.

A small man walked up from the ropes and leaned on a musket before holding out his hand to pull her up, "The name's Dist, and you are?"

She contemplated using the name of the angel of the sea but recognizing a sailor from the far west in his eyes, she found herself drawing a blank. She couldn't lie. She found she couldn't tell the truth.

"You're not mute," said Jacquelina, "We just heard you speak, so you can answer Dist's question, can't you?"

"Turn the ship to GoldArrow and let's make it there as fast as we can Jack," said Prince Eduard after he had finished eying their new passenger thoroughly. Dist looked from the prince to the princess, and Ivette felt, in her gut, like he knew what she had wanted to keep hidden.

"Who's in charge here?" asked the princess, looking from the young man who had swooped down to the deck now far behind them to save her, to the woman he had called Jack who she had thought captained the ship.

The captain looked at the prince. The prince looked at the captain. They both shrugged, having never established a formal hierarchy.

He turned toward the young woman, and smiled, "Admiral Jack

runs the ship. I'm along for the adventure." He looked back over the rear of the ship at the Santisma that had circled and descended to the wreck of Ricaldi's galleon.

"Admiral Jack. We have to go to Albion right away."

The captain looked at the young prince as if awaiting orders, and Ivette grew a little impatient as if they were playing some kind of game with her.

"What's your business in Albion?"

"That's none of your concern."

"Correction. It is mine and only my concern with respect to you," said the prince, advancing upon her. "When I saw a woman on board, I thought you had been a passenger of that ship. But, I saw you trying to heal one of the Imerians who raided it. Were you one of them?"

"No."

The captain looked at Dist, who nodded, as if he were some kind of lie detector.

"He seems to think I should trust you. Why?"

"You have no reason not to."

"I can tell you right now we're not going to get to Albion soon."

"Is there somewhere we can talk in private?"

The prince looked around. The deck was almost clear. The nearest man was Dist. He was about to say something when Admiral Jack pulled the two of them toward her captain's quarters. Ivette took a moment to admire the extent to which the woman had filled it with trinkets and treasures.

The trio left Dist outside, and after weaving deeper through the suite to a rear office, the princess relaxed, convinced that he couldn't hear through two sets of doors and rooms.

"I'm on a diplomatic mission to Albion on behalf of Menetoris."

The prince and captain barely flinched a facial muscle, and during the silence, the captain began to tidy up her desk of things that had shifted during the rescue.

"I'm the princess of Menetoris."

There was still no reaction.

"Well, one of them at least."

"And you're on a diplomatic mission to Albion specifically?" the prince asked.

"Yes."

"Why is that exactly?"

"We were informed that the kingdom of Albion is to be re-established by the Lord Stone."

He seemed to be contemplating the news, unsure of what to make of it. He had been away from the mainland for some time, but he wasn't sure what to make of this turn of events. One of the princesses of a major trade partner of the Coltari's, who barely ever communicated directly with him or his father, had been lucky to survive an ambush by a ship that had devastated the countless merchant ships alongside a handful of Albion privateers. Not only that, he had possibly retained the title of prince in full and not just in mocking jest. A move he would never have expected his father to make unless something drastic occurred.

"So, you see we must go to Albion, so that I can finish my mission."

"We're not going to Albion," he replied.

"We must."

"We're not. At least not yet."

"And who are you to deny a princess her request?"

Admiral Jack whistled and looked up at the two of them from readjusting a globe.

"Prince Eduard of Albion at your service, my lady," the young man smiled.

"Am I supposed to believe the prince would risk his life like that?" Ivette asked.

"Well, he did, because I'm he. The one and only prince of Albion. There's no other," he smiled and looked to Jacquelina who was also keenly aware that something sudden and strange had happened while they were away.

"I must complete my mission."

"And, I must complete mine."

"And what is that?"

"To stop that ship, we just saw."

"Are you worried it could attack Rorik?" Ivette asked.

"No," the prince sighed.

"We wouldn't make it to Rorik without refueling princess," said Jacquelina.

"We're going to GoldArrow to hide and refuel," the prince admitted. "We now know what we've been chasing, and we are over our heads. The fortress at GoldArrow will offer us some safety while we figure out how we'll catch the Santisma."

"The Santisma?" asked Ivette.

"The name on the side of the ship," said Jacquelina. "We had heard the name, but now we've seen it."

"It's been harassing our ships for possibly months off the coast, in between here and Menetoris. Now, that you've updated me on some news, I'm starting to think some bigger objective is underway in a coordinated effort by Imeria and Akre, though I'm not sure why."

"What do you mean?" asked Ivette.

"Who sent you to Albion?" Eduard responded with a question of his own.

"I still don't know what you're trying to get at."

"What prompted you to leave St. Egrivan for Rorik?"

"An ambassador from Valgaard said that Albion was interested in an alliance."

"An alliance with Valgaard and setting off on our own? I'm confused. How long have we been away?" the prince looked a bit stunned and needed to find a chair. "I wonder if Erolin is behind this."

"You didn't hear?"

"Hear what?" Eduard looked up alarmed at the tone in the princess's voice.

"If you're talking about Erolin Ardrada, the king. He's dead."

"Dead? That can't be."

"His ship crashed into the side of a mountain after being attacked by dragons."

"Dead," Jacquelina breathed out, convinced.

"Well, Princess?" he paused, waiting for her to fill in the blank.

"Ivette."

"Princess Ivette. It was a pleasure to meet you, and this discussion has been fruitful. It seems we will have much to talk about in the coming days and weeks. For now, we're on our way to GoldArrow."

"And after that, Albion?"

"Yes, most likely. I'll need a moment to process this." The prince sat down while Captain Jacquelina took the princess to show her a guest room within her suites that the woman could take, leaving Eduard alone and in a stupor, at a loss for words with the sudden deluge of information.

He was sure he hadn't been away for even a month, and though he had missed Frostmas, his father was never one to celebrate it much. He had caught the ship preying on trade lanes between Menetoris and Albion, but it had turned out to be monstrous. On top of that, he had apparently saved a princess of Menetoris's life.

He had been just behind the Imerian airship time and time again as they had attacked the Coltari merchants, his allies, and while he had wanted to deal swift vengeance for the loss of life and gold, it was clear that he had to return to Rorik as soon as possible to deal with recent events.

He had believed a pseudo-war over trade between Albion and Imeria had already gotten underway and had wanted to sniff it out and prove to his father it was true. However, now he knew what fire and flames his opponent ship could unleash, and that the stakes were potentially much higher. If his father was contemplating an alliance with Valgaard, then a much larger war might be imminent.

GoldArrow would be a great temporary resting place in the safety of its hillside star fortress, nearly impregnable to cannon fire.

1513 - Chapter 18

"How did you do it? How did you stop the dragon's fire?" Erold asked Kahron as they rested in the morning light, beside the deep lake. The dark purple and black of the dragon's carcass blocked the view of the fortress ruins from the lake where they sat. Its tail dangled into the quiet lake.

Erold knew the fortress from many stories. It had once been used as a last bastion for many heroic victories and had later been the site of terrible massacres. It had also been a waypoint for travelers headed south through Pili's Pass after the ice finally took the north completely and forced the three major tribes of Normen, who had lived in the cold lands since well before the Otum fell, to find homes in the southern lands just under one thousand years ago.

"Angel magic is what it was," Kahron said. After coming down the mountain, following the battle with the dragon, Kahron had revealed it was he who Erold had helped on the mountain side, and he who had returned the favor when Erold took on the dragon.

"Can you teach me?"

"Yeah, I could teach you Angel magic, but it is not easy to master. It takes patience, foresight, and willpower. It's the magic of constitution and of fortitude, but most of all, serenity. And your power was a fountain of rage and fury."

Erold nodded, "I want to learn."

"We, me and the other survivors, owe you our lives, so it's the least I can do. But, you have to understand that you might not be able to pick it up. It's not like this stone," Kahron picked up a small pebble and threw it into the deep, still lake. Somehow, Leif, Lathin, and Angela had ridden their rams off the castle keep and away from the dragon, only turning back at the sound of the thunder, seeing the flash of light from Erold's blast melting the dragon's face in vengeful fury.

"If it's not that easy, where'd you learn it yourself?" asked Erold.

"I grew up in Menetoris and attended one of the great academies on one of the smaller of the eight major islands. You probably have never heard its name, but its one of many mage academies in the islands. It doesn't matter much though for our purposes. What does matter is that it took a lot of work at every stage, and I was naturally inclined to angel magic. Whereas others work with entropy, time, or in your case, fire and lightning, I used the power of grace."

"How do you know?"

"How do I know what? That I used grace?"

"No, what you're naturally good at?"

"Sometimes, it is just a feel, and for example, I can see you, you're a Normen. The berserk rage thing of the Normen is legendary, which touches along the edge of desire and immediate results, whereas you want to learn an ancient and slow power. Each tribe of the Normen is a little different, but generally, your people are better known for taming dragons and riding them into battle. But, the same argument can be made in your favor, depending on what ancestors you hail from. Many of the Varanorian tribe are known as the most gifted among angel mages, and many of the spells I learned were from Varanorian texts rather than translated elven."

"So, how do I get started? I was going to the school in Albion, but we never learned any angel magic. Is there a way that I can learn the way you did?"

"That's way too much reading if you ask me, but to expand on a point, do you know any elvish?"

Erold shrugged and shook his head, "a few words. Why? How is it related?"

"Angel magic is not traditionally elven magic. It's angel's magic, but a lot of the work done between them was done during the elven ages. The common tongue at the time was generally elvish and so are the texts. That's probably why your school did not teach you what I learned. Translations can be hard to come by and those that circulate may not be very good. Many old, elven tomes have yet to be translated. It was part of my final research projects to translate a few of them."

"How long did it take you?"

"Well, those ones, only a couple years, but I ended up spending another twenty years on the project."

"Twenty years? How old are you?"

"I'm an old man, though I may not look like it. The old blood of the Menetorians keeps one young. You might have some Menetorian in you. Many of us settled here millennia ago, but that's a side story for a different time."

Kahron paused and looked off into the distance in a solemn moment of silence, thinking about those of the Menetorians, who were among clans that had not found a new land of their own. Even millennia after the flooding of the lands, following the end of the first icing.

Many had settled, here, near to the Menetorian islands on the

West Ahrian continent, while others went similarly close to South Olympus, and those who learned to get along when the peace treaty was signed, despite the shrinking land stayed in Menetoris. While two millennia of conflict he had studied in classes between the Otum, the blights and Domiscus occurred, peace had reigned in Menetoris and blights had been prevented or eliminated for almost three thousand years.

Today, even with all their modern conveniences, technology, and steam power, there were those Menetorians still out there, who were like Atara, may the twilight shepherd guide her to heaven, had described the Kederan. Even though the ice had returned, the land did not. It was why Kahron had first left the modern day Menetorian islands, but not why he ended up here as a mercenary, doing odd jobs like this.

Kahron stood up, "Come on, let's get started. First, I'll teach you to use a simple blocking spell--

"Like the one you used to stop the fire?"

Kahron ignored him, because it was more like a weak version of how his troop had opened against the dragon. The spell he had used was one of the most powerful angel spells. A level of mastery, he doubted he would ever see Erold achieve, so instead he raised his voice, "For now, you'll listen. Once you've mastered simple blocking, then I'll teach you to walk on water, and finally, you'll have to master both at the same time. Until, you can fight with offensive and defensive magic while walking on water, you'll never have the patience needed to master angel magic and become an angel mage."

"Walk on water?" Erold had heard stories of Fros walking on water to sneak by the Otum, but he was skeptical as to why it would mean anything now.

"Let me show you how it's done."

* * *

The stone walls of the fortress were covered with moss, and it had been abandoned long ago. Only the strongest fortifications at the center of the castle had stood the test of time. Where arches and stone bricks didn't support the floor, the building had caved in, leaving behind a pile of stones. The wind whipped through the open doorways and glass-less windows, which from the second floor had a view toward the valley and the lake, where the duo had begun slinging soft white spells at each other in curling arcs that looked like slow comets, trailing through the early morning daylight.

Inside the castle walls, in one of the deepest and quietest rooms of the ruins, Moon sat in a catatonic state of shock, wrapped in blankets and beside a fire, deep in the ruins of the abandoned, crippled fortress when Volstad brought her some coffee he had brewed and that the mercenaries had bought when their route had passed through the rain forests of Miranda.

"Here, drink this, it will perk you up."

Moon reveled in the smell, which she hadn't had much of a taste of since her days in Akre. Even in Seylil, it had not yet become a common trade item, and she'd become used to only seeing beer and water as her only two choices lately. Since beer was often cheaper and they had to be conservative, she had grown used to waking up and downing an atomic pint before heading out on the trail for the day.

She took a sip, and the bitter taste surprised her. After a few more, it almost tasted tangy and sour like chocolate, which she began to crave. Chocolate was another taste that she had not had for weeks but hadn't even thought of.

Instead, flashes of the size of the dragon, the speed at which it killed, and her complete helplessness kept entering her mind, unwanted and vivid, simultaneously casting her capabilities to herself in a new light and reminding her to be thankful that she had not been separated into pieces.

Moon hadn't seen the carnage directly. Volstad had been the one to clean up. He had gone through the deads' belongings, collected what metal and trade goods he could, found loose change and salvaged whatever else there was to salvage; but he could not clean all the blood marks off the castle's main keep on its second floor. They would have to take a different route down and out of the ruins.

The man was methodical about the cleanup, and she realized it was because he had to go through similar before. Any ironwork or metals could be sold to a blacksmith. Anything left in shape enough to eat, or in this case drink, like coffee would be better served by the living, but she didn't want to ask any more questions. Boiling the water from the lake for the coffee rid it of potential disease and made it one of the only ways they could safely drink water that hadn't been purified for them.

In this case, as she sipped the coffee, when it was this cold outside, it was a good use of the flint and fire, when otherwise drinking boiled water would have been act of desperation, considering how bland and strange tasting it could be, depending on its source.

Desperation. Moon thought of how desperate she had been to get away the night before, and how easily Volstad had moved her, out of harm's way, his arms surrounding her; and how calmly he had been to cast spells that she couldn't and didn't even know the names of.

She had plenty of skills that he hadn't seen yet. She could, no doubt, take on a mage or a warlock, like Volstad, and be able to stop their spells, reducing their advantage to a match of physical prowess, where she would instead have the upper hand through special training. Of the many things that she had collected as an inspector in Akre, charmed trinkets that granted the gifts of speed and the ability to diffuse direct magical attacks were just two.

She had been so confident that is all that she would need, coupled with her disguised arsenal of weapons that she had been trained to use by the last one to hold them, that she had felt an air of invincibility.

Moon looked at Volstad who was watching her, wondering what she was thinking about. He sipped his coffee. Dragons were different up close. No two dragons were alike either, and it was just as well that they had the mercenaries there. They could have made it through the pass just fine or they could have been captured like mice by a cat.

Only in this case, a dragon was--

Volstad had to stop thinking, because Moon had set aside the coffee, crawled out of her blankets, and pushed him down beside the fire straddling him.

She leaned in, to kiss him, snatching him quickly in a tight embrace, pinning him down with her knees on either side of his arms.

"Elara," Volstad began, wondering if at any moment the kid and the Menetorian would return, "Elar--" but he was forced to shut up and stop thinking by Moon's mouth, which pressed into his as a cold wind rushed through the ruins and pushed her hair out of the way of her black, jewel-shaped eyes.

The warmth of the fire permeated, replacing the cold draft, and Volstad began slipping her out of her undergarments while she undid the tie, holding up his trousers.

* * *

A couple days passed and the remaining ramriders, led by Angela, the new captain, had not yet returned. They were out looking for a merchant or combined group of merchants willing to help ship the dragon to the capital, Peth, which without the proper equipment to separate dragon scales, could be a lot of work. What was impervious to their weapons would similarly be impervious to standard instruments made of iron and steel, but anyone with a knowledge of the soft spots could help to break the dragon down and ship its parts. For a nominal fee and cut of the profit, of course.

The whole endeavor was a lot more complicated as they began to talk about it than any of the history books about dragon slayers had made it seem, because there was a lot more dragon than one or even ten people could carry alone. The simple answer was to hire help, but this was cross country shipping. The concept of a cross country train didn't cross anyone's mind as the idea of even a train had barely existed.

The only consistent goods trains were near Akre, spreading through Ithlin, Verdas, and the Solgra of Normany, and then likely slowly to Ingra, and even then, were only in their first years of shipping industrial goods like Orichalc.

The capital of Valgaard, Peth, was just over seven hundred atomic miles away, which walking at a fast, even pace, pushing hard, and yet allowing for some slowing down, could take three weeks at a minimum.

That meant it was a question of capital. The merchant or merchants, because this was a large dragon, would have to put up a lot of initial capital like any typical overseas shipment, but unlike in a city like Akre, Cardane, or even Rorik, where an investor might be on-hand to fund the initial outlay, they were in a nearly desolate area of Valgaard.

No one without the money would help with the dragon because they'd risk more than they had or owned on the goods being delivered on time and retaining value. The dragon skin and scales had value (as strong as the strongest dwarven metal if not stronger), but the bulk of the money was in the dragon's meat, especially with a specimen of this size and its rarity, considering the lengths through very public beheadings that the Valgaardian government had gone to prevent dragon hunts from continuing.

Now, where this was concerned, they had some luck that it was autumn, or the dragon's meat--which tasted like salty chicken (think tying a shrimp to a chicken and frying them both), because they often swept over the ocean to digest plankton, given their size and high caloric needs not necessarily satisfied by rock ram, elk, deer, moose, or scavenged mastodon alone--would have begun to rot a lot faster.

The cold weather helped, but they would need to dry and cure it before shipping, salt it, or ice box it. Ice boxes were generally too heavy and curing it would take too long. They couldn't get cross country when winter came, so the goods needed to be shipped now or bought now and if shipped, they needed to be salted.

Which, meant a lot of salt, something Valgaard was known for from beneath their giant, inland lakes, but getting a lot of salt was expensive and it was produced on the other side of the country, which brought it back to a question of capital. And finding the capital was beginning to feel unlikely here. Being in a less densely populated, they would need to rely on good will and handshakes, and since the deed from the mercenaries' guild had been melted along with most of Captain Dale, they didn't have a direct bill of worth for the contract, meaning it was void unless honored elsewhere, which meant government, which at the scale of ten thousand gold meant the capital, Peth, and that was why "cross country shipping" had become such a key consideration.

It was all very complicated, and the loops of bureaucracy could get even more complicated, but Erold was at least glad that Angela had survived for explaining how this all worked. Volstad would have gone to sell the salvaged goods using the horse to help distribute the sale of goods and fund the endeavor, but having grown up in Valgaard, he knew that he was unlikely to find anything at all nearby.

This had always been wild country even though over a thousand years ago, it had been the only populated area. Moon's map didn't show a single town nearby, and even if it was mainly a map of Normany, Volstad knew this was likely true. He hoped that the mercenaries knew this too, and trusting that this was their biggest possible pay day at the lowest risk to life and limb, now that the dragon was dead of course, he expected the soonest they would be back was a couple more days, or even three or four.

This gave Kahron time to train Erold, and disappointing to them both, he needed it. He couldn't walk on water, and he couldn't throw a convincing shield up. After a few days, for such a basic defensive spell, Kahron's foresight about Erold's disposition being toward fire and rage, appeared archer-ly accurate.

It was during one of these training sessions, Erold yet again swimming in the lake, when the entourage accompanying the mercenaries returned. There were pipers piping and drummers drumming as hundreds upon hundreds of men descended on

Helmun Loch to see the dragon kid. Leading them were the three mercenaries, riding the three rock rams that hadn't run off or been eaten whole.

"This is the boy that slayed the Hammer of the Night!"

"I sen it wit me on' tue eyssss! I did!"

"You wasn't even here."

Erold had swum out of the water to find an impressive looking tall gentleman, a little fat and a little muscular, give him a once over up and down and say.

"Right. To be clear, this is my impartial statement on the matter as I am a public official, and therefore, because I am a public official, have no issues in me taking on the actions of said public in this account of facts. Hunting a dragon is against the local articles as well as illegal under the, while successful, still very important, conservation statues of the king. Therefore, if it's a matter of the law then, you don't have proper authority by the decree of the king to have killed yonder dragon, and after paying a nominal fee for attacking a protected, local species, thy will be hanged."

"If you lay a finger on him, I'll cut you from end to end where you'll live another fourteen days in hurt," said Moon, with a different passion than Erold was used to seeing from her. She looked different too, as his companions gathered around him, and the crowd booed the official.

Angela stepped in to the rescue, "By imperial decree of the crown, this dragon was deemed a menace by article 215 section b of the statutes on dragon-human interaction, going to the treaty of 1311, and the division of mountain to valley interspecies interference, in the act of self-defense or in the defense of other person or persons in the vicinity of a dragon marked as a public nuisance or deemed to be marked as a public nuisance on a review of the facts as this one was, then the killing of a dragon is no longer viewed as a criminal act without trial necessary. If you had checked the list of dragons marked as a public nuisance you would have seen specimen 4953, nicknamed 'Thief of Life', properly named in old Normen as Grimr Njol, was tagged as a public nuisance in 1512 on Norain, the thirty second, by King Hughgar."

"Riggghht. By rights of the government as this is unpopulated land and you have not issued a claim to the dragon, it's my official duty to inform you that I will be requisitioning the property until further notice."

"I made a claim," said Erold.

"You did?"

"Yes, I said, I claim this dragon as mine, the minute I killed it."

"I heard him."

"I did too."

"You wasn't even here!"

The official shushed everyone, and then turned back to Erold, "Did you file a claims form at your local constables or other such government officials' offices, including but not limited to local mage's affiliated boards, army conscription offices, or regional or other such state assembly?"

"What now?" someone said.

"It's where you write in whether the dragon was flying or not flying and state evidence to the facts like did you aggravate it, was it old, was it already sick," another explained to the question's asker.

"Quiet!"

Erold stared blankly at the official.

"I didn't think so. So, back to the original statement. You have no right to the property, and I will be claiming it on behalf of, well myself."

"You said that this was unpopulated land. I claimed the land as mine under the right of conquest as the true King of Normany and heir to the throne in Akre."

Gasps went through the crowd.

"And by that claim I--"

"Have you any proof?"

"Yes, I heard it. Right before he killed the dragon."

"Proof?"

"Yeah, a ring, or a family 'eirloom. Something to show you ain't making this up?"

"I second him as king," said Volstad and then Moon and the rest of the mercenaries agreed.

"King of this measly little hill?"

"And everything on it."

"I don't honor the request without tangible proof. Unless you have a proper deed to the land or was a squatter, there's no way that you are allowed to have rights to this land, serving in my duty as the principle justicar of local affairs and on behalf of Valgaard."

Groans went through the crowd.

"Oh, come on," the official said, clearly having hoped for support from the locals in his quest to rid the dragon from the kid's hands.

"Squatter's rights?" asked Erold.

"Yes, if you have lived on a property for more than seventy-two days, then you have rights--"

"That's just great, because I've been here for exactly eighty-three days today, so by squatter's rights then, I claimed the dead body of the dragon on exactly the seventy third day!"

Everyone cheered.

"Do you have any proof or a witness?"

"We were all here for all eighty-three."

"Yep, that's right."

"Yes."

"Indeed it's true."

"That's right, eighty-three days in there."

"Are you a pack of loons to live in that heap of rubble with this thing flying around?"

"Everyone saw me kill the dragon." Almost the entire crowd assented despite not even any of his companions having seen it directly, Kahron having passed out and no one else having a direct line of sight. "And therefore." Erold hushed the crowd with a wave of his hands, "and therefore, my claim is valid, under my authority as leader of this side of the lake, in fact of the whole of the pass where I have been living these..."

"Eighty-three."

"Eighty-three days. And that is longer than seventy-two, where I claim this ancient territory again by squatters' rights, which all of these people can attest to."

Again everyone assented.

"And therefore these few territories are being collected under the nominal authority of the greater Normany, by my right as king."

"Get on with it," said the official.

"Therefore, the dragon is mine."

"For future reference," the official said behind his hand as the people cheered around him, "just slip me a few gold coins and we could have avoided this whole chat. You're making me look bad and I have a reputation to uphold." The official rubbed his fingers together and turned to the crowd. "Well, you heard 'im. It's his dragon by rights!"

More cheers.

A few men approached him, well-dressed in ostentatious outfits of clashing colors embroidered with gold.

"Wonderful display of the 'slaying of bureaucracy'. Might we have a word. You see we represent the trade organization in the nearest town, and well, we'd like to split the dragon into parts, you take the skin and scales, we take the meat and bone."

"No dice," said Angela as she stepped forward, "We get the whole thing.

"Yes, well, someone needs to pay for it to be moved and dissected."

"And, the meat and the bone is the best part."

"I assure you, you won't get a better deal. We are the collective merchants, representing the guild. Everyone else here is just here to watch and quite possibly just to get paid."

Erold pulled Angela aside.

"Can we pay wages in meat?"

"Whatever someone would eat in a day, we could get ten times the value of them standing around, pissing on the dragon, if we can get the dragon to Peth."

"Of course, you do the talking." Erold nodded and they turned back to the merchants.

"Who's doing the dismantling of the dragon?" asked Angela, but no one raised their hands or came forward. "I'll rephrase. Who is our dragon specialist who will be assisting in the design and oversight of the dismantling?" She clapped her hands together when one man stepped forward and raised his hands. "What is your name sir?"

"Brian, the butcher."

"Okay, Brian, the butcher--"

"Just Brian is 'kay."

"Okay, Brian, please tell me, do you have any dragon dismantling experience."

"Yes, well," he looked around shyly and then said in a too loud whisper, "My pap used to bring home a dead 'ne at least once a year back in them 'ld days before the law was passed and he g't his head ch'pped off. He sh'wd me how."

"Great, perfect. Sounds lovely. How much would you like for your work?"

The merchants' eyes lit up, realizing she was going to outbid them and work directly with the specialist.

"Well, these fine f'lks were's going t' give three silvers, but I guess I'd like m're."

"Three gold pieces, sold. How long is it going to take?"

"I reckon we could have it d'ne in a day."

"A day? This big?"

"Judging by the angle 'f the wing, which l'ks about sixty degrees slope up th' vertical r'ck face it's lying over, and about f'rty at'mic yards from the base. Y'r luking at abut eighty atomic yards t' just a wing. A wingspan 'f one sixty atomic yahrds, not conting the body." The man spit and looked her dead in the eye, "I ain't stupid."

"How long do you think that means it will be?"

"Two hundr'd in sixty. Mos' likely. Falling previ's experience. Not the biggest un' I seen, but the biggest 'un I seen dead of unnatural causes. Meat's still good even if they been dead a while. Trus me."

"Perfect, you're clearly the man for the job."

"Much 'bliged an' 'n the matter of help, we must be cutting into the belly sen 'r it likely will expl'de."

"We'll discuss how much help you'll need and how much to pay everyone here."

Excited murmuring cut her off, but she yelled loud enough over them.

"And, before we get to that, if anyone takes so much as a blade of grass with dragon's blood on it, we will kill you, in some violent way I can't be bothered to simplify right now, in front of everyone else as a warning to the rest of you lot! Now, back to you three. Who wants to bid to ship the goods and divide the profit? I need to get as much of the meat as possible to Peth, and bone, skin, scales, what's left of teeth, each talon, and each claw. If you want to negotiate pay in pounds of flesh, maybe we have a deal, but it better be sweet."

"I can do covered ice wagons in exchange for half!"

Angela resisted the urge to say something snarky. She relished in the opportunity to negotiate.

1513 - Chapter 19

Laughter filtered through the air from the ramparts below as children played a silly game. Prince Eduard watched them run, playing with short sticks. He watched them keep the brown rods away from each other and then trade them as if there were two sides to a game he didn't understand. He had been giving them candy just minutes before, and after a couple turns and staircases on the winding hillside wall, the children were now miniature men and women far below.

His mind was spinning quickly. He could barely think about anything but the possibility of war. The wind cut across his face, and the laughter picked up louder. The sky was a blazing, brilliant blue that in the heat of the sun and warmth of the island wind seemed somehow more colorful.

Princess Ivette's long, red, curly hair caught in the wind and brushed across her face like a tornado of fire, traveling upward. Then, it collapsed just as suddenly, leaving her to fight to rearrange it before the next violent gust. The young prince could only stare, mesmerized.

The ship had been docked, and the crew quartered. The star fortress of GoldArrow dominated a large hill that split through the center of the bustling port city, a door to the western water world of Menetoris, the Fire Islands, and the far west and places like Gakayon, which could be reached much easier and more profitably by island hopping across the great ocean, Argal, than by passing south of Roon Kalada in the east in one long trip.

Sea ships could not easily pass north of the great island nation, and man could not live on its southern shores. The invention of the airship, which was only beginning to make longer trips promised to turn even trips to Sinma and the spice islands south of the Yin kingdoms into mere days. Today, even a distance almost a quarter of Frost away was impossible for most existing aircraft.

After a month of little rest aboard the prize of the Albion fleet, the Secondwind and now standing atop the central castle of the star fortress overseeing the ocean and city in every direction, prince Eduard had begun to rethink what was possible. Half the world away, the great southern island and its dragon riders rested as the last stop before the spice islands and Sinma on the western tour.

A trip that crossed more than half the globe to the west, filled with danger and profit, long dominated by the Coltari black orchids and yellow crest could be shifted overnight in favor of the East Cardane who despite a smaller geographical footprint already controlled half or more of the world's trade in the smaller Otum ocean.

In a little over a quarter of the world where the ancient elves had reigned from for many millennia and enslaved much of the world, a corporation operating on behalf of a city leading a vassal state to the senate of Akre turned quite the profit. Where elves and men once worshipped the frost, which provided power in the form of common crystals, gemstones offering the gift of nearly unlimited magical energy, man traded goods and services for sometimes not even gold coins. Power crystals were of the past and Orichalc was the new currency.

The Otum had created monuments to the aura of the frost that had produced these gems and hidden them with magic in the densest places of Frost's magical auras. The lost city of Ramelon, for example, somewhere in the heart of the Dyvan desert according to his father's friend Theodore Everett, was rumored to hold a diamond the size of a man's fist.

The old cripple, in a wheelchair as long as Eduard knew him, had always entertained the prince with odd stories when he was a child. With each year as he had grown older the tall tales of the lost cities had become less and less meaningful and he had not thought of the brief children's stories for quite some time. That was until the last few months on the Secondwind when he had met some of the old crew old Theodore had run with.

Sometimes in passing, the few older crewmen, who still worked for Admiral Jack like Thomas and the quartermaster Cheval, would mention in the days long ago how they had crossed the world this way and that under Jacquelina Catalina Ferrara's fearsome mercenary flag, following Theodore Everett, now the last of a once famous family of Akre, and his little red journal. No one had the full story to give because they didn't know.

All they cared for was the fact that they had gotten rich. Just ask Theodore they would say. Now, the pieces of the old man's tall tales were coming full circle for Eduard, prince of Albion, standing on this impregnable fortress's castle keep, with the dark blue of the Bacine sea, sweeping as far as the eye could see to the north, only broken by the large white crests of tunneling waves whipping toward the shore.

Something had happened in the lost cities of the frost even if they had all seemed so fanciful. He could feel it in his gut. All while the greater world entered into an age of chaos.

The lines on the map between nations were being re-drawn by the old King Hughgar's vengeance for the massacres of his father and mother and centuries of war against the southern kingdom of Akre and by the power struggle of the Akrin monarchy against the senate it had established fomenting into a brief revolution in what was often called the Akrin spring of 1495.

In a day, the rebels and the coup achieved the deaths of King Karles III, the Queen Edriana, and prince Matthias. Today as prince Eduard, almost twenty years later, Erolin, a man the young prince had known as the most noble of men, was dead, never having fully ascended to the throne by decree of the Akrin senate, a liquid body of populist-elects who held sway in the court of public opinion.

Battle lines were being redrawn still, as prince Eduard was standing there, beside princess Ivette, who pleaded with him to move on to Rorik and make progress on a treaty with Valgaard to the north. All former enemies in some way. He didn't want to make any rash moves, but it seemed something had forced his father's hand.

He hadn't yet received the news from Rorik in GoldArrow about what had all transpired. All he knew was that there was an attack, and while he could understand what was happening on the surface, he was growing more worried about the silent struggles beneath the obvious that could be pulling the marionette strings behind the scenes. He did not want to be a clockwork puppet like the theater dolls whose gears the puppet master wound and greased.

Ivette was right. They were too close to Imeria. They were on the peninsula after all, but they were safe. She was quiet now, watching the waves too. He looked over at her. Her petite, slender form seemed small against the magnificence of the miniature hilltop city with its sprawling, crisscrossing walls of stone and mud, having been built into the frost. A cannonball would not be firing against stone as much as it would be slamming into a hill that would return fire in all directions.

From where the trio stood, Admiral Jack with the prince and the princess, the commander of the fortress pointed out the landmarks of the city below. The sprawling catacombs of the large old town that lined the golden sands of the long beach to their northeast. The monuments and manicured gardens of the new city to the west.

The princess turned away from the tour and walked to the other end of the square shaped castle rooftop. Prince Eduard followed her slowly, carefully. Her floral scent caught the wind, and he was acutely aware that his attraction to stand beside her was not purely political.

"My father needs to know about the attacks on the trade ships coming directly from Imerians, not from hired privateers or even pirates. He could explain those away, but he would have to believe me this time."

"It sounds like you're trying to convince yourself that he would."

"I saw it with my own eyes," she said but she also nodded slowly.

"He could argue it was a false flag."

"Painted on its side?" She nodded again, and then turned to look at him, staring deeply into his eyes, her pupils swelling as she stared, "When can we leave for Albion?"

"Soon," he smiled and looked away, back at the deep blue ocean with its serene horizon below a cloudless light blue sky. After a moment, she turned away from his bright blue eyes, the color of the sky, and followed their gaze to the horizon line.

"I don't know what to make of this. Any of this. What is happening in the world?"

Prince Eduard weighed the circumstances and he realized that it was impossible for him to ever truly know if she was on the side of good or evil in a grand scheme where there may be no true right or wrong. He would have to decide quickly whether to trust her or not. The fate of their kingdoms hung in the balance right at this moment.

They both could sense it. The future weighed heavily on them both. They could decide now to trust each other and stand together, come what may. Eduard wrapped an arm around her shoulder, and the tension fell from her shoulders. She leaned toward him, falling briefly through the air between them about to collapse against his chest and into his arms.

He caught her, pressing her into his arms, holding her tightly, and the horizon moved. Dark shapes came out of the thin line, separating out from the blur of distance and forming into their own line like black gnats advancing across the Bacine sea toward GoldArrow.

"We have a problem," Admiral Jack remarked from behind them.

"The citadel will never fall," the commander remarked proudly, but Jacquelina was pointing at the sky to the south and the east while the prince and princess pulled their gazes away from the enemy rushing toward them from the north. They were surrounded by at least twenty battleships of the air, led in a circular advance by the Santisma.

Dist appeared on the top of the stairs to the small town below and beckoned to the trio.

"We must leave," he said.

"The citadel will never fall," the commander remarked again proudly. He nodded over to an adjutant who had climbed the stairs beside Dist and arrived just behind him, panting, "Man all battle stations and fire at will."

"Yessir."

"I will help them to safety," Dist said, and he nodded when instructed to take them into the hilltop fortress's catacombs. As they went, they collected what they could find of the Secondwind's crew, but instead of turning toward the hilltop town's inner workings, he led them toward the cemetery at the rear of the star fortress.

He opened a tomb in a swift, easy motion, before the others had fully arrived, and then beckoned them inside. Someone lit a fire ahead, and at a momentary loss for where to go next, they waited until Dist appeared and picked path after path through a maze of underground catacombs beside countless tombs and empty shelves.

The prince realized that they were descending quickly. The cold became nearly unbearable, but suddenly it was not cold. There was a rush of air from behind them that felt as hot as a summer day.

It dawned on him as they exited the catacombs into the old city even before he looked up at the hill behind them to see what had happened. The ships of the line had bombarded the star fortress and set the entire hill ablaze, leaving nothing that could start on fire safe.

Even his shoes, standing so far away from the blast, felt warm in the wind, and he fought the urge to rip them off. Had he been on the hilltop, even away from the flames, they would have melted or started ablaze just by proximity to the heat.

* * *

Captain Graneuva placed a small grip of tobacco carefully into the paper wrap. He could smell it in the cool air that whipped past him as the ship thrust forward into the wind toward their quarry.

He rolled the paper and lit it with the fire of an Orichalc lamp on the edge of the outer deck. He looked out over the sprawling city that had long been a city state allied to Imeria before coming under the control of Albion across the Bacine sea below.

Graneuva smoked quietly. He let the flavor stew in his mouth and leave his nostrils. The soft gray smoke filtered from his lips mixing with the steam of his breath, practically one and the same and also completely different.

He and twenty newly built air battleships of the proud Imerian air navy, enclosed upon the legendary fortress of GoldArrow. The intricate architecture of its central castle, a building older than the Akrin Empire, seemed to mock him from below, and he nodded to his second in command.

Vintillo, the cartographer, had been temporarily imprisoned in his quarters for protesting what was about to happen. All Graneuva had to do on this morning was give that nod, and the orders had been distributed.

He did not know what had truly led to the destruction of Gangüt far to the north in what was now the modern day Orichalc hills. He did not know what had led to the destruction of Vilshala in Emira. He had heard many things about red dust and legendary stones, which he assumed to be Orichalc, as well as wars between elves and dwarves that upset the angels and raised demons. But, he knew now what would lead to the razing of anything that moved on that anthill of Albion below.

He let the paper butt of the cigarette he had rolled and smoked fall of the side of the Santisma. It fell quietly, slowly toward the sea below, catching the wind like a feather as the freshly shaven captain, rolled another.

The fortress had been said to be able to withstand a thousand cannonballs from the sky and house well over one thousand people, men, women and apparently children. But, could it withstand the fire of a thousand cannons of the sky?

As the paper cigarette butt hit the water and softly submerged into the salty sea, the first wave of fiery breath of the Imerian navy burst forth, answering the echoing shots of musket and cannon that had come from the star fortress. Graneuva watched the wave of one thousand cannons travel the distance from sky to frost in the blink of an eye and slam into the exposed top side of the walls, detonating after many balls had sunk through the muddy ceilings and into the cavernous hillside walls beneath.

Others exploded against the exterior as shards of stone and steel went flying. Explosion after explosion rang out in the morning air as wave after wave of skyborne cannon fire fell upon the castle, town, and hilltop walls, which suddenly burst into flames that licked the air and ate the very metal below like dragon's fire.

Graneuva watched as the hilltop itself, began to cave in, and the flames grew until the hill was a house with its full top ablaze. He let his second cigarette drop from the side of the Santisma and watched the paper burst into flames in the very air. He looked up at the sky. He watched the birds frantically fly away. He peered back over the town below, full of Imerian people, and he wondered melancholically if they would view him as liberator or unjust villain.

In what might be the most profound, pivotal moment of his career so far, he would later learn that the prince of Albion and possibly a princess of Menetoris had both arrived together in GoldArrow, after witnessing the Santisma in an attack on a Coltari vessel.

History would long debate the start of what would someday become known as the First Alliance War, but no one would debate whether or not to include the battle of GoldArrow, a crushing bombardment that wiped the ancient star fortress GoldArrow completely from the frost. Future generations would walk a shorter hill with only the faintest memory of the stone walls outlining what had once stood there. The bricks and metal would melt and burn. The waterfall that fed the catacombs within would boil and turn to lava like heat, bursting from beneath the ground as the hill succumbed and crumbled beneath the fire.

The glint of light off the telegram tower just to the north of the old city caught Graneuva's eye, and he began to grow paranoid. He ordered the ship around to blow it to smithereens and then he saw that sea ships too were fleeing from the city in droves.

Satisfied that the castle had been completely devastated, he began ordering the men to relay between ships an order to encircle the city below and embargo the whole of the town. Not a soul would leave to tell the world what had happened here until they had determined how such a move would be viewed in Akre.

Graneuva knew it wouldn't be long before he would soon see his wife after being long away from the Imerian shore, but he hoped that there would be few reasons to leave after a short war could end the supremacy of Albion over the Bacine Sea. And now defeating Menetoris, too, in a battle over the sky began to circle in his mind.

* * *

Docked within the lower chambers of the castle now ablaze, the glorious frigate, the Secondwind, gift to Admiral Jaquelina Catalina Ferrara, Jack for short, was no doubt beyond rescue. The old woman, suddenly feeling her age, laconically stared into a beer at a small tavern in old town, with the few of her men that had escaped the blaze, somberly contemplating the luck that they shared to not be burning alive atop GoldArrow hill.

Eduard sat alone on a second-floor balcony that wrapped around the inside of the tavern, looking out a window at the hills surrounding the city. Ivette was quietly sobbing into a tavern bunk, having temporarily colored her hair with a spell she had never thought to use.

The prince watched as the ships disbursed from the fire that still torched the hillside fortress and would possibly last days, billowing black smoke into the air and filling the formerly cloudless sky with ashy clouds of black that would rain soot in the days to come.

The Santisma eased through the air in a wide arcing turn until it found a place just above the telegram tower. Eduard thought he was going to see cannons burst it into flames, but instead a party of men leapt from the ship. They were merely specks against the monstrous ship in the distance, swarming on the unseen building below the tower, taking control of the airwaves and any communication with the outside world.

Eduard looked away and drank a bit of cold beer. He was tired but no longer filled with uncertainty about his place in the fate of the world. If he could survive, he would do everything he could to band with Menetoris and Valgaard against a senate that would condone an offensive attack of such devastation. He could not get the faces of the children out of his mind, who had barely begun to experience life before being snuffed out by the evil of man. There was no justification.

The door of the tavern opened below, and the quiet of the room went quieter. Dist had appeared, and he looked up at Eduard sitting on the balcony alone. He nodded to Eduard, and Eduard nodded back.

It was done. A telegram had been safely sent to Albion. In an instant, a message could travel across the ocean by wave to alert his father in Rorik through channels that did not exist twenty years ago of the devastation. Now, all they could do was wait and lie low, praying for rescue.

They were trapped in GoldArrow. As they began to filter out from the tavern to accommodations arranged by black market contacts of the former pirate, Ferrara, with strict orders not to contact or see each other for many days, Prince Eduard could only think to himself in disbelief.

He should have listened to Ivette. They should have left for Rorik as soon as they had refueled. There was no ship to use, nor money to get. They had to rely on the goodwill of Imerian men, who would put their allegiance in peace above war.

Ivette relied on him to make good decisions now, and he relied on her. They had established trust, but they had to be careful who else they could. They would see no one but each other and whichever Imerian family sheltered them in the maze of old town.

First, he said goodbye to Admiral Jack, who disappeared to her own shelter, and then to Dist who stayed behind last. Then, the prince went on his way, holding Ivette quietly against his side, following the shrouded figure of an Imerian man, wrapped in a shawl against the ashy rain, between buildings and down alley ways. Muddy brackish water dripped in between the cobblestone and pooled at the edges of the street, steaming and hissing just by proximity to the distant flames.

Imerian troops from the ships descended onto the city, and the distant musket fire of the last executions of a brutal attack rang out in the darkness that would have been just after the high noon sun.

He had never wanted his father so bad as he wanted his father to swoop in and save him in that moment, but he knew if any help was to come it would not be immediate. He had to trust the man, leading him through the maze of city streets with his life and now Ivette's, who he kept wishing he had listened to. He relied so much on trust. He had to trust that Dist had sent the message. He had to trust that if the message was received in Albion that his father would do anything about it, or that it would even get to him.

1513 - Chapter 20

King Stone's castle tower had not stopped buzzing since the coup. Concerned citizens and motivated guards coalesced as the thin standing military supporting the Coltari along with the militia became a formalized division overseen by King Stone himself. The Coltari, though formally private, recognized quiet fealty and service to lord of the silver coast, and taking stock of the state of the nation, the now sudden King realized quickly that his strength was in the navy alone, both by sea and by air. There were not enough boots on the ground so to speak to defend the coast against any kind of land invasion, but Albion could dominate by sea or air.

New positions to govern the nation were established, and empty floors in the tower were requisitioned as what had been essentially a largely empty vertical estate for the lord and his family, when he had one, became instead a formal headquarters for the establishment of the independent nation. The excitement of controlling their own destiny outweighed the fear of any retribution by Akre far too far away to threaten Rorik before winter.

Despite all of the shuffle and hustle around him, Stone had felt the crushing loneliness of life more than ever. He had lost his wife many years ago, and he had made no effort to pursue another life, another love. Now, here Onya had come and though he felt something for her, he had also discovered he was more than likely a mere mark for a spy but her spying had a perhaps fortunate twist. He had made up his mind on the matter, but as so too can stones grow cold, he felt hardened and weary like ice had returned in place of his heart.

Loneliness and solitude had made him what he was, but he had not wanted it forever. He had forgotten what it was like to love again, to touch and to taste. He had forgotten what it was like to run like a wild beast, to let the animal within him win and to take control.

The weary King, slouching in his old, lord's desk chair, turned into modern throne, looked at the cabinet where he had kept the silver medication he had used to prevent his transformations for years. He had moved most of his yesterday life to the old Bowery Place Estate, which had long been the seat of the kings in the days of Albion past.

Merely the office furniture and an elegant overnight room that had not been damaged in the coup, along with some gentlemen's toiletries remained in the stone tower. He was thankful that the damage he had done as a beast had been covered up. He could not imagine allowing the general public to know the extent of his condition, and now that it was abuzz with life when it had once been so empty for so long, he had been sure someone would have discovered something until he saw the damage himself.

Stone lifted his hand slowly before him, his eyes transfixed on the mystical device that he had used to save Onya's life, which she had turned into a blessing rather than a curse: a rhodium scepter, not even large enough to be used as a significant weapon. The Scepter of Lyse had a thin line of white tape wrapped around the center where it might be held. The weakness of the werewolf transformation had always been that it either occurred once under moonlight or as in the days of old Albion as a painfully near permanent condition for those turned too strongly by a white demon.

It was one of the things that had led him to a solo life. As he had grown older, the symbol of the lone wolf had become a persona he had mentally adopted as his burden in life. His son, Eduard, would become like him some day. The transformations, now, in his youth, were weak and easily prevented. With each year, the King Jack Stone's transformations had grown ever more powerful to the point that if he were to need any more silver to prevent his transformation, he would merely be replacing his blood with metal.

Onya, belle of the north, had come into his life, and by unfortunate circumstance become a monster like him. He couldn't abandon her, and he feared deep down that she would abandon him as soon as her mission was accomplished. He may be a beast, but he felt something for the woman. She churned his insides; she calmed his animal side. It was as if she were a smell that he had not yet sniffed, but when inhaled, subdued him. If she were to leave, then that intoxication would leave too.

He was making many assumptions, he reminded himself as he returned the scepter to rest on the desk and stood to look out the new window at the old city as he had done many times before but with fresh perspective. Airships lifted off and landed in the distance to the north while sea ships moved much slower out to port, and in the space between buildings horse drawn carriages trotted in long lines while red smoke from the trains out to the mines farther north billowed slowly across the twin bays toward where factories fires burned red Orichalc.

The city was alive. He was alive. He could feel the blood of the beast turning within him, longing to run, longing to fight. He wanted

Onya, and he had summoned her, and perhaps the greatest of assumptions had already been made. If she didn't want to stay, he would make her stay no matter what. He would soon be taking a chance and asking her directly on the matters at hand, whether she wanted to stay and if she could message the ice princess.

The door opened behind him, and the snide frown of a suspicious Miss Logan let Onya in, motioning to a brown leather seat across the chipped, slightly darker brown desk. As Onya sat, she traced the char marks from the blunderbusses, pistols, or muskets that had been fired. Onya was well aware that Stone had officially become king, but he had not changed his attire or taken up a crown. He appeared in a formal lord's suit with the old flag of Albion stitched into the left chest and golden Lyse flowers set into each of the buttons with resin.

When the man turned, she saw the intensity with which he had been mulling over the problems of the world. She felt suddenly safe, but also as if she were being judged by trial. It was an uneasy feeling. She would have lay on the desk if he had asked her, but now, she wondered if something had changed. She could not tell if these were two sides of the same man, or if a day had made the legendary iciness of his stoney heart grow cold once more. If the future that she had seen had also flashed before his eyes, maybe he had turned from it and away from her.

King Stone stood in silence, watching her twitch and sink into the chair in her mind. In reality, her shoulders had frozen in place out of fear or experience, making her appear to him as if she suspected nothing. His eyes never wavered, and his eyelashes blinked in long, slow movements, barely fluttering with each movement. She was taken momentarily aback when she realized again just how large a man that he was compared to her and her small frame. His shoulders were almost the width of a normal doorway. The bustling city in the window framed him as airships drifted by.

Stone had to take some time to work up to it as the two stared at each other. Their eyes dancing as lovers' do. Each pair of pupils finding the other's then swelling and rescinding from dark, black pearls into tiny dots, shying from the light of the day, casting the room in full color.

"Don't mind how I've come to ask this question but answer it honestly." He mulled over it once more, whether there could be any punishment better, for him or her, than imprisoning her in a place where he could see her every day.

"What is it," she paused and added, "my king?"

He scoffed and a moment of rage at her play-acting, caused a half-growl to stir in his throat, "if you are able to put me in touch with Princess Valessa of Valgaard or her father, it's best you do it and soon."

"What do you mean?"

"You heard me. I know you're just a spy. You're being placed under permanent house arrest as we speak." His anger subsided as he saw the strange hurt appear in her eyes, and while the strength of his voice faltered, the hurt did not in hers. "Your belongings are being searched and moved to the Bowery Place Estate. You are not to be out of multiple guardsmen sights. As I said, I've taken the liberty of moving your things to the palace, my normal home in the city," he added soften.

She took a moment to recover, realizing that while her love was in question, her mission had succeeded. For better or worse, she was stuck with him. Perhaps as a prisoner, instead of a lover, but she imagined few women had dug their claws this far into the hide of this king. The way she saw it, the estate would be hers to redecorate, for as long as she was there.

She let the tension of the moment release, weakening his resolve and giving her time to work through her words, "Yes, I can pass a message to Princess Valessa through the smugglers that cross the Evorul mountains, and we better send a message soon. It's getting cold fast."

"Good."

She checked the door and stood slowly, leaning forward to within a foot, and then in a chillingly seductive whisper, "You are right, of course. I am a spy. I was sent here to work to form an alliance between our nations, but you already guessed that didn't you. And that's not all that I am. Not anymore, is it?"

Stone stood a bit taller, leaning slightly away from her, out of fear of his own feelings overtaking him, "My friend Erolin spoke of it to me before his death if that is what you are referring to, and I would like to accept. We both need allies after all. That much has been proven to me. However, until an official delegation is received, and formal treaty is signed and counter-signed, you must not leave Bowery Place."

Miss Logan knocked on the door, and Stone ushered her into the rectangular office, "What is the news?"

"We must respond to the King of Menetoris. The next Coltari ship to Saint Egrivan has sent a messenger to leave without further delay." Miss Logan paused when Onya was not dismissed from the room and Stone glancing between them both unbothered, urged her to continue, "We have received a desperate communication. It seems that one of the King's daughters has gone missing, and he fears she has come here to make peace. If she has not come to the capital, he wishes to have that known as he has begun to fear the stories of merchant ships being attacked at sea."

"Onya if you will please leave us, I must respond to this," the king motioned for a guardsman to take her and commanded she be brought directly to Bowery Place. As she left, Onya heard the last few words spoken by the king.

"We must open a dialogue with our trade partner. We don't have the best history, but to confirm a formal alliance would be more than profitable. Send an ambassador with the ship and inform them that my son has been tracking privateers in the Argal with success. We will update him soon that she has no doubt arrived safely." And with that his voice trailed off, but she could still see the image of his desk in her mind's eye. Where there had been scorch marks there had also been ink spills, and with the stroke of a pen, he had declared independence from the Akrin Empire.

The loyal Miss Logan had smiled as she had taken the document and had hand delivered it to a printing press where she had overseen the copying of the original and the creation of a simplified flyer for the mass printing of the formal declaration of independence. All of Albion would now see the Lyse flower as the sign of independence for the crown from the distant senate and know that times were changing.

It was when Miss Logan had returned from the morning errand with the document that she had seen Onya, who had been summoned and filled with jealousy, but still let the younger woman into the king's office. The news from Menetoris had given her the perfect opportunity to interrupt whatever was being said between them, but she had never expected the woman to be moved to Bowery Place Estate of all places — out of her sight.

* * *

Onya was soon left alone in a large blue gray estate in a gated world of its own, after a brief tour of the interior and nearby grounds. She was driven in a horse drawn carriage up an ancient gravel road between slightly overgrown but still patiently manicured gardens to a large two-story building, separating the Bowery Place market, which lay across the river, from the cemetery to the palace complex's north. The small river ran served as the formal boundary between Piruma and Rorik, running along most of the north side of the Ash Vale..

The tour she was given of the grounds was barely more than a few pointers on where not to walk lest she join the myriad of visitors who have disappeared in strange circumstances over the years and become yet another ghost of days past. She had much to decipher from the groundskeeper's mumblings. The main campus at the complex's center housed all of the necessities of daily life and entertainment, and the rooms in its wings were mainly unused, unmaintained, or empty bedrooms and their attachments.

Behind the palace stood a dense thicket of forest that King Stone had no doubt used to hide a transformation in his past. As they approached the oversized dark brown double doors, Onya found her breathing strained by a rolling fear that seemed to ooze from the dark, old building. The two wings were perfect mirrors of forty windows in either direction, stretching to almost the edge of sharp sight, making it appear as if it met the spiked wall at the edge of the grounds.

Once inside, she realized that the ceilings of each floor were almost twice the height of a normal floor. The enormity of the entry way was breathtaking. A giant, crystal chandelier hovered over a ball room the size of four throne rooms from the white palace in Valgaard. To either side a curved staircase stretched from the floor to a high second floor balcony along the rear wall that overlooked the large foyer floor, where the decal of a Lyse flower had been set into a bright wood. The dark mahogany color of the rest of the floor accentuated the simple elegance of the design.

As Onya explored, she found herself slightly dizzied by the strange structure. Its exterior cast the illusion that the building was as normal as any other. Within the quiet estate, the floors descended quickly upon entry and sometimes dipped further down depending on the room. The second floor extended high above the otherwise normal placement of the windows.

There were no pets or people to introduce herself to. She was quite alone in the old estate except for the groundskeeper who had showed her in and the guardsman, who waited outside. The reality of her predicament began to seize at her chest. What if Valessa never received her message? Would she be okay being stuck here for the rest of her foreseeable future?

Her things had all been placed at the back of the ball room near to the closest bedroom. She noticed it had been meticulously filled with everything a woman could want. There were perfumes from around the world, different sized mirrors with which to admire herself from many angles at once, and creams and dyes labeled with all sorts of magical wonders.

There was no doubt that this prison was unlike any other, but a prison it remained. She felt like she could get anything she wanted, but for the moment, the voice of someone to talk to. A small voice within her reminded her that it was late, and the next morning or evening, arrangements could be made for staff that could liven up her day, but that did nothing to quiet the turning in her stomach that it could be more than a day, or that she would remain lonely even if Stone were to arrive. As cold as he had been, she hoped in her heart that he may not arrive at all this evening, giving her time to explore the quiet, old house on her own.

No, not quiet.

She could hear the rustle of the wind from what sounded like an open window down the hall. There was the groan of the floorboards, creaking under what sounded like footsteps of an invisible man, traveling through the upstairs hallway. The very walls shook, and when she listened closely, it seemed to be saying something in bellowing yawn.

Raahhgghhnnn, it sounded like.

Run?

Her heart fluttered, but then she smiled to herself. There was no way that the house said just that. Just now. She waited silently, feeling watched, but confident in her strength. Facing the window, she could see the groundskeeper who had let her inside, wandering between a row in the hedges without a thought at all to the house.

She was alone.

She slowly twisted to look behind her. The door was ajar, but she remembered it had just been nearly closed. Had the house been trying to warn her, to scare her, or had it all just been in her imagination?

Had she left the door fully ajar? She stood, rooted in place, straining to hear, but it was quiet now. Onya let herself relax and tiptoed quickly to the hallway, looking both ways. A part of her wished she had claws and could run without worry, howling at the moon.

She pulled her hair up into a bun and rolled up the sleeves of her dress, then went into the hall. She felt a little naked without a larger weapon in hand, but she had a handful of hidden daggers for the living. As a werewolf, she knew she could deal with the trespassing dead.

She had heard of haunted houses, especially from tales of Valgaard's north. Wraiths and banshees were tethered to places or people due to unfinished business, and a mercenary warlock from Imor Valsen would lay them to rest. She had always doubted their validity as invented tales for gaining fortune, but here she was seeing dancing shadows climb the walls, wondering as she slowly eased her way through the hallway between closed doors whether each shroud of black fleeting through the halls was a formless banshee looking for a place in the world to reveal itself and steal her life's force.

There was a broad ray of light brightening the dimly lit hallway from an open door near the end of the long hall from where a patter grew slowly louder like a knock on a door. There was not a sound near her beside each seemingly thunderous creak from the floor when she pressed her heel slowly against the carpet, which was so dark a blue that it was nearly black in the shadow.

When she peered into the room, she found it empty aside from a painter's easel. An empty white canvas stood at the center of the room with a stool hidden out of view behind it. There were no brushes or paint. She neared the open window cautiously, only to find that it had begun to rain. The rain on the window made the sound she had heard. The whoosh of a gust of wind blew the curtains toward her like two ghostly arms reaching for her from the window frame.

She pulled the window shut against the rain just as it began to grow stronger, and the thick gray of the storm blotted out her view of the front gardens. She could just about see where the groundskeeper had been, but she could no longer tell if he still stood there or if it was just a statue.

Onya turned around slowly, and something flashed before her. For a moment, it was as if a small child as white as a sheet had stood in the open hallway door. She blinked and looked again. It was gone.

Onya stood, rooted in place. She could not get the image of the child in white out of her mind's eye. The image in the doorway remained even when she closed her eyes, but there was something else that made her move and made her look about, re-examining. A gut feeling that something had changed in the room.

A bright, red line had been swung across the canvas resting on the easel. A sheet that had rested over the painting had been strung across the floor. She suddenly wished Jack, King Stone, was there to comfort her. Had he sent her to a true prison after all, or would he suddenly arrive to save her from whatever ghastly sprite was playing tricks on her? She couldn't move, but she wanted to.

"It's going to take more than that to scare me away!" she cried at the lonely darkness. "I can't leave. Even though I could try, I don't want to." I want to see him again with his eyes burning with desire for me as they did once as beast, she thought to herself.

A warmth suddenly filled the room. A bright, white light, a will of the wisp appeared in the air in the center of the room like a lamp floating alone, the object of a spell. It twinkled at her, playfully.

It hovered and slowly drifted out the door and then came back suddenly through the wall. Was she supposed to follow this poltergeist that had just spooked her to somewhere else in the house?

It made the motion again and again until she followed it out of the painter's room and toward a vertical staircase at the end of the hall. It twisted in the air playfully in front of her as it beckoned her downward. There was a myriad of paintings on the walls of the staircase but none with people.

When the two reached the bottom of the staircase and a large steel door, braced and locked, she the sprite appeared to be begging her to open. It furiously rushed through the wall over and over, growing more and more desperate the longer she stood and waited. She reached a hand to the bar. Her curiosity overcame her as she suddenly realized she wanted to know what would be locked in the basement of a haunted palatial estate.

There was a crash upstairs, coming from the first floor. Onya froze to listen. The hairs on her spine were like razor thin spikes that grown longer from standing on their ends attempting to leave her body.

Instinctively, like a scent on the air, she knew that Jack had come home, and he was not happy. The sound of his monstrous footsteps fell away from the entrance where he must have slammed through the exterior door. The crashing continued, however, as he threw anything in his way.

The wisp was gone. The hallway brightened from the shine of Orichalc lights lit from a distance as night fell. Onya took her hand away from the door and ascended the staircase. She felt, once again, timid, as each step she took gently glanced against the ground and she neared ever closer to where Jack as merely a man had thrown a table through the plaster of a wall. She wanted to know what had happened more than she still wanted to see what was in the basement of the south wing. Was he tearing the house apart looking for her?

The crashing sound stopped. She began to sprint, no longer worried or afraid of the strangeness of the home. She heard a man biting back tears, questioning the air. She turned the corner of an empty door frame off the hallway to find him on one knee, his head resting in the crook of his elbow and his fist clenching a miniature portrait of a young boy.

In a flash, she saw the face of the child ghost and wondered if this were some kind of memorial for the beloved deceased. She walked into the room, and as she drew closer, he looked up. His resolve stiffened and the emotion left his eyes. Onya knew instinctively that the child in the photograph had not been the sprite she had seen in the south wing.

Jack made no move to stop her as she reached out a hand to place it on his back. She thought of something to say but held her tongue. Whatever inner peace he was trying to reclaim after the shock of the coup, it had been stripped after learning that she was a spy and whatever news he had just received. She could see it in his eyes.

She could sense, like second nature, that he longed for her touch and as her hand hovered, she realized that she was passing through a threshold between them. She could feel it like she could feel the spirit of the house. There was a place for souls that sought each other.

She could turn back, she thought. Something inside her felt fear. More fear than from the basement door. He looked up at her again. His eyes also afraid—afraid she was turning away from him--then she placed the hovering hand on his shoulder, and a rush of emotion overcame her as if she were feeling the weight of his burden falling from him to her.

They sat like that in that room for a long time. Him kneeling as if in prayer with her hand on his shoulder and his hand, clasping hers to him until she could not stand in one place any longer. She kneeled beside him and hugged him. He turned toward her, looking in her eyes, again with love.

She felt the urge to kiss him, but he turned away from her and looked at the carpet. He closed his eyes. She wanted to know if they would ever make love in human form like they had as werewolves, and she felt she might have her answer soon. The pulse of his shoulders slowed as he relaxed in her arms, and she could feel the hard muscle of his arms and back beneath the soft underbelly of her arms. Only her thin dress and his half-undone tunic separated them.

He held up the photo, "My son."

She relaxed, disappointed. She wondered if the sprite she had seen had indeed been the boy in a past life.

"He's stuck behind enemy lines. GoldArrow has been attacked. They were able to send a telegram out before going dark. I didn't get it soon enough to send word to Menetoris today, but we now know that the missing princess is there as well."

She fell to a seat beside him and rested her head on his knee, looking up at his fierce, stony blue eyes. They were full of a range of emotions. Anger, fear, perhaps love. They blinked from one to the next, unsure what to be at any moment. Whenever he looked at her, they turned bright until again he cast them away, afraid to trust.

"He's lucky to be alive."

She listened to him continue on.

"They bombarded the garrison there, laid waste to the star fortress. There is nothing left where the castle town once stood, protecting it for so many years. It even acted as a bastion for the men of Imeria during the Domiscan wars. It's unclear how many may have died. Over three thousand, possibly up to seven."

"All those people," she whispered.

"They long wanted to reclaim their land for years on paper, but Imeria never controlled GoldArrow. It was a city state that welcomed all and only joined the state of Albion in the last one hundred years. It's been a part of our nation for longer than we were a part of the Empire." The representative republic his family had once joined was now anything but. In less than a month so much of his world view had shifted, and here was a woman from a faraway place that he had never thought of as more than anything dangerous, resting her soft hands and head on his shoulder.

"What do we do now?" she asked, watching his eyes. She sensed that he had decided something. The gravity of this turn of events weighed on him. Any move to aid his son would be a clear attack on Akre and Imeria, but in the same reasoning, the bombardment had been a clear act of war.

If he attacked, his two main adversaries would be further bound together, closer together than they had ever been, even closer perhaps during the wars against Domiscus. The King he was now had to act, but he could not stand alone. He would need Menetoris and Valgaard, just as they needed him.

For the life of his son, could he risk opening his kingdom up to retribution? He had also gotten word of the nightmarishly large ship, the Santisma, leading Imeria's fleet. How was he to deal with that?

"What can we do?" he thought out loud, and she frowned, disappointed.

"You can fly down and get him."

"The city is under siege and embargoed. No ships are coming in or out. He's trapped by a fleet of Imerian airships."

"You can fight."

He grunted.

"You can fly to GoldArrow and get revenge for all those innocent people whose only crime was living."

"Revenge on who? If we fight them over the city, we might not save anyone at all. We can't just shoot cannons from afar, even if we have better range."

"No, obviously not, but what's the risk that a ship crashes in the city. What if you board the ships?"

"We would need more men."

"Or you use this." She reached around his waist and grabbed the scepter of Lyse from his side. "We can board the ships as werewolves and take them by force then steal them or steer them clear of the city until you can escape."

"I can barely control myself when changed. When I received this gift, if you will, I was told that it can only activate the power, not control it."

"I can. You can learn."

"Are you sure? And even if I can control it, you expect me to be able to use that to change more than me?"

"I believe it. I was drawn to you. You were my guiding light, a force more than human. I needed you, to follow you. To hunt with you."

He laughed. She playfully bit at his shoulder in response. He lightly placed a hand on her cheek and turned her face toward him.

"Onya."

"Jack."

* * *

Soon, they were running in the woods of the estate as beasts, searching for each other. The scepter in the monstrous hands of the turned Stone. He had often found solace in the woods near the cemetery as a boy when he would turn into a wolf, but now it had new meaning, running with her.

She helped him to control his animal side. The larger world out there, beyond the walls of the estate, may have been complicated and on the precipice of war, but whenever he commanded her in that tiny sliver of forest, she obeyed. It was thrilling how she followed him unquestioningly and yet, she guided him to without words.

If they could band together the wolves of the silver coast, her plan could work. If there were any more wolves to band. He would not merely change a man for the sake of this adventure. It would still be a curse to many.

He was no longer a lone wolf, friend to few. He was a king of his grandfather's nation, running alongside a beautiful wolf from the north. He had friends in the world. Even if they too needed him, if they came together in time, it was possible to divert war entirely.

He could see that now. Just as he could see that his curse had become a blessing.

Not even a sliver of the moon appeared in the sky as he dove and jumped and pushed between trees and through the unkempt brush. He ran as a beast with the cold night wind in his white hair, and this time no matter how dark the night, he was not alone.

1513 - Chapter 21

Trumpets roared and bass drums thumped. The pipers who had piped doubled and tripled, joined by flautists fluting in quarters and triplets. The drummers drummed along with each step they took. Hammers banged on cowbells and others slammed books together in thunderous clapping.

In groups of five, in lines of ten, it must have been five hundred men. Next, four hundred more on horseback rode, carrying eight dragon scales up the road. Then, two hundred men on elks, carried dragon skins, each worth eight bear pelts.

On and on they came, and as they marched through each town, ten or more joined the parade. Thirty violins and other strings followed one hundred singers, singing praise.

No one knew who the fun was for, but everyone recognized the glint of a scale, and could see the wagons coming, packed full of salted dragon. Past every place they went, they sold and sold, gaining a mountain of gold. Ahead of the tower in the seat of power, was just a boy, a pretty and tall but normal boy, who despite his simple appearance led the column on a simple horse, trailed by the dragon's bones and the skull, the only part of the beast still wrapped in skin, which sagged further with each passing day of decay.

And still the parade went on as one hundred dancers sauntered past. The entourage grew, and the countryside came to life. The dragon slayer was on his way to the capital where he would meet the king.

Every night, Erold lay awake, wondering if the next day would be the same. Every morning, he'd sleep off and on as the train of people grew and grew. It felt as if the line of men and women that followed him stretched back to Helmun Loch. That no one had moved, except for him, and new people joined just by running ahead of the growing parade, but that's not how it happened at all.

Keeping a tight watch of every speck of gold at night and his few followers flanking him as he went. Wherever he went, even to use outhouses along the way, were at least one, usually two of them. Over the long trip, he began to only trust the three riders with rock rams, the mage from the islands, Kahron, the guard captain, Volstad, and the always mysterious Moon, who Erold still knew little about--but he, like his father, trusted more than anyone else.

They came upon Peth from the northwest, almost in a straight-line route from Helmun Loch, except for a few river crossings rivers and Valgaard's mountainous hills. Peth was built along the lake at the intersection of three rivers--one smaller running from the north and a large river running west to east--which formed into a confluence at its center and then ran into a wide inlet from the north, while the smallest of the three rivers fed the lake from the south, creating a natural harbor where the three rivers combined. This was separated from the sea by rock cliffs that ran along the whole of the lake.

Many of the crowd had never seen the capital of Valgaard, Peth, before and many spoke of the wonder that it was to behold, with white-stone walls and towers of gold. Erold had never seen a city with such a large sprawl. It spread out over the foothills that surrounded it, which rose to a natural plateau among the bluffs on the shore of the north river, where the palace stood, a low stone wall around the campus of the modern building, looking down at the world around it.

"They've made changes since the last time I was here. That palace is new and there are more churches," said Volstad.

They descended the hills, leading to the city, and crossed the north river before taking the main road, which ran around the lake, through dense forest and on top of the bluffs, looking periodically down through the trees upon rocky beaches and wind-swept shores, void of sand, and the rare view of the city before them, which began to form well before they reached the hills below the modern castle.

It had taken almost twice as long as it would have otherwise, but they had arrived at the white-stone city, where the 'ice' palace of king Hughgar had been newly built and almost any resemblance to the ornate white-stone columns of Akre and Elessia that dominated in days of old had become mere parts of new monuments, re-adorned with gold and re-decorated with new heroes and statues.

Volstad pointed out the missing places of old heroes that had been lost to time, while in their place stood trees decorated with gold and candles. They had arrived only a few days before the Great Day of Thanks, which was held annually in the middle of Halthi-eld on the fifteenth to celebrate the old country and the beginning of the great migration of Normen to the south.

Every year on this day, when winter had neared, new groups had burned a dead tree to a cook a great feast and remember the old country and the good things they had received, before setting sail or out on foot, never to return from their journey south. The exodus had lasted for a few centuries before finally all the Normen had left the great cities of Nole.

The north had always been inhospitable from the mountains, northwest of Valgaard, which the Visgollans were said to have followed south, to where the old country had once started, perhaps fifteen hundred atomic miles north; but, when the glacial ice returned, it was impossible to stay any longer. Some few people still lived toward the south and central of Nole, but the Normen sought out larger lands and the beasts of the ice in the north followed them south, forced by the same cold.

In this year, though, a new tradition, the parade, was born when the dragon slayer and his entourage entered the city from between the trees and down the hills and from the north bluff, bringing an entourage of over one thousand men and women from all of Valgaard. Every year after he first visited Peth, a parade was held to commemorate the Great Day of Thanks.

As he walked through the city, inviting stares, Volstad pointed out more that had changed. Church towers now rose higher than old gazebos that still dotted the city. As it was after Frostmas, and the day of the Lord on the twenty fifth of Vetfal quickly approached, Frostian decorations adorned every oil lamp on the street, public trash can, bench, and bathroom. Gold and silver foil, giant bells, and garlands of pine with bright gold and green bows, were hung on every corner. Within the capital, as long as Hughgar remained king, no decoration ever used red, the color he associated with fealty to the Empire in the south.

Almost all of the city's old walls had come down, and the harbor, which they could see as they rounded the bluff to head toward the palace, perched on the central plateau, had received modern docks where both sea ship and airship still loaded and unloaded passengers and goods as winter fast approached.

The old castle, a fortress for another time, stood quiet, forlorn and empty, just beside the harbor on a bluff south of the confluence and near the mouth of the east-west river into the harbor. It had now been converted into a garden garrison, still called a southern name, the 'Presidio,' the last of the monuments to the past, a forgotten relic near the entrance to the bay with white-stone columns as tall as fifty men wrapped around a quiet park, open to all.

If Erold had visited, he would have read a plaque there that referred to its once more useful days, when it guarded the port with three thousand men, a quaint number in modern times. Erold's entourage of civilians alone dwarfed it.

To Erold's right as he followed the river walk, against the current, back to the northwest and rising through the heart of the city, to where a ruined temple to the old gods had once stood, the modern palace shined in the light of the sun. It was not much more in appearance than an ornate manor or a library, built out of the pieces of the past in the same white stone and marble as the rest of the city. Within Valgaard, no other city, used white stones.

There could have been four hundred windows in three stories, each with the lights on, as it waited for visitors, flanked on all sides by pristine gardens and open grass. As Erold approached he caught a daily presentation of arms, where unicorns paraded in a choreographed routine across the palace's foregrounds, guided by riders in forest green jackets, with yellow-gold detailing. Infantry men, in similar colored tailcoats, followed in briskly marching lines before firing muskets loaded with only black powder into the air.

* * *

Seeing the approach of the dragon slayer from a rear window of the palace, and then a north facing one, and finally a south facing window was the princess, Valessa. The size of the dragon's skeleton could be seen from when it first crested the far hill over the north river as the procession filtered in after the coming king, and she could follow the parade with her eyes from the next window by just looking for the skull and bones of the dragon being led through the city.

Soon, she could hear their music too. She had heard that he was coming from those who rode ahead, and now she saw that their stories were true, as the parade neared the palace. The people that followed the kid king, still stretched from where she had first seen the dragon, to where he was now, rounding the bluff, and following the river to the palace's front door.

She was sure that he did not realize the size of the crowd, because he wouldn't be able to see it like she could. The whole of the walk they covered was well over twenty atomic miles, maybe closer to forty. There may have been fifty or sixty, maybe one hundred or possibly even close to two hundred thousand villagers, descending upon Valgaard's capital to see the dragon slayer, of whom the rumors said many things. They had said the boy had eaten the dragon's heart while the beast was still alive, held down by just one foot, and also that he had climbed upon the dragon's head and killed it by pulling its tongue so hard that he ripped out its stomach through its mouth.

Since Valessa had been helping her father run the kingdom, roughly five years before, there had almost never been a case where a dragon had been killed. Her father, a long friend of the dragons, since his days at Imor Valsen, when he said he rode them like his childhood idol above the clouds--a possible lie she never directly questioned--had instituted a policy early in his reign that no dragon should be slain on the punishment of death, except for those allowed after council with the dragons. If quite possibly only for his own desire to have more dragons, it was one of the better moves he had made, as dragons were notoriously vengeful and otherwise passive. The nation could quite possibly thank half of its northern population's survival to his love of the airborne beasts.

Valessa realized she was in front of the vanity mirror in her bedroom, mindlessly twisting at her blonde, almost white, hair, evening out the waves, straightening out any curls, and tightening the braid in an effort to look absolutely perfect. She was thinking too much. Her head was spinning.

She was glad that she had worn a nice dress--both befitting the holiday season and the nation, which her father would appreciate-- custom-made forest green with gold lace on its delicate sleeves and long, cage-less skirt. It almost fell to the floor and followed her form and legs when she walked. She grabbed a thick white and gold shawl, made of yeti pelt, as well to wrap over her shoulders.

She exited her bedroom after having her handmaidens help apply her makeup in accordance when attending court with foreign officials. Realizing she had forgotten her princess tiara, she ran back to get it.

As soon as she was back in the hallway, she snuck a peak at the foreyard, momentarily caught looking at the daily demonstrations of the royal cavalry on their unicorns, when she realized that the dragon slayer was almost making his grand entrance.

She took off her shoes and ran down the hallway, making sure to stay on the carpet rather than risk slipping on the polished floor. She put her shoes back on after descending the three flights of stairs.

She put them back on and came around the corner, nodding to the guardsmen at the door, who opened them for her. King Hughgar was again taking open court when she arrived, and for a moment he looked over at her in fear.

She gave him a quick look to assure him that she was not there to stop him, but a look of confusion flashed across his face as if to ask 'then what could it possibly be that's it's serious enough for you to come here.'

"Daddy," Valessa said under her breath so no one else could here, "sit there and look intimidating." To which he shrugged, wondering, 'didn't he always.'

Valessa pursed her lips, sucked in and let out her breath, she smiled, and she stopped smiling. Seconds ticked by while she waited at her father's side, watching the door, waiting for the dragon--

Erold pushed open each door with one hand, leaning forward as the doors crashed open. His long blonde hair, waved in the wind as the cold wind off the lake followed him into the courtroom.

He walked with purpose, flanked by an expression-less woman of far western descent, dressed in civilian clothes with a pistol around her waist, a heavily armed and lightly bearded older man she barely recognized with a graying brow who wore delicate, merchant's clothes, no doubt recently purchased, and a black mage, carrying a white staff, dressed in blue with brown leather greaves and gloves, and gold-painted armor reinforcing his shoulders and upper arms--on which Valessa recognized the twin angels of Menetoris.

Behind him as the guardsmen closed the door, Valessa could see the pile of gold, guarded by the remaining mercenaries, still riding their rock rams. The men carrying the skin and scales brought up the wares and placed them next to the gold in a growing pile in the courtyard.

"I have come to claim the contract on the dragon, the 'Thief of Life' and to buy an army to take back my kingdom."

Hughgar turned to his daughter first, "am I supposed to know who this is?"

"It was in your daily briefing," she whispered back quickly adding the specifics, "this is Erold Ardrada of the line of Arandil, chief claimant and only known, remaining male heir to the thrones of Akre, Normany, and of Galdir."

"He doesn't look like a man of the Arandil stock. I thought they had darker hair and eyes too," said Hughgar speaking under his breath into Valessa's ear.

"If you're referring to whether he is a Normen, you'll like him." Valessa did not state the obvious that it was Erold's mother who was of Normen descent.

"Are you going to continue to chat amongst yourselves, or are you going to honor the contract for the dragon?" Erold said, before giving a slight bow to the king. "I am Erold, son of Erolin, it is an honor to meet you King Hughgar of Valgaard."

"Honor the contract for the dragon, yes," said Hughgar, "By will of the king, see to it Bouvedere that whatever was brought along is divested and paid for." Hughgar placed his hand on the edge of his throne again and turned to Valessa another time, whispering, "could you tell me what it would cost to field an army equal the task?"

Valessa whispered back, "About one hundred times the value of the dragon, parts, pieces, and at the value of the contract."

Hughgar grunted a bit.

"This was in my daily briefing father," she said.

"We can't give him that, but I like his air. He reminds me of--"

"You."

"Yes," Hughgar stroked his chin. "My daughter, here, will have worked up some sort of plan in the event that you graced us with your presence Erold."

"I came to negotiate with you, sir. Will you honor the contract and allow me to fight for my kingdom?" Erold asked, and he kneeled before the king, looking up momentarily into Valessa's icy, sapphire eyes. It was her turn to feel chills as if her own magic had run a hand along her back to her neck.

Hughgar stood up from his throne, made of gold, pearl, and green, embroidered velvet, and stepped down the short stairs to place a hand on the boy's shoulder, squeezing tightly as if feeling him for muscle, "Yes, the value of the dragon is extraordinary, and I'd ridden a dragon about that size as a younger version of myself. It might have been an old friend of mine, but I knew this one to have always been a difficult fiend among the great giants of the sky. Come, my boy, get up, follow me to the inner sanctums, where we will discuss particulars. Valessa, are you coming?"

Valessa nodded, remembering herself, and turned to Erold's companions, who seemed caught unsure what to do, except for the expressionless woman, who had moved quickly to Erold's side as the king guided him through the side doors of the court, saying, "If the other two of you could stay here and sort out the particulars of the arrangement with Bouvedere, he is more than capable of assigning values to the materials you've collected, and requisitioning them on behalf of the throne of Valgaard."

As Valessa followed after her father, she heard Bouvedere begin describing the undertaking, "Yes, as the king and princess have authorized me on behalf of the crown, before all witnesses here of the royal guard, I will now distribute to you the effecting of duties to be taken on behalf of the exiled prince, Erold Ardrada of the line of Arandil Ardrada. I will see to it that the collection of gold, presented in the courtyard, has been counted, recounted, and transferred to the treasury at the bank of Valgaard, where it will be counted and recounted. Under the assurance of the bank of Valgaard, acting in the king's name, any lost funds will be sought after by the constables or professional detective liaisons of the king on punishment of death by public execution. In addition, we will purchase at market price, the values of the goods seen in the court and courtyard, of which we will confirm by weighted average to be conducted in accordance by no less than three mages of mathematical training. The value for which will be directly added to the account at the bank of Valgaard, under Erold's name. From which he can distribute said funds as to the ways that he sees fit to those who served with him in this undertaking, or whatever use--"

The door shut behind Valessa as Bouvedere continued to speak and the work he described began to be undertaken by associated staff members. She, on the other hand, caught up to her father and walked slowly behind him as he described how dragons are good omens in Valgaard and how killing one was like plucking the largest tree out of the deepest forest, one that had been growing for hundreds of years. It was an essential part of the ecosystem, the food chain, and while it was worth a lot of money, he turned to Erold in a very serious manner and said, "Don't kill any more of them," while pressing his fingers into Erold's shoulder.

Then, he turned to Valessa and said, "I leave him in your very capable hands, of which I have no doubt you planned. I am going to take a bath, because I can, and I want to."

Erold and Valessa stood next to each other for a second, each wondering if the other really had needed to know what her father would be doing and momentarily, at a loss for words. The woman, Moon, cleared her throat and spoke.

"Would you like it if I gave the two of you some space to discuss next steps?"

"Yes," said Erold as if a trance had been broken and he was brought back to the moment, "but please remain on hand Elara, and don't go anywhere just yet. Princess?"

"Valessa," said the princess. "Pleased to finally make your acquaintance." She mentally froze thinking she sounded like a fanatic, but he seemed overjoyed that his reputation had preceded him somewhere.

"Pleased to meet you as well." He paused for a moment, looking around, the sky still bright outside. The banners that had hung in the halls were continued throughout the hallway. Even the carpet was green and glimmered as if little diamonds had been woven into the fabric. Marble busts of Hughgar and other figures of Valgaard's past that Erold wouldn't have been able to place lined the hallway in either direction. He looked as if he was trying to find a public bathroom at a museum that had no signs placed on where to go. "Your father said you have a plan?"

"Yes, follow me. Elara, was it? You can come as well."

"Please, call me Miss Moon, your grace."

"As you wish Miss Moon."

They walked down the path toward the meeting rooms where her aides met in a loose association often referred to by her father and staff as the 'inner chamber' as if she had hand selected them when appointed to run things behind the scenes.

"He was impressed by you," Valessa said.

"Didn't seem like it."

"He has a soft spot for dragons. They are special to him, and it is true that they are generally only aggressive when attacked and rarely seen outside of the mountains anymore, though equally are quick to avenge another's death. You shouldn't have to worry about that in this case though."

"He made those points very clear."

The route required a few turns, angling them back toward the middle of the long palace, and eventually through the inner chambers to a small hallway, where Valessa asked Moon to wait outside, and that she could be assured no one else would be in the room, this being the only entrance of a room with no windows.

The princess keyed open the door and locked it behind them, showing the exiled king to one of her secret delights, a map that stretched from further north of Valgaard in Nole, west to the east coast of the Menetorian islands, south of even Imeria to the Miranda rain forests near the equator, showing almost all of the Haruphtian peninsula, and then finally east, beyond the boundaries of the Akrin empire to Emira and through about half of Central Ahria, complete with miniature forests, painted rivers, the borders marked in strings, and the geography of the nations displayed.

It was possibly a full third of the northern hemisphere and roughly the boundaries of the continents of West Ahria and North Olympus, though each were missing small, but relatively less important pieces such as the full extent of the sparsely populated Westernlands that stretched off the side of North Olympus. On the map were positioned clear markers set like miniature blocks, in the main color used on the flag of the different nations.

"These are the known troop positions and estimated strengths of each nation. It's how I have helped to determine international policy goals."

Erold pointed to the blocks in the center of the Akrin Empire, nearest the border with Valgaard.

"It's our current information on Akrin's forces that have not been deployed into the Westernlands. They currently have a central army force positioned in the vicinity of Akre that is believed to be nearly one hundred and fifteen thousand men after receiving recent reinforcement. It is the force your uncle fought at Elksits hill." She pointed out the red blocks scattered across the board in order.

"They also have sixty-four other divisions distributed across these four positions. These are thirty-six divisions, groups of six, three, or one noted by the type of piece, that sit in Elessia, where we believe, they are attached to respond by airship to threats in any direction."

"What types of threats?"

"Centaurs or minotaurs in the mountains here or here; yetis and giants along this line in the north of Mondelvania; ogres and trolls in this range that are not friendly. Orc settlements that are attempting to establish independence on Altonia's border with Haltvia along the south side of the Atlan. Not to mention rebellion, coups, and trying to remain close to the defense of the capital at Akre."

"Do you have those types of threats here? Why are all your troops stationed in this region?"

"We have to keep consolidated in the case that Akrin forces attempt to invade. And no, we don't respond to those types of threats. We have too many small ones, almost all north of these hills. Instead, there are independent mercenary organizations run by warlocks like your companion that operate throughout the region, and overall, have succeeded in reducing life lost to threats to almost--err--close enough to zero."

"And what about the rest of Akre's units then?"

"Here, these are twelve units in Verdas near the Valgaardian border along the Atlan River, three on the southern border with Harupht, a trade alliance ally of theirs that utilizes Akrin army attachments to respond to military threats. And, these are ten that they have positioned throughout the gulf in the east, supporting the East Cardane trade network, protecting the nation from attacks by the independent tribes that control most of the massive Mondelvanian and Emiran wild territories. We believe that, in addition to this, the private army in the employ of the East Cardane through the Akrin military, excluding these divisions, is likely in excess of two hundred thousand military personnel, which we have placed here at the south end of the gulf as they are distributed across East Cardane Shipping Company assets and highly mobile."

"Putting the total Akrin forces at?"

"Over five hundred thousand on this board alone, which doesn't include the west army attachment fighting the elven rebellions in the Westernlands. For comparison, we, in Valgaard, are nearing about two hundred fifty thousand men currently stationed in these five units as you can see," Valessa had possibly gotten too excited at being able to describe the board to someone else for the first time as he stood there not even moving to rub his cheek, "Any other questions, you seem speechless?"

"While not the main question, it's the one I want to ask first. How much does my dragon get me?"

"I estimated that you can hire one thousand regulars, possibly supported by artillery. Definitely half a mage squadron."

"That is not a lot. How did my uncle put together his force so quickly?"

"Mainly volunteers based on reputation, which frankly you don't have. Not only does no one really know who you are, despite defeating the dragon, Sven also could mobilize the local network and recruit from the militia. He still didn't have the money to support a long-term engagement or utilize cavalry units."

"Okay, and what if I purchase cavalry? How much do those cost?"

"Currently not an option."

"Isn't the Valgaardian nation historically known for its cavalry? Why not?"

"We're working on it."

"What does that mean?"

"We're in a colder weather climate." He just stared, so she continued, "that can no longer support horses. There hasn't been a military engagement north of the Atlan River that has utilized cavalry for at least five hundred years, maybe more. That's why the land you claimed, which don't think I didn't hear about, was abandoned. It had been a horse kingdom in the time of Fros."

"What about the horses I saw parading out front?"

"Unicorns."

"Ah."

"Which are one of the things that you could help with," she said, injecting a hopeful note in her tone of voice, as it was an important passion project of hers.

"I see. I'm sure you'll explain. That is the major question though. Where do I come in? One thousand troops and nobody knows who I am, up against what, five hundred thousand? What is this plan you've put together, and how does it make me more than I am?"

"First of all, don't discredit yourself, and you don't have to fight all five hundred thousand to reclaim your kingdom. They will always have some portion at sea to deal with the Coltari and other threats, as long as there are other threats. The dragon is key in multiple ways to me. Just not maybe the way you thought."

"How then?"

"One example is mercantile routes."

"Mercantile routes," he said, disappointed.

"Since my father attacked Akre, we've been cut off almost completely from international trade, which hasn't been such a bad thing but will be. In reality we are a huge country. From that line of hills to the north mountains, it's about fifteen hundred atomic miles, possibly closer to sixteen. With reductions in taxes, we are relying on increased volume, which relies on trade. Our treasury would make even more if our citizens had access to international markets. We're doing well, but we're locked out of either of the two major networks until we hopefully form an alliance with Albion, and therefore, we are unable to scale up sale of products like salt that could be shipped anywhere that doesn't want to buy from the East Cardane."

"What does this have to do with the dragon?"

"That pass, the dragon had begun to block, was the only route that we could regularly and easily move goods through to Albion and the Coltari network that feeds almost anything west of the Central Meridien."

"Doesn't Akre block the pass with their wall?"

"It doesn't matter. For now, it certainly doesn't help, but once Albion accepts, if they accept, our proposal of an alliance, which I am hopeful they will, we can sneak goods through on foot and pack mule and back again. Especially, when Lord Stone learns you're alive, I think he'll negotiate something, though he might not see us as enough yet, in which case we hope to ally with Menetoris to help cement our alliance. Are you with me?"

He looked at her with a blank expression for a moment and then he nodded his ascent, so once again she spoke, filling the silence, "And back to the question of cavalry. The cold has almost completely wiped out the local horse population, but unicorns thrive here more than anywhere else in the world. If you allow us to utilize the funds as an investment in subsidized breeder awards--"

"Slow down, aren't unicorns rare?"

"Elsewhere they are and long have been. They prefer a cold that is not quite too cold and over the long-term, require access to frigid fresh water, near ice temperatures without forming into ice, which they have in our unique lakes."

"So, you plan to institute conservation efforts like with dragons?" he asked.

"Not exactly. When we tried similar conservation efforts, we saw a reduction in population. Unicorns have difficulties in the wild, and their habitat loss was devastating their breeding pattern and reducing available food. However, once we instituted a subsidized breeder test program and promoted trade in unicorns over horses through additional subsidies, we saw a four thousand percent increase in unicorns over a five-year period, allowing us to reduce the subsidies. In short, we are effectively on track to have a heavy cavalry be once again, a pride of Valgaard."

"So, if I invest in breeder awards?"

"We believe that further embracing competition will inadvertently cause breeders to oversupply the market with unicorns, which is just what our country needs. Few people can afford unicorns or horses at current prices, and horses are still cheaper, especially because of the high mortality. They rarely survive the harsh winters and snow of Valgaard, and once again, three fourths of our population lives north of this same set of hills I pointed out earlier."

"I get it, okay. It's too cold for horses. How does this have anything to do with the plan? If you're planning to ally with Albion and Menetoris, I don't see, looking at these troop positions why you would need me."

"An allegiance between the three of us would only buy us time. Combined, we could muster a standing army of just over one million troops, excluding the private army of the Coltari trade organization, which would likely follow Albion, and would therefore offset troops of the East Cardane. Without Normany's independence, we project, using a simple mathematical exponential slope analysis on the population, that the army that the Akrin empire fields could be close to two and a half million troops by the late 1520s. They would most certainly attack Valgaard at that point, resulting in a devastation the world has never known.'

'The last battle to be fought in current Valgaard was in 1495 in an engagement of roughly eighty thousand men total, which at the time had been almost twice as large as any previous engagement in the north. My father used the victory to double his number and galvanize northern men--tired of years of defeats to the kings who sat in this very city supported by the Akre military. They marched south, took Seylil and sacked Akre, before falling back and later moving the capital here. After two years of war against the now Emperor Polesar, they were forced to surrender the mountain palace, which emphasized the need for increased conscriptions, which my father achieved. When southern troops decided not to pursue--a wise decision--the 'war' if you can call it that was over, but Akre has been looking to strike back ever since."

"Why?"

"For revenge and because Valgaard has a lot of land and resources to tap into for profit."

"I see. So, you think that if I don't retake Normany, Valgaard and Albion, especially, are doomed to be attacked and most likely fall under the control of Akrin?"

"Yes, I know we will, and that's a worse fate than it sounds."

"I've seen some of my country's conditions. I know that my people need better."

She wanted to mention what she had heard about what secretive things were going on throughout the Akrin Empire underneath the façade of the senate, but it felt outlandish and there was already enough at stake. The potential of war clearly had an impact on Erold. Talking about secret initiatives of a foreign government to run inhuman tests on its own people of particular backgrounds, based only on the allegations of secondary sources seemed empty and false.

Instead, she simply said, "In short, the fate of the world rests on whether you can take back Normany."

"One war to prevent a greater war."

"Yes."

"You've avoided it for a long time, giving me reasons why I

should accept whatever plan you propose. I'm instead thinking how could I not have accepted from the start? What do I have to lose?" he joked.

"Your life. Limbs. Sanity."

"Of course, but let's hear it already."

"I propose that you join the Varanorian Guard in Cardane and earn the money."

"Okay."

"It's not that simple."

"What choice do I have?"

"Do you want to hear the risks?"

"Not really."

"Don't you want to know how dangerous it is?"

"Just point me in the direction of what I have to kill, and I'll do the rest pretty--I mean princess."

She blushed. "Our proposal is to send you with the men and supplies you will need to get to and begin your quest as a mercenary on behalf of Cardane."

"Great," he said.

Annoyed that he seemed entirely uninterested in the dangers of the journey or of fighting for a foreign government allied as a vassal state to the senate that tried to kill him, she continued, "You will have to travel far, but if you make it to the 'city of the brass flower' you have a chance to make quite the profit. In at least ten years or more, you should make what you need in gold, which is about one hundred times the amount you are to receive in net from the proceeds of the dragon, bones, meat, and all. You will have to act as mercenaries on behalf of the enemy, but in the end, you will have your army."

"What do I get for men and supplies in this case. Much less than one thousand I suspect?"

"That's part of my plan as well. Every spring, we allow one hundred fifty Valgaardians to travel to Cardane to serve in their ancient Varanorian Guard. It has been capped at that for hundreds of years due to how many would go for the money and women. It's lucrative, but dangerous and too many people were dying. Almost every Visgollan that could go, would go, and our nation's population had suffered greatly. This year, the one hundred fifty volunteers will be a specially recruited personal elite force. The enemy must not learn who you truly are, so no more stunts like claiming territory."

"Of course. What about gear?"

"We will fashion you armor fit for an outfit of at least two hundred men, in the case you need to recruit in Cardane, from the dragon's skin and scales you provided. I have already contacted the best blacksmith and tailor to do the combined work needed to fashion the battle armor. Traditionally, the Varanorian Guard would wear dragon armor, because it is lighter and as strong as the best dwarven metal. It is only fitting that you would too. Of course, the king's staff and I will negotiate the costs for all of this from your earnings from the dragon. If you return, Valgaard will provide you with an outfitted army, and hopefully, heavy cavalry with which to take back Normany. You can think of the dragon as an excellent down payment on our alliance. And if you're capable of taking down one dragon, maybe you're capable of taming the dragon lady of Cardane, 'Empress' Zosin. Do you accept the offer?"

"Yes, it's a deal."

* * *

Three days after Erold arrived, they held a feast to celebrate the Day of Thanks on the fifteenth of Halthi-eld. The Good King Hughgar Wenselclaus had a fire built in front of the palace, on the same site where twenty men were to erect the tree of thanks the next morning to celebrate the season between this day and Lord's Day.

Hughgar felt that it was a particularly fitting way to celebrate as if they were burning trees just as they did in the homeland centuries ago, before their Normen ancestors shipped out before the winter would soon come and prevent all travel out of the old valleys now covered in ice for over a millennium. Each of the three tribes of the Normen had different cities in the old valleys, where they believed in death they would return.

Hughgar let all of the palace staff join in the feast along with the adventurers and declared that a public festival for all the travelers that had come to Peth with the dragon slayer cover the whole town. While it seemed the whole city was singing "Good King Hughgar" this Day, he also secretly hoped that any increase in sales from those who had journeyed would help the treasury, which after building the new palace, and upgrading other aspects of the city, needed to be rebuilt with the same shrewd efforts he had once used to build his first army.

"Erold, my boy, sit down, here have another beer. You know it was once customary only to kill and eat meat as a sacrifice before the day of battle. Our ancestors preferred to love their animal friends until battle was a necessity. I much prefer it this way, eating bits whenever I like except dragon," Hughgar bit into the tender dragon meat and smiled, "It's been a long time since I've eaten dragon, and I can tell you with certainty, there's nothing quite like it anywhere else, on sea, land, or in the air. Not even leviathan."

Erold sat down next to the king and took up the pint of beer guggling it down and letting out a satisfied sigh. He had had enough of the salty, strange chicken lately and instead, shifted to the lamb legs and roasted hams that the King had lain out dressed in rosemary, thyme, and sugar around the fire in a wide circle. Lamb leg, ham, lamb leg, ham. With the width of the circle of fire in front of them, Erold counted that there must be forty of each. He was certain they wouldn't be able to eat them all.

"Anything not eaten will go to the poor at the end of the day," said the King, noticing he was counting. "We have them delivered to families that sign up ahead of time on a list outside the palace, which is checked for fraudsters, and then the feast meal is delivered before the end of the night. Princess Valessa set it up."

"That's very nice of her."

"Yes, now, lad, tell me, the Varanorian Guard! I wish I had gone back in my day, but I had a rebellion to start and buildings to set on fire with evil people inside. All very exciting. But, you, you killed the biggest dragon I've seen maybe ever. Tell me what excites you the most about the thrill of a kill?"

"Your highness, I've only ever killed the dragon."

Hughgar seemed to be waiting for the next bit of the story, where Erold let out a battle cry, so the boy made something up.

"I guess it was the fear in the beast's eyes when it knew my bolt was going to make it bleed from them!"

The king let out a cheer and drank another beer in one gulp before slapping Erold on the back.

"You know, little Erold, I think you are a true Normen, like me, and that means I like you."

Erold tried to say something in thanks, but the king had had another beer given to him by an adjutant and was finishing it as quickly as possible.

"In truth," said the king, "I only had dragon once before. An old dragon who had passed away, and we had burned it in a ceremony in the north, where everyone in the fortress--Imor Valsen. Converted from a dark wizard's old tower," Hughgar burped and put the glass down. "We were all invited to taste a bit. Just not in front of the dragons, who patrolled the mountains around the fort. It's been so long since I tasted it."

"Yes, I think you might have mentioned that."

"I'll send you to Cardane with twenty warlocks. That's what I'll do--from Imor Valsen. It's where the greatest legends of Valgaard were trained for battle, the most loyal men of all. I only knew the most loyal men were from the far north, so I went there when I was young."

"Thanks," said Erold and he started on his second beer, giving up on keeping pace with the king.

The old king seemed to be fighting back tears of nostalgia and continued his tale. "It's where I learned to fight too, as a young-in. I drank their punch when I was eight after walking for forty days from Canari, because. You see. Most of them aren't magic, but I was, just didn't know it yet. Coulda died. Instead, I became more than a Warlock. The greatest of warriors. I miss the man I was then. Do you see?"

The King drank yet another beer. Start to finish as if he was drinking water. Erold was surprised the King didn't have to piss yet, given how clearly drunk he was.

"See what?" asked Erold, while watching the king's bearded face grow dour and thoughtful.

"My family was murdered before my eyes! And I couldn't be seen north of the great Atlan River, so I walked along the mountains in the south through the abandoned lands, eating once every two days, sleeping where I found places to sleep. I drank from iced over streams I plunged my hand through the ice to drink from. You see I'd done a trip like you did when you came here. And, I crossed the country on foot all on me own. Forty days and forty nights. I didn't know if anyone was chasing me, and I didn't know yet that I had the gift of the Lord's magic in me. But, when they dropped me on the glacier, in my test of prowess, to fight my way back through the snow, ice, yetis, bears, and sabretooths, I learned that I had the blue flame, because I burned the face off a tiger, to not, you know die. And, I ate it's cooked remains in front of the other tigers--cooked it with my own magic. And they stalked me and tried to get revenge, but I burned them all. The whole pride. And, I vowed then to burn the outposts of the Akrin empire that covered my ancestral land just the same way."

Hughgar finished another beer and put his hand on Erold's back, "Did I tell you about the times I rode the mammoths? Down the ice mountains?"

Volstad came by and whispered in Erold's ear, "You'll be in for a long night with the king if you let him start telling his mammoth and mastodon stories. And don't let me catch you drinking too many of those beers, either. We're not off our next run across the countryside quite yet."

"You're so little, Erold," said the King. "Look at you, look at me. I'm twice the size of you, and you took down a beast of a dragon. There are many beasts just as dangerous, and some of them are tiny too, but it's hard for me to imagine. What must have been going through that beast's mind?"

Erold drank some more beer and watched Volstad go talk to Moon as they gave some distance between Erold and the King as Valessa approached from nearby.

"You know the problem with Cardane is that you have to sneak any gold out of the--"

"Okay, father, I think that's enough of talking to--prince? Or would you prefer King--Erold, who just wanted to enjoy his beer and lamb. He's probably heard the same 'was it a mammoth or mastodon story' one too many times. Erold, can you walk with me, please? Father, did you check on mother, yet? I haven't seen her here, and she never comes to court anymore."

"She's around, somewhere. She just takes away the fun." The King Hughgar drank more of his beer and got up to walk off in the other direction, looking for his wife, the actual queen, who didn't seem to do anything but sit in her room and whine about there not being enough Bohemian salt, coming out of Haltvia these days. She needed her baths colorful.

"What was the king saying about gold and Cardane?"

"Nothing that I'm aware of, but he has more experience with it than me. Everyone goes and either comes back rich or doesn't come back. Maybe ask him when he's sober."

"Is he always like this? Serious and threatening by day..." Erold trailed off.

"Completely different person at night? We rarely do things like this. With such a large dragon, a fire this size is the only real way to, I guess, celebrate."

Erold took another drink of his beer, while looking into the princess's beautiful sapphire eyes as if ice had a color and had been placed like diamonds in front of the fire, sparkling in the same way.

She could have been saying anything and he would have

listened, but he also needed to remember to ask more about this thing about Cardane and gold, he couldn't remember that. He meant, had to remember to forget--not forget. He took another drink of his beer and focused intently on the princess's lips, watching the princess talk...

* * *

"It's been a good run kid, but we need to get moving north before the winter comes," Leif said, he winked and placed a hand on Erold's shoulder, "You're a good looking, sweet kid. I hope everything works out for you. The trip to the gulf and the getting back your kingdom."

"Don't get too sweet on him Leif. I'm watching you," said Lathin, "We'll miss you. Dragon king. Hang in there."

"You three can still come with me, if you like," Erold told them, looking at the three of them, having eaten their fill in recent days, washed, gotten clean clothes, and upgraded their weaponry before shipping north.

"I think it's the other way around. You can give up this whole king business and come be mercenaries with us in the north. We heard this is the time of year when it just gets fun," Angela was testing the bags on the side of her ram before getting ready to hop on.

"Yeah, all sorts of things start to get spooky in the winter night," said Leif.

"And what about you Kahron, are you sure you want to go back to the gulf, especially after this whole dragon business? I feel like you'd rather go for easier jobs."

"I'm not sure this turned out to be as easy as I thought it would be coming in. Besides, I have unfinished business in Cardane. Not to mention, my girl ran away from me." the Menetorian said, and he embraced the three other ram riders, who then turned to embrace Erold as well.

"Funny that this is the first time I haven't seen your shadow around," said Angela. "Make sure you don't lose her. She looks like she'd burn down a city looking for you if she thought they had you as a prisoner."

"I'm sure she would too," Kahron laughed.

Erold nodded, realizing that he had just thought that Moon might need a break from chasing him wherever he went, but maybe there was another reason she had gone off.

"Last chance to come to Cardane with us and stay here for the winter instead of going north," said Erold.

Angela jumped up and onto the back of the rock ram and settled in, "We won't go to Cardane. It's often as dangerous as this dragon hunt was, which is why we left in the first place. A lot of friends died, and we thought we were the 'survivors.' We'll have a new nickname for the band the next time you see us, but we'll be looking to make our names in northern Valgaard. We appreciate the money--you didn't have to share so much--seeing as how you were the one who killed the dragon."

"You negotiated all the deals to even get this stuff here. If you stay, you can get the armor too."

"Yeah, well, I think I speak for Leif and Lathin, who already appear to be inching to the edge of the courtyard, we don't want to be living with the shadow of our dead friends draped over our backs. I'm guessing Kahron understands that better than any of us, if you ever feel the need to ask him about why he left the 'city of the brass flower.' Besides, there are a lot of farmers and innocent civilians that need our help in the north, not the 'Empress' Zosin and her schemes. Remember Fros walks with you always."

"And with you as well." Erold said. He apologized for Moon and Volstad not being there, while the mercenaries yelled one last time, that they 'were thankful for their lives, because they certainly would be needing them where they were going' before laughing and riding off.

"It seems like we'll have a lot of time to train now," Kahron said, and he guided Erold to a room that had been set aside for the two of them to trade mage magic at any level of power. It was one of King Hughgar's favorite rooms to have designed, because he had gotten to see how many types of material, he could blow a hole through or start on fire with his sorcery. In the end, he had been able to blast through them all.

* * *

Moon thought it was suspicious that Volstad had business to attend to at the same time the mercenaries planned to leave, so she trailed him around the palace while he went a round-about way to sneak into the princess's inner chamber. He came out, clutching a bag of gold.

1513 - Chapter 22

Erold found Valessa on a rooftop balcony on the east side of the palace as the sun rose over the Lake of the Elms, the Great South Lake. The core of the city lay out before her, surrounded by the low pine forests of the green bluffs beside the lake and curling with the river through the center of the city, toward the high hill, covered in snow, where the palace sat where the north river met the west river.

"I thought it was you I saw coming up here every morning," Erold said as he approached. She turned to smile at him, wrapping herself tighter in a pelt as the icy wind picked up from the lake and rushed across the city, which began to glint in the yellow light of the sun and the bells of the churches rang to tell the city the day had begun.

"Yes, I just love this place. It's so beautiful when the snow covers the hills in white. It feels as if the entire world is glowing with light."

Erold turned left to look to the north and then craned backward to see the color of snow having covered the entire countryside for an unnamed number of atomic miles, all sparkling like one magnificent river of white.

"I spent the last two winters in Albion. They don't get much snow if any."

"Really?"

"It's true. It's almost always around thirty-two on the Odin scale, but if it snows, it tends to melt on the ground when it lands."

"I'm not sure I believe any place on this planet somehow doesn't get snow."

"I feel like you'd be the one to know."

"What does that mean?" she snapped playfully, truly unaware of what he meant.

Erold looked at her as if she was being facetious and then back out at the lake as he rested on the balcony banister with his elbows and said, "It feels like you know everything. The way you described those troops, the dragon, the trip to Cardane."

She blushed a little, but he didn't notice. He continued to stare out at the city, just the way that she liked to the past year or so and especially in the late fall and winter, to feel the cold wind across her face, easing the tension as the days of navigating advancing technology and thwarting war wore on her.

"I take it you are impressed?" She surprised herself with the way it came out as if she was trying to flirt, but he seemed oblivious and absorbed in his own train of thought.

"More than impressed."

She blushed further, mouthing but barely able to breathe out the words thank you, while they stood together and watched the lake glimmer in the rising sun.

"How far does this lake go?" Erold sounded in awe.

"It's just over two hundred atomic miles across in the direction you are staring now. If you look to the right, it's much shorter, but most of the lake is wide, especially as it gets further north."

"How do you know how big it is?"

"We had to figure it out for the room that you saw. In the end, it's just a question of simple mathematics, but it starts as just those two questions you asked me just now."

"It looks like an ocean."

"For a long time, the people who lived here thought it was, but this lake used to be multiple rivers. Each riverbed widened gradually, and when a natural dam formed at the southern end of the lake, empty lowlands were filled with water."

"How do you know all this?" Erold shook his head and rubbed his temples, glad of the icy wind, "Wait, let me guess, mathematics."

"Yes, actually, which we corroborated with records from a few thousand years ago showing how these were lowlands and marshes that the river gradually took out to sea."

"Took out to sea?"

"The river still connects through the White River to the Atlan and the Evorul at Akre in the south.

"I see, and how far north does the lake go?"

"Are you asking, because you want to know more about the path to Cardane from here, or just curious about the country's geography?"

"Both," said Erold and he looked north along the coastline again. Valessa watched him quietly.

"Two of the 'Eight Lakes,' as they are called, are connected by a thin gap of water just about six hundred atomic miles north of here. They seem like the same body of water, but they are actually different colors of blue."

"Which are these?"

"They are the Lake of the Elms, also called the Great South Lake, here, and the Great North Lake, Lake Sarafsel." He nodded, so she continued, "You won't have to go that far north though, you'll have to portage--"

"Portage?"

"In simple terms. Pick everything up and carry it across the land from one lake to the next."

"Okay, and then from there?"

"From the east shore, it's a few hours to Lake Brünn, where you'll have to row across to the city of the elves. One of the reasons you have to wait out the winter is that this time of the year most of the lakes other than the Great South and North are most likely frozen over."

"Why doesn't this one freeze over?"

"There are ice bergs in the water, but it's big enough to not freeze despite the cold of a long winter, here in the north. The lakes to the north, no matter how big they are, freeze solid as the winter wears on."

"So, we leave in early spring of next year then?"

"Yes."

"And we can't go up the Atlan from its nearest point?"

"A few reasons. The first, you'd still probably freeze to death. The second, you'd never be able to row against the current, and the third is that it technically lies in Akrin territory. They would never let you pass."

"What about Mondelvania? Isn't that Akrin territory?"

"Most of the populated parts. That portion is under Cardane's duchy and therefore jurisdiction. And, because they require the Varanorian Guard to do the ample mercenary work around the gulf to keep the core of their business moving, they look the other way. The Varanorian guard has fought for them for centuries, and these mercenaries are considered the best even if they come from Valgaard, a sworn enemy of Akre."

Valessa watched Erold's face as he seemed to visualize the route or begin to contemplate the risk. She felt he was being too nonchalant about the downside even if he had no choice.

"They will have a chartered ship waiting for you to take you south through the Iron and Emiran seas."

The door to the balcony behind them opened. Erold took one last look at the princess before seeing that Bouvedere had appeared, saying that Kahron had requested that he be found for another round of lessons. Erold nodded and departed the princess's company, following Bouvedere down the stairs.

He wanted to ask her more about the trip, and especially what they were going to be rowing across the lake, but he also didn't want to keep his master waiting. Kahron's patience with him seemed endless, but his own disappointment in his progress grew every single day.

Bouvedere escorted him through the hallways while he contemplated what if anything he could do to improve.

* * *

Day in, day out, he attacked the walls of the training room, and sparred with his master, Kahron, who moved like the wind and water, and hit like an icy rain. Their battles were ethereal, mental, and physical, testing his willpower, focus, and his endurance.

No matter how hard he tried, it never mattered. When Kahron told him to sling one hundred aura balls at the wall in twenty minutes. He threw two hundred. The next day he threw three hundred, and the next day four.

But, when he asked him to cast a simple shield spell, nothing happened. Not even a sputter.

He learned the ancient elven words of things, and he began to practice reading aloud; so that he could learn the secret names of defensive spells and of objects to call upon the forces beyond the boundaries of his skin and mind, pulling in energy and power from anywhere it could be found.

Yet, he could not achieve what he wished to achieve. Kahron remained patient, reminding him that lessons were short, but patience endured. He told him that it was easier to find the rage in response to pain, but it was harder to endure pain with patience.

Erold felt like he understood this, but at the same time, like he didn't understand enough. He read as many books as he could find on magic in the palace. Books written by scholars from all over the realms. From the Great South Island, from here in Valgaard, and from Imeria and Albion.

They spoke of simple words for moves and pulling magic from beyond himself. That it wasn't as simple as saying the right word or having the aptitude. It wasn't about belief. Instead, it was about conceptual knowledge and correct execution after achieving technical mastery over time.

Yet, how much time was the question. He read books from the Menetorian islands that were over thousands of years old, nearly original printings, with bits of paper that flaked off as he turned the pages and covers so worn that he could not read the names of the writers that spoke of auras and counter-magic as if they were second nature.

He understood the power of will, but technical mastery did not simply follow whether he put his foot in the right place or spoke the spell in the right way. He understood, instead, that sometimes a spell wasn't there to be called upon when one needed it.

Therefore, searching inside one's own mind was a skill that must be mastered. Learning and finding, waiting and adapting to the moment. He read of ancient battles between dragons and dragons, demons and angels, vampires and werewolves, between wizards in duels, and any competition interchangeable between them all.

Battles and war seemed to write the history of the world before him, wherever he searched, including that of his home, Normany and in Nole. Many of the names he recognized as names of places and tales from his mother's ancestral home in the north, and others from the history of his father's people in the south.

And even though, many names he did not recognize, he still learned from the battles of old. There were examples of simple spells and hard spells, but there were so many variations that he had not considered. Some had, once upon a time, used spells to make the very walls talk and walk. Others, such as vampires, had used spells to make people do their bidding. Still others had used them to search into the ocean's depths and wake up the monsters of the deep.

He learned that more than anything there was some kind of magic imbued in all places, and tapping into this, the power and kind of spells one could conjure were only limited by the imagination and not by what had been achieved before.

There were also warnings of old magic that even the mages of their time dared not conjure and of artificers the world over that had assembled dangerous devices, they could never control, causing catastrophes throughout ancient history. Erold had reflexively touched the orb while turning the pages.

The texts that he poured over, especially of the great duels of master wizards, made him want ever more to be able to use those same defensive spells as Kahron had. It seemed that the secret to power was not to overwhelm an enemy, but to subdue them and eliminate them as a threat. The power to give and to take power, to dictate the terms of battle, altered the course of history, whereas simple rage was a blunt instrument that could be used by an enemy's deft hand and cunning touch.

Each day he returned to the training room. No matter what the disappointment was, and no matter how many defeats Kahron dealt him, because he knew that he would discover the secret powers within and beyond himself.

Kahron would repeat, "Focus! Control! Focus! Control! Attack!" and the master wizard would lash out with a blast of sunlight that Erold would have to block or dodge while he had been in the middle of conjuring his own blast or lifting rocks by hand or throwing them as hard as he physically could. With each day that he trained, he became physically and mentally stronger, but still, no attempt at a blocking spell fizzled on his wrists or in the way of an oncoming blast, which often landed, leaving a red burn in its place, a temporary reminder for him to remain vigilant and try harder.

Soon, King Hughgar began to come daily in the early evening to observe these training sessions, and he would comment on Erold's footwork. He would tell him that he wasn't keeping his eye on the opponent. That an engagement between a beast is different than an engagement with a witch or wizard. They could strike at any moment, and even an offensive spell could be used defensively if the target changed.

He, had often fought a dozen or more mages at a time, never more than twenty, and the key had been to force them into a single engagement of force, rather than try to face them all individually one by one, when they could send five single spells instead of one big one.

A beam of sunlight grazed Erold's cheek leaving a sizzling burn, and he let out a gasp of pain.

The King chuckled, "At least you're not dodging one of my blasts, it would have taken your cheek off."

Erold wasn't amused as he felt for blood and sat down against the wall, tired at the same time as feeling as if he hadn't been working at all. It had been almost two months since he had arrived. Celebrations had come and went. Preparations were being made to leave in only a few months.

And yet, no matter how much he read or worked at it, it felt as if it had only made it feel even more like defeating the dragon had been luck rather than skill. He was no great mage. Where other people saw skill and achievement, he felt as if it had been a fluke. What's more, Kahron had actually saved his life before he had been able to use the power of the orb to overwhelm the dragon with brute force. Not skill.

"Come, my boy, there is much to learn certainly, but plenty of time. Come with me, it seems like you could use a break, and well, you'll see."

The King pulled Erold to his feet as if he was as light as a feather, patted him a couple times on his shoulder, and then he began guiding him through the halls of the palace just as the princess liked to do.

"I see you've been spending a lot of time with my daughter this winter."

"Yes, sir, your daughter is a great teacher. Is that what this is about, my liege?" If the King had turned around, he would have seen how bright red Erold was, worried whether the king who could take on more than ten mages was planning to give him a threatening speech about giving his daughter space.

He had been speaking a lot to Princess Valessa, who was not as rigid and all-knowing as she had first appeared. She had shown him the palace and some of the city, which was strange as it seemed many city-dwellers paid her little attention, despite the security that followed her.

She showed him different courtyards within the palace limits and described to him what was housed in each hall. They also sat by the fire and watched the snow fall together. They were indeed spending a lot of time together.

"I have no doubt that she has talked your ear off. My daughter and her Queendom." The King laughed shaking his head.

"Excuse me sir, if I'm being blunt, but don't you run things?"

"I do, and I don't."

"So, you mean you have her running things on purpose? I thought you were the one who helped write the organization documents for the country to be a better monarchy."

"I never had a mind for the political game she plays. That's what the country needs right now."

"As opposed to what they needed, when you did things?"

The King laughed, "Me, I'm a different kind of ruler, and I'm sure they're waiting for me to die or get much older before they come knocking again. I rained blue fire down upon them once, and I could do it again."

They continued through the hallways toward an inner chamber room and sanctum, almost identical to his daughter's, possibly right next door to each other, but entered into from opposite directions, within the palace.

After they had walked in silence and come to the door, the King stopped and sighed while he slowly prepared to open the door to the room, "But, I won the land back for my people. Not for me to play war games with their lives. There are perks, though. I get a salary, which I can do just about anything I want with. For example, my trophy room!"

Hughgar opened the doors, displaying his favorite artifacts of violence. The secret rooms didn't just have adjoining walls but were similar in the fact that each housed a personal treasure of either the King or his daughter.

"I figured I might as well finally provide you with a tour, seeing as how I never let anyone but me-self in here. And in a way, being 'royal' Normen alike, we're kin."

"Wow, this is amazing!"

King Hughgar appeared to wipe a tear from his grayish blue eyes, "I've been meaning to show you this since you arrived but wasn't sure of the right time. Most of these are the originals. I had to get some custom made. They are my hand-selected favorites from history."

"Is that--that can't be--an original of the shield of Elessia?" Erold asked, almost touching the shield as he got close to inspect the painting on the front. "There's debate as to whether it's even historically real, but this is beautiful."

"This is indeed that very shield, not a replica. This one here was custom made, out of bronze like the original, original to be battle ready, but I'd hate for the paint to come off of it."

Erold continued into the room, and upon seeing a section labeled dragon slayer, he said, "I thought you preferred not to slay dragons?"

The King laughed, "Well, I haven't but others have. Do you recognize any of these?"

"These are the twin axes of Hughgar of the Southern Isle."

"Me namesake and another Normen, though of the Norlander tribe," the King smiled, "A dragon slayer, like you, and a dragon rider, like me."

"I heard he killed the king of the southern dragons with just one swing."

"Two, just one from each axe. These very two axes."

"And this one," Erold's eyes grew wide, "This must be Brutallius's mage-blade, which he used in the battle against Domiscus in Verdas! I didn't realize he had slayed any dragons before then."

"Yes, yes, it is; and yes he did, in Imeria during one of their many blights. The only problem with a straight blade like this is that if it isn't curved, you can't cut off a limb. It becomes a blunt force instrument, which made this more of a defensive close-range weapon, helping to funnel his magic for long-rage."

"What's the point of showing me these?"

"Erold, my boy, what you may need is not something in books or in training. You might just need a good weapon!" The king laughed again and displayed more.

"You can't be thinking of giving me one."

"I have and I am. It's just a matter of appeal at this point, so take a look."

"I can't even use the spells I'm trying to cast. Shouldn't I just use a sword?"

"Erold, you have to slow down for a moment. Sometimes the greatest achievements a wizard has achieved have not been the scale of the spell, but the timing that it was delivered and the knowledge of how much of a push to apply."

"And you think that a weapon is going to help me--" Erold looked again through the hall, filled with swords, shields, staffs, and even a bow with arrows, "--How, exactly?"

"It's a conduit, you see." Hughgar touched at the edge of a display gently, poised to stroke it, "to help you focus and channel your power. Such as this one, which I used. My baby, the Hammer of Nole."

"So, this is what you rode south with into battle against the Akrin legions?"

"Yep."

"When you rode the mastodons?"

"Yes."

"Did you really?" asked Erold, skeptically.

"Indeed, we did. We must have had more than one hundred riders. We took one step over the Akrin fortress's walls, and they ran for the hills."

"So, how exactly does a conduit work?" Erold looked over all of the items and wondered if the orb would qualify for a display like this.

As if reading his mind the King said, "Some things, such as a wizard, create or exponentiate power, and then others focus it, like for example a magic wand. Who hasn't heard of a wand? I don't use one, but some do. Others use staffs. Even Kahron uses a staff, but you didn't notice, did you? You are so focused on the result and doing everything yourself that you are not thinking about the process."

"I didn't realize. I didn't even think I could use a staff without knowing the spell first."

"At this point, I think you know the spells. You've read about them and worked so hard to apply them. Sometimes, a tool such as a staff is just a way of helping guide your application. Once, you have cast the spell more often, you should be able to cast it without the staff, through experience with the type of spell you are casting."

"I see. What is the point of not using a staff then?" Erold looked at a bright, white staff on display.

"That there, is an artifact of Old Galdir, where your father is from. This staff was said to be blessed by angels. Unfortunately, you can't use it."

"Why's that?"

"The magic's left it. They say the magic leaves the item if you don't care for it long enough. It's one of my older pieces, and unfortunately, you'll need to look at another one. I have one from an ancient hero of Valgaard around here somewhere, but..."

"So, back to what you were saying, why am I not using a staff, or wand, like you said in my training?"

"Kahron is training you from the ground up, so that your spells will be much more powerful when cast."

"The books I read seem to describe that everyone already knows the spells, and they are easy to use once you have achieved the right level of focus and put them to the front of your mind. I can't seem to connect how it works."

"The old books that you have been reading are partially fiction. You can't know if it's all true. The world is still here, despite the doom they foretell or describe. Besides, that's not the point. You're one of my own kin, I wanted to give you a legendary weapon to match dragonskin armor that you'll go into battle with. Perhaps, a sword, such as this."

"I recognize this one." Erold pointed out a different blade than the one Hughgar had presented. It gave off a strange glow, "It's Io's sword, who fought for Akre against Domiscus before leaving to help rebuild Albion."

"That's not going anywhere, mind you. Though, it's mostly from my own obsession. It's rather dated. Only twenty years ago, you could get by with just a weapon like this one, like when I sacked Akre."

"Why's that? Has this one lost its power as well?"

"Yes and no. This one is a replica, so not much power. It's also the changing of the battlefield. Now, a pistol, a rifle, or a stray shot from an artillery position could kill a mage not on their guard. You'll need something that can focus your defensive magic while providing close range combat capability, like the mage blade. This next one would be perfect for combat if it worked as a conduit."

"I recognize it too. It's the 'fang of dawn' blade from the Yin Kingdoms. Is it made of a dragon's tooth? It doesn't look like any dragon tooth that I've ever seen."

"I have my unfounded doubts, but it seems legitimate. Besides, your spell shattered the dragon's teeth." Hughgar stood there admiring the blade, "It has that curve, though slight."

"Are there any that you haven't collected that you wanted to collect?"

"One thing I didn't collect that I had hoped would be easy to find when I was down there razing Akre was the legendary Kalsvebir, blade of Akre, but it was evacuated from the city along with the senate when or sometime before I arrived."

"That must have been awe-inspiring to have a city emptied out as you strode up its gates."

"Yes, though, I was also driven out of the city by Polesar, and we've been in a stalemate ever since. A stalemate your charming friend and my daughter, Princess Valessa, won't stop reminding me of."

"I couldn't take any of these. And if it's true that the methods of war are changing, shouldn't I adapt too?" He was beginning to think a pistol might be an easier option, even if they often misfired.

"Where you're going, you'll be in the fire. For centuries, men of Valgaard have made fortunes in Cardane as mercenaries. I might have gone myself if I didn't go north instead."

"Given how hard it has been to master a simple shield spell, I am a little skeptical I'll be ready to go this year."

"Nonsense. You slayed a dragon! A big one too. We all start at the floor of our potential, but your growth from there is unlimited."

Erold remained unconvinced while Hughgar seemed to be deep in thought.

"How about this, I have a mage's staff custom made for you, to go along with some modern armaments. We'll also get you a standard issue Valgaardian short sword. Something else might be too heavy, and of course it has a curved blade. My design. Along with two officer's pistols, which have a longer barrel. It'll be as if you're the head of a division."

"How much is this going to cost, and shouldn't I be using weapons without the branding on them? We shouldn't be using officer's pistols."

"I'll have two made without the markings imprinted upon them, so they aren't confiscated by foreign authorities. You'll have to figure out whatever else you need as you go. I'm sure my daughter told you that she'll be providing your force with weapons and supplies. There will be plenty of ammo."

"And what about this custom mage's staff?"

"You've made a significant down payment toward the crown with what you brought in from killing the dragon and trust me we pay a lot more money to a lot less interesting propositions. Plus, this one strikes a chord with me. A king seeking to win back his crown from the Southern Empire, though in your case, you're going east. It's my own story all over again, though my path was a little simpler. And, I didn't get you a Winter's gift. Consider it a combination of all of the above."

"Thank you," said Erold. They turned to leave the room when Erold looked again at the weaponry, "There is one thing that confuses me, though, about your collection."

"Yes, what is that?"

"You have so many weapons from unifiers, but didn't you split from Akre?"

"I like to see it as I unified my people despite Akre, rather than the other way around, but I've thought about that a lot myself lately."

* * *

"Elara, hey," Volstad grabbed her by the arm. "What has gotten into you lately? I rarely see you unless you're shadowing the kid, and you're not even doing that as often." He had finally caught her alone in one of the palace hallways, and made sure to catch her before someone else appeared.

Moon shook his grip off her arm.

"Abrim, if you haven't noticed we're in the safety of the 'Ice Queen's' palace. He doesn't need me as much right now."

"What about me?"

"I could ask you the same thing."

"Explain this to me. We seemed to have something between us, and now, I'm not sure what happened."

"I'll make this simple. Was the kid just a job to you, and I just a perk of the trip. Or was there, like you said, something else here?"

"What are you talking about?"

Someone walked by, so Moon leaned to whisper in his ear, "I saw the money you got for bringing the kid to Peth."

He whispered back, "So what if I got a little extra for being on the good team. I've learned I have to rely on me."

"I could ask the same thing to you. What about me?"

Volstad pulled her in close to him and kissed her. She pushed against him angrily and then relented. He let go for a second, and she escaped his grasp and slapped him.

1514 - Chapter 23

It was almost Ninstar, late in Gardus. Both Vetfal and Halthi-eld had come and gone with the crew of the Secondwind stuck in the city of GoldArrow since the early days of Narsi-eld. The Day of Thanks, Diamonds Day, and The Lord's Day had all come and gone as the new year had begun with quiet celebration between few members of the crew joining each other in secret throughout the twisting old city.

They had lived for a time there in relative obscurity in the catacomb-like maze of tightly packed low buildings, hiding each other from the cold spray off the Bacine sea. It became a second home.

Eduard and Ivette would slip out of the home that sheltered them and find space to laugh beneath the trees as they had lost the last of their leaves later in the warmer climate of the Imerian peninsula. In the early days, swirls of red and yellow and some green would drift around them in the slightly damp wind of the ocean.

Traversing the quiet city as enemy airships circled above, they discovered centuries old bakeries, serving chocolate and churros. They shared coffees on iron tables set along the edge of the river running through the center of the old town and watched long boats ferry patrons from one end to the other, who quickly disappeared.

The world swirled in uncertainty, but the two of them could awake each day in each other's arms and company, learning the smell of the other and enjoying forbidden fruit. In the shadows of the low buildings as the sun hung overhead, they could kiss in the corners beneath lonely arches, dripping with yesterday's rain and stand hand in hand on the quiet shore, watching the sea ships rock back and forth in the waves.

Up from the beach, between a portion of straight roads, across a quiet main street, through a narrow road that curved around an old cathedral wall, then taking the center right path out of five that met the little square at the north end of the church before taking that to where it met a path back at an angle to the left, then right at the fork, then where the path went left, they took the first right past a smaller, older church, and then followed the cobblestone along the side of an open air market, where women shopped quickly and quietly, then it was a left just before the main square, which they followed until the road had passed the old man selling iced cream where they took a right and then the first left passing many old taverns, quietly empty but for a handful of old sailors, and pretty soon the two story house, just like any other they had passed along the way was sitting quietly on their right.

Inside they found the family that had been sheltering them hard at work. The father was mending the staircase. The mother was re-sewing the children's clothes while minding a stew on a steam stove that warmed the room. They could hear the children reciting lessons to a tutor in the drawing room.

"You have guests," said the father with a smile, tanned from the sun and dark haired but for his sun-kissed long locks, like any other Imerian. He wiped sweat from his neck and forehead with his loose-fitting shirt. "They're in the back room. Keep your voices down."

Prince Eduard and Princess Ivette, exhausted from the steady climb of the walk back from the beach, reluctantly followed the corridor beyond the stairs and into the back room to find Jacquelina and Thomas sitting by a fire. Thomas stoked the logs in the rear fireplace with an iron poker, idly watching as the dying embers of an old log caught fire of a new edge of wood and began to consume it anew in bright golden and orange strands, emanating heat.

He heard them come in but didn't look up as he put another log on the fire. Jaquelina eyed them with a smiling wink and folded her hands together, slouching deeply into the plush, old chair. Ivette and Eduard sat one after the other on a velvet sofa between the two chairs, facing the fire and away from the door behind them. Thomas put down the poker, stood and after walking slowly with a slight limp closed the door.

Eduard looked between the three others as Thomas sat, and then he held Ivette's hand as she spoke, "Is there news?" It was the first time they had been visited since Jacquelina had first come to check on them.

"We came to warn you."

"About what?"

"We know you've been out and about."

Thomas and Jacquelina looked at each other, the way that parents might when trying to tell children that they shouldn't misbehave in a way that they had every right to.

After a long silence, Ivette asked, "So?"

"So, we've come to learn that they are rounding up Albion citizens along with any sailors that might have worked for the Coltari and shipping them south by train."

There was another long pause and Jacquelina spoke, "We didn't want to worry you until we were able to confirm, but you have to lie low."

"Right."

"How did you find out?"

"Some of the crew have already gone missing."

"Obviously I feared for Tom's safety. He's the most Albion looking man if I ever did see one."

"I haven't run into any soldiers. I haven't much left the flat they'd arranged for me. But, I had been keeping regular contact with my old mate, Cheval. He was investigating the disappearances when he went missing."

Jacquelina picked up where he left off, "I did some digging and the soldiers have been given orders to start going door to door with no warning. We don't know when they started, but they've been removing families from their homes, leaving everything behind just as it was. I've been to some of their houses. Children's toys all over the floor. Chairs tilted as if someone were reading the paper with a half-eaten breakfast on a table. Not even touched yet by maggots."

"How much time do we have left until they come here?"

"We don't know."

"The family has already risked so much for us."

"We have plenty of old smuggler holes in this home and others, but we'll have to be more careful."

"That's it? No other plan."

"We've been coming up with something," said Jacquelina before she nodded to Thomas.

"We've been thinking of stealing an airship and running. It seems our best option now, but — "

"Time is running out."

"Precisely."

"How many men do we need to pilot the ship?" asked Ivette.

"If you're wondering whether we can still pilot a ship despite the disappearances. The answer is yes, but barely and not for much longer the way things are going. If we lost Thomas, we might need a few more than otherwise, but even then," Jacquelina looked over at her highly regarded second in command who was well built and had hunched back over the fire, "We could manage. For now."

"Ideally we could have waited out the full winter," said Thomas, "I was getting ready for the long haul in GoldArrow, but now, I'd suggest getting ready for a different reality. We might not be getting out. No one has found a way. We're stuck between the mountains.

Every road exit is guarded by troops and just leads to more Imerians. The sea is heavily guarded, and the battleships circle the sky every day. We might not be getting out," he repeated and looked down at his hands that mindlessly poked at the fire with the black iron poker, kicking powdery gray soot into the air.

"So, how do we get an airship?"

"We don't know. The Secondwind is buried. There weren't that many in the port to begin with. Anything we could find that isn't one of the Imerian battleships itself would be merchant class. It would be slower, much smaller, and under gunned. Impossible to fight our way out with that."

"The only option is to take an Imerian ship?"

"And that would be suicidal, but possibly our best option. We might have one hundred sixty to two hundred odd men, but one of those might be staffed by as many as five hundred. They look small from the ground, but they are almost twice the size of the Secondwind. Slower, but we're stuck under the dragon's eye."

A fear gripped Eduard when he realized that his supply of silver to stop his transformations wouldn't last more than a couple more full moons.

* * *

Tom carefully picked his way through the city roads. His coat upturned over his chin. He couldn't avoid a slight limp that had been worsened by the steepness of the old town in the foothills of the mountainous coast.

Something about Cheval's disappearance didn't sit right with him. The old man, just a bit younger than himself, had been looking at the crew's disappearances from another angle. While the families of Albion men and women had been taken by soldiers in the broad light of day from the outside of town, inward. The crew had been placed throughout the city at old smuggler's haunts, and he was convinced that they were disappearing at night.

Cheval had been checking in on a couple of the younger guys almost daily. He had seen one just the day before and come to his room to find it looked as if he had never been there at all. It was as if he had been spirited away, but Cheval, from his own family experience before shipping out to sea, had known ghosts to show signs of possession like dark signals. He hadn't seen any of those, and to be targeting only the crew?

Tom may have been getting old, but he could put one and two together like anyone. He recognized the same pattern that Cheval saw.

He found the tavern where Cheval had been staying after he had decided to start moving locations, knocked on the door, locked for a midday break, and said the password to the owner with a white handlebar mustache who let him in.

"Time's is getting dangerous fast for Albion men like you and me," he said before locking the door behind him and returning to his lunch behind the bar where he munched on a bit of dried, salted fish dressed in the last of an imported mustard and wrapped by one stale slice of rye bread he had tried to fold.

Tom climbed the stairs and passed the emptied rooms, waiting for one-night patrons or the hours long shifts of night women. He eased open the door at the back of the second floor and found the room undisturbed since its patron left. The bed had been slept in, the sheets were in disarray and the bottom sheet half pulled off. The desk had a few vials of ink. One still open, coalesced around the tip of a white feather quill that had been used to fill a notebook or write a letter. Neither of which Tom could find on a first glance.

If the man had been getting paranoid, he might have been carrying it with him. The room didn't look searched, nor did it look like it had been put back to normal the way that Cheval had described. The bed would have been made and Cheval had made it a point to place all the candles in the room on the floor in a line beneath the window.

Tom opened the desk drawers. He checked under the mattress and inside of the pillow. He felt around the floorboards for a replaced piece. There were no nooks in the walls, or self-made hiding holes. Tom brushed at the sweat building at his brow and got up from the floor.

Wherever his friend had gone, the man had taken his two trusty firearms with him. He had spent a lot of money on a pair of multi-barrel pistols and there was not even an empty shell to be found. Even if Tom hadn't found a clue as to where he might have gone, he knew his friend would have gone out firing a bullet or two.

He tried to remember if he had heard a gunshot recently. He didn't live too far away from the tavern. That was one of the reasons Cheval had picked it. Safety in numbers, but it was a big city. There were rarely guns fired, and often a sound echoed through like the sound of one. Even if he could pin down a day or think of a direction with which to search, those types of sounds had a way of disappearing from memory.

When he came down the stairs, the old barkeep waived him over and handed him a half sheet of parchment paper blotted with ink on the outside like a black spot, "Almost forgot that your friend left this for you if he didn't come back the other night. He said you'd be by."

After the moment of fear passed and Thomas realized that it was just spilled ink from a shaking hand, writing fast he opened the soft wax seal and read a single line. The old barkeep sat chewing on the sandwich as Tom left. There was only a half sentence of a few words scribbled shakily, but it didn't leave much room for the imagination.

"Vampire in the sewers. Going down." It read.

Thomas's mind could not fully grasp it. They had dealt with vampires before, the two of them. But, they had been much younger then. Why he had insisted on going alone against a being more powerful than man, Tom didn't know.

He turned the letter over in his hand as he left the tavern and then recognized that the blots were not absent mistakes but a bit of a treasure map of the sewer head entrances where water poured into the city beneath the city. Tom followed them along the street, checking against the map. Even if he wanted to rush, he couldn't.

His free hand found his own two-shot .54 and where it appeared that treasure map indicated to enter, he gripped onto the handle. He had to trust that a few bullets would at least weaken the beast of legendary strength. It couldn't live in the sun, or so the legends told, so it must be in the sewer now, hiding from the entrances like this one where the sun shone through like a wall of light.

He took the pistol out as he pushed his way into the undercity and stayed in the sun, looking both ways. He checked the map while he still had the light and deciphered where to go. He couldn't understand how the beast had come to know where they all were. Had it been living with them in secret on the ship, or had it been in league with the smuggler's guild of GoldArrow to feast on the crew members passing through?

He momentarily took a break from thinking to start quietly down the side of the rushing water at the center of the sewer. It wasn't much of an underwater river, but the sides of the bank were a bit wet where it must have overrun the central walls during the light storm, they had a couple nights before.

It seemed the most likely that the vampire must have been living in the city and preying off the smuggler's guild. It made him think about the barkeep idly chewing the sandwich. So much and so little was known about them that he couldn't be certain, but he knew that they were creatures of the night who didn't eat the food of man.

Or it could have been one of them. Someone who knew all of their faces and would normally be trusted. The only two new members they had picked up since leaving Albion had been Dist and Ivette, and he had seen both of them out in the sun. Dist on the ship and Ivette...on the castle walls.

He was thinking back to all the times he had seen her in the shade when he came across what he knew he'd likely find but didn't want to see.

Cheval's face drained of life, stacked atop and beside at least forty other bodies that lined the wall alongside the rushing water. It appeared to all have been former crew, some of their bodies wet and decaying in a strange stench that seemed to be missing some of the usual rot and only smelt oddly like wet leather and building mold.

Tom closed Cheval's eyes and sifted through his jacket. He didn't find anything. Not even a bullet left behind. When he pulled at the collar and turned it down, he confirmed what his friend had surmised.

A vampire.

They had one more thing to worry about. If the Imerians didn't get them, if they didn't run out of capital, and now, whether they were sucked dry while half alive by a vampire stalking just them, one by one in the dark.

He thought he heard a noise behind him. He flipped around, gun up. How much could that do in the semi darkness. There was nothing there.

He left quickly from the way he came.

* * *

It had been almost four months in the city, and Dist had been paying close attention. The Imerians had been excavating the collapsed star fortress, clearing the rubble. To what end, he did not know, nor did he care about their initial purpose. They were doing the heavy lifting that needed to be done if he were going to be able to leave this meaningless city.

Sneaking around the dig site, between heavy equipment and stacks of rubble being set on pallets and tied together with rope or increasingly with double locked chains to be shipped away, Dist had neared the center of the work where torches and lamps lit the crater-like dig.

They had found the Secondwind weeks ago and increased their speed, sifting through the rubble. The ship had somehow remained almost unscathed by the collapsing castle around it and the frigate sized ship most certainly was being considered a prize for the admiral of the armada that had lay waste to the castle from the sky.

The Albion built ship had out run the much larger Santisma by a great deal, and that kind of speed in the open air could not simply be ignored. Ever since that the main deck had been unearthed, engineers that might have designed Imeria's latest fleet were diving into the wreckage in teams, investigating the design.

Blue copied specs had been pored over by multiple teams of men, but Dist had never stuck around when the guard had begun to swell and someone important appeared. Instead, he felt that his minor annoyances such as spilled tea, a misplaced blueprint, or untied rope around a rubble bundle were good enough.

At the center, he stood off to the side, acting as if he belonged in a suit of a miner, slightly covered in dirt like he had been working on the dig.

There it was, being readied for a test run, still filled with Orichalc. The Secondwind had been fully extracted from its formally eternal tomb.

Dist was aware that the clock was ticking for all of them in the city, even him, a survivor, and as he had watched the ship slowly be uncovered, he realized that their collective best bet would be to take it by force one night and attempt a moonlight escape to Albion.

It would be helpful if they had some sort of distraction, because even though he was sure the Imerians did not know they were here, the guard was substantial and there wasn't a man in that navy that didn't fire straight.

They would only get one chance to escape and would have to be ready. He looked around the dig, turned his head way from a few guardsmen passing that might have noticed his far western eyes and not his tanned skin.

The catacombs below remained covered for now. They couldn't sneak in that way without a lot more excavation. He could enlist a group of men to help out, but it was dangerous. If someone was picked up by the guard, the whole scheme could be revealed. He had to figure out some things for himself.

Dist had seen Ivette do magic, but he was unsure how much or what type she had. She seemed to have been a healer. She may not be much help. At least in the case of stealth.

They needed the element of surprise, though. That she might be able to help with. With a little bit of luck, something would happen soon that would give them a window to act. They would have to come up with some sort of mobilization signal that he could trust someone high ranking in the crew to coordinate throughout the ranks. Then, as soon as the best opportunity came, they could fight up the hill on either side where the Imerians had flattened the crater for the movement of goods and people between the ruins and the surrounding city.

He began to feel weak and tired, and slouched onto the pickaxe that he carried. It had been a long day and a hot sun burning brightly overhead. He had pushed through without eating, because it was getting to the point where he was doing himself more harm than good by not rationing better.

He would have to make do with what he had, especially given recent events. He touched his sore side where his belly ached and looked at the glorious monstrosity of the ship above him. Its open-air deck wrapped around the central balloon, which had survived, encased in the ancient, white dwarven metal. Considered a rarity except for some pockets deep in the frost such as where Gangüt had once stood, it had been more and more often reworked in modern times from old armor and jewels into larger and larger airships.

The old three-ram design and small island-hopping merchant ships that had long been common in Menetoris and the other islands of the Argal were being replaced by monstrous battle machines that made most dragons look small.

As if on cue, the Santisma hovered above and behind the Secondwind in the distance. If all the ships of battle began to loom as large as that object did in the sky, the wars of the future would rewrite the history books in damage wrought. Even the flying devices of the angels, hidden eternally in their floating city, would pale in comparison. While he had heard stories of their battle machines like parhelions on the edge of the sun falling from the sky within blinding rays of light, he could see this and understand that even the clockwork armies of Domiscus might fall before its cascading flames.

Men were dangerous creatures if left alone to their own devices.

* * *

"Hurry, out of the room, take the bedding with you. You must hide."

They pulled the bedding up and off the bed and followed the father of the house through the closet. He clumsily pulled a fake back off the rear to reveal a small room. He pushed them inside and then indicated a false lamp that when unscrewed could be pushed open to reveal a drop-down staircase. He pointed them upward and then disappeared while Eduard helped Ivette up the small entry way to a room filled with contraband.

Eduard pulled the small ladder stairs up into the room with them and then screwed in the light bulb, which locked the door in the upright position. After a few tries, he recognized the order of things, locking the door from the rear and screwing the last of the light bulb in from above.

Whoever had tipped the father off to the raid, he was below at the door, stating that there was no one but his family living in the house. The neighbors had seen something suspicious. He replied he may have had tenants, but they moved on before the embargo and blockade. He's only had friends over since then, but they might have stayed the night once or twice. No one likes to travel through the city these days.

A group of soldiers fought past him and began searching the rooms while the family hid in the corner of their second-floor bedroom, watching, hushed, when the soldiers came through, searching for anyone that they would interrogate further as potentially not Imerian.

So much of southern and central Imeria was fair skinned, but the north of Imeria tended to be tanner where the heat from the Argal kept it warmer in the winter months. Most of the civil wars of Imeria had been between the two halves of the nation, north and south, with each side believing in a slightly different version of the same prophet's vision of the world. At the core of each was a Chancery with similar chants and a long history with the magic, elves, and the blights that had also endlessly rocked the Westernlands before Domiscus.

Therefore, as they tore through the house, kicking out the backs of closets, they were searching for anyone with fair skin that may not know the chants of a Chancery by heart. Anyone from Albion would surely be a worshipper of the divine God through Fros, who Imerians did not completely deny had saved men, dwarves, and the free elves from the long, slave rule of the Otum. In effect, they also blamed that event for the creation of the blights as if the thousand years of suffering before the rise of Domiscus could be placed on the hands of Fros alone.

They pried floorboards up in the kitchen, started the fires in the fireplaces and inspected the basement, leaving walls, floors and ceilings torn up where they went. One of the soldiers found the empty bed, missing its bedding and when kicking out the back of the closet, found the hidden room.

He looked around once inside, sniffing the air and listening for movement. He turned on the oil lamp screwed into the ceiling, and it lit in a bright yellow. There was not even a seam in the walls of the empty, rather large secret room, making him wonder what might have been here.

"Old smuggler's haunt. Doesn't look used for a long time," the soldier said, inspecting the ground for dust but finding not even a trace of a dust bunny. Instead, it looked like it was covered in a fine layer of paint dust but it was actual paint.

"Go back down and ask the man of the house if he knows that this is here."

Eduard and Ivette could hear them moving around below. It was early in the morning, and it was the only sound beyond the creaking of the external walls. They seemed to be safe when the door to the closet shut, but Eduard held Ivette's mouth. He didn't dare breathe at all.

"Who's there?" said a voice from below with a smirk. "Did you think I left?"

Eduard kept his hand on Ivette's mouth, even though he could feel her tense in panic. He didn't dare move. After a long pause, he could even feel Ivette's body begin to slacken in his arms, succumbing to the situation. Knowing to move or breathe might be exactly what the soldier below was waiting for.

Then, the door opened again.

"Let's go. We have more houses to hit tonight."

"Yes sir."

The boots tracked out slowly, making loud impacts as they went, sending a shiver through Eduard's spine as he too began to slacken. His vision becoming heavy and dark, he let go of Ivette and pulled her sleeping form against him in the dark like a large doll.

If he hadn't been passing out, he would have thought more about time and it running out. About how the man of the house had saved their lives and likely his own as well, but the darkness of sleep overtook him.

The pair awoke later in the early morning, confined for the rest of their time in GoldArrow to this little attic. They whispered to each other, found each other and grasped at each other's bodies. Their lips found other lips, and the fear gave way to exhilaration. They had been spared, and that was all that mattered.

The exhilaration of freedom. The pleasure in each other's nocturnal form. It shook them at a spiritual level as half asleep their mouths locked again and again in sweet embrace while Eduard thrust inside of his Menetorian counterpart. There was no decorum to their sudden love.

They had slept together many times, but in the early morning, having escaped death a third time, they felt a fatalistic certainty to each other's embrace.

The night blurred into one of passion and sleep. Of making love and of holding themselves together, clinging in the sheets spread out on the floor of the small, dark room with no windows and no light but what would filter through the cracks in the walls in the morning.

Eduard held himself inside her as they fell asleep, and he had given up the fear that they might have a child together. It would only be if they were lucky. It would mean they had to escape or survive, and his duty to that unborn soul was to protect Ivette, who turned in his arms and molded her form to him. His arms curled around her from behind and he kissed her neck, sniffing her hair, and pressing himself deeper inside her.

1514 - Chapter 24

King Stone knew that the enemy would see them coming. He needed them to. They had to empty the city of soldiers to allow his men to search for his son and other survivors. Dusk was falling quickly on the fifth of Ninstar, and the ships lit the forward lights at first, coordinating their attack lines. As the last rays of light cast their dull golden glow on the edge of the horizon, turning the sky into a grayish blue hue in final light, the ships of Albion could be seen on the horizon from the beaches of GoldArrow.

The alert went up quickly. They may have been hardened soldiers but went night fell and battleships met in the dark, moonless night, would they breathe fear when the wolves of war were unleashed by the alpha, keeper of the scepter, king of the coast, Jack Stone.

He remembered the speech he gave. He had touched the shoulder of each man with the scepter, watching them change before his eyes and then commanding them. They had trained for four months to become a fearsome boarding unit. It would be ten battleships to ten, and then the Santisma perhaps more than a match for his smaller, forward brig.

They had an additional element of surprise in a squadron of three-rams that would run a first pass on the city to alert any survivors to climb aboard and escape. This second wave would hopefully catch an enemy in disarray additionally confused. On strict timing, the entire fleet would disengage no matter the cost of the battle, even if the air above GoldArrow was theirs, and escape back to Albion as one unit.

As they neared the city, in the dying light, the enemy ships had begun to form into a line of battle five to a side of the Santisma in an arc around the city, forcing the confrontation to occur above the city or for the Albion ships to disperse and attack in a scissor formation.

They were too slow in their movements and unprepared for the closing speed of the Albion ships. Some had made it to the rear hills, others were caught above the city at odd angles, attempting to run to the rear. Unable to fire openly without damaging the city, the Albion ships assigned to that battle line circled their escaping prey from their rear. Stone with the last light of day ordered the remaining ships to rise above the fray, so they would come down on the enemy in the rear in the dark as if a horse hurdling a fence.

Musket fire began to ring out from ship to ship. The odd cannon exploded, shredding ship and man from point blank. He could hear the roars from beneath him as wolves began to jump the gaps, landing on the outer decks of the Imerian battleships alongside sporadic cries of terror.

Men were thrown overboard, shrapnel ricocheted into the dark night as splashes of red fire lit the black, showing body parts flying from open holes in the hulls. Ship and ship could hardly be seen in the black cloud of war apart from chaotic flashes of pistol or musket bursting briefly through the cloud filling the sky and obscuring the carnage.

Werewolves quickly forgot their initial objectives, but still accomplished disruption, barreling through hallways and steel doors, cutting through swaths of enemy men, who had to turn inward and run for their lives. The Imerian ships drifted off course and left the battleships of Albion, largely unharmed, to turn back toward joining the fight in the rear where the battle lines of each nation began to turn and position ready to engage in a fiery display of molten rain.

As the two main lines neared each other, with reinforcements from the first engagements following swiftly behind the Albion ships, the three-rams began to sweep over the city with bright white lights. The quick losses over the city shocked the proud Imerians who could not see what had happened to their men, and until the Albion ships closed in could only hear the distant screams, the gunfire, and then the white lights drifting over the city like specters.

The firefight began. Cannons and howitzers sprouted red and black flame as black orbs of destruction flung through the air at high velocity between the battleships of Imeria and Albion. Far too many of the shells bounced off the hulls of their enemies, falling to the mountain top below. An odd cannonball shredded the ceiling of a mountain top home.

The advantage of the early battle for Albion was quickly lost above the mountain top. The Santisma cut forward and shredded a battleship that turned and attempted to ram what was left of itself into an enemy hull.

As the ships closed together, Stone attempted to separate the Santisma from the rest of the line by joining a battleship in cutting toward it. The Santisma turned and unleashed a broadside, twice the height though similar length to the smaller approaching ships. Few shots hit their mark and those that did caused minimal damage.

As ship to ship, the melee began to rage, he could feel the tides shifting further and further in his favor. He could see the forms of wolves triumphantly climbing the outer shells of Imerian ships with men in their teeth, slinging them over the edge and onto the mountain below.

Stone turned his attention toward the Santisma that retreated further and further upward and away from the ground. He followed, unsure as to what game it was playing until it had become lost in the clouds.

He stood on the forward deck, hidden by sturdy glass from the elements, watching as the dark gray clouds began to hit his ship and disperse as formless as the water they held. He had lost sight of the Santisma but could see the tail of the battleship that had gotten ahead of him.

The sounds of the battle below drifted off and the quiet of the clouds began to engulf him. They were far above the world below now. Nothing but the sounds of the ship nearby reached him, and he wondered if this is how the dragon riders of the Great South Island felt. Perhaps they felt something different in the open air, or maybe they felt more afraid that they might fall from their perches. He only had the mechanical beast to carry him ever forward into the chilly, black air.

They burst through the clouds to find the Santisma engaged with the battleship above the clouds. The starry night sky and the purple of the galaxy were behind the battle as the two ships traded muskets and cannon fire in close quarters.

The battleship's central balloon was punctured in the onslaught and in a fiery rage it began to fall into the clouds in a slow drift that looked almost like a ship sinking into thick, gray mud.

The flaming ship disappeared. Just the tips of the flames above the clouds and the fire lighting up the gray edge of the wide expanse that hid the frost below. Stone could see that the Santisma was not unscathed. Fires engulfed decks on a few levels, and he assumed that werewolves must be wreaking havoc. His heart raced.

The two ships would go to battle, and the winner would take all. The vengeance for GoldArrow would be retribution. He could hear the chanting start to grow from below deck, yelling and howling Remember GoldArrow.

The sound of the chanting grew. The Santisma turned broad side challenging Stone's brig. Then, as Stone issued orders to close the gap and strike from close range, the magnificent opposing ship, under the stars, turned and ran, taking advantage of Stone's move to port.

Stone blinked. He believed he could still overtake it, but it had left a series of small boarding ships, headed toward the approaching brig. Without having the broadside to fire upon them, he knew that he would be boarded as the Santisma began to disappear into the distance.

The three ships rammed into the side of his ship, attempting to take him down by force rather than allow him to engage the injured Santisma. His ship shuddered but it remained stable. He could hear the fighting begin, and he ordered his men to command the deck and turn toward the city of GoldArrow where they would regroup with the rest of the Albion men, and hopefully escape with his son aboard.

As he left the bridge, he took the scepter from his cloak, dropped his overcoat, and turned into the beast. He had become so much more used to it now, that the white fur bulging from his bursting naval uniform no longer surprised him or hurt.

He felt as if he was becoming just as much beast as he was already man. He followed the sound of the fighting, and he breathed easily. Some of his wolves might arrive, but he also knew what he was capable of alone.

The corridor along the long end of the ship stretched away to where the first enemy ship had stuck into the side. He could see his men fighting in front of him. Bullets, knives, and swords traded, but his men were outnumbered.

Stone advanced forward and when the opposition, ducking behind the cover of the corners of the hallway, saw him in his enormity, they began to run. The white beast lunged from the shadowy hallway, slicing forward with enormous claws, ripping legs away from those who had tripped and arms away from the few who dared to stand against him with guns.

A stray bullet sunk into his skin but then fell to the floor as he shredded the front half of an opposing soldier whose gun bounced against the ceiling still held in dismembered hands. The men fled before him for the ship that had breached against his hull.

It was all over in seconds as he tore from man to man faster than they could react. Man after man, those that fled or who tried to, he caught them and emptied the enemy breach ship. He pushed the small boarding craft, lodged into the side of his, out of his way and onto the mountain below, and his men ran before him to attack the boarders from the next ship.

He peered out the hole on the nearing city where the battle raged on the hill, apart from the Imerian battleships that could be seen retreating just off the edge of the firelight. From ship after ship, either waved the flag of Albion or was actively being glided into the mountains around the city.

The sea ships were scattering. Albion had broken the blockade on the Coltari ships. The city was at war too. On top of the hill where the castle had once stood, there was pockets of gunfire and mage blasts as two sides fought for something in the dark.

The lights of the Secondwind came on, revealing the frigate, patiently sitting within the crater of the old castle. Stone did not know what to think, but then atop the hill on the front end of the ship, there raised the flag of the Coltari with its two orchids and he knew it must be his son or Jacquelina.

Upon sight of the flag, empty cannon fire erupted from every Albion ship in celebration. The exploding flash of clouds ricocheted throughout the sky and then the ships in the bay began to fire muskets into the air in response.

Ahead of him, on the brig, the fighting had taken a turn for the worse, and he turned to see his men being caught again in a close quarter fight. Even in this beast form, he was at risk of being taken by too many bullets.

Stone turned to face the boarders, and suddenly Onya in werewolf form strode forward to join his men and began to tear apart the enemy soldiers. He had told her to stay in Bowery Place, but she had not listened. The little will of the wisp that had not stopped following her in the building was at her shoulder, and the two began to wreak equal havoc sending body parts flying. They fought ahead clearing the ship until the third breacher had jettisoned itself into a terrific freefall to escape the claws of Albion.

As they descended, he could see the Secondwind was out over the bay. He turned back to man as Onya changed back as well. The fight had gone well, but it was because they had surprised the enemy. His men were regrouping and turning their ships to follow the Secondwind as the Brig descended toward the center of the city.

Stone held Onya close to him and briefly thought about attempting to hold GoldArrow before he saw the glint of light in the distance revealing that the enemy ships were waiting to potentially take a run back at the Albion force floating above the city.

Stone returned to the bridge and ordered the signal be distributed to retreat. He hoped all of the men who had boarded ships would not be abandoned like those who had allowed the

Santisma to escape his brig. They had strict orders on how and where to return.

He could try to end the fight once and for all now, but there was more risk than he was willing to take. They may have lost GoldArrow, but if his son was one of those piloting the Secondwind then they had accomplished their goals.

Once the city had begun to disappear again into the distance, the wind of the open holes in the hull began to worry him less and he held Onya close, looking down upon the black Bacine sea as it rushed below him back toward the shore in tall, white cresting waves.

1514 - Chapter 25

"GoldArrow was a victory!" Polesar yelled to silence the crowd of senators that watched him, waiting like sea monsters or sharks, for him to make a false move. He took a moment to settle himself while surveying the crowd.

Senator Karlson who was acting as chair for the meeting, motioned for one of the senators to take the floor. The man brushed off the invisible lint on his trousers, shrewdly smoothed his mustache and puffed on a lit cigar, "It doesn't matter if you feel that way. What matters is significant damage done to a port that we control. Reports state that the castle was destroyed and the enemy." He paused puffing again on the cigar, "absconded with all the goods on the trade ships in the port!"

Polesar watched the man where he stood. His black eyes staring back through the smoke. The thick gentleman's mustache on the senator's upper lip was neatly groomed. Polesar had heard a different sequence of events, but Tanneran had spun the story brilliantly.

"What have you to say to that?" Karlson glanced away from Polesar, as he tapped the char off the edge of his cigar, "Emperor, your majesty." The new Emperor stood before the senate, unarmed and in white, regal dress with a gold eagle on both the front and back of a tightly fit tunic. His yellow eyes caught the light.

"Yes, the attackers destroyed much of the city in their attack as well. Debris from the air battle was scattered throughout, injuring thousands of civilians. But, the battle was won. Three ships were lost. Four were destroyed."

"That seems hardly a victory when the port was lost!" yelled another senator.

"Might I remind you, we didn't lose GoldArrow, but we might have. Loyalists acted fast and seized the port after the rebel king seceded Albion from the union of our nations. If Captain Graneuva had not won GoldArrow on behalf of the empire, our position in the Westernlands may have been jeopardized long term."

"There's nothing in those lands. They are empty. The blights wiped them all out."

"Precisely why it is a land of opportunity for the empire. We vote today to embargo goods shipped by the Coltari to the east, cutting them and effectively Albion off from profiting any further off the lands of the empire."

"Yes, yes. We were provided an agenda," said another senator, who spoke out of turn, not having waited for Karlson to select him before standing and addressing the crowd gathered to gain clarity on the crisis in the west. "And what of GoldArrow? If it's such a strategic position as you imply, how can it be defended? A cursory force of Albion ships destroyed the fortress there and were able to escape. I have reliable reports that the *now* royal family of Albion was there, under our noses, and that the implied heroic efforts of your Captain Graneuva do not make up for the fact that as we dither away here, a treaty may be being signed between our once splintered northern enemies, old and new."

"GoldArrow will be rebuilt better than ever and now fully under our control. With respect to, as you say, your implication of risk with respect to the alliance in the north, for the safety and security of the empire, the states of Imeria are a far more important ally in the wars to come."

The senator, seemingly satisfied though perhaps doubtful of the validity of the emperor's assertions, sat down. The concept of wars to come seemed to be a rainbow in the dark that left him deep in thought.

Senator Hammel now stood, "And what of trade now? Explain how we overcome the loss of any shipments of Orichalc coming from Albion."

"I am pleased that you ask that question," the emperor smiled at the planted question and the old friend. He nodded carefully and met Hammel's eyes. They both knew that trade with the Coltari had almost dwindled to nothing, except for a few parts of northwestern Imeria and the most remote northern towns, on the border of Normany. They did need to address the issue of limited Orichalc supply as the technology was increasingly adapted, including city lamps in Akre itself. In closed meetings, they had decided to expand military operations in Mondelvania.

"There's been a rebellion in Mondelvania in the northwest, stretching to the border with Emira. Normally a fractional force could suffice to respond, but we plan to use this as an opportunity to annex the Orichalc hills from the dwarves of the seven kingdoms. We can do this after carefully expanding the northern borders of the empire through establishing new garrisons in the north in response to recent crimes against the senate by the rebels. The dwarves have traded freely with both us and Valgaard for years, and it is time for retribution if they do not side with us of their own volition and kneel to the eagle. The dwarf clans are splintered, and while Mondelvania is a key, resource rich nation to their south, the Orichalc hills are the real prize. We will take the hills and permanently control the largest mines of metal and Orichalc in the world."

He had been surprised at how much of an uproar the battle for GoldArrow had caused among the elected men who sat in the Lion's Den on behalf of city guilds and localities, but he was not in any way prepared for the sheer jubilation with which they appeared to approve of beginning phased military operations in the far and icy north.

They clamored to speak and raise praises on their Emperor, who they had known from the start to have the best interests of Akre in mind. There were many remarks of the greed of the Dwarves, who never shared and did not participate or join the cities of men. Their underground churches and clandestine services to Fros were orthodox and did not follow the supreme priest and the missive of the church of Elessia, whose message had finally begun to supplant the wild views that had come to dominate the Church of Akrin in the days of King Karles II.

Polesar could not keep track of all that the senators said, but in short, their admiration and exultation crossed every facet of the nation's industry, economy, and future. He was soon dismissed to roaring approval, and in the hallway, he stood alone to soak in the sound of continued cheering through the thick doors. The small events of Albion, which had occupied them for months as an inevitable failure to have acted soon enough in relinquishing legacy rule in a small but rich region, and GoldArrow, which the senate had only known of for days, had disappeared into old news to be revisited as a victory in future stories.

Tanneran exited the room moments later and motioned him to take a walk through the halls surrounding the main chamber, "An exciting development. Before you worry too much about whether their enthusiasm is less pronounced as it appears, it is not. They are hungry to put the war machine you've built to the test, and any excuse to flex the might of the empire, may soon be met with similar, as I said, enthusiasm."

"Is this what you were meaning to talk about, and should we wait for Alger?"

"The less a mage knows about some things the better, but I assure you he's been briefed on the subject."

Polesar nodded as they passed all the meeting rooms and came to the back hallway, which meant they would soon be halfway around the central auditorium where they had begun.

"GoldArrow may have been a victory, but we received intelligence that it was more than the royal family joining a raid on the city."

"I'm aware that the city was besieged for a few months. You did an excellent job in containing and redirecting the prevailing story."

"No, that's not what this is about. And I do thank you for the praise. It appears that both the now crown prince of Albion and a princess of Menetoris had been trapped in GoldArrow during the siege."

"How did you find out about this?"

"As some say, I have my ways," Tanneran played with his sleeves awkwardly and looked slyly at Polesar who returned a warm grin.

"How long have you known?"

"Not long."

"You've done well to contain a volatile situation, but learning of this in the way that I have has made me wonder if someone knew this sooner and could have acted on this information, why didn't they?"

"Good point," Tanneran grinned again. "It doesn't bode well if information like that was withheld when it could have aided in decision making on how to proceed with let's say, a delicate situation."

"Though on the other hand even if we had known, we couldn't have done much else than take them prisoner without further aggravating our new enemies, and that would have accomplished nothing different."

"Perhaps you are right, but someone's been keeping secrets from you. Your quick rise must have ruffled some wings. You would do best to focus on the task at hand, or perhaps evaluate how else to win the senate over to your side."

"Perhaps I can accomplish both. To ensure the success of the mission in Mondelvania, I plan to oversee it personally," Polesar smiled widely and slowed their walk as they neared the final turn, back to the entrances to the chambers where deliberations would continue for perhaps hours.

"Is that wise?"

"Many of these missions have been meeting stiff resistance while our mages are unable to subdue competent locals in various

disciplines. There is not a mage in the world that could defeat me."
Tanneran chuckled darkly, and Polesar had to wonder if there was
something else, he hadn't shared.

"We can't have you fighting all of our battles unfortunately,
especially as our borders continue to grow. Even then you should be
careful."

"Being too careful is the sign of a weak-minded man. Once the
reforms go into full effect that Alger and I have designed to
systemize university education for all our nation's mages, there will
be no need for me to test my staff on the field. Until then, I am the
best."

"You may be right, indeed, on all accounts" Tanneran touched
him playfully on the shoulder and instead of shaking his hand,
bowed low. "I hope to see you a few more good times before you
travel north."

"Certainly, master Tanneran. Good day," Polesar nodded curtly
back to the backpedaling gentleman as he made his way to a side
exit.

"Give my best to Empress Aurelia." Tanneran said and he
disappeared in almost the same moment that Hammel and Alger
exited the chambers.

Hammel smiled broadly, "What a job well done today. I've never
seen someone handle their talking points so well in front of the
assembly."

"Thank you, and why aren't you in there?"

"I'm not a voting member and there is an odd quorum today, so
I am not required as a tie breaking vote."

"I see," Polesar looked over at Alger as they exited to the marble
steps overlooking the city directly to the east. The emperor was on
his way to the rebuilt palace compound in the north to see his
blonde-haired beloved. "Archmage Alger, did you have time to
discuss the standards of mage training to be instituted at
universities, starting this fall with the high council of Justicars?"

"No, I'm afraid I did not, but I am still amending and reviewing
the document. I don't know how you wrote it all in one sitting."

"Please revise it at the soonest my good friend. We must ratify it
to begin training professors before I leave for the summer."

"Yes, yes, I hear you, my emperor. I will address it with those
members of the council that are on the campus now. I will have
copies made, and we will review it together. Now, I must take your
leave."

"You are dismissed archmage," said Polesar, nodding back as the man bowed and took his leave toward the high council building at a brisk walk.

"Still planning to build an army of wizards?" asked Hammel, mockingly.

"Always," said Polesar in a monotone note like a pan being struck with a mallet, as he watched Alger walk away. Off to the right, the factories were in full effect just across the river, pumping black smoke into the air, which fell off to the east away from them. The largest of sea ships circled in the river to go northeast or southwest. The ancient castle of King Karles I lay to the southeast across the river. The old town surrounded it on either side of the river just to their south, beyond St. Drosef's Cathedral.

It was there that Polesar went every morning and twice on Soldays to pray. He could be a part of the people and hear the Godspell of truth. It troubled him today, with what he had heard of Graneuva's actions in GoldArrow, that the faiths of the Akrin Empire were splintered. Even if Cardane followed Fros like them, he did not trust that the will of the supreme priest extended within their realm too, and the states of Imeria followed their own prophet.

He was not as concerned with the limited paganism throughout the nation, or the Utaurans who long awaited their own prophet and their own land. These were small groups, but while glad he had easily consolidated the church leadership of the Church of Akrin under the supreme priest in Elessia with the help of all parties, he could not easily do the same with the distant vassal states.

"What's troubling you?" asked Senator Hammel as they rounded the building through the gardens that filled the campus of buildings with green vitality during the summer months.

"Nothing, nothing," smiled Polesar.

They walked together in silence through the gardens. Polesar examined the curious fruits, frozen on the outstretched branches in a state of living death, iced over in the night and juicy in the afternoon sun of a particularly warm day.

"They're beautiful, aren't they?" Hammel remarked and motioned to the Lyse flowers lining the walk as they were now halfway around the northern exterior of the senate hall, mirroring the same path that Tanneran had walked with him inside the building. Polesar looked up to the sky before glancing at the flowers that bloomed even in ice.

"I'm sorry my friend. I've been in my own head. I wish I could be more talkative."

"The nation doesn't run itself," said Hammel. He turned to the side to look at Polesar under the intermittent shade of trees, devoid of any life save the frozen fruit.

"Precisely."

"And it's your first year of being Emperor. It makes sense that it feels as if there is more pressure than you would have felt before accepting the coronation."

Polesar nodded. The sound of galloping horses grew louder as they neared the busy street of Newkassel Avenue, which was the old road south that ran along the old river to Newkassel and was now being replaced in importance by the train lines. Many new money players had entered that new dominion, and it remained to be seen how it altered the City of Gold, Akre. There were many sayings of the city, but all amounted to a city of perennial change.

The galloping got louder, and Polesar tensed ready to unleash a mystical barrage. It was nearing them around the corner of the great marble building. A horse neighed, and the rider became visible through the naked trees as the beast burst forth at a hard gallop on the gentle curve of the ornate marble path.

"It's Murdot," Polesar almost laughed.

"Who?"

"One of the field marshals in the legions."

"Ah," nodded Hammel.

"He's a rising star. Maybe the best. Not including myself of course."

"My emperor," laughed the young mage as he neared, "I've been looking for you." His long, curly black hair flew in the wind like a little cloud. His piercing blue eyes matched the color of the western sky, unblemished by the smoke of the factories that lay behind the emperor.

"What is it?" Polesar stood attentively, ready at a moment's notice to spring into action.

"Only that I've just arrived for my commission. I was told I could find you at Saint Drosef's or the Den. And if not there at the palace," cried Murdot, happily.

"I thought this was an emergency."

"Nothing of the sort. I'm looking forward to serving with you in Mondelvania."

"Your position is well-deserved Field Marshal Murdot. You will be one of the three highest ranking officers to assist with the operations."

"Will there be enough for us to do?"

"I am sure Master Murdot that like any mission you are tasked with the for the legions of Akre that this is of the upmost importance," said Hammel.

"Precisely," nodded the emperor, "And to satisfy your curiosities as to why we're moving so many troops north. It is not just to ensure success. At the core of this mission will be the final tests for establishing a modern system for the field, never before used, that may end up being the defining factor in the military history of not just our nation but all nations."

"Ah, I appreciate the clarity," said Murdot fighting a yawn, "Do you have time to discuss now?"

"The empress is expecting me home soon, but we can ride to the palace together and speak there. She may be upset, but it is no matter."

Polesar hoisted himself onto the horse behind Murdot and looked back at his friend Hammel below. He presented himself as the perfect gentleman standing near the Lyse flower trees with one hand in a pocket and a slight smile.

"Before you take your leave, my emperor, I should say your request to increase conscriptions in response to news out of Valgaard that their military has potentially doubled has been approved."

"Excellent, thank you. Now, Murdot, let's be off. My lady awaits. I told her not to wash until tonight."

The boys laughed and Murdot turned the horse around to rush to Newkassel Avenue and north to the palace gates yelling, "Make way for Emperor Polesar, the great!"

* * *

Later in the evening, he and Aurelia were alone in the enormous palace bedroom. The stars shone brightly, illuminating the glass windows that overlooked the small White River, running off to their left in a curling meander on its way from the north to connect those many lakes to the great Atlan River that ran from far to the northeast in Mondelvania and the mountains even beyond the Orichalc hills.

Only a small, glassy trickle remained of the glimmering water, but the wide basin it once carved turned it into a work of natural art in a softly descending canyon, visible as many shades of purple in the soft light. A natural dam of sorts had fallen many millennia ago in a place whose name time had forgotten, creating two of the great, eight lakes that now filled much of the elven lands.

On this night, Polesar, resting on the bed, was transfixed by the black water as it twinkled white in the shadowscape as if it caught only the light of the stars above that filled the sky. A pianist, violinist and concert bassist that Polesar had the staff hire were still playing pieces in the gallery below. Slowly, they played, and the music lofted lazily from below filling the quiet, cold winter air with something other than the rattle of the windows or the brush of the trees in the breeze.

"My violet, why must you go?" asked Aurelia as she stood, wrapped in only a dark blue silk blanket with white embroidery, near the open windows that led to an overly large balcony, almost the size of their bedroom.

They had already made love, and Polesar came up behind her and hugged her with all his might, nibbling on her ear, taking in her nocturnal smell. The scent of her skin. The faintest touch of perfume that remained in her hair. He could taste the sweat when he kissed her shoulder and then traced a line back to her ear along her shoulder blade with his lips.

"I will be back before the summer is over, my darling."

"And what if you are not?"

"I will be."

"How can you say that with certainty? How can you love me and go away?"

"By the power of truth, I, while living have conquered the universe," whispered Polesar.

"Mister Rolard, you've conquered nothing and don't quote Domiscus to me. I recognize her words."

"I've conquered you and you are the universe to me."

A chill ran down her spine, "Hold me tighter."

He stared out the window beyond her. He had expanded the empire considerably since first becoming a general in its ranks, but it wouldn't be his legacy as general that would stand the test of time. It would be what he could now accomplish as emperor, and he thought to himself, looking to the left into the endless black of nothingness that stood between Akre and Peth, the capital of Valgaard, almost directly to the north from their palace, where their bedroom faced due east: "history would ultimately judge him on whether he could conquer the white city in the north."

It didn't matter whether he had defeated elven tribes and coordinated colonization in the Westernlands, purposefully distributed overseas colonies on trade routes across the Otum Ocean to take advantage of the East Cardane, or negotiated absorbing Cardane as a formal vassal state while fighting uprisings and border wars across the empire. Only his ability to take back that which was taken would prove he was indeed Polesar the Great and not Polesar the Fool.

"I don't want you to leave."

"I must."

"I think I'm pregnant Polesar."

"When will you know for sure?"

"I don't think. I know."

1514 - Chapter 26

Valessa kneeled in her dress carefully, feeling the soft carpet beneath her knees and making sure not to tear the tight fabric, stretching across her heels. The dark room smelled moist with a touch of lavender and iron.

The young princess took up her mother's hand as she often did when visiting alone. Her mysterious illness, consumption, had overtaken her quickly, and her father, in denial, had merely called to her the best mages in the land. None could yet solve the riddle of the body giving up on itself.

Valessa let her head fall slowly to rest on the lukewarm, overturned hand of her mother. She looked up, hoping even to see the listless, gray eyes, register life.

They did not. Instead, her mother coughed, squirmed in her sleep as her eyes darted back and forth beneath her eyelids, and then she coughed again. A thin trail of red phlegm flung out from her thin, unpainted lips. As she breathed in, it slowly drifted along the pillow, being swallowed back until Valessa lifted a handkerchief to silently dispose of the bloody spit.

Valessa had prayed for many things, but this one, she felt powerless to convince a higher power to intervene on. She had asked so much already, and while she knew that God did not trade in miracles, she believed that she had already asked so much on behalf of her nation.

"Valessa."

It was her mother's voice. Weak, but she was alive.

"Mother! I've missed you!"

"I heard you were hanging around with a boy. What's he like?"

"That's the first thing you ask about?" Valessa reddened and then felt ashamed at herself for being upset at all, as her mother's eyes grew grayer and the recognition of light faded faster than she could speak.

"Find a nice boy my princess, like your father." Her mother trailed off and closed her eyes. The princess kneeled there, waiting for more, but the realization that she may have missed her last chance to speak with her gripped her heart, and an icy chill ran up her spine.

"Valessa."

The princess's eyes shot up. Bouvedere had entered the room and quietly waited at attention near the door. He didn't seem in particularly a good mood this winter, and she watched him from the corner of her eye as she stood. A blank expression had replaced his once smiling face, and he hardly seemed to notice that the lights in the room weren't in the same positions they had been the night before. It was a game they used to play when she was a child, and even though she didn't always feel like one, she wanted, today of all days, to be treated like she still was that little princess and not the ice queen that they called her behind her back.

"What is it my dear Bouvedere?" she asked. She watched his eyes. He made no expression in the limited light from the open doorway and that which filtered in at the edges of the long window curtains.

"Odessa has a message for you," Bouvedere whispered into her ear as she followed him out into the hallway.

"What is it? Did she say?" Valessa asked, attempting to mask her excitement. With Arla still stuck under temporary house arrest in Menetoris, despite not being the reason the princess Ivette had gone missing, and since Onya was likely due to get married any day now in Albion, the princess's usual chain of strict rules had been slightly relaxed, but mainly to allow her personal handmaiden, Odessa, to help her be in two places at once while she spent time with Erold and Seaspirit, who he constantly attended to during the long, dark and cold fall and winter months. With the weather also slowing the letters from the west, Valessa was desperate for news.

Odessa waited at the end of the hall with the slight curve of a smile at the edge of her delicate lips. She nodded to Bouvedere who returned to Valessa's mother's door. He had followed her for a few steps but nodded and returned to his place.

The two women walked further toward the front facing windows of the white palace's third floor to overlook the forward lawns where a unicorn practice dance took place under the supervision of a young lieutenant general from Normany, Garold Milton, who had defected from the Akrin army after serving for a number of years in the Westernlands, defending settlements from the attacks of the elven tribes that were wary of and violent towards men.

They walked in silence along the windows for a time, watching the large unicorns parade with their sparkling, soft pink horns, strut about the lightly snowed over courtyard. The green jackets and the gold detailing of the cavalry looked crisp and pristine. The young Milton looked intently on, absorbed by his work rather than the pageantry of the exercise.

Finally, the pair of women came to a point far enough from the staircases, or other members of the house to step into a statue's nook and discuss whatever turn of events had prompted Odessa to interrupt Valessa's time with her mother. The young woman fit neatly behind the bust's head and her petite form slouched against the wall with her blonde hair falling against her shoulders in a nonchalant manner.

She appeared for a second like the picturesque beauty, molded as if from the same cast as the marble beside her, comfortably settled against the wall like just another statue with one arm pinned against the wall to hold her there. She looked at Valessa with her smiling, bright blue eyes as the princess stood closely beside her, leaning into hear her whisper in her ear.

"King Stone of Albion launched a surprise attack on GoldArrow and has successfully rescued the prince of Albion and princess of Menetoris. Onya confirmed the news upon landing in Rorik. They sustained some losses but were able to inflict a significant blow upon an Imerian air fleet."

"This is incredible news. We'll have a treaty at last," Valessa smiled, and she leaned in to awkwardly attempt to hug the woman stuck into the corner. The two pulled apart and looked at each other in the small alcove. Valessa felt for a moment, eerily, that she was looking into a mirror.

"I have to tell Erold," Valessa thought aloud. Odessa's smile was unwavering, but her eyes appeared to drop slightly as if she had relished in the opportunity to share in this private, good news with the two of them alone.

"He'll appreciate the news my lady," said Odessa.

"It relieves a lot of pressure," Valessa said, thinking of Erold and then thought of herself as well.

"He's a good-looking boy too. There are worse men and worse princes in the world."

Valessa nodded and though she tried to appear aloof, she let a touch of emotion show in her voice, "There is a lot of time before anything of that sort needs to be decided."

"Quite," smiled Odessa, with a knowing smirk.

"Come, let us stop by my mother's bedside once more, and then we'll climb to where he's attending his fitting." The two women briskly followed the hallway back to where Bouvedere stood as stone-faced as ever.

Valessa nodded and Odessa curtsied as the pair quickly went

inside the room. Valessa leaned over her mother's body, half revealed by the light of the doorway, fully clothed and mostly tucked beneath a plush, purple comforter. She whispered the good news into the woman's ear that war would not be coming to Valgaard this spring after all, but when the princess watched the queen's face, it seemed that she was fast asleep. There was not a movement on the mature, yet still beautiful face or from her wan limbs to register that she had heard her daughter enter the room at all.

* * *

Valessa found Erold still with the tailor, getting fit for dragonskin armor. She spied him from the doorway, admiring his increasingly toned physique. The tailor was struggling to fit the dragonskin armor over his arms, so she could see his tight chest muscles, bristling with short curls of blonde hair and the top half of his abdomen in four sharply defined abs. She found herself idly wondering what the rest of him looked like.

The tailor hadn't been putting the suit on. He had been taking it off. The old man had worked it upward to get it over the shoulder of the much younger man and was now sliding it down Erold's back while the two of them were half turned away from the door left slightly ajar. The armor went lower and lower, sliding down to his midriff where trousers disappointingly began.

"My lady, what can I do for you?" asked Volstad from behind her.

"I tried to stop her," said Odessa.

Erold looked up with an idle glance to see the princess and her maid standing there staring at him. He seemed unbothered in the slightest and it mildly infuriated her.

"Valessa," Erold nodded, as the old man pulled the dragonskin cleanly over a pair of baggy, brown full length trousers that had been hidden beneath the armor.

"Those look a little big on you," Valessa said, stammering for a moment in search for something to say.

"So was the armor," said Erold and then as he slid a shirt on over his toned body, he motioned to the purple and black suit and asked, "Did you happen to see it on?"

She shook her head, "No, I just arrived."

Erold could see Volstad's amused look from behind her, but he simply shrugged, "It was a little big."

The tailor waved a hand, "It takes a skilled blacksmith and tailor together to make this armor for you. It was as close to perfect as it could be without ruining it on the first try. We could take it in, but we think he'll grow a little more. He's a young man."

"Thank you, sir," said Valessa, "We appreciate your efforts, and perhaps you're right."

"Of course you do, and of course I am. I know that, but he needs to know that. And, he's lucky he's got a few more inches in him at his age. He could be stuck that way," he grinned, revealing a pair of fake golden teeth. Valessa chuckled when Erold blushed, and she stepped into the room, running her fingertips along the edge of the armor, resting on a headless mannequin.

"Is this the final color?" Valessa asked as she stepped around Erold admiring the way the shirt hung over his shoulders.

"We wanted it to look as close to the natural color of the dragon after working with it. It's hard to keep any paint on scales anyway."

"I see," said Valessa.

"I like it," said Erold.

"You heard him then. That's all that matters," Valessa smiled at the old man. "If you have all you need then, you are free to go."

The old tailor nodded, "I'll make an adjustment or two, but he should be able to wear it for years without it wearing it out. If he grows too much taller, he'll have to exchange it for one of the spares, but it will last him a lifetime if not." He whistled as he packed up his things. "Dragons aren't exactly like snakes you know. They don't shed their skin, otherwise the trade of dragonskin wouldn't be so difficult. You won't have to kill another one for your life though. Not good, not a good thing to do. In general, I mean. I know this one had it coming, but you don't have to kill another. If you do though, let me know, and I'll do the work for a fair fee."

While the old man blabbered on, Volstad came into the room and sat in a chaise set beside the window. Odessa waited patiently at the door to the room.

"What is it that you wanted to tell me?" asked Erold once the old man had left.

"Albion has bought us time."

Erold looked at her dumbfounded for a moment and simply asked, "How is that?"

"I'd presume it's because they were able to do some damage to the Akrin war effort. Is that it?" Volstad said, crossing his arms and watching the princess.

"At some point Erold you need to stop asking questions and start answering for yourself. You're a king, you better start acting like one soon," Valessa said, a bit annoyed at Volstad for ruining the moment when she shared the good news, though Erold's facial expression did not change. She wondered if that's because he didn't understand the meaning of the news, "Do you know what this means?"

"Abrim," Erold said in an assertive tone, "Can you please leave us?"

"Certainly," the old man stood and went to the door, pulling Odessa out with him and shutting the door. The two young royals stared at each other for a moment, then Valessa stood and walked to Erold, leaning her lips close to his.

"You wanted to get me alone?" she asked, and she closed her eyes, imagining this was the moment they shared their first kiss as the whole of the world stopped crumbling around them and for the first time in all her years of memory everything seemed perfect.

"Yes, princess," he said, "I appreciate everything you've done for us. I really do." He grabbed her shoulders and looked deeply into her eyes as her lips began to slip further back away from his as he strongly moved her away.

"Is there something else you want to say?" she felt herself cringe and her stomach turned over a bit.

"Yes, as a matter of fact. There is."

Valessa stepped back and then couldn't keep still in the silence, waiting for him to speak. She circled Erold once more, as she had when she entered the room. Erold remained in the center, surrounded on all sides by mirrors trained on his physique. He watched her as she passed in front of him and then followed her in the mirrors as she circled behind, admiring and judging him all at once.

"As you've said, princess, I've been asking a lot of questions, since I came here."

"You have."

"But, I feel like there are some things you've been intentionally withholding from me."

"Pray tell," she said and smiled, flirtingly.

"Don't mock me," he crossed his arms, and his biceps bulged at the edges of his tunic. "We could talk again about the fact that the Ithlin states are rich. That the Verdasian and Altonian lumber mills are working overtime, or that gaining Albion as an ally gives us access to their Orichalc supply as well as that of the dwarven kingdoms, but none of that matters if I can't trust you anymore."

"Where is this coming from?" she asked. He looked at her,

slightly amused.

"You have information on almost every meaningful place in the nearby world, I start asking a lot of questions, and you don't stop to think that I might eventually ask this one question?"

"And what question is that?" she asked and stopped right in front of him.

"Answer honestly now," he said.

"Ask," she replied, looking up into his ocean blue eyes. Her mind swirled.

"If you knew so much. You must have known where my father was on the night that he died."

"Doesn't everybody?"

"You know what I mean. You knew ahead of time, didn't you?"

The princess hesitated, thinking of Eleanor and how she had been betrayed and just when he was about to speak, she blurted the word, "Yes." A woman so close to her for many years had been the one to be working against her this entire time. It still pained Valessa to think about, but the reality was that she had gotten Erolin killed. She couldn't reveal that to Erold, who had luckily survived.

"You knew that he was on his way here, didn't you?"

"How did you know that?" She was astonished.

"I overheard him speaking on it in a meeting before the flight here. It's true then?"

"Yes."

"Did anybody else know he was planning to come here that might have not wanted that to happen?"

As if she had already given away the information she didn't want to, she felt her gut twist back the other way, and his eyes went dark.

It took him a while to speak, and when he finally opened his mouth, he only said, "I see."

"We need each other Erold," she said, as if trying to convince herself as much as him that she had more to offer him than he to her. "The alliance needs you."

He waited, watching her eyes. They both knew that he could walk away at any point and leave Normany to become just a part of Akre's core for good.

"What are you going to do?"

"Right now? I'm going to rest."

"No, I mean about the alliance?"

"When, or if, I return, I will cement Normany's part in our alliance and join this fledgling coalition of nations alongside our northern brethren in an effort to ensure a permanent global peace."

"That's good," she said.

"It is for you," he gave a half smile, "And, it is what my father would have wanted."

"But it's not what you want?"

"That's irrelevant. To repeat something along the lines of what you just said. I'm a king, I need to start acting like one," he smiled, stepped forward to place a hand again on her shoulder, and then he turned to leave the room.

"Where are you going?"

"I need some time alone," he smiled.

"That's it? You didn't want anything else," she asked, hoping he'd come back to kiss her, but he just shrugged and continued out of the room, opening the door carefully.

"I think I've gotten all I need for now," he said and left in the direction of the stables.

* * *

Erold kneeled beside Seaspirit, who lay with her legs curled beneath her. She had not moved much throughout the winter, other than to walk from one end of the stable to the other. He came every day to bathe her in warm water and talk to her.

He dipped an oversized towel into steaming water that was just beneath too hot to the touch and then rung it out, feeling the sting of the hot water pour over his hands until the towel cooled just slightly. He pressed the towel over the back of the horse as it seemed to shiver from a long night alone despite the stable's heating sources and the blankets that she had been given to sleep under overnight.

"It's okay, I'll be back," he reassured her and himself. The day fast approached when he would not just have to act like a king, but that he would have to be the warrior he was training to be on the field.

He pulled the orb out from beneath his tunic and looked at the white, crystal ball. He had hidden it nearby in the same room when the tailor had come by. When she had closed her eyes, he had grabbed it. It was something he still felt he couldn't even show to Valessa much less give to anyone. He wasn't sure that he fully understood the danger of the object, but he remembered how quickly the power had come and how quickly it had gone too-- through him and then through the *Thief of Life*'s skull.

Erold had been lucky that when he had used the orb, no one had been around to see it but him and the dragon. He had seen the form of Kahron, where he had passed out on the hill just after they had saved each other from the beast.

No one but him knew how he had defeated the monster, but everyone was surprised at how hard it was for him now to summon a fraction of that power. They sometimes said, in a reassuring tone, when they saw him struggle that it must have been the adrenaline and fear. No one wanted to tell him that it was a fluke, but he had begun to think it for himself.

Sitting there now, taking care of a horse that seemed too sad and upset to stand some days due to the cold instead of casting thunderous lightning, made Erold feel like he would never be the type of warrior that King Hughgar was.

Then there was Valessa. She was more beautiful than the words he knew how to describe her with. She was also as wintry and cold as any winter night, but she had a warmth of spirit that he felt intoxicated by.

The only problem was that she would always be the type to prioritize Valgaard, and she would stop at nothing to get something done if it meant the nation was stronger. He wondered idly as he brushed Seaspirit's back, if there would be any time in her life when she wouldn't make decisions based on what was best for Valgaard.

Erold wasn't as upset at her about it as someone else might have been. He didn't blame her for his father's death, even though he could have. Instead, he felt lucky to be alive. If it hadn't been then, the enemy in Akre might have found a different way to attack him and his father. He might not have been so lucky. Now, he also had a purpose in life that he hadn't had before, and he could write a new destiny following in the footsteps his father would have wished were his own had the circumstances been different.

He hid the orb away within his tunic.

* * *

Valessa knew that Erold had gone to comfort Seaspirit, so she had tried to spy on him. Sometimes, she had listened to him talk to the horse she waited outside before joining them. Today, he had few words for the horse, so after peaking at him through the window, Valessa eventually crawled away, paranoid that any second, he would turn or she would step loudly and in the silence of the stable, Erold would hear her. What if Volstad came up behind her now?

She would already be terrified of speaking to Erold for weeks, and all she had wanted to know was if she had ruined her chances with him. She went to speak with her father. He was the only one in the palace other than Erold who was not in some way, paid to speak to her. In fact, he was hoping to earn enough to pay her.

Thinking of it this way, she suddenly felt depressed. She found her father in the training room that he had built for himself and was letting Erold use.

He had taken his shirt off and in loose pants, he was casting growth spells on tree saplings before violently chopping them down with a wood axe.

King Hughgar seemed to sense her presence, because in the middle of attempting to chop down the tree, he stopped and looked directly at her.

When their eyes met, she couldn't stop a few tears from flowing, and in the next moment, she was being held in her father's arms while he patted her on the back.

1514 - Chapter 27

For whatever reason, he had regressed. Erold tried to call upon the simplest of spells, and he couldn't.

Kahron's call outs continued, begging him for focus and control, but then, when told to send aura balls at the wall, his hand kept slinging forward empty.

"Attack!"

The bolt came at him, and he dodged.

"Throw those aura balls! Focus!"

Erold threw empty handed again.

"Attack!"

The beam of light caught him square in the chest, and Kahron let the bottom of his staff hit the floor, signaling they were done with the session. Erold took a knee. Despite it still being early in the day, he was tired and there was a lot on his mind other than training. He was simply too exhausted to try dodging Kahron's last strike.

"Erold, you still need focus and control. Put the spell in your mind and hold it there. You need to control your emotions and feed them into the spell. Once you have mastered that, you can expand from there."

"I am trying."

"Trying is the enemy of doing. Just do."

Erold looked down at the floor. Sweat was falling off of him in thick droplets. He had been running sprints, and doing pushups, whatever it took according to Kahron, who now that Erold noticed, seemed only to swing his staff and yell out commands. Erold opened his mouth to say something, but Volstad walked in, likely saving him from a painful demonstration.

"It's time, soon, for the first planning session. We leave in less than a month for Cardane."

"We'll be there," said Kahron, and he came near Erold to stand above him, "I told you that angel magic was going to take patience and time. You wanted the training. Don't give up on yourself when it isn't easy."

Erold nodded, "I did, but I feel like I'm struggling with even my most basic spells. Ones I've known as long as I can remember without having to name them."

"Sometimes, we need to forget before we can remember. It's the cycle of the inner mind. You had great power on the mountain, where is it now?"

Erold didn't say anything. If he couldn't conjure a simple ball of light, then he was really taking a step back. Sure, maybe focus and control was all he needed according to a master wizard, but he was increasingly beginning to think that the only reason he had defeated the dragon was the orb. And, after reading about the artificers' creations in the library, he had taken a different look at the orb.

Theodore had said in the study that it was dangerous, but Erold felt like there was no one he could ask directly the simple question, 'what exactly is the danger of the orb?' Worse yet, when he had used it, he had tapped into only rage and anger, and those felt like opposites of what Kahron taught him now.

They had trained all winter, and he was simply looking forward to getting back to taking action rather than waiting around, training. A trip across lakes and down rivers didn't sound as arduous as a dragon-guarded pass, even if it went through the legendary lands of Haltvia, where giant spiders were said to reign. At least his training with gun and sword had gone well, he thought.

He had practiced angel magic, when he could have tried getting fury magic lessons from the greatest of them all, King Hughgar, whose legendary fights against the Akrin mages changed military confrontations forever.

At the same time, times had changed. Mage attachments were now being not only standardized across all infantry units in the Empire but professionalized. Valgaard was working to do the same. The fights of mages that had so often been duels in the distant battles of the past, were now going to be massive confrontations of hundreds of mages at a time. He had trouble visualizing it, but he knew that every battle, there would be the risk of death coming from out of nowhere. There were too many variables and too many opponents. Without the shield magic of angels or similar counter-magic that Kahron suggested was almost the same, Erold would die easily in a fight.

Erold followed Kahron around the palace and into the meeting room dejected until he saw a familiar face. Curly black hair, rugged sideburns, and smooth eyebrows, with a strong jawline and hooked nose between his large crystalline brown eyes.

"Braddach!"

"Erold! I didn't expect to see you signing up for the Varanorian Guard. It makes more sense why we're in the palace then."

Erold made a motion to be silent and pulled Braddach into the hallway, "I didn't expect you to be here either. You made a huge impression on the teachers in Albion. They couldn't stop talking about the great Patr Braddach."

"Hah, that's the first I've heard of that. I feel like I barely escaped there with my life, let alone having been ordained a mage by the guild mages. What are you doing here? Don't tell me it's true that you were the one who slayed the dragon at Pili's Pass."

Erold didn't say anything, still frustrated about the day's training session. The reminder of his only success stung as much as it filled him with pride.

"You were, weren't you!"

Erold nodded and said, "Keep it a little quiet though. We will all be on the same page soon, but Cardane will be a serious situation. No one abroad can know who I am."

"We haven't left yet."

Erold nodded, "One thing I've learned in my short time as the last Arandil standing, is that there are spies everywhere. I've only been privy to the ones fighting for Valgaard at the moment, but there must be Cardanian spies here too. Only some of our men may be in on the secret, in time. Now, tell me, what made you sign up for the Varanorian Guard?"

"I'm with the twenty warlocks sent for by King Hughgar. He made a decree that he wants to keep the Warlock units battle tested against enemy mages and believes from reports that rogue mages in the gulf should be the perfect test of our mettle."

"That's where you went after Albion? I'm just glad that you survived. I've heard no end from the people in the palace, including the king, how dangerous becoming a Valgaardian Warlock is."

"It's easier for some if you're already a mage because it's traditionally forcing the non-magical to be able to fight with and against magical forces. It takes a different kind of stamina, but you never have to worry about drawing a blank on a spell. Do you ever get that feeling when you just can't seem to find the right word, and the spell doesn't come?"

Erold nodded. He had been dealing with that the entire morning, and it felt like every session had been another opportunity for him to fail to find the right spell. He was beginning to see why the ancient tomes said that surfacing a spell from your mind was one of the most important skills for a mage to learn.

"Let's get into the briefing meeting. I'm sure they'll start soon, and it will be a long trip to Cardane. We'll have plenty of time to talk on the way. I'm looking forward to hearing if you faced any sabretooths on the glacier."

Braddach laughed and put his arm around Erold's back as they joined the briefing meeting. Braddach sat down in the back, while Erold went to the front to stand beside Volstad, Moon, and Kahron, who each gave him varied looks of impatience.

They weren't technically his royal guard anymore, but they still acted like it. Even if they were technically instead his future companions in arms, heading off for dangerous mercenary work in the gulf.

He realized that he needed to respect that they were trading momentary danger for constant danger with the additional risk that he could be discovered as heir to Normany on top of the threat of 'rogue mages.'

Volstad cleared his throat, "I'm going to give a short speech before we split into longboat teams of twenty soldiers. Each boat will also have an extra ten of the guard who will take the ships back to Peth around the same path that we go. On the Lake of the Elms, we will have a knarr accompaniment, but they will return to Peth from the first portage. I will be leading this expedition and as a warlock and former Varanorian guardsman, myself, I can tell you that the dangers of the gulf are real, and that I and Kahron, here, have seen many men die alongside us amongst the sand."

There was some rowdiness, but Kahron put out a strange sound with his staff, without even a word, and the group focused. Erold couldn't tell if he had cast a spell, or just caught their attention with a neat trick.

"When we are in Cardane, Erold, here, who some of you may know--" Volstad looked to Braddach in the back. "--is my beloved son. Some may ask about our company, and it should be known that we are the leaders. Father and son. There may be a lot of people who ask."

Someone raised their hand and Volstad shrugged and nodded at him to speak.

"Is he the kid, who killed the *Thief of Life*?"

"Yes," said someone else.

"From now on," Volstad said, "If asked by anyone outside of this room. No one knows who killed the *Thief of Life*, and it was none of us here."

Everyone nodded.

Volstad continued, "No one, and I repeat no one is to be trusted in Cardane. We must remain vigilant and secretive about all aspects within our unit of the Varanorian Guard, and if we have good strategy, follow these and additional, basic warnings, and do everything efficiently, we have the opportunity to make a lot of money, and that should be our main goal."

There were cheers throughout the room, even from what Erold assumed to be the Warlocks, who seemed even a little shaggier than the ragtag group of rough, tough Valgaardians that the princess and king had assembled for him to go into battle with.

"Now, we are going to split soon into the teams for people to meet your rowing companions. We will row out of Peth about three weeks after the start of spring, taking longboats across three of the Eight Lakes. We are going to be doing just over one hundred atomic miles a day, stopping seven times until we reach the elven capital in the woods. Then, it will take an additional five stops before we reach Helsingstein in Mondelvania, where we will board a chartered frigate of the East Cardane Shipping Company to sail down to the city over a few more days. The whole trip will take almost three weeks or a little more. We will only cross the Atlan River in the north, so that we completely avoid any risk of getting caught by Akrin forces, which heavily patrol the river to the south. I think it goes without saying, but given that we are getting additional armaments than usual, I will emphasize, that there is no way Akrin military forces, would ever let such a heavily armed group go through."

There were cheers to that as well, despite Volstad's even tone, as if the men were ready to slake their bloodlust as soon as the first night fell. Volstad held up his hand and waited for the bloodthirsty lot to quiet down.

"There may be icebergs on the lakes or flowing down the Eldin or Atlan Rivers, so we may need to adjust our plan. To anticipate any questions on this, if we leave in the summer when the ice has melted, the storms of the gulf are much more violent. Any questions? None? Good."

Volstad broke them into teams, putting Erold with Braddach, Moon, Kahron, and himself. Meaning he had only twenty-five new faces and names to learn on the first day. Fifteen of which would be soldiers destined for the gulf and the other ten were the longboat crewmen who would take their ships back again, leaving them only one way forward, Cardane.

"Veleon," said the first man, who had a trimmed blonde beard, and clean-cut hair. Erold had taken a personal vow to leave his hair uncut like the Normen of old after the death of his father until he suffered a defeat, so he wondered if Veleon had recently lost something.

There were some more introductions, and then Volstad and Moon began leading the planning. Erold was glad that he'd have Braddach on the ship.

His father had taken the toddler, Patr Braddach, in when Braddach's father had been killed in the line of duty during the spring of 1495. Erold's father had never told him exactly what had happened, but it was Erold's understanding that Patr's father was killed by Akrin men who were using the cover of the evacuation ahead of Hughgar's attack on the capital, to attempt to kill the royal family, including Erold's mother and father, Erolin and Valeria. Erold was born a few years later after Erolin had moved back to Seylil, the once upon a time capital of Old Galdir. Braddach had grown up with Erold and shown him how to use his very first spells.

Erold's father had been impressed by each of them, fawning over Braddach, despite him being an adopted son. On the other hand, Erolin had always been deeply concerned about Erold's skill as if he had read dark portents in the runes, which given Erold's lack of capabilities in his recent training sessions and difficulties at school in Albion, never made sense.

It became clear who had done the trip over the lakes before based on who was talking the most. They were hopeful to avoid ice, because a walk around the lakes, like the days of old, would be almost impossible.

They could have used the elven canoes, but the south lake would take them six days of hard rowing by itself. On a canoe, they would have been in teams of four to six and had to row for twelve to eighteen hours straight to make it to their targeted camps. They'd be able to cover more than that distance in a longboat and be able to carry their gear, which would include guns and ammunition.

Most of the fighting force would be traditional Normen fighters, trained in hand-to-hand combat with battle-axes, swords, or battle-hammers, as well as modern weaponry, including long-barrel rifles that used advanced shot, the mass-produced .54 caliber. The twenty Warlocks coming along would likely be their only mage support other than Erold and Kahron, meaning if they were to indeed fight rogue mages, they would need to form supplemented battle lines where their warlock forces defended the other heavy rifle infantry from ranged and area-of-effect spells, while the group advanced forward.

They would still have to be careful about how much gear they could bring, because food would likely be difficult to forage for on the first leg of the trip. On the second leg, they would have to hope that they could buy additional supplies from the elves, when they were deep in the heart of West Haltvia in Anpol with limited access to any other outsiders. After that, they would most likely be able to forage for additional food during the second leg of the trip and then make purchases once they reached the towns on the other end of the lakes.

With thirty men carrying the boat, they would still be testing their strength on three twenty atomic mile land bridges along the way. The portages would allow for an additional day of camping, and possibly more depending on how fast they were able to make it through the generally dense forest across the lake, but a path should still be cut through the trees at the marked spots, allowing them to navigate between the lakes.

Erold flashed red, realizing that Braddach might not have heard of his adopted father's death. He would have to pull him aside after and let him know what had happened. It's possible he had read it in a paper, but even if he had remembered to send a simple telegram, there were no telegram towers yet outside of the empire. Erold had no way of knowing how to reach the young warlock, who had been off on his own for almost five years. He looked more regal than Erold felt he himself did, and for a brief moment he felt ashamed.

Erold looked from man to man, wondering what their stories were, compared to his own or Braddach's. From some of the other men like Ragnar and Thein, it became that much clearer like frost on the water that the trip was not made by people who had many options. It was do-no-gooders looking for a second chance, who were running out of money and had few or no other options. Almost anything was going to be less dangerous than this.

As they spoke and introduced themselves, asked questions, and looked excited to be doling out bloodshed for money, he realized like an epiphany that this was his path too.

He may have been born an heir to the many thrones his family of kings had won in days of glory long gone, but it sunk in now that he truly had no people of his own, save maybe Moon. He may have slain a dragon, but it only bought him what he had now, outfitting a troop of thieves and brigands with dragonskin armor and new weapons before traveling to the gulf.

He wouldn't be traveling in style in an airship bound for glory.

He had done his research on it just in case. If he had wanted to buy the airship instead of outfit and formally hire on the additional volunteers he was given, he would have only been able to afford the smallest, military grade vehicle, a three-ram, which only carried seven people, six marines who covered the "three" guns that gave the ship its name and a pilot.

So here he sat in a pre-adventure meeting that felt more like a dinner party in a chandeliered, brightly lit room of the palace with social circles in plush green, cushioned chairs, meeting his rag-tag group of bloodthirsty marauders, who he'd be embarking across three lakes, three rivers and two seas with, as they would have otherwise done had he not even been there, albeit with less equipment.

He knew that they would give him a small airship in Cardane to begin to his missions. If he proved himself in the Varanorian Guard, he could get an increasingly larger one.

Ultimately, that was the answer, he would have to prove himself again. This time he didn't just have to slay one dragon though. He needed to prove himself one hundred-fold to earn more than ever to come back to Peth, walk up to the princess in the court at this 'palace of ice,' and buy himself a real army to take back Normany.

It was the only way that he could bring his people a better life like he had seen throughout Valgaard and had known in Seylil, sheltered, and once cut off from the daily needs and struggles of his people.

* * *

Valessa didn't want to be caught spying on Erold again, given how their discussion of espionage related activities had recently gone, but there he was petting his horse, Seaspirit, who he had cared for through the harsh winter.

The young king in exile stroked the horse's forelock and brushed down the dark hair of the mare's mane. He seemed lost in thought or absorbed in the moment. She continued to stare as he moved to get water for the horse.

She decided against being caught in the shadow's staring and walked in boldly, "Erold."

"Yes, princess?" He said, without turning, putting warmed water like tea up to the horse. The stable air was brisk, but much warmer than the world outside, where ice and snow covered the land in a thick sheet of white, and the air froze your nostrils and flared your eyes even without a hint of the icy wind that often streaked over the lake.

"I wanted to apologize for what I said the last time we saw each other," she looked at him closely. He had smoothed and pulled his long, blonde hair behind his head and into a loose braid, like the pictures of the Normen of old times, who lived in the cities now burned, left behind, and iced over.

"You have said a lot of things," he said, which felt a little as if he was twisting the knife that he had already placed into her heart. "They were true though, and I forgive you for what happened with my father." Erold continued with a sigh, "I haven't been the king I need to be. I have been relying on other people to show me everything this winter. It's a lot to take in, and I haven't had much to add. Old magic, mythical weapons, the reality of the economics and militaries across the globe. I was upset about my father's death, but it was wrong of me. It wasn't your fault. I should still be thankful that you have the information that you do, however you do get it. Because it will be how we avoid the type of total war that would devastate the land and cause so much needless suffering."

She listened to him speak, watching the way his lips moved, and how he remained focused on Seaspirit. She didn't know what to say in the moment, and it left her stunned. She was so rarely at a loss for words, feeling as if any situation arose, she always had the answers.

"If you will let me ask another question, though, I'd like to. It's personal and important to me," he said.

She froze in place, wondering what could be on his mind that he wouldn't merely say with just the two of them there, "Yes, of course. Like I said, I'm sorry. Ask away, ask anything that you want to." She could hardly help but wonder what it might be as he tenderly rubbed down his horse trying to make sure it was warm and well fed.

"Will you," he sighed, "It's stupid."

"Just ask," she said.

"Could you take care of Seaspirit for me while I'm gone?" the prince looked at her with his fiery blue eyes that caught the dull glow of the oil lamps that lit the stable.

Valessa was surprised at how disappointed she was that that was all he had asked. His arms had grown thicker from all of the training that Kahron had put him through. His jaw had tightened, and even though he was still just the same age as she was, he seemed so much older. His shirt hung loose over his muscular chest, as he went back to working at caring for the brown beauty.

"Yes, of course, I will," she said, fighting the urge to sigh. Instead, she moved closer as he bent over and began soaping the mare's side, where she couldn't see him. "I will protect your horse from the cold, no matter how cold Peth gets. She'll be an indoor horse from now on."

"Thanks," he replied, and she watched him work. His brow furrowed and his eyes, tired and sad looking. He had worked so hard on everything to catch up on the situation, to understand the mathematics behind her researcher's calculations, and to see the need for modernizing the military to meet the demands of changing times. How it worked in the Empire, how it would begin to work in Valgaard, and how he might be able to apply those same changes in Normany someday.

Then something dawned to her. Perhaps, he was beginning to worry that there would be no Normany someday, and that he would fail in his quest to regain his kingdom. Slaying the dragon had been circumstantial and without that money, he'd have even less than what he had now, forced still to do the same trip to the gulf, but without the armor or additional weaponry. Maybe it was beginning to weigh on him, especially with how the training had gone. It was her turn to start asking the questions of him, rather than always the other way around.

"Erold," she said quietly, leaning around the stable door between them to look at him closer as he kneeled against the floor, rubbing the mare's hind leg gently with warm water and wiping it way with a thick pelt of soft fur. He had been advancing the daily ritual he had kept to help warm his horse's muscles and keep them loose.

"Yes?"

"Is there something bothering you?"

"I had to tell my brother about our father's death today," Erold looked off into the distance and before she could ask about a brother she had never heard of, he continued, "Not a blood brother. An adopted son of one of my father's guard, who had been killed, protecting my father."

"Was it hard?"

"He took it worse than I did, and I don't know how to feel about that." Erold turned to look up at her, "Part of me feels like I've been focused on next steps, what I can do better, how to improve. I never stopped to wonder if I'm following my heart and being the right person."

She looked at him, wondering what he meant and watched him look back down at the floor, let his hair loose from its braid, shake it and pull it back across his forehead and behind his ears, taking in a deep breath.

"I've been going where the wind takes me. I've been upset that I haven't been able to spend time with my family, but it's been about me--not about them. They passed on, returning to the homeland. Dying so that I may live, and hardly a moment has passed when I have mourned them or even celebrated their memory."

"You've been coping and adapting. You didn't have a choice," Valessa said.

"That's the easy excuse. I'm glad I didn't sit there and feel sorry for myself, or wallow in self-pity."

"You took action. You did what you had to do to move forward," she pointed out. "Your father and uncle would be proud of you, and they didn't throw away their lives for nothing, they believed in you and in the future of Normany."

"Maybe, you're right." Erold sat down against the stable wall, despite the dirty floor. Valessa watched his now tender eyes, as she came near him as he looked at the horse. She wiped at her gown and sat down next to him.

"You're not worried about anything else?" she asked, careful to not let her shoulder touch his, even though she wanted to. She glanced just briefly against his arm, his bicep visible in the high cut of the sleeve that ran to just above his elbow. She could see the shirt tighten against his chest as he looked up toward the ceiling of the stable.

"Not really, no."

"Not the elves in Haltvia, or the old forest they've grown across all of Ahria for one thousand years where it is said that horrors lurk and dangerous beasts feast on helpless travelers in the night."

"When you put it like that?" Erold chuckled, "still no."

She blushed, suddenly worrying for his sake. He'd be traveling into so many places where men larger and stronger, with more battle experience than him had perished despite their valor and the ancient call to battle of the Normen warrior.

"You're even not worried of Cardane? No one can know who you are. They are trade affiliates of the Empire and are sworn under numerous treaties to provide intelligence and to release prisoners across the border to Akre that are wanted in the capital for crimes against the government."

"Is that all that could go wrong, or is there more?" Erold turned to look at her.

"What about if you fai--"

Erold put his lips over hers, and for a moment, left frozen, he merely pressed against her, until she warmed and returned his tender kiss.

* * *

The spring equinox, a day that changed year to year with the movement of the frost, rotating and traveling through space. It was strange to think that, here in the northern hemisphere, the winter was the shortest of the four seasons by a couple days, despite the ice that stretched across almost all of the northern land.

The men of many lands had, in olden times, tried to split the calendar by months into equal days, but the stewards of the Lord's time, upon recognizing that winter was two days shorter than summer, moved an extra day to the summer and reminded people of the shortness of winter by celebrating the spring equinox, Iodawn, as it came.

The Prophet's Resurrection Day ceremony, on the other hand, would be in a few days, always just after any possible day that the equinox could fall, which was as late as the twenty fourth of Áevonstar, the last month of winter.

Erold knew the ancient tale of the death and simultaneous rebirth of Fros on the twenty fifth when the Otum fell, but he, like many, did not know if the tale was true. Iodawn marked the beginning of the golden days that lasted until the celebration of the end of the Otum in the name of the prophet and the Lord, above. This year, they were lucky, and the equinox landed on the twenty second, so the golden days were followed by golden nights, when they broke out the beer and even wine for four total nights.

The celebrations were bittersweet as the men of the volunteer guard drank in their fill, before they would aim to leave before the great day of Forgiveness in less than three weeks.

During one of these days, King Hughgar invited Erold and Volstad to a final, nearly private unveiling of the dragonskin armor that he and his troop would be taking to Cardane. The King had some attendants on hand as the tailor and the blacksmith presented their work.

They described what they did to even out the coloring and reinforce the joints and spaces in between the skin and scales, improving over old, dated models with white dwarven metal, stapled within to an internal layer of the dragonskin that wrapped around the body like chainmail by dwarven metal staples that had to be hewn in forges made specifically to work with the hardest of metals. The natural black and purple of the *Thief of Life* was therefore accented by strips of solid white metal hidden mostly beneath and between the scales, depending on the angle, covering gaps in the shoulders, armpit, along the sides of the torso, and around the waist.

"What do you think?" The quartet, including the king and Volstad, looked at the boy who would be setting out in a matter of weeks for endless battle.

"I like it. It's not the traditional red of most dragons, or even the green and rarer gold that I've seen in pictures of the Varanorian Guard of old. I think the new look with the addition of the dwarven metal makes it look highly advanced." He remembered how the bullets had bounced off the dragon when the mercenaries had attempted to bring it down. Something he had learned was rare among armors and skins that could often be easily pierced by bullets, "How does it perform?"

Hughgar blasted at the armor with a streak of blue fire, and the blacksmith and tailor mutually screamed in terror at the possibility of their work being turned to dust like the walls they had seen coming crushed out of the palace.

When the smoke of the blast hitting the armor cleared, it remained pristine. The blacksmith and tailor smiled and congratulated each other, patting each other on the back and laughing.

"It was a light blast," said the king, inferring that he would have been able to take the dragon down and then he confirmed, "It will stop a bullet."

Volstad looked on, stroking his chin, thinking perhaps this trip to the gulf would be smoother than his last. He remembered how he had shared stories with members of Sven's military who had served more recently in the guard. The dangers had been increasing, and even the mercenary group that had suffered greatly at the hands of the dragon had echoed a similar sentiment. Something had put a fear into them that even legends of Evorul dragons and the fearsome creatures of northern Valgaard had seemed less dangerous.

"There's one more thing," the King smiled. He flicked a finger behind him, beckoning his attendants to come forth.

Two men came forward delicately balancing a case that looked better fit for a lyre.

"What is this?" asked Erold, wondering at first if they would actually be performing a song.

"Don't just stand there. Open it!"

Erold undid the clasps, lifting the front over the top as what was inside, gleamed in the bright light of the room. A sheen crossed over it as he picked it up.

"A battle-axe."

Two heavily curved blades at the top, larger than the standard size of parchment, faced either direction. They were sharpened to the finest of angles, which you could barely see in the darkness of the object despite the glare of the light in the room. The axe heads were completely black, as was the staff of the blade ran through between them. Only grips on the handle and a metallic guard that ran around the staff to protect one's hands from being sliced was pearly white and the plush grip itself a dark purple, matching the armor made of dragonskin.

"Not just any battle axe either," Erold said, wondering at it. "What is this made out of?"

"I had a bit of an epiphany when I was showing you the great weapons of the sacred past. I did not see any two-handed battle axe among them, and when we discussed the 'Fang of Dawn,' I thought we have a wonderful material with which to work that I had never seen so much of."

"Dragon--" Erold thought for a moment what had been so black as night on the dragon and tough as, "talon?"

"Precisely," said the king, "It's been chiseled and worked like metal as no other material I've ever known. Some of the talon had to be discarded, but theoretically it could be reforged like iron."

"This is to be my staff as well?"

"Try it."

Erold pointed the axe blades at the dragon skin armor and sent the same light aura blast he had been struggling to throw in the training room. A blast of blinding light came out the end covered the room in light as if a cloud of smoke had erupted instead.

Erold smiled shyly at the masters of metal and cloth, thankful that no damage had been done beyond a second moment of fear and a little light show.

The king patted him on the back, took the axe from his hand gingerly and put it back in its case. Erold admired it as the case lay open in the two men's hands. The king had been right about needing a staff after all. The training had been working, even if it felt as if it hadn't.

"The handle is the focus staff. Many tools of wizard and

witchcraft have used dragon materials to enhance magical potency, and this is no different. For ease of use, it has been directed toward the top between the two blades of the axe. You'll have to be careful of course not to hurt yourself. It's a little shorter than a standard staff for that reason, so that it's easier to maneuver."

"And, the curve of these blades, should be perfect for shedding limbs?"

"They will do just that indeed," said Hughgar, proud of the handiwork. "Make sure no one else gets their hands on it though, as it is a potent weapon."

"Thank you, King Hughgar," said Erold in awe. "This combined with the armor and the twenty warlocks from the north. This is amazingly generous."

"I had a son of my own once, just a few years older than you, but he passed away unexpectedly. My wife hasn't been the same since. Neither have I. It seems like I've been waiting to do something like this for my next kin."

After a long silence, Volstad put both hands on Erold's back and said, "I appreciate it as well my King. We'll also need all the help that we can get, and being that so much is on stake, these gifts really are extraordinary."

The King partially snapped out of a momentary reverie about his fallen son and said, "Yes, yes," in nearly breathless whisper before nodding to the attendants and everyone in the room then departing quickly.

* * *

Sitting beside the fire with his companions on the Resurrection Day celebration, Erold could only watch the princess, Valessa, who appeared to be avoiding him, talking to any other guest.

When he had kissed her, she had kissed him back, and then run away, even freezing his hand against the stable wall. He hadn't known she could even use magic, but in that way, she was like her father.

To escape the ice, he had grabbed the bucket of warm water he had been massaging Seaspirit with and poured it slowly over the ice over his wrist until he was free.

If he could have read her mind, he would have learned that she had begun to question sending him off to the gulf, because it had been an opportunistic plan that she had envisioned could rebuild the Valgaardian treasury if it worked, while not risking any assets they didn't already have. She was glad her father had added the warlocks, but the likelihood of Erold coming back alive could be slim.

Princess Valessa did have feelings for him, but she couldn't let them overcome her better judgment. If she gave into the feelings for the exiled king, she would make him stay, and the enemy would learn of him soon and make a push at Peth either in secret or in force, to capture or kill him. Or, if they didn't, it would be impossible for her to support both her local military endeavors to delay an invasion coming from Akrin and field a force destined for Normany. She gave up her own feelings, holding them inside, for the good of both their nations.

Erold sat between Braddach and Volstad, who was flanked closely by Moon. Everyone held a drink in hand. Erold downed his beer quickly. Braddach was telling the three of them stories of the north, and Volstad asked him questions about whether the same masters were teaching there.

Volstad reached to get another drink, coming close to Moon's ear, and said, "You can trust me Elara. I'm with Erold for you from now on. And maybe a little for him. We do this together for the good of Normany. And for Erold, we will both remain vigilant and secretive at the same time."

A chill ran up Moon's spine. She knew more than Volstad did about the way the Empire worked. It was far more than Normany that suffered at the hands of the Empire. There were many secrets that she had uncovered while working in Akre. Secrets that, because of the spring of 1495, she was never able to fully explore to discover who was playing puppet master with the strings. She had once followed their symbol, a red mark, up to the secret coup against the royal family, investigating it with her master, the Akrin Phantom, who had taught her more than the ways of silent darkness.

In the end, she was only able to save Erolin and his wife, Valeria, as well as Theodore and his future wife, Anifiel. When she had discovered her master had died, an impossibility she had never imagined, she let the city disappear from her mind, watching it burn from afar as the King Hughgar who sat here with her now, playfully drinking beer and shouting stories, razed the palace to the ground, unknowingly burying any trail of darker evil in his blue fire.

1514 - Chapter 28

Eduard and Ivette shared a carriage in Rorik from Angel Bay to the far harbor, Piruma on Burlgate Bay. The old Bowery Place palace, named after a city in the north, was on a large, forested plot of land, in between the two sister cities that had become an enormous wedge-shaped bastion of nature on the coast that was slowly being enclosed into the interior of one combined capitol metropolis. If someone saw it from the dominant bluffs south of the larger of the two cities, Rorik, the palace campus appeared to be a perfectly triangular dense forest between the two.

As they rode in the carriage, Eduard found himself missing the open ocean. He never missed the piles of horse manure stacked on the side of the road that were actively being shoveled away into carts or into piles on the side of the road, even as the dusk began to settle on the city.

It didn't hurt that the Santisma was still out there, and Eduard believed they needed to do something about that ship to prevent it from continuing to attack their merchant ships throughout the Bacine Sea. He had personally caught a few privateer sea ships that had been caught attacking the Coltari, but he was almost positive that the Santisma had been the only airship to hunt on the wide expanse between Albion and Menetoris. Despite no leads on the enemy ship's latest whereabouts, Eduard longed to be back out there, chasing down that monstrosity with a quintet of frigates or even battleships like those that had saved him in GoldArrow.

The entrance to the palace was a rather simple gate of painted iron just on the edge of the road that ran along the coastline's edge before the old road reached the walled pathway that connected the two harbors across the small isthmus between the two bays. The meandering pathway, through the gate, wound on a slightly upward incline, between trees until it came, to the long, low, and flat gardens that stretched across the center of the complex and up to the main entry of the estate.

Once they had crested the hill, the gravity of returning to Bowery Place began to weigh on him. He turned to look at Ivette, who was soaking in the sight of the city and the palatial estate, which was unlike the far more ancient stone castle of her father's in stony Saint Egrivan.

"What are you thinking about?" she asked him when she noticed he was staring.

"Nothing."

"You want to be back out on the ocean still, chasing down the Santisma?" She grinned at him.

"Yes, do you?"

"Yes, but I'm glad that we stayed now that I see this," her smile broadened, and she turned to admire the gardens and watch the house as the carriage closed in on the enormous building. Its windows were full of light and the shadows of party goers could already be seen through the glass in the darkening night. Had they not received an invite at the perfect time, they might have already been back out on the open ocean.

Admiral Jacquelina Ferrara had accepted the invitation immediately, and the prince still held the heartfelt, hand-written letter from his father tucked away within his jacket pocket, resting against his heart.

As it stood, it wasn't a bad opportunity for the two of them to mingle, and Eduard had wished to get an answer or two out of old Theodore while he knew they'd be under one roof. The prince thumbed at the letter and thought again to himself, perhaps that was the only reason he hadn't left Rorik already. A chance to see old Mr. Everett.

The black carriage pulled by four horses came to a rest at the front door, and the prince paid the driver a handsome tip despite being a chartered man. He wasn't sure how to go about the whole adventure of transitioning to a royal, but he wouldn't let it change the things that he liked the most about himself.

Eduard helped his lady down from the carriage in her shiny, new dress that made her look like a mermaid and then held her hand to help her climb the stairs up to the front doors. He knocked twice and his father's new butler let him inside. There were somewhere between one and two hundred people present, so the party wasn't too large, but large enough that you could only understand the people talking nearest you.

As soon as he saw the giant figure of his father near to the back of the dance floor, just beyond the chandelier, the prince had an uneasy feeling about his father meeting his soon-to-be betrothed, Ivette. He had avoided it until now. The old man had always been a traditionalist when it came to matters of love, and the two young lovers had already sinned. Beside him was a stunning young woman, not much older than himself, in a gold and yellow dress that made her look like a gold dipped sunflower. Her brown hair caught the light from the chandelier in shimmering waves.

Eduard tugged Ivette lightly by the hand and guided her through the dancing and mingling lords and ladies of the newly founded independent state of Albion to where his father stood entertaining guests with a story from his younger days when he had met Jacquelina, who stood off in the distance drinking rum punch and Theodore, who Eduard didn't see.

Eduard had never heard this story before, so he spent some time listening as it had suddenly taken on new meaning with his recent adventures among the accomplished Admiral Ferrara's experienced crew. Unfortunately, when his old man noticed him, the story ended midline.

"Eduard! My boy. My prince!" the King picked him up and swung him around. "And you must be Princess Ivette," the King bowed daintily and kissed her hand. "I have heard much about you from your father, who has officially countersigned a peace treaty. Today, is a celebration to peace!"

"Huzzah!" the crowd yelled, "To Peace!"

"We've been doing that all night. I'm glad to have you home my boy. The North Alliance has been formed. And where are my manners, this is my betrothed bride-to-be, Onya Wilde."

"Miss Wilde," Eduard bowed, shrugging off the embarrassment of his drunk father's celebrations.

"Pleasure to make your acquaintance, Miss Wilde," said Ivette to the beaming young woman whose deep brown eyes, sparkled in the light ricocheting about the room from the chandelier crystals.

"How are you dears? The pleasure to meet you is with me," she smiled.

"Is this what you expected of Rorik?" asked the King lightly touching the princess's shoulder.

"Not in my wildest imagination."

"I'm also new to the city," smiled Onya.

"I never would have imagined a place as beautiful as this when I left Saint Egrivan."

"Your father has been begging me to send you back," laughed King Stone, heartily, sounding almost like a wolf.

Eduard stepped in and touched his father's chest gently, pushing him away from his woman, "We planned to go straight to Menetoris after arriving here to refit the Secondwind, remember?"

"And miss this party?" the King smiled and took a step back, wrapping his arm around Onya's thin waist, "We must celebrate the peace."

"The peace!"

"We're here aren't we father?" Eduard smiled.

"And you should stay until the wedding," said Onya, "Even if your father wants you home."

"Perhaps we will."

"And what about you two? Are you getting married?" the King asked.

Eduard blushed deeply, but Ivette said, "Yes, I believe so, though you'll have to get him to ask me."

"Great news," said Onya. "You must have the wedding here."

"My father might prefer it that way," Ivette joked. "I was on the merchant ship to come here to help form an alliance, and instead I found myself a prince, who rescued me like something out of a fairy tale."

"It's a good thing he was there," said Onya.

"Yes," said the King Stone, "he was on me often about being more defensive along the shipping lanes as he had heard stories of ships being attacked by privateers. I never would have imagined the size of that ship, the Santisma."

Eduard simply nodded.

"The Imerian actions in the Bacine Sea were not unnoticed, and I'm glad my father finally signed a treaty," Ivette agreed, but when she turned to look at Eduard for agreement, she found him distracted by something in the crowd.

"If you'll excuse me," the prince smiled, "I have someone I want to speak to about something important."

As he left, he could hear his father and Onya asking the beautiful woman who wanted to marry him to share stories about where she was from. Eduard felt a touch torn, but he had seen Theodore being pushed in a wheelchair by his do-it-all staff member, Mr. William and standing by his wife, Anifiel Coltari, whose father had been one of the most brilliant minds in trade in the fifteenth century AF, after Fros.

As he passed through the crowd, Jacquelina grabbed him by the shoulder, "You should have seen this man, your crown prince. We wouldn't have made it out of GoldArrow on the Secondwind without him. His effort to take back the ship was nothing short of extraordinary. He's a master with a sword, he is."

"Thank you, Admiral," smiled Eduard. He tried to follow Theodore with his eyes as she began telling the story of storming what had turned out to be a well defended castle hill. Eduard looked from Li to Thomas, two of the old crewmembers who were nearby, wondering if they could distract their drunk captain, but Thomas was locked in a passionate conversation with Miss Logan and Li seemed more amused by the farce of watching Eduard try to escape her clutch.

"I haven't seen Dist," said Eduard.

"He's not here," said Li as Jacqulina took a swig of rum punch.

"Where is he?"

The admiral shrugged, "I don't know. I haven't seen him much since we touched down in the city."

Eventually, Eduard was able to turn away from the vice grip that had been placed on his shoulder. He thanked her for the praise and tried to follow the trail Theodore might have cut through the crowd by looking for gaps between people. He luckily caught him near the hallway where Mr. William was pushing him toward the back of the crowd.

Anifiel Coltari still had the same long and black hair as she had when Eduard had met her as a child. She glanced his way and smiled. She looked just as young too. Her eyes like dark oval diamonds, characteristic of the women of the far west, had long eyelashes and her teeth were bright white. It was almost if she hadn't aged a day.

"Prince Eduard, how nice it is to see you again," she said with her hand on Theodore's shoulder. Prince Eduard bowed and gave her a short hug.

"I've heard you've spent some time in South Albion along the coast," he said mechanically.

"Yes, with a pet project of ours," she motioned to Theodore, who smiled and turned his wheelchair around.

"Prince Eduard! My, my, even in a year as a young man, it's as if you've grown that much taller."

"I'm glad you're not getting any shorter."

"Yes, well, that's funny. My darling and I have been telling everyone about our first grandchild."

"Our daughter, Charlotte, just had the most adorable baby boy, Victor."

"That's wonderful. Congratulations!" Eduard smiled, "I'd raise a toast, but I haven't had time to grab a glass. I've only just arrived."

"Don't let us keep you waiting. I'm sure there are plenty of young women interested in meeting a future king now," smiled

Theodore.

"Being handsome doesn't hurt either," teased Anifiel.

"That's a very nice thought of both of you, but I was hoping that we might have a chance to speak in private, Mr. Everett. It's rather urgent," the prince smiled.

"Suddenly, I'm Mr. Everett," laughed Theodore, "I must have done something wrong. Mr. William?" He looked up and behind him at the patient butler.

"Yes, Mr. Everett."

"Could you please take us to that study old Jack was showing us earlier?"

"Of course, sir," Mr. William said and turned the wheelchair, guiding it into the quiet, south wing. He smiled, kindly at the prince, "I hope you don't mind me joining you. It's so nice to see you."

When the prince didn't speak up, Theodore chimed in, "Mr. William knows more about the world than most Prince Eduard. He may be good to keep us company, but Mr. William, perhaps it is best that you stand by the door and allow the two of us to have a heart to heart."

"Yes, sir, as you wish," smiled Mr. William and he guided them to a study with a blue velvet couch, a handful of chairs of the same design and wall to ceiling shelves full of books. There was a small writing desk between the two windows at the rear end of the room. Theodore wheeled himself around until he was between two of the chairs and facing back toward the door.

"Now, my young prince, what is it that you wanted to speak about?"

"You know those stories you used to tell?"

"Yes."

"About all the travels around the world? Those were true, weren't they?"

"Of course, they were."

"Then, can you enlighten me about what exactly happened?"

"What do you mean?" asked Theodore, cautiously.

"Did you make something, and if so, what did you have to give?" Eduard could feel himself getting angry at the thought of how many might have died at the hands of a man who sat there smugly, rich and innocent in his wheelchair.

"I still don't know what you mean."

"You know exactly what I mean!"

"No, I don't."

"You created something in your travels, didn't you? I don't think I'm far off to assume that you were chasing a philosopher's stone. How many died to do it like the stories of the alchemists and the red dust in Vilshala?"

"My child," Theodore said, holding up a hand. The door behind Eduard had opened and his father had entered. Ivette, Anifiel, and Onya joined them as well, and then shortly after Jacquelina instructed Thomas to replace Mr. William at the door, and came in, standing behind Theodore. Eduard watched, wondering whether they had come to cool him down, or to watch. He was seething, shaking in rage.

"It's fitting that everyone join us for this discussion," said Theodore, calmly. "It's high time we all got on the same page."

"Are you going to tell us that you're a monster?" asked Eduard, feeling his fists clench, growing angrier, the calmer that Theodore acted.

"No, Jacquelina was there, but she doesn't know the full story either. Perhaps this will clear up some details. No one died to create this object, which you, and perhaps I, once foolishly thought of as a mere philosopher's stone. What it is, is much more than that."

"What could be more than that?" someone asked.

"The combination, fusion if you will of six such stones," Theodore stated plainly and looked around the room. "If you ever wondered how Domiscus had powered an endlessly large clockwork army that enslaved almost all of Ahria and some of Olympus before she was stopped by a secret organization, this is part of that story. It's a short tale. Deep in the lost cities of the world, the elves collected the natural Gaia powers of Frost, in hidden temples to the glory of nature. Before this, these powerful gems were said to be as common as rocks but broke easily. These new gems did not break and granted power for nothing that could be used for almost anything. There were said to be six such orbs created by Domiscus to enslave the world. However, in the City of Angels, high above the sky, in a battle with a secret enemy, I made a new one, with the same power to create like nothing you've ever seen before. It was near limitless power, in the palm of your hand. Whatever you imagined power to be, this was a power unlike any other. With it, I theorize, that you could destroy a city a day, an hour, faster than the blink of an eye, it would all be gone, leaving only shadows behind of what had once lived a full and beautiful life. No, creating it was easy. It is not how many died to create an object. That moment was innocent. Its creation was nearly effortless apart from the moxie filled journey to find its pieces. Now, that's it's been created, again, the question becomes how many may die, because of its existence?"

"Destroy it."

"Don't you think I've tried?" Theodore almost laughed.

"Give it here, let's try now. We'll smash it on the ground, all of us together."

"It's not here," said the king.

"Well, then, where is it?"

"Don't you think if you realized that the orb in question might have been with me that someone else might have?"

"The secret enemy?"

"I only knew her as 'Lady Black,'" said Theodore, and Jacquelina nodded.

"Is she still alive?"

"No."

Jacquelina confirmed strongly, "We made sure she was dead. Her ship crashed in the walking mountains of Yin, and not even her clockwork friend survived."

"She brought it upon herself," said Theodore.

"She was the embodiment of evil," said Jacquelina.

"So, she's dead, then what are we up against?"

"More of her, I would assume," said Theodore. "Unfortunately, I don't know anything else about them. Chief Inspector, Moon, an old friend of ours," he motioned to Anifiel, "believed this secret enemy, I call simply the dark, was behind the coup in 1495. She was investigating me on request by the senate at the time. I believe her, but even if there was evidence, what does it matter? It's not like fighting a hydra with regrowing limbs. It's like fighting a shadow. When you deal a blow, you find you've only struck air. Nothing has changed, and whatever the result, they've somehow won."

"What do we do? What can we do?"

"You mean, how do we fight an enemy that we cannot see, that we do not know, whose goals we can only guess, and is only waiting for us at all times to make a wrong move?"

Eduard nodded.

"I don't know."

"They do have one calling card," said Anifiel. "Some minions of their order are marked by a red mark. A tattoo that they place in hidden spots. It's as much as Elara, Inspector Moon, was able to discover."

"Where is the orb now?" asked Ivette, unable to explain a sudden grip of fear that came over her. The red mark sparked a memory, but she couldn't be sure.

"Right," said Eduard, "This Lady Black is dead, and maybe, you thought, what? That you were safe, but you weren't, and you found this out in 1495 in Akre. You've been hiding the orb ever since?"

"I entrusted it to Erolin to take it to Valgaard with my ideal goal of it eventually being moved further north to the fortress at Imor Valsen."

"But, his airship crashed," said Jacquelina. "Should we be worried?"

"Indeed," said Theodore.

The king, Stone, held up a hand, "Let's not panic on our announcement day. We know that Erold survived, and that the former Chief Inspector, Moon is with him."

"That she is," said Theodore, "We have to assume that the two of them have the orb as Inspector Moon has known of it since 1495. She didn't achieve her rank for no reason. If the orb was to fall out of their hands, then we would all be in grave danger. It could be used to restart the pinnacles of Domiscus, powering a new infinite, clockwork army, or theoretically any new doomsday device. In many ways, I'm glad that I was never able to discover how to use it. The corruption of temptation may have overcome me, but what I say of the power it wields is true. It is the power of particle fusion. Of that much, I'm sure."

There was a bit of silence, followed by Jacquelina cracking a wide smile and after regaining some self-control, stating, "Is that what you did in the City of Angels? I had always thought you got up to something else."

No one laughed but Jacquelina, but the two briefly reminisced on days long past while the rest of the room remained in quiet contemplation. Their brief tales of yesterday ended with the pair agreeing that the sea would never be the same after the invention of the airship.

"Perhaps this is the best time for us to discuss what the two of us have been working on," said Anifiel and Theodore clasped onto her hand, which had remained, resting on his shoulder. "A much more practical matter of the day is how do we defend the long coast of our nation from raids, or any other form of airborne attack."

"Did you plan that I would secede from the Empire before I actually did it?" asked Stone.

"We didn't think they would give you a choice, and we bet on you to survive whatever was coming," said Anifiel.

"Fair," Stone nodded, "What new technology did you come up with this time?"

"Even though you're hard to impress, I think that this will impress even you."

"Let's hear it then."

"I've recently returned to the Ash Vale after negotiating contracts and planning the distribution of a lightning defense array that Theodore and I have designed and invented, channeling the same magical powers that mages are able to tap into, but to be operated by any man. We calculated the maximum effective arc and have begun the installation of outposts in the south on the rim islands off the coast and also on the coast. Any ship that comes near can be most definitely rendered inert with just one blast of lightning, which acts as a destructive force to electronic tools aboard, or if necessary, a continuous salvo of multiple towers. It will delay any invasion, prevent raids on coastal towns, and hopefully limit the bombing of these same areas."

"I couldn't go with her, on account of my condition, so that's the real reason she has been away. Any enemy ship could be tagged as it approaches, and then if it gets close enough, zapped by a bolt of lightning, as she said. It helps shield Albion from a surprise attack from air or sea."

"Akre could launch an attack through Normany," said the king, "But we, have the alliance now."

"True, at the moment, we believe that they wouldn't be able to launch an attack on Albion by land without leaving themselves open to a counterattack from Valgaard."

"Counterbalanced," said Eduard, stroking his chin, and having calmed down, gone to stand beside Ivette with his thumbs pressing gently into the crease between her shoulder blades.

"I'll have to spend more time at your new Redbridge in Ash Vale, so that I can pay attention to all that you're doing," remarked the king, Stone.

"You're always welcome with us, and the city would love it."

"They've already begun chanting, 'God love the king,' all about town."

Stone beamed and blushed at the same time. He had never expected such an outcrying of support against the senate far off in Akre.

"Until the lightning array is operational and even by itself, we are not prepared to fend off a full-scale invasion. Are we?" asked Eduard.

"I've spoken at length with Ferrara on this," said King Stone, "We are instituting a plan to begin building battleships, based off of the Secondwind's frigate design. They will be much larger than a frigate, but still faster than the Imerian battleships we fought over GoldArrow."

"We have also always had longer range guns, but we will now emphasize this even more so," said Ferrara. "With the help of a team of engineers, we hope to extend their range. We'll ensure that we can strike faster and from a distance with just as much potency. We have battleships, but few. And, our experience in GoldArrow with the Santisma has shown that we have to adapt."

"What about three-rams?" asked Ivette.

"We have no production in effect for three-rams," said the King. "We understand that if we were to face a full-scale invasion, we would need to balance the smaller airships with larger ones to prevent being overwhelmed, but we have to focus our production capabilities where we can."

"Menetoris can supply the three-rams," Ivette smiled, "A coordinated attack of three-rams could devastate a coastline with raids and bombardments. My father has talked at length about how to defend our island whatever the cost, in the case something was to happen to him. We would proudly make that our military contribution to the alliance along with our powerful mages that guide them."

PART THREE: THE GULF AND THE BRASS FLOWER
1514 - Chapter 29

On the ninth of Solsri, two days before Forgiveness Day, they shipped out of Peth, on longboats like the Normen warriors of old, who left the north in search of warmer lands. Nine longboats flanked by two knarrs rowed into the rising sun. Their sails were brought up, because the wind was high against them. The cold lake waves were high too, but their boats split them like sharpened knives thrust through fresh meat, splashing great sprays of foamy white in the air in the place of blood.

The coast behind them sloped off gently from northwest to southeast, and they followed a track just off of east, a hint south and nearly perfect east to Moon's compass, pulled to the right by the natural drift caused by the magnetosphere.

They had said their goodbyes already. Now, Princess Valessa watched from the rooftop balcony of the palace, where she spent most mornings, far away from the shoreline as the dark ships, cast in shadow by the low sun, pulled away in the great strokes of the oars to the left and right.

Two hundred sixty-four men across those nine warships. One hundred fifty volunteers, twenty warlocks, ten extra boatsmen per boat, three companions of strange repute, and one king in exile, Erold Ardrada.

Her mind wasn't all figures and facts. Numbers and political games. There was swirling emotion in her as the icy wind blew against her face. She just let emotion drift away with the wind as much as she could, because the gulf had taken a lot of people over the years.

She knew that as well as her father. They both understood the dangers that Erold undertook. For the good of Valgaard, she had to let what would come, come. Inevitably, the alliances she had already made would fail to outpace the Akrin empire, whose armies grew with each passing year, month, and day. The fate of the young northern alliance and its chances to avoid a war that would cross three continents, drawing all of the planet into the crossfire, hinged on a boy her age.

Just a boy, younger than her brother had been when he passed away.

King Hughgar stood on the shore beside the harbor south of the core of the city and had reminded Erold, "Fros walks with you always."

The huge pillars of the white-stone 'presidio' stood behind him, and from this angle, Erold could see the open middle, so it looked as if King Hughgar was the center of the monument behind him, like a bronze statue to one of the great, old Kings of Elessia who towered above the rest of the city. He was flanked by his honor guard and his wife, the queen, who had worked up the strength to attend. She waved as if she were attending the wedding of a foreign dignitary.

Erold responded, "and so he does with you," and had looked up at the palace on the hill where he thought or imagined he could see the princess, watching them leave.

The ships had pulled out from the harbor and spread out into the lake, stretching from the south end of the city to the north where the bluffs rose with colors of green, their evergreen trees being joined by the first leaves of spring.

The shoreline rapidly disappeared from behind them, and Erold rowed as hard as he could, letting his hands feel the rip of the oars underneath each thrust of the great oak wrapped by his fingers, trying anything to keep the memories of the recent weeks from entering his mind as not to dwell on the strange coldness of princess Valessa, and instead turn to the task at hand.

The 'city of the brass flower,' awaited them, and they had weeks ahead, traveling through Haltvia, the lightly settled, land of ice, elves, and further north than they would be going, the kingdoms of the dwarves beneath mountains where it was too cold for even dragons to roam.

Before they left, Volstad had given them all final reminders as the troop had dressed in travel gear, packing the black, purple, and white armor and their other gear into chests on the ship, placed as the chairs on which they would sit on their voyage across the lakes.

"This is a final reminder that you must live in Cardane as the Cardanians do. Even at the most basic level. You must use the days of the Akrin Empire whenever we are in the city or near anyone from the city. We are all under one God in heaven, but if they suspect you of following the heroes of the north instead of the heroes of Akrin, they'll cut off your hands as a non-believer and ship you back to Valgaard."

Erold had realized that the day was Freyday in the Normen tongue. The day of unheralded beauty like the fairest maiden of the old country, who had helped to lead the people south when the ice returned.

Beauty like Valessa's beauty. Beauty he could not escape even in the name of a day of the week. He had said goodbye to her days before in such a way that he wanted to forget. They did not fight, but she was cold.

Perhaps it was for that reason that people called the white-stone palace that they rowed away from, the 'palace of ice,' and not because it looked as white as the snow that fell across the land each winter. It got its nickname from her, and not the other way around.

For now, Volstad was the one in command, but Erold vowed to learn everything that he could just as he had. He hoped that Cardane would give him an airship large enough for his troop, but he knew he'd earn bigger.

He didn't feel sixteen. He felt much older. He looked up at his 'father' from here on out, Volstad. And behind him, Moon, was still his shadow. She watched the lake and the trees and the shore, and the way that the men worked at the oars.

They would soon be suited in the black, purple, and white of the new Varanorian Guard's dragonskin armor. They may not have come as his men, but they would be soon. The troop that came with him knew him only as Volstad's son, the dragon slayer. They would fight, dressed as the best of the legendary Varanorian Guards ever had been, and Erold wondered at how might the same legends of 'berserk bravery' be tested in the coming years.

He looked over at Kahron, who rowed near him, likely knew better than even Volstad. Kahron had been the only one to not don the dragonskin armor, preferring to remain in his armament from Menetoris.

He wondered what business Kahron had to return to in Gor'mondell's Gulf, north of Cardane. He hadn't spoke of it, and among everything going on, Erold hadn't pried into the mind of the master mage. The old wizard, however old he truly was, rowed along with the rest of the men, one stroke at a time.

The men began to sing an old Normen song:

If I die today,
Valhalla surely awaits
I long to see the shores of home
Old Asgard and the Sovnstone
But today is not a day for death
Give me life, not a final breath
Though if there's somewhere I must go

Tell my wife I loved her so

They switched key to an upbeat tone and left behind the notes of the solemn reminder of old homes:

For the girls are fairer in Starholm
Yes, the girls are fairer in Starholm

Braddach, broke off from the chorus to sing a solo verse with a beautiful tenor:

Doesn't everybody know
Whose time it is to go
That if death awaits
There's just one place

And the rest of the crew joined in:

It's Starholm
It's Starholm!
Where there's the kind of girl for me!
Long ago they locked their gold
We took their wives and left their homes
And now if it's time to go
Well my wife is on her own
Because the girls are fairest in Starholm, hey!

And another solo singer sang:

And if your wife's not pretty
Just take her to Áelin City
Where with their knives
They'll change your lives!

"Okay, now, that's enough," yelled Veleon, "All right, I said shut it! If you don't start singing about killin', I'll send you all back home to the old lands myself, and leave your stinking, singing bodies to rot in the lake!"

"Did that hit too close to home?" asked Braddach.

The whole crew laughed, especially Erold, who was always fond of Braddach's jokes.

"Oh, I'll get you for that," said Veleon and then to soften his vague threat, "It'll be dirt in your beer for the week. Just before you drink, I'll sprinkle it in there."

Some of the crew continued to laugh.

They had to cut across to the opposite side of the lake here in the south where the lake narrowed, to help give them the quickest route north as the next day they would be able to launch to a deserted island in the center of the east part of the Lake of the Elms.

As the day wore on, the city of Peth disappeared behind them and slowly the shoreline ahead of them became less of a gray blur and a difference in the clouds. It began to resemble the flat, endless land of dense pines that appeared to be the only thing that survived north of the lake.

Some of the men who had taken the lake route before, dropping off previous volunteers, assured them that there would be more than just flat land in the coming days. Although there were few hills in this region, there were a few and even some that were conflated with mountains by elven tribes that had not ventured far enough north or west.

It seemed the elves of the woods, never ventured south of the lakes, preferring the life of their ancestors, who had guided the forest to grow and were said to have moved the rivers and made the lakes.

There were even some elves among the Valgaardians, and some men with elven blood. There had been many tribes of elves throughout the land and the ones that had lived where men settled too had varied histories of either war or cooperation. In the end, many bloodlines were crossed across nations that eventually united under a local banner, especially as the wars of empires like Akre's spread across continents.

The cape became clear on the eastern shore where the land came up from the south and then fell away sharply on the northern side just a touch in the northeasterly direction against their heading, giving the appearance of a peninsula as they closed in on the trees of elven land.

When they reached the shore, they jumped into the shallow water, and pulled the longboat onto the rocky beach as a team, careful to find a flat enough surface not to deal with a difficult heave the next day.

One by one the longboats landed and did the same. The knarrs followed slowly after, carrying much of the food that they would rely on while they were on the first lake.

Erold grabbed his gear that had been wrapped in a day bag out of the dark, wooden chest he had sat on for the row across the lake, as the rest of the crew hopped out of the longboat one by one and found the remnants of last year's camp.

He then grabbed the lyre case that held his axe and hopped out after them. It appeared as if the camp had been frozen in time, and Erold wondered if they would all look like that. There was a wide expanse of flattened ground, still cold from the winter's frost, where the trees had been cleared away, and fire pits that had been dug out had left black stains, colored by the ash that had vanished as the year wore on.

"You bunking with me, Erold?" Braddach asked as he claimed ground for a tent.

Erold looked over at Moon, who shrugged. Erold had seen Volstad and Moon lately having numerous chats, so he wasn't surprised when it appeared the two of them would be sharing the same tent.

Erold nodded to Braddach, "That sounds good to me. You still haven't told me whether you tried to ride any Mastodons in the north."

"I'm no King Hughgar," Braddach laughed, "but maybe we can catch up on some more positive news than lately. How about that princess?"

"It's not happening."

"She seems taken with you."

"Just drop it," Erold snapped, but that seemed only to entice Braddach more who continued to needle them as they set up their tent like the rest of the crews. Then, the knarrs began unloading food, and different teams of tents began re-clearing the nearby ground for kindling with which to light fires to cook their food.

Barrels of beer were rolled out of one of the knarrs and Erold heard the excitement of some of the men, including Veleon as they went to get their ration.

Each leg of rowing was about one hundred atomic miles, but the first day's trip had been the longest. After setting up camp, helping to get the fire started, and speaking about old times with Braddach, Erold was exhausted but couldn't sleep. The men at the nearby fire couldn't stop sharing horror stories about the woods.

The worst was the story of a dense fog that covered the town, and each day a child would appear lost, and the townspeople tried to help the child find its way. But, the child never did and they would let the child stay the night. The child would be gone in the morning, but a new child would come. And, soon the townspeople realized that townspeople, who had helped the children, were missing too, and they tried to not let the children in. But, the more they refused to help, more children began to appear. Until, finally, what was left of the townspeople ran to escape the fog and the town, but none were heard from again.

As a new story began, Erold turned over to Braddach who had his own blankets and his own makeshift cot to keep off the cold ground, "You think those stories are true?"

"Not a word, get some sleep."

Erold dreamed of the princess.

The next day they ate breakfast before the light of the sun had broken through the trees. When they pushed off the shore, they were able to catch the wind that ran again from the east to the west. It caught on their square sail and helped them as they broke away from the eastern shore to find the island where they would make their second camp.

It was closer to the south of the lake's bay, which would help in case they had made a wrong calculation with their heading as they should make it in its vicinity early enough in the daylight that they could see it to the east or west. For this reason, they made a slight over correction toward the east to not be carried toward the center of the lake, where they wouldn't want to spend a cold night if they didn't have to.

They were lucky to have the daylight as well, as they had been slightly pushed by the waves in all directions across the lake, and they were able to correct their heading into an alcove of the island, where they could tie their ships down against the stone and not worry that they would be pulled out by the waves at night.

The island was almost purely rock, save for forested bits that stood on a hill that ran up toward the north of the island, obscuring its length and hiding everything else from view. They repeated the same process as the evening before but skipped the beer to avoid losing one of the heavy barrels in the lake. The men had tried, but the distance between the knarrs and the boats made it hard against the rocky shore not to lose one's footing and someone did have to be pulled out of the water.

Getting out of the boats had been hard enough with the steep incline of the rock, and they ended up forming a chain to unload their gear for one person at a time. Erold had been able to balance barely as he took his axe with him.

He admired the way that Kahron might have actually glided on air as he used the edge of the longboat as a platform to run and jump from onto the rocky shore. Kahron bunked by himself and seemed at one with everything around him.

Underneath, the man sat in a circle of mental entanglements related to past promises. He had left Cardane. Now he was going back.

He both wanted to and didn't want to go back. When he had grown up in the islands, where people of all colors lived in harmony, he had heard stories of the Black Menetorians, who had not yet found a home. They were like the Kederan whose home had been destroyed by war that poisoned the land, and yet it had been many millennia, not a few centuries, and they traveled as one, not in small groups or as individuals.

They were now called the uncounted people, and they didn't belong to any particular place. Kahron had gone to see if he could change that. To convince them to come back to the islands or move to South Olympus, where many tribes had gone. The leader of the tribe at the time had thought him foolish, and instead preferred to stay in Cardane, where they worked alongside the Varanorian Guard just as the troops from Valgaard did. However, in Cardane, they would never become full citizens.

Kahron meditated on this while the camp swirled around him, eating when everyone ate and otherwise, left deep in thought. The group cooked salted beef at night and had salted pork in the morning. Some of the men tried their hand at fishing in the lake, and a few were eating a side of fish with their rations as they sat around the fire with bread, canteens, and boiling water that they would let cool overnight to fill their canteens with in the morning.

The next day, they repeated the procedure, following the coast of the small, circular island slightly to the northeast for about forty atomic miles until they came around the massive boulders that marked its corner and caught what was left of the wind, trying to make up falling behind on the morning row.

They had about seventy atomic miles slightly to the northwest to go and fought hard without much help from the dead wind that the day before would have pushed them almost exactly where they needed to go. The shoreline beside them became visible sooner than expected, because of forested hills that ran along it from north to south, which the guides pointed out. Soon, the hills disappeared from the distance as the shore ran back to the northwest, and their heading changed accordingly.

They missed the old camp on the coast, forced to pull into a muddy, gray beach they found as the sun came down. The gear was out, and the tents were set up against the tree line as fast as they were able. The darkness of night would be on them fast, and they needed to set up fires before they lost the ability to find kindling in the dark.

As the knarrs rolled in, having struggled to keep up with fewer oarsmen, the men went to grab beer in the shallow water, while campfires were still being lit. The knarrs lit a pair of oil lamps to help them work as dusk neared, but they didn't provide much light beyond the front of the ships. Finally, the group secured the ships and had the beer out to make up for the day before.

The group didn't have to worry about tides on the lake, so the longboats' perch and more importantly, their camp were safe from being caught drifting in the water between then and the morning. Instead, the lake's height changed from year to year, and it looked like in previous years this lake had been a few feet higher and had covered this beach from previous troops of travelers, as it had made a great, inaugural camp.

Erold asked Braddach whether he had found a girlfriend up in Imor Valsen among the Warlocks, or even in a town in Valgaard. The older boy laughed about how busy he had been and how he hadn't had time to think about it much.

"She would be no princess, though, that's the God's honest truth."

"Come on Patr, you got to stop harping on that. She's in a different world, a higher one."

"If she's in a higher world than you, then what luck does a guy like me have?"

Erold beamed in the dark, "Father always said you had the most talent. I was always just a wild card."

Patr shook his head and said, "Nuh uh," so that Erold could hear him disagree. "We both would talk at length about how scary it was that you seemed to pick up anything anyone showed you. It came so natural to you."

"It doesn't feel that way lately."

"The true process has just finally caught up to you. That's how it's been for me this whole time. If it's not the princess, who would it be? What's your perfect girl?" asked Braddach, as he tightened the blankets around himself. The fire had died down and the wind had picked up on the low beach.

Erold thought of Ti-Enna. The girl from the Leidyn ball. He had thought that he had gone through an ordeal then when survived the crash. The ball had been so fun. There were a lot of similarities between Ti-Enna and Valessa in how they looked, but not how they had acted.

The princess was something else entirely. She navigated everything in front of her, as if she knew all the answers before the questions. He found himself wondering if she had ever made a mistake in her life.

"So, do you have one?" asked Braddach again.

"Not sure. It's hard to say."

"It's the princess, I knew it."

Erold would have hit him in the arm if it wasn't too cold to leave his blankets, so instead he disagreed loudly and asked, "What about you? Who's your perfect girl?"

"She'd have to be a redhead first."

"Why?"

"I like redheads. Always have. And, she'd have to be brave and kind."

"Anything else?"

"I haven't thought much about it lately. I've been so occupied with training. Did you meet anyone in Albion at school?" Braddach felt as if he was beginning to fall asleep, but he yawned and tried to force his eyes open.

"Nah, did you?"

"Yeah."

"Was she a redhead?"

"No. That's not why it didn't work out. She just wanted to go to school in the islands, which is hard. It requires a lot of back and forth and money, because they don't have a direct agreement with the Empire, and Albion does things their own way too. They have different criteria too, which is why she wanted to go. Also, I wanted to do things on my own rather than get help from father, and I was able to join the Warlock school for free. They provide room and board."

"Well, they may be getting an agreement soon. They plan to sign a formal alliance. One I aim to be a part of someday. When all this is over, you could go to the islands, with your cut of the money."

Braddach sat there thinking as Erold spoke. Each sentence was a new revelation to him about the circumstances of the adventure, so he asked, "Is that what this is all about? That's why they sent the warlocks to the gulf?"

"Yes, it is," said Erold, "I want to fight for peace in the world and a free Normany. It seems that this is the only way to do it."

"Count me in," said Braddach.

"It may be a long road" Erold said, wondering to himself if his friend would remember this conversation in the morning, and thinking maybe he should leave the rest of the conversation for a future date.

He wasn't really worried about anyone listening from the crew of Valgaardians that were among them, but maybe he should have been. He listened to the wind howl through the tent, thinking he might have heard a distant howl at the moon.

* * *

Erold had finally approached the princess, who had clearly been avoiding him at all costs, the day before he left, cornering her on the rooftop of the palace, where he wanted to say goodbye to her and express his feelings.

"You should go," Valessa told him.

"Valessa, just listen to me please."

"Erold," she began to walk back inside, but hesitated, and mulling over her words said, "Fros will walk with you always." She dodged him as he tried to grab her before she scurried back to within the palace walls.

He didn't understand. She had kissed him back, and now, it was like she wanted nothing to do with him.

Beneath the icy façade, she was internally confused. What was best for Valgaard was not what she wanted. The best way to deal with it was to push it away.

Erold was left standing, alone in the morning sunlight as the wind drifted lazily over the city and the bells of the early morning began to chime.

* * *

He awoke with the fourth day of rowing ahead of them, and the camp was already alive. He rushed to get ready and catch up as the sun rose ahead of the camp's progress. He ate salted pork as fast as possible and he threw his axe case at his feet, tossed his bag as quickly as possible into the trunk and helped heave the longboat into the lake through the muddy sand. Water splashed all over his baggy pants, sinking into his last change of cloth undergarments that would begin to smell foul as the day wore on.

They were soon back on the lake, whipping with the wind, as they rounded the cape and had to bring the sails down. They had made good time following the shoreline with the wind, and with the sun shining brightly ahead were able to pull into the sight of the previous camp ahead of time, even the knarrs too had benefited from the strong wind, making a large tack north of the camp and following the wind down, almost beating the longboats to the beach, where they pulled up on the shore and made camp.

They planned to stay there for a day of rest and also to use a large, clearwater stream near the camp to wash clothes, so in teams of four, the men started hustling over to wash quickly, hoping to not miss out on beer. They had salted beef as the stars began to shine with a sky so clear the galaxy's purple mouth crossed the entire face of the night. Some of the bread had gotten stale sooner than expected, so stale bread it was.

In the morning, Erold and Braddach helped to make tent repairs and build new fires. Moon and Volstad had become inseparable, and Erold felt happy for them. Moon had followed him almost wherever he went, and she had never seemed more content. Yet, no matter how many times he looked over, he still never caught her smile.

On the other hand, with each passing day, something seemed to weigh heavily on Kahron. Not only had the training stopped, but he seemed intent on meditation. Every day before they set out to row, he would sit under a tree, facing the lake. On their planned rest day, Kahron remained under the tree as long as the sun shined in the sky, and Erold thought he might speak with him.

Before he could though, it was his turn to wash clothes, and he needed it badly. He and Braddach found their way to the stream, where they set up within eyesight of each other, and waded into the slow, cold water with their packs.

"I never thought I'd get tired of salted beef," Erold said, after he'd been washing his clothes for some time. Braddach looked up but didn't speak.

He tried to mime at Erold to be quiet, but Erold continued to wash his clothes, and looked over, "Braddach?"

Erold saw Braddach pointing, luckily in the direction away from the camp. Between the two of them, a wolverine was dragging the carcass of a half-eaten moose. Erold paused, he was unsure what to do here, and was still half naked in the water. The two of them watched the animal drag the dead carcass across the ground bit by bit as Erold grabbed up his clothes and quickly left the water.

Braddach watched the animal to see if it would be aggressive, and then followed Erold. They each checked for leeches and ran back to camp laughing at the small creature's appetite.

The next day on the water was as smooth as ever, as they were headed back in a northwest direction and were able to catch the wind. On the following morning, the knarrs turned back to Peth as they had run out of the beer in the night, leaving any remaining food for the longboats, and the crews got a late start as they had an easy last leg of the Lake of the Elms with the wind almost fully at their back.

They landed at the marked portage point, where it appeared either elves or Normen had placed down wooden spikes through the lake to act as a mooring point or indicator where they should round the correct miniature peninsula to the shortest walk between the lakes.

They camped on the isthmus and Braddach told Erold more about Valgaard, and Erold told Braddach about the zodiac signs, and how they followed the frost's orbit around the sun. If you traced the suns path through the night, over the course of the year, you would recognize that the zodiacs followed the same line.

After a warm night, the crews had their hardest task ahead of them yet. They had to complete their first portage, lifting their ships, clean out of the water, and walking them along twenty atomic miles of thankfully, flat ground, where the trees had also been removed by previous travelers, cutting through the thick Haltvian woods.

They packed their stuff in as if they were going out on the lake. Took off any extra clothing that would make the lift uncomfortable, had sentries posted along the way, in case of danger to call them into action, and then worked in teams equal on each side to heave the ships into the air. At first, it didn't seem so bad, then it began to wear Erold down. He felt fortunate that the whole team was lifting it, but he worried if he didn't do his part that the whole thing would fall to the ground.

Up ahead a crew was resting, and as they saw Erold's crew near, they picked up and went off. Moon had marked it as the halfway point and someone directed them to stop and rest as well, which Erold greatly needed. They ate as quickly as they could, because in the distance the next crew had appeared.

Back up the longboat went, and they trudged through muddy ground and over tufts of grass, dodging tree stumps that hadn't been removed and decaying logs, as they made their way to the edge of Lake Brünn, where some of the longboats had already been placed in the water, and tents had been set up along the shore and ice could be seen floating in the water.

After they let down their boat in the water, Volstad and Kahron who had been in the lead were laughing and congratulating themselves, and others began to unpack their belongings to set up camp. It'd be another night and day of rest before one last ride where they would be at Anpol, the stronghold of the Haltvian elves on the isthmus between two of the 'Eight Lakes.'

After they set up camp, Erold rested on the shore, like many of the men, looking out at the quiet lake that had barely the ripple of a wave, or the sound of wind through the trees. The pines were even bigger this far north and lifted into the sky seventy and eighty atomic yards high.

Erold wished that he had taken one last look at the Great South Lake, but he had been too focused on lifting the ship. He tried imagining it, and instead, he found himself thinking of the white-stone walls of Peth, that reminded him too of his own home, Seylil, the mountain fortress.

If he was to ever have a kingdom in Normany, his capital would look different than both those cities, but he couldn't picture it. It wouldn't have walls, or marble columns, and he couldn't picture a palace either. Not in the traditional sense or even like the modern example in Peth.

Braddach came up behind Erold as he sat on the tiny rock near the water, with his feet almost touching the glass surface of the murky lake. He placed a calm hand on his shoulder.

"What are you thinking about?"

"Whether elves are any good at mage-ball."

"I'm being serious. It's the girl, isn't it?"

Erold blushed, even though, for once, he wasn't right. He had finally had a clear thought that didn't involve princesses and their schemes. In the next phase, he would have to deal with an 'Empress.'

Braddach gave up pestering Erold for what was on his mind and sat down next to him, their shoulders touching. He picked up a rock and skipped it on the water. It went five skips.

Erold tried too.

They stood back up and made a competition of it until the night fell.

The camp was abuzz the next day as they prepared for the elves and tried foraging on the isthmus. Some of the men were surprised that they hadn't come across any of the dangerous monsters that were said to be lurking in Haltvia, but it was a big country. From one end to the other, likely over one million square atomic miles and the chances of running into even an elven settlement were considerably low unless you set out looking for one.

The men were also both excited and cautious about meeting the elves in Anpol. Even the elves among the crews were wary and suggesting that they remain careful with what they say or do. The men who had made the trip before downplayed the rumors, but even Volstad, who perhaps had come through at a different time, suggested caution and tight lips.

These were the elves that lived without men among them for centuries. They lived very different lives and had subtle differences in creed of right and wrong, whereas their ancestors had been Valgaardian since before Valgaard, once helping to forge the nation as one nation of men and elves after centuries of conflict between the two species.

The row across Lake Brünn was the easiest one yet, but one of the longest. They rowed past the ice that floated near the shore and then out into the lake beyond the melting islands. The lake swirled beneath their paddles as they rowed, and their ships left great wakes trailing behind them. The waves crawled along the lake, shifted the floating white ice, died, and left the surface like glass far into the distance behind and ahead of the ships.

As they neared the elven fortress of wood and stone, he began to hear chanting for his ears alone. Kahron must have heard it too, in the language of the elves, whispered through the áether like a spell.

"Welcome Erold Ardrada son of the king of Galdir"

"Welcome Erold Ardrada son of the king of Galdir"

Then, the crews heard the drums beckoning them forth, and as if they weren't worried enough about impending battle, trumpets blared. Kahron whispered into his staff and let out a note of calm through the men just as some reached for their swords.

Moon looked to Volstad, both annoyed as subtlety had currently not been the elves preferred touch. Lyres and harps, made of gold, played along the walls of the elf-made harbor, as the elves opened the water gates, allowing the men of Valgaard to enter their humble fortress.

1514 - Chapter 30

Valgaard regularly traded with the elves starting midspring when the ice was guaranteed to have thawed. The volunteers to Cardane marked the beginning of trade every year with one of the largest elf towns in Haltvia, Anpol.

The men set up camp at the edge of town, within the walls, in the same way they had throughout the trip, and Volstad worked with Moon between the two camps to barter goods and refresh supplies. They also made sure to reassure the elven guard captain that there were no werewolves on any vessel, given the full moon that night, and the rapidly descending sun. They had been more aggressive than ever the last few years.

Something caught Moon's eye. She noticed a poorly dressed man in rags, breaking quietly away from their camp as the dark of the night neared. She began to follow him. At first, slowly, but he was speeding up, racing for the south gate.

"Stop! Where are you going?" she yelled, realizing that she didn't recognize him from the troop.

He began to run. The dusk began to settle. Moon couldn't take the chance that he would change.

She took her pistol out and fired. The flintlock smashed down, the powder exploded, but the bullet died in the barrel. She threw the pistol down angrily and pulled out twin throwing knives, breaking them from vials of deadly poison. A poison that she was immune to.

One knife to the back is all it took.

"You killed him?" accused Volstad.

"Werewolf," Moon said, sniffing the blood. She would have tasted it had he not been there. It had been one of her first cases as an inspector after the clockwork theatre that she had stumbled upon a werewolf lab that had started her battles with the agents of the red mark.

Volstad didn't question her. He turned to the elven guard and began to discuss battle orders. The man was racing for the south gate. They must be coming from the south. They were hoping to get through the elf defenses before any one was aware. They couldn't leave the north walls undefended. The east and west of the city, being protected by the lakes, would still have elven defenders too.

"Veleon, you take half the men and cover the north side of the wall. I will cover the south side."

"What about Erold?" asked Braddach, who had also followed the commotion from the camp to the street, where the body now lay, still beginning to change, writhing in death, as the moon rose, and the night began.

"Do not alert Erold or Kahron. Move to the northern wall with Veleon." Volstad ordered. The men began to ready their long rifles, glad that they wouldn't have muskets and would instead be able to load a bullet at a time from the muzzle without having to pack in the powder.

No one at the fort yet knew how many bullets it would take to bring down beasts twice the size of men. As people disbursed to take battle stations, Volstad leaned into Moon.

"What do you think?"

"They waited for us. This man must have snuck into our camp last night and joined the row this morning. There's no saying how many there will be, but there could be hundreds of them."

"We'll be on the south wall. The beasts will know that they'll have to fight their way in."

* * *

Kahron shadowed Erold, who went to meet the tribe elder and voice of the town amongst the council of the elves of Haltvia, though it was known by another name among elves. Staff members met Erold at the docks and led him through the city, which was formed in orderly rows of houses and shops that split from a central circle in the shape of web or a wheel.

The yellow, wood houses had short red doors with tall facades that stretched up toward the sky, covered by steep rooves made of thatched sheets of painted-green wood. Snow still rested in the nooks where it had gathered like clumps of permanent paint and was piled high in the courtyards between the rows.

A belltower stood at the central square and behind it, Erold could see what looked like a lighthouse, which must have been for the bigger lake to the East. Some of the white, snow elves were guiding elk through the town like horses. The town steadily rose between either lake shore toward its middle on top of a flattened hill.

The staff showed Erold in to meet the councilor in a wooden building off the central circle, that looked much like a modernized version of an old Normen grand hall, given modern finishes and stone foundations. Perhaps, they had traded secrets once upon a time. This far north it had to be hard to get more than wood and stone shipped, but the dwarven kingdoms that mined metal and jewels weren't much further north.

As they entered the elder's office, he stood up happily and greeted Erold and Kahron by the door.

"Erold Ardrada, the king of Galdir, pays us a visit," said the councilor. "I am Councilor Blue Shroud, in the common tongue, which doesn't sound as pleasant to me, and who are you, sir?"

"Kahron Yuvek of the Menetorian Islands, a mage, councilor Blue Shroud."

"For convenience's sake, call me Louie. I wish my daughter had been here, but she's on her way north to meet with the dwarves about a land dispute they want our help with. It's a pleasure to meet you."

"Pleased to meet you as well. Sorry, to be so blunt about it, but I didn't expect a welcoming committee."

"Why's that?"

"I don't currently sit on the throne of Galdir. I am setting out to win my kingdom back now, your highness, and we are passing through your lands on the way."

"I am an appointed official, so councilor is fine. I never did much understand the way that it works among men, considering there always seems to be a dispute over power, but I have been hoping to meet you at some point, as an adult."

"If you don't mind me repeating your own question, but why is that?"

"No bother, no bother. Really, it's nothing." The councilor played with something on the desk and then briefly glanced at the window, "You see, I heard a rumor that there was a prophecy about you. One that was hard to read. I dabble as a seer, myself, in my spare time. I'm a bit of a hobbyist, sleuth of the future, and I had hoped to read your runes."

Kahron put his hand out to indicate for Erold to hold his tongue for a minute, "Are you suggesting that, since the future nears and the path has become clearer, that now would be the time to re-read the signs?"

The councilor nodded, "Yes, I'd be honored to read a difficult prophecy. One that hasn't been deciphered by even the greatest oracles in Elessia."

"It's like a solving a puzzle game, only with real stakes, and you want to be the one to solve the game?" Kahron stood back and let his hand down, "Erold, I don't know about you, but I'm curious, having never seen a seer work."

Erold spoke, "I've met many seers, and they all say different things. The future is murky, but much will happen before its done unless death comes first. Or, between the ages of thirty and fifty, all they see is prosperity, but then darkness. None have read either side of the coin into what it means. I've already lived longer than has been foreseen."

"So, it's a no?" asked Louie.

"I didn't say that. Just that I fail to see the point. Yes, you can read my runes."

"Great," said the snow elf as he motioned for Erold to follow him through to an antechamber. He held up a hand for Kahron to stay outside, but the wizard laughed.

"I'll either watch through the wall in ethereal time, or you can let me join you in the room where I can observe you at your work."

The old, snow elf dropped his hand and shrugged, "It may make it harder to read, but Erold, first we'll talk, I'll get to know you, and then I'll see if I can be possessed by the spirits of the future. Mr. Yuvek if you could quietly observe, I would appreciate it."

"As long as the boy's safety is guaranteed, you have my word, I will be silent."

* * *

As the moon rose, casting its glow over the trees and the wide swath of open ground between the walls and the tree line, howls began to rise in the night like sirens' songs. One, two, two hundred.

The duo of Volstad and Moon were beside the gate on the wall along with over one hundred thirty of their own men and at least two hundred elves.

"They'll be going through with the attack," said Volstad, making sure he had his pistol with easy access in case of close quarters, and checking his rifle a couple of times, ready to load the ammo down the front and fire.

The men had the new .54 ammunition in cartridges set beside them near the wall to load as quickly as possible, and the elves had a combination of elven longbows and muskets, with barrels of black powder hidden beneath the wall alongside more ammunition, .54s and iron balls. Support teams would run packs up the stairs to those who called for it.

The long bows had a much longer range, but an arrow on a werewolf could be like a bee sting on an elf unless they took the arrow to the eye or chest. Even a silver tipped arrow wouldn't be completely deadly. The long bows would fire at the tree line, while the rifles waited until the enemy had moved halfway across the field to begin firing.

* * *

In the antechamber, there were two low couches, with plush pillows, and dim lighting. The walls were covered with blue, purple, and gold wallpaper. An oil lamp hung in the center, and Louie turned the dial to a dim glow.

He presented one of the low couches to Erold, and motioned for Kahron to stand in the corner, where he leaned on his staff and watched.

"First, are you aware that you are part elf?" asked Louie as he sat.

Erold shrugged, "I might've been told that before."

"It's from your father. He comes from an ancient line of elves, one even more ancient than mine."

"Why does it matter for the prophecy?"

"It'd be easiest if you let me ask the questions," Louie sighed, but he shrugged, "In many nations, the tale of elves and men is one of anger and strife, some yet to come."

"So, you think that the secret to the prophecy could be related to whether Erold is part-elf?" Kahron asked.

"Both of you, seriously. Erold, don't ask questions. Kahron, silence. This isn't airship science. I have to get some sense of the facts before trying to read images from the future! Do you know how hard that is?"

Both of them shook their heads.

"Believe me when I say, it's hard. And it's harder if you don't follow some simple ground rules. Okay, Erold, are you aware that you were given an elven name as part of your lineage?"

Erold nodded and spoke his secret name.

"The man with no path." The councilor grabbed some ink and a quill and wrote this down next to the word elf in swirling cursive and black ink that seemed to shrink after he had written it on the page.

"And, you are aware that you can use magic? You have self-actualized?"

"Yes," said Erold.

"Fascinating, yet simple. What do you know of the Otum Elves?" Louie looked at Erold closely, "this is a bit of a history test, so speak freely."

"The Otum Elves," Erold thought for a moment, wondering which direction to take the question. There were many things said

399

about them. Many things and many opinions. He had to carefully weigh the words before he spoke, even in such a private setting, with just the three of them there. With a question such as this, the walls have ears and secrets have long lives.

"The Otum were known as many names across the lands. We call them the Otum. They conquered and colonized across the world. They took over an empire that is rivaled by only Domiscus. With the help of Fros, the Otum and their evils were defeated over fifteen hundred years ago, but in this land and in many lands their influence lives on, for good and for evil."

"And the not facts? What about those?" said Louie, "The opinions. Who were they? Were they good, or were they evil?"

"The Otum were evil. Many were defeated in war and the Otum seduced them with the promises of technology, and enslaved men and elves across all the lands, twisting their lives into property," Erold replied quickly.

"Were they also good?"

"No," said Erold.

Louie thought about it as well, "if it was the slavery that made them evil, for they enslaved men across the world for centuries, what was the rest of their society?" Before Erold could respond, Louie continued, "You see, some believe, we elves are all the same; and that we resent men for the Otum's fall; but we fought that ancient battle just the same. Your savior is our savior, though not all men know his name. We, the elves do, and we keep it now."

"Fros," said Erold.

"It might be, it might not be. The true name of the prophet shall not be named, confirmed, or denied. But, back to the point of good and evil. I believe the Otum elves were both, evil and good. But, as great colonizers they shared their gifts throughout the world and that is not what we found evil, for spreading trees, seeds, and knowledge, is not evil."

"But, you say your forefathers fought with Fros, as mine--I mean, as humans, elves, dwarves, and all our kith and kin, did against the slavery of all."

"True, we, the free elves, fought against the Otum, because of their evil, alone, and not weighed against their good. Our northern tribes of free elves allied with men, though some free elves in other regions did not, not because they thought the Otum were good, but because they didn't believe it was their fight. We did. We, the elves of this endless forest, cherish the Otum's defeat. We, of your shared ancestry do not make war, we protect the forest, for we have decided to stay; and for many generations our young would like to leave for foreign lands and cities, but often they stay too. For this is a quiet life and despite our desire for strong borders, a peaceful one."

Peace, Erold thought, is though only thing anyone seemed to talk about.

"Something about peace doesn't ring true?" asked Louie as he scribbled down more notes.

"We all talk of peace? Peace? Yet, it seems the destiny of the world is written in war."

"Destiny. What an interesting choice of word," Louie jotted notes furiously. "It is true that men often sought to escape or blame the Otum, and this led to many other, great wars. War is an animalistic trait though. Innate, but not fate."

"What's the point of all this?" asked Erold, becoming annoyed, wondering out loud, "Are you reading my future or are we discussing the ancient past?"

Louie thought out loud as he reviewed notes, "Often understanding the past is the key to understanding the future, and often the past is chosen to be simplified and overlooked, rather than investigated and explored."

"What does that have to do with me?"

"In your land, unlike all others, was a tale of love, between a free elf queen and a free human king. When many elves left this land, we stayed as she did, and we kept this forest as those who came before us did. You, now pass as many generations of your past did, as elves and men, through this very forest, who decided whether to stay and keep it safe. Many more left for further on, to the north, and to the west, and to the south too, pushed by wars against the Otum Elves who landed in this land, to the east; and in other lands, to the north, south, or west. Direction is both meaningful and meaningless and as all things, relative."

There was a silence, and Louie realized that he had let Erold do the questioning, so he asked, "What about magic? What do you know about magic?"

"Okay, so as you say I'm descended from an ancient line of elves."

"Ancient and powerful line of elves."

"Yes, and I am touched by the divine gift. Most elves are, naturally, and some men, with or without elven blood, but almost all with. I know from recent reading that every nation has their own legacy with magic. Some darker than others. You point out that mine is a legacy of love. Interesting." Erold stopped, noticing that for once there was a piece of history that did not revolve around endless war.

"I find that interesting too," said Louie, and then he turned the attention back toward magic. "The mythology of magic is itself another mystery as long as the history of time, and the tales and explanations of how it's used and why are just attempts at understanding something not naturally gifted to the fraternity of men. For elves, on the other hand, understand naturally, how to draw power from the land without tapping into the darkness that waits inside. It could be that your nation's legacy has yet to be determined by the forces of darkness and light."

Erold didn't like Louie's answer, so he said, "It could be that my nation's legacy is key in some other way." He didn't want to be the one to unwrite the past, especially when it was the only example of love in a world of war.

Louie put away his quill, and said, "I think I'm ready to read the runes."

* * *

Moon could see the werewolves begin to slip from between the trees. She looked at Volstad, hoping he knew what he was doing as much as she hoped she did. She had only ever fought one werewolf, and she had gotten lucky.

She had decided to grab a rifle too for this fight. She hadn't fired a gun in a long time, and the size compared to a musket was daunting. The kick of the gun would leave a bad bruise, as she had to heavily brace it down to shoot it, but she wasn't going to leave defending the wall to men who didn't notice the stranger among them while worried whether the elves of the village were dangerous.

Some of the elves let their long bows loose, reaching the tree line. They had doused the lamps on the high wall, to help the shooters adjust to the way the light would track across their field of vision. Some of the field had patches of snow, while most was muddy and dark green. No one could completely see the shadows beneath the trees, even in the gray light of the full moon. After a few blinks, the shadows of the grass, like waves of dark tufts rather than blades of needles grew out of the empty ground, revealing that there was always more to see.

If the elves had seen their arrows hit, their morale may have shaken as the werewolves ripped the arrows for their arms, hungry for fresh meat and foregoing reason, intent to attack an entrenched foe.

As one, with a tremendous roar, they leapt from the trees, landing on all fours in a dead sprint at the wall. The first line from the trees was at least fifty strong. The second another fifty, then sixty and seventy. Then a fifth line of eighty, and finally, the last line of one hundred, pushing for the wall.

"First line fire. Second line fire!" yelled Volstad, commanding the riflemen to stagger their shots and then realizing the speed of the enemy, changed tactics. "Fire at will!"

He pulled up his rifle and fired at the hundreds of wolves that tore across the ground, disappearing between shadows, their skin covered in mud to match the darkness. The arrows flew and muskets fired too, at first in unison and then in desperate fury, unleashing as many silver balls as they could on the oncoming beasts.

It took ten arrows or more to fell a beast and as many as six bullets. On they came, in a space of less than five minutes they could close the gap and leap to the top of the wall. Even three hundred hands couldn't unleash enough salvos in time to stop more than the first line. The arrows of each quiver were used before a single beast had fallen.

"Warlocks, gate spell!" yelled Volstad.

They made marks in the air and a barrier was unleashed, which for a brief moment allowed the elves and men to reload their arms and refresh their arrows, neither side able to cross the threshold until the magic had been beaten away by the gathering werewolves, readying to avenge the few of their number that had fallen.

"Warlocks, let's give them a push!" yelled Volstad.

The gate began to visibly weaken as the werewolves began to tear through the veil. Rifles fired on the encroaching limbs, and a shot split the hand of a werewolf that screamed in agony as blood and skin flipped into the air.

The eleven warlocks readied to unleash a push in unison across the battlefield. The ethereal gate came down, and they let it loose, the air rushing across the field and throwing the werewolves back.

Some few strong enough to brace, or far enough away to not get the brunt, held their ground, and the rifles and muskets on the wall took aim and began eagerly to greet the oncoming waves intent to feast on flesh.

The fire of guns lit the night in pockets from the top of the palisade, and the angry wolves, pressed on, their numbers thinning, until the first of the wolves met the walls, leaping until they were half up. Their claws clung to the wood, pulling themselves up to the top in one rush of brute strength.

Arrows turned down at their faces. Rifles fired away at more werewolves that swarmed. Some on the wall fell back, dead, covered in arrows across their heads like needles. Others were able to tear the heads of elves with their bows from the walls with huge fists, clenching and tossing the creatures into the night behind them.

"Warlocks, cover the walls!" yelled Volstad, knowing that only they could challenge the raw power of the werewolves and hoping upon hope that the werewolves wouldn't be able to break their line on the wall and begin to swarm among them. The battle would shift in favor of the attackers if they could get behind the defenders.

A werewolf climbed over the wall, dwarfing Volstad and about to swing at him. Moon, stepped in the way and put the muzzle of her rifle between its chin, jettisoning the shell up through the beast's brain at point blank.

Warlocks across the wall began to defend their brothers in arms as some werewolves began to retreat, taking what elves had been thrown from the wall with them. The last on the wall were brutally executed by sword and rifle as the elven men watched their own be taken, knowing they would soon be ripped to shreds and eaten.

No matter how much beast a half-man was, be it wolf, bull, elephant, rhino, panda, cat, or any other type of half-man or near-man creature lived in this world, a true elf or man could never eat it. One could only hope for a swift death for the captives had already come, and be thankful that none of the women or children were taken.

* * *

"This is a process called a peace quest, and there are many processes like it that people use to look forward and back, together at once. With this information, hopefully I can help you understand your destiny, Erold."

Louie took a folding table, hidden behind his couch, and placed it between them. He checked that it was sturdy and pulled out a sleek box of polished wood. He opened it revealing stone dice of all sorts of shapes with runes etched into the sides of an ancient language that the snow elves once only shared with the Normen, not even other elves. Erold recognized them from items his father had kept of his mother's.

"The process is simple," said Louie. "There is no sulfur, mushrooms, or other enhancers involved. It's a roll of the dice and a sprinkle of my own magic."

He gathered up the runes and scattered them across the floor, with Louie seemingly unbothered by whether they were visible from where he sat. After the last die had rolled into place, Louie stepped toward the circle of scattered dice.

As soon as his foot hit the center of the room, his eyes lit up ghostly blue. Then orange, then red, then green. Each changed colors as smoke began to rise from them toward the ceiling. His mouth drooled and his right eye stopped on red.

His left eye continued to roll and roll again, as if someone had pulled a lever to make it spin.

Finally, it stopped on white, and the smoke of different shades of color gathered in rainbows above his head.

Louie spoke in an even, controlled tone, as if he was reading the book of ages, that had been presented before him alone to read before its pages had been filled in, "There is a dark and a light in the story that can't be unwoven from a casual glance. I will speak as much as I can to understand, but it is true, your destiny is difficult to unravel. It may be your secret future, and ours to behold. War, peace, each in equal measures. Love, hate, both fill your life. Victory, defeat, that is where the path splits. Yes, that's it."

Louie stopped speaking and began to look in either direction as if he was turning pages or looking for another book in a library, "Maybe, I shouldn't try to read your future, but read the possible futures of the world just beyond yours. It is so clouded, but I can see something. If you are to die now, in fifteen years, twenty million will be moved from their homes, more than two million soldiers dead, and fifty million more will never have been born. There's more to it that I can't see. I see it now, wars stretching endlessly and more nations that suffer with more death and strife. At least ten million dead and then thirty million. I can see the spirits of the near future form and disappear in the mist. And if you are to live, there will be a different war, but its fate. It is too clouded. Perhaps, you are right, and the destiny of the world is war for I cannot read beyond it."

The elder council member sat down, and blinked furiously, clearing the mist from his eyes, and disappointed in himself, he said, "It seems the secret of your prophecy continues. We are still much too far away, and much has to be determined through the actions of many men must run their course until the path before you can be determined."

Erold nodded, "In other words, my destiny is my own to make."

"I have never heard of a case where it would appear such as that. Most often there is at least a part of the future visible in the mist. War could be in any one's future. It's unclear what part you play in it, but without you, war is inevitable."

Kahron had been curious of the visions for Erold, not actually because he hadn't seen one. It was because he also had visions of his own life presented before him once, and he had thought that future was gone and forgotten, untrue, until he had seen the boy stand up to the dragon on the mountain. He was not yet sure how it might relate, but he had to return to Cardane to discover whether another prophecy once foretold would come true.

As they left Louie's antechamber, he pulled Erold outside and threw a spell of silence into the air, hiding the two of them from Kahron.

"Your path remains clouded, but I confirmed in my vision the object that you carry with you. It is no small trinket. With it, you have the power to do great good, but great evil will come from it."

"What did you see?"

"In your possession, you hold a powerful tool--we have long known of these orbs, yes--keep it secret. That device is built upon ancient power with a technology not that old, but its devastation is legendary. It is said Domiscus built many of these orbs by tricking the angels, and the resulting wars lasted more than a century and engulfed the world. We hid from that war because we knew its danger. The orb wields a power that must not be used. The forces of darkness are still seeking it now. They seek that very orb. We here in this deep part of the forest, where the noise of the things that cannot be seen, can be felt, have sensed its presence. Others in the quiet world, might find it too if they choose to listen. Others with darker motives. There remains evil, pure evil in the world, despite the fall of the Otum, and there may always be. Be vigilant."

Erold felt at the small, white object hidden away against his side, in a little pouch wrapped beneath his armor.

"Can you teach me to wield this power safely?"

"No! You must never use it. Instead, you must learn to balance good and evil, if you are to avoid either path alone, each of which fills the future with darkness."

The spell was fading and soon, Kahron would turn to discover the two of them speaking, so the elder let his fierce grip of Erold's arm go and relaxed.

"I'll have one of my best staff members assist you in your

endeavors to combine the elven ways that come naturally with you with the magic of the islands I can sense master Kahron has been teaching you. Remember there is power in all things." He looked as if he wanted to say more, but Kahron had turned and appeared confused. He seemed to wonder if he had missed some question that Erold had asked about magic. Perhaps both Kahron and Erold had underestimated Louie.

Louie had them meet his attaché, Eche, who would be guiding Erold around the town for the remainder of his visit, and if he would so choose, help him to practice magic for however few hours or days he remained in Anpol.

Eche led Kahron and Erold back toward the camp the Valgaardian contingent had made. It had gotten dark and old, oil lamps that dotted the city came to life, lighting their path. Eche didn't say much. He left the two of them just outside the tents, where Erold could see men cooking beef beside the fire.

"It might be helpful for you to learn something from the elves," said Kahron. "I have been teaching you simple magic because simple magic built up, becomes complex. Defensive magic like the magic of the islands allows you to respond quickly and strike fast. For me, I had to learn the process of converting energy into spells through movement. Perhaps, with your elven blood, as I have now learned, you need to learn how to bridge between the natural power you can gather easily and the world around you."

When Erold joined his companions, he could see the black powder residue all over their shirts and sleeves, "There was a battle?"

He joined them as they sat around the fire and ate. They passed him some cooked beef.

"Werewolves," said Braddach, who listened in from the tent that he had set up close to the fire, "They attacked the south walls while I was guarding the north."

"No casualties," Moon informed Erold, "Among our men, at least. The elves were lucky we were here."

"The rifles we were given were a much more accurate model than even the old, long barrel muskets. The elves will be buying some now," Volstad said.

"Our first real horrors of Haltvia and I wasn't there to fight," said Erold, disappointed.

"I've seen this kind of werewolves before," said Moon, having confirmed they looked identical to those that she had first seen more than twenty years before a detective in Akre. She was certain that the encounter was anything but random. A trained dog strikes where its master tells it to.

"Not many have and live," Volstad commented, looking at her with a renewed respect.

"What did the elder want?" asked Moon, changing the subject quickly while her mind silently traced through possible theories.

"To read the runes," said Erold.

"What did he say?" Volstad asked.

"Best not to discuss it further," replied Kahron. "It can wait for another day."

* * *

The next day, they lifted the ships out of the water, using a pully system that the elves used in their harbor to take the boat up on a platform. After carrying it across to the other side, they let the boats into the Alf Lake side harbor and went back to their camp.

It was a much shorter walk than it had been from the Great South Lake to Lake Brünn, so it didn't take all day. But, it was still exhausting. Even the elves helped despite seeing how the Normens lifted their ships with apparent ease.

Afterward, Erold and his companions sat and lay around a fire beside their tents under the afternoon sun. Erold took his watch out of the bag that he left it in during the trip and saw that it was only three.

Perhaps, he could train with Eche, who had helped with the ships, but he didn't want to.

"Aren't you going to train today?" asked Braddach, "I wouldn't waste this opportunity."

"I'm too tired," Erold said. "I'll train tomorrow on our rest day. We've only taken two breaks since we got on the lakes, and we still have half the trip to go."

"If you want my advice on all this magic business," began Volstad, who was drinking a beer he had bought at a local tavern and carried over, "it's about seizing opportunity. Not just about an opportunity to train. You have been working hard, now you have to apply that to opportunities. Be opportunistic."

Erold studied Volstad, looking from a loaf of fresh, elven bread, smelling of garlic, rosemary, and thyme, that he was tearing through to the old Normen across the fire. Volstad being a warlock had surprised him, but he knew now. His advice as a man who forced himself to gain magical powers, was likely spot on.

"It's not that I can't use the spells. You saw back in the palace. When I had the axe, the spells that had been such a challenge when training with Kahron, came easy." Erold took a bite of bread and thought for a moment, "But I want to take the next step. I want to be as powerful as you are, Kahron."

"As I've said from the beginning, it is about controlling your emotions and channeling them forward."

Erold nodded.

"I may not be a mage," said Moon, "but from my experience, it is important to always be ready for anything. You need access to your power always."

"Yes, that's the issue. It seems like I need to learn how to have the access to my power at an instant. What do you think Braddach?"

"I didn't train in the islands like Kahron, so I don't know how it's done there. I succeeded in Imor Valsen by charting my own course and letting the feelings of independence and freedom guide me."

It began to rain, so Erold didn't search out Eche. It was a convenient excuse for how he felt. In truth, he was upset that he had been left out of the battle against the werewolves, and he felt, knowing that it wasn't likely true, that his lack of skill was to blame.

The next morning the rain continued to fall, so the elves beckoned the Valgaardians into the taverns to wait it out. Beer was more expensive than water, so most of the men had to go without until the elves lowered the prices on account of the battle the day before. Erold and his companions, including Bradach, sat around a small, round table, looking at glasses of water for most of the morning. Their day of rest had turned into a day of waiting.

When the rain had finally subsided, the streets were filled with puddles and mud. Eche appeared a couple times, but he could sense that Erold did not feel up to it. As the sun finally started to shine in the late afternoon, Eche took a different approach and asked Erold if he would like to go for a walk.

"I heard from the Councilor that you are trying to learn defensive magic from the Menetorian islands."

"Yes," said Erold. He wasn't sure if it was going well, or poorly, and he wasn't sure if training with an elf would make any difference.

"Have you ever trained among elves?" asked Eche.

"No," Erold shook his head.

"I could see why you might not want to, considering we weren't very strong against the werewolves."

"That's not it, but why not? I thought the councilor said that all elves have magic."

"Elves are magical, but untrained, we only have access to the limits of our initial skill. Many of our higher-ranking elves in Anpol are the strongest mages, but they aren't our first line of defense."

They walked in silence through the streets as wagons and carriages pulled by reindeer passed by. Eche hoped that Erold would open up to him, but Erold said nothing.

"Did you know that you were part elf?" asked Eche.

"I still don't fully understand what that means. My father never told me," replied Erold.

"Where did you study then?"

"I trained in Albion, where we learned mainly offensive magic like fire and lightning. There wasn't even much on magic theory or history class. I learned a lot of that from the palace library in Peth. I realize now that there's a lot more to magic than just controlling the elements."

"Yes, there is. Did spells come easy, or have you found it a struggle?"

"It's always come easy before."

"That's the elf in you!" Eche exclaimed.

"Maybe, explain it for me."

"Elves draw naturally from the world around them. Human mages tend to gravitate to different schools of magic, accessing their own power first rather than that of the world."

"I had read a little bit about the delicate balance of good and evil, but I don't read elven."

"Yes, across all things there is a balance of forces of evil and good. Elves access the natural forces innate to objects. All things, even the smallest things, have power."

"So, it's not related to the balance of forces?"

"With any magic, you must beware of crossing the threshold, known as many names in many places, all meaning the touching of the other side with your inner being. If you fail to tether yourself to the world of the living, the darkness can grasp a firmer hold of your undefended soul, but it is not all evil. Some mages, whether known as wizards, warlocks, or witches, have no problem with the power that they wield, and it spills forth naturally."

"How do I have it become like that?"

"Naturally, as part-elf, you should have a center of balance that you can access. When it comes easy to you, that is the same thing you are looking for now. You are trying to think like a human mage to use human spells, but you need to draw the energy from around you and not within you. Then, you can use the magic like a human mage. It's the difference in where the energy comes from that matters."

Erold agreed to train with Eche and surprised himself. When he stopped thinking and just let the magic flow, he threw powerful aura balls and even colored them in all different shades. Kahron looked on impressed that he was starting to improve again like when they had first begun together.

When the training session was complete, Kahron caught up to Erold, "Now, all you need is to test whether you can use defensive spells?"

"We can do a training session tomorrow."

"I don't mean another training."

"I mean a practice duel with only non-lethal spells. Not against me of course, but perhaps Eche here would like a go."

"I'll do it," said Braddach. "I'd like relish a chance to push your limit, Erold."

"Loser does the other person's laundry next break?"

"Deal."

"We'll do it tomorrow morning near the Alf Lake front."

"What about the plans to ship out tomorrow?" asked Eche.

"I'm sure Volstad wouldn't mind watching a duel even if it means leaving a few hours late," Kahron said.

* * *

They set up on a natural beach of gray sand on the shore. A few men came to watch including Veleon, but most hung out in the camp, using the extra morning hours to sleep in. Volstad and Kahron came up with the ground rules after discussing differences in how the two schools trained. Eche and Moon watched on from dry rocks, near the tree line south of the elven city walls, that gave a slight view from above.

The mage to leave the first mark from a charged aura ball would win, meaning that it couldn't be lightly tossed. It would have to be thrown hard enough to singe the skin, or the hit wouldn't count. There was some debate on whether they would be allowed to fight in a circle, or if they had to stand on opposite sides of a center line.

In the end, they decided that Volstad and Kahron would joint enforce distance between the fighters, and they would have to stay at least five atomic yards apart, or a gate spell thrown by Volstad, which was more subtle than an aura wall thrown by Kahron, would pause the match.

Kahron started the match with a blue light flashing into the ground in front of the two shirtless challengers, and the duo for a second stood there without their guard up, readying spells, as if they were going to play mage ball.

Braddach tested Erold with a slow ball, Erold hit it with his own faster one, fizzling it in mid-air. Then, they began more earnestly.

Erold found that he still didn't have the blocking spell, but he could knock Braddach's aura blasts out of the air by shooting them with his own.

One almost caught him though and he had to hit it with an aura ball still wrapped around his fingers. He tossed the broken shard of white at Braddach, and it snaked through the air like a spinning knife.

Braddach narrowly dodged the beam as it spewed sand everywhere, and the battle picked up speed.

Erold had to run to dodge, and Braddach chased. As he neared the water's edge, Erold began to get pinned in between the field limit behind him and the water to his right, which was technically not off limits. He made a move to try to get back inside, tricking Braddach, who launched blasts to Erold's left.

Erold dove toward the waves and sent two aura blasts up at Braddach. One hit in his bare chest, the other shoulder. Neither left a mark. He hadn't put enough power into it.

Braddach turned and began hammering a furious bout of aura balls at Erold, who rolled backward. He got a second to stand, and slipped, realizing too late that he had gotten onto the ice. His friend stood on the beach, preventing him from getting back to dry land and had an aura ball ready.

Braddach threw the ball and Erold, slipped, dodged, and partly dove toward the water at his right. The aura ball caught him on the side as he naturally braced himself with his arms.

He looked at his side. No mark. He was still in it.

Kahron cheered from the far side of their field of play, and Erold looked down.

He was standing on the water, just like Kahron had tried to show him at Helmun Loch.

Another aura ball came at him, too fast for him to try to get out his own. A shield spell countered the blast, leaving Erold's arm glowing with the yellow aura and the aura ball fizzled into thin air.

He began running across the water left and right, throwing spells back toward the beach, using his blocking spell to counteract

Braddach's spells.

Braddach ratcheted up the intensity too. He used push spells with one hand to blast Erold's aura spells every which way while unleashing an endless salvo of aura spells on Erold in a circular pattern, trying to catch Erold's defenses out of line.

Braddach kneeled under one of Erold's spells, used the push on the water, and threw four aura blasts in a line.

The water whooshed out from beneath Erold's feet, and he fell into the sand at the bottom of the lake. Two of the four aura balls hit him, leaving red singes, while the ice-cold water rushed back over him from behind.

Braddach had won.

Volstad congratulated Braddach, while Erold climbed out of the water and Kahron conjured an imitation of a towel and lit a fire on the beach to help Erold dry off in the morning sun.

"I didn't realize you could conjure objects," said Erold after his teeth had stopped chattering.

"A wizard never reveals all that he can do. Besides, it's not my specialty. A functioning towel is a requirement to pass the Menetorian licensing exams."

Eche came up to Erold as he huddled close to the fire, feeling soaked and cold, "You performed well. I'm proud to have helped you access your power."

"Thanks Eche. I didn't win though."

"Winning is temporary. Ability persists," said Kahron.

"Hopefully, you will now be ready to fight against the sharp, brass flowers you'll find in Cardane," Eche smiled.

1514 - Chapter 31

Valessa and Arla stood beside each other, looking over the large map. In many ways, they were opposites and, in some ways, similar. Valessa stood, blonde and with blue eyes tall and thin, with her icy, sapphire blue eyes, staring at the board like two peaks of the eternal blue flame that burned at the center of every fire. Arla was a bit stockier, but she too, was thin, and her red-brown eyes did not pierce like ice but warmed like fire.

Arla was glad to be back in the palace after her months in Menetoris, and with the success of the alliance and Onya staying in Albion, she had suddenly become the best and only real option to work alongside Valessa. Her efforts in mage school had paid off, and she felt confident that the position was not only well deserved but that she would be able to reward Valessa for her trust in the long run.

Valessa appreciated the company more than she ever had after Eleanor. Her first two friends, Eleanor and Onya, had assisted in developing her information network. As things had gradually settled down following the frantic rush to delay and prevent total war, engulfing Valgaard, she had begun to question anything that Eleanor had ever touched. Arla had never worked with Eleanor, and she had proven her loyalty considerably by showing good faith in Menetoris.

It was the two of them, alone, practically running the show for the whole country. With her mother's health quickly deteriorating and her father sinking into solitude, the two of them were left to coordinate the administrative daily tasks and deal with anything major that happened. One such major event had taken place in a bit of a shocking twist.

The forces of Akre that had been mobilizing and preparing on the fields south of the city for the last few years, had begun to ship up the Atlan River toward Mondelvania, where a sudden rebellion had attacked Akrin strongholds. Valessa had occasionally backed organizations financially in nations across the empire when they had attempted to establish a new local rule such as previously in Emira and for a long time in the Westernlands, but she couldn't send anything to Mondelvania, even if she had anything left to give. Her relationship with the nearby dwarven kingdoms was far more important as even with Albion's mines, her people relied heavily on the northern Orichalc. Not to mention, the rebellion had already attacked them. For that reason, she wondered if this had been a rebellion backed by yet another player on the world stage, Instra, the cold, dark nation that held most of the Ahrian northeast.

The frustration of the sequence of events was that Erold was to be passing through Mondelvania almost at the same time as the emperor and his men might be. Every time Valessa counted the days that it might take Erold to finish his trip, she believed that there would be a few days overlap of the two, passing through the same country.

She could only hope that the vast wing of the army that was on the move wouldn't make target practice out of the small militia in the longboats, shipping to Cardane. She had begun to pray that the enemy would be delayed, if only by a day. It was all she had left, but to hope that he would be safe. She wouldn't even be able to know, for however long, whether he would survive the journey or not.

If he arrived in Cardane, it, too, would be dangerous. He may not have realized it, when he was here, as much as she did right then, looking at the map, but she felt suddenly that she may be betting the future of her nation completely on whether Erold could make it back to Peth alive.

Until then, whenever that was, the empire had plenty to deal with or without Valessa organizing or aiding anything. The fringes of Emira, like many of the nations under Cardane's oversight, had long been pushing back against the brass flower in the east. Emira seemed poise to burst again and Harupht to the south, one of the world's largest suppliers of Orichalc, had not been able to reach quotas, according to reports, referencing dissatisfied workers. The fighting continued in the Westernlands too, but she would consider herself delusional if she thought the small pockets of wood elves that she funded could do more than upset the colonies' shipping lanes for much longer. The attack by the Ispiardans had been lucky. She hadn't planned for good luck, only bad luck.

She was running out of money, though selling the parts of the dragon she had bought from Erold would help, she had to empty much of the remaining coffers to fund his expedition. The reality remained that if she wanted to make any impact on the local results of nations vying for independence, she needed more money. For that reason, as well as needing the manpower of Normany and the breadbasket of the Solgra, Erold had to return from Cardane, rich and willing to purchase from her the army and weapons necessary to retake and re-establish hereditary rule in Normany, which remained virtually empty of troops, just across the Evorul mountains.

Valessa traced the lines on the map mentally. Arla was entranced by the magnitude of the room as well. They both watched the silent figures move in their imaginations, representing millions of soldiers and people.

Things hadn't played out exactly the way that she had imagined them to, but in the end, a necessary alliance was formed that protected each of its members in some way. She hoped only for peace, and as the opposing nations struggled internally to keep it, she began to look at the many nations that formed together to make up her own. Right now, the leaders of each state, understood banding together for the greater good, and in relatively recent memory, could call upon the betrayal of her grandfather in the massacre at Canari Valley to not trust Akre. She contemplated moving all of the leaders to Peth to govern from the center, or instituting many annual celebrations so that she could appease everyone.

"Nothing we can do, is there?" Arla mused.

"We can," said Valessa.

"What?"

"We can celebrate the peace. That's what all this is for, after all."

* * *

The sun rose on Lover's Day of 1514, and Valessa was spending it alone, except for Seaspirit in the stables. The horse was happy that it was warmer again but had kept looking for Erold. Valessa stroked the mare's back. The unicorns were much larger and often hard for a woman, even of her height to ride, but this beautiful mare was the perfect size.

"You're thinking about him too, aren't you, Seaspirit?" Valessa cooed into the horse's ear as she brushed her hair. She could only wish that he was safe as he passed through the dangerous territory of Haltvia. She had begun to spend every day with the horse in the stables, but especially on Lover's Day, she thought of him, braving the dangers of the ice forest.

The horse neighed to Valessa, and stretched her legs, tired of being trapped in the building. Valessa felt it in her core, the trapped feeling. Oh, how she longed for the old, innocent days, not so long ago, when she ran through the palace halls with her brother, Lanhyr, who was killed by the princess of Cardane, Zosin, after Valessa had seen her with the commoner named Safu. It had turned out to be the defining moment that turned Valessa into who she was today, but it was also why she worried constantly for Erold's life.

"You want to go for a ride, don't you?"

Valessa felt as if the horse was talking to her, saying that she wanted to see the city, so she took the saddle off its resting place and hoisted onto the back of the cooperative horse. She walked her out the stable's front gate, and then hopped on her back.

At first, she trotted out of the palace calmly and alone, and she nodded to the royal guard, who joined her on the back of their unicorns. She eased Seaspirit out the front gate and began to follow the main street through the city, looking at the green of spring, filling up the cracks and spaces between buildings. The calm, blue lake glistened under the bright yellow sun, stretching to the horizon into the distance, and the white and gold of her city welcomed her, shining equally, as the people came out to greet their princess, lining the streets and calling out her name with adoration.

They threw white flowers at her, and she smiled and waved, flanked by the head of the guard's cavalry division, Milton. He was always serious when in his officer's uniform, but when she looked at him, he had cracked a big smile too. She realized that tears were coming down her cheeks. She hadn't seen so many of her people, since Erold had marched the dragon up to the palace steps, and the spring bursting forth from a long winter inside, invigorated more than just Seaspirit.

1514 - Chapter 32

They rowed away from Anpol before midday with a better view of the city than on the way in. None of the pines blocked the hill where the city rose up gently away from the lake; its large main hall and its central spire, where Louie worked, were visible from the glassy water.

Anpol was the furthest north they had been, and they came out onto Alf Lake facing to the north before they would cut back to the south when the lake widened to camp on the southern shore. Alf Lake was a little less than twice the size of Lake Brünn, which they had crossed to get to Anpol. Ice still covered much of the shoreline of the lake and in thick sheets across every inlet. A cold wind sprayed ice into the air like a fog of sharp snow.

The lake was no longer protected from the coldest of the winter wind by tall mountains in the north, far away, that pushed the wind east. The lake had mountainous hills on its northern coast that made it impossible to use any of the northern shore to camp, so they followed the line of the ice slowly.

In the end, Volstad made the decision that they couldn't risk being stuck on the lake for three days of rowing if they couldn't make camp on the southern shore, so they began to row hard where the lake had been melted across its middle.

The sun soon fell, forcing them to tie the boats together and huddle in their same clothes in the boat while the temperature dropped to below freezing on the Odin Scale. The days of spring may have begun to warm above freezing, especially on sunny days, but until the summer it would never get close to seventy in the day.

This far north, drifting along on the water, curled between his oar and his trunk against the wall of the longboat, Erold imagined warmer days. His fingers felt cold enough to break off, but at least he could feel them.

He felt responsible for them being stuck on the water, because of his duel. He had wanted badly to beat Braddach, and although training had become a chore, the idea of facing his friend had reinvigorated his spirit.

It didn't make a difference to the trip in the end, because taking the direct route across, it was still almost a two full days journey to the other side of Alf. They would just have to hope that if they drifted it would be toward the east shore. Given the lack of waves, Volstad wasn't too worried and night watchmen kept a log on the current.

Ocean travel would have been different in the times of the old legends who lived on in the people that they had guided from old Nole to their new countries.

The backs of Erold's hands began to feel almost warm, which worried him. Erold pressed his hands beneath his armpits and blew warmly into them, curling under his blankets, that like everyone else, he had taken out the ship chest they used as windbreakers. He felt pain in his hands again, which kept him awake. He lay there, worrying if his hands were going to fall off, and he'd never be a mage as the moon, having been full those three nights before, lit the lake in silver.

It was the twenty first of Solsri, the thirteenth night of their trip. Lovers' Day was two days before for citizens all around the Empire and nations where the Empire's influence had spread. So much of the world was celebrating new beginnings and continued passion.

Here he was freezing as he clutched himself beneath the blankets, hoping ice wouldn't splash cold water over the ship's side where a painted wood and steel shield, gifted to him by King Hughgar, was held in place.

He imagined what Princess Valessa might be doing. Perhaps she was thinking about him, but most likely not. He was still the king of nothing, but at least now he could sling the more advanced spells that Kahron had taught him.

He briefly channeled magic into his fingertips, seeing the glow shine through his blankets and feeling the tingling sensation of the warmth of power, despite the cold world. There was still a long way to go to reach the gulf.

The last night watchers woke up the ship's full crews as the day broke the plane of darkness that circled them. The waxing moon still hung in the sky with dots of the stars that shined as brightly.

They ate cold bread and drank from their canteens. No one wanted to risk a fire out on the frozen lake. The rowing began shortly after and those that had kept the night's last vigil, napped in the back of the boat.

Erold had trained physically in the palace, but the journey was beginning to exhaust him completely. His head hurt, his side ached, his fingers bled. Callouses were born and broke. On he rowed, as hard as ever, hoping to do the work for two men.

They took their usual break at midday to eat more bread, which felt like a bad omen when they couldn't save it for later when they might run out of salted meat. Some of the food had rotted while rowing across the first two lakes. They had to take what they could barter for from the elves, which would have to last almost another week.

The guides began to warn them about the river that lie ahead, telling them that if the river was low for the season that there would be rapid water, and even if it wasn't they would have to portage past a number of waterfalls that broke across the length of the river.

It would be the most grueling part of the journey yet, with stops and starts to the rowing, lots of lifting, and only one extra day of camp to make sure the return group had enough supplies to make it back to an elven city.

The far bank of Alf Lake came into view and Erold held in a sigh of relief as they heaved as fast as they could. The sails weren't out, and the sun was fading quickly. Once again, they rowed against the wind.

Faster and faster tempos were called for. They rowed harder and harder. The men grew excited as they closed in on the pine trees of the eastern shore. No matter what the guides said, they had almost made it the whole of the way through Haltvia, and once they were on the river, it would be all south from there.

When they got into camp, had set up the tents and built the fires, Erold could not believe how excited he was by the smell of searing beef and of the campfires that boiled water and unfroze his hands that still ached from the night before.

It felt like the entire camp did nothing but eat with silent praise for the gifts from God. Few words were spoken. The night was just a touch warmer, and as soon as the sun went down, Erold wrapped himself tightly again in his blankets.

His first battles would be soon. They could be attacked at any moment. These were the trees of the Endless Forest, that stretched from Haltvia to the other end of West Ahria through every kingdom in between. He was almost itching for battle. His muscles clenching and unclenching involuntarily.

His axe was beside him in its case. His shield was ready to be plucked off the ship. The orb, which he must not use, was still tucked tight to his body anyway, a memory of his father. He had trained with all kinds of weaponry, but the double-sided axe made from talons ripped from a giant dragon's claws, would be the first true weapon he took into battle.

The next morning, the sweet smell of salted pork after just one day of maggoty bread, the elven bread being saved for future days, was divine. He ate as if he had never eaten anything like it before, knowing full well they would be portaging again to where the Eldin River neared Alf Lake.

One by one, the boats were heaved out of the lake by the teams from the beach bank and lifted into the path cut into the trees. Sentries continued to keep watch. Erold forced himself to focus on his part of the ship's edge. He had stopped caring what his clothes were going to look like as he stepped through puddles of mud carefully and looked ahead to the rest point and food with desire.

The nine boats with their shields, mastheads, and cargo were left side by side, one by one on the bank of the river, which ran too quick for the boats to not be shelved on the shore. They would repeat the process down river, hoping to use one of hundreds or thousands of side streams to pull the boats out of the river's current.

Another day of rest.

Erold cleaned his and Braddach's clothes after losing the battle, in a stream too small for the ships. He looked down the stream at the Eldin River. It flowed into the Atlan many atomic miles away, which marked the end of the enormous elven nation, Haltvia, and the start of Mondelvania. According to Princess Valessa's many lectures, Akrin worked through Mondelvania to ship the dwarf kingdoms' metal and ore to Akre while Valgaard, used a longer but easier route, running near the mountains in the northwest, that could also accommodate the deeper droughts of the frigate and cruiser-sized sea ships that would be carrying the ore on the Atlan as well.

Before he left the stream, he found a rusted clockwork arm on the edge of the water. He lifted it up and looked closely. It must have been one of Domiscus's machines. He hadn't realized they had ever come this far north. He put the object back down on the side of the river and rejoined the men at the camp.

They slipped the ships into the river, holding them by rope to the shore, with men and gear inside, who then worked with the land-side men to ferry people onto the boat. The ships let go of the shore once everyone was on board and they began as much to row down the river as to guide the ship down it.

Spotters marked their point on the river by turns and noted stone, and soon, they were shelving the ships again on the shore, pulling them on through the muddy bank of a side stream, where the ship wouldn't be pulled by the current and lost. They lifted the ships up again and found footing in a large loop to get around the cliff face of a giant waterfall.

At the base of the falls, where the path had looped, Erold looked back up at the water tumbling down the wide crescent moon of black stone that rose like a cliff away from its base in the shape of eagles' wings, delivering the river to the water below like a faucet. Only time could know when the strange plateau would break and come tumbling down.

They may not have covered as much distance, because of the falls, or even rowed as hard, but for the fact that the day had required both and was toward the end of the long journey, they broke out the only barrel of elven beer they could acquire at dinner.

Moon came to check on Erold, and they both talked about how nice it had been to be out in the quiet air of the far country without the daily concerns of revolutions and what that might mean for daily life if they could escape the axe.

The wide riverbed sunk below the distant scenery, leaving them to look at the tops of pine trees, encircling them except for the shelved boats and the river, almost giving the appearance that they were completely ensconced in another world, transported away even further from the old concerns than they truly were.

Erold agreed but didn't tell her that he was beginning to see politics everywhere. The elves claimed this land but had no towns along the river. Mondelvania or the orcs in the south might push into the north if the weather would warm. The tall trees would make good lumber trade and the Eldin running into the Atlan meant the goods could be shipped to Akre.

Protecting a land for its own sake in the fading light, cutting through the trees from the fires dancing between white tents, became a question of the alliance. It became a matter on the table of objectives when considering the implications to both Haltvia and Normany if he were to fail.

Braddach woke him up early in the morning to make sure he could get some of the salted pork. He had recognized that it was running out and went to wake up Erold. Erold dressed quickly and ran to join the gathering swarm, just barely getting a half portion that he had to fight for.

They'd have two more camps and on that final morning, they'd go their separate ways. One crew north and a longer route home, planning to resupply in a town on the border shared between snow elves and dwarves.

The other crew, his crew, the one hundred seventy-three plus him, were in for a short hike to Helsingstein, a city with a rich history of violence, that stood as the nearest port town to the confluence between the Atlan and the Eldin, and housed the Cardanian frigate that would carry them south across a different river.

Whatever portion of the pork, he got, it was worth it. The day was hard and long. Brutally cold for a spring day, and they had to cut past multiple smaller waterfalls. It felt as if they did more walking than rowing.

The boats slowed into a curve of the river, and Volstad and the guides were speaking at length with the boats ahead. The river was too low, and the water would swirl into whirlpool death traps. Their boats were shallow enough to not get caught and twisted onto the rocks, but they would need to row hard.

The calls were made to push and pull with all their might, and they thrust their longboats forward in the same long line of nine, hitting the edge of the river, passing the swirling drain of dark water in a tilt.

Erold's axe shook a little bit below him, but he thrust his foot against the case and pulled twice as hard. Their long rows hit the river disappearing on the left right before Erold's face and threw it back, lunging the ship out of the wake. Pulling it up the same way the ship before it had gone and then following that too as it meandered its own route through the river, navigating around the black rocks that cut out of the white, blue, and dark shadow of the river.

Another portage and Erold felt like he was holding the weight of ten men on his own. Rocks and streams, creeks and trees, passed on his left as they heaved the dark brown ship over the path, now overgrown. Perhaps not used in year's past when the river was running higher, or perhaps they were far enough south that the days were not as frigid.

His feet got wet in the spray of the rapid water, and the creeks so small they'd had to wade the ship through. He rested them now beside the fire, bare and purple from the bruising of the long journey. He let his shoes dry too, hoping they'd be ready by the morning.

Braddach did the same, sleeping beneath the twilight. They were thousands of atomic miles away from home now, or at least it felt like they were. It also felt as if they were on a normal trip down the river, running it like the explorers of old. Yet, they were really sneaking in one big arch around the biggest Empire in the world, passing soon into the northern reaches of enemy territory and going humbly into their lands as journeymen mercenaries of ill repute.

They pushed off the next morning for the last time, and Erold became nostalgic for the feel of the wind in his hair, and the tension in his arms and chest as he pulled on his oar, despite still having a day's row left. The river had run through its hardest course and now widened as it neared its confluence with the Atlan.

The trees began to melt away, leaving them within a growing canyon that sloped away from the river.

"On your guard men!" yelled the guides. "We still may be in Haltvian territory, but these are highwaymen borders."

Rifles were placed at the ready, and they watched the quiet, stone hills for even the movement of a mountain lion. A goat jumped from cliff face to cliff face, looking the size of a silver piece held at arm's length.

Erold looked now at the white-stone carved away by centuries of water and noted the swirls in the façade like black galaxies of shining stars, riddling the cliff walls like mold riddles through cheese. Little sprigs of crooked tree split at odd angles at less than an atomic yard a piece and between them little green bushes, so hungry for the sun that they were almost only a ghastly, pale white.

"We're almost into the Atlan boys!"

Cheers went up.

"We have to launch across as fast as we can! The current'll pull us too far south if we let it."

They would soon leave the Eldin River behind, but there were no markings on the edge of elven land, just the mystique of the canyon giving way again to the forest up ahead, where the opening in the distance, signaled they were nearing their destination.

The cries and calls for even strokes went up, and the men pulled as hard as they could.

"Slow! Stop!"

It was too late, they were going full bore into the river, and had to dodge the ship in front of them as it tried to swerve to the right.

Ice bergs rushed past on the Atlan, coming from one of the Eight Lakes far to the north. They wouldn't be able to make the low beach camp off the river just across the way. Then, he worried they might sink and be pulled all the way down to Akre by the current as frozen dead.

The first ship cut into the Atlan, unable to come to a halt, and the current sucked it in, pulling it toward the iceberg. The men put up their oars and poked them into the berg at once trying to keep it at bay. The oars that touched the ice splintered, sending wood over the side of the ship.

Erold could hear the man at the head of the ship yell, "Row back you ninnies" as he tried to get them to push against the current of the river. The ship started to slow, but the nose of it where the head man stood, swung toward the port-side as the stern of the ship fought the current.

Whoosh!

The dragonhead on the bow swung just past the ice, and the ship's heading switched to navigate for the nearest shore on the Mondelvanian side.

Erold's ship followed next, waiting until they could slip into the Atlan at an angle with the river, then paddling to match its current and shift to a southeasterly heading following quickly after the first longboat.

The rest of the ships followed suit, and they had soon found a new place to camp with a large enough stream cutting away from the river on the eastern shore to hold the boats through the night. As Erold's ship pulled in a bloodcurdling scream split the air.

"Fight!" the first ship yelled.

They had to get out of the boats and push the attackers into the woods or risk being burned alive while the rest of the ships would fall into the same ambush. Erold had his axe out of the case just as an enemy's hand gripped the side of his ship, jumping from the hill flanking the ship. They must have been attempting to board them and force close combat.

Schlop.

An armored forearm fell against the floor of the ship, wriggling.

He slipped his axe out of the divot he had left in the ship, unhooked his shield, jumped over the side of the ship and decapitated the highwayman, landing above the stream bed on the hill, blood flying against the side of the ship and filling the stream.

An arrow came at him, he used the shield. Then, he sent an icy magic spike out of the head of his axe, whistling through the air, catching the man in the stomach and pinning him to the oak tree behind.

The rest of the longboats began to pull into the stream, while the battle shifted toward the hills. The enemy was forced to retreat to the high ground in a defensive U-shape. Rifles began to fire as the Valgaard forces fought up the hill on the enemy's right flank. Erold took cover against a tree, searching for his companions.

A minotaur, half-man, half-bull, broke forward from higher up the hill, and sliced at the tree where Erold had hid. The tree almost snapped completely in half as Erold dodged.

Erold slid onto his knee, bracing to not slip into the stream bed, and sent a mage spear hurtling through the air from his axe, aimed at the minotaur. The beast broke the spell with one quick swoosh of its mighty arm.

A crossbow dart whistled at him from his right. Moon caught it with a shield and at the same time sent a poison knife through the shooter's throat.

The minotaur charged at the two of them, downhill. Erold ran at it. They met in the middle, the minotaur swinging its scimitar through the air. Erold used the shield spell he had just learned to break the blow at the minotaur's elbow. He shoved his axe into the minotaur's neck and speared it through.

As it fell to its knees, gurgling up blood. Erold twisted the axe and sliced once back away from his body, splitting the beast's head from its body. He grabbed it in the air and raised it in the air.

"Yess!" He screamed.

"Don't feel too good," said Moon, "I saved your life."

They followed the battle up the hill as Volstad and Kahron bolstered units that pushed the enemy away from the ships.

"We likely got lucky that we were pulled off course," said Moon as they caught up to Volstad.

"Yes, looks like they had set an ambush at the site of last year's camp," said Volstad.

"They might've been staking out for weeks," said Kahron.

Erold threw the minotaur head down.

"I have a unit circling back along the stream to see if they're going to attempt to double back and make a second attack, but they suffered heavy casualties," said Volstad.

"How many did we lose?" Moon asked.

"At least ten, run through. Clean kills. We have three wounded," Volstad replied.

"Where's Patr?" asked Erold.

"None of the warlocks went down," said Volstad. "Valgaard'd be in sore shape if our special forces could be at risk to a group of highwaymen with mixed arms."

"And us," said Moon. "We would be too."

"Yes," Volstad agreed.

"Cardane won't be easy even with their help," Kahron said.

"Erold, you and Moon head back to the ship, and begin

organizing the camp. I'll finish rounding up the troop and setting stricter watches. We still have to try to make the walk to Helsingstein and the Raudren River tomorrow."

"Will do," Erold was annoyed that he had to miss out on the rest of the battle, especially after Anpol, but two kills, and one being a minotaur, was a good day's work. He helped the men clear away the dead to be burned, to avoid plague and for their souls sent back to their ancestral lands. Few graves could be dug deep enough in the hard ground of the frigid north.

They looted the remains, stripped them of goods worth selling, and put the gear and loot among the rest of the food to be shipped back the northern elf route with the longboats.

After shelving the ships on a low shore off the stream, they broke out the elven bread and extra portions of beef for one last feast as a unit.

They slept tense that night as large crews watched the fringes of the camp for a redoubled attack by the large band of highwaymen that had attempted the ambush.

None came, and in the morning, the teams split. Those of the Valgaardian army contingent that had helped them along this far, portaged the ships up stream, taking much of the gear with them, and the best of the men, not attached to the warlock squads. With only ten they could lift the ships and Erold wondered if they had let the others struggle to give themselves a rest for their own long haul north and back around to Peth. At least Mondelvania was relatively flat compared to across the river in Haltvia.

Erold looked at the rest of the crew, ragtag, hungry, and thinner than in Peth. Thein and Ragnar were two of the only men with any thickness about the arms. They were well armed but had little training. In less than a week they would likely be in Cardane. His contingent formed into loose ranks, cleaned up the camp and packed the rest of their gear.

Erold didn't know what awaited them, but if he was to be fighting the equivalent of a dragon once a month or more for the next ten years, this sorry brigade would need to be stronger as a unit. He unhooked his shield along with the rest of the men and put it over his back as they went to leave.

Erold was sure that the rowing they did across the north would have helped them become stronger and form a common bond. He also knew that they had empty armor to fill with new recruits, and the ones they had would need to form tighter, more disciplined battle lines or risk more empty armor.

They reached Helsingstein at about midday. There were square-sailed frigates, cruisers, and schooners moored in the harbor of the town. The ships were, no doubt, part of the Orichalc, iron, and salt trade that the East Cardane Shipping Company ran from the hills north of the Raudren River through the Iron Sea to the many gulf nations.

He could see them before he could see the port. Their masts protruded from the break in the short rocky hills and thinning pines that blocked the low town, which sat along the shore, from view.

The town had a sign as they approached that described some of the history and noted it as the "City of Black Roses" and beneath that a single line explanation, "the only town in the world where black roses grow naturally."

As they came down the slope of the hill, the path closed in on the river, and then it took them back around to the north, where they viewed the city from low to high.

It nestled in an almost closed circle around the harbor, where a watchtower doubled as a lighthouse over the water dug away from the river by man's hand. It must have snowed the night before, because the buildings were dusted lightly with white.

Most of the buildings were loose wood, encircling the harbor and a large town square with a brilliant fountain, shooting fresh, clear liquid into the sky, that sat adjacent to the water on the northeastern side. Stone and brick made up the rest, as there were Akrin arches and Cardanian turrets, high wood walkways stretching over intersections, and Normen-esque pointed roofs, and in between these church towers. Some roofs were thatched, some shingled, and the roads were paved stone.

Volstad found a modern hotel he had jotted down, where he bought rooms for the night for the remainder of the crew. He found the merchant captain, who owned the chartered ship at the hotel's own bar.

It was interesting to him that the taverns he'd stayed at made little comparison to the 'Grand Mondelvanian Hotel' when sitting at its exquisite tables and staying in the rooms just overhead. The old format for the wayward traveler remained the same, but the destination changed.

The old merchant might have been a man Volstad recognized from the first time he'd made the trip. There was no way to know for sure. He excitedly bought extra rounds of drinks for the two of them as he was thrilled for the easy payday when the waves of the ocean would be light.

The merchant tried to haggle for the Valgaardians to pay too, but in the end, he relented. The trip was easy money, and though it had him resting and waiting in Mondelvania for a couple weeks of the year, hoping that some, if not most, of the Valgaardians would show up, it was the type of risk he could afford to take.

In the morning, the merchant crew helped the mercenaries load their gear on a large frigate-class merchant's vessel, void of almost all guns. The merchants filled in empty space with more goods from the local market. When Erold loaded his gear, keeping his axe case and the orb, he peaked at the rest of the cargo hold and noticed most of the ship was filled with Orichalc from the mines in the north. 'Red Gold' the merchants were calling it in idiomatic code.

Afterwards, they shipped for the south, following the Raudren down through the Iron Seas, then out into the Emiran and across that to Cardane, the 'City of the Brass Flower.'

Three days, at the longest, the merchant captain had said as the ship left the old port behind.

1505 - Chapter 33

The solemn chants of eight men and eight women, one for each of the first followers of Fros, filled the grand banquet hall accompanied by a lyre and a flute. At the rear of a long table, in the shadows cast by fire light, emanating from candles lit in bowls lined along the center of the table, the eastern emperor, sometimes referred to as sultan by his own people, Alalwee Zosin stood. His mocha skin looked almost black like the color of his eyes and beard. He stood, tall and powerful in his best white robes, fit snugly around his powerful physique, with a blazing red sash and his long beard meticulously trimmed and shaped to show off his impressive chin.

His face was full of mirth as he held his brass cup before him, ready to raise it to his honored guests at the end of the slow song of sanctity. The chants of Cardane were unique to the country and recalled the eves of ancient battle. They had evolved since they were first sung in the days of Otum invasions. The rising feminine tones set amidst the deep voices of the men invoked a chill in the spine and they had become symbolic of the deliverance from great evil by Fros.

Alalwee closed his eyes as the men's voices rose to higher notes, and he let out a light sigh through his nose. He was eternally grateful for the acts of Fros, who having surrendered his own life, gave all men a chance to live without falling under the slavery of the Otum elves. The lands of Cardane that he had inherited, long after, were much of the core of the Otum during that time, and it was the territory just across the Unedette Sea in northern Elessia where the mountain vale of the ancient holy land resided in the shadow of one of Domiscus's ancient pinnacles. Cardane had suffered more than most kingdoms under her reign. She had once again shackled men like the Otum had under her ruthless clockwork armies.

She had also set out to destroy the free elves. For Alalwee, when Akre had fallen to King Hughgar, his honored guest, he had taken it as an opportunity to reassert the power of his fatherland and its commitment to the sanctity of Fros. Though elves had long since dwindled in his desert lands, he also reasserted a welcoming to the free elves as pilgrims, traveling through his territories for they too had followed Fros to cast down the Otum. Despite his devotion, he did not hate those who did not believe. He did not hate the Utaurans who did not follow Fros but believed in a hidden path to the unclaimed land of Zion, nor did he harbor any resentment to the followers of Estelaide in Imeria.

It was a sticking point with Alalwee, during long negotiations over the years, that Valgaard, who had been plagued with hatred for the free elves in recent centuries, renew their own commitments to internal peace. At the same time, negotiations had become more tenuous for them both. Akre had regained its footing beneath an increasingly powerful senate. After a few years of skirmishes and finally ceding northern Verdas, also known as southern Valgaard to the northern kingdom, the golden city had begun to reinforce the claims of King Karles I, the conqueror, who had captured Cardane in the fourteenth century as a vassal state.

His great grandfather had been allowed to remain as the emperor in the east, in title, keeping the independence of his state in exchange for military servitude and tribute. Alalwee did not relish returning to a position of being a puppet of the foreign city, but he would do what it took to avoid a war he could not win, even if it meant surrender. He was running out of time to pick a side.

Bright white banners had been hung along the sides of the banquet hall emblazoned with the red flower of Cardane. The table had been set with dark blue and dark red napkins and cloth, adorned with brass plates, cups, and cutlery. His guests, the King of the north, his son, Lanhyr, and young daughter, Valessa, had been seated with their retainers and their glasses were filled with red wine.

Four lambs and ten rock chickens had been sacrificed and a Celadonian boar from the east coast of Elessia had been hunted and shipped in across the Unedette sea. The steam of its roasting meat still drifted into the air from the center of the table where it lay. Sweetmeat confectionaries, exotic fruits, and spices from far flung lands filled the room with smells that the foreign king and his children had never imagined. Golden syrup from the trees of southeastern Mondelvania dripped down towers of golden Kouign-amann cakes that had been layered in successively smaller cylinders.

The chanting subsided and Alalwee raised his glass, "To my dear friend and guest, King of Valgaard, Hughgar Wenselclaus, may your days be filled with feasts and friendship for all time. It is a pleasure to have you return here--."

Reena Zosin, his daughter, had finally decided to enter the hall, followed by the stern disapproving look of Varce Kidel, leader of the Varanorian guard and his right hand, a young Valgaardian, who had spent too many years to count in Cardane already, Abrim Volstad. On her left was her personal guard and assistant, Jrasood, the 'tiger.'

"Ah, my daughter has graced us with her presence at last,"

Alalwee's smile grew, "To cement the alliance between our two great nations, as we have agreed, my wonderful daughter will wed the crown prince of Valgaard. Lanhyr, please stand."

The tall, blonde man, seated next to the old king Hughgar, stood. He was much thinner than his enormous father and younger than Reena. Reena Zosin smiled and bowed. The man was good looking, but she was still upset at her father. She was tied to convention, but that did not mean he should be allowed to choose who she married.

Lanhyr bowed, "My lady, it is a pleasure to make your acquaintance." His full, white smile oozed an aura of smugness, and Zosin had to calm a flutter of anger that rose into her. He was just another outsider who wanted something from Cardane's slice of the world.

"She's just as beautiful as you described," smiled King Hughgar and raised his cup to complete Alalwee's toast. Brass clinked strongly like metal swords as the wine sloshed about and the feast began.

Zosin was sat next to her betrothed, and while she could not stand him, she conversed with him in the common tongue and behaved in a manner befitting Cardane's royalty. He was vain, but unfortunately charming. He didn't win her over, but she understood the circumstances placed on her father. She was twenty now, and she had figured out how to live in private one way and public another.

Jrasood stood behind her, and she glanced back at him as she dug her teeth into a bit of lamb leg that had been served by one of the staff. Zosin knew that Jrasood was one of the few that she could count on to be by her side, even after she married the foreigner or if.

While her father would be adamant that the move was to guarantee independence from Akre, she also knew that he was upset that they had not taken his side, or any side, in the long-standing trade war with the Coltari in the Otum Ocean. She wondered how much of this event, today, was merely an empty gesture, some kind of farcical show, to force action by the senate on behalf of the East Cardane trading company.

Princess Zosin stole a quick glance over to her father to see if he was still talking to the captain of the city guard, Alil Nessah, who had become a de facto advisor in recent years. The two were locked in some kind of debate by the looks of it, but when Alil looked her way, she had refocused her attention on her would-be groom.

While the Cardanian princess refocused her attention on the blonde prince, the young Valessa watched the older princess intently. Her long, dark hair gleamed in the light as if it had been soaked in oil, and the way she walked caused the long, thick plait to sway side to side. The older woman was practiced and mature, whereas the young Valessa had only been taken along by her father to see a different part of the world. She stared intently at every movement the woman made, down to the way that she sliced the lamb and the boar that was given to her.

The older Zosin with her dark skin and manicured fingers, painted purple, sliced her own meat with no hesitation, and while she appeared dainty with her thin wrists, she did not act that way. She talked and acted forcefully, except that to every professional of her staff that waited on her, she praised and demurely stated a graceful thanks.

Valessa's father had never cared, nor tried to make her behave in any particular way. Her mother was far stricter, but neither had the grace or tact of royalty that Zosin exuded. None of the houses of Valgaard that ruled the many fiefdoms throughout the countryside could boast such an example of fine living. The woman made being a princess a performance art, and the child, Valessa, was in a way, starstruck.

* * *

As angry as she was, Zosin knew that she had to let things play out. If her father wanted to try to marry her off to the highest bidder so be it, but that would not stop her from living her own life.

She nodded to Jrasood as she wrapped herself in a cloak and stepped from her balcony up and onto a three-ram, hovering over the white stone. Manning the contraption was the young, Safu, a simple soldier in the navy, who she had fallen for. Every night as darkness descended on the coast, he whisked her away to enjoy the magic of the stars away from the city lights.

He once said that a three-ram, fully stocked, could even make it as far as Elessia in one ride, but they had never tried to go that far. He had stopped her in the market one day when she had gone out for a stroll and bought her an apple when she had no money.

She had fallen for his kindness, and when she had later seen him among the naval soldiers in a parade at the palace, she had Jrasood track him down. She had loved most of all that he did not expect anything from her, or even guess at what she wanted with him.

Zosin curled up against Safu's arm as he stood, guiding the small aircraft over the city with deft hands. Their one headlight lit the darkness ahead. A few other airships whizzed past as the shadows of boxes and men aboard did not even glance from their own work.

She turned to look at her love. He didn't glance back. She kissed his neck and pressed her forehead into his shoulder. His heartbeat was patient and slow, and she tightened her grip on him, looking forward to making love in his little flat, where they could sip tea and laugh in secret.

Safu didn't guide the ship there right away. Instead, he followed the city streets from above until they came out over the beach on the western shore. He slowed the ship and let it hover forward slowly where they could watch the last of the sun disappear over the horizon.

He let go of the wheel and sat with his feet dangling over the edge. He beckoned her beside him. A few people stood on the beach below, tentatively enjoying the shallows as the last light of day lit the world.

In the semi-darkness, it did not feel as far as it might have been to the dark sand. It was far enough that they couldn't get back on the ship if they fell, but not far enough to get hurt. He draped his arm over his shoulder as a chilly wind danced along the shore, kicking up a bit of sand and teasing her neck. When she turned into him, his lips found hers, and she kissed him back as beachgoers, who did not know her, cheered from below.

* * *

"She wants to meet the princess tonight?" Alil asked, thoughtfully.

"Yes," Lanhyr replied, holding his young sister's hand as she nodded.

"Not you, correct?" Alil looked at him, skeptically. "There is protocol. You do understand this."

"Only my sister," Lanhyr nodded.

"Fine. I will take her personally," Alil stood from his desk and nodded to his adjutant to take over. Varce Kidel, who had advised against the outsiders making the request was surprised at the breach in protocol. He knew that the princess was not there, but when Alil commanded him to escort the prince back to his chambers, he was stuck.

The King Hughgar was back in the royal guest chambers, where Kidel was headed. Jrasood was manning the door to Princess Zosin's chambers. Even the 'Tiger' would not say 'no' to Alil. If the young Valessa found that Zosin was missing, or worse yet, Alil did, what would happen next?

Kidel motioned for Lanhyr to lead the way, and then pulled the young Abrim Volstad aside, who had stood waiting at the door to the stairs downward, which would go to the guest chambers, "Follow them, make sure nothing untoward happens to the little girl, and report back to me of anything that occurs."

Volstad nodded and jogged to catch up with Alil, who had grasped the little girl's hand and began leading her toward Zosin's floor. When the young mercenary caught up to them at the stairs, he explained that Kidel had asked him to take the Valgaardian back later that night.

Alil led the trio between the guards at the top of the curved stairs that ran along the outside of the curved walkway of the old central palace tower and along each floor in a wide, half-moon shape. On the newer towers, they had installed new technologies, which might someday change the shape of the palace tower, but Alil did not mind the stairs even if he had to help the young girl climb them.

The last light of the sun poked through the circular windows that overlooked the city to the west on the princess's floor, casting beams of light into the hallway that were separated by dark gray silos of shadow. Jrasood waited patiently outside the door into Zosin's chambers.

"May we see the princess?" Alil asked.

Jrasood shook his head, "She is not available."

Alil smiled and under his hand cast a simple spell that no one seemed to notice but the young Valessa, "If just the girl could take a peek?"

A simple charm of some kind was cast to weaken the resolve of the stiff Jrasood, he immediately relented, cracking the door for the young princess. Volstad was surprised that Jrasood had not put up more of a fight, but before he could say a word, the tiny, foreign princess had disappeared through the grand door, alone.

Valessa looked around, a little scared. The room was as dark as night. Once her eyes adjusted, she began to find her way. It did not appear any one had lived in it for some time. The pillows were placed elegantly on couches, untouched. The chairs had been pushed into a table that appeared waiting to entertain no one. A candle stood unlit at its center.

The young Valessa neared the inner chamber, Zosin's bedroom, where the door was open a crack. She saw the young princess, unmistakable from her profile even though she was wrapped in a cloak, hovering over the balcony on a three-ram and kissing a strange man, who then took hold of the small airship and guided it away from the palace.

Valessa stepped away from the door. She was alone in the apartments, and she suddenly felt very sick in her stomach. She felt she had to tell her brother, but she also wondered if she should tell anyone else. Perhaps, she should tell the young guard outside from Valgaard, who had followed her and Alil, or maybe she should tell Alil?

She left the room in silence, smiled, and said thank you to the guard who didn't seem to recognize her. Alil took her hand, and Volstad looked at the two suspiciously as soon as they had turned toward the stairs back down.

Volstad wasn't sure what had transpired, but he would report the exact sequence of events to Kidel.

1514 - Chapter 34

A light, cold spring rain drizzled over the Saint Egrivan as thousands still lined the streets to welcome the princess home. A fleet of five Battleships from Albion appeared as high as the clouds on the horizon a day after pamphlets had been distributed, celebrating the princess's imminent return. At the head was the newly frostened Thirdwind flanked on either side by two other battleships that had fought at GoldArrow. Airship schooners and three-rams scattered in a frenzy like birds of prey escaping predators while fluffy white snow melted in the warm spring air and filled the sky with gray mist.

A soft breeze filtered down into the bay from the large island's distant mountains, cutting into the descent of the enormous ships that drifted menacingly downward. Even though airships had been invented in Menetoris in days long past--even before the great civil war and the great flood that affected the whole world but forced many Menetorians to move to the Ahrian and Olympus continents--and still hopped between the island empires, many civilians suddenly stopped what they were doing, leaving cakes half iced and furniture being moved, lingering in the rain. They looked up to the sky to see the modern ships, larger than dragons growing with every moment until they docked above the port.

If the people had not heard the news of the princess's return, they might have thought this was an invasion party, and the way that the soldiers of Menetoris swirled about on their own three-rams added a bit of trepidation. When the five ship fleet had finally docked and shaken to a complete halt at the airdock spires on the bay that looked overwhelmed by their size, Orichalc lights from ship and shore began casting long beams into the gray mist of the rain and the ramps of each ship began to lower, screeching out the scream of metal on metal as gears turned.

From the ramp of the flagship, the Thirdwind, the clear center and lead of the fleet, the princess, dressed in all white, was led by battalions of red coated musketeers, marching in lines of four by five. The sounds of trumpets blazed, and drums tapped the beat of each step. These were answered by welcoming salutes from the trumpets of the Menetorian guard. The purple of the Saint Egrivan peacekeepers, not much above citizen soldiers, appeared in broken formations on the edges of the procession to clear the paths.

It was like a parade of summer carnival, where the whole of the city was out in the streets, but it was not to party and sling clay at each other while well-dressed but to see the princess returned. Instead of washing each other in the summer with icy water, they were slowly getting soaked in the soft rain. The princess, glorious with her red hair tucked in an impressive multi-layered bun stood atop the driver's seat of a carriage to wave as she went, flanked by a well-clad gentleman, who some knew to be the crown prince of Albion.

Ahead of the carriage, the redcoats marched and behind them too. Though most of the soldiers stayed at the ship, it still had an irksome appearance to some, who felt as if this unnecessary pomp was some excuse by Albion to show their strength. The brass band continued as the men of Albion paraded up the winding stone streets of the city to the palace where cranking iron chains lifted iron gates and opened iron-reinforced, old wooden doors.

When the princess passed, the people cheered as she waved and smiled, making eye contact with as many as she could. The women of the city chattered from one to the next and some few followed the procession to confirm the obvious while others went home out of the cold.

The news filtered through the crowd like the rain drizzled over them. The princess was obviously pregnant. Some had not known she was gone until the pamphlets had gone around and by decree of the king it was announced that Menetoris had joined the Northern Alliance, and the princess having been saved at sea from the hands of Imerian privateers would soon return alongside an escort from Albion.

A peace that they had not known was at risk was suddenly saved, and most were glad it was sorted. That was the king's job after all. The disparate news had come at once in the same notice, and though a few of those engaged in shipping had known of disappearing Coltari ships, few had been overly concerned before learning the truth.

It could have been merely an uptick in piracy or kraken attacks rather than Imerian privateers. As soon as the curious spectacle had passed, the citizens of Saint Egrivan began to disperse. The city went back to work, from dusting confectionaries with powdered sugar to repairing boilers and sweeping Orichalc ash out of exhaust pipes from steam engines where the red dust mixed with racing steam that hissed when it hit the cold air of the spring storm.

The parade went through the outer wall of the palace, over the high, stone bridge, made of four towering arches, that split a gap between the natural moat of the rocky white bluffs where the gray palace was built and the city that surrounded it. Then, through the inner wall, where the white and gold armor with dark blue cloaks of the king's army stood, gazing solemnly down with eyes hidden in shadow by impassive golden helmets, dulled in the misting rain mixed with a flurry of thick snowflakes that drifted over the high walls and tower like a thousand glittering dove's feathers. The soldiers' gloved hands held halberds vertically with muskets slung over their backs.

The redcoat musketeers stole glances all around them at the legendary sentinels. They were walking where no men of Albion had maybe ever walked, seeing the cloaked warriors of ancient legend, who had won ancient wars between the islands and even fought back the machines of Domiscus.

The parade entered the court and circled a sculptured fountain that spit water into the air, then fell in line. The sweat of the walk began to cool in the shade of the castle, and the men in redcoats shivered while the prince helped the princess down from her perch.

Admiral Jacquelina Ferrara stepped out from the carriage followed by Thomas Clayton. She nodded to the adjutants from the palace who had begun to spill from the forward doors. The driver guided the horses away while the Albion men were directed inside to a feast hall where roughly eight months prior, a smuggler crew had waited for a Valgaardian information officer turned ambassador to finish an impassioned speech to the king.

Another adjutant nodded to Ivette. She had forgotten his name but recognized him. He guided them up the series of stairs to the main door into the throne room. A brief wave of worry washed over Ivette at what her father might say upon her return or that she returned four months pregnant, but she had no time to ponder. The grand doors were already open, and King Mitas stood, resting on his golden trident and smiling down at his daughter.

"My wonderful darling Ivette! Finally, you've returned. And, welcome, my guests of Albion, come inside, let us eat in my private hall. There is much to discuss!" Instead of waiting for her to come up the remaining stairs, he stepped down them lightly and embraced his daughter. His large white fur cloak, made from the hide of a polar bear engulfed her. One hand still clutched the solid gold trident.

"Father," she said, partially stunned by the tenderness and warmth of his embrace.

Before anyone could say a word, he lifted his hands and a side door flew open, "Come, come! We must enjoy a feast of seven fishes. I hunted a kraken personally, just for this meal. There is plenty to go around."

Soon, they were eating and enjoying the feast that her father had prepared. Ivette did most of the talking, telling the old island king about all that had transpired, save for some romantic details from leaving Menetoris to escaping GoldArrow. The others chimed in intermittently with details, but having begun the conversation over hunted kraken, even Admiral Jack had been unable to find many words.

"Did she show off her skills?" The king asked Prince Eduard, and then glanced at the other two. "She's an accomplished shield mage, one of the finest in Menetoris." Ivette found herself blushing. The last time he had spoken to her about her skills, he had called her just a healer.

"Yes, when we fought to recapture our ship and escape GoldArrow," the prince said. His voice nearly failed him as he tried to fight through his fear of King Mitas.

A guardsman entered the room. He adjusted his uniform and stood slightly away from the table between the princess and her father.

"Ah, Fastian. You have arrived just on time. This is Ivette's personal guardsman."

She smiled, wondering if this was some way to cheekily point out that she had put him to sleep, "Of course."

"I will permit you to leave the island again, because let's face it, I must have no choice, really."

"Thank you," she said in almost a question.

"But, I ask that Fastian accompany you on all journeys outside of the palace walls."

Ivette looked to Eduard who shrugged, and she nodded, "Thank you father."

"I just want you to be safe, but I can't stop you from being like your mother either. She was brave more than anything, and you're more like her than your siblings."

"Where are they now?"

"Off doing what it is that they do now. I've asked them to be my eyes and ears overseas, and they may visit the Ahrian continent soon."

"What about me?"

Her father couldn't stop a glance at her stomach and then sighed, "Your siblings are older than you and as such, they will be running the kingdom someday. You, on the other hand, seem to have already made your decision though I hope you have made it official."

"We have," Prince Eduard almost choked on one of the seven fishes.

"What about Sandra, can she come with?" asked Ivette, blushing a deep crimson.

"She disappeared the night you did. I thought she may have left with you."

* * *

The next day the sun was partially hidden by clouds, but the rain had subsided and a bit of warm air from the fire islands drifted over the city from southwest to northeast.

Princess Ivette led Prince Eduard out onto one of the battlement balconies of the citadel. There were innumerous towers in the castle with an inner and outer wall. It felt like an impenetrable fortress out of a fable. From their vantage point, they could see almost all of the expansive complex. There was an inner wall that surrounded the inner castle and an outer wall that was beyond a ravine that encircled the gray palace. The inner citadel alone was larger than the Stone Tower in Rorik. Though none of its towers were quite as tall, they appeared that way from where they were positioned on the outcropping.

"It's enormous," said Eduard.

"Yes, but it feels so small to me now that I've seen so much more of the world. More than I ever dreamed of," sighed Ivette, looking out over the city in the distance. "You get a wonderful view of the port from here, see it?"

The trade ships, sea and air, arrived and left from the harbor surrounding where the five battleships were docked. Eduard studied the city in the distance where even in the light of day, one could see the Orichalc lights flickering when they burned particularly bright like stars blinking on and off.

"Yes," he said.

"And look there," she said and pointed, directing him to the expanse of the sea that stretched into the unknown. The storm had gone that direction toward Albion and sent large waves back that roared into the rocks of the bluff where the outer wall rested far below. He could see the white where they turned over, but then they disappeared from sight before the rushing crash could be heard from where they stood.

"And now here," she said and guided him until her lips met his. They embraced, interlocking lips as the waves crashed below and the warm wind from the west rushed over them. Then, together, they looked out over the sea, and each thought of the mission that lay before them to run down and capture the Imerian cruiser, the Santisma.

Neither said it out loud. They had spoken about it so much already, but they knew that unchecked it would continue to wage its trade war on the ships traveling across the Bacine between their two kingdoms.

It wouldn't be long before they launched the fleet together with the aim of cornering the massive Imerian brig and capturing or destroying it with all five battleships working in unison. They would have to plan their trips carefully to avoid stalling with no Orichalc to guide their dwarven metal balloons, but there were many days in the air above the sea ahead.

They would be working to cut off the head of the dragon, as it were, to interrupt the flow of communication, but more attacks had already been launched by new Imerian ships. Her father had told them in the wake of GoldArrow that Imerian cruisers had been spotted as far west as north of Ispiarda, and they continued to harry shipping lanes wherever they went.

* * *

Captain Graneuva looked at the maps of the Bacine Sea and sighed. Vintillo was standing opposite him, drinking some beer while watching the captain think. A red mark had been made over GoldArrow to show that it had been taken under their control but looking at it made Graneuva slightly sick.

"The Hero of GoldArrow." Graneuva didn't realize he had said it out loud with a tinge of disgust until Vintillo gulped. They hadn't had a full conversation, since the old star fortress on the hill, surrounding a centuries old castle and small village, had gone up in flames at his command.

"I can't control that, that is what they call me now," said Graneuva. His hatred for the emperor, the empire, and all things not Imerian seethed, but then calmed. He had rid the Imerian peninsula of any non-Imerian control, but he would never be able to shake the shackles of the empire, and now the emperor, himself, was calling for him to be commended, promoted even further, and had bestowed upon him the moniker.

It angered him how much he hated the empire but was beholden to it for coin. The Imerian Inquisition had once fought to rid the nation of mages while defending the elves, and yet the Empire had made witchcraft the pride of every university in their command. He believed in the chanceries, but he hated the free use of magic. It made him afraid and angry. He couldn't protect his wife from some of the spells men created. And, it was part of his pride as an Imerian!

Vintillo still said nothing.

"Do you have nothing to say!"

Graneuva looked at Vintillo, who for a brief moment as an elf looks like an elf, reminded him of his wife, who he so longed to see. Graneuva hated the face that Vintillo made. One of stunned fear. An academic who did not seem to understand that wars were fought with bullets, and you couldn't always be right with every side you pick.

He looked down ashamed but then in a flash of anger, ripped the map from the table, leaving only the pins and sending instruments flying.

He crumpled it and threw it against the wall, "There's nothing there. We can't go north!"

Vintillo took a step back. All of their work may have just been destroyed right in front of his eyes, and he was just a simple cartographer.

"We must--"

"You're needed on the bridge, sir," said an adjutant who entered. Graneuva nodded, grabbed a warm beer, chugged it, wiped his chin on his sleeve and rolled a cigarette as he followed the adjutant to the main command floor, the forward bridge of the Santisma.

"Commander on deck!"

Graneuva received an update as he surveyed the bridge. His men were in their positions along the outer edges of the large glassed-in room. He could see out the front glass, exactly what the issue was as the navigator told him positions and the head scout communicated bearings of the enemy vessels.

There were five battleships off the portside bow and closing on them. He had been on one of the outer decks for GoldArrow, but after the force from Albion had struck back, he had not strayed from the bridge during operations.

"Turn to broadside."

"Commander?"

"Do it now!"

Commands were issued through metal pipes. The sound waves were bouncing through copper running throughout the ship as steam hissed and the ship turned harder to its right to open up on the five encroaching ships.

The enemy began to move into position, copying the move by turning to their left to run parallel to the Santisma and engage it with fire.

"Wind again?"

"To southeast."

The ship had turned to broadside facing the enemy ships with its guns, which had not yet evened out their own position. He could sense cannons being readied far off in the distance.

"Turn downwind. Turn downwind now! Now, now, now!"

The same communications filtered through the ship, clinking and clanging like water through the pipes. Graneuva could see it in his mind.

They were running away, opposite of the direction the enemy ships had turned, but they had no choice. Besides, he had work to do mapping out the Westernlands that extended even further south than the current colonies. No one, not even the wood elves dared to venture past the Land of the Fae by sea, but to make it to South Olympus, the land of the dark elves, and the fabled islands of Bermulla, he could go by air.

He looked down at his hands, palms sweaty. He had crumpled the cigarette, and the tobacco was moist. He put it in his pocket to hide the shakiness of his nerves. When the call went out that the enemy ships did not pursue, he smiled while the men congratulated each other and him.

* * *

The Thirdwind had turned to open fire with the Santisma, but the Imerian ship had then turned to get the wind at its back and jetted off riding the current. In a straight-line race with the wind, they could only hope to match the Santisma's speed, not to catch it. From the outer deck of the Thirdwind, Prince Eduard watched the ship drift away to the south.

Ferrara stood at the door to the bridge. She could sense his disappointment, but she suddenly felt like things weren't quite what she had signed up for any longer and didn't know how to say it. She may have given the commands today, but he was acting like the captain.

She had grown up on the sea as a pirate, not beholden to the navy, and running from armed trade ships. When it had just been working for Theodore, his wife, and the Coltari it had been one thing, but war. She was doing it, attending the meetings, directing the flow of where ships could go, but it was much different than running the first airship she had ever captained, the Firstwind, when she had first met Theodore.

The missions Theodore had taken her on to find lost cities and thwart evil had felt so meaningful, but war? Today, they were defending the coast, but what of tomorrow? Tomorrow, would they attack?

She drew the line in her mind right then. If there was ever a day when that changed, when Prince Eduard changed, or any one of them changed, she would take her savings, buy another air schooner, hire a young crew, and go in search of Bermulla beyond the land of the Fae.

Ferrara went up to put a hand on Prince Eduard's back as he leaned on the high, iron rail of the outer deck, and saw that Princess Ivette was coming to do the same when Thomas approached her.

"Jack, you got a moment?"

She nodded, "Yes, Mr. Clayton. I think I just might." She took one last look at Prince Eduard, dejected but not angry and followed Thomas below deck.

He turned this way and that, opened doors, went past the main boiler room and the red soot covered workers in overalls fanning flames, followed iron and copper pipes that ran the length of the ship, went into the sub-engine rooms, and then began to climb up a metal ladder when she stopped him.

"Thomas, we've gone the length of the ship. What is it that you want to show me?"

He held a finger to his lips.

She whispered, "I'm not going any further until you tell me where we're going."

"Just a little further," he whispered back.

She shrugged. He helped her to climb up to one of the maintenance tunnels that ran back the way they had come through the center of the underbelly of the ship.

Eventually, he stopped, and motioned for her to sit there and listen. At first there was not a sound, and then one could hear the steam engines roaring and the fires burning Orichalc crackling and the creak of the metal of the airship.

"Do you hear a patter?"

"Thomas, what are you on about?"

She spoke in a whisper, but he grabbed her arm and looked at her menacingly to talk even quieter.

Then, he whispered into her ear, "I had to wait until there was no rain, but don't you realize, in a normal ship there is always a patter. The rats of the ship, Jack. We have no rats. We did. All ships do. I knew we did at the start, but now none. No rats."

"What are you on about? It's a new ship."

"New ships have rats. The Secondwind had rats, plus I brought some."

"You what?"

"I brought some."

"Are you tired? Maybe, you should retire like you were saying you would."

"I will. This is my last trip. I'm not crazy."

"You sound crazy."

"There was a vampire hunting us in GoldArrow. I think it's on this ship."

"Eating rats?"

"Jack. I'm serious. You didn't see the bodies of our friends, but I did. In that sewer in GoldArrow. It followed us, or was with us the whole time. I think the question is who and who do we know and not know."

"A lot of new faces on the ship, since GoldArrow."

"Yes, maybe, but how much do we trust Ivette?"

"It could be anyone," she couldn't believe that she was entertaining his fantasy, but she was.

"Could it really?"

"How many vampires do you know that have gotten pregnant? Did you think about that?"

"No."

They heard a clank, and each jumped. She motioned to him that they could continue the conversation elsewhere. If he was right, she didn't want to be stuck in that fight. She felt embarrassed that she was giving credence to his delusions, but she had grown to have a special hatred toward vampires.

They were people-sized blood-sucker bugs with superior strength and speed, which unlike the needle-nosed could survive in super cold temperatures. Besides, she had seen enough vampires in her life.

She, and Thomas, both had.

1514 - Chapter 35

The large wooden sea ship, a simple trade galley, swept over the ocean, under its square sails at speeds unachievable when riding into the wind on the lakes aboard the longboats. They followed the river for most of one day, then were in the Iron Sea on its north side and by day two had crossed through the narrow, southern gap in the land that separated the smaller sea from the larger Emiran. About midway through day three, the city, Cardane, appeared to them as if out of a dream of future possibilities.

The city itself, surrounded by a high white wall, stretched out across the bright green oasis of the coast, ahead of the arid land behind it, that grew out into large sand dunes that ran south to southwest. Thirteen white towers stood in a long horseshoe shape around the center of the city from south to north, with five on either side and three thicker towers making up a curving semicircle on the south end of the tower formation. Closest to the sea on the highest hill in the northwest was a large church with rounded domes, facing due east into the rising sun.

Beneath this was a central stadium where horse and chariot races were run and other ancient games were played like mage's javelin, the spell Erold had used against the minotaur, and above these towers were hundreds of airships encircling the air around enormous bronze balloons, docking and undocking, ferrying citizens from one tower to the other. In the distance, six more, far towers stood, serving as docks for the outer reaches of the vast, sprawling city of unknown millions, for even the great Emperor Alalwee had never counted the many Black Menetorians, who lived among the Cardanians, and were largely used as a supplemental military force.

At the center of each hub, these bronze balloons lingered like watchtowers, surveying and directing ship traffic. The effect did look a little like brass flowers with white stems, blooming toward the heavens. Erold would learn soon enough that one could, and many did, live their entire life without ever leaving one of Cardane's towers.

The harbor wrapped around a natural bay to the southeast of the city that was given additional protection from the harsh weather of the gulf through a man-made barrier of thousands of rocks. On the edge of this were no less than four long, tear drop shaped towers that mirrored the enormous central towers in color though not quite form.

The very tip of the pointed copper tops looked like bishops' hats of the great Church of Elessia and reflected the strong sun onto the sea. Within them were strong lights powered by Orichalc that could shine through the darkest storms, directing traffic carefully into the harbor.

The merchant frigate pulled in around the harbor barrier and toward docks with innumerous wooden platforms built to accommodate shipping more than to disembark passengers. The platforms themselves rose above the docks to twice the height of the ships and could be seen loading and unloading cargo from frigates, brigs, cruisers, schooners, cutters and more. Many of these sea ships of the East Cardane were built for both warfare and trade.

Erold looked up at the colors of the ship he was on and now knew the flag of the trade organization. A symbol he had only seen in seal stamps made on cargo being delivered to Seylil when he had been up early enough to see deliveries made inside the compact castle walls. Now, he could tie the red wax or paint depending on the item or letter to the white flag with a red flower.

"It's something, isn't it?" Kahron asked Erold as they neared the dock, the towers stretching into the sky above the cliff wall as it blocked the view of the low city.

"Yes, it is. What's it like coming back here?" asked Erold, wondering about the details of Kahron's personal journey first here and then back.

"Strange. I used to say that the Menetorian islands were my home country, but Cardane was my home. That was before many things happened though. What about you Abrim? You were here once?" Kahron asked, avoiding directly answering. He would address his goals in the future in bits, starting from the smallest of endeavors and hoping that would spread.

"Strange as well," said Volstad, "When I finally had earned a decent amount of money, I thought I'd gotten my ship ticket out of the city for the last time." He would have mentioned that warlocks predated the military wing that they had now become in Valgaard and that this had once been the best way to earn the most money, but he was worried about listening ears and didn't want people to tie the once rare warlock in the east to service under king Erolin in Seylil.

"How'd you get your money out of the city?" asked Kahron, curious as he had to leave much behind to move on for different pastures.

"I'm sorry?" asked Volstad. Before they could speak more on the subject though, the ship eased against the dock and gently tapped the wooden guards set along the side, giving the ship a jolt. The next conversation about the past, money or otherwise, would have to wait until after they had disembarked.

Their gear was hauled out by the merchant crew ahead of them and placed on trollies that were then guided along beside them toward a customs house on the bank of the gulf.

"What's this?" asked Erold, Kahron walking beside him.

"It's a customs checkpoint. They count any goods that enter the city, stamp them in and account for them."

"What does that have to do with us?"

"We're the cargo in this case, besides civilians are required to check in as well, when you enter Cardane. It's a standard part of the entry--and exit--process."

The mercenaries and their belongings filed into the long house and were met with, one by one, by an officer in red, who appeared to oversee the checkpoint's security. He was flanked by two soldiers in similar red, with white hats, who never spoke.

"And what fine day is it today, young sir?" the officer asked with friendly eyes. A trick question and a friendly demeanor to throw him off. If Erold had been in Normen territory, including the northern states of Normany it was typically Venday or Vendagr, more specifically. In Akre, and across most of the rest of the East Cardane Company's expansive footprint, it was Zenday. While this letter difference was trivial across the five of the seven days that were different, it was the sticking point Cardane made to find non-believers.

"Zenday."

"Very good. There is only one God, and he is God. Now, be on your way."

Attendants in white with red hats then checked and re-checked every item that they had brought along, including Erold's axe and the dragonskin armor he was wearing. He was given a stamp of goods, which included the total value of cash in hand.

Erold read the paper, thankfully in translated common tongue as well as Dune-hand.

"Keep that as safe as anything you own," Kahron told him, "If you want to take anything out of Cardane, you'll need an official slip like this with that item on it. Any gold you brought, you might as well kiss goodbye."

"What does that mean exactly?"

"You'll see."

As they continued through the customs house, Kahron gave occasional pointers. The number of armed soldiers increased too, until they were being ushered through hallways to an open arena, seating possibly five hundred on stone benches with the harbor behind the speaker before them.

The podium at the heart of the stage lay empty, and the troop with their gear waited elsewhere while re-assured that this was a standard part of the procedure. Kahron nodded at Erold, who was glad that he hadn't entrusted his orb to his bags but got antsy whenever his axe was out of sight. He didn't want to be caught in a fight without a weapon on hand. They let Kahron keep his white, mage's staff.

An armed guard of thirty riflemen fanned out at the front of the amphitheater and an escort of ten more men entered ahead of a dark-skinned woman with black hair, dressed in dark red and light pink. Although her dress was not ostentatious in its lace or frills, she wore numerous golden pieces of jewelry that glittered in the early afternoon sun, including gold loops for earrings, a simple golden crown, and a plain golden necklace along with a diamond band around her left arm. From above she seemed short, but her eyes could be felt from the stage to any of the seats where the men sat.

The woman appeared polite to her guards as she quietly thanked them for their having led her there safely, and she nodded to those that she passed as she stepped up the stairs to the podium. The wind was soft, and the blue ocean glittered behind her. The balcony and the stage appeared to give the speaker the appearance of standing on the water as she spoke, without having to resort to magic to do so.

There were no trumpets or tambourines, and there was no parade. She appeared in a business-like manner as this was a job to do. The purpose of which, Erold still wasn't sure he understood, but he hoped would be explained.

"Welcome to the Varanorian Guard. First of all, I'd like to compliment the very impressive dragonskin armor that you have. It recalls the best of times among the precious guard. For those who have not served before, I am the eastern emperor, Sultan Alalwee's daughter, Reena Zosin. My apologies for keeping you waiting. I received a telegram as soon as you arrived, but I wish I had earlier notice, to have met you immediately. You have a very important purpose in Cardane, and I wish you all to know that I am glad that you will be serving with the guard.'

'These soldiers before you are members of the guard as well, having come from Valgaard many years ago. If you are not aware of the purpose of the guard, I will explain it to you now, as these will be the duties you are likely to fulfill. For the last few centuries, my family has controlled the city, and the shipping business that has come to dominate much of the world. There have been many forces that would attempt to take that from us, and those that stand to benefit the most, are the ones within our own city.'

'Centuries ago, it was decided that the defense of the royal family would be handled by mercenaries that had been contracted from Normen regions as an elite force that once supplemented the military. Today, that has evolved to include the local defense of the business efforts of the shipping company and the internal defense of the Cardanian controlled regions. The guard no longer serves the formal military in any capacity.'

'I would like to say that times have changed and that we could trust that there aren't those of our people that would come for my father and I, but I know otherwise. It is more dangerous than ever, and it is imperative for the safety of many people beyond just my father and I for the Varanorian Guard to continue its brave service of Cardane.'

'With that, I bid you good luck on your assignments. Maybe, I will see you as members of the Varanorian Elite Guard, like these men before you, someday; perhaps a few years down the road, serving Cardane in the defense of the royal family."

Erold watched the beautiful woman exit the stage, accompanied by the men of Valgaard. Now, he knew what he would have to set out to achieve by rising the ranks to Elite guard. His men were better equipped with their dragonskin and newer rifles. Hopefully, it would be sooner for him than a few years.

They were ushered out of the stadium and marched to one of the towers where they were given a unit barracks for up to two hundred fifty men, in the event that any unit would have to absorb the remnants of another. They were brought up in groups of twenty at a time on a steam powered lift that practically levitated to their floor. The operator assured them that nowhere else in the world did they yet have steam lifts.

Erold couldn't catch much of the offered tidbits on the city rules from any of the attendants who showed them around, but he doubted they would say anything useful about what he most wanted to hear. His future gold.

Many of the staff didn't speak common tongue, so Erold's outfit ended up distributing about the barracks while Volstad followed an attendant out to meet with their commandant about orders. When Volstad returned, he motioned for Moon and Erold to join him alone, showing them the way to a tavern on their floor.

"These are indeed all the same layout," said Volstad as he led them to a table in the back of the tavern. "This isn't the tower I was in, but I'm glad they finally installed the steam lifts. There used to be just a shaft there while the things were still being invented. They only finished building these newer towers about thirty years ago."

"What's this about Abrim?" asked Moon. Volstad motioned for the barkeep to bring the three of them beer.

"It's a game of good and bad. Problem is that the good is also a little bad."

"What's the bad?"

"Cardane is not letting any gold out of the city once it has arrived. We will either be earning money on the job or looting it, and we'll get an additional fee from Cardane in gold. These will be set aside in a locked and guarded vault at the city's center. The only way to take money out of the city is through Akrin dollars, which are no good in Valgaard. Or, in five hundred pieces of silver--"

"--That's nothing--"

"--in a year."

"A yearly limit of five hundred silver?" asked Moon.

"Per unit there is another limit," said Volstad.

"So, we need to find a creative way to get gold out of the city," said Erold, "I'm sure we'll think of something. What's the good news?"

"We were given an airship to use on official business."

"That's great," said Moon. "What's the bad in that?"

"It's only a three-ram, meaning--"

"We can only take seven people on our first missions, if one of them is also the pilot."

"Yeah," said Volstad, "How did you know?"

"Read it in Peth," smiled Erold, "To recap, we need to figure out a way to get our gold out when we want to get it out and have a limit on how many people can come on mission one and until we earn a bigger airship."

"How do you know they'll give us a bigger one?"

"I read it, but what's more important than that is this: did we get our first assignment yet?" Erold looked over at Volstad, who nodded.

"It must be finished within the week. There is a group of rogue mages that are apparently terrorizing a local town. We need to execute them as they've lost their minds and can't be returned to the light. I haven't heard of this type of thing happening in over a hundred years, but..."

"How many?" Moon began asking questions.

"They wouldn't say."

"Why did this fall to us?"

"I'm guessing it's partially a test and partially that no one else wants to go in on a group of pissed off, high mages, likely possessed by demons, taking refuge in a desert town that they're defending to the death."

"Who assigns jobs like this?" Moon sounded like she was just now in disbelief about the strange line of work that they had fallen into.

"A combination of the local military, the Akrin military, the royal family, and the East Cardane send in possible jobs through the commandants' office here, which are old members of the guard that never left. If you're wondering how these jobs come up, that I don't know. 'Something's in the water' is what people say about the gulf. And, they mean that literally too. As in Leviathans are in the water."

Moon nodded, trying not to roll her eyes. The three drank their cold beers suddenly relishing in the fact that they'd have beds for more than one night, and once they started getting jobs, fresh food.

* * *

Kahron investigated the modern barracks, looking at the rooms one by one as the mercenaries filed in, generally selecting to bunk with their tent mate. Kahron had tented alone, and the barracks were built for many more than the roughly one-sixty odd men, with living quarters, separated from a joint-use space with kitchen and the unit's armory, into a two-story catacomb of sixty, four-person bunks with a commander's and a quartermaster's quarters.

The commander's quarters were taken by Volstad, who was joined by Moon, and Erold would likely bunk with Braddach in a four-person room, leaving the quartermaster's room for Kahron, if he wanted it, but he didn't.

He took a four-person bunk to himself in the front left of the second floor, hoping to be as visible as possible to the team and for them to be as visible to him. After he had left his clothes and the luggage, he carried just his staff and looked back at the team filling out the rooms before exiting their quarters.

The steam lift operator required a silver piece to take him to the airship ferries, and as he slipped the silver over, he took another look over his shoulder to the door of the room, which couldn't be directly seen from the curved hallway. The steam lift, sitting at the center, closed its brass gates and began to rise quickly.

No one saw the direction Kahron had left in, and he didn't want them to. He hoped that he hadn't yet garnered the attention of the team for them to care where he went or not.

At the ferries, he asked how much for a trip to the south side tower. It required an exchange at the fifth stop, and would be a long ride, the man behind the glass said. Two gold pieces for a round trip if he had it. Kahron gave the money and received an empty punch card with a round trip stamp on south tower.

He gave the punch card to the ferry operator as he joined the crowd of people entering the airship that would be hopping the towers that covered the core of the city and the outer reaches of the sprawl like southside.

Kahron stood on the deck, listening to the announcements and advertisements that came through iron tubing that distributed through the passengers seating room and the viewing deck that wrapped around the outside of the ferry, which was a closed oval shape, above a cylindrical balloon. A slightly different and less agile make than some other builds, it made airship travel more appealing to general travelers who didn't like the idea of there being nothing between them and the ground.

He watched the city descend and the next tower appear and the process of travelers getting on and off, repeat, looking out over the red roofs of the low city with their cream-colored brick, stretching for atomic miles in every direction that wasn't ocean blue.

The evening sun had come, and the darkening dusk of the sky colored them in deeper colors, while the constant brass of airship and metal fixtures in the sky and across the city still glittered like a shimmer on the ocean.

He exchanged at the fifth stop for the southside bound ferry and was now one of the few remaining passengers. The advertisements changed to a different selection, catered to clientele with other daily concerns. He smiled as he saw the south tower appear, with many airships parked for the night that wouldn't make trips into the thousands of towns and handful of cities in the oases of the Andure dunes to the south, or possibly the other outer towers of Cardane, until morning.

Kahron followed the red line of the sun across the sky with his eyes, seeing chariots in the streams for the first time, where the land met the distant light of the star. The land extended into almost every direction except mainly to the northeast, as the cape of the greater peninsula on which Cardane sat, jutted further into the gulf and cities of the nation lined the coast on mainly the gulf's coasts, one to the east that ran southeast and the other to the west that ran north to south.

This was land where the Black Menetorians, who had not gone to South Olympus, had lived for more than an age but had never been granted citizenship. Given the tumultuous political climate of Cardane through its desire to maintain independence from the senate in Akre, citizenship was unlikely to change in modern times. The city was far enough away from Akre that it could self-govern, but granting citizenship to the Menetorians could simultaneously make Cardane a more powerful threat to Akre and more dangerously grant the Menetorians the ability to leave.

Kahron left the airship ferry, took the steam lift down to the first floor, and headed in the direction of a house he once visited before a falling out with the sons of Tullthro, one of the main elders who oversaw the innumerous clans of Cardane. The streets here were filled with Menetorians as if they were the only people.

It felt strange, for when growing up in one of the six to eight major islands of modern Menetoris, depending on your criteria, and its thousands of smaller islands, a landmass of in the vicinity or over four million square atomic miles, though much of it ice, there was not a town or city that was only White or only Black Menetorians. It was only those that left for the continents of West Ahria and South Olympus during the floods of long-ago ages that had separated in this way.

The old leader lived on the top of one of the three-story apartments, often called townhouses when they weren't sixteen units or more, that the people had built from the cream-colored brick over the centuries.

Kahron couldn't discern it from the sky but knew its general location. As soon as he had left the tower, he remembered the general path, following the mix of cobblestone and dirt paths, and passing through one of the many open-air marketplaces that existed throughout Cardane's neighborhoods.

"That gold is mine. Now give it here!" someone yelled. Kahron looked up and for the moment ducked away.

"It's ours. We came to buy fish," said the oldest of three little girls.

"I say you took it! You took it."

"You're lying," said another little girl.

"Let's go get the guards and see what they have to say about it. Do you think he'll believe three who loo--"

As the man turned around, forcefully grabbing at the littlest girl, Kahron stepped in, waved his white staff over the man's face when attention might be diverted elsewhere and whispered, "Do as I say, not as I do. Walk the other way and no harm will come to you." A simple diversion and a simple spell of mind control on an unsuspecting villain to make him walk blank-minded to the end of the street, allowing the three girls to escape. Kahron winked at them, the smallest clutching a toy doll. He had only added the words for their ears. He walked with them to the end of the long row of stalls, quickly purchasing fish with his own gold, and then shepherding them as the whispers of those who had seen but not comprehended were left unsure if they had seen anything at all--an effect of the spell.

When the quartet had left the row of stalls behind, they continued in the same direction that he was going, "Where are you going little ones? Can I take you home?"

"We're going to that building," the oldest pointed ahead at what Kahron instantly recognized to be the apartment of Tullthro.

As they went in, they went with him to the third floor, where he asked for Tullthro by name.

"You can go see him, but he might not have much to say," said his wife, who Kahron had rarely seen open the door.

"Why, what is wrong?"

"There was a raid to take the men and forcibly conscript them into the military. They took all of our boys, and he hasn't been the same since."

Kahron was let into see the old man, who rested on a sofa in a sunroom, flanked by many treasures from his many years. He slept with the sun drifting over his face, his eyes closed, and a tattoo of the star in black encircling his right eye.

"Tullthro, I've come to see you," said Kahron. "It is I, your former servant, Kahron." The man opened his eyes, but they were gray as if they had lost the light to see and he did not speak, leaving Kahron to bend his head further, sorry that he had not been there to use a spell and save the man's sons.

Five, six, not that many years ago, he knew their leader well, and now he lay dying, given up on life.

"I'm sorry," said Kahron. "I'm sorry to have left."

"It was not your decision to make," croaked the old man, "I am the one who should be sorry for being angry with you."

"You should leave," said a familiar voice from the door of the room.

"Fros walks with you always," said the old man, ushering Kahron to follow his daughter's angry command.

Kahron stood up and turned around, "Xipartha?"

She had been much younger the last time Kahron had come, and now she had the scar of a blade traced from above her left eye, down through her cheek and across the bare part of her shoulder, to her leg, slightly hidden by her threaded shirt. It must have covered the whole of her left side.

"Why have you come back?" she said, angrily when they had left the sunroom.

"To ask for men to join the Varanorian Guard."

"Hah," she laughed, "The notion, the nerve, you would have to ask such a thing, when our men are being taken to serve instead of Cardanians."

Kahron had to admit that it was poorly timed.

"I am tired of men like you coming here with their appeals of good will of my father for his riches and from other tribe leaders when they have their own sons and mouths to feed. This has to be the worst of them all! Asking for men who have already been taken away to die."

Kahron simply stared. He had not known what might come, but he had hoped that he could bridge the gap by having them work together.

"Not to mention how impossible it would be to get Menetorians into the guard in the first place!"

"Be nice to him," said the oldest of the girls from the market, "He's the one who helped us."

She looked at him skeptically.

Kahron knew the answer was still no, but potentially, he could be of help to the people of the southside in other ways. He looked into Xipartha's fierce, black eyes. There was only hurt there and frustration.

* * *

Ragnar and Thein had already picked the fight when Braddach and Veleon arrived, but the newcomers were the two to end it. Planning to do a drinking competition, which Braddach was sure Veleon would win, they had explored further afield than the bar on the floor of their tower barracks.

Problem was, they weren't the only ones, and one of the other guard units had decided that hazing the rookies--who had all left in their plain clothes rather than tour the city armed--would be a good idea. What they hadn't realized was that the some of these rookies were warlocks, who rarely left Valgaard for service in Cardane.

"What's going on here?" Veleon looked around at the bar as a loose fighting circle had started. Ragnar was coughing up blood, kneeling down in the center of the tavern. Thein was knocked out and lay staring face up at the ceiling in a chair near the ring.

"More rookies," laughed one of the old guard.

"We don't want a fight," said Braddach. "We came here to drink, eh."

"Screw that," said Veleon, "You touch one of our boys, we split your skin from chin to shin." He cracked all eight of his knuckles against each other.

Braddach grabbed Veleon's arm, "Come on, let's not do this Veleon."

"Aight, you heard what he said, boys a pus--"

"You'd be dead before you could lay your hand on a beer you queer."

Braddach still with his back to the door, and his hand across Veleon, mulled things over. Lose face in front of Veleon, Ragnar, and Thein, or leave a pool of blood and guts on a Cardanian tavern floor.

Braddach let the mage's spear loose using his back hand form slicing it through the air as fast as a bullet and severing the man's face clean in half before anyone could whisper a word. The yellow-orange bolt of ethereal power fizzled as it devoured its own energy against the wall, leaving the body to sag to the floor as its legs stopped receiving messages from the brain.

"He threatened my life. By city rights, I had license to respond in equal measure. Anyone else who wants to die today--"

"We didn't know you was mages."

"Let's be clear on one thing," said Veleon, "I would have done the same had he not been in my way."

458

"I say we leave the fighting for outside the walls of Cardane."

There were murmurs through the crowd as they assented. Veleon helped Ragnar up and threw the massive Thein over his shoulder like a ragdoll.

"Let's find another bar to drink at now that this one's stained."

1514 - Chapter 36

The Andure sand dunes were a near endless stretch of sand hills, split frequently by oases where villages built simple houses of white clay bricks and covered with the odd patch of tall, thin grass that looked like reeds.

The three-ram buzzed low along the dunes, following the map and compass, counting the number of villages and comparing size and estimated time of arrival to judge how far they were from Pergana, a city on the map, that wasn't too far from the village where there were either captives being held, or the entirety of its population vanquished.

They spotted Pergana from afar due to a city monument that was also on the map; a statue of one of the old Angels the Normen had spread through many of the other nations. Erold couldn't make out which one she was, but they had carved her with her wings spread wide and a sword held high in the sky--more than likely one of the battle seraphs.

After they took a wide right back toward the gulf and the west coast, Moon spotted the town in a pair of binoculars, replacing the brass spyglass that she had once borrowed from Erold. She directed them in a high circle around it while she tried to judge the enemy's number. Their intel had said anywhere from three to eight, but she counted six twice, which would put them at even numbers.

Braddach, Veleon, Moon, Volstad, Kahron, and Erold had climbed on the three-ram with its two side guns and its forward gun likely to remain silent. They hired a local pilot, as they were tricky to fly, especially in hot air. Though, it was a cool day, they were sure the summer heat would require the soft touch of experience to guide the brass dove, which looked like it had tiny wings of its own that helped to achieve lift along with the propeller at the rear and the steam balloon over the top of the small ship. Orichalc burned in the steam engine below, and mixing with the excess water, left a light trail of glittering red mist that disappeared quickly after them as they went.

Volstad motioned for the pilot to let them down after they'd circled it a couple times from afar, at about the max length for the binoculars to be useful. Hoping that they would have been hidden by distance from the naked eye of their quarry and maximizing the limited range of the instrument by not going for full detail on approach.

Erold was glad for once that there weren't that many gaps in the armor despite the general heat of his body because the sand would have slipped in through every gap. Surprisingly or unsurprisingly, the dragonskin despite being black as night and darker purple than wine kept the heat of the sun from penetrating the shell of the creature.

Up a dune, down the other side, and trying not to run, Erold couldn't help but wonder if the others were having as much fun as he was. He kept gripping and un-gripping his axe, wondering what the battle would be like.

There were rules of engagement among professional mages, but in a battle with rogues? How would his crew stack up with three warlocks of which only one was a battlemage, Kahron a master, Moon--who he still hadn't completely figured out--and him, a new mage? He hoped that he wouldn't be the weak link, but then he hoped none of them were.

They had only been about ten minutes walking when they reached the edge of town. Moon and Volstad leaned over the top of the dune beside the town, looking south to north, with the sun on their right and the town's houses built along a clear, blue pool that had formed like a long tear drop in a crater-like valley between the dunes.

The others waited for the suggested course of action. As the sun beamed down, getting higher in the sky, they drank from canteens slung over their shoulders and shielded their eyes, looking at dunes upon dunes in the distance. Erold tested the handle of his axe again, still cool to the touch, despite it being as black as night.

"They're flagging us down," said Moon.

"So much for going unnoticed," said Veleon.

"Hard when we have black armor in a desert of golden sand," pointed out Braddach.

"What do we do?" asked Moon, "What do you suggest Abrim?"

"They must want to talk it out," he rubbed his beard, and thought deeply. His hazel eyes narrowing. "It's risky for us, but they've already seen us coming."

"I think we could take them," said Kahron, "if you're worried about risks, I can defend and we can split the warlocks with Patr in the middle, and Erold and Elara on his left and right."

"That's what we'll have to do. Form up. Kahron, you'll take the back. We stay dune side and move left, don't let them encircle us." And then under his breath, "if we can help it."

"We didn't hurt anybody! We just scared them off, so we could we go our separate ways!" The one waving them down called out as Erold's team came down the side of the dune.

"The information we got says you murdered the entire village. Judging by the emptiness and no sign of people on the sand, it looks to be true." said Volstad, from the right flank. The other mages in the village fanned out, surrounding them in an arc. Seven total, including the leader.

"It's not exactly true," said the mage.

"What's the truth then?" asked Volstad, "looks to me like you aren't planning to be friendly."

"We couldn't stop our friend when he ran off. A couple people might have gotten hurt, but it's not our fault."

"Sounds like he went over," said Volstad.

"He's just sick."

"Then, why don't we take a look?" Volstad nodded to the others as he took a step.

"We can't let you do that."

"Of course, you can't."

"It's not that simple."

"If it's all a misunderstanding, let us kill your friend, and you all can walk."

"We don't want to kill you like we killed the last guards that showed up here. We outnumber you."

A black axe spun through the air and split through the face of one of the mages and then flew back into the waiting hand of Erold.

"Easy, now it's a fair fight."

"That was our healer!"

Volstad wasn't exactly happy with Erold, but it sure beat talking about fair fights and letting rogue mages dictate terms when they had a possessed mage about to burst in the village.

He used simple spells to frustrate his opponent who kept trying to whip him with an ethereal flame whip, hoping that the others would be able to make quick work of their opponents and then circle back. He knew Kahron had his back, but he had never been one for the most offensive of spells.

The mage did a back flip and kicked the air, sending fire his way, and Volstad used a simple push spell to block it out of the air, sending his opponent to the ground at the same time.

Pistol, bullet inside, hammer pulled in advance. Trigger pulled and scissor kicking fire mage was dead. That was much easier than he thought.

Moon, caught the lightning bolt thrown by her enemy in a move no one could see. As she reversed the ethereal bolt, she let her blades fly. The mage blocked the bolt, but not the blades that slipped through the ethereal shielding and split her skull through her eyes like darts.

Erold deflected his enemy's spells as he moved in, closer and closer. The enemy continued to try to lift him or manipulate him, but a deflection spell nullified this skill. Erold swung the axe as he closed in on the mage in nothing but a cloak and otherwise nonexistent armor. The mage's head rolled across the ground, mouth open, looking at the sky.

When Volstad turned to look at the battlefield, Veleon had snapped the enemy's strong man in half, Erold was cleaning the blood off his axe, and Braddach was picking the pockets of the mage he had killed whose hands were still on fire as if ready to throw a fireball.

Kahron brought the last of the mage's down between his friends after he had trapped her in a blue sphere of light. His staff glowing blue at the tip.

"Where is this sick friend of yours?" asked Kahron.

Before she could answer, a black light exploded from one of the two story houses behind them, shattering the building into rubble and extending to the sky above.

There was the mage. He began to levitate. His eyes as black as the night, spewing black and white sparks along a stream like the milky way.

"I am the end and the begin--"

Erold's axe throw chopped off the possessed mage's head, and then swung back around to him.

"It's easier if you don't let them talk," said Erold. "She's killing herself."

Kahron looked back at the sphere where the mage was imprisoned. She had ingested poison and begun to writhe in agony as she died in front of their eyes.

"I'm sure there is some bigger explanation for this, but let's take a look at the bodies. See if they have anything on them to see why they'd come out here for a rogue mage."

They searched the bodies but found no indication of where they had come from or trained. The only mark was emblazoned on the neck of the possessed mage in dark red. Erold only caught this, because when his body began to dissolve into black ash, his head remained long enough for Erold to see the tattoo and make note.

He kept it to himself, wondering if anyone would believe him or if it was a mark that signaled possession. None of the other mages had any markings of any kind, save for those that his band had dealt, leaving Erold with little clue beyond the mark he could still see in his mind's eye.

At least he was getting paid for this.

* * *

"I was told I could find you here," Kahron said as he came upon a windmill at the outskirts of Cardane's southside, near patches of grass and a small stream creating a small pasture for goats between the last few houses of the city, barely more than tents built of mixed materials, and the growing dunes dwarfing the stone and wood building.

"You're back," said Xipartha, continuing her work, trying to fix the mechanics of the windmill, which were to convert wind into a limited supply of electricity.

"Can I help?" asked Kahron as he watched her struggle with the components.

"You going to wave your magic stick and make light," she grunted as she couldn't force a tube out of the wall of the windmill.

"I used to build machines like this," said Kahron, "let me take a look inside."

She looked at him, skeptically, and pointed to a small hatch on the wall of the windmill.

He put the staff down, untied a purple cape that he had worn around his neck and attached it to the staff, then took off the greaves, leaving them on a stone bench in the sand and climbed up the side and into the hatch.

"What's this used for?" he yelled back as he looked around the interior components, using a simple spell to cast a temporary ball of light ahead of him.

"We use it to power our wind bikes, which make deliveries across settlements."

"No Orichalc?"

"This doesn't cost money like Orichalc."

"It's not as powerful though?" asked Kahron as he found the problem. Someone had cut the wires inside the windmill, leaving whatever Xipartha had been working on outside useless.

"Have you ever seen a wind bike?" asked Xipartha, "It doesn't take a whole lot of power."

"Two fans, a seat, and handles to turn it. I did live in Cardane once before," Kahron said as he pulled himself out of the hatch, covered in a bit of grime that had accumulated inside the machine.

Xipartha looked at him unimpressed by where he'd lived or when he'd lived there, only waiting for him to either gloat or to say he had given up after just five minutes inside.

"Someone sabotaged the windmill."

Hmmph. She put her hands on her hips. When she needed another problem, it arose.

"They cut the wires on the inside."

"I could figure that out from sabotage, and I didn't need your help either, I would have figured it out when I took a look inside."

"I fixed it," he said as he wiped the grime off the tight muscles of his arms.

"I know why you keep coming here," said Xipartha, still staring at him.

"Hmm? Enlighten me, why do I keep coming here?" he took his cape under his arm and put the greaves in his lap as he sat down, suddenly feeling the heat of the summer sun, maybe eighty degrees on the Odin scale.

"You want our people to move to a new place to live. We have lives here, homes. We can't just follow a stranger from an island no one cares about anymore to a place that won't be any better than this."

"I know," said Kahron. She continued to stare at him, believing that even if he knew, it didn't mean that he would give up his strange quest.

"We are not slaves. We are free people."

"The freedom is relative."

"How so?"

"You are not free to walk down the street without being accosted."

She stared at him blankly as he for the first time referred to when he had helped her younger sisters.

"Your men are taken to war but can't serve as police. Even if there was a parliament or senate in Cardane, they sure as hell wouldn't get the right to vote."

"What does it matter to me if men get the right to vote? Nowhere do women get the right yet. Tell me, how does it make a difference to me?"

"Let's say women of this nation had the right to vote, wouldn't you want it too then? You wouldn't get it here. None of our people would."

"So, thinking a step ahead, you think you can trick me into helping some long-term plan by proposing we send more of our men to die with the Varanorian scum. One of which, did this?" She displayed the scar that ran across her body, throwing an open palm into the air at him as if throwing sand.

"Xipartha," he had tried so hard to ignore her scar, but there it was now presented before him along the edge of her breast down to the top of her thigh and presumably further toward the edge of her bare ankle, "how could I have known?"

"I hate them, and I would kill them myself! They made me ugly and took away my brothers, leaving me to die."

Kahron set his things down, slowly on the stone seat beside him and then pulled her onto his lap, pushing her hands behind her back and looking up into her eyes, beyond the scar that split her left eyebrow and cheek.

"You're beautiful Xipartha. That's why I come here. To see you, even if you never want to speak a word of soldiers or fighting ever again, I want to hold you in my arms, and make you know that you will never be ugly."

Her arms pinned behind her back, she let out a scream of frustration before kissing him and pressing her hips against him, using him despite her anger and rage.

"You're not using your magic on me are you, wizard?" Xipartha gasped.

"My staff's over there."

"Uh huh."

* * *

While Kahron went off again to visit the southside of Cardane, the other five let loose after another successful mission, drinking beers in the bar in their tower. A habit that Volstad had picked up in his first stint in the gulf for similar reasons. Guards got anxious in the city and often played the game of who's a better fighter against other guards.

After the incident with Braddach splitting a head open, they were keeping a low profile. At least as long as Volstad could keep Erold from exploring the further delights of Cardane. Keeping people in groups when not in the barracks until further notice was hard enough, especially with how few had gotten to work yet.

"I think we should institute a rotation model until we get a bigger ship," said Erold.

"Why's that?" Volstad asked.

"We need a rest, and we can't get sloppy. Plus, we could take on more odd jobs." Erold held up a hand to have Volstad let him finish. "Our men need to be trained. They need practice. They're getting antsy, and we haven't been here that long."

"Training? How hard is it to shoot a rifle?" asked Veleon.

"I agree with Erold," said Braddach. "The two of us have been talking about it."

"The two of you talking about something other than women?" Moon doubted.

"At some point, we'll definitely have to leave the tower to see what the city has to offer," Braddach looked around the bar at the few patrons from their floor that weren't part of their crew, "because you may be able to get whatever you want to eat or drink on one floor, but there's more to life."

"What are you proposing?" asked Volstad.

"I suggest that our main six start by going on missions in pairs or trios, based on the mission we feel we can handle with four of the other guards coming along. Because we have one hundred sixty left after the highwaymen incident, we'd have forty rotations--we could run two missions a day--maybe three if they're close to the city. If we lose anybody we'll recruit--"

"All sounds fine," said Volstad, "but, please don't tell me you've been listening to Kahron about recruiting from the Menetorians."

"Why not? We need men, men that we can trust, and we can't trust that if we poach from any of the other Varanorian Guard units that they won't just raid the armory and ditch."

"Let's see. They aren't typically trained or mages. They are historically separate units that work with the army directly. And, let's see, they hate our guts and the empress would have to sign off on them being allowed near the palace."

"Have to try to figure out how to meet her at some point, anyway. So far, the only way we're getting gold out of this city is by asking nicely."

"I think that's not the best move either," said Moon. "It draws attention to us and limits our chances of promotion to the Elite Guard, if as Volstad says, they aren't trusted within the confines of the palace."

"How are we going to recruit otherwise?" asked Braddach in a matter-of-fact tone, "The situation is simple. We need to start running more jobs to make any real gold. We're exhausted as is, and none of the other men have been battle tested. Would they have survived the mage job from a few weeks back? No, not unless they shot first and asked questions later. We only spoke with them, because we thought they might actually have something important to say. We need the men trained to seek, identify, and execute, within reason. There has to be some criteria for pulling back, but this is just my opinion."

"It's my turn to say I agree," said Erold, "We need a recruitment plan, and we need to start getting more men into the field."

"If it comes down to me, I'm siding with the kids," said Veleon, "so, let's not waste everyone's time, by putting this to a vote. I don't care so much for tradition and these jobs are getting boring when it's the six of us. I want a real fight, like the Normens of old. One on four or against a wall of spears. I want to--"

"Okay, that's enough. We don't want you being killed off, because you get too much bravado. But, I see your point," said Volstad, "about the training. With respect to the Menetorians, you'll have to make that decision for yourself, but ruffling feathers here may draw you the wrong kind of attention, and we'll have to see how that plays out."

* * *

"She's agreed to meet with you, because we've worked together" said Kahron, "but that doesn't mean we'll be able to recruit the men like I suggested."

Erold stretched his back, looking out over the red roofed city below, as they took the passenger line between the towers and toward the southside, "So far, we've suffered few casualties, but the losses will mount."

"I know," said Kahron, thinking of his own experience in the gulf, "Especially as we get assigned more difficult work such as leviathans and more troublesome rogue mages."

"That's what I'm worried about. We've taken hundreds of missions. If one unit was wiped out. If we lost Patr or Veleon, Moon or Volstad, you or me, because we didn't have the men to have that extra gun..."

There had been little risk thus far, but not only had they been careful, their armor was resistant to simple bullets. If a round could pierce armor, or something more dangerous was deployed, such as artillery in the form of cannon or howitzer, there would have been many more casualties than they already had. A mage could stop a bullet only if the right shield was up before it was fired, but artillery was an even greater risk on the battlefield.

It felt as if Erold had blinked, and Kahron was already navigating ahead of him through Cardane's southside. It was strange to come from a nation, which had almost no people that were non-white, to suddenly living in Cardane, where the only white people were the Varanorian Guards. The refugees from the constant dynastic wars in the three Yin Kingdoms, such as Moon, were largely required to remain in a handful of select major cities within Akrin's core empire by law.

Here, the young, Erold, pale as the white towers and as blonde as the sun's light, stuck out like a lone dandelion on a grassy hill rather than the other way around.

They navigated through open air markets, selling delicate pottery and ornate rugs, as well as fish and hot peppers in barrels of green and red stretching twenty atomic yards or more. There were stacks of books and of mechanical toys, as well as jewelry and exotic candles. Many things he saw, he had never imagined, and couldn't help but think would be just as out of place back home as he felt now. Everything felt new, and the world became brighter and more sensational because of it, as if there was nothing here that he had ever seen before, despite having certainly seen a different kind of urn or a carpet in his life.

The stalls, too, were brightly colored, as they played with his senses in sight, smell, and sound. The awnings were various colors like purple, red, orange, and blue. The wood had been painted to accent the goods, and the shopkeepers, men and women, Cardanian and Menetorian, called to him and Kahron as they passed slowly through the thick midday crowd.

Kahron pulled Erold off the main road and guided him up flights of stairs made of the same cream-colored brick, a few cracks here and there patched by a material in another shade of white. After three flights, they were at a large mahogany door where Kahron knocked politely.

A tall woman, with an ample bosom and sharp featured face, along with dark black hair, braided in rows, opened the door; her face scarred on the left side. She grabbed Kahron and forcibly kissed him, which caused Erold to smirk. Now he knew why Kahron really was out here, all the time.

"Xipartha," Kahron half-gasped, half-mumbled when he was

able to regain the use of his lips, "This is Erold and Erold, this is Xipartha."

"Erold," she said and nodded lightly.

"Xipartha," Erold half-bowed as his father had once taught him to do for foreign dignitaries. Xipartha almost laughed, though she held it in, and a big smile crept across her face.

"Kahron has been telling me all about your exploits. Three mages in one job. One of them taken."

"Yes," Erold blushed.

"I could see you walking from the end of the street. You are as white as they get, and you blush as red as I've ever seen a man blush." She motioned for him to come inside, where a table had been set with fruits of the desert and fish in a thin, yellow and very spicy curry. The three of them were left alone by the rest of the family, but the little girls watched the stranger from a doorway that led to a kitchen. Erold tried his best to not let his eyes water, but he had never had anything as painfully spicy in his life, worrying that this was a first test.

The silence grew heavy as they ate, and Kahron began talking about the winter weather soon coming. Xipartha clearly wasn't interested in discussing an end to the storm season, and instead watched Erold eat.

"Why are you interested in us, the Menetorians?" Xipartha challenged Erold.

"We need men," said Erold.

"Seems that there are many places you can do that," Xipartha shrugged, and gave herself some more fruit.

"We need trustworthy men," Erold emphasized.

"And you think we're more trustworthy than the other white-folk?" Xipartha retorted, just as she was about to take a bite.

"Kahron suggested this plan, and I trust Kahron. We've had our run-ins with the other groups of the guard. We've been making waves. We're more successful than most. Better trained, better equipped, and succeeding where others can't."

Xipartha finished chewing, "Having Menetorians join you won't make you any more popular."

"That's not my main concern," said Erold.

"What are you hoping for?"

"We're looking to expand our troop and augment our force," he replied, looking over at Kahron, who appeared to visibly sit further and further from the table.

"You won't find many mages like Kahron among us, if that's what you're hoping for." Xipartha had watched Erold's eyes move to Kahron and looked over at him too.

"No, we're not looking for mages."

"Standard troops, then. We don't train to fight here. We train to be farmers and herders."

"We'll provide training to some degree."

"What kind of training?"

"Rifles and blades."

A silence fell over the table, and for a moment it seemed as if Erold had answered all of Xipartha's questions, "You're aware that I'm the decision maker? I speak on behalf of my clan."

"Kahron informed me."

"Did he say my father recently passed away or why?"

"I'm sorry to hear that and no, he didn't."

"I don't care how you feel. All I'm concerned about is what I know about you, and I know very little. How can we trust you? A white demon gave me this scar."

"I could give you that white demon's head."

"Revenge doesn't help. What does your word mean to me, if you would kill anyone that I ask you to? Someone could ask you to kill me."

"You have my word that your people will be in good hands."

"And how are you going to get approval from the emperor or his daughter?"

"I need to meet with her at some point to discuss other matters. Bringing this up now would help that along."

"I see. Well, it's still a no."

Kahron closed the door behind them as they left, looking one last time at Xipartha who cleaned up with her sisters and tired mother.

"Sorry, that it didn't go better," said Erold barely above a whisper to Kahron as the two of them took a few steps away from the door and down the stairs.

"Don't be disappointed," Kahron smiled, "That was a good first step. Xipartha was impressed by you, even if she didn't appear to be."

1519 - Chapter 37

Valessa--now twenty-one and a little taller even before adding the green crystal high heels that waited by the door for when she left her sanctuary--leaned over her large map of the world, with a set of notes taken from numerous reports and through discussions with many of her aides. She worked to re-distribute pieces and add more, comparing relative strength on the board between the forces in and around Akre and the forces in southern Valgaard.

Akre had moved an additional one hundred and twenty divisions into just the region surrounding the capital along with the return of the west army forces, making it an additional three hundred fifty thousand men. After having formed a central army in Polesar's first days of overseeing the full distribution of forces, Akrin forces were now mobilizing again, following new battle orders. Deciphering their movements was essential to figuring out if they planned to attack.

The old form of the empire's armies of four equal armies in the north, south, east, and west had begun to reformat immediately in 1513, but it was becoming clearer how Polesar's new structure worked. Each battle unit was expected to work independently and therefore reform within a larger group at any time without Polesar's own orders.

This would make it possible for Polesar to hold one force in Akre, no doubt poised at striking Valgaard while keeping loose forces active for the defense of outer territories--something that they had seamlessly done over the last five years. They had successfully responded to the rebellion in Mondelvania between 1514 and 1516, and in Emira between 1517 and partially, still ongoing in 1519, as well as having largely ended the elven rebellion in the Westernlands that had run off and on for about eleven years, ultimately ending in 1518. Valessa had backed the wood elves in the Westernlands until Imeria had consolidated their navy south of the Bacine sea shortly after GoldArrow.

Valgaard was largely on pace to meet her goal of having a standing force of eight hundred thousand troops by 1522, but the enemy had already reached the considerable number of eight hundred seventy-five thousand, including the two hundred thousand in attachments to East Cardane Shipping but not including Imerian forces, which she had failed--so far--to insert a spy within. In combination with the East Cardane company's forces, Imeria had continued off and on engagements with her own allies between the Bacine and Green seas, Menetoris, Albion, and the Coltari.

These extended naval engagements had largely stalemated due in combination to Albion's superior steam work and the lightning defense array that had successfully nullified numerous attempts by Imerian ships to conduct raids along the long Albion coast. The Imerians could not yet utilize their superior numbers to their advantage, and Albion wouldn't risk a catastrophic offensive after losing GoldArrow. Imeria had not pushed for a full engagement yet, which prevented the Menetorians from moving their airships out of the islands.

Valessa contemplated changes to the board to alleviate pressure. She was locked in a strategy match, seemingly alone against what felt like more than one mind. Ultimately, the safety of Valgaard came down to maintaining pace with Akre's increasing force--something she knew Valgaard wouldn't be able to continue to do for long--so she had to hope the enemy would continue to wait for an opportunity to strike at both ends. This would make the most sense for them as a possible loss in a naval engagement on the coast by Imeria would put Akre's consolidated force at risk of having to split to respond to any Albion counterattack, making it possible for Valgaard to finally outnumber their force stationed at Akre.

A knock on her door interrupted her train of thought.

She went slowly to the door, holding the skirt of her dress over her ankles to walk and looking over her note sheets one last time before crumpling up anything she had already used and depositing them in a waste basket to be burned, leaving what was left on a side table near the door.

Valessa slipped on her custom-made shoes, gaining a tenth of an atomic yard in height, four inches in archaic terms. They were a gorgeous dark green, studded with emeralds across gold emblazoned straps that fit snugly on her feet. Her form fitting dress, that had dragged slightly behind her on the floor, now lifted off of the ground.

She opened the door, locked it behind her and went through the small hallway to the inner chamber, where Arla, who had become her most important aide, was waiting. She had been more than adequate over a number of years and become more than just a temporary replacement for Onya who having stayed in Albion, was a much better queen than spy.

"We have another message from the spy in Cardane."

"Oh?" Valessa tried to not perk up too much. News of Erold had been sporadic over the many years since he left, but she hadn't always appreciated the activities that had been attributed to the boy she once knew and, admitted only to herself, still had feelings for.

"Would you like to hear the report here?" Arla looked around and added, "this may be the most private place right now. I've swept it just before speaking with you."

"That good?"

"I decoded the message myself, mam. Can't say it's everything you'd want to hear, but there's quite a bit at once."

"Let's sit here in the chamber and let me read through the material as you speak it. You brought a copy?"

"Yes."

"And burned the original?"

"Of course. I took down the message myself as it was transmitted and burned the notes after decoding."

Valessa admired Arla. Arla was efficient whereas Onya had relied on her guile and charm. Valessa appreciated that Arla had been able to communicate effectively in Menetoris, but now, she would think twice about sending Arla on a foreign mission. Once upon a time, Valessa had perhaps been more carless in her desperation and while she had been the one to hope Onya's feminine charm would wake Stone into action, she didn't want her to risk a friend's life again.

Valessa nodded for Arla to begin.

"First, we confirmed that his units were indeed engaged alongside Akrin forces in both Mondelvania and Emira over the last five years. We're hoping that they were not able to identify him, but we have no confirmation there. It is additionally reported that he most likely did work in the holy land, but this has not been confirmed. It has been confirmed that he has helped Cardane to consolidate formal power along the sea routes to Roon Kalada, including in Malervna."

Valessa turned to the next note sheet.

"Second, he has continued to shut down rogue mage activity in the region, and as a result has been promoted to an adjacent unit of the Elite Guard. He has expanded his regiments to multiple airships and is now completing numerous major contracts per day with few losses or casualties among his men since his arrival over five years ago."

Valessa turned to the next note and shook her head, realizing again it had really been that long. Her life had remained so unchanged as she continued to fret about war and host dinners for state officials from all over Valgaard as well as keep up with the allies whose alliance in the increasingly near future would hinge on Erold's return.

The prospect of his return now seemed much more likely than it did then when he was just a young boy having first gone into exile as heir to the thrones. That spring when the sun had returned was far away from this winter now, with a blizzard dropping a third of an atomic yard of snow in early Vetfal.

"Shall I continue?" Arla asked.

"Yes, sorry," Valessa said.

"I lost you there for a minute," Arla said and then she continued, "He also recently applied to have Black Menetorians inserted into his unit of the guard. As an aside, I don't know how he's done it, because intelligence suggests that this mixing has never been done. However, he received immediate approval from the Empress herself."

"There must be some reason for that beyond merely recruiting troops, as he could have selected from those that we've sent bit by bit over the years," Valessa wondered.

"I can't comment on it specifically but moving to the next sheet. There seems to be the same negative reputation as well that we had recently received in the update last year. He's begun to take as many courtesans as he can afford to," Arla looked up at Valessa wondering how Valessa felt, but the princess remained stoic. "I know how much that news disappointed you when we first heard it."

"It's no matter," Valessa smiled, "Just a matter of good principles. Burn these, please."

"Yes, your majesty. And thanks for the Frostmas bonus. I didn't get a chance to thank you before. You are as generous as your--"

"Don't go spreading that type of nonsense. People would be asking me for everything," said Valessa, who continued to contemplate next moves while her aide departed the room, quickly and quietly. Once the blizzard's snow had been cleared away, they would send final invitations for a Lord's Day ball, which she'd have to express her extreme desire to have certain parties in attendance for.

Most of which had already been invited, but naturally a couple names now came to mind that she had neglected to send a second invite to. This year they would have something else to discuss than the ordinary trivialities that came up when friends gathered for the holiday season.

To get started, she would go see her father. She stood up, using the arched table of the inner chamber to help herself stand easily and for a moment, let the blood rush to her overwhelmed forehead, before letting out a sigh.

Princess Valessa walked through the hallways, over the familiar green carpet, passed busts of legendary wizards and warlocks, and through the door to the open court. She prepared to use the excuse of the first classes of mages successfully graduating from the northeastern colleges since the near-blight incident of the 1200s to get past Bouvedere at the door if he tried to stop her again. The only problem is that Bouvedere had heard it before, and it had happened in mid Norain. When she neared, she found him absent from that post.

She took a moment to admire the new emblem her father had designed with the gold sun now behind a unicorn tilted slightly from center as if it were rearing up at you. He always thought that she didn't appreciate these things about him, but she admired his creativity.

When she nodded, the two guards opened the door. She expected King Hughgar, her father, to turn immediately toward her, but he was enraptured in something. She had long given up trying to get him to stop taking open court.

When Princess Valessa turned to see who had appeared at court, a strange pleasure tickled her shoulders. Louie, a councilor from the elf city of Anpol among the lakes was strangely on his knees asking for assistance with a heartfelt plea. He had dressed in a well-fitted jacket and trousers, both a combination of yellow and green, to visit Valgaard, eschewing his typical blue or even red, commonly worn by snow elves.

King Hughgar, very interested, nodded and made affirmative noises as Louie explained his situation, "And why haven't you gone to Valgaard's parliament about this?"

Princess Valessa could have almost hit her father. Sending a foreign dignitary away when he's come to him for help, when she more than anything would use this opportunity to cement a formal allegiance rather than a handshake agreement to conduct trade between their borders.

"I did go to them. They told me to come to you. More specifically, they said," and he stopped to read from a thick letterhead that he had copied parliament's remarks upon, "your daughter would be the one interested in making comments on any formal response to the matter."

"What seems to be the matter?" smiled Valessa, attempting to look concerned and polite, despite her enthusiasm to be meeting with someone who could, with increased cooperation, satisfy not only her nation's lumber needs for centuries, but also that of the northern alliance. They not only had the reserves but a substantial supply in their enchanted forest.

"King--"

"Councilor," Louie corrected.

"King councilor Louie, here," Hughgar cleared his throat, "has been telling me that his daughter, Glo, has gone missing in the north on her latest trip to the dwarven kingdoms."

"All contact with the dwarves has gone dark--well--darker than usual," Louie added, and the two of them looked expectantly at Valessa.

"Would you care to comment, princess?" asked the king.

"Let's start with finding a quiet place to discuss what it is you're asking for Councilor Louie, and then I can let you know how we may be of assistance."

Princess Valessa nodded at Bouvedere, who had arrived behind her and began to lead Louie toward a private room. The king lightly motioned to Valessa before she left.

"Was there something else that you wanted to discuss?" he asked her.

"No, not at the moment."

He looked at her sternly.

"Just that we have happily graduated the first class of mages from the northeastern colleges that have not been open for ages," she smiled as he recognized it would have to wait for a later moment and likely involved military matters.

After the elf had gone out of view, the king said, "I used a deshroud spell just in case. Can never be careful, not just because it was an elf visiting. You should be safe, but Valessa, remember to remain vigilant."

"Yes, father," she said and put an icy hand on his shoulder to remind him, she wasn't to be trifled with either.

As soon as she was in the meeting room with Louie, she asked politely, "What is it that you think happened and assuming you came here for military support, what are you willing to do to make sure we do help?" She offered him an ornate oak chair, with overly plush cushions on its back and seat, across a desk from an identical one that she took, resting her feet on the spikes of her heels.

Louie partially groaned, though he also knew that he had come here for just this type of negotiation. He had long avoided negotiating exclusive rights for Haltvia to Valgaard, preferring to stay neutral, but knowing that he couldn't let Akrin forces into his territory or they would never leave, he had come here for help.

"I believe bands of highwaymen formed together in the north after being displaced by the recent anti-rebellion activity and attempted to kidnap my daughter or take an Orichalc mine by force while my daughter was nearby. Either way, we don't have the resources to spare to devote to the required military activity in the north."

"And the guns that we requisitioned to put into production a number of years ago, they won't help?"

"They have been very helpful in assisting in the defense of the walls across our settlements in the north. We don't have the ability to mobilize enough troops to defend the territory without putting our homes at risk of that same type of attack."

"You'd like military assistance, then. I'm guessing you have some idea of scale if you aren't willing to mobilize to meet this aggregated force."

"Military assistance of some considerable kind, yes, but without putting my daughter at risk."

"How does a search and rescue team of elite soldiers and warlocks sound for starters to identify your daughter and to bring her to safety unharmed, while we follow up that success with a military detachment?"

"That sounds great."

"Do you have a number in mind of the attackers?"

"Estimates put it at ten thousand men."

"Ten thousand men is hardly a band of highwaymen," said Valessa, feigning exasperation. "Sparing let's say twenty thousand men for such an engagement, just to be sure of success, the criteria for this would have to be no less than a formal alliance between Valgaard and the elves, with exclusive rights to forestry in Haltvia--"

"Without hesitation."

"I wasn't finished." She watched him contemplate what else she might ask for, "And, assistance in negotiating with the dwarves for exclusive rights to their share of Orichalc mines that fall within Haltvia's territory."

"They may not be happy about it."

"We have a large alliance that needs steamtech powered. They have the Orichalc, and there is plenty of competition across Mondelvania for them to not miss dealing with the East Cardane squeezing them."

"I can bring this up at the next council meeting," said Louie, trying to push it off.

"If you want my assurances now, then I need better than promises to possibly confirm something. If you came here for help, then you must have been given some decision-making authority, or I can't help you."

"I was. Yes," said Louie.

"Then what will it be?" She leaned forward pressing her toes hard against the floor like a predator, prepared to snatch at its prey.

"Fine, I accept."

* * *

"I know you don't like being cooped up here during the winter, Seaspirit, but it's what is best for you."

Valessa sighed and soothed the horse with a soft brush and a warm towel, dripping wet. Every time she came here, she thought of the time she had first kissed Erold. She had thought he was upset at her, and then it had just happened. To this date, it had been her only kiss. He, on the other hand, had been taking any courtesan with nothing between her legs.

Valessa knew she shouldn't be upset about it, but she felt a range of emotions, across the spectrum in a combination of upset and happy. Upset at his behavior and happy that he had enjoyed so much success in Cardane. He would very likely return. The question was quickly becoming when, rather than if.

She had spent the morning on the castle rooftop, overlooking the lake as she had done so many times with him while he had stayed. It had been her tradition, but now it was a memory of a happy time.

Times were still happy now, she reminded herself. Only, they continued to live with the threat of war. The constant posturing of Akre was wearing on her, and she recognized that they must know as much about her as she did about them. One wrong move and life as she knew it would end.

She felt that she needed a break from trying to prevent total war, but at the same time, she considered that to be her only real job. Her people, and the people of her allied nations, counted on her to do it well.

She had long stopped getting too excited about the good news that came either. Louie appearing unannounced at her father's throne room, asking for her, and promising everything she could have wanted. Something bigger was amiss in Haltvia and the northern dwarven kingdoms, and while she felt she needed both as allies, she couldn't shake an ominous sense of foreboding.

"Mommy, can I help take care of the horsie?" a small voice came from the other side of the stable door.

"Elenia, how many times do I have to tell you? Please do not call me mommy. I'm your auntie."

"But?"

"No buts," she replied.

"You hurt my feelings."

"I'm sorry," Valessa stood and went to the stable door to see the sniggering face of the child entrusted in her care. "Do you want me to let you in to take care of the horsie? Will that make you feel better?"

"Yes," the little five-year-old girl said, and the two of them worked to keep the horse warm together.

* * *

A white carriage, pulled by two unicorns trundled up the long wide road that wound through central Peth, shaking in the early snow of Vetfal. In the rear of the carriage a figure cloaked in dark green hoisted thickly wrapped tobacco to his scarred lips and breathed in.

The light of the Orichalc lamps on the street passed through the window in arcs and the driver exposed to the cold glanced back at the passenger whose scarred eye glistened in the liminal light breaking passing shadow.

A streak of white flesh in a line from through one eyebrow and underneath the sharp eye, gray in the night. A gold ring glinted in the night, and the driver snapped forward as a bounce of the road caught him by surprise.

The cabin of the carriage filled further with smoke, and the patient rider looked out the window to watch the white palace grow ever larger, ever nearer, lit by a thousand lights like a beacon of daylight in the longest night of the year. The red bulb of the end of his cigar flashed brighter with each breath and then returned to faint embers.

The carriage turned along the wide arc of the street and ahead the driver could see detached carriages lined along the side of the street nearest to the palace. He breathed a sigh of relief that he would earn a warm coffee and a bed near a palace fireplace for the evening.

The cloaked figure yawned and finished the cigar as the carriage turned into the large circle below the gates to the palace compound. Six guards rushed about to corral the unicorns and relieve the driver. The man in the rear stepped out of an opened door to a wave of salutes. He paid them no heed and continued up the stairs.

The gate's doors were opened in front of him, and after fighting through the snow, finding his footing on the shoveled stone felt oddly shaky. He climbed the palace gates, admiring the strings of fairy magic that shone like white spirits floating along the top edges of every wall, and on the Lord's Day trees.

The old man wiped his brow and took the hat off his head, revealing his white hair, slicked back by sweat and cream. The doors flung open before he could touch the wood, and there she stood, the Ice Queen, princess of the north, awaiting him, the straggler.

"General Mikael Kutzbek, welcome to Peth."

"My lady," he nodded, and when she reached out her icy, gloved hand in a dark emerald-green gloved hand, he took it and placed a soft, delicate kiss above her wrist with a bow.

"Your room is on the second floor. An attendant is waiting for you at the bottom of the stairs with a candle. As requested during your last visit, the Orichalc lights have been shut off, and a fire has been lit."

"You're too gracious my lady," Kutzbek bowed again.

Another attendant clad in green with a slight touch of red, for the season, appeared and handed him a red box wrapped in a thick blue ribbon with gold edges.

"Please accept a token of our appreciation for your service to the crown."

"My lady," Kutzbek gasped, and he kneeled, placing his lips against his own wrist folded one over the other on his raised knee with his eyes closed, he gave a silent prayer to the lord on behalf of the princess.

She smiled down at him and placed a hand on his weary shoulder, "My good man. Please rest. We will celebrate Lord's Day ball tomorrow evening."

Kutzbek nodded and climbed the rear stairs, following attendant after attendant. There was no doubt that all of the twenty-five jurisdictions of Valgaard had arrived as well as the other military leaders of Valgaard's combined forces. For days, Valessa would have stood out front, greeting every guest as they entered through the main hall in elaborate outfits of red, green, white and gold.

In the same way that he had been greeted, they would be handed a coordinated gift and directed to one of the many palace rooms meant for the royalty of Valgaard to winter together for a time in the nation's capital.

He could see the exhaustion in her eyes, so he arrived just after the last guest from far north would have, waiting in the wings, watching their carriage ascend to the palace ahead of his own. Throughout the palace as he went evergreen trees glittered with Orichalc lights, fairy charms, garland, and crystal rope. In every hall and every corner, there was at least one. He could sometimes see three at a time. When he entered the warm room, he sat on a plush chair facing the fire and fell quickly asleep, entranced by the shape of the flame.

The next morning, he awoke to hear that the party had already started in its nascent stage. The first orchestra of the day had begun to loft heavenly melodies through the hallways from the expansive ballroom where as many as three orchestras would be distributed through at different points to play a stream of music throughout the day until the ball of evening gowns and flashy dances. Kutzbek would only stand, watch, and listen. The families and guests of the eight largest provinces would compete in every way but physically to win the attention and adoration of the rest of the ever-expanding crowd.

Princess Valessa had begun these parties five years ago, and while she had added a celebration for each of the other seasons, the Lord's Day ball, despite the beginning of heavy snow was always the largest of them all, even larger than Frostmas.

Kutzbek spent the day wandering the outer walls, receiving salutations from the posted guard, who everywhere he went, stood at attention immediately, gasped, and ran about to attend to him as if they recognized the presence of a living god. He refused their extra kindnesses and reminded them as he notified them to continue as they were that he was to be treated as an ordinary officer of the rank.

When he finally arrived to the ball, he entered unannounced and surveyed the crowd, unable to yet recognize the heads of one house of a province over another. Each having once been a kingdom of its own in days long gone, they had retained, regained, or won by proxy their ancestral lands when King Hughgar defeated the empire. The nations once united by treaties in their many wars with the south that began almost three hundred years before were once again united against a common enemy.

Kutzbek, a portly old man, watched the lords and ladies dance until he spotted the princess Valessa who was locked within the crowd of dancers vying for the best dancing pair with the young, handsome General Kienber. The passion between them was fitting, thought Kutzbek, watching from afar. He was an inspiring flame mage, who some believed had generational talent to be unrivaled, even by the king himself. She, the legend of ice.

When the song stopped, she nodded and he departed, replaced by Andreas Wermack, who had taken over as lead general of the cavalry. He was an expert unicorn rider, and had a bit of flair too, daring to spin the princess to the delight of a clapping crowd.

After the spin, when the princess was looking around, flushed and red, clinging lightly to the beaming Wermack's shoulders, she caught the eye of Kutzbek and tapped the shoulder of her dancing partner. He turned and nodded to the old general as the princess whispered something.

When the song stopped, the princess gathered a handful of the usual suspects and led them through the corridors to her private sanctuary.

"Gentleman, it has been a long time since we all formally met," began the princess. "I have never shown any one of you the sanctuary room. Not even General Kutzbek. Behold."

She displayed the large board before them, letting them soak in the feast for their eyes. It had been lying there under their noses the whole time.

"Mikael Kutzbek, Andreas Wermack, Ivan Plaski, Karl Dave Gavo, Petr Eichlen, Mikael Kienber, Andral Borgoron, Garold Milton, Doctor Arne Pasan, and Andiere Blaggard. You are the chosen generals with which to strike into Akre and take the land of Normany from the Atlan River to the Ash Vale."

"Madness," said Eichlen and others concurred.

"If you've stared enough at this board, you would know that we don't have much time before Valgaard strikes at us. When they do, we will have almost no chance. Our one opportunity to attack, may be our only hope. In a few short years, we may have an opening to strike first, raising a militia out of the defectors from the south."

After the objections, Kutzbek raised his hand ahead of his face,

"I see. The emperor has moved the rest of his men out of Normany, and you consider this an opportunity to take the land with minimal effort, only requiring a strategy to keep it."

"A force could theoretically fight through the fort at Pili's Pass and take much of the country right there by capturing the city of Gulldalr," mused Wermack. "It's a simple plan, but it is the most likely to net positive results."

The princess nodded in agreement, "Pili's Pass is no longer guarded by the 'Thief of Life.' If the emperor doesn't know this yet-_"

"He definitely knows," said Kutzbek, and the princess frowned a bit but agreed. "The problem is that he's still baiting us into a trap. We just have to make him regret it by holding the land that we occupy."

"You're a brilliant tactician General Kutzbek. How do you propose we accomplish this?"

"We will need to rely on cavalry to hold this open plain here in Gardnor. That's our only advantage over their forces, but we could also use the hills of Dalvalles to our advantage to force their troops into fights where we have the advantage."

"I will personally lead the cavalry," said Wermack, "I say we can muster forty thousand strong additional troops that can be spared from the defense of Peth. That is if we are given a few year's time."

"I was counting on you. Your determination and foresight are appreciated General Wermack," said the Princess, triumphantly, stepping forward to hover over the board. Wermack blushed and Kienber shifted. Eyes had begun to wander to the princess rather than the to the tasks of war.

"And who will be leading the infantry divisions, your majesty?" asked Kienber.

"Well, it will be General Kutzbek, of course."

Everyone turned to look at the legend and only non-mage in the room. It appeared he may also soon be the last non-mage officer to serve in active engagements.

1520 - Chapter 38

"Do-ba-dee, do-ba-da, I'm going to live forever if I can just find Shangri-la."

"Kahron, could you stop singing that song for Frost's sake?" yelled Veleon, over the sound of the airship, cruising along at a top speed high above the sand dunes, burning Orichalc in a bright red blaze that trailed after them like a comet's tail.

"You got a problem with it, sing your own song!"

"We've been riding in this hull for hours, and all you've been doing is singing that same song," Veleon walked over to get in Kahron's face.

"I just want to get this job done."

"You and me both. Erold, when are we dropping?" Veleon yelled back at Erold, who stood closer to the steam engine. He shouted as loud as he could.

"You want to drop?"

"Let's go!"

Erold hand motioned to Volstad who was manning the ship, while "mage team one" ran this job south of Cardane. Everyone braced and adjusted their goggles--despite still being in the belly of the new airship; its deck reserved for low flight missions--as Volstad dove the ship, carried by a large balloon on dwarven metal chains toward the dunes, cutting through the air like scissors through paper and sending cloud across the bow and sweeping behind them in great swaths of white like spiraling cylindrical wakes on a lake.

Volstad cut the throttle back, evening the ship out over the dunes to get them ready to drop. Erold peered out the window and saw that they were coming up on the dark tower, which had become the sight of some recently normalized possessed mage activity: moving dunes, visions of giant spiders and other psychotic hallucinations induced by prolonged exposure to the 'other side.'

Erold nodded at Veleon and Kahron, who saluted each other with a quick nod, and opening emergency hatches on either side, jumped out, dressed in mage flight gear that would help them land when they hit the sand.

Erold looked around at the rest of the eighty men. Rifles and pistols at the ready, they would soon follow Veleon and Kahron in to give support. The dark mage was sending sandstorms across the dunes, and the mercenaries had been informed to expect an army of undying sand monsters that would reassemble if cut down.

"Take us lower!" yelled Erold, worried that the non-mages were still too high to rappel off the main deck. "And spin us back around the tower!"

"Aye aye," winked Volstad and he hit the air brakes, lurching the airship in an arch, sending its forward end left and its rear end right, causing it to slide through the air in the shape of a scythe. The airship shuddered as it split the air, and as they came around, Erold could see the assembling sand armies closing in on Kahron and Veleon who were charging spells at the center of a swarming sand warrior circle, readying for battle.

"We go now!" yelled Erold to the men, deciding then and there that this mission needed him too. Forty Menetorians and forty Valgaardians, split into teams of one warlock, with a pistol, and seven riflemen, dove off the left and right, with rappelling gear and ropes tightened to a harness.

The airship swung in with the men rappelling down, watching as their final approach slowed, before the airship would take off again.

Erold, waited until the last possible moment, watching them detach from the ropes and land in the circle, giving Veleon and Kahron support. When the airship was just pulling away, he ran to the back of the ship and jumped off.

He let the air fly through his hair, his axe and shield tightened to his back. As he neared the ground, he used a spell to blow a hole through the sand warriors freezing them into little towers of frozen sandstone then pulverizing them into melting liquid glass.

Erold landed at the center of his team and pulled his axe and shield off his back. It's not quite flying, but it sure feels like it, he smiled as the wind caught his hair and the separate teams arrayed in a circle of ten with seven gunners in closed ranks around a warlock who would keep their enemies at bay.

They needed to draw out the mage into a direct fight, and it would require cutting through the swarm of the sand warriors until the mage who probably wished upon a djinn for unlimited power came out for a direct fight.

The problem with a djinn is they only knew how much power they controlled, and Erold had learned that a collection of trained mages could subdue almost anything, including himself. There was no djinn in the gulf that hadn't wished to be put back in the bottle after facing his men.

The sand swarm swirled and formed into more shapes like

hollow zombies. There might have been a line three deep at first, and it slowly grew line by line as more sand of the dunes was collected and distributed into form.

"Men, let it rip! Warlocks, do not let them near!" yelled Erold, and rifles began to fire tearing the sand into strange shapes, as they began to advance forward. Once they reached, an outer circle, they were stopped by the warlocks gating spell and easy picking for the rifles that tore apar their legs and limbs, leaving them to disappear with the wind on the other side of the ethereal wall and reform.

"Kahron, Veleon, anything gets close, do anything you need to, to eliminate the dark magic, poisoning the sand."

They nodded at him, readying to throw fire, wind, water, or control the very sand itself in response to draw out the enemy mage. It seemed to Erold that each time he had fought off a horde of sand soldiers or zombies, that some wizard came along and tried the same trick again.

His men might have been eighty. The sand-soldiers may have numbered eight thousand and reformed again to another eight thousand, but his men were worth well more than an empty shroud of dust or dead tissue.

Kahron and Veleon began firing fireballs and banishment spells as a few sand creatures broke through the edge of the shield wall the warlocks formed. Erold used his axe staff, to give himself a high field view with a momentary levitation spell and began spitting ice at the forming sand clouds watching them crash down in heaps behind the thinning line.

The mage wouldn't be able to do this forever, though his men's bullets wouldn't last either. Even possessed, the mage would run out of stamina soon, and whatever souls had been forced into these sand figures, would be released back to their ancestral grounds.

"Formation two now."

His team below him collapsed slowly back into a tight circle, as Erold's levitation spell wore off, and he gently floated back to the ground.

"Kahron, you got this. Unleash an ultimate judgement."

Kahron, an experienced, expert mage, cast an angel spell that sucked the formed and formless sand warriors into a single ball above the field and then with a blink of yellow light, banished them into nothingness.

The sudden reduction of sand, revealed the dark tower again, black as night but appearing as only sand-brick, tainted by the dark magic encircling it.

Erold blasted the front door open with a sun beam spell, tearing through the aura and reducing the walls to nothing, revealing the demon-possessed mage. He was so far gone, that his soul appeared to dissolve before their eyes. He was little more than a zombie already, face contorted, eyes white and mumbling incoherently in a catatonic state. Black and purple clouds, like the color of the armor of Erold's men began erupting from the mage's eyes.

The eyes turned on Erold as he continued to mumble something, then the axe hit the head, sending it crumbling into ash. Like the pendulum of a clock stroking the final hour, the axe ended the spell before it could be written into the book of ages.

The rest of the body began to dissolve away in the same black-purple cloud of smoke as his eyes had, and Erold flashed back to one of the first possessed mages he had fought.

He quickly ran up to the body as his axe returned to his hand, noticing the edge of a red mark tattoo adorning the mage's pale white skin. The number of rogue mages in Gor'mondell's gulf had continued to increase, and he was sure he had seen this tattoo even another time. There was no mistaking the symbol as the shadow of a soul went to meet its eternal judgment in the eyes of the one true God.

Erold could sit here and say that as the number of rogue mages in Gor'mondell's gulf continued to increase, so too did this mysterious red mark, but he hadn't seen all of the bodies quickly enough. He knew it couldn't be a coincidence.

Volstad circled the ship around to pick them up and take them back to the city, where they would meet up with the others who had been piloted out of the city by Moon and swap stories from the day's battles.

They swept back into the city in a long arch, so that Erold could stand on the deck and watch the approach with the sun setting at their backs and casting the whole of the city in a golden hue, with the ocean to the north behind it.

The airdocks at the top of their tower had become so many of Erold's own ships that the officer in charge of officiating the tower had threatened citations. They pulled the ship in to dock alongside the other similar sized airship, fit for about eighty men and disembarked.

Erold had his eye on a particular model of ship called an air schooner, because it was as fast as a three-ram, despite its size and could carry as many as two hundred men and cargo. It was no battleship, or even the equivalent of a frigate or brig that could run over one hundred guns to a side. But, it was twice the size of the ships he had just had his teams run out across the dunes and could theoretically fit anything he wanted to in it with his men, while flying at top speed.

He would be able to afford one soon, while not cutting too deep into his growing money, but he had been methodical about his approach. Getting around one hundred Menetorians on his side also allowed him to finally maximize his barracks and though some people had to swap sets of armor, he had thankfully been able to recover any from a lost man, unless they drowned at sea.

Erold joined Braddach and his other senior officers, which they didn't object to being called, at their usual pub hangout in low city, that sat near where the hill that the main city towers sat on dropped off on the southwest side, allowing a view of most of the west and south sprawl.

"Here's to no casualties!" yelled Volstad, and the men that had joined them cheered loudly, including Ragnar and Thein, who had become something akin to Braddach's disciples. They followed him wherever he went.

Erold scoped out the women that had appeared for the evening, dressed in thin veils of all colors that only pretended to be modest, except for face coverings that hid their smiles. It was up to the beholder to decipher their gazelle-like eyes as they looked across the room. Women from across all six continents made their way to Cardane to make money as courtesans, just as the men came for mercenary work.

"Is it possible for a job to get any easier?" Kahron asked, drinking his beer across a long table from Veleon.

"Hey, we've had some challenging missions over the years," Veleon replied, inspecting his hand to see if he had lost some eyesight over the years.

"Name one," said Braddach as he joined them with a beer of his own.

"This dragon on an island, with like the six cities. You weren't there, because it was after we split into two teams," said Veleon, nodding to Ragnar and Thein as well. He took another swig of beer.

Kahron laughed, "You killed that with that giant spirit axe you conjured, using our combined force in one soul blast. All we had to do was stand there and cast an empowerment spell. That seems pretty easy to me."

"That was harder for me than you seem to think. It took a ton of stamina and the right timing. A spirit axe is not that good unless you have the right opportunity. We knew the dragon was cocky, but that spell takes a ton of stamina."

"Ah, I've seen Erold kill bigger," Kahron took another drink, and slapped Erold on the back.

"Yeah, I know the story," said Veleon, "You've only told it a thousand times."

"It was twice the size easy. He didn't even have a mage's staff. He just--"

"The way he tells it you helped," said Braddach.

"Yeah, well he needs to learn how to lie. Erold, Erold, you want in on this round?"

"Nah, but I'll tell you a lie right now."

"Eh, what's that?"

"I'm not going to use this money to get lucky tonight." Erold put a handful of gold coins on the wooden table in front of him, while Moon scoffed, sitting across from Veleon on the other side of him.

"You're a dog. How many times do you get around, and you still have money left?" asked Veleon.

"Why do you go around with those girls anyway, when there are plenty of nice-looking girls in Cardane that give it away for free?" asked Kahron.

"Said by someone who is spoken for," said Volstad. He looked over at Moon, who smiled at him.

"Yeah, Should I be telling Xipartha what you have to say?" laughed Erold, "Anyway, I've got my reasons."

"I doubt they're good ones," said Moon.

It could have just been an excuse to start getting lucky in a city far from home with girls from all over the world, but he had learned a little secret about Zosin. She had her own nocturnal habits that needed satisfying, and she had associates scouting for willing sidepiece applicants from the elite of the guard, which he was now one of the leaders of, based on numerous sources. The main source being what she could find out indirectly about indiscrete abilities from less savory sources.

He had the beginnings of a plan to get his gold out of Cardane, but he needed a figure out a way into the vault or to get his gold out of it.

Erold nodded to Braddach and motioned to the girl he was going to take upstairs to the adjoined rooms. At first, he had played it safe, especially when he hadn't yet earned close to half the money, he would need to buy an army from Valgaard for a mission he hadn't forgotten. However, he still needed that key to the door to the safe.

He didn't have a full plan yet though. He was winging the whole thing, and he couldn't admit that to anyone, even Braddach. Everyone had heard stories of Zosin churning through men. Despite that she always seen alone, carrying on as the most proper of women, dressed elegantly, kind, and often demure. It was no secret though that her father had become sick, and she had long been overseeing the administration of duties while he lay dying.

When Erold took his girl, dressed in blue, with reddish skin up to the second floor, Braddach took a girl too, and went into the adjacent room.

"I wonder how close we'd be to going back to Peth, if Erold stopped spending money on courtesans," said Moon, looking at the water in front of her and the beers of her companions.

"Hard to say. We've been buying and selling equipment, exchanging airships. I'm not sure if a piece of gold is drop in the bucket," said Volstad.

Moon kicked his shin, "That's not the point."

He grunted, "I was just going to say that." He took a long drink to hold in the pain, "I'm not sure this doesn't have something to do with gold."

Volstad looked over at Ragnar, Thein, and Veleon who were arguing about who had the bigger arms and could lift the most weight, "You know, I'm thinking of leaving this mercenary life for good, and the sooner that happens, however that happens, I'm ready to have a house in the hills or something, listening to the sound of the wind through the trees."

Moon had stopped listening. She was following some movement with her eyes. Awkwardly delicate movement that she had seen few times before.

She took another drink of water and checked to see if she had any good weapons on her. She slipped around the table and checked Volstad's hip for his pistol.

"What's this?"

She started dodging through the crowd, maneuvering to the stairs that Braddach and Erold had disappeared up. She caught the glint of its porcelain-like, fake skin, sheen from the top of the stairs as it went into one of the rooms.

Moon ran. It came back out, the room was empty. Moon hit it across the head with a knife, but its fake face swiveled and looked back at her.

The machine pushed her through the locked door behind her, splintering the frame. Braddach was sitting, with his jacket off and his trousers on, talking to the girl in her bright pink lingerie.

"Clockwork assassin!"

Braddach looked up and sent a spear at the automaton. The bright orange-yellow light dissolved across the glassy surface of the machine.

The glassy eyes of the porcelain face looked from one person to the other and then went to find the next room. Braddach grabbed his jacket, searching for a knife or a pistol and ran to the door, where he tried a warlock's push. The whoosh of air momentarily pushed the assassin back.

It turned toward him and lifted its hand, which spun around a pair of gears, revealing projectile needle darts, filled with poison.

Moon had been looking for a weapon. Having picked up a lamp that she had tied to a stick with a belt, she turned to leave the room. She saw Braddach frozen at the door and made a split-second decision. She used an assassin's dash to push him down and out of the way.

A dart caught her arm. Moon took her makeshift hammer walked toward the assassin, whose arm reloaded another needle and smashed its face and the lamp before she crumbled onto the floor. She could feel her mind spinning. She could still see the room. Hopefully, it was a poison she was immune to, but damn, it still hurt. It was painful enough that she blacked out.

Volstad had used a spell to lock the fractured automaton to the wall at the top of the stairs, while Ragnar and Thein who had gotten there ahead of him through the crowd, ripped off its arms and legs. As soon as he was by them, he saw Braddach standing in the doorway and Moon on the floor in the hallway with a feathered dart protruding from her shoulder.

Kahron looked on from behind them all with Veleon, though while Veleon felt like the others had stepped in, Kahron, not yet knowing Moon had been wounded, blamed himself for not having been as aware as Moon or as quick to react.

* * *

"Hello, pleased to meet you. I'm Jrasood, Chief aide to the emperor's daughter, Reena Zosin."

Erold had opened the door to the barracks, where everyone had collected after the clockwork automaton's assassination attempt in the low city.

"As your unit has now been promoted to the elite of the guard, I've come to congratulate you on your achievement. From now on you will be receiving work directly from my office. One such task, I have for you is no easy one. We have need of someone of skill to take out a white leviathan that is attacking cargo ships, sometimes devouring their shipments whole. If you are to succeed in this job, which we believe you specifically can, I have been told, when the job is complete, you will be invited to meet personally with the lady Zosin. Before I leave, I must have confirmation that you will leave immediately. The white leviathan is not to be taken lightly and recently devoured the last ship sent to go after it by pulling it down using the very harpoon meant to spear it. The only trace that was left was a sole survivor that was picked up on a beach in the east, and a sighting off the shore near Panorma is almost beside Cardane!"

Erold notified Jrasood that he would leave in no later than thirty minutes, thanked him and shut the door of the quiet barracks. Their unit had wanted to celebrate the promotion to elite of the guard as one, but now the tone was somber. One of their own had gone down.

She was in critical condition, fighting for her life, with Volstad by her side, secured in the captain's room they still shared together.

Erold couldn't pull Volstad, his best pilot, away from Moon's side, but he couldn't miss this opportunity to get closer to Zosin even if it meant a night flight, something incredibly dangerous in an airship. So many things could go wrong when flying, but traditionally, airship flights were during the day to watch out for obstacles. Kahron who could have provided them light had gone to spend the night with Xipartha.

"I can fly us out," Braddach put his hand on Erold's shoulder, "if that's what you're thinking. Moon." He paused, "let me take the wheel a couple times to practice."

"She'll pull through lad. She's a fighter like us. Now, let's hunt big fish," said Veleon.

"What size ship are you thinking, speed or power?" asked Braddach.

"We need to run this thing down, but we also need to haul it out of the water. That means it's the Top Knot, our biggest ship," Erold said and went for his axe. "Light crew on this one. Let's bring our harpoons across all ships aboard and latch 'em in. That makes twelve, each operated by four men."

"We'll have to hope that's enough to lift the beast from the water to prevent it from escaping," said Braddach.

"Before we spear it through the skull!" laughed Veleon.

* * *

They had detached and installed the harpoons in a matter of hours, and the air cutter, a size below a schooner, took off, out and away from the tower after the moon had risen and the stars dotted the sky, mirroring the low light of the oil lamps, glistening below them.

The Emiran sea to their north shimmered, a long line of white cast across its center by the moon, causing the sea to glow in the darkness and guiding their way on the clear night as the engine hummed and the red gold burned. Braddach guided them softly and easily, shifting them down through the sky, toward the ocean and then up over the harbor, and clearing enough space that even the largest of leviathans couldn't leap the water and grab at their ship in the sky.

Veleon commanded the harpoons. They were to ready and keep night watch if anyone could spot the white beast against the black of the night ocean. While others slept and rested, the ship followed the beast's last known heading away from the beaches, east of Cardane.

They swept across the dark night, looking for any sign or shimmer of the white beast. Leviathans were usually a minimum of twenty-seven atomic yards, but if one could brazenly attack and eat a sea ship, then it must have been much bigger. Erold had hoped his ship would be big enough at just under sixty atomic yards in length to carry the beast. He'd never have been able to lift a seventy atomic yard dragon.

They sailed the air through the night and dawn crept up over the sea, with them having left the sight of land and cut up further north than expected. Taking a reading of the last of the stars with a little math and a compass, they were able to pinpoint an approximation of being slightly east of Panorma.

They rounded in a curve north, sighting a heading west, noting the dots of merchants' ships on the horizon.

"Ready the harpoons Veleon," Erold called, while looking through a pair of binoculars that gave him about twice the sight of a spyglass.

"You see something?"

"Might just be imagining things," Erold said under his breath, watching the glimmer of the ocean in the morning sun. A sea schooner was perched with its sails down, quietly getting ready for returning to home with the morning sun. Its walls were painted blue and black, with a thin white line, running the length of the rim at about twenty atomic yards, it would be the height of three men in less length than the regular size of a typical leviathan and would have to be on guard if a larger beast was on the loose.

"Braddach, take us lower!"

"Aye, aye, Captain!" laughed Braddach. He was doing well but shouldn't get cocky, thought Erold. He planned to hail the ship and let them know to be wary of the 'White Leviathan.'

The crew members on the ship began to take action, likely curious whether they were being tagged as the target of a pirate's raid.

"Hoist the colors on the port line!" yelled Erold.

They took out the white flag of Cardane, with the red flower, which should be visible half an atomic mile away. Erold peered back into the binoculars. They were still readying the guns. He checked their flag, it was Cardane's. He scanned the water but couldn't see another ship for miles.

He looked back at the ship.

"Veleon, ready the guns on the port side."

"Aye, sir."

"Braddach, ease her over starboard and give them broadside at thirty degrees!"

"Aye, sir!"

Erold could see that the guns on the schooner were pointed at about them while they came in from the southeast to northwest angle.

They began turning to curve around the ship as if circling like a predator with its prey. The guns of the ship let fly sending plumes of smoke into the air.

"Brace for possible impact!" Erold ducked against the iron side.

Erold still couldn't tell the exact direction of the guns, but expected they were well out of the ship's range. At almost three times their size with twenty guns of their own to a side, despite a light crew to have packed in more Orichalc, he couldn't believe they would fire on a ship from distance when their shot could ricochet harmlessly off the metal hull.

He looked back up over the side of the ship in time to catch that some of the cannon fire landed harmlessly in the water toward where they had vacated the air in the water.

"Harder to port!"

"Aye, sir!"

"Off the guns, ready the harpoons!"

"You heard him, men! Back to stations!"

There were collective groans as the guns were returned and the men ran back up to the top deck where the twelve harpoons had been stationed on either side of the ship.

He had only seen a ripple.

Erold took up the binoculars again, and there it was, the faintest sliver of white cresting the water. The ship's men were arming the ship and readying for war to take the fight to the beast in a matter of life and death. For as the water ripple grew, so too did the beast. Just its formless shadow developing on the surface of the water as Erold's ship turned and the water dragon that went in for the kill was twice the size the schooner, sitting dead in the water.

Having chosen flight or fight, they had chosen wrong.

The mouth of the beast split the water, dwarfing the ship, looking like shark's teeth on the body of a whale. An arm came out of the water, like the claw of a lobster, and landed on the center of the ship as the beast tore and ripped, trying to snap the trapped wooden vessel in half.

Muskets fired at the white beast. Black harpoons, the size of dragon's talons, already stuck out of its white hide like natural spikes, and the round bullets drummed against its skin, angering the beast, which turned its eyes on the men on the vessel, squirming its mouth toward them, leaving the front of the ship half sunk in the water, sucking men into the vortex of teeth like ants.

"Come around men, harpoon the beast before it takes the ship under!"

Erold's airship came in, drifting lower over the stern of the trapped sea ship. His airmen mesmerized by the death as the beast fought still against the front of the vessel. As their view of the beast came into full focus, the six harpoons on the port side were fired into the back of the beast, digging into the back of the beast that let out a terrible roar and brought its claw down again on the center of the sea schooner, splitting its hull.

Braddach angled them around as the beast began to try a dive, and the right harpoons shot into the beast's back, leaving their giant talons like two great claws clutching the beast from through its skin.

"Bring her up!" yelled Erold.

"I'm trying!" Braddach worked at the wheel of the ship on the top deck, forcing it to move to his whim, but the beast below fought against them.

Braddach slipped on the wheel, and the beast below rolled, pulling them toward the water, where their ship could land but would have no defense for an attack by the beast, save for their iron sides.

"Get her back up!" Erold yelled, but when he realized they'd hit the water if he didn't act soon, "Release the harpoons!"

"Release the harpoons!" Veleon echoed running down the line of men. One by one the tethers connecting them to the beast, let loose and slithered like snakes into the water, encroaching quickly.

The last of the harpoons released, and the ships angle began to even out. They splashed into the water, sending great spews of sea spray in either direction.

"Get lift!" Erold yelled, wishfully.

They had no way of sailing through the water. They were dead in spot.

Braddach worked furiously and began to pull them up in a slow reverse, as the airship engines pushed back against the water that began to create a wake in front of the ship.

Erold saw the beast's face in the water, returning toward the surface. As it increased in speed and neared where sky met sea, the face of a seal with great crab-like claws, and shark's teeth, grew in size.

As the airship left the water behind, the leviathan leapt after them, catching air, and beginning to clear the water.

Erold had pulled out his axe. He had run down the length of the ship toward the foredeck. He had heard the legends of old, of men who had stood on the heads of the leviathans and plunged their harpoons through the skulls.

He gave himself a boost pushing with magic off in a temporary levitation spell to leave the deck behind and clear the teeth that neared the hull. The wind whipped up through the long braid of his blonde hair, tied together now by leather straps and reaching to the middle of his back.

Landing on the head of the beast, he slid slowly down, catching himself in the skin, using the blade of his axe. He stood, turned, and plunged a massive mage's spear through its head, looking through the center of its skull as the innards steamed and melted and the beast, jaws slackening, collapsed toward the water.

The ship turned to collect the dead body of the leviathan, floating lifeless on the surface of the ocean as sharks tore into its sides, feasting on the meaty belly of the beast. The few surviving sailors of the wreck that hadn't climbed aboard the last longboat were doomed.

Erold stood on the white beast's back as if it were a little island in the ocean, waiting until the ship neared to climb a rope ladder let down for him.

After re-harpooning it, the ship lifted the forty-six to forty-seven atomic yard man eater out of the water, and pulled it to shore at Panorma, as sharks, dangling for their meal, fell with flesh dripping from their jaws back into the water.

* * *

Disappointingly, the Empress-to-be, Zosin, did not invite him for a meeting despite the slaying of the white leviathan. With the amount of sea monster oil obtained from the beast, he would have thought before Orichalc that the creature would have at least provided a hefty pay day, but it was still adequate. Still not enough to change his timeline. Ten, maybe eleven years in Cardane and he'd have one hundred times a dragon and hopefully a little more, perhaps in the form of his ships, in case the requirements raised.

Erold tried desperately to suppress a yawn while he waited on Emperor Alalwee, who had been sickly in his late years, and had taken to remaining in his room almost permanently. His men were scattered throughout the palace. He and Braddach shared the duty at the 'high sultan's' door.

The hallway of the emperor's was much like the hallway of his own tower. The curved white walls were the same. The main difference was the Cardanian emperor's path had gold baseboards running around the length of both the inner and outer walls. With few changes to the layout or architecture, the inner workings had been touched up elegantly.

The rooms still ran along the outer wall with any access to windows or balconies. Their men hovered in three-rams daily outside and in crisscross patterns to avoid anyone getting within one hundred atomic yards of any windows in the palace tower, the largest of any of Cardane's towers, though only really felt from the inside. It was big enough to have desert orchid trees, planted in urns larger than Erold's chest, sitting on either side of the door that Erold and Braddach guarded.

The men guarding the Empress came into view, and Erold and

Braddach prepared to kneel. While none of the Menetorians were allowed in the palace, many of his own men were among the rotations of the elite guard that traveled throughout the palace. Though these weren't his men, he recognized them, from the distinction of their red dragonskin uniforms.

The Empress, in thin pink and turquoise dress, with more gold than usual adorned over her body, being carried along by bearers, turned slightly toward Erold as she was brought by.

"Please exchange guards," she commanded.

Braddach and Erold nodded and fell into line behind the Empress's escort as the two nearest stepped in their place.

They moved through the palace, to the enormous steam lift at its center, where the forward guard operated it and brought it to Zosin's floor.

Erold examined the chair from behind Zosin, only able to see her long, black hair, snake down the edge toward the floor of the platform.

When she reached the door to her apartments, she asked that the other guards stay outside, while her new men, Erold and Braddach be entertained within.

As they entered, her handmaidens escorted Braddach away, and Zosin lay down on a long divan of soft purple satin and let the sandals off her feet, smiling at Erold as she did so.

"I've heard many things about you Erold Volstad. An interesting last name. You're the son of a former member of the guard?"

"Yes," Erold replied, "He is working with me now."

"And he lets you lead?"

"I have taken over leadership duties."

"Impressive," she said, stroking her legs. Erold relaxed his eyes, trying to keep them level at her.

"Thank you, my lady."

"Please sit beside me," she said, beckoning beside her toward the dark tan of her sleek, shaven legs, glistening under lamp and day light as if they had been rubbed thoroughly in oil. Her lips still hidden by a thin sash that linked between her ears. When he didn't comply, she added, "It's a command."

He sat beside Zosin, turned toward her as if preventing a cat from ambushing him from behind. She was older than he had initially realized, though still clinging to many of her youthful features, age had sharpened her jawline, catching behind the loose mask that wrapped around it, and darkened her eyes. She may have been in her late thirties or early forties.

"It was also impressive how you took down the white leviathan so easily," she looked at him, batting her thick eyelashes, "I had never imagined someone could kill a beast, so large, all on one's own and so easily, I hear."

Erold smiled and said playfully, "Is there something that you would like?"

She smiled coyly and brought her knees toward her body, clutching them in her arms. Her soft, draping clothes hid any bit of her except her bare feet and painted nails, which Erold could see from the corner of his eyes.

"A bit of business," she said. "If you're up for it."

"And what that might be?"

"I imagine you've heard that my father may pass any day," the princess stood up and went to a long table against the wall, where she poured red wine from a golden pitcher into two gold cups, one for him and one for her.

He sniffed at it.

"It's not poisoned."

"I prefer beer."

"Drink it," she ordered, and he obeyed.

She stood over him, drinking from her glass, holding her mask above her cup, watching his eyes, hanging her lips, tenderly, against the edge of the gold cup, still hiding her face from his view. Only her gazelle-like eyes could be seen over the rim.

"By the will of my father, I am to marry a man by the name of Alil Nessah. I'm sure you've heard of him?"

"Yes."

"It's a move to placate the Cardanian people more than anything, not just my father's traditionalism. The issue is," she took a sip of her wine, "I don't know as much about him as I'd like to, and I've come to be concerned that he might not be the same Alil Nessah that was born in Cardane almost sixty some years ago."

"You think he was replaced?"

"By an imposter or a shapeshifter, I do not know or care, but I want you to follow him and report to me his whereabouts until I can determine how to proceed. If you tell anyone about this, I will kill you myself. Do not engage him in any way, and if he is to discover you, your life may be forfeit, and this time, not by my hand. Are we in agreement on terms?"

"Yes, I understand."

"Good, you can finish your wine and leave. Leave your cup on the table, or you'll lose a hand."

She left the room to where Braddach had been entertained and sent him back in. The two men looked at each other, unsure of what the other's experience might have just been.

1522 - Chapter 39

It took a few days to fly to a city called Clio. At several stations along the coast, they had to refuel on Orichalc to get out to an area just south of the Lisrakul shifting rock hills in Emira, where enough rock sheep and cattle had gone missing that local towns and cities had paid to have the Elite Guard investigate.

They were meeting a shepherd and cattle rancher on his ranch about fifty atomic miles northeast of Clio and a similar distance from the base of the hills further east, where the rancher controlled most of the territory in every direction.

The ship flew in over the smaller hills, dodging between cuts in the land, following the streams toward a river that flowed from the higher hills, where few people lived as a result of near constant seismic activity. The coast and country itself were large, if not spread out, so Cardane's control in the area remained essential and especially with Akre having fought recent battles on behalf of Cardane throughout the gulf, responding quickly to requests like this had been increasingly emphasized by Zosin through Jrasood.

The ranch sat off the main river that ran southwest to Clio and on the largest side river, which stretched further to the south. The main house was nestled in between a number of trees, while a collection of buildings including a mill, collecting hydropower, sat on the river. The mercenaries could see teams unloading salt from a sea ship that lived on the river, owned by traders who networked local goods from Clio to the surrounding towns and businesses.

They connected to a boot-strapped, private airdock, near the stone mill at the riverside, that stretched into the sky like a lightning rod. Because of its nature, they had to extend their rope ladder and climb off one by one with weapons strapped to their backs and most of the team would figure out how to unload ammunition while Erold, Volstad and Moon met with the rancher and his family up at the house.

Moon was glad to be back to work after Erold had kept her off missions for a while. Madame G at the orphanage where she grew up, before she had moved to Akre and followed her dream, had always told her that she would amount to nothing. She had thought long ago that she had proved that old hag wrong, and while maybe she shouldn't blame herself for the end of the general peace that had existed throughout the 1400s, she wanted to be there when they could put an end to the wars.

She hated getting shot, but she hadn't died a thousand deaths, drinking poison every day for three years, while working as an apprentice to the legendary phantom of Akre, to not be prepared for a moment such as that. She had eaten scorpions until they had become her painkillers, endured numerous snakebites, had strange compounds inserted into her at near lethal amounts, all acting as vaccines, homeopathic preparations for increased chance of survival.

Erold led the way up the hill to the house between the trees, the foothills surrounding them covered in short grass, kept low by the teeth of the rock sheep. They reached the door of the house, and went to knock, but it had already been left ajar.

"Come in, we know you're here," said an older man, Erold assumed as the rancher.

"Erold Volstad and my men," said Erold, introducing himself to the rancher who sat with a long rifle over his lap in a quiet room. His wife knitted near the window and two kids in the kitchen hand-washed dishes with water collected from a red pump that could be seen out the window, "We're members of the Varanorian Elite Guard, dispatched by Cardane. We were told you need--"

"To kill a cyclops."

"You're sure it's a cyclops?" Erold asked.

"I am."

"What makes you sure?" Erold looked at him skeptically.

"I just is."

"Sir, do you have any clues that it's a cyclops, or any clues of any kind for that matter?" asked Moon.

"How am I supposed to know?"

"Cyclopsi are extinct, sir, so it'd be helpful to have some place to start," said Volstad.

"Just because they was extinct, don't mean one ain't survived and is out there right now. It could have been frozen in the ice for heck I know."

Moon relaxed and let herself get back into the right mindset, where she wasn't focused on having to prove anything, "Sir, please start from the beginning. Where you first saw the cyclops attacks and when they have since happened?"

"See, I'm not crazy," the old man told his wife at the window who rolled her eyes and looked at Moon, wondering if this was some mind trick she was playing.

"Please, continue when you're ready," said Moon, wishing she had paper and a modern fountain pen, sweeping the world since the late 1510s. Erold handed her a pencil and a loose sheaf of paper on which to write.

"It all started a few months ago. We noticed we were missing one of our youngest sheep, Sheila. We went into the hills with guns to see if we had a case of wolves. If you can imagine, you don't see many of them 'round here. Not this far south of Instra in the farther north. Well, shoot, I ain't never heard of one in all of Emira. Where was I?"

"In the hills, you found something?"

"Yes, the lack of something. It was like the blood of the lamb had turned black and oily. It smelled of blood, but it wasn't no blood. That's how we found the spot where the sheep was taken, and if you can guess, we keep finding that same pool of blood gone black wherever this beast has been feeding. Whether there's anything left of the slaughter'd animal, or it's been completely removed, hair, skin and bones. Cyclops'd do that. Eat it 'n one bite I read in 'em old history books."

"Anything else you can tell me? Have you seen one of the sheep taken?"

"Geraldt did, sorta. What'd you say it was?"

The younger man, who was still in the kitchen, came over wiping his hands and tipped his cap where it would have been, then recognizing they were all waiting to speak began, "Pap was getting worried, so I staked out the hills, sitting on the old grain silos. I saw this bright light like an aurora, green-blue and yellow all at the same time."

"And what was there?"

Geraldt looked over at his father, a slight look of shame in his face, though the old man nodded, "I was too scared to go look that night. When I went over in the morning, that's where the smudge was."

"Had scared all the sheep too," his father said.

"And you said this has been going on for months? Why bring us in now?" Volstad looked at him questioningly, having heard strange lights stories before in Valgaard when working briefly in the north before chasing more money in the Varanorian Guard.

"The beast is getting more aggressive," said Geraldt. "At first, we could bring the sheep in close at night, but now, it is coming by near every week no matter how near we keep them."

"We didn't see any sheep when we came in," said Erold.

"The beast only attacks at night. We'll bring them in a few

hours."

"And if we take a sheep into the hills, you think it will probably be taken."

"Reckon so," said Geraldt.

"You ain't taken any of mine," said his father, "Not unless you pay me first."

"How much?" asked Erold.

"A couple gold pieces a sheep."

Erold pulled Volstad and Moon aside, "a sheep can't be worth more than forty cents in Akre."

"Looking to gouge us to make up for his lost flock."

"We'd still make money on the deal."

"Let's still negotiate some," said Volstad.

"Okay, let's see how low he'll go."

They ended up getting the sheep for two silvers, which was still almost eight times the value. Geraldt gave them an okay looking sheep that didn't appear sickly. He then pointed them toward the path in the mountains.

Erold, Volstad, Moon, and Kahron brought a group of about ten men out in the hills to help build hidden fortifications, dugouts covered in camouflage such as wood and other debris with space where they could prop guns out the front of the hole--nicknamed foxholes--before night fell and to build a pen to keep the sheep in as bait. The rock sheep were notorious jumpers, but typically, didn't fret unless provoked.

The first night that they staked out, nothing happened, and the next day passed lazily as they watched the river and the clouds above, taking sticks and dragging them through the ground, making marks for games to be played with stones and snail shells.

After a few nights, Erold was beginning to contemplate a new plan. They had already had to buy food, and had not even heard of another attack close to Clio, making it longer than a week since the 'beast' had fed.

The wind whistled through the trees, with the same constant monotone. The river glittered in the night, or it didn't, depending on the sky cover. Their rifles grew cold in the cold nights, as the world neared winter in autumn nights. The leaves would start to color and fall.

They had to hold their breaths and they had to watch their minds to keep them sharp. They had to fight off the verge of sleep that called to them, drifting ever nearer, waiting for them to close their eyes.

Bang!

The blazing light shined through the sky in a roar, swirling in all colors just as Geraldt had described and through the light, the wings of darkness, red with blood, a creature of beauty, fallen from God's perch.

"Hold your fire," said Kahron, "It's a fallen angel." He held up his hand, as if to catch a feather that fell through the sky, only soon a beam of light began to spin through it and send shockwaves of glowing yellow through the night. At first just breaking the darkness around them, but then dissolving the shroud of light, surrounding the angel, breaking the dark reverie of the twilight that had fixed her mind on the sheep below.

Kahron used a levitation spell, and Erold watched in awe as the master wizard went bravely to battle the beast with white feathers stained with red and black blood. Its hair was so tainted by a shadowy aura that the vision of its color was gone. Her eyes turned a bright searing gleam of red. The white of her skin so pale that she had become ghostly white. The only remnant of her essence was in the luminescent waves of light that had emanated on arrival and the gleam of her celestial armor.

Aaaah!

She let out a screech, a howl like a siren, and dove toward the wizard, striking at him with talons growing in place of her fingers. A thin blue forcefield pushed her strike back, and she pulled out a sword, dressed in white fire and began attacking at his shield.

With each strike the shield began to falter. Erold was not sure what his plan was, but he watched the angel's every move, intently.

In uneven moments, Kahron let the shield down to shoot sunbeams of cleansing light at the angel, only to have the quickness of her flight dodge each blast.

He caught her in the wing, and she howled again at him, shrieking through the night and slamming into his field, sending him shooting through the sky, until he had regained control, his forcefield blinking out.

The wizard tried to bring it back, but he may have drained his stamina, attempting too many spells at once. Volstad stepped in, jumping himself into the air by throwing a wave of force into the ground, and pushing the master wizard out of the way, with the same move.

The angel streaked through the air, the sword blazing a trail of molten cosmos where the wizard had stood. Moon dashed to Volstad's side, where he had landed hard, and yelled at Erold, pointing at Kahron, struggling to get his defenses up as the angel swooped back in, sword raised, for the kill.

Dawn began to break, and the angel shielded her eyes. As the sun broke the plain of the horizon, Erold ran to defend the wizard, casting the simple deflection spell he had worked so hard to learn as the angel's blade pierced through the sky, momentarily delayed by the sun's light.

The angel's blade was thrown from her hand. She went for Kahron with hands, scratching at his body, shielded well, but blood ran down the warped fingers.

Erold brought up the axe, the angel turned to him, and he swung at her head, catching the talons that separated as fingers as his axe cut through the air.

She flew to grab her sword with her unhurt hand and came back at Erold, swinging the sword down as he met it with equal might with his axe, shattering her blade, and then following it up with a bolt of lightning that sent her crashing into the side of the hill. Erold leapt across the gulch, ready to swing the axe down upon the bent head of his fallen foe.

"No!" yelled Kahron, blood dripping from his armor.

"She would have killed you!" Erold yelled back.

"No, it's tainted, can't you see? Hold it there!" Kahron used the last of his energy to cast one last beam of light. Erold held the angel from behind her arms as it tried to squirm away from the blast.

For a moment, Erold regretted taking Kahron's advice unsure any changes would take place. She coughed black, and her wings shook. She looked back at Erold, who still pinned her, and he relaxed his grip, feeling the serenity he knew of angels.

He may have been no healer, but as Kahron lay passed out on the hill in the early morning light, the angel's purple hair no longer had the black tint of ash, and her eyes turned to the black pupils, reminiscent of her human similarities.

It must have been a blight-like infection, but not one that Erold had ever heard of. Erold had thought the creature was gone beyond saving, but Kahron had cleansed from her soul what had tainted it.

An oil-like black substance remained on the ground, smelling of iron and blood, just as the rancher had described. It seeped off of her as if running, leaving a black mark like a spot where she had been afflicted and touched the ground.

Erold let go and she stood, before falling, looking at her hands. Fingers gone from one.

"I'm sorry," said Erold.

"No." She sobbed, pressing her forearm against her eyes as her fingers bled, "Thank you to you both. It was a waking nightmare."

"What happened?"

"I was taken by something on a mission from the floating city of Angels. Where am I?"

"Emira."

"That's not where I was supposed to be. I must return home, or they will look for me soon," she said, casting a glow on her hands, healing over the open wounds but leaving her fingertips gone.

"I'm Erold," said as he watched the Valkyrie lift her wings and in a large gust of wind from one flap, return to the sky; the aura of red disappearing as she rose, returning to blue and green with a golden halo.

"Mine's Kina," she laughed and soared away. "Maybe someday I will return the favor."

* * *

Erold had tailed Alil over the course of the last year. He wasn't sure how much time he had to figure this out, but Alil was a paranoid target. Erold noticed a pattern of regular excursions, and once he had found that pattern, he moved a little bit further down the route.

Alil sometimes changed his route, but there were only so many directions one could take to the low city. Through the airships, through the streets, Erold had inched a long over the year down the path, watching Zosin's groom-to-be go somewhere for something.

It was hard to be inconspicuous with blonde hair in the city, but he wasn't the only one of the Guard out and about, nor was he the only Normen. He instead opted to make the sections of the route a daily habit, and if he succeeded in moving the section further down the line so be it.

Erold stood near a street vendor, eating an apple he had bought and looking at foreign newspapers. Some were dated more than a few weeks ago, but others were more current. Not much of interest.

Alil crossed through a mirror in his field of vision and passed into an alleyway behind him. Erold slipped among the crowd and saw the door of a nearby pub close, with the heel of Alil's boot disappearing.

Erold tensed. He felt like he was close now. He could walk into the bar. He hadn't been there yet but knew what it was after scoping out the neighborhood.

He walked through the alleyway, alone, discarding the rest of his apple, and as the door slowly shut, he grabbed the edge with the palm of his hand.

Erold slipped into the seedy dive. There was a long cream-brick bar with a hot stove behind it bellowing smoke. There were patrons at tables along the walls. Erold saw a few closed doors at the back and no Alil Nessah within the bar.

Erold asked if there were rooms to rent. It wasn't a tavern he was told. He ordered a beer and got as close as he was going to get to a lager, flipping a silver to the barkeep, who went back to tending to the meat and fish on the open charcoal flame.

Erold sat down at one of the tables along the wall, and drank his beer, listening to the pub and letting his eyes closed and open as if he was half-asleep.

"I heard that Akre's been planning an invasion of Valgaard for quite a while."

"I'm glad that they finally caught the guy who was a fake doctor, working in the slums."

"A tip on that is going to cost you."

"I'm not sure what this meat is."

"I heard he had made some money, working with some crime boss. I wonder if he'll ever get his money back."

"I can't believe that Emperor Alalwee is still alive."

"No, if you get arrested, they take your gold. They put it in the detention center. I seen it in boxes."

"I'm glad he is. He was great. His daughter though--"

"This seat's mine white boy."

Erold looked up at the tall Cardanian man. He finished his beer in one gulp, nodded and left.

* * *

Zosin's handmaidens let him into her apartments while she was being bathed and massaged with oil. She sipped on a glass of wine and then lay face down as attendants dipped towels in warm water and massaged her muscles, then lathered oil onto her.

"Leave us," she spoke, glancing over her attendants as she closed her eyes and rested against the cold marble where she had been receiving her massage.

Erold looked around at Zosin's attendants as they went, who glanced at him with smiles hidden by thin fabric but obvious in their brown eyes and thick eyelashes.

"Do you have anything to report yet?" she asked, eyes still closed.

"I have found the location where he meets."

"Do you know any of his associates yet?"

"No."

"After all this time, Erold. Nothing, really?"

"The location--"

"Locations can be changed!"

He watched her, skin glistening and naked under the warm light, except for a thin towel that covered her rear. She breathed quietly, thinking.

"Has anyone seen you?"

"No."

"Then find out who he is meeting with, or something I can use." She thought for a minute and then added, "If you don't find something out soon, you will be dismissed. Permanently. Now, leave me."

1523 - Chapter 40

They were tracking a pack of orcs that had been raiding villages throughout northern Bohemia. The orcs had been fighting to establish and keep independent towns through the southernmost corridor of Haltvia along the Atlan River and to extend these to the southern shore of the river as well.

Cardane had put the Elite Guard on the task after having been previously helped with re-establishing dominance over their holdings in Mondelvania and Emira, despite the successes of Akre's armies shifting the power in the region further toward Akre.

"Two days ride east," said Ragnar, inspecting campfires and feces left by animals and orcs. He had been a tracker for much of his life, until running afoul of the law.

"We push on!" yelled Erold, smelling blood, after having followed the trail of blood the orcs had left for weeks, camping with light packs throughout the heavily forested country, carrying shield and axe, eating blackberries off the vine and foraging odd-shaped potatoes, growing like weeds on forgotten farms.

A trumpet roared.

"Positions."

The men closed ranks into a loose circle. They were a small unit of only eleven total, mainly riflemen. Volstad, Kahron, Braddach, and Erold led. Moon and Veleon were back in Cardane, overseeing the daily operations.

A messenger in Akre dark blue and white approached flanked by two guardsmen, "Telegram for sirs Volstad of the state of Cardane's Varanorian Elite Guard."

"How'd you find us?" asked Thein.

"Downwind by the smell most likely," said Ragnar.

"We've been attempting to catch you at every town, east of Bisan."

"Bisan? That was a week ago or more."

"We're express messengers. By order of the Ki--excuse me, the Akrin Senate adjusted the pledge a while back. Express messengers are to deliver anywhere unhindered, under penalty of death. New messengers have been sent with fresh horses."

"I'm not sure orcs play by the rules of the senate," someone remarked.

"Probably why there's so few of them left," another joked.

"What is the message?" said Volstad, ignoring the men.

"It's for your eyes only, sirs, either an Abrim or Erold Volstad, king's names I see. If you could sign here that our message has been delivered. Here's a fountain pen--if you could be careful with it."

Volstad signed while Erold looked on. They nodded as the messenger and guards left for the safety of a city's walls as quickly as their horses would take them.

"What's this?" asked Volstad, "We're off this job. A more urgent one. Sermbra's been attacked. They fear the whole city's up and disappeared. We're to investigate immediately and send a telegram from the city's tower back to Cardane."

"If there's power," said Braddach. "A city getting attacked probably means that the telegram service and more has been shut down."

"Good point. We'll have to be careful," Volstad mused.

"A whole town's been taken out. We're ten men. Careful?" said one of the Menetorians that had come along.

"We'll have to kill as many as we can!" yelled Thein, shaking his shield.

"If we're going to make it to Sermbra any time soon, we should leave now. It may still be a few days' hike to the coast of the Iron Sea," Kahron mused.

"You heard him men. Start packing up your things. We'll have to leave the orcs to escape judgment. Perhaps its divine intervention on their behalf," Volstad said as he kicked at the ashes of the fires."

Rifles strapped on backs, shields, axes, swords, they were ready to hike within ten minutes and were back on the road south and east, moving through the dense elms and pine trees that made up this portion of the same forest that stretched to Anpol and well beyond it.

They marched for almost a week through the forest. As the trees thinned and the wind howled, the towns and cities of the coast grew closer. The ground was thick with the brown of dead pine needles and sloped ever so gently toward the coast, so it felt as if the world had tilted beneath them.

The men kept night watches and doused their flames early, still wary of orcs. In the dying light of the evening fire, Erold checked the weapons he had rarely used, an officer's pistol and a short sword. His black axe was sharp, his shield marked where it had been tested by mages, knives, and arrows. He had always been able to get a deflection spell or shield spell up before shots were fired.

The titled ground evened out and the trees had all but gone when they came upon Sermbra near where the two seas met on the west coast of the Iron Sea. They could see the telegraph house on the top of a hill near the outskirts of the city, but they had to cross into the town to get there.

The buildings were a mix of stone, brick, and thatched wood like Erold had seen in Mondelvania. There was a church at the center, whose bell tower was obscured by the height of the two-story houses until they were nearby.

Erold had lost track of the days, but it didn't matter there was no one about. The town had not been attacked. It had been abandoned. There were newspapers flapping in the wind on the street and children's toys on a covered boardwalk that ran along the rows of houses.

He looked into the windows and saw lights flickering out above food rotting on shelves. Goods on the counter of a general store waited to be bought. He looked at Volstad, and then motioned to the store front.

The main group waited outside while the duo went in, found the back door locked. The floors were covered in flour and tipped over bags of dry beans. A bag of potatoes looked as if it had been dropped in place. The pair raided the limited supply of .54 shot before emptying the register and grabbing dry meal and continuing the journey up the road.

As they climbed the hill toward the telegraph house, Erold could see the dark blue of the sea, a slightly darker shade than the blue near Cardane, but it was a welcome sight after being surrounded by green and brown, only broken by the occasional trickle of streams so shallow that they were as black and gray as the color of the rocks they pooled into. Few things able to live in them through the cold of winter.

At the top of the hill, Volstad kicked open the door of the telegraph house, aiming his gun forward and holding his free hand at the ready to cast a spell. The others fanned out around him, six looking back in the wide of arch at clock positions and the other four watching Volstad's back.

The team then filed into the house, covering their backs with two men standing at the door. The house itself was a three-story converted mansion that overlooked the town. There were papers strewn across the floor, and the telegraph operators' chairs where they received and sent messages had been moved against the back door of the house.

Volstad moved around paperwork on the desk while Braddach inspected the machinery. Erold looked through the first floor of the house as teams checked whether the rooms were clear. There was a smoldering fire in the stove that choked on the ash and wood that it had lit. Erold tried an oil lamp and found that it had run through the oil.

"Everyone back into the main room!" yelled Volstad.

"What is it?" Erold asked as he appeared.

"Beside the obvious that this might be a trap?" Volstad asked as he continued to investigate paperwork.

"Trap?" someone asked.

"Look around at the windows, the doors. I don't even want to see upstairs. Someone barricaded this place and the last messages--."

"--are cries for help," Braddach said as he read the tape from the machine.

"What happened?" Thein voiced.

Ragnar started checking at the floors, looking for signs of struggle rather than seeing what had been left behind, "It looks like they left voluntarily in the end."

"They couldn't have," said Kahron, "Volstad's right. Look at the windows in the back. They've been punched out from the inside, and there's powder marks along the sill. They were firing at whatever was coming from the tree line."

"They were sitting on top of a recent Orichalc shipment," Volstad said. "Either someone wanted it for themselves and needed the key and exact location or they had planned to lure us here. Or both."

"Why us?" asked Almo, a Menetorian rifleman who had joined a few years back. The Valgaardians among them couldn't help but look at Erold.

"Kahron, you Thein and Almo, check the upper floors. See if you can find anything. Be ready."

"For what?" asked Kahron, readying his staff.

Volstad had a guess, but he didn't want to say, "The rest of us, we split into two teams. Braddach, you take Ipel, Werkel, and Shein. Re-fortify the rear windows. After that make sure the foundations on both sides are the bricks leading to the chimneys and set the fires if we haven't done so."

"Erold, same thing, with Maru and Ragnar. Any materials that were blocking out the windows, reinforce them with anything that you can find on hand not paper. I'll work on the front door."

Night would come soon, and Volstad was certain that it was a necromage that had called the undead to do their bidding. The entire town, but undead, would likely be descending on them as night fell, including children that had been bewitched by the evil sorcery of the faithless.

Kahron returned from scouting the second and third level, "Blood stains throughout the top floors. The windows were similarly knocked out and it appears many broken through."

"Did you find anything we can use here?" Volstad asked.

"More ammo."

The teams had gathered in the central operations room. The power to the facility had been choked out as all the Orichalc had been removed from the furnace room. They filled it with scrap wood and discarded belongings that couldn't be used for barricading entries, waiting to use it to turn the lights on at the last minute. The only light, as the evening fell, came from the reflections from the fireplaces through the open hallways; the house being the length of three rooms and two rooms deep in either direction.

"It will be a night of the undead," said Volstad. "Kahron, you cover each side from the middle. The rest of us, we will split into five teams of two. One team will split the middle defense and the others will stay on the wide side. We've barricaded what we could on the top level, but they'll make it inside. We'll have to fall back in waves when I call. Each team will have a rifleman and a pistoleer. Rifles take out what you can from range. Pistols, follow up anything as it closes in. Mages, save your stamina for when we must fall back. Distribute melee weapons and save them for any limb that gets through the window."

The only pure warlock among them was Volstad. Braddach, Kahron, and Erold had been split up, and Volstad took the center room, on the same side as Erold.

As dusk fell, they heard the wind through the trees, but soon knew that it was no wind. They could hear the sound of the drones once as lifeless and cold as statues now gathering in the sparse trees that lined the rear of the hill and across the roads that they had walked in the light.

It was a new moon, sparing the troop from seeing the thickness of the horde, packing into one mass of death, the color of dirt and mud where stolen from their graves and as white and pale as the most recent of their number.

Rifles plumed and sent sparks, momentarily revealing the faces and eyes of the evil, glittering like fireflies as the light collected on the glassy whites of the unfocused balls. The black clouds of powder obscured the oncoming mass again, which sent feverish chills through the defenders' spine. A city of twenty thousand or more advanced from the trees.

The defenders' bullets shattered and crumpled them, flipping decayed torsos and heads into the dirt, as great holes opened following the track of the thick lead. The zombies ran toward the house and began climbing the walls. They packed into the chimneys and worked at the glass on each floor.

The pistols began firing now. One shot at a time, still front loaded. A bullet let go from the hammer, sparking the powder packed inside its shell. Another bullet pulled from the box, slipped down the front of the barrel. Aim, pull the hammer back, fire. Maybe they had carried two thousand bullets up the hill between them. Certainly not enough.

The arms and faces of the dead hit the windows, staring at them lifelessly and began slamming their fists, cratering into shattered bone against the repaired wood and glass. Erold stuck the short sword through the frame into the face of a zombie and it was sucked away from him into the frenzy. He followed it with a shot from his pistol. He didn't have to see what it hit, because the undead body was replaced as soon as it crumbled below the window.

Specks of dirt flung into the house. The smell of the undead baking in the fires of the chimney as the fires grew and also risked being put out, alerted the defenders who now swung sword and axe at flailing limbs that it was time to pull back.

The eleven fell into the main room as the weak defenses shattered across all windows almost at once and the bodies of the undead fought to pile into the house. Bullets continued to fly from rifles and pistols.

"Gate the rooms!" Volstad yelled at Braddach.

As Erold ran to the middle, his axe filthy with the black dust of the undead, a crawling torso seized his leg. Volstad's bullet split the face and crumpled the body.

The gates went up, but they would not hold for long against the sheer mass that now began to crowd the doors. The sounds of walking from upstairs grew and parts of the barricade at the top of the long, thin staircase tumbled down the stairs. Volstad grabbed Erold, fired his pistol at bodies crawling by their arms through the heap, detached at the hips. The heads and eyes of every kind of face stared at them with hunger.

The defenders fell back to the staircase to the furnace room where they had stacked debris to restore the lights in the night, and they abandoned more packs of bullets and rifles, opting now for the last of the swords. There were no bullets left for Erold's pistol, so he threw it on the stone floor of the basement level as they retreated.

The last of the riflemen came down the staircase, covered by a few more shots. Kahron put up a shield as Volstad and Braddach worked out what to do, and the men at the top of the staircase shut and locked the door from below, pushing a wooden bar over the frame. The sound of the dead digging at the floorboards above them trying to lift the entire floor and fall through the ceiling frightened everyone in the near complete darkness of the basement.

Kahron lit the furnace. They had pooled what was left of the oil and he sprayed it there now.

Volstad and Braddach set new warlock gates over the floor as Kahron's forcefield on the door broke and what was left of their rifles, not abandoned, or shattered by undead hands, aimed at the bending door.

Erold retightened his grip on his axe. His shield, useless on his back. He brought it down, ready to smash with it whatever he could. He wondered how many spells he could cast. He reflexively felt at the orb at his side. Was this a moment to use it, and would it even make a difference.

The door broke in a spray of wood, and the riflemen fired as Braddach and Erold tossed mage's spears into the fray of zombie limbs that rolled and pushed down the stairs.

"Retreat into the far corner! Quickly!" yelled Volstad who threw his own spell of slicing air across the threshold, sending limbs and bodies momentarily back only to be crushed to dust by the weight of the horde behind them.

More reloading, putting bullets into rifles one at a time and firing at the dead walkers that found their way through the doorway and clamored toward them.

One, two, three. Few came for a moment, but then it was ten at a time, twenty, thirty. One hundred, undying, filling the basement. Erold swung his axe and used his shield to defend their feet, smashing zombie faces into dust with the sheer force of the steel.

Braddach cast fire balls, abandoning his hesitation and Volstad fired the massive pistol slugs through the crowd, while throwing the last strength of his warlock spells with each flick of a finger.

Riflemen reloaded desperately and shaking, shot into the crowd. Then, felt for bullets at their side that were no longer there. They turned the butts of the guns at the horde and rammed the iron plate against them.

Erold stopped swinging for a moment, grabbing at his side for the orb. A creature seized his axe and tried to pull him into the crowd to be torn apart. Volstad shot it at the shoulder sending it hurtling back as the bullet tore its way through the lifeless limbs.

Kahron, having waited for the right moment, the final moment, cast a spell. One ball of white fury rose from his hands into the center of the room and then furious light, burst forth like guided beams, streaking through the air and disintegrating the undead.

"Why didn't you do that before?"

"We had to draw them in."

"Are they all dead?"

"If they were near the house."

"We need to move and get more bullets now," said Volstad, pushing forward. He reloaded his pistol. He had only a few shots left, himself.

He had his spell hand ready to go and navigating the filth left of the dead, forgotten limbs and cratered cores, ash of judgment and the grime of the land, eased to where the door lay broken at the bottom of the stairs.

The men followed him. Erold just behind, readied his axe and shield. Kahron was almost out of stamina. Braddach too, had used everything he had in desperation. The riflemen with empty barrels followed last in the line of eleven.

Dawn had begun to break while they had been below and Volstad relaxed. There was not a trace above ground of what had happened, save for the caved in windows and destroyed barricade on the stairs.

He went to the door to see if he--

An arrow whizzed from his right, and he stepped back just in time as it grazed his right shoulder. A blackness steamed into the air as the wound opened.

Erold ran to the door. Another arrow pierced it. Kahron kneeled beside Volstad, who slumped by the door in agony, and tried to heal the darkness of the wound before helping him to a chair and stitching and bandaging up the bleeding shoulder.

Men found rounds and loaded their rifles. Erold nodded to them, pulled out his shield and led the party after the shooter, who was also likely the necromage.

They fanned out but stayed close to the house. The necromage was gone.

Volstad's arm would heal, but Erold was uneasy. Someone had bewitched the dead and purposely led them here to try to kill them off.

They searched the town in the daylight, and then stole a small ship from the docks to get to the next town. Whoever had tried to kill them, had also used the horde to collect the Orichalc and haul it off via the docks.

Erold would give the information to Jrasood to see if he could help, trusting only that he was closer to the Empress, who still said she needed Erold than he was to whoever had been behind the attack.

* * *

Erold drank his beer at the pub where he had once seen Alil Nessah, the potential future emperor of Cardane's controlled territories, a trade affiliate and subordinate of the larger Akrin empire to the west.

He hadn't seen Alil back here since then and the new year had come. It was closing on six months since. Zosin could have been right, and the location could have been changed. Erold was beginning to wonder a lot about whether it could also be related to whomever had tried to catch him with the undead.

Some regulars came in that Erold recognized. Some left. He ordered another beer. Zosin was getting impatient, and so was Erold. It was closing in on ten years since he had left Peth, and he had earned enough gold now to buy his army. He just needed a way to get it out, and he had a plan. Staying on Zosin's 'good' side was key.

A pattern of use for the back doors had emerged. One was a bathroom. One was the back storage room for the bar. The other, Erold, could only assume led to where meetings were held and today, it was in use.

Erold noted that a commandant of the Varanorian Guard had entered and exited. A leading merchant of the East Cardane who had been sitting at one of the tables for the last hour, checked his watch and went inside.

Erold fought the urge to check his own watch. Instead, he sipped his beer and closed his eyes. When he opened them, he noted a couple clergy members of the Church of Elessia, speaking in hushed tones. They went to the door, spoke to the commandant and were ushered in.

The commandant looked across the large room. Erold leaned to wipe something off his pant leg. When he looked back up, the commandant was greeting a bishop Erold recognized from service as one of those visiting from the Akrin Church.

Now, he was only missing Alil and anything else that might connect this group together. Seeing different denominations that believed in fundamentally different things at one meeting likely meant an organization that crossed the borders of nations like the Taivaan Vartijat once did hundreds of years ago, though under many names that Erold did not know.

Churches were a complicated subject on Vatna, and Erold had a headache just thinking about it. Most churches followed the words of the prophet, Fros, transcribed by those who walked with him in fellowship.

There were some who did not believe there was a prophet, Utaurans, they were called, but they did not openly preach against Fros. There were also many denominations of the followers of Fros, including the Akrin Church, which Cardane publicly followed. This had split from the teachings of Elessia in the last century. The Church of Elessia, which many viewed as the original and widest spread, was established quickly after the fall of the Otum and the freedom that event had granted from slavery throughout the gulf and then to the other regions that had not yet defeated the Otum. Because some nations had fought off the Otum Elves before Fros such as Imeria, those nations may have followed their own path to the true God and divine builder of all.

Before Fros and the light of God, many men of Vatna followed the Old Pantheon, which had in turn superseded the worship of fallen heroes. Harupht and Elessia had followed their own old heroes before they each fell to the Otum. This was partially the case among Normen, who still revered those who led them south after the ice covered the old land. They also had spread the names of the Valkyrie, who many viewed as God's answer to the demons that many believe still plagued the world in secret. Modern Normen followed Fros through the loose authority among Valgaard's churches.

There was Alil! Erold privately rejoiced. He finally had something concrete to tell Zosin. He planned to wait to get up after another beer, but as Alil disappeared into the back, he saw something else.

Alil had flashed a red mark tattoo to the commandant before the door closed; a similar symbol to the one he had seen on so many rogue mages throughout the gulf, which was the group he had assume had sent the undead after him.

Erold could see just the edge of it as his sleeve came down over his wrist after Alil's quick wrist motion.

* * *

"That's quite a list of people in attendance at a clandestine meeting with my betrothed," said Zosin, she stood up from the divan where she had first spoken to him and beckoned him to an inner room.

Her bedroom.

"And you're sure about these people?" Zosin asked as she sauntered toward a white four post bed, low to the ground, with large white curtains that looked like silk.

Erold's eyes couldn't leave Zosin's hips as they swayed away from him, "Yes."

"Is there anything else you want to tell me?" she asked as she lay back, opening her legs for him and drawing him toward her with a nod, grabbing his arm and undressing him before he joined her on the soft white sheets.

"No," he said.

"Nothing at all?" she pressed as she guided him inside of her.

"No," he said, as he tried to kiss her. At first, she refused but then she kissed him back, passionately.

"I'm going to need you to do something for me." She said, in between deep thrusts that caused her to moan involuntarily, "Once my father passes away."

"Yes, anything," he gasped, trying to enter her deepest reaches to cause her pain and pleasure with each thrust. He had been abstinent since she had first called him in many years ago, knowing word would get around. Now, he unleashed years of pent-up thirst, anger, and lust.

She whispered into his ear, stroking his long hair, and pulling him into her, relishing in his pent-up frustration being set free inside of her, "I'm going to need you to kill Alil Nessah before the marriage is confirmed. I can only prevent it while my father is alive, and no one else can be allowed to take his place by influencing my father."

1524 - Chapter 41

A lonely tower stood on a mountainous island between Cardane and Elessia, just south of Amotra, the largest island that rested in the Gulf, nearer to Cardane than the coastline of Altonia, its mother nation.

The tower, dark and quiet, stood on a natural plateau made of lava rock that jutted off the mountain and above forests that decorated the island like a deciduous paradise of oaks and maples, already lush and green in the early spring.

Stone seaside docks rested along the edge of a rocky shore, hidden from the wind and the rain by an alcove of barren rock shaped like a bat's wing. It sat at the base of a forested path that wound around the plateau and up to the tower. Two ships, about the size of small frigates, not much larger than the faster schooners, tethered to the docks, trembled in the choppy sea, cut just enough by the small harbor's low rock wall.

"Take us down near the forest. Let's have a look at the docks before we call at the house!" yelled Erold.

"Jrasood better be right about this," said Moon.

"Whoever wanted us dead at Sermbra probably wanted us here too," said Volstad.

"That's what I'm hoping," said Erold, eager to dish out some payback. His pistol at his side again. The sword reclaimed from the undead field in which it lay. The mage's battle axe and shield attached to his back, ready for battle.

"Don't be too eager," said Braddach.

"Yeah, save some for us," laughed Veleon.

"We'll go ahead and scout the shore and tower. You keep the engine warm, but don't run it too hot. If we need to make a quick getaway, we will signal you," said Volstad.

"Got it, boss," said Veleon.

As they came around the island, they got a better view of the estate attached to the tower, which appeared nothing more than a converted light house as they neared. Whatever it had once been used for, not a light in the mansion was on.

Erold flexed his fingers around the handle of his battle axe, over his shoulder. The airship swung over the docks, and then near the shore, as the dark night crept on. The dawn could not come soon enough.

They rappelled down the side of the ship, hanging onto the rope ladder as a guide, and let off their safety lines once they had hit solid, grassy ground.

The four of them had faced a dragon, but the only one confident approaching the docks from the tree line was Erold, itching to unleash fury. When they reached the docks, they could see the Orichalc, not yet completely unloaded from the old frigates. Erold leaned over a box that sat at the base of the walk to the tower and scooped out the red gold, which left a trail of chalky dust on his hands the color of rust.

"So far it seems like Jrasood has found our target," said Erold and he began up the hill. Moon couldn't help but feel that something was too easy about this.

They climbed up the steep path to the tower, feeling the burn in the back of their legs as they ascended the gravel path. The wind rushed past them and the sound of wine-colored waves crashing against the side of the island filled the night.

There was a large knocker on the door in the shape of the head of a bull, but Erold kicked at the door instead. When it didn't open, he sheepishly, twisted the knob and then kicked it open.

The wind blew through the house, swirling abandoned papers along the ground and rustling curtains that hung over three-story windows, opening up to a view of the water. In the daylight, other islands could be seen spotting the distance, but in the early morning hours, the glass was only black.

They kept a tight formation, checking one room at a time, looking for any sign of recent life. Dishes had been cleaned and set away. The cupboard was almost bare, save for wheat flour from Normany and a jug of olive oil from Elessia.

There was a violin sitting beside papers strewn about the floor and a piano by one of the open windows where it looked as if a duo had readied to play for an audience. Chairs sat empty beside water pooling against the wall.

"It hasn't rained recently, has it?" asked Kahron.

The first floor empty, they checked the second and the third with similar findings. Stark bedrooms, waiting to be used for numerous unknown family members. Not a single painting of one of them had been hung about.

The group circled back to a two-story library on the second floor that looked back out on the island's forests. There, Erold began trying to find a secret room while the rest of the group felt too uncomfortable to take a seat.

"There's a door right here Erold," said Moon who could not stop looking at every corner as if something was waiting for the moment, she stopped being careful.

"Didn't we try that one?" asked Kahron.

"No," said Volstad. "That looks like it must be the door to the tower above."

Erold opened it and led the way up stone stairs that wound along the back of the tower, taking his axe off his back, while Moon and Volstad pulled out pistols and readied whatever else they had at their disposal.

At the top of the stairs, they found a lab where rare tomes were strewn about a crowded desk with the accoutrements of vile sorcery. Rat tails and bat wings as well as sabretooth fangs and crushed mastodon tusk.

"This must be vampire's teeth and I guess this is werewolf's fur."

"Shh," said Moon, investigating markings on the floor and tables.

Erold twisted the knob on an oil lamp, which revealed glass chambers with large iron fixtures colored by brass, that could fit two men. One of them had been cracked open completely, oozing black sludge onto the ground.

"He was attempting to conjure djinn and other spirits to help him reach a higher plane of existence," whispered Moon.

"How do you know?" asked Erold.

"Keep quiet. It's his diary," she said.

"He stumbled on something. There are plans to control leviathan and notes on resources need to feed a Brazgul here," said Volstad, tightening his grip on his pistol.

"What's a Brazgul?" Erold asked, this time in a quieter voice, shifting where his hands were on his axe. For some reason, they grew clammy despite the cool breeze.

"An ancient demon that feasts on power," said Kahron. "I've only heard of its legendary battles with a wizard of our angelic order centuries ago."

"It appears that he was breeding the Brazgul in these lab tubes," Moon whispered, backing toward the wall and nodding at them to do the same.

"It must have freed itself and gored him," said Volstad, taking short steps after Moon, realizing that they were likely already in the midst of the demon.

"Show yourself!" Kahron tapped his staff against the ground.

"No!" yelled Moon.

Laughter echoed through the room, "Do you think I would have let you leave if you wanted to, little one?"

A black cloud formed and collected into the body of a corrupted wizard, possessed. His eyes and face looked as if they kept the last look of horror that had been on his face. The opaque eyes looked at nothing and yet the demon could see.

"I had to discover my enemy once my leviathan was killed, and it seems the plan has worked. You've come right to me," laughed the demon. "Now die!" he pointed a crooked, broken finger at them and shot bolts of purple lightning, tinged with the shadow of darkness through the air.

Erold knocked it away with a deflection spell while Kahron backed him up.

"Do you think that worked?" the upper lips of the demon's possession smiled but its broken jaw hung there still dead, despite being nothing more than a shape.

Volstad let out a scream of terror. His arm began to blaze where he had been caught by the arrow. Kahron had thought he cleared the corruption, but it began to take hold, morphing Volstad into a non-human.

He grew fangs, his fingers became pointy talons, a barbed tail shot out from his back, as evil energy collected matter around him, to shape him and re-form him into a half-lizard Vishgra. His angry eyes snapped at Erold, and he sliced at Erold's throat, frozen in place.

Moon batted away the blast.

"Snap out of it!" she yelled at the beast.

Kahron cast a spell to cleanse Volstad's spirit, but the Brazgul's magic was too strong.

Volstad knocked over a table as he came after Moon and Erold, as Erold yelled at Volstad to come back to them. His fury growing, while the Brazgul watched patiently above.

Erold yelled and shot a bolt from his battle axe, which prompted a clap of enjoyment from the audience circling above, but to the beast's surprise Erold had imprisoned Volstad in a cage of jagged, yellow light that forced his limbs against the wall, tighter and tighter as if he was being tied to the wall by a force perpendicular to gravity.

"These markings! This circle! It must be a runed banishment spell!" yelled Moon, over the growing noise of the demon and the growling anger of the Vishgra.

"Can you complete it?" asked Kahron, while he took up a

position beside Erold, both watching the beast.

"Only if you buy me time!"

Moon found the chalk, the images in the book that lay open on the desk. She recognized that circles upon circles had been placed across tables and across the floor, only easy to view from above, and she would have to guess as to not make a mistake.

"I'm not just going to sit here and watch you try to put me back into the áether. Now that so much power has been collected for me by this silly wizard, why should I stay in this simple form?"

The demon began to morph, growing, bursting out of the tower above them, sending stone, brick and wood flying. Kahron shielded them while Erold helped to knock away boulders that got caught on his shield and magic.

As he got angrier, worried for Volstad, upset at the beast, he began to feel different, as if he drew power from the very surface of the frost. He knew he must avoid the orb. He had called unnamed spells that he had never imagined before. The very áether as the beast called it felt as if it was rushing through him, just as Louie had said was the way of the elves.

He yelled, lifting his axe, and swung out at the beast, growing above them sending a bright blade of white light crashing through the air. The Brazgul looked down at him and grabbed the light in his hand, appearing to enjoy the feel of Erold's power, smiling as it ate the energy.

Kahron tried to hit it with a focused banishment spell, but the beam of white light flashed and faded into nothingness. Moon looked up for a moment from her work to see the whip of a tail hurtling through the air at Erold, and she dashed into him, pulling both him and her away as Kahron tried to keep the tail from landing on the floor. He failed, and the tail crashed into the ground, shaking the stone tower.

Erold jumped into the air, casting a levitation spell, attempting to draw the demon away from Moon, who was now defenseless. The demon grew a basilisk arm, and Erold fought at it, smashing the snake in the face with his axe and gouging its dangerous eyes.

Kahron defended the tower with his blue forcefield as the great beast smashed its opposite hand down at the wizard. The beast continued to grow larger, climbing to the air.

Their airship swung around and began to fire cannonballs, rifles, and mage blasts at the Brazgul. The attacks landed in pocks and marks but phased through the beast's skin like a cloud. It lashed back out at them with its tail.

The ship pulled away. Its passengers desperately cast spells with all their might just barely avoiding a similar fate to the tower as the tail missed the ship. The Brazgul reached its hand at them, but Kahron had abandoned the tower, rising to meet the beast in the air and defend the ship. He batted away punch after punch, while Erold still fought the basilisk arm that lashed out, biting at him in the air.

"I'll save the ship! You try to keep the attention of the demon!" yelled Kahron.

They each knew they would run out of energy soon. Kahron landed on the ship, unable to last much longer with the difficult levitation spell, and guided them away, knocking away tail and fist.

Erold looked back at the tower, where Moon clung to the wall, and Volstad in his twisted form remained locked to the other side while the foundations shook. They had been his parents all these years.

His real mother had died in childbirth. Moon was all he had ever known. His real father had driven that ship into the mountainside to save him, and Volstad had stepped in to raise him, though as a mage-hunting mercenary.

And, Braddach, his brother though also not of blood, was on the ship.

They needed him. He drew strength to him, pushing himself as far as he could go, pulling energy from the mountain, the trees, the island, the grass, the wind, the sea. He threw the axe back, and with each swing, uprooted trees and sent them at the Brazgul, luring it toward the mountain side, where he would engage it one on one.

He landed on the mountain and called at the beast. The basilisk arm flew at him through the air. Erold threw a bolt of lightning, stunning it and then jumping in the air, threw a slice of white light that this time snapped the arm in half, sending blood into the air like rain.

Standing on the mountainside, he stretched his energy inward, calling again to the mountain, feeling its strength, and he lifted the axe into the air, conjuring the spirit of a dragon the size of the one he had once killed, white like lightning. The Brazgul screamed through the sky at the demon, that shuddered in pain as it grew a new hand in the place of the dead one.

The dragon of energy ran into the beast, but the Brazgul caught it in the air, and held it by the neck, squeezing it into nothingness and then smashing its bits into dust as the power, dissipated.

The sun began to shine in the distance, but clouds began to touch the Brazgul as it grew and it turned gray and caused them to rain, blocking the sun.

Erold needed to use the orb to win. He had tried everything he could imagine, and the beast had just grown that much stronger with each moment.

Either feeding off his power, or inevitably showing its true strength it did not matter. Erold wrapped his hand around the orb and said a silent prayer to God.

"Don't use it," came a voice in his head; one he recognized.

An angel swooped in. Kina.

"You would only be feeding the Brazgul. The demon feasts on power. You have to steal it back from the Brazgul or it will continue to grow."

Erold stood on the mountain watching the battle above. The wind kicked through his air. The axe in his hand. The shield on his back. His clothes torn to shreds.

The Brazgul went to go for the airship again but was stopped by Kahron. It went to go for the tower, but Kina cast white blasts of light at the Brazgul, causing it to lash out angrily as the angel siphoned life away.

Erold watched the spell, and with the uncanny ability his father once noted as dangerous beyond words, he copied Kina's magic, pointing the axe at the Brazgul and he cast his own beam of light at the demon to steal its power.

He could feel the power resonating through him. The power of the mages on the ship. The power of the Orichalc the demon had eaten. The power of--

His axe shattered into two.

He heard Volstad's beast form scream, released when the blade broke. From where Erold stood on the mountain, he could see the freed Vishgra Volstad and Moon fight as the tower, shook and swayed beneath them.

He lashed out at her with claw and tail, but she was the speed of the wind, snapping his hands away with hidden daggers and a curved blade that appeared around her left fist. The blood of the lizard creature splashed through the air and yet on it went, lusting to slake its thirst on her blood. It was as if she only needed a pebble floating in the air on which to stand as she caught the lizards jaw with a hidden stiletto knife that stuck inside as she ripped herself away before his counterattack could land.

Erold looked at the two pieces of his axe. He leaned down, readying to leap at the demon as it fought against the ship and angel, both defending themselves and attacking the beast at the same time. The Brazgul reformed, believing itself a cloud of all-knowing, all-powerful energy that could devour anything it wanted to.

Erold jumped, launching himself into the side of the demon, readying the staff in one hand and the axe in the other. The beast laughed as it had, annoying Erold.

"If you're trying to find the wizard inside. There is no wizard. His human form has dissolved. You are going to join him soon!"

Erold powered a spell with the staff of his axe, as he could feel the demon eating away at him, attempting to possess him while he tried to counterbalance the beast's energy, devouring it as it devoured him.

He could feel them joining. He could feel their souls intertwining as the pure evil of endless lust for power joined with his soul. He could feel it as if there was an Odin scale for evil that rose like the degrees.

Ten percent. Twenty percent. Fifty percent.

He knew that the beast had over-extended itself. He knew that it was mindless energy, reaching out, soaking into him. The soul of the beast itself had not yet crossed over, but Erold couldn't wait any longer. The angel and Kahron fighting for their lives and to help him outside. Moon and Volstad locked in a vicious battle to the death.

Erold felt the energy of the demon focusing on his staff, and he cast another spell with the other half. With a bolt of light, much like the one he had shot at the dragon, and yet different, as it was purely his own, borrowing on the power gifted momentarily by the unwitting demon, he brought the axe down in a battle of souls and will power, swinging through the air, and the hit landed, snapping the demon's soul in half, putting fear into the nightmare where no fear had been.

The Brazgul had been emptied. Half of it was gone in a flash, and it could do nothing in response. The young man that remained fell in the air and the angel caught him and pulled him away, as the demon, now half black dust floating in the air, and a wayward soul that had nowhere to go, latched on the closest face. The woman in the tower, and regathering the black cloud rushed toward her.

The beast struck its target, only the target didn't feel quite as alive as the woman had looked.

The lizard Volstad, beaten, covered in blood. His hands sliced by knives. His body ripped to shreds. His jaw still split by a long, stiletto knife that hung from it, accepted the demon intent on possession.

And as the life of Volstad faded, so too did the Brazgul for its newly possessed soul was gathered by the twilight shepherd who brought the human eternal rest in Heaven alone while bringing the Brazgul to be judged on harsher terms.

* * *

When Volstad had died, his body slowly morphed partially back into his human form. Enough to be recognizable as who he had been, half his face still lizard and the wounds were impossible to unsee as little was left of him, save for the form of a man.

The crew collected him and Moon off the tower and the angel brought Erold down on the ship before leaving. The two were even as far as she was concerned. They had defeated the beast she had been sent to track years ago, and now, he lived.

When Erold woke up, he could not help but feel the pain of loss and anger at himself for rushing into the battle without knowing what dangers they could have been up against.

They let the airship hover over the bay while the crew collected the shipment of Orichalc. Erold and Kahron took a lifeboat off the frigate, also often called a longboat, a smaller version of the old Normen ships they had also rowed across the lakes. They built it up with sticks and lay Volstad down in the ship just as the Normen had done for centuries.

Everyone gathered on the shoreline, a rocky beach, as they lit the ship on fire and pushed Abrim Volstad, the great legend of the Varanorian Guard, into the water one last time. He would make his journey to the homeland of his tribe whether he was truly Varanorian, or had been Visgollan or Norlander instead, there would be a town in the old land where his soul would find heaven.

Moon cried quietly to herself after they had all gone back to loading the Orichalc or to eating and drinking. Erold sat down beside her.

Erold watched the ship burn and begin to sink as the day grew into the afternoon, taking the closest thing he had ever had to a real father away to God's hands.

"We'll definitely have enough to leave after this job," Moon said as she forced herself back to being the woman, she felt she had to be. She had married Volstad. Even if they had never told anyone their secret, it had been official in Peth.

"Yes."

She wiped at her face, "We've been lucky enough not to lose many people. We've lost more to retirement than death. Abrim had always talked about retirement. We shouldn't get any greedier, or we could lose more good people."

Moon had heard Volstad talk about retirement so much lately that despite her desire to see things through, she had begun to contemplate it too. At least from this line of work. For the first time in her life, she suddenly felt her age. A higher number than Erold would ever believe.

"You're right," he said, not sure what to say, hearing her words, and understanding that they were both sensible and frustrated. She really wanted to know deep down, why they couldn't have just left already. She knew that they had enough money a year ago to buy the army from Valgaard.

It might have been Erold's job to figure out how to get the gold out of Cardane, but it didn't matter to her how much money they had or didn't have.

"Did you figure it out how get the gold out of the city?" asked Moon, holding in her contempt.

"I have an escape plan, yes. With the Emperor Alalwee expected to pass away this week, the plan can finally be put into action," Erold said.

1505 and 1514 - Chapter 42

The eastern emperor walked out onto the lowest balcony of the palace tower and waved to the people who had gathered in droves in the central mall to witness the spectacle. There was a matter of bloodlust to be satiated as well as curiosity. Unlike the days of old, it was rare for a public execution to take place, but this man, a soldier in the navy, had been assigned both a religious and treasonous offense. The rumors of what transgressions he had committed made the people sick with anger.

It was a bright day. The event had almost been postponed on account of yesterday's rain, but the rain had relented. The sky was a pure blue but for a few powdery white clouds hovering over the white towers with their transit balloons, drifting high above like brass clouds from tower to tower as if they were trading places in a children's game.

The eastern emperor had on a regal dress of red, blue, and gold, and his face was unquestionably more stoic and grim than anyone ever remembered. He had always been the cheerful leader of their strong, underestimated city, urging them on with consistent positivity as the world around them grew ever more chaotic. Today, his face was one of disappointment.

Far above, the princess, Reena Zosin, had been locked in her room under house arrest to be overseen personally by Alil. Even Jrasood was barred from entering. In the emperor's eyes, the man was lucky to have his life, but he would never again be able to make children.

Far below, a puppet princess in a dark teal veil with gold trim, hid her face, averting her gaze from the scene that was set before them. Their guest, Lanhyr of Valgaard, who had stayed behind to complete the marriage on schedule despite the concerns of his father, and the Varanorian guards, Kidel and Volstad, stood quietly on the balcony.

A man was carried in black, wrapped in cloth and rope up a series of wooden stairs onto a makeshift, high wooden platform that could be seen throughout the mall, from the towers, the drifting balloons, airships, and those standing on the yard where horses still raced on weekends for sport.

He was kneeled in front of an automatic axe, and the signal was given to the emperor who raised his hands to quiet the clamor of the crowd, "This man has committed the most heinous of acts against our city. May he pay the price."

Alalwee lowered both hands at the same time and the axe shot down at the tug of a lever by a masked executioner, ending Safu's life and removing his head, hidden from the world by the black cloth into a small basket. Far above, the young empress-to-be, wept bitterly.

She hated her father, but she did not blame him. He was bound by tradition.

It was Lanhyr, who she blamed. He had been the one to discover her secret, though she did not know how and he had told her father. As such, when Alil spoke to her in these moments of agreeing to be the future chief advisor of the city at her father's request, she nodded her ascent. She would no longer challenge the man who had grown up here. He was a staunch supporter of Akre despite the fealty it required, but she no longer trusted Valgaard.

After the last of the ceremony was conducted, Lanhyr was escorted by the two Varanorians at his request, and the princess's agreement to see her in her chambers. Alil left her as they entered and smiled to the Valgaardian as he departed for the floor below where he would be spending more time in the coming days.

The young Reena looked up at Lanhyr, who looked at her with a strange mixture of concern and pity. She did not see the same love in his eyes that she had seen from Safu's. Behind him, the two Varanorians stood patiently.

"My dear, we can overcome this," he said, and he approached her to help her from the bed where she lay, wishing for the light of the sun to disappear from the balcony where Safu had once visited her.

She did not respond to him at first, so he placed a hand on her shoulder, "My dear. It is as simple as trading places. I can still be the man you need me to be." Volstad stepped forward instinctively, but Kidel placed a hand in his path and gave him a stern look.

Lanhyr looked up at the two men, "It's all right. If she's not interested, she will be in time."

"No, please. It's okay," she said, and Reena looked up at the two men who watched on.

"That's a good girl," Lanhyr said and caressed her cheek tenderly. He turned and rested his hands on his knees, readying to stand, but she grabbed him.

"Don't go," she said quietly. "Please stay."

Lanhyr looked down at her pleading eyes. She placed a tender hand on his chest and began to unbutton his tunic. He glanced at the two guardsman and shrugged, motioning for them to leave. As Lanhyr began to undress her and himself, she sat up and looked at him, seeing a red mark on his upper chest just below his neck as he took off his shirt.

He leaned in to kiss her, and she turned away. He began to kiss her neck. She wondered oddly if this was some kind of game to him as she re-wrapped her shawl and climbed out of bed. She said nothing, but looked at him, sitting there on the edge of the sheets.

"If you don't want to, I can leave," he said.

"No, it's okay," she said and interrupted him with a kiss as he had almost squirmed out of his pants. As he struggled to take them off, she went slowly to the door just as Volstad was leaving it and swiftly pulled the sword from his sheath and throwing her whole weight against it was able to close the door into him, shutting it just long enough.

"What are you doing with that?" the foreign prince said, holding up his hands. If he had been magically inclined like his prodigious sister, he might have thrown a spell even if just to freeze her hand, but he was not.

Before Volstad had instinctively turned to open the door and stop the princess, Zosin had plunged the blade to the hilt through the blonde man's chest with two hands right through the dark red mark.

In the chaos that ensued, Kidel gave Volstad his sword, and stole his subordinate's belt, telling him to not say a word. It was Kidel who had defended the princess's honor while she sobbed on the corner of the bed with the dead man's blood spilling over the pearly white shimmering silk sheets.

* * *

"Alil, my love. I have it all under control as usual," she kissed his cheek. "I know you feel safe walking among the people, but it was once a very risky thing to do. I wanted you to have extra security." The two stood in the outer chamber of her bedroom in the palace, embracing in a loose hug and looking into each other's dark eyes as if looking into each other's souls.

"Yes, I understand, but he's a barbarian," Alil replied, hiding any concern that he may have for being followed. She could not read him, but she didn't trust him.

"True, that he is," she said, "but it does not change that he is motivated by coin, and we have the biggest purse. Even if we didn't, he also can't speak the local language. No one in Cardane could persuade him from protecting you."

"True, my love," he returned and leaned into kiss her on the lips. She allowed it briefly, returning the kiss as his tongue touched hers, and then turned away.

"Soon, we will be partnered forever," she said and pressed her forehead against his shoulder, looking to where she had seen the red mark quite by chance. The same red mark tattoo that she had once seen on Lanhyr that she could never forget. She did not know what it meant, but even if she had done no research, she would have assumed the two were somehow linked. While they had not come to her directly, whoever was behind the scenes of this scheme to gain direct power over Cardane, they had played both sides, Valgaard and Akre in their effort. She would do her best to 'inspect all the dragon's eggs' as it were, but it had an added bonus.

"Besides, he's not just any barbarian. We believe that he is Erold, the exiled king, do we not?" she said, "We have made sure that Akre know that we will take care of him when the time comes, but he remains a bargaining chip."

"Yes, that is true," said Alil, and a strange look flashed over his face almost uncontrollably. It was one of a thoughtful man who had some other side concern as if he had a secret that he wanted to share but had then thought better of it.

"What is it my love?" she asked.

"Oh, it's nothing," he smiled.

"You can tell me anything you know that, right?" she smiled as Jrasood entered the room.

"I will tell you in due time. It is a trivial matter that I do not want to bother you with." Alil looked at Jrasood and sighed, "Is it that time already?"

Jrasood nodded.

"Back to work running things my love," Alil bowed and kissed the back of her hand before departing. He then bowed to Jrasood who returned it, whipped his sash over his shoulder and exited the room.

"Much to discuss?" the princess asked Jrasood.

"I could ask you the same," he replied.

"Let us come to the bedroom."

When they had passed through the outer chamber and into the inner chamber, she closed the balcony doors and looked out one of the windows before shuttering it while he turned on an old oil lamp that hissed loudly.

"What news is most prevalent?" she asked. "Has the senate conferred on anything?"

"The grand army is yet again set to increase," he replied.

"By Fros. A one point two million person troop has already been assembled across the empire. How much larger could it be?" she asked.

"By Fros indeed," He nodded. "My estimates now assume it may be larger than that, but I don't know the target."

"And they see Erold as a threat to their plans," she mused as he nodded again. "If we knew their goals, we would be able to make a real decision on whether to keep him alive or to continue to use him as a bargaining chip."

"You've kept him alive this long to be of more than one use," he replied sarcastically.

She frowned.

"I should remind you that there have been some assassination attempts despite their promises," Jrasood said.

"Yes, it is only more proof than we needed that he has upset someone, who we might want to keep upset. Perhaps, we need to take further precautions to keep him under our control," she replied barely above a whisper. Jrasood had to lean in to hear her over the hiss of the lamp.

"You must decide fast."

"Only one thing is for certain," she paused, watching his eyes and waiting for him to ask.

"What is that?" he looked at her, knowing the likely answer already.

"I can't marry Alil no matter what happens, so if Erold can succeed in at least preventing that then he will have fulfilled his most important use." Zosin bit her lip and looked off into the distance imagining another fantasy fulfilled.

Jrasood rolled his eyes.

1524 - Chapter 43

Erold pressed his hands firmer, strengthening his grip, against the curve of Zosin's hips as he held her lying prone on the bed below him. He dipped inside of her as her feet arched up and pressed against his back. Her face relaxed against a pillow tilted slightly toward him, revealing the upward curve of her painted, red lips in a smile of simple amusement, as he left his seed inside of her once again.

She turned to look at him, covered in beads of sweat as he lay back against the white bed, the sheets pushed to the sides, and she grabbed him and thrust him raw inside of her again, letting herself feel him, still dripping, throbbing and ready. She grinded against him while he watched her, a firm hand pressed against her side.

He admired the dark tan of her beautiful skin, glistening with oil and soft to the touch. The posts of the bed framed her. With the curtains drawn, they were left in a white oasis alone, as if sharing a cloud.

For more than a year, they had met as secretly as they could meet in a palace full of gossip. To most, he was just another Normen toy of Zosin's. When she had foregone a skin sheath to separate them, he couldn't resist the desire to fill her and still couldn't, despite the risk.

Each time he did this, he wondered about what the consequences could be. He, a king by rights. She, soon to be a queen. In the end, it didn't matter, he had to--needed to, yearned to--slake his lust, and she had begged him for his Normen liquor, as if selecting a wine.

When she had her fill, she let herself rest, looking up at the ceiling while he still panted softly beside her. He looked through the thin veil of the white curtain at the pillows and divans of her room as white as the towers, with the expansive balcony, closed off by a brass-colored, metal screen, looking over the southwest of the city that would have gleamed in the early morning sun.

"My father passed away this morning," Zosin said, softly. She loved her father, but there was much at stake that he would never focus on this late in his life as his health failed and his only daughter, half his age, had yet to give him another heir, male or female, as she neared the last of her child-bearing years. There were more voices like Alil's in his ear that had played upon his beliefs.

"You need me to kill Alil?" he whispered into her ear in a breath heavy with the scent of her own love.

"Yes," she said in barely the movement of her mouth, "And if you can, his compatriots too."

She wouldn't tell him why exactly, and though he didn't ask, he wondered about it. There was a threshold of trust that neither had ever crossed. For the same reasons that he didn't tell her who he really was or that he suspected this had something to do with the red mark tattoo he had seen adorned on so many rogue mages over the last ten years.

"Will you do this for me?" Zosin asked quietly, leaning over to kiss him, mixing the taste of him with the taste of her. Her tongue glancing playfully against his.

"Yes," he said as she kissed down his abdomen, scarred by battle, and leaned down to awaken his resting dragon with her lips, greedily helping herself.

Erold rested his head, his long blonde hair--still not cut since his father had died well over ten years ago--wet with sweat, feeling her love or lust with a mix of pain and pleasure, having been worked hard by her already and yet willed on by her desire to bend him to her will.

* * *

Erold knew that the group would likely meet that night, the night of the king's death. He let few people know where he was going.

They were rarely allowed to carry weapons within the city even as the guard. He brought the short sword, a few bullets, and the pistol, hiding them within plain clothes.

He donned a disguise, much like the one that he had worn to get on the Vagalla with his father, years ago, and he tied his hair up within a turban, making him look a Cardanian man.

Erold generally relied on the opponent getting greedy and overcommitting to whatever plan that they had. A final confirmation of particulars, handshakes over agreements.

He watched Alil enter the pub, followed him slowly, saw the red mark tattoo and knew it was him. Quickly, his blade was out and in the man's back. He had pulled his pistol and put a bullet in the heart of the commandant as the man's hand twitched to draw his own.

Erold kicked the dead body out of the way after sending a mage spear through the heart and head just in case, found a flight of stairs, climbed it by two while reloading. When he reached the top floor, it was an empty, one-room meeting hall with chairs waiting and candles burning.

A window had been opened. He looked out, seeing the trail of his quarry. Old men taking off, desperately, over the roofs of buildings into the distance, likely crying in fear.

Erold couldn't follow. The constables had been set on him, and he watched them point at him from the street. He waited for them to climb the stairs, and arrest him by the order of Empress Zosin, who had anticipated his act and if only, she had sent them sooner, they would have arrived to stop him in the act.

The constable's men pulled off his disguise, threw the turban on the ground and kicked him in the back, kneeling on him as they tied a rope around his hands telling him he was lucky the princess had ordered him alive.

Erold was picked up by airship that took him off the roof of the pub, hovering above the city with Orichalc powered lamps turned on him. Once on board, the ship flew directly to Cardane's main prison, a portion of one of the towers.

He had been there before, seeing vicious men he had put into chains on behalf of Cardane as a mercenary, tracking them over the desert. They were lucky he had not chopped off their heads like so many others. Now, they yelled and jeered at him as he laughed to himself at how typical they were like every other sad, sorry group of inmates. And like any other chained killer, he could still end them now if he so chose.

Too basic a story for him to waste his time adding it to the book of ages. The guards cut his hair and took his clothes. They looked for jewelry but found none. They pushed him into a bath of ice water and lashed him for the joy of turning white skin, pink and then red with blood.

They kicked him into a cell with barely a loincloth on, his hands still tied in front of him. Once he was alone, he tested the ropes with fire, smelling them smolder and then put it out, grabbing the melting material with his hands. He looked between the bars at the window that led outside. Somewhere below the city, the constables greedily packed his gold, jeweled and molded, of all shapes and sizes, bars and coins into two thousand boxes.

Some snuck a coin into their pants and then thought better of losing their hands, putting it back even quicker. After the prisoner's head rolled, the money became the Empress's, and no one stole from the royals without twenty-five years of torture in a cage hung above one of the towers where the city could see you die if they looked hard enough.

Five hundred trips of four boxes, heavily laden with the gold, flew up the steam lift. They had to clear out the storage rooms, moving shipments of other contraband into the constable's offices and the armory. The gold boxes packed the windowless room that had never been half full, and then filled part of the hallway, and then began filling the hallway nearest the airdocks, many of which were empty, waiting for his air schooner, just big enough to fit without being too big, to slide inside. The full force of the guards were outside packing the boxes gleefully while Erold awaited his next move.

* * *

Before he had gone up to see Zosin, Erold had informed select parties of his plan. With others being informed of portions only when they were being called upon.

His unit of the Varanorian Guard would be leaving Cardane once and for all. Braddach and Veleon would round up soldiers when it was time to make their move. Moon would gather intelligence, and Kahron had to stay behind.

In the small room where they had swept for bugs--Moon ever paranoid about clockwork listening devices--the five senior members of their elite force met for one last time before their leader, no longer sharing a title with the beloved and sorely missed Volstad, would be arrested by design.

So many rogues who thought they were tough, knights who thought they could get away with anything, dreamers who upset the lords were thrust unfairly in jail only to wallow in self-pity, or to fight their way out and act as if they were great kings among men. Erold needed his gold transported for him, and whether the doors to the cell were mage-proofed and reinforced with steel or not, he knew he could leave at any time, axe or no axe, orb or no orb. He had unfinished business in the city.

"I have to stay and none of the Menetorians can be seen as helping you," said Kahron, grasping Erold's forearm near the elbow and hugging him with his other arm, one last time.

"I respect your decision."

"It's not a decision I can make," Kahron assured him, "If we were seen as helping you, more than just our lives would be at stake. There have been many genocides over less. We would be risking our own people."

"I understand now." Erold hugged him closer.

"I have a family now too. I can't risk the repercussions to my people if even one Menetorian is believed to have helped you in anything you might have planned. Besides, I should congratulate you.

"On what?" smiled Erold.

"You can use angel magic now. That siphoning spell you used to defeat the Brazgul was masterful. Continue to foster the angel spirit in you to truly master it, and you will be able to defend the people you love."

"Thank you master," Erold bowed, "Say goodbye to Xipartha for me." He brought Kahron in for one last embrace, "Thank you for teaching me everything you have my master."

"Good luck," were Kahron's last words as the team headed for their stations and Kahron readied to protect his men in an as careful way as possible.

Moon pulled Erold aside and looked him in the eyes, partially regretting thinking his plan would be less complicated, even if it was also simple.

"Don't let them kill you," she ended up saying, weighing each alternative carefully.

"Take this," he whispered into her ear, and handed her a small object still wrapped in the blue velvet his father had given him. She knew it at once to be the orb.

1524 - Chapter 44

Polesar returned to the city on horseback accompanied by Murdot and a cadre of the royal guard. He had returned many times to the city through the Brandon gates due west of the palace, near the Union Square steam train station. The large, marble gates were five massive marble arches where a circular road had been placed like a spindle at the center of the new sprawl of the city. Eight roads traveled away from the center, with the two largest going to the station and the palace on directly opposite ends.

There was little fanfare this time, unlike the first time he had returned after defeating Greenski in the Solgra. The people had gotten used to him traveling to and from the station on his way to or back from the southern fields that hosted the grand army's training.

This time, as every time, Kalsvebir rested at his side, bounding lightly with every step of the horse. In ten years, he had never thought to return the red blade to the stone, nor had any one in the senate asked.

They had voted on many things over the years with or without him present, but usually they left him alone to manage the armies of the city. This time, they had called him to return for a special meeting.

He gripped the hilt of Kalsvebir. They were getting close to finally pressing their advantage and striking north. It would be the summer or winter of this year, barring any unforeseen developments, though he had long made plans to bait his northern opponent into an attack on Normany.

He passed beneath the Brandon Gates and then at Orion Square, another circular court that had not shaken the square moniker, he took the right path, as he always did, to the southern Lucherene Cathedral gate, one of five gates, into the Chelsea Palace compound.

Polesar rode through the gate to the trumpet of his men on the wall in the early morning light. The sun rose slowly over the palace to his east. It was so bright and low over the ornate palace ahead of him, he had to put his hand in front of his eyes. As he passed through the gates into the 'high city,' as it was sometimes called, he fell silent, seeing the empty place, to his left, where the Lucherene Cathedral had once stood, until it had burned in the fight against the northern invaders as the city was sacked. In its place, after having taken seventy years to be built, temporary gardens had been erected, but nothing could compare to the majesty he had once seen as a child.

He felt it meaningful in many ways that he now took Solday service with the people that he represented in Saint Drosef's between the Old Towns north and south of the Atlan River. It stood, as it had for centuries, on the Abrim Plaza where the statue to the angel, Anifiel, stood facing the north.

He looked that way now, away from the sun, and saw Everett's Hill, blocking his view of the north wall of the center square and palace compound. There used to be houses on the hill, but they, too, had been burned in the sacking. Most of the central city had not survived. Only the palace remained, for it had been said to have been defended by a battalion and soon after the city had been sacked, Polesar, himself, had led the southern army into the old town, forcing the Valgaardians to flee to Seylil the following night.

In retrospect seizing that moment to defend the city from the barbaric horde had launched his political career. He had saved most of the city's key landmarks and its leaders, including Lion Den's Hill and the senate. He had also been the first general to turn back King Hughgar, whose lightning-fast campaign to take the north coinciding with a tumultuous spring in Akre in 1495 shocked the entire world. Polesar would eventually rout Hughgar from Seylil after numerous engagements in what was then Northern Verdas forced him to surrender the mountain fortress without a direct siege.

Polesar jumped off his horse in front of the Chelsea Palace to see that Tanneran was waiting for him. He nodded to Murdot that he was dismissed, but the man and the guard lingered while Polesar pulled off his riding gloves and put them in his left pocket. Adjutants came and went to take his horse and then someone took his gloves and brought him a hat for the sun.

"For what reason, do I owe the pleasure to seeing you on my morning ride?"

"Private news, sire."

"Sire," Polesar repeated and looked off at Murdot and at the adjutants, "Then, let us proceed inside." He displayed an open hand to the door into the palace.

Tanneran hesitated as if he didn't consider the palace to be strictly private but then he agreed and went up the steps ahead of Polesar. As soon as they were through the front door, they were guided into a sitting room, which Tanneran followed Polesar through to his study that overlooked the front gardens, which had once been the site of central square apartments for the senior staff of the palace and had also been burned. Some had wondered if he would rebuild or build a new palace offsite, but instead he had installed ever more complicated gardens in their place.

"Now, pray tell me, what has you worked up this morning old friend?" Polesar asked.

Tanneran looked around nervously and stood as close to Polesar as he could before whispering, "The senate grows restless. They've agreed to a force of one point five million, but they find the results lacking."

"Lacking? Before I took over the deployment of the armies, Cardane had almost signed a treaty with the north."

"Yes, well. That was before you became emperor, and the failure to secure any Orichalc mines from the dwarves has become a partial tragedy to your reputation."

"Even if I reconquered key portions of Mondelvania and reopened trade with the dwarves?"

"Yes, well, a promise given, and delivery failed, has begun to worry some. With the standing army pushing ever larger, some wonder if we can continue to afford it without retaking Valgaard or Albion. It is well known that each have been able to manage their finances."

"As have we. Their salt is profitable, but we've controlled the world's gold."

"Yes, but the senate looks ahead to debts promised and wonders-_"

"If I might fail to deliver?"

"Precisely."

"And they do not wish to raise taxes?"

Tanneran shook his head, "They are elected men."

"On the provinces?"

"We are becoming ever more beholden to Cardane, and their trading company."

The emperor nodded and after a slight pause, he said, "Let us not forget that they owe us for taking ground in Emira."

"It does not matter. Not to the senate, when the concern is you may have lost sight of the goal."

"Valgaard?"

"Yes."

"So, you come to me with vague demands, wanting to know when might we go to war in the north?"

Tanneran shrugged, then started nodding gradually faster in return, "Precisely yes. That's close enough to the truth of it my liege."

Polesar stared blankly at him for a moment, and then simply said, "Barring any complications, this year, or next, now that the increase in the army has been approved."

"You may pray that it is this year."

"Tanneran, is that a threat? Should I be worried about something? I'm the greatest military mind this world has ever seen, and I've won countless battles. Valgaard has done just enough to make it too risky. The whole empire could fall. As it stands, I've been from one end to the other just in these last ten years. With Valgaard increasing their army size to nine hundred thousand, we may need the grand army to stand at one point five million before we can guarantee success."

"It will be that by year's end."

"Good. Now--"

"But what of complications?"

"By what do you mean?"

"What kind of complications could disrupt you?"

"Why do you ask?" Polesar said, suspicious of the way that Tanneran had begun to fiddle with objects in his study. Polesar walked around his desk and stopped him from continuing to spin his globe and then repeated, "What, pray tell, could you consider a threat to this invasion that I have not been told about?"

"Nothing--"

"You're not a good liar Tanneran."

"That you won't learn about in the senate session tomorrow."

"That's closer to the truth." Polesar watched the man fidget, lift a hand to the globe and then put it away. Tanneran took a step back and then forward as if he was going to say something and then didn't. "If it's that Valgaard might attack, I am counting on it. We've purposely left Normany undermanned to bait them into attacking with enough of their force that we can pin them their while we attack Peth directly. If it's that Harupht's pharaoh may need our help to stem the tides of rebellion, I've been planning that counterattack for years. Valgaard has been lucky that they were able to make strong allies, but they have reached their limit, and we haven't."

"Right, well, I must take my leave."

"Tanneran?"

"It appears you have everything under control?"

"Tanneran?"

The old man opened the door and didn't look back."

"Tanneran! What aren't you telling me?"

Polesar stood at the doorway, watching his old friend sweat and leave. As the old man left, he saw his son in the doorway with his blonde hair and blue eyes, so like his mother's standing there looking at him.

He was so young. He had not yet turned ten, and yet, if his mother ceded her birthright to the throne of Arandil as queen as she had agreed to when he married her as emperor, their son was now first in line for the ancient throne. The senate had never fully left the royalty behind by protecting Aurelia, who had become a symbol to the people of the city.

As soon as little Drosef saw Polesar, he bolted for him, screaming, "Daddy!"

Polesar embraced his son, picking him up and kissing him on the forehead. Whatever happened, he believed his son would one day be emperor of Akre too.

His other son appeared in the doorway, sucking his thumb and Polesar beckoned him nearer. He was shy unlike his older brother, and Aurelia had said afraid of his father. But, he came closer and Polesar scooped him up to kiss him on the cheek.

1524 - Chapter 45

"Get up you vermin," said the lead guard. "Empress Zosin has sent for you."

"Put this on him," said Jrasood, giving him a simple robe to wrap around his near-naked body, covered in the filth, dirt and otherwise, from the floor.

The guards unlocked the iron door, and it swayed open. The guard through the wrap over him after testing the bindings on his wrists. The guard motioned for him to follow Jrasood, who waited patiently in his formal, regal attire with no look of surprise and barely a hint of recognition in his brown eyes.

Erold was escorted by mages, readying spells and guards holding rifles at attention. They took him onto a small airship, not much larger than a three-ram, and flew to the palace where he had been so often to see Zosin intimately.

The ship landed beside a large, metal dock that stretched away from a central pillar above the tower, tethering to the side, with a large platform beneath the ship, suspended above the white of the tower below.

The escort pushed him over the walkway that the attendants on the airdock stretched out over the small gap and tied into place on either side. He followed the route that he knew well, over the dock, toward the central iron tower, plated with brass and bronze, giving the city its namesake.

* * *

Through her binoculars, Moon saw the ship leave with Erold on it, and hand-motioned to the men who had loaded armor, ammo, and supplies onto the same ship that still held the crates of Orichalc they had not yet sold.

Braddach, a black axe and its counterpart staff, strapped to his back and a second steel shield at his side, started the ship's Orichalc-powered steam engine, sending clouds of steam and red mist into the air.

They had communicated overnight, bit by bit, that they would be leaving in the morning for a mission, and then as the morning had come and the sun broke through the glass of the windows, they had changed that communication to robbing the guard of their own gold and busting out of the city. There was no nobler purpose for a mercenary than spilling guts for gold and glory.

The ship launched into the air, a normal occurrence for any

mercenary unit, and then rushed quickly in the early morning hours to an empty landing dock above the prison tower. Before they landed, they distributed rifles, loaded them from the front with the .54 shot. Strapped on ammo pouches, tightened their black and purple armor, and readied their weapons.

With grappling hooks and lifelines, men rappelled onto the dock, quickly as men covered them from the top. Warlocks in the forward line helped silence cries for help as bullets began to split the air.

Light-armored guards on the top of the tower rushed at them with cutlasses drawn only to have their attacks thwarted by dragonskin and their stomachs pierced by sword and pike, their arms lopped off by the swings of sharpened axe, and their bodies left, discarded to fall off the dock and onto the safety platform below.

Before any ships could leave for help, they were secured by the first squad as a second descended onto the docks and moved on the guards defending the prison.

Guns had been pulled out of the armory, packed with contraband, and the round bullets of the common musket glanced off of dragonskin harmlessly, or dented steel.

Some shots landed on soft tissue, gouging out eyes and dropping mercs, whose bodies would be dragged off on top of boxes of gold, to be buried or burned in Peth, by whatever Valgaardians survived the attack on the tower.

The squads of mercs kept coming, breaking through the doorway, and clearing the rest of the guard out, executing them with pistol, rifle, and blade in battle.

Second units began to count the boxes of gold and find the same dollies that the guards had used yesterday to hoist the boxes to where their schooner had been docked and the deck of the ship lowered to be ready for loading.

* * *

Not a sound of battle could be heard across the distance between the towers. The buzz of the airships readying for the morning was too loud, and the sun still too low for the slowly gathering black powder, lingering in the air, to yet alert men on the palace tower to the battle at hand.

Most watched as Erold, accused as the jealous, jilted obsessive fiend who desired the pristine Empress for himself was brought before her to face her wrath. The armed escort walked him, barely clothed over the bright walkway, catching the horizontal sun.

They pushed him down the stairs that wrapped around the

central pillar, connecting the docks to the white brick of the top of the tower.

He stumbled slightly and men laughed and pointed. His shortened hair could not hide his ugly face.

Before him, the bronze doors opened, and he was ushered forth to the steam lift. The men sent the contraption in motion, hissing steam and hurtling downward to the Empress's apartments. Still, the same ones he had visited so many times before.

Jrasood waited beside him, quietly, making no indication of his thoughts on the matter known. His hands were clasped in front of him, hidden by his white and red robe.

The steam lift stopped, and the escort prodded Erold forward.

* * *

Prisoners cried to be let loose, but the Valgaardians of Peth, laughed and began pushing carts loaded with gold up to the loading level of the airdocks.

The same process they had just completed for the weapons, armor, and their personal effects at their old, white tower, sitting quietly and never to be returned to again.

For ten years, they had worked and fought, bleeding, some dying, to help Cardane cement its authority over the islands, coasts, and seas of the gulf.

They had fought every creature they could have ever named, and many they couldn't have known existed. They had fought every type of mage, and they had all bled the same.

As members of the Varanorian Guard, these men of a distant land, some blonde-haired, some brown, had earned this gold. In their minds, they were being paid in full.

Bodies of the guards, dressed in white or red, were stained with blood and left for dead. The men that had survived Cardane, numbered little more than one hundred ten, worked quickly and had the gold loaded before cries of alarm could be put out at other towers.

Soon, though, their ship would have to be on the move, pursued by Cardane's own airships fit for battle. Erold and the men had installed only a few large guns on the ship's sides, knowing in advance of the weight of their treasure trove for this daring flight.

* * *

The escort pushed him past members of other units of the Varanorian Guard, who smirked, many younger than him, brought to the city after he had been, knowing the rumor that he had been the dragon slayer. Now, the 'dragon' of Peth had her way with him and was leaving him discarded and used. Four of them, six, the final pair in front of the door.

"He is to come in alone with me," said Jrasood, quietly confident in his own abilities.

The two of them walked through the princess's main guest room, where she had lounged on the divan, and gave him purple wine from the golden urn, still waiting on its perch. They passed the room where she had bathed on marble while he waited to hear what she had to say.

Now, he was presented before her in her bedroom, where she stood alone, looking out the open balcony as light shined through into the pearly white of her palace room, feeding the trees, living in pots and bouncing across every inch of the room, including the bed where they had held themselves together just the morning before.

"Leave us," said Zosin.

"But Empress--"

"Leave Jrasood."

"Yes, my lady," the man bowed graciously and closed the door behind him, where he waited, ready to pounce if he had to save Zosin.

"My tender love," Zosin said, "How could you have betrayed me so?"

Erold felt as if he smiled within, wondering who this performance was for.

She neared him, whispering in his ear, "I used you, my love, to do what was necessary. To get Alil Nessah out of the way. Just as you had planned to use me."

For a moment, he wondered if she had anticipated his plan to be arrested, but she continued.

"Erold Ardrada. Heir to the thrones of Normany, Galdir, and of that golden city, Akre. Do you think I would not learn who you truly were?"

She pulled away from his ear to look him in the eyes, while her hands ran down the length of his body perhaps feeling it for the last time before she would have him executed for being jealous of her betrothed, the perfect cover.

He looked at her, carefully, wary, waiting to see what was truly on his mind. Perhaps, she had used him in more ways than one.

"Perhaps, you want to know how I found you out," she asked, pulling the robe away from his body. It fell to the floor at his feet while she continued, contemplating whether to take advantage of him one last time. "A simple trail of evidence that you had been on the ship with your father when it crashed in the mountains, including witness, bank records, and gliders recovered weeks after the crash. A shootout at an inn in Hafhamarr and finally, the dead dragon in Valgaard. My spies alerted me to it before you had even arrived in Peth. But, you offered me a convenient way to root out Alil's local allies, to a degree. Something I needed done by an outsider who wouldn't die. I've been protecting you from Akre, though there has been the occasional assassin that has had to be cleaned up, I needed you politically in more ways than one. Not to mention you made a great..." She broke off and stroked him, smiling, "mercenary."

"I used you too," Erold said, and he caught the glint of bronze and white in the window. He hoped it was his airship, or this would be a long fall.

"Oh?"

"Goodbye, Empress." He melted the binds, ran for the window, and boosted himself as high into the air as he could, soaring above the city, as Braddach twisted the ship, laden with mounds of gold beneath him.

The race was on as Cardane's navy was put into action. Guns fired off the fore deck and aft. Rifles blazed at three-rams that raced to catch and board them, outmatched by the sheer size of the air schooner, unable to ensure a cannonball could dent the iron and dwarven metal.

Some three-rams had mages who sent powerful spells back at Erold's men, catching them off guard and sending bodies hurtling toward the awakening city below.

Warlocks pushed men off of pursuing ships that closed in with well-timed spells while the larger battleships of the Cardanian navy began to burn Orichalc in pursuit. Unable to match the speed, the battleships pulled their seventy-four gun broadsides wide to take fire.

Bullets whizzed across the deck as men rushed to grab the loin clothed Erold and pull him below. A bullet ricocheted off an armored arm and caught him, as lightly as a bullet could, in the side, but surprised him as he angled a levitation spell to land softly on the deck. He fell instantly to the deck shattering his ankle and a bullet caught him in the forearm.

A line of fire opened up from the side of one of the battleships as

Erold's ship cleared the central city limits, and push toward the air above the bay.

Erold was pulled into a doctor's room and treated by healing magic. Moon and company worked desperately to pull the infectious, iron shrapnel from his body and close the gaping wounds. His ankle, where he landed, hung off of his body like a large round ball with a dangling foot attached was forced back into place with pain searing through his body like a million needles were stabbing him.

His side ached as blood drenched an iron bed on which they worked. When he felt his shattered right wrist, he moaned in agony. Any movement or vibration of the ship sent excruciating pain up his forearm and into his shoulder.

Outside above the dark water of the bay, seventy-four plumes of the battleship joined into one rising smokescreen of burned powder.

Braddach expertly turned the ship for only its narrow, rear deck to face the slower navy, coming to life in pursuit behind them, and then grabbing the staff half of the black axe, charged it and sent a powerful spell of ice in one single blast to knock a thousand cannonballs, despite how near or far they were from striking them, down to the sea. For a moment, the air between the pursuers and the pursued was clear, and the distant faces of the Cardanian men could watch as the speed of the Varanorian Guard's ship lengthened the distance between them.

Beneath the deck, Moon found the bullet in Erold's side had not penetrated deeply; she pulled it out with what simple healing magic she knew, and then patched up the wound. He was lucky the momentum of this bullet had nearly died on its ricochet. He might have been killed.

The surviving three-rams of Cardane regrouped above the edge of the water, awaiting word from the larger ships on whether the air navy would pursue.

They were told to stand down. The higher ups had determined that their fire could be a risk to the city and the gold on board could be lost to the sea if the ship went down. However, as the ship grew smaller in the distance, it was clear that its speed outmatched the Cardanian air navy.

Zosin had called them back personally too, speaking it over with Jrasood, who stood in frustrated disbelief after echoing her order to the lieutenants in the tower guard. He was sure he could have stopped Erold's escape had he been allowed. Erold was a talented mage, but he was sloppy.

Zosin thought to herself that perhaps this could work in her favor. Inside her might be a baby boy, who could claim the thrones in the event of Erold's potential death in the west.

Hopefully not a girl, who would have to scrape and manipulate as she had, fighting off anyone who would try to marry her, fuck her, then leave her buried in a shallow grave.

She had seen his naked body. He had, unhesitating, killed a member of her real enemy--the forces behind the red mark--who they had worked so hard to put in place to manipulate her. It was clear that he was no friend of whatever force attempted to orchestrate the fate of the world through secrecy and devoted minions. Jrasood was a faithful protector, but there were many ways that Erold's survival could turn out to be a boon for both her and for her people and city.

Finally, Moon got to work on Erold's wrist. He would have difficulty walking for a bit. His hip would give him issues beneath where the bullet had struck him. But, if she didn't work quickly and successfully there was a risk that the boy, now man, she had protected for so long and shivering in pain before her would never be able to use his strong hand again.

1524 - Chapter 46

The ship swerved hard to port back to the north. The crew saw that the enemy did not pursue and let out cheers! Below deck, Erold writhed in pain, but Moon assured him that he was no longer bleeding after cauterizing the surface wound. Without a mage who knew how to truly heal on board, he had to do with her methods, though he should be more careful the next time he didn't wear body armor.

"I'll try not to jump out of a window naked anymore too," laughed Erold as Veleon helped him upright.

"We'd have a potion for this whipped up if we were in Valgaard to help restore your stamina, but it won't help if your dead," the old warlock said.

"Thanks," Erold smiled, "Let's get above the deck and see the ocean from here. I want to look back on the city one last time now that we're leaving it for good."

Erold climbed to the open top deck of the ship, eighty-five atomic yards long, crates of gold, sitting against the walls that ran along the deck.

"How are we doing for weight, Braddach!" yelled Erold after he had watched the city grow smaller in the distance.

Braddach gave him a cheery salute and yelled back, "Just fine captain! Once we start burning the Orichalc reserves, we'll be even better!"

"Well, take us higher then! I want to see what this thing can do!"

"Aye, aye! Let's ride the clouds!" laughed Braddach and he rung the engine bell for the crew to stoke the fire with more Orichalc. They were going to aim for the clouds.

Before anyone in the harbor had heard the news of the tower heist, they had watched the ship soar over the bay, unaware that on board was enough coin of the shining, glistening kind to coat the ship twice over or more in melted gold.

As the ship climbed slowly higher, Braddach shifted the heading back to the northwest. Valgaard was a good distance away, but in a ship, laden with Orichalc too, they could make it within the day.

As they burst through the low clouds, dew rested on the deck, causing the whole deck to become awash with a yellow hue from the bouncing light of the sun, unencumbered by the smog of burning Orichalc from the city below, reflecting off the water and the glittering gold.

"Fasten your safety ropes gents and lady! When's the last time we were this high!" yelled Veleon.

"Let the engine burn, Braddach!" yelled Erold, but the sound of the wind had grown too loud, and they all had to enjoy the view from where they were.

Quickly, Braddach dropped them back down below the cloud level as it had grown too cold, even with the brightness of the sun. An Odin scale was not needed to tell them it had gotten below freezing.

"We should be careful still, sir!" someone warned Erold, "We don't want to run out of Orichalc."

Erold knew they probably had enough Orichalc to make it twice the distance to Valgaard, but in his mind, he wanted to say they could get around the globe.

For once though, it was not the great Elara Moon who was issuing him a warning though. She had just been right behind them when they had roped themselves in.

He found her near the front of the ship, leaning her elbows on the side, looking out at the sea, calm in the early spring, before it would become stormy and dangerous as the summer grew closer.

Erold watched her for a moment as she enjoyed herself. She smiled, for he believed the first time. He wondered what she was thinking about as they soared near the clouds, well underway, and never to return to Cardane.

Moon noticed him staring and beckoned him closer, giving him a hug, "I wish Abrim was here."

"I'm sorry," Erold said.

"There was a moment not that long ago, where I wanted to fight forever, but there's more to life and he knew that."

"You're not leaving my side now, are you?" asked Erold.

"No, but there will be other people that need me. I've been in this fight for a long time, and there are a lot of times when I don't feel like I've been successful. But, I have been, even if the fight's not over." She looked out over the ocean, remembering the relieved looks on Erold's parents faces, Erolin and Valeria, when Akre, though burning, was far below them. Now, here Erold was, having lived to be a man, because she had stepped in to save the day well more than once.

"I'm not sure I even know what the real fight is or what I'm fighting against," said Erold, leaning next to her and thinking of the red mark rather than the Akrin Empire that he had long ago stopped thinking about daily.

Moon, too, thought of the red mark, her own nemesis from her days in Akre as an inspector, and for that reason she knew that one of the many places the red mark was hardest at work was the city of gold.

"Maybe, it's not as real for you. The fight against the empire, but it should be. Not just for what they have taken, which yes, from you, they have taken a lot, Erold. The Empire killed your grandfather's brother, your father, your uncle, stole a nation you never really knew, a capital city built over the generations by your family that you have never even seen. And, yes, there are other enemies out there, but you more than anyone have a reason to fight."

"If that's the case, then what's in it for you? Why are you willing to fight?"

"Because it's not just about what they've taken. Not just because of those things that are gone before you ever really knew them. That's not what this fight is about. It's about what they will take, because they won't stop until they have to. And sure, it's better if no one has to fight a war. But, war is coming or is already here, and when the two of us, return to Normany," Moon put her hand on Erold's shoulder and looked him intently in the eyes, "This war is personal, not just a profession, and that will make the difference."

"Is that's what has driven you all these years, when you could have left back in Normany?"

"Call it disillusioned idealism if you will."

Erold looked out to the sea where she was looking. In a rare moment, Moon let her shoulders relaxed, and it looked like the porcelain, doll-like mask that she wore began to crack, revealing the older woman who lived underneath.

"When I first moved to Akre, a lot of things were different, including me. The world was at peace, and the king was the reason why. Only I didn't know it then. No one really did. I started out on stolen items in what was called 'the Pound' in those days, then moved to investigating missing people, and wound up, trying to stop a coup with a senator who had once vowed to kill the king himself, but instead fell in love with the king's son, the man you know as Karles III."

"Sounds complicated."

"Every bit of this path has been complicated, but I won't get into all the details, because you don't want to hear it. That's not just why I fight against Akrin. I fight against Akrin, because war is their agenda. For nearly a century, the Akrin Empire did not go to war. That all changed, because the senate wanted it to. And you could say that there is a darker power at work, behind the scenes manipulating men; and to an extent there was, I fought against it, them, when I was that young, naïve detective. And yeah, that force is still at work behind the empire."

"The red mark?" asked Erold.

"Yes. How do you know about them?"

"I don't really," said Erold, "what do you know about them?"

"They are agents of chaos. It's not always something you can see on someone's skin. You can't know who everyone will turn out to be. Even if you found every one of those tattoos, whoever is playing puppet master, already has a new army built in plain sight."

"How do we stop them?" asked Erold.

"I used to think it could have been stopped long ago. Maybe not by me, but by the senate. But, when the time came it was votes by men that killed the king and ended the peace, and I wonder now if they even needed a push. Maybe I was the only one fighting."

"Didn't Valgaard attack first?" asked Erold.

"If you hear the story from Valgaard's perspective, they will say war was inevitable. No doubt you have heard of Canari Valley, which was a horrible massacre of men. Not of elves, which for some reason are often the first to be attacked, but men, women, and children. I knew someone who lived it as well on the Akrin side, and he then swore to end the line of kings. But, history is complicated and the senate had pushed for all-out war against the people of the north."

"The senator you worked with?"

Moon nodded, "The king at the time, King Karles II, is generally who people think of as the bad king, divorces, beheaded wives, and mistresses. He was easy to blame, but he had the bigger picture in mind and avoided full mobilization of troops. He is also the man who modernized the economy of the empire and made it possible to have airships and steamtech. He let trade organizations compete; he helped the common man become the modern man. And yes, he did horrible things too, but he wasn't the one who paid the price, King Karles III did, and his family, and you would have too. I saved you from that. Your father and mother had been called back to Akre, and I rescued them with Theodore Everett and his wife, who you met in the Ash Vale. We watched the city burn at the hands of Hughgar's Visgollan attack, but the senate just used him to wash the truth of history away."

Erold watched dragons, dwarfed by the size of their ship, possibly between fifteen and twenty atomic yards in wingspan fly in a flock of about thirty down to the water and scoop up gulps of plankton from the sea. They must have flown from the mountains in southern Verdas.

"We have a chance to put a stop to this before it is too late, or at least, I hope. There's no telling what the future will hold, but the plan of the Northern alliance is solid. It would have the potential to be more powerful than the Akrin Empire, and that's the first step," he said. "What waits in the shadows will have to wait."

"I'm not sure you should completely trust Valgaard in this war, but I agree, it's the place to start. No matter what, I'll always have your back."

"Like with that assassin," said Erold.

"Or that crossbow shot near Helsingstein, or the Brazgul's tail on the wizard's tower, and...I'm sure I'm missing a few." Moon looked over at Erold who was silent and chuckled when she saw he had reddened. "Do you think that was Zosin in the end? What did she say to you all those times you saw her?"

"No, I don't think so. Akre likely knows I'm coming. They may have known all along that I was still alive," said Erold.

"I guess it's always best to assume they're coming for you however safe you feel," said Moon.

"Like they came for my father..." Erold trailed off, thinking about what Moon had said, about all the things the empire had already taken.

"Before I forget," Moon said, and handed him back the orb in its blue velvet bag. "I'm sure the closer we are to Albion, the more likely old Theodore checks in on whether giving this up was a mistake."

"Still have it, don't I? Now I just need to get the pieces of my axe and my shield back from Captain Baha over there."

"True," Moon laughed.

The ship would soon cut across Verdas after hitting land over the Altonian, far too high above the entrenched borders below for them to stop their track to Valgaard waving the white flag of Cardane. Zosin could have alerted Akre by telegram, but even then, it would have taken time for them to move large enough airships to catch them.

When they reached Valgaard, they would switch colors and fly lower toward the much quieter airdocks in Peth, a nation too cold most of the year for the hot air of steam flight.

Erold checked a few times to see if they would indeed enough Orichalc. They had barely touched the extra stores they had. As they flew between low clouds, he began to contemplate the return to Valgaard, calling a meeting of the men.

Below decks, Moon taking over the wheel, the survivors of the long years abroad in Cardane, who once set out together from Peth in ancient longboats, now sat in their dragonskin armor after ten years in the Varanorian Guard.

"We are safely away from Cardane and have outrun any chance of pursuit. We are all going home rich, with the share of the gold, we earned in Cardane."

They cheered with each word, but he quieted them down and refocused, putting his foot up on one of the benches of the wooden tables gathered into three rows of a semi-circle in a lower deck room of the airship that held a small break room for bored travelers on a long fight. The ceiling was high and made of iron and the walls were dark and had bronze hue. All of the men had to lean in to hear him speak.

"My fight is not done, and there's one more job for you if you'll take it too. A job not finished. The reason I fought for all this gold, and why we return now to Peth is to purchase an army from Valgaard to take back Normany. We are all Normen, whether Varanor, Visgollan, or Norlander, we are Normen, and we either fight now, together, for Normany, or we die apart in our separate nations. Men, are you with me? To win back Normany and defy the Akrin hordes?"

No one spoke. Eventually, a man got up and patted Erold on his back, thanking him for his portion of the gold and the dragonskin armor.

Then another man did the same.

Then another.

Werkel and Shein.

Ragnar and Thein, too.

Soon almost everyone had, gotten up, thanked him for their armor, some for weapons, and their share of the gold. Almost all one hundred that had survived of the original one seventy who had left Peth, had walked out the door.

Finally, Veleon stood up and approached him.

"I'm pretty sure, me and the rest of the men, being of Valgaard, and not even caring much for that, have risked enough. We're all truly separate nations underneath. I won't be making that trip south. It's not that we don't love the gold and the stories we've gained, because we do. I speak for everyone when I say we love that we earned so much money working with you over the years, but any of us, including you, we're lucky to have made it alive through the gulf. The mage battles have been legendary, but you know what's deadlier than any mercenary campaign, where you're usually fighting at most one rogue mage or giant monster?"

"War?"

"Yes, war. Us warlocks have been training to counteract war mages more and more specifically over the years. The modern battlefield will have thousands of them. I'm not even sure how that would work. But, I am worried that the combined power of those mages would unleash exponentially powerful spells to devastating effect. We're not our Good King Hughgar Wenselclaus. What's worse is that we know it all too clearly, especially after Cardane. He once defeated twenty mages at a time, but the enemy's training is even better now. Could he do the same?"

Erold didn't answer out loud. He could only think of Sven at the battle of Elksits Hill near Leidyn. He knew Sven as a powerful mage, and also knew that old Greenski wouldn't go down with a fight. What had happened on the battlefield, he didn't know.

Erold hung his head, and Veleon patted him again on the back before thanking him for the armor, the weapons, and also, for the memories. Veleon hugged him once as strongly as he could and then went out of the break room too, leaving Erold alone amidst the loosely assembled furniture they had packed inside for this meeting alone.

Erold looked up.

There sat Braddach, waiting. The only one of his men from Normany, and Erold knew that Braddach too, was a true Normen by birth. Even though they didn't look much the same, his father had known the lineage of Braddach's father. A true Varanor, the callers of the Valkyrie, like Erold's mother. Just like those first mercenaries of Cardane that formed the original guard.

"I'm not sure you remember this Erold, but I once promised you in a tent long ago on the shore of the Lake of the Elms, I think it was. I promised then, and I promise it again now, I will fight for my homeland, Normany, and not just for my king, but for my brother, Erold."

They clasped hands.

"For Normany," said Erold.

"For Normany," Braddach echoed, then he sang an old fight song of the Varanor, loosely translated, "You can try to take my hands, or come to take my land, but I don't care, I won't bend the knee, you won't take my breath from me."

1524 - Chapter 47

Arla decoded the message and checked the time. Almost ten in the morning. Telegrams, which had been slow to develop in Valgaard, were instant if direct, but this message had to be routed through a network, using machines in secret across multiple nations.

Valgaard's palace was lucky it had arrived quickly. Adjusting for the length of time it took for an international flight if the mercenaries left Cardane at eight o'clock and had to fly across the sea. Arla wasn't sure of the distance, but she reasoned through the problem to herself, digging the edge of the graphite pencil beside her lip.

'Let's say it was one thousand atomic miles at the most. One hour of flight per one hundred atomic miles would be aggressive, so most likely not accurate, especially if they had an overladen ship, making the flight. They would possibly be here before eight in the after noon hours or even earlier, before the sun had set over the mountains that ran along the length of the nation's southwest.'

Arla had to let Princess Valessa know immediately. The woman had a tender heart despite how cold and unforgiving she could be, and Arla knew how she took each piece of news of the exiled King, Erold, that she had received. If the man showed up, landing a ship on the foreyard, she'd be devastated that she hadn't been notified of this development first.

Arla walked briskly through the halls of the palace, glad that she didn't share the princess's desire to always wear tall, sharp-heeled shoes. The thick green carpet alone had tripped her on her shoes more often than she would have liked to admit while running between rooms.

Valessa was speaking in front of the inner chamber when Arla knocked and entered quietly. The princess shot her a concerned side glance, but Arla tried to exude some measure of calm. The princess and her shared a lot of features. They were both tall, for example, with sharply cut cheekbones, but the princess was slender whereas she was strong. They had different hair and eye colors too, and Arla liked looking at the way Valessa's eyelashes fluttered like velvety butterflies when she blinked.

Valessa's blue eyes dashed back and forth across the page, reading it multiple times while Arla's red eyes watched on, admiring her. In many ways it was a shame that Valessa didn't feel the self confidence that she might have when the princess saw herself in the mirror each morning while maidens did her hair.

"Could we please have the room? On second thought, we'll continue the meeting tomorrow. Please note that Operation Lucherene is now in effect."

There were a few murmurs. Everyone knew the code phrase and that it meant Princess Valessa would be disguised until the operation was terminated, as the Valgaardian Archmage Cherene--loosely named after one of the Queen Valkyries of the old Eldrnor tomes.

Most, remained slightly relieved to be leaving the room near the halfway mark of the meeting rather than having another thirty minutes to argue between the limited responses to Akre's determination to reach one and a half million troops by year's end, or the following spring at the latest. The meetings had grown stale after the information had come in. Doom felt, once again, near at hand. The year of 1525 would be marked with blood. A war unlike one the world had ever seen before, involving millions of men was: inevitable. Their lives were most likely some of the first at risk, having led key affairs of the northern nation.

After everyone had filtered out, Valessa found a place to sit and leaned back to stretch her tense shoulders, "How long do you think it will take them to arrive?"

"I'm guessing eight in the after noon hours at the latest."

"Middle of the evening. Possibly just after sunset."

"It depends on how fast they fly, but I don't know enough about airships. Just making the general assumption that their military craft would be faster than a passenger ship. I know the fastest passenger crafts generally fly between fifty and sixty atomic miles an hour."

"Yes, that sounds reasonable. I wish we could develop something that worked year-round here. We're having enough trouble with developing trains."

"I don't mean to bring you back to the point at hand, princess, but shouldn't you change and alert Odessa?"

"I'm worried more about Elenia right now. She's always known me as her aunt. Her mother's about to arrive. I am certain that the news that Abrim not having returned to Cardane on a recent mission means that he passed away, leaving only her mother alive, who will not soon vacate Erold's side," she didn't want to seem fatalistic, but she was confident, "Maybe not even after Normany has been freed."

The royal family had taken in Captain Volstad and his wife Moon's daughter while they fought in the gulf. Abrim had come alone to deliver the girl in a rare trip away from Cardane on an indirect adventure, almost mirroring his first path to the city.

Princess Valessa had taken to the girl immediately. She had never told the girl that she had helped to raise, with the help of the entire staff of the palace, the full truth of her parents. She had only told her that they were still alive and coming for her when they could.

Arla hadn't even thought of the little girl. If Valessa and Elenia's mother went to war and were to, Heaven forbid, pass away, the girl would be alone.

"I'll let Odessa know that Operation Lucherene has gone into effect."

"I'll speak with her myself," said Valessa, "Inform the king that we'll have guests and notify him of Operation Lucherene, immediately."

"And if he asks who?"

"He should be able to guess," said Valessa, who left to speak with Elenia and then begin the transformation into an alter ego fit for battle.

She told herself and everyone else that this was about being able to see the front lines from the forward officers' command, but she knew completely now as Erold's return neared, that it was an opportunity to see him again and see if a spark she had once felt long ago was something natural between him or a foolish childhood fantasy.

She didn't want to imagine how many thousands of missions he might have been on over ten years, or how much that had truly changed him. She knew that she too had changed, and perhaps that was what distinguished the years and would help her refocus her mind away from the exiled king. After ten years, she believed that he wouldn't even recognize her, especially with the makeup removed and the hair let down and cut to her shoulders.

After she had spoken to Elenia, she went back to her rooms, which would soon be vacant. After dressing only a touch more masculine, she would take over her brother's old quarters as Cherene, the tough, female lead archmage of Valgaard's advance army.

She would dress in uniform daily, fit for battle. Attendants took away the turquoise dress she had been wearing, and her favorite spiked-heel shoes that looked almost like crystal. They brought her green and gold fitted armor, made of the white dwarven metal and then painted like canvas, crafted to be flexible with joints at the arms and ankles moving naturally like the knights of old ages.

Traditionally, suits like these were worn with light chain mail underneath, but that was too heavy for her, so they invested in combat vests that had proven to dull direct bullets. She wished she had tailored a dragonskin suit for herself but believed it wouldn't look good with her own people, considering dragon hunting was outlawed.

The attendants stripped off her makeup, taking the white paint and fake rose coloring off her cheeks. They wiped off the eyeliner and the eyeshadow and her light lipstick, leaving just her long, black eyelashes and the dull, natural tone of her thin, pink lips. It was as if her eyes were suddenly the only feature on her face and yet not as attention grabbing as they had been when surrounded by color.

Valessa watched herself transform into Cherene in the mirror until she began to believe that this was who she really was underneath, a warrior first, a princess second.

"You may excuse us," said King Hughgar, entering the room and dismissing the staff who had almost finished tying Valessa's hair in a bun behind her head as if she were a Varanorian man or a Gakayonan samurai, going to battle. "Valessa, are you sure this is necessary?"

"Cherene, please, father."

"Okay then, Lady Cherene. Is this level of precaution necessary? It's a risk you're taking being among the command even if the enemy doesn't know who you are."

"I want to go to the front lines. Besides I can handle myself," she said.

"That's not the point. You've built this army to fight. It will succeed without you risking your life."

"I can't sit and wait while men risk their life for the good of Valgaard in a foreign country. It's not right."

"At this point even I would wait until the enemy was at the gates to enter the foray."

"That's different."

"No, it isn't."

"There wouldn't be a Valgaard without you. No one cares about me."

"That's not true. You've run this country, since you were thirteen."

"No one even knows how much I do for this country! No one cares. What I do. What I give up. What I don't take. What I leave behind. To try to keep so many of us alive."

He waited. It was difficult to see her crack when she had always been stronger than anyone he knew. He watched her, as she wiped at teary eyes.

""It's been ten years since King Erold has been here, and now that he's arriving today, you think he won't recognize you? Is that what this is about?" said King Hughgar, thinking of the good-looking young man, who he had once taken under his wing like he had wished someone once had for him when he was alone in the frost of the north.

"I've prepared the essential staff for almost five years," said Valessa. "I'm doing this."

"I'm going to miss you running the nation behind my back, but we'll manage. I can understand your need to see this plan through, and though there's more to it than this, I know you've been negotiating the northern alliance for as long as you've been working at the palace, Va--Cherene."

* * *

Erold's air schooner flew in as the dusk settled, casting the world in half darkness and light as the sliver of its golden hue disappeared over the distant mountains, over three hundred atomic miles away.

The Great South Lake still shimmered and the white palace on the high hill still caught the edge of the sun's light. The rest of the city, stood in liminal shadow, caught between day and night for minutes on end, shrouded by the light cover of snow that still dusted the northern world despite it being more than halfway through Solsri.

Erold wanted them to touch down in front of the palace, with the bow facing the doors and the rear of the ship, extending out over the city, but Braddach talked him out of it. Instead, when they neared the city, they found that the palace's private airdocks facing southwest had been vacated and were waving them in with bright oil lamps.

In the end, the ship had burned through a lot of Orichalc on the trip including some of the reserves, especially as they needed more heat, the further north they went. Orichalc weighed too little for its use to make a considerable difference to the weight of their ships.

Erold went ahead, dressed in his black and purple armor, with the broken axe and handle crossed in an X over his back, and the shield tied in its harness over his shoulders. Moon followed behind him, similarly outfitted. Braddach and Veleon stayed behind to begin speaking with palace staff about unloading and disbursing soldier's dues and the shipment, on the whole. Bouvedere stood waiting at the docks.

Erold followed the dock to the low castle wall that ran around the palace's grounds. He jumped the last set of stairs, trying to hide the wincing pain from his ankle and grinning sheepishly at Moon. He breathed the air in heavily as he circled a walk, limping slightly, around the outside of the palace, shoveled out of the snow that glistened in the sun like marble.

Ten years since he'd walked this very path with Princess Valessa by his side to go to the stable where he'd cared for Seaspirit, and where they--. Seemed so long ago. He wondered if that old horse was still alive.

He had left as green as the stem of a day lily, and he'd come back a seasoned killer, who'd earned gold the hard way, having learned quickly what it took to take on a rogue mage, eyes filled with darkness and soul devoid of light. Some were far more difficult to catch than others. Some battles had left his mind and body scarred.

Yet, here he was, circling the palace, around to the foreground, where perhaps a larger cavalry of unicorns would be paraded. He almost chuckled. He'd hardly seen a horse, since he left on that longboat. Unicorns seemed suddenly as fantastical as if a whale had a horn. What could he even call that? A sword whale?

It was absurd to even picture. Though, perhaps, they wouldn't have to fight as hard against leviathans and sea serpents if that were the case.

Before he could touch the doors, they were opened for him from the inside. The sheer warmth of the palace, suddenly hit his face in a rush like sitting directly beside a fire. He felt drowsy, winded. He felt the years and their toll as he entered the hall with its arches on either side.

The banners now had unicorns on them. Green and gold was everywhere to be seen. Glittering and shimmering and yet, somehow it felt restrained and particular, refined, and almost modest, compared to some of the statues and places he'd seen around the gulf.

There she stood. Princess Valessa, beside her father. Younger looking than he expected. He had remembered her as sharp and deadly as ice, but she returned his smile and nod with an inviting smile of her own.

There, too, sat King Hughgar on his golden throne, watching with his chin, held on the palm of his hand, bored with the day, ready for beer and revelry in the night. Flanking his right was a strangely beautiful newcomer, who looked like she could've carved the cuts in the moon herself. A true Normen warrior woman.

"King Hughgar, Princess Valessa," Erold bowed deeply after he had approached the throne, and then he kneeled.

"You're right on time as per our agreement. Ten years. We'll move your gold to the treasury, but you have your army," smiled the princess, Odessa in the place of Valessa, standing in a shimmering green gown, with emerald heels, enjoying the feeling of being the center of attention.

"Thank you, my princess," said Erold and he bowed his head again, still on the knee.

"You may get up," said King Hughgar, somewhat lost in thought and not as concerned about the court pleasantries, "Yes, you've earned your army. You've done the people of Valgaard a great service, we will not soon forget, and you will have more than you set out to receive delivered to you."

"Thank you, my king," said Erold as he stood.

"You're your own king now," said Hughgar, "And when you win back your throne, don't let anyone take it from you." He walked over to the boy and admired the man he now saw before noticing the axe had been broken. "What did that?"

Erold pulled the axe and staff from his back. The broken dual axe head was in his right hand and the thin staff of the broken handle in his left. For the first time, he felt the true weight of these weapons as the pain in his wrist increased with each second the axe pulled his hand back toward the frost below them. He held the pieces out for the king to see, "A Brazgul, an unnamed demon of immense power, summoned by a hapless wizard appeared in the islands against us. I smote it with the pieces after the axe had been broken by the demon."

The king touched the broken weapons of war, tenderly, "Good, they haven't lost the magic, not yet. Did you try using the shield I gave you?"

"There were times that I used the shield, yes. That battle required more direct magic." Erold had not expected the old king to be more interested in the damage done to the blades than the fact that he had survived Cardane.

"This blade will be reforged." King Hughgar looked around for Bouvedere, and then remembered he was sorting out the particulars of the gold. "I'll have this done before the end of Solsri. Mark my word."

"Thank you, my--"

"Yes, yes. That's quite all right. I know I'm the king. Why don't you--"

"Mother?" asked a tentative voice of a young girl, who had come through the doors earlier than she was told to.

Moon looked over at the little girl, she had never wanted to let go of so many years ago, "Yes, my sweet. Please forgive me for not coming sooner." The two rushed to embrace almost cautiously before Moon broke into tears, and the girl, whose jet-black hair and jewel-shaped were so much like her mother's, held out her hand to wipe them from her cheek.

Erold glanced at Valessa, who seemed predictably aloof and at the warrior woman on the right side of the throne, who seemed strangely touched, as if she knew the particulars of the tale as well as Erold did.

* * *

The mercenaries were given beds split between the servants' rooms and guest quarters of the palace where they rested overnight, and then in the morning, in a surreal dream, Erold's men began to depart one by one, taking their share of the gold, armor and weapons, and just as they had thanked him on the ship, gave a final goodbye and left.

Only the warlocks that had survived, stayed in the palace, readying to take orders to join special forces units that worked separate to the main combat battalions, if more was even required of them after Cardane.

Erold, on private invite from the princess, walked through the hallways to Valessa's sanctum room, where he assumed an updated war board waited to be discussed. Arla, who he thought he should have remembered from his first time in Peth but didn't, guided him, asking him about the cities of the gulf, which he answered in simple explanations.

He wasn't sure how relevant it was whether he had seen Phoesa, Crossa, or had ever visited the Elessian peninsula or any of its greatest cities. It definitely didn't seem relevant to the task at hand, which felt a bizarrely solitary prospect. It was just Braddach, Moon, and him left, from all the people he had met and fought with over the years.

They entered the inner chamber and could hear arguing and muffled frustration beyond the rear doors that entered into Valessa's sanctum.

Arla smiled at Erold and asked him to step back into the hall for a moment. He acted as if to shut the door but left it slightly ajar as she went ahead of him. He could just make out the archmage speaking with Arla.

When Arla returned, she noticed the door ajar, but found Erold inspecting a marble bust down the hallway. She imagined he would have had to run to have made it that far if he had been waiting at the door, which seemed silly but possible. Arla beckoned him inside, and she led him to where the princess and archmage waited.

"Princess Valessa," Erold bowed to Odessa, the beautiful, tall blonde woman with blue eyes, wearing a well-tailored light blue dress almost the color of ice. She curtsied lightly in return, impersonating the Valessa who met foreign dignitaries and not the way the one beside her, Cherene, would have longed to embrace an old friend in at least a hug--once worried he would die like her brother in Cardane, never to return.

"And you haven't yet met my archmage, who will be assisting in the coming expedition into Normany, Cherene."

"Cherene, like the name of the angel? It is a pleasure," Erold bowed and took her hand, kissing almost just the air above the back of her ungloved hand tenderly.

"King Erold," Cherene said, slightly thrown for words, but appearing a mask behind her equally glassy blue eyes, much like that of the Princess's.

"Ahem," said Odessa, "Let us get to speaking on the war board, shall we?"

"Yes, there is only one thing I would like to bring to your attention first, princess." King Erold said standing tall and addressing Odessa directly, "I would like to have Patr Braddach appointed my second-in-command and given the highest rank, equal to that of the archmage. I would like him to be in attendance at all meetings of this nature going forward."

"Impossible," said Odessa, quickly.

"Impossible?"

"Cherene, please explain it, as you said."

"We have strict military procedures as regards to mages King Erold," said Cherene, "He must work his way up just as all the other mages have done."

"He fought ten years with me against rogue mages of all kinds in the gulf. He is adequate to the task."

"It's not a matter of adequacy. It's of principle. He must show that he can handle a large distribution of men and guide them into battle." retorted the archmage, whose eyes began to show a passion Erold, admittedly, liked to see.

"I can't imagine there have been as many battles for the men who have waited at home. Besides, what is it that he has to prove to be capable of? That he can get them well-timed in parade and that his mages can make coordinated dance moves with fire? I have heard the stories."

"Timing is a key function of battle. Can you imagine a troop not being at the assigned flank at the right time? It is of no consequence anyway. Many of your men have seen large scale military action in the Akrin military, including many of your senior commanders, who, as men of Normany blood, have defected from the southern corps to fight for you. You would do well to show them some regard."

"Of course, Cherene. I'd prefer to have my way on this. I do not want my man being engaged on the front lines."

"You can't always have your way. I--we--have heard of the galivanting you have done between missions in the gulf. Those were not full-scale engagements either." Cherene motioned to Arla and Odessa as she spoke.

"Galivanting? Yes, quite. Well, while you've been sitting in your crystal palace, I've been killing a lot of people on the way here to fight even more battles for my people and kingdom. Patr Braddach has done the same."

"He has volunteered for service in this expeditionary force and has been placed under my command. He has been given lead of a division as a mage of second rank. If he is talented, he will work his way up from there. If we act swiftly, we anticipate that the engagements will be limited." Cherene directed his attention to the board, where the army's had been redistributed.

"Over one million in troops on the Akrin side?" Erold said in disbelief, reading the board he had spent a lot of time at with Valessa so many years ago.

"Yes."

"I'd say I returned with little time to spare. They may have been preparing to launch north this year."

"Unlikely given the nearing winter."

"I fear Polesar cares little for anything but the destruction of men. I see this force has pulled south."

"There are rebellions in Harupht."

"I wonder where these rebellions get the funding," Erold looked over at the princess.

Odessa simply smiled, "Let's focus on what troops you have at your disposal and what your likely moves will be. Firstly, well done in earning more than what we had previously agreed upon." She began the rehearsed lines, pointing at the correct pieces on the board and in authoritative manner, appearing for the first time to Erold like the princess he had once known, "To summarize, we've delivered in excess of expectations, having drafted a force of forty two thousand infantry, supported by mages in excess of the eleven men squadrons per division as we look to expand the force through conscriptions once we enter Normany. We have delivered thirty thousand armored, heavy cavalry units of unicorns. The breeder awards, thanks to your financial assistance, were able to re-double the previous work of subsidies, and create a stable population in the north. And due to your increased contributions today, we have organized three hundred mixed artillery pieces in an array of howitzer and cannon, which will support full artillery units as well as mixed units, pulled with cavalry."

"One of these mixed units is where Braddach has been assigned," Cherene inserted. "With luck, he will not be directly engaged even if we see battle in the field."

Erold nodded, "So, these troops positioned north the old fortress at Helmun Loch are mine. I assume that the plan is to move south through Pili's pass, to take the old Taivaan Vartijat fortress, Ämelin. There are only two divisions stationed there, and the wall, though large, could be decimated by artillery from distance."

"Precisely the plan," said Odessa.

"How heavy is a heavy unit of the unicorn cavalry?"

There was a moment of pause.

"Unicorns of the cavalry are at least five hundred atomic pounds. Why?" Cherene replied.

"Heavier and larger than a horse. When fighting against mages or artillery, how does a cavalry charge fare? From your description it sounds as if the cavalry go in with few mages in support. Do any of the generals know the results from experience?"

Cherene answered, "A well-positioned infantry unit with mage support can effectively repel and in many ways decimate a cavalry charge. A well-timed cavalry charge can rout enemy infantry even with mage support. There is only so much a mage can do. The cavalry of Akre will be similar.

"That's what I was wondering. The weight of a charge would be impossible to repel by only a few mages. We'll have to focus on limiting enemy cavalry advantages and avoid committing forces forward against mages unless we have to."

"Only in the case of a prolonged engagement," said Archmage Cherene.

"Isn't it clear? This is a trap. A lightly defended forward position with easy access over the mountains and only a wall of future rubble in the way. They are baiting Valgaard into overcommitting, so they can split the northern force into two."

"Are you not willing to go then?" asked Odessa.

"I don't see how I have a choice. It may be a trap, but it is also the best option. If we don't move on Normany, Valgaard will be outnumbered as soon as this detachment returns north. We will have to immediately conscript, placing forces at Gulldalr, and expect that a portion of the force from Akre will move if they continue to have numerical superiority over Peth. It looks like we'd be facing as many as one hundred thousand with this three hundred still in the south."

"Kutzbek, the general, we appointed, said almost the exact same," Cherene remarked thoughtfully.

"As noted earlier," said Odessa, "the enemy's troop will be at one and a half million, potentially by the end of the year, including the estimate of forces deployed in Imeria. We have nine hundred thousand in Valgaard."

"Currently they are over one point three million soldiers worldwide." Erold paused for a moment then asked looking at the vacant space, "And how many in Albion?",

"Possibly as many as two hundred thousand not committed to the navy, but with a threat from Imeria, it is highly unlikely that they move their troop away from their borders."

Erold nodded, "As for Akre, I expect the same caution. I doubt they would ever risk moving under a ten percent advantage. We can safely assume that they would keep one million at all times in the capital. That might mean we could move on Normany before they can respond if this force remains deployed in the south. How high can the military of Valgaard be additionally stretched?"

"That is as far as we estimate we could go. It is already over conscripted compared to ancient wars of the Otum. We expect him to remain in the south through 1524," said Odessa.

"It also may be worth it to mention, it is a similar conscription rate to Akrin's current targets."

"And they're target is one and a half million. We must attack soon, or their conscriptions could outpace our ability to manage a response. They could split their force to attack in Normany and defend in Akre simultaneously, then wait to regroup before counterattacking North."

For a moment, they all looked at the board, even Odessa, who had until speaking it over with Erold had not recognized what the numbers meant and that the grip of war had tightened around them while she had been excited to wear the princess's dresses. Cherene may not have looked at Erold, but she recognized that he had changed much. He was no longer just asking questions as if everything was left to learn.

"It is estimated that the Otum elven hordes had as many as forty thousand attack Seylil in the battle of Annpel fields, compared to a defense of possibly thirty thousand, including reinforcements," said Erold with his eyes cast downward. "It was one of the largest battles in my nation's history."

"In Valgaard, too, it would be larger than any troop confrontation ever seen. Correcting for braggadocio, the wars of unification included three separate forces of over thirty thousand on each side in closely linked campaigns. The attrition of the first war greatly reduced southern Valgaard's population, causing it to turn to Akre who offered independent duchy, in exchange for rebuilding their army, ultimately leading to the unification of the north under southern Valgaard."

"What about King Hughgar's attack on Akre?"

"He could have conscripted a larger force, but the numbers were similar in size. About forty thousand to a side, and at one point, he had eighty thousand. In the intervening years of peace that the north had enjoyed under Akre as an independent duchy before the events of Canari, the population grew by roughly eight times, which is a typical peacetime number for a united nation over the course of three hundred years without suffering from blights. However, Akre did not divert resources north, so he had no reason to force conscriptions. Valgaard's historically low population due to its icy, northern climate means that a total war would devastate us."

"Even without diverting total war, the size of these engagements could exceed any battle ever fought this side of the Atlan River. My uncle's force at Seylil fought against an army more than five times its number. By far the largest army that had moved on Normany, and we would likely face the same or more in retaliation."

"More than just Valgaard needs you too. The alliance needs you, Erold. Your people need you," said Cherene.

"When it looked like you were actually going to survive in Cardane, we started building the army out of the refugees that came here through the pass you cleared of the dragon over ten years ago. They snuck around that old wall in droves," said Arla.

"How many people came north?"

"Two and a half million."

"Why?"

"Arla?" asked Odessa after seeing Cherene nod subtly toward the intelligence officer.

"I could say that I knew, but I don't. Something isn't what it seems about the Empire lately, but it's beyond the reach of our spies. Many people, men, women and children, came north," Arla explained.

"When we called for volunteers, even without saying the true king may return, there were many among those that had left that were willing to join the fight," said Cherene.

"The return of the exiled king will surely galvanize men already willing to fight for their old homes and way of life," Odessa added.

"Do we know anything about air and sea ship placements?" Erold asked, pulling his hair back over his head and feeling at the sides of his temples.

"We believe that all airships are consolidating under Imerian leadership," said Odessa.

"We do not have spies within the states of Imeria," Arla interjected.

"We may not know the positions of their ships directly, but Albion and Menetoris have the sea and air covered. We'll only be concerned with winning Normany and the ground response that is issued from Akre."

"There is considerable risk," said Erold, calmly. "They could send as many as three hundred thousand men. In which case, the war would begin in full and to our great disadvantage. I see no choice but to chase the fish. We shall move into Normany as soon as possible and hope their forces do indeed remain engaged in the south until the winter, allowing us to conscript enough troops to prevent the trap from closing."

* * *

"Hold on there, girl," said Erold, laughing as Seaspirit, whinnied loudly as he approached, "at least someone seems to care that I've returned."

He stroked the horse along her back. She seemed more muscular than he remembered and to be in good spirits, despite the princess's once dire proclamations of horses not surviving a single winter in Valgaard.

Cherene stood up, as stoic as in the board room, from beside the horse and wiped away some dirt that had been kicked onto her face by the excited horse, "Surprised to see me here?"

"Well, yes," said Erold.

"The princess commanded that I take care of the horse, so here I am. Usually I have help, but she's occupied."

"Elenia, Elara's daughter?"

"Yes," said Cherene, wistfully.

"Were you close to her?"

"I helped take care of her too."

Erold nodded and continued to stroke the horse.

"I apologize for giving you a hard time earlier today. The argument, I mean, about Patr, and also about Cardane."

Erold smiled, "Seems like word gets around, sometimes further than intended. Perhaps it explains some things." Erold looked off into the distance, thinking about how much fun he had and yet how he was now shifting his focus to acting like the king he meant to be.

Cherene watched him, having not known what to expect about this plan of hers, or what it would feel like to him when he returned. She hadn't at all meant to make him feel forgotten and alone.

He also didn't seem like the womanizer he had heard stories of, and it was weird to look at an older version of the boy she once knew. His hair had been cut shorter while he was gone and he needed a shave, but otherwise he looked much the same. She hoped she wasn't as obvious to him.

"I'll leave you two alone," smiled Erold, "I'll be back to prepare Seaspirit for returning to Normany soon." He left, not looking back.

* * *

True to his word, King Hughgar had the bellows worked and the Orichalc burned, the forges lit to the highest flames, hotter than the fire of dragons, and though it would not be quite the same as it had been new, as it was not true metal and required magic to seal its power in and steel to reconnect its pieces, the double-bladed black axe of King Erold Ardrada was re-forged to await future glory.

PART FOUR: THE END OF THE FIRST ALLIANCE WAR
1524 - Chapter 48

They flew the air schooner, emptied of most of its gold, to one of the larger cities in central Valgaard, east of the fortress at Helmun Loch. They flew low to see the country, crossing over two sets of high hills, some of the nation's finest cities, and six or seven different rivers that Cherene described from the air, as they covered the almost six hundred atomic miles in just under nine hours, taking a little longer due to the cold air, which would halt air travel north of the Evorul mountains in early winter until spring.

They were to stay the night in a hotel, not much larger than a tavern in the city, and then planned to part ways. Erold and company--Braddach, Cherene, and Arla, who came along to be the princess's eyes and ears--were to ride out the next morning to cover the near fifty atomic miles to the training fields, aiming to get there, not too long after midday.

Moon agreed to drop Erold off at the airdocks within the city before making a run with her daughter to Albion to deliver the ship and remaining gold in exchange for additional arms and artillery. Moon wanted to spend the summer with her daughter in the Ash Vale before linking up with Erold and forces, well after they had crossed into Normany and closer to end of Ivanssun at the latest.

Portions of the army had occupied a space for almost five years roughly halfway between the city and Helmun Loch on a stretch of the abandoned foothills of the old horse kingdom, using the cover of larger hills that extended north from the Evorul spine to help hide from potential spies.

Troops fiercely guarded Pili's pass and three-rams buzzed anything man-made that got too close to crossing the mountains, acting as escorts for merchants and the few passenger ships, flying this far south, from Albion, hoping to warn off enemy reconnaissance without appearing like full scale defensive maneuvering. Erold assumed the precautions that Cherene described were to avoid giving away the size of his force, because he remained convinced the enemy baited them to attack and knew they would.

It was the first time he and Moon would be apart for a significant stretch of time in his life, but Erold rode Seaspirit confidently, ahead of the trio flanking him on unicorns, a touch larger than his own horse. He had to look back a few times to believe it.

He rode with his black and purple dragonskin armor on, the reforged axe tied to the side of Seaspirit, back in a case like the one he had first taken to Cardane. The iron, painted shield had been repainted too, and that hung off the other side of Seaspirit, hiding his left leg with its immense size. As if eager to prove herself to him, the mare pushed hard across the relatively flat, barren terrain.

As they had made good time, they decided to cut across the hills to come in on the training grounds from the heights. Erold saw the bright, butter yellow uniforms with blue hats and white pants, and a half smile grew across his face.

Cherene couldn't tell what emotion had crossed Erold's face, so she explained, "These are a yellow jacket that we had been using in Valgaard briefly to separate different units until we standardized forest green. We could get enough blue hats made to keep them Normany blue and yellow, but until you can order your own uniforms, this was the easiest option for us."

"How long have they been training here?" asked Braddach.

"We set aside the space about five years ago, but the consolidated force is just over two years old. We have our own uniforms to make as our force has continued to expand."

"I like the yellow, but it will stick out."

"In the fog of black powder that crosses over the field, you have to be able to tell whether someone is friend or foe. These will be easy to tell apart from Akre's blue and white. It is also why we have banned all forward position inspections. The Akrin army still does the practice, but it's the largest historical cause of casualty among their mages."

"Noted, I will stay behind the lines," said Erold.

"You'll do more than that," said Cherene. "You shouldn't be anywhere near the front lines at any time."

"What about you?"

"I intend to fight."

Erold would have questioned her on that, but they had come across the troop, who paraded across the training grounds in tight formation with muskets over shoulder, directed by mages in similar attire to his archmage friend.

"Most of the mages in your force are on loan from Valgaard!" Cherene yelled over the sound of marching men who began to present arms and coordinate with empty artillery salutes, "We'll speak on it later!" She tried to say, but when the black powder rose, the men cheered, upon seeing the king return, having only heard the rumors.

"Hail to the King! Hail to the Sun!"

Guns fired.

"Hail! Hail! To Normany! The kingdom of the West!"

Artillery fired on the range.

"Hail! Hail! Hail!"

The men continued to cheer for him, and he sat stunned as the uneven clouds of black broke and the bright sun shone on the field. The men took it to be an omen. Erold could tell from the sheer size of the demonstrating force that this would not be anything like his tour in the gulf.

He was only looking at about ten thousand men and therefore forty-four mages. They had fifty guns test firing blanks toward the southwest. It was just less than a fourth of his infantry, an eighth of his artillery, and he had yet to see the cavalry. He could hear the commotion that the men had caused in their salute, coming from beyond the hill.

He nodded and raised his fist into the air. Ten thousand fists joined in unison as he rode onto the next short hill, walling off the troop from additional demonstrations. Riding along the top of this hill, he could see the other three units clearly also separated by what must have been man-made mounds. They were watching for him and as Seaspirit galloped, they cheered his name and sang to him. One hundred howitzers sat silent, resting off in the distance, and yet those two hundred that boomed black powder into the distance sounded like the almighty voice of thunder. A chill ran down his spine, looking out over the collected troop.

Erold could see the edge of the cavalry running tight demonstrations across the field in the distance. One thousand men at a time, galloping across the field in ten lines of one hundred, practicing the stride and the height of the gun in their hand, before they broke off, circling left or right depending on their side of the field, heading off to rest at streams that had been dug in the ground.

There were fortified grounds far off into the distance, where wooden buildings and tents had been erected. Erold imagined that they must have wintered elsewhere. From a cursory glance, they appeared ready to fight, but he wondered if they knew what they would be in for if the enemy took to the field, likely outnumbering them by thirty to sixty thousand men or even far more.

Cherene yelled to him again over the cries, pulling in close to his ear, "This is why we believe that you could build a substantial army once we've crossed the Evoruls. Rumors of your exploits in the gulf and knowledge of your heritage as the true king of Normany has begun to circulate among the men recently, courtesy of the princess!"

Erold nodded, "We should go meet the officers." He raised his fist as he led their horses on toward the camp. The men cheered in return.

Cherene turned to Braddach as they neared the buildings, "Lt. Master Mage, you can find your station in the administration office, which is clearly labeled. Just there, second building on the right."

Braddach nodded and went to rode up alongside Erold. They shook hands and hugged across horses, unsure when they would next cross paths in the coming days as Braddach got to know his squadron of sergeant mages and infantry men.

"Remember Fros walks with you," Erold said, and then he leaned beside Braddach to whisper, "keep the dragonskin armor on in battle if you can."

"I will," said Braddach quietly, though he expected he would join the rest of the men in wearing the uniforms of Valgaard's master mages as he didn't plan to stick out, "And also with you, Erold. Good luck with the egos."

Erold shrugged, nodded, and followed Cherene to dismount outside of the officer's command center.

"What can I expect?" asked Erold.

"What do you mean?"

"I'm assuming they've been alerted ahead of time?"

"Yes, they have been alerted by telegram that you are on the way."

Erold nodded, "Then, we shall see what they have to say."

He entered the wooden building. There were ten officers awaiting him. Most bowed their heads as he entered, which he thought was curious if they were all men of Valgaard.

"King Erold," the first man bowed, fat, white hair, and his eyes not quite looking the same direction, likely due to the large scar through one, but he appeared sharp of mind, "I am Field Master General Nikolai Kutzbek. Head of the combined infantry and a true Normen. I grew up in Thordyn in the Normendin province."

"Pleased to meet you, sir. Is there anyone else who is from Normany?" Three men raised their hands in salute. Erold nodded for them to speak.

"Andiere Blaggard. I am Quartermaster General, and I will be additionally helping to conscript, train, and outfit additional soldiers when we've crossed into Normany."

Erold nodded to the next man.

"I am Arne Pasan, a former doctor who is now one of the Brigadiers for the infantry."

"And, I am Garold Milton, Lt. General of the Cavalry."

"Ah, great, pleasure to meet you all. And, who is the head of the cavalry then?"

"That would be me," said one of the younger men in the room with smooth styled brown hair and piercing gray eyes as well as a well-tailored green jacket, "I am Andreas Wermack, General of the Cavalry."

"Pleased to meet you as well. And the rest of you, name and rank? Anyone else from the cavalry? No."

"First Major General Mikael Kienber, sir."

"Major General Andral Borgoron."

"First Brigadier General Dave Karles Gavo."

"Second Brigadier General Petr Eichlen."

"And I'm Brigadier General Ivan Plaski."

"Great, men, General Kutzbek, I will defer to you. Have you prepared an attack plan to discuss now? I'd rather not delay too long. The sooner we get into Normany, the sooner that General Blaggard can recruit troops."

"Sir, yes, I believe we could leave as early as tomorrow, though we could issue orders in the morning and leave the next day. I only want to warn you that I believe we are walking into an obvious trap. No one else seems to agree with me on the considerable danger."

"I agree with you General. I thought as much myself. We have to spring it now, or we won't have another chance. Perhaps, then it is better to ask different questions. Do we have a plan of defense once we are in Normany and the strength of the possible counterattack?"

"We have options on the table." Kutzbek brought Erold over to a map that they had hand-drawn in pen of Normany. "I agree with Andiere, General Blaggard, that we should be staying in the north, perhaps focusing our force in Gulldalr, central to each of the three northern provinces and then training as one cohesive unit before moving into the south in the spring after we've had a chance to recruit troops from the populous Normendin."

"Yes, well the majority of the population is in the south, and we can't lose them to secession."

"Perhaps you would prefer my plan, then," said the cavalry lead,

Wermack.

"Please do explain."

"I believe that we could hold a strong defensive position in the Dalvalles hills, given their heights and our large supply of artillery."

"And Kutzbek, your objection to this is?"

"I believe it puts us too close to Akre in the event that they move a sizeable force out of the city. We have limited routes to retreat if we move south of the Ohrin."

"And what if we don't retreat?" Wermack re-joined. "The hills would be defensible."

"Yes," said Erold, "And it is my desire to begin laying foundations for bridges and plumbing quickly once we enter Normany. It will win favor and help with the logistics of the troop. The Evorul River valley is long and one of the most significant farming zones outside of the Solgra. It would be a great place to start, and if they do move forces outside of the city, we should have time to retreat."

"It is possible that we get caught within the river valley," warned Kutzbek.

"How so?"

"We can't retreat north through this forest. We would never be able to move our artillery through fast enough, and they could cut us off if they're able to move out of the capital fast enough through the passes in the hills."

"Yes, I know them, but we could empty out the Erstber River valley and force them into an engagement where we have the high ground," Erold pointed out on the map.

"Please explain," said Kutzbek.

"There are limited resources in these hills, and they'd be forced to forage on the north side of the river. There are limited bridges across the river. We could attempt to hold them on the south side and force them to retreat to resupply or find a bridge too far north."

"Might I suggest Umfell then?" asked Wermack. "It has high ground and is a walled city. They would need a significant force to rout us from there, and it is close to the key bridges that run along the Evorul north of the Erstber."

"That's a great place to start after moving on Fort Ämelin, and it would give us the ability to recruit from the Solgra and send men north to Gardnor."

"I think it's a risk. If Emperor Polesar marches out of the city, retreat would be unlikely."

"I certainly think he will march out," said Erold. "It's a matter of the size of the army now."

"Why do you think that?" asked Wermack.

"Because it's a trap," said Kutzbek.

"Yes, so we'll have to force him to delay as long as possible by having a secure defensive position. Neither the fort nor the city of Gulldalr are going to provide that."

"I see," said Kutzbek. "You want him to reconsider the risk until the winter comes and allows us a chance to recruit unhindered by a potential fight."

"Precisely, or at least, I think we have to expect that as soon as we move into Normany, a counterattack is likely. No delay."

"It's a risky plan," said Kutzbek. "But then again all plans are risky."

"Stepping in for a thought. The risk is worth it if it means we have a more defensible position and access to the Sudryn provinces," said Kienber. "We won't be able to last this year or next if we don't get more recruits."

"I agree with that," said Blaggard. "Improving the size of the army should be our first consideration. If he attacks as soon as we enter Normany, the battle will be close to even now. But, without considerably more troops, we will be defeated the following year if the southern detachment rejoins Akre's main forces."

"Cherene and I spoke on this." Erold nodded to the silent archmage who had the faintest bit of color on her cheeks, and a few of the men nodded adroitly.

"We expect that Akre wouldn't risk leaving themselves open to attack from Valgaard, meaning we have some time. Hopefully, until the end of the year," said Cherene.

"The sooner we deploy, the sooner you can get started General Blaggard," said Erold.

"Thank you, my King," the general said.

"If you would please continue, please explain the current situation regarding the distribution of arms as well as the management of mages and officers."

"We have plenty of guns and ammunition to sustain a fight if that is what you are wondering. Cherene," Blaggard emphasized, "has seen us well-supplied in every facet. With respect to mages that is a more complicated discussion."

"Why is that?"

"We have an abundance at the current moment. We were given

three hundred and fifty new and recent graduates from Valgaardian schools as well as many who have defected from Akre's armies, but we won't be able to recruit mages in Normany. Any force deployed by Akre will likely outnumber us in mages as well."

Erold reflexively grabbed at his axe, but it was outside. So, as he brought his hand back slowly, he thumbed the orb underneath his tunic instead.

"How do we currently have mages deployed?"

Cherene stepped in, "We've distributed mages across infantry divisions in the same way as it is done in Akre."

"Which are all Normany refugees?"

"The infantry are, yes."

"Are we able to get more mages from Valgaard once we cross into Normany?" Erold asked.

Cherene shook her head, "That will not be possible."

"Could we at least ask the p--"

"I will be the voice of Valgaard during the campaign on authority of the palace," Cherene said. Arla concurred. "I am here to enact orders on behalf of Valgaard."

"And what about fighting? If you go, I go," said Erold.

"We will discuss this at another time."

"Fine then. How is distribution done in Akre?"

Cherene smiled, "Mages are heads of divisions with ten sergeant mages that act as a squadron leading two hundred fifty men apiece. Every mage including the senior mages here has their own divisional unit, and then oversees units within the corresponding chain of command."

Blaggard leaned forward on the board, "With our current force, we could field fully staffed divisions up to seventy-seven thousand five hundred infantry."

"And we should be expecting to see more than that on the field," said Erold, thinking to himself. "General Kutzbek, you're not a mage, what do you think of the current structure?"

"It's precisely why I'm here and not in Akre as a senior leader if you permit me to say it," said Kutzbek. "There are a lot of talented non mages who would be fit to lead men, but in a tactical sense, a battle-trained mage is an extremely potent weapon of war. With access to summoning spells or like some who have the ability to conjure thousands of spikes at a time out of thin air, rearranging matter at will, the battlefield is getting more and more dangerous. The only way to counteract this is to ensure each division can negate the potency by counterbalancing their spells, with spells of their own."

"I understand your point," thought Erold, remembering the night of the undead. If he could have seen that mage, he could have thwarted the spell before it could be written in pen in the book of ages. "So, explain to me, why you should be in command now?"

"I may not have magical powers, but I rose the ranks due to my battlefield success within the Akrin army. I was dismissed by the emperor when it was determined that no one without magical talent would be an officer going forward."

"Before you worry about it, you're at no risk of dismissal here, and I will continue to rely on your foresight over the course, of hopefully a very short campaign. Everyone else, thank you for your time. Kutzbek and Cherene, Arla, as well, if you could stay for a moment. Before I let you go Kutzbek, what can you tell me about Akre's changes among the mage force?"

"They were making general changes in line with the church as the anti-magic religions are considered to be pagan. The modern mage is seen as the religious ideal. I see myself as a Godly man, first and foremost, but I don't abide that you have to be a practicing mage to have been given a gift from God."

"I agree, that satisfies what I wanted to know. Thank you General, you may go, yes. Now, Cherene, I thought Valgaardians held a number of superstitions about magic. Is there some issue with promoting schools of magecraft? Am I at risk to face similar resistance in Normany, is what I'm asking."

"Answering your first question first. Despite that most Valgaardians consider themselves Frostians, there is hesitation about magic. This is not the case in most of the Empire, except for Imeria, where they have split chanceries, each following the same prophet as the other but not Fros. As for Normany, I'm unaware of the feelings among Normen. As you probably know most of Old Galdir and the current Akrin Empire follow the same religion but in different ways."

"Thank you, Cherene. Yes, I do," Erold said and looked down at the flat map that lacked the detail of the one hidden in the ice palace. If he got too close to Akre, they would certainly launch a force of one hundred thousand, but they wouldn't risk it if he were in Dalvalles. He was positive, but he would have to remain careful about whether they were able to return their army from Harupht.

When he looked up, Cherene still stood there, "Something else,

Cherene?"

She shook her head, and then nodded, "Valgaard is stretched tightly with its mages, most certainly. Many of the mages in your force are also refugees that were trained in Valgaard, or they are mages that defected from Akre that were from Normany and trained in either Akrin, before scholarship from Normany was reduced on account of too many Normen, or in Albion, which I believe is where you studied."

"Yes," smiled Erold, thinking of his first time at school in the Ash Vale as a thirteen-year-old, "You seem to know a lot about me."

She reddened and Arla seemed to relax back onto one foot as if waiting to hear the response.

"It's no matter," said Erold, "What about this territory we're in now. Has the princess reconsidered giving me the fortress at Helmun Loch?"

"Valessa told me that you should consider the old fortress and path to Normany, your first official territory. Though it was never very fertile land, it's history is rich with the three tribes of Normen, since the first days of the ice."

"Anything else you can tell me like that?" he asked and looked into her blue eyes as the oil lamps began to be lit in the command center, where he would also be quartered for the time being.

"I'd be worried about the hilly terrain with the heavy cavalry and dragging the artillery pieces along with munitions for your troops. That seems difficult through Dalvalles."

"It's no concern, the passes are wide, and I was told a long time ago, that there's a convenient pass that would make a quick escape if we needed it in the end."

"Well, then, I think I should be going. It sounds like we move in two days. I will ride with you. Have a good night, King Erold Ardrada."

"Thank you, Cherene..."Erold paused, but she did not fill in the name, "you too. Have a good night, and you too Arla. And, Arla, please speak up if anything comes up as a concern of yours."

* * *

Braddach tried to remember the names of his men, but it was difficult. He had even thought that it might be easy to remember the names of his mages, but it was not. There were too many men of the same name.

Many were the names of kings, of course, like Abrims, Erolds, Ivans, and Karleses. But, also fourteen Olgafs, twelve Olafs, thirteen

Svens, six Frostofers, ten Arnes, thankfully only sixteen Daveys, there were also three Daves, and that wasn't to mention Mikaels, Nikolais, Petrs, Patrs, and Arnes.

Of his division mages, he had written them down in fountain pen, but it was hard to remember the face to the name. Two were named Sten, one of which had an S for a last name and the other a C; one was Sven; there was another Patr, he would call Patr D; he had a Frostofer, nicknamed Frof; and then an Arne, an Ivan, an Avael, a Honter, and then Nido, his second in command.

It was important that he learned these names, because they would be the ones promoted with him as he was promoted, which he wasn't sure seemed fair for the front-line infantry. As non-mages, even if he had overheard them speaking intelligently on battlefield maneuvers over the fires at night, they had no chance of being promoted beyond the levels of private.

His unit reported up to Wermack in the cavalry, but as most of his division was an infantry unit as part of the horse drawn howitzer, mixed unit, acting as a defensive unit for either advance or rear-guard action, he had to learn the parade maneuvers in one day before they marched to Normany.

Nido took it very seriously, which was just as well. Braddach had studied all night but couldn't remember the moves when marching in the lines. Before even the first maneuver, Nido had said the moves to Braddach in advance, so Braddach could yell them as Nido said them.

Braddach couldn't help but think that it was merely that Nido wanted the unit promoted, but there were far too many levels between them and General to get excited. To Braddach the whole exercise seemed pointless. For most of the time, they marched in lines back and forth across the meadow, the commanding mages, Captains and then above those Majors, weren't paying attention at all.

Everyone seemed lost in thought about how they were going to prove themselves worthy of promotion. It wasn't until Erold toured the lines in his own yellow jacket, which for some reason made Braddach smile, for he too had succumbed to wanting to fit in among the men, that the commanding officers began to bark orders, almost shadowing the actions of the lines, rather than anticipating them, trying to make it look like every motion was at their whim, if only a mare's hair width late.

Braddach marched at Nido's calls, left, right, forward, and back.

Five steps, salute, show the flame of a fireball to the left, display an icicle to the right, melt it into water before five more steps.

At times, the cavalry commanders came over and discussed items with leadership. The cavalry commanders appeared just to appear to be issuing orders as the captains began ordering a new display of formation, which Nido described to Braddach as they went, once again.

Most of the leadership wore forest green for Valgaard, in vibrant, well-tailored uniforms with gold trim. Only a handful of the infantry commanders wore yellow. Braddach wore yellow, but it felt like he was going to dinner or a party than going into battle, like in the gulf. He began to realize that the lack of direct armoring was because especially the artillery they would soon face would shatter and scatter the iron--and possibly even the dwarven metal that could despite its strength be bent or hewn through by mage's spears--of old battle armors.

Back, left, forward, right. Display arms. The men shot black powder from their muskets. Braddach made mental note that the accuracy and destruction power of the long rifles his compatriots had used in the gulf would also be missed.

He would make sure his men learned or mastered a simple shield spell, he knew from his days in Albion, but it was not nearly as effective as the disruptive magic that Erold had been able to learn from Kahron and would do little to help the men who could not use magic.

They drank beer and broke bread that night around the fire, singing songs and swapping stories. Braddach didn't directly mention that he had served with Erold in the gulf, but it seemed like the men knew as they looked over at him as if for approval or comparison after each story they told.

Braddach cooked a ration kit and saved his bread, preferring to eat the salted ground meat, mixed with some kind of unrecognizable shredded vegetable that had become the consistency of hot wheat cereal, while he could cook it a bit over the red flames.

His hands were cold. Some of the men spoke about infantry maneuvers. His mages continued to watch him. He had left his uniform jacket on near the fire, but many of the men had shirked them as soon as they neared the tents. He had grown too accustomed to the heat of the gulf, even if a temperature difference of only twenty or so degrees on the Odin scale.

He drank his beer in slow gulps, cherishing the liquid, and

knowing that as soon as that ration had gone, they'd be boiling water and placing it in canteens. Soon, the taste of iron and other metals would linger for days on end like those few weeks they had rowed across the lakes.

With luck, they would only be doing this through Vetfal, and then could build proper fortifications and get a night's sleep on something other than a set of blankets carried on their back before year's end.

He wished he had spoken more to Erold about it now, as he sat there, looking at the men. The fire danced across their faces, shadows growing and receding under and behind their eyes. He had a feeling they were in for a fight but had no sense of the size or scale of the battles that approached.

He was sure Erold did, and he had to trust that he was leading them toward victory without throwing them headlong into battle to face shell, bullet, and mages' fire.

Spring 1524 - Chapter 49

The army vacated the training grounds on the morning of Lovers' Day in 1524 and climbed Pili's Pass, relatively easily, if not slowly. Led by a detachment of cavalry scouts and the vanguard artillery.

They held no banner as the eagle had long been taken by Akre and Erold had foregone Valgaard's standards, golden suns. They were fighting for Normany and though he knew the significance of the standards for troop movement and point of reference, he had not chosen beast or object that fit the men of Normany for he did not know what it is that they believed themselves best fit to be.

In the early days of battle, it mattered not whether they played capture the standard with enemy troops. They were drilled and ready. He would adjust tactics once he had to. New troops wouldn't be as well trained.

The mountain pass was as wide as he remembered. It looked as if they could pull ten howitzers up the mountain side by side, but they kept space on the sides, in case a unit needed to pull off and rest.

The hills gave way completely and the steep assent became pebble more than dirt, stone, or gravel. It looked like watching wheels spin on a beach as they continued the long, slow climb that he remembered very differently on foot.

When they crested the mountain, there was the widening field before them, but they could not yet see the wall or the old castle towers, where guardsmen stayed. He could no longer see the full length of the line of men behind him, but he trusted that they would follow and if anything should go wrong, they would be alerted in the front of the line.

From time to time, he spied the sky, remembering wild dragons, large and small, claimed these mountains. Only birds flew in the air, possibly moving back to Valgaard from warmer lands like possibly even Albion after a long winter. Red birds, blue birds, white and yellow birds. None of which he knew by name, but all fighting in the air as they swept over the pass that cleaved the mountains.

He had strapped his axe around his back and had received a new pistol and officer's sword. Both had been taken when he had been imprisoned in Cardane, and he wanted to be prepared for battle even if he would not be engaging directly. Cherene rode beside him.

It had been a cool, dry day at the base of the mountain, and as the air thinned, it grew cooler. He shivered in the wind as it kicked up over the mountain and was sucked through the mountain pass.

Soon, the wall came into view, and he spoke with Cherene, Arla, and Kutzbek about relative distance. There were trebuchets on the top of the tower.

"They have a range of only one hundred atomic yards, sir."

"And our howitzers?"

"Good from six hundred. More deadly from four."

"We'll wait until we can line up forty in two lines and fire on the wall like two hammers striking a nail."

"Yes, sir."

The troop moved forward at Kutzbek's command, and Erold followed him off to the right as the field began to take shape. He could see the enemy attempt to set the trebuchets and fan out at the top of the wall.

Part of him wished they would run, but for some reason they did not. They wouldn't be able to reach the height nor the distance with those antiques fit for battle fifteen hundred years before now.

"It appears they wish to engage, sir."

"I agree. We shouldn't waste men, sending them to be thrown off a tower by those who won't sue for peace."

The artillery filed into formation as additional pieces crested the hill.

"Shall I give the order?"

"Wait, just a moment." Erold held his hand, "Cherene?"

"Yes, King Erold."

"The likelihood of a mage on the wall? Should we be concerned that they could stop the artillery?"

"I can answer that," said Kutzbek. "Many a mage has tried to stop a prolonged artillery engagement, but a cannonade does not simply end when one ball is pushed to the side. We'll have forty and another forty shot at once. If you believe that you could stop them, standing up there, I'd urge you to reconsider."

"Very well General Kutzbek."

"The order sir?"

"Bring the wall down," Erold almost laughed, trying to help himself, remembering to sonder on the way all men's lives lead them to one place or another. It could have been that the men on the wall had no choice but to stand there and die.

The cannonade had little effect at first, but quickly when the stone began to churn in vibration and crack as the iron slugs thundered through the air and slammed against its base. The whole of the tall fabrication began to visibly shake. Fresh rounds echoed their counterparts devastating the stone, sending huge chunks beyond the wall, leaving it to crumble in on itself like a sandcastle under foot.

Erold imagined the rubble itself would delay them longer than the wall would, but Kutzbek assured him that they had a process for moving bricks aside as long as they were not delayed by additional defenders to allow the men to get beyond the pass to make camp. He then asked if they should turn the guns on the castle keep where it appeared more men had set within the keeps waiting to dish out rifle and crossbow fire.

"Deliver the thunder," Erold nodded. "If they shall fight, they shall have a fight."

Polesar would likely be deploying artillery as well, Erold thought. They must have been desperately baiting Valgaard into this move themselves, but with any luck Akre wouldn't field a large enough force until next year. By that time, the combined power of the northern allies would have caught up with Polesar's in number.

"We knew that a high wall, no matter the thickness, was a structurally unsound artifact. We could have assumed that it was built to keep out Domiscus's clockwork hordes, but we know it has stood since long before that."

"Perhaps we should save the bricks for the historical society," Erold smiled. He nodded as she further explained how they had come up with their initial plan.

A detachment of the cavalry rode ahead to see if the enemy had dispatched a rider to alert Fort Ämelin. They preferred that the emperor did not know they had launched their attack, until they had reinforced a position as discussed two nights before when Erold had met the commanding officers.

The army camped in the same hills where Erold had once camped with Moon and Volstad, only desperate to make it north as the money dwindled. He went by to see if Braddach wanted to play cards, but he was laughing with his squad and having fun. Instead, Erold spent time with Seaspirit while survivors were searched for, and the night began to fall.

* * *

"Have you tried to speak with him?" asked Arla.

"Yes," said Cherene, "of course. I have spoken to him, multiple times." Cherene paced their shared tent as they were the only two women in the field. Part of what Cherene wanted to learn from the upcoming battles was whether she wouldn't feel heartless sending female mages, colloquially known as witches, into the field like the Akrin military had begun to.

Arla, sitting on the edge of a cot dressed with blankets, couldn't help but imagine that Cherene still hadn't realized that normal women weren't often treated like princesses in any way shape or form, and she, meaning Cherene, couldn't just expect a man, or anyone for that matter with a lot on their mind, to start up new conversations with essentially strangers when the war could escalate any day.

"It's just not like him to forget a day," said Cherene, "He used to bring me things and meet me in the morning with them. He'd make them himself. Little sculptures of ice or sometimes he'd find a stone that reminded him of a jewel. When we celebrated the Lord's Day together, I just..."

Arla nodded, "He used to do those things for the princess, Cherene. To him, now, you're a stranger."

"Part of me thought he'd just recognize me anyway, and then I'd let him in on the secret."

They heard rustling outside the tent. Arla instinctively readied a spell. It's why she was really along anyway. Enhanced protection for the brave princess, who could be putting both their lives at risk for the sake of any excuse she could make to rekindle a forgotten flame. Seeing as how her hand, too, had turned blue with ice, it could take something more out of character than she was used to, to get Erold's attention.

Wermack--and Kienber.

"Were you two ladies doing anything special this evening?" asked Kienber, pushing Wermack ahead of him. "We could use a pair for a game of cards, and I snagged this bottle of wine when we passed through the city last week."

"Now might not be the best time," said Cherene, coolly. She touched her cold hand to move her hair as if she had never readied a spell.

"Just one bottle, maybe two," said Kienber. "No one's around, pri--"

Cherene flashed her ice over his skin and said quickly, "you never know who is listening Kienber. Did he put you up to this Andreas?"

Wermack shrugged, innocently saying, "I didn't see how it could be wrong to celebrate the first day of the campaign."

Cherene nodded while Arla internally rolled her eyes, because Lovers' Day had nothing to do with it. She was sure the bottle of wine was sent for when they learned the princess would be there only a few days before.

Cherene looked at Arla and then at the gentlemen. Wermack was good looking, sure, but he was an officer in her military. She had flirted with him in the past, sure. She couldn't deny herself, simple fun. This was clearly a romantic pass disguised with the most basic excuse.

"Another time," said Cherene. "Another time don't you think, Arla?"

"Yes, I agree with the archmage on this."

"Suit yourself, but we'll hold you to it Cherene," Kienber bowed and pulled Wermack out with him, patting him on the back and when out of earshot, giving him a bit of friendly advice to try being more suave and less weak. He was one of the highest-ranking officers in the military after all.

Cherene continued to pace. Her face contorted as she appeared to chew at the insides of her mouth and then press her thin lips together. Alternating between one of the two.

Arla turned on the oil lamp and watched her friend think. She imagined that Cherene was disappointed that her visitor had been Wermack and not Erold. It would be a long night if she continued to wait on him to call. Arla imagined that if Erold bothered anyone, it would be Kutzbek to ask about possible battlefield maneuvers.

* * *

The ride south to Fort Ämelin took almost as few days as it had taken back in 1513, but through the hills, up and down, pulling artillery made for hard work. Cavalry rode ahead and attempted to gauge whether the enemy had discovered their advance or sent scouts ahead.

The towns on the route, shut their doors and watched them cautiously from windows. Erold after discussion had callers go forth and warn the people that the king of Normany had returned, but he received little welcome. Only a few children who ran into the street before being called home.

Cherene said that they might be skeptical, but he imagined that they'd seen enough dead kings in their time to concern themselves with yet another. Four dead kings in the last thirty years. Besides, they'd had the emperor for almost eleven years now.

Erold saw all the things he wanted to change were still unchanged. The roads were still disheveled, but at least kept clean of trash. There were few bathrooms--little more than troughs--and few bridges that could fit more than one artillery piece at a time, and they had to place down patchwork bridges rather than fjord some of the smaller streams. He could not see any indication of plumbing, and because they were in the east of the Dragnor hills, where lumber was sparse, he wondered how the houses without chimneys kept warm when snow fell. Even at the border of Normany in the Ash Vale, the temperate weather of the warm air current had largely worn off. Below freezing, possibly to zero, and snow piling up outside, he could imagine heating stones--or whatever other method they used to distribute heat--only went so far.

He wondered if that's possibly why Gardnor was as empty as it was. There were forests in the east along the mountains, but not a tree nor a hill for much of the center of the country. It would be difficult to break the winter wind without finding a hill to build beside.

On the twelfth day, they stood on the hills, overlooking the fort, which appeared to be in working order and to have put up a guard.

"We should send men this time to ask if they'd like to surrender the position," Erold said, "There's no cover from these low walls with the hills. We could bombard the internal cavities of the fortress without facing their resistance."

"Of course, sir," said General Kutzbek, who issued the orders through attendants. A smartly dressed adjunct of the cavalry, on plain horses rode across the hills in a diagonal line and then put up the flag for peace.

Bullets rang out through the air as one of the men on horses, fell into the hills. The others looped around and rode back to the hills where Erold watched as the man, struggling to get back up and trying to find his horse was mercilessly shot at by the men, picketed within the small fortress.

Before the horses had returned, Erold had made new arrangements, pressing one hundred howitzers to the edge of the hill. Their ability to aim within a considerable arc made them lethal from the hills.

"Light them up," said Erold and the cannons let fly.

Explosions riddled the fortress. It was hard to imagine anyone surviving as clouds of smoke covered the hills, thicker than fog and the buildings within the low walls of the fortress, built for a different time, burst into flames.

After ten salvos of one hundred shots, Erold ordered an infantry detachment to charge the base. They found few survivors, all with casualties, likely mortal, who under the torture of knives pressed on wounds, told Erold's men that the main contingent had already gone south, hoping to escape the Valgaardians and rendezvous with Polesar.

Erold asked if they knew that the king had returned, but he was told that none of the men were from Normany that were found still alive. They removed rubble from the base and planned to use it as the camp. Erold met with the other officers in the command tent after the cursory engagement. After some pleasantries the focus shifted onto what to do about the detachment that had fled south.

"How far do you think they might have gone?"

"Hard to say. We've been marching in the hills for just over ten days. We can't know when they got word of our movement, but they could be halfway through Gardnor in a few days if they're moving only infantry supplies."

"General Kutzbek, what would you suggest in this situation?" asked Erold.

"I'd say ride them down and attempt to capture them. We could send them to Albion or back to Valgaard as prisoners of war," said Braddach.

"And if they choose to fight?" asked Wermack, recognizing that he'd be the one doing the riding if the cavalry were to be put into action.

There was a short pause as everyone looked between each other before focusing on Erold. He had templed his hands at the fingers and was deep in thought.

"They gave us no mercy at Elksits," said Erold.

"At the highest, there could be as many as five thousand, given the size of the fortress, but it could also be as low as one hundred," cautioned the Brigadier General Pasan.

"If they fight, they've made their choice," said Gavo, another Brigadier.

"If they are men of Normany, I would hope that they would side with the true king," said Blaggard, thoughtfully.

"If the enemy engages," Erold thought carefully, wondering if his words would be weighed as a moment that defined the engagements to come. Whether history would look kindly at him for fairness and just action. He could not and would not let them escape.

Prisoners of war seemed fair, but what if they intended to fight?

"Valgaard would happily take the prisoners of war," said Cherene, suddenly looking a touch pale. "I am sure they would lay down their arms if they were outnumbered six to one if we are to send the whole cavalry."

"Without a doubt, we would," said Lieutenant General Milton, second in command of the cavalry and in general charge of forward maneuvers unless engaging with Wermack, "We could not risk that they hold the line steady, and we lose an equal number of men to theirs. A cavalry charge against entrenched men is risky, but with numbers on our side, they'll be easy to scatter and then easy to finish."

"If they engage," said Erold again, "destroy them as you say Milton. Do not assume that they will yield if addressed by a larger force."

There was a hushed silence as everyone thought through the potential field of battle in their heads.

"By rights of the Storr Ríta, I claim this land for the men of Normany. If they are not men of Normany and wish to engage war on foreign land, assume no man will yield after they have issued a challenge." Erold announced the name of the constitutional documents yet governing Akre that had bound the senate and king together long before.

"One man could cause the death of thousands," said Pasan.

"We're at war until we're not," said another Brigadier General, Eichlen.

"Arne, my good friend," said Blaggard, "Do you forget that at the battle of Elksits, as King Erold mentioned, our brethren were outnumbered by the same six to one and when suing for peace, the messenger was shot in the head?"

"Two wrongs do not make a right," said First Major General Plaski.

"Who said we are in the wrong here?" asked Kienber, "If they massacred Normen at Elksits, then retribution is at hand. Let it be swift."

"What do you say Andreas?" asked Blaggard.

"The cavalry will take the field and if we catch the force, we will act on orders and leave no man safe from iron or steel, whether by blade or shot."

"Aye," said Major General Borgoron, "Best to catch them now, or they'll join the force in the south and attach knives to their rifles against us again."

Erold nodded. He listened to the men, but he watched Cherene during the discussion. She was new to the field of battle, whereas many of these men had seen combat. The only way they could parse through it in their own mind was to detach death from the men behind the face and look at the statistic. Not because they were brave or strong of will, but because it made the experience capable of comprehension.

He had gone through the same in Cardane. In ten years, three hundred sixty-five days in a year. He couldn't count the number of missions he had done. Few missions were to face beasts like wolves or minotaurs, or to warn off orc raiding parties. They were often fighting men, many rogue mages, but also thieves hiding in the woods, considering themselves champions of the people. A job had to be done, but war expanded even that scale by thousands.

* * *

Braddach cooked his salted beef at the end of a stick over the fire, having forgotten how dull it could be to eat a rationed meal for weeks at a time. He assumed that they'd probably be active through the end of the year, but he hoped that they would stay in a city for much of the duration rather than making do with cheap meat in the woods. They were camped in and around Fort Ämelin, which he had heard the name of from some of the members of his infantry unit.

It was strange to no longer have access to that information regularly. The Varanorian Guard used to plan their missions with the entire crew involved. Now, he was waiting to hear where they would move next or make camp. They could march back and forth ten times and end up in the same place that they started, and he wouldn't know whether the officers had a plan or merely couldn't figure anything out.

He had begun the process of boiling water, taken from a nearby stream; after it had boiled, he would need to wait until it had cooled before he could pour it into his canteen, but the steam had the added benefit of helping to warm his fingers as he sat beside the fire. He hadn't realized how easy it was to feel as cold as he felt.

Cardane was still not as warm as the equator, but he had a bed indoors most nights and the gulf could be considered temperate most of the year. Sitting in mid spring in the Normany north, nights like this felt like they were in the thirties on the Odin Scale.

"I heard you had spent time in the gulf," said Frof, "but seeing you shake in the cold makes me believe it."

"That obvious?" asked Braddach.

"Yeah, it is. Sorry for the lack of formality," said Frof, as he tore into his own ration of cold, salted beef.

"As they say, a dragon doesn't tend to sheep," said Braddach, drinking a bit of rationed beer. He had finished the water he had decontaminated the day before.

"True, true. So, the gulf. We was swapping stories the other day, but you didn't say anything about it," said Frof. Braddach eyed him as he drank some more beer, and he noticed a couple of his other squad mages circled nearby. They might have put Frof up to asking about it.

"No, I didn't," said Braddach. It wasn't that he didn't want to talk about it necessarily, but none of his men would have gone through the same experience.

"Is it true some of the things they say?"

"About what?" Braddach looked up at Frof, and then glanced at the Stens who had seated themselves within ear shot.

"Werewolves or vampires in every town or city of Mondelvania?" asked Frof, finishing his beef and starting on his own ration of beer.

"Something like that," said Braddach, eating a bit of the salted beef he had let cook in the fire. He hoped they'd get another bit of bread soon.

"You must have some good stories," said Avael, sitting down on the other side of the fire from Frof, flanking him. "We heard King Erold killed a leviathan five times the size of a schooner, almost swallowed the ship whole."

"I was there. Not sure it was quite that big," said Braddach, "but, if you're looking for stories about the king, it sounds like you've already heard plenty."

"We want to know who our leader is. What kind of fighting you've seen," said Nido, joining the group, opposite Braddach, chewing on something, hidden from Braddach by the fire, licking up into the darkness of the cold night.

"Yeah," said Frof, "We was all wondering what kind of experience you have."

"What types of missions did you go on? We heard the mercenaries fought against guerilla rebels and hunted mythical beasts."

Braddach shrugged, looking at the men. He hadn't thought of himself as the focus of their attention, and he didn't want to come off as callous or vague, but it was hard to contextualize.

"Maybe, I'll get into more details at another time, but. It was, if anything. Harrowing," said Braddach, and seeing as that didn't satisfy their curiosity in the least, he continued with some detail, "Most missions we went in with no accurate information. We'd drop off the side of an airship that would swing away like a bird while we fought for our lives against summoned beasts or conjured colossals ten or more times the size of a man. We usually had just rifles backing up one mage, often me, and sometimes with a warlock."

"From Imor Valsen?"

"Shh, let him speak."

"The mage doing the summoning might have been incoherent, just off his mind as if he'd eaten toadstools. The beasts we fought had no direction and just crashed through buildings and trees, while we saved kids and brought the things down. The mages were always beyond saving themselves. Just husks of a human being. Other times you didn't feel like the good team on a mission."

Braddach, nodded, and left for a moment to clear his head, and when he came back, he saw that all his squad mages were still sitting there watching him, likely wondering if what he said was true. Mostly legends of the danger and the types of risk had filtered back to Valgaard over the years. Few men returned. They usually stayed in Cardane or died there.

* * *

Milton pointed out the low terrain and lack of streams along the flanks of the opposition.

Through his own pair of binoculars, Wermack could see that the enemy had taken up defensive positions with a wooden picket line on the opposite side of a stream, where it narrowed to about the length a unicorn could leap in one stride. The stream wasn't large and just under what a horse could do, too, given a full run.

"It appears that they are hoping we descend on them from the marsh, avoiding the need to either fjord or find a bridge on either side of the encampment," Wermack could see hoof prints in the light green grass that their unicorns had left as they ascended a low hill to get a view of the enemy that scouts had notified them had begun to dig in.

"I think we could easily cross the stream north or south of here at about an hour's ride. If we feign the frontal assault that they appear to be trying to hem us into and loop the flanks, we should be able to run them down."

"So much for taking prisoners," said Wermack, adjusting himself on his saddle and pulling his canteen from his waist to quench his thirst.

Milton pointed along the low hill they stood on, in sight of the opposing line, "I say we camp here tonight, and send contingents out just before break of day. If the enemy has scattered in the night, we should be able to run them down on the move. If they are still entrenched, they will wake up to the thunder of hooves with the morning light."

"True, without the infantry here, our men should be able to make adequate timing to meet on positions. We'll target having them rendezvous at center by seven in the morning."

The night came, the day broke, and the opposing infantry had stayed entrenched, having even attempted to build up fortifications along their flanks in the night, but the stakes were driven in too shallow, and the cavalry too heavily armored. The unicorns broke through weak points in the line, and the defenses became the infantry's own prison.

There were no rousing speeches as dawn broke or the clatter of metal, other than that of the colted hooves, shattering the helmets that some of the enemy wore. The fire of the bullets and the cries to battle of Akrin force caught the dewy air of dawn that lifted a light fog over the fields at about the height of the knees, slipping over the camp and obscuring the bodies of the dead, falling between tents.

The blue and white jackets scattered and fought equally, either abandoning tents, guns, and food, or grabbing up arms and being taken through by iron halberds before the musket powder could be packed. No one had seen a unicorn cavalry ride and the few mages, mostly powerless without the infantry at their side against the combined weight of such terrific beasts, abandoned their posts more than the Akrin infantry.

The few thunderbolts or fireballs thrown were doused by the mage officers of the unicorn cavalry who led the charge, but many attacks, whether bullet or bolt, ricocheted into the dirt off the iron armor.

When the two halves of the cavalry met in the middle, the opposing force had been reduced to nothing. Those who abandoned their posts would be searched for as deserters to be sent to Valgaard as prisoners of war as Cherene commanded.

Though the cavalry had lost a few of their number, the day had been easily won.

Summer 1524 - Chapter 50

With the resounding victory at Tavyfjord, Normany's north ceded to King Erold. From Ohrin River to the Ash Vale, the free men of Normany--for there were no slaves and no slavery in Normany for all of time--and the few regional leaders, came to the great assembly place to represent themselves, their towns, or just their families at the great thing--the original use for the term thing at a stone pillar called Frosta in Gulldalr, a monument to Fros, built by the men of the north who came south.

As far as the men of the northern provinces were concerned, Erold had set the nation free. There had been a darkness over the land, and he had lifted it, returning to them their sense of national pride. They roared the traditional hail to the king above the mountain.

"Hail! Hail! Hail to the sun of Normany!"

At the back of Erold's mind as he looked out at one hundred thousand faces or more, representing over four thousand cities and millions of his people, was the Akrin counterattack. The south knew it too. From Dalvalles through the Solgra, the men did not come.

But, word of his return spread quickly by merchant, letter, and telegram. In newspapers in Albion, Akre, Cardane, Menetoris, Imeria, as far as in Yin and in the Great South Island, and even among the men of South Olympus, voices whispered, the voices of nations echoed. Whether they cared or not, they still spoke of the mercenary king who had returned to take his kingdom back from the largest empire in the world.

"King Erold Ardrada, the lost son of Erolin and last of the line of Arandil had returned."

And many around the world said he would not last, but the men of Normany who saw him that day at the assembly speak like he had the voice of one hundred men, believed that the truest king since the kings of old, who built the empire of Akre, had taken the mantle from his father with grace.

Blaggard stayed in Gulldalr with a cursory force with a mind to conscript and train enough men across Nordryn, the north lands, to reach a combined force of one hundred fifty thousand before the year's end, an ambitious goal without the Solgra. The old Quartermaster General believed it could be done, but likely only if he had both the summer and fall to recruit. If they were attacked before Frostmas, it was unlikely he would reach one hundred thousand strong in Gulldalr.

King Erold marched the men to Dalvalles, and he entered the rocky hills through the pass to Hoenheim valley as the merchant had told him long ago. He went through the city of Snajrberg, where the men raised their fists at first sight.

He walked with his men, guiding Seaspirit by hand, through the valley in the light of the sun of summer to each of the old towns of Brechtinn, Langholm, Nordlind, and Odinheim, which combined made Hoenheim a municipal region of over fifty thousand men.

The houses sat on the small stream that cut through the hills to the Erstber river, and they stretched into those same hills on both sides of the grassy riverbed, like an arena, where men and children stood watching the procession of the king. The soldiers paved the road as they went and built bridges of stone that had been taken from the fallen wall at Pili's Pass and placed in wagons pulled by unicorn.

The men of the valley soon filled the streets that ran along the hills from left to right up into the sky like a stadium, they watched, perhaps twenty thousand strong. When Erold raised his fist, they raised their fists there too.

Hail to Normany!

After passing through Odinheim, he crossed into the Erstber River valley, filled with its houses and sleepy little towns, following the wide road beside the riverbed, the very same one he rode through with Moon and Volstad long ago. Now, he was flanked by Cherene who smiled at him in the summer light, Arla and Kutzbek who wiped sweat away from his scarred eye and brooded, thinking not of the men of the valleys but of the soldiers who walked beside them, working at the roads, breaking stones, and laying strong foundations down.

Wherever Erold went forth along the Erstber, the men upon seeing him, dropped their things, threw up their fists and chanted the hail. Days and nights, they camped as forty thousand men in tents, eating what they could forage and the remaining rations of salted meat, beef, pork, and lamb. They found blackberries, strawberries, and blueberries throughout the hills and carried them in baskets and caps to the camp, where the men ate and laughed together after long days in the sun.

They passed the pass to Godrland that opened, invitingly, toward them. Though Erold longed to return to the beautiful Solgra and see Normany's largest cities, which he had never visited, they instead went left. They could not get too close to Akre before Blaggard had finished building the targeted force of a combined two hundred fifty to three hundred thousand men by the beginning of the following spring.

Soon, they arrived at Elklin, a beautiful city of wood and stone, surrounded by a low wood wall. The city sat on a natural plateau that jutted out from the mountainous hills and the low riverbed, overlooking the valley that fell away in a long slope beside a large waterfall in the river. The road wrapped around the cliff through the town and followed the edge of the hills in a long low slope.

Elklin's main city had a second, inner wall of stone, where fortifications overlooked the pass, both south and north. Heralds went forth to tell of the king and they were greeted with raised fists.

As they entered the large city, the houses sat in neat arrays like the leaves of a fern, and at the center of the city was a large stone cathedral to Fros, whose single, massive belltower could be seen from the road for atomic miles around.

Shopkeepers and street vendors raised their fist to the king as he passed. Erold spied eggplants, olives, oils, and wine. He spoke with Cherene and Kutzbek, and they requisitioned a supply for the army, almost selling out the city of over fifty thousand.

To ride into Umfell from the south, they had to cross to the west side of the Erstber. Before they would build bridges nearer to Umfell, the nearest bridges to the largest city of the Evorul River valley were themselves inside of large cities along the Evorul that stretched from Umfell to the west, Donworsh, Werentinn, and Günz.

Coming out from the Erstber, heavy woods forced the army to follow the looping road east toward Donworsh, which was the only one of the three smaller cities, each of at least fifty-five thousand souls, on the south bank. The yellow army marched to raised fists cheering them along as they cut back through the city, along the stone roads of Donworsh. They cheered back and raised their fists as the men pressed on day by day and night by night, camping and doing what they could to help the common folk as they went. Braddach toiled among them to shovel and pitch.

They rested across the river from Günz, able to see the city lights across the water during the night. In the morning, they crossed the double-wide stone bridge, capable of wagons going either direction at the same time, and after a short walk from the bridge, passed through the cheering city, where people hung out of the balconies of multi-story houses along the street to see the king, tossing flowers and chanting hail.

They followed the Ilsa River north, where Umfell rested quietly, blue and yellow flags raised atop tall stone keeps that rose up to about four times the height of the city's wall, dwarfing the many trees that ran along the river. For a few atomic miles, a red brick wall, neatly kept with ferns and shrubs at the top, surrounded the city. The nose of a pair of old guns could be seen on the wall from across the river. Beyond the wall, tall houses with steep roofs, waited with quiet windows. And behind the houses, a tall cathedral with bronze metal work along its edges from bell tower to great hall, could be seen.

* * *

Braddach picked up a stone from the back of a wagon and carried it a few atomic yards, before placing it lightly on a growing pile of bricks that would make up the bridge, crossing the Evorul River on the west side from Umfell, where they would start putting in an alternate road from Umfell to Elklin as the summer wore on.

It had begun to grow warm, and Braddach was convinced that the temperature had risen as high as eighty degrees on the Odin scale in the sun.

The river water sparkled. The birds chirped. The wind cut through the dense oaks and ashes of the mountainous hills but did little to deter the heat of hard work.

The stone blocks were larger than each of his hands, so he had to lift them by rolling them toward him and catching them as if in his arms like a basket. When he had moved them, someone else on the chain would deliver them the rest of the way to the growing bridge, which would have a central foundation in the middle of the river and would be made up of four stone arches that supported a walkway with solid stone walls.

It was their most ambitious project yet and would require most of the summer as they would have to collect more materials from the mountains on the other side of the Evorul and ship them back along the Ilsa to Umfell, where they worked.

Braddach stopped for a moment when his pile had grown taller than expected to drink from his canteen. The water tasted like iron and tin, and yet it was refreshing in the heat. He could see from the wagon as the men lowered the heaviest stones from multiple small boats into the water at the determined points, guided by mages, doubling as engineers.

He took a second to make sure no one was around and then let out a sigh. A combination of frustration and exhaustion. They had built so many bridges and helped to flatten so many roads, laying down the framework for even more modern improvements, from here to Gulldalr. Throughout that entire time, Erold had spent almost every waking second with Cherene, who doted on him.

Braddach took another swig of water and watched the river glitter in the light of the summer sun. He could see the reflection of a small dragon, no larger than fifteen atomic yards, dart between the white, snowy mountain peaks in shadows on the water. The men laughed and joked on the river.

It was like seeing a dove. Rare but common, especially along the Evorul River, where it was the shortest distance to the Normany coastline for the dragons to get their fill of plankton, krill, and fish. He had once heard that a dragon was the whale of the sky, but had to eat like bird, consuming at least a quarter of its body weight in food from the sea.

Braddach saw that the mound had reduced, so he got back to work, lifting the rocks from the wagon, walking them down to the river and then placing them on the pile, so that they could slowly fill out the foundations of the stone bridge.

Later in the day, he joined Nido and Frof, who had become his drinking pals in the long summer nights as they toured Umfell's taverns one by one and then repeated the loop.

This evening, they rested at a pub in the central city, where a bard played requested songs and recited old tales of heroic warlocks, Fros, and the tall tales of other long dead heroes, like Io. When someone requested a song about Erold, Braddach almost groaned.

"Don't hear much from the king, do we?" said Frof.

"He's been at the other end of the chain of command," said Nido.

"I know, but it would be nice to get a rousing speech. A congratulations or something. He hasn't spoken much since Gulldalr," said Frof. "He's always with that lady mage from Valgaard."

Braddach drank his beer but nodded.

"It's not my place to say anything, but it's my guess that the war's not over yet," said Nido.

"That's no excuse for spending all your time with a woman," said Frof.

"Merely pointing out that he won't be giving any speeches espousing victory when we could be attacked by Akre any day," said Nido.

"You think so," said Frof, thoughtfully. "What do you think Patr? You used to spend a lot of time with him, right?"

"Used to. I wish I had more direct knowledge, but not even First Majors, which are a few promotions away, are being told anything beyond making camp in and around the city, and then of course, building bridges and improving roads."

"Dull work," said Sten C, who sat down with an atomic pint, grinning over it, "I was wondering where you three were this evening."

"Didn't mean to run into you fellas on purpose," said Arne, "Just tired of the usual haunt. The same, few local girls been whoring there, and I seen so many men go with them that I'm glad I never had a try."

"Sure, you didn't," joked Frof. Arne merely raised his beer in response and winked.

"What's it like here?" said Sten C.

"Look around. Quiet except for the bard," said Braddach.

"Is the food good?" asked Arne.

"Bread and butter. They might have some meat or stew, but we never asked," said Frof.

"I heard you guys talking about the king being sweet on the archmage from Valgaard," Arne smiled as Sten went up to get bread for the table.

"She seems sweet on him too," said Nido.

"It seems strange to be a king and spend all your time with one woman," said Frof, "I thought he had a reputation as a ladies' man in Cardane."

Braddach shrugged, "People change."

"It seems a little like he's playing the role," said Arne. "He wants to do the right things."

"Speaking of people who have changed, you don't seem yourself as much lately Patr," said Sten as he sat back down.

"What do you mean by that?" Braddach drank some of his beer.

"Always moping, shrugging and sighing," said Nido.

"Yeah, not even playing those pranks the way you did when we were on the march down here," said Frof, "coming to think of it."

"You got something on your mind?" asked Sten.

"I don't see how much of a difference it makes, but I can't stop thinking that we're in Umfell for a reason," said Braddach, reasoning with himself what to say.

"Suit yourself for not telling then," said Arne, "but laying foundations and digging holes for pipework is good enough reason for me."

"Yeah, word is that we'll be helping to build schools in the river towns soon as we're done with the bridges," said Sten, eating some bread.

Braddach ate some bread and listened to the four of them talk as more soldiers began to filter in from the many divisions. He wished that he could recognize whether some of them were his men, but he had given up trying to tell them all apart. That was his squad mages job for their individual battalions of two hundred fifty.

Braddach left some extra gold pieces for his squad before he left the pub. The sun was just setting, so he still had a good view of the mountains. The river was hidden by the low wall, and the oil lamps lit the walk as the chilly wind howled and the moon began to rise in the early dark. The tents appeared in the distance and Braddach retired to solitude, waiting for the light of the day to fade against the cream color of his tent. Even the king had chosen to sleep under the stars in the summer nights, looking up at a cream-colored roof.

* * *

"This city is lovely this time of year," remarked Cherene as they walked down the lone, long main street, that wrapped in a wide oval around the city and joined with the circle where the church stood, facing the rising sun.

Erold watched as the barest fog of winters breath lifted in puffs of white from her pink lips, chapped by the wind. It would begin to snow soon, but at least they had the last few weeks of summer to look forward to. In the early morning of late summer, it was still rare for it to be this cold. The early fall would also hover around freezing for a few more weeks after the coming equinox.

"Look at the decorations," Cherene said, noticing that Erold watched her instead. The people of the city had become used to seeing the king walking about and raised their fists when he passed to which he often simply nodded in response. When he looked up to spy the silver and gold tinsel and ornaments adorning the street as well as decorating spruce and fir trees, he saw many such fists as shoppers enjoyed Merchant's Day in Umfell in anticipation of the coming Frostmas.

Erold had taken Cherene shopping in Umfell to celebrate the second Zenday of Ivanssun, 1524, among the people in the same way his uncle Sven once had taken him. First, they needed to buy gifts and then they would walk through the cities, from Umfell to

Donworsh and maybe further northwest, donating them. Most likely to the churches rather than from home to home.

"They're nice," said Erold, looking back at the young, blue-eyed archmage. They had spent a lot of time together, going over maps while he learned more about Normany, and she had watched, often explaining things. After a long summer of patience and mental growth in the valley with no news from Akre or from Valgaard, he let the books alone.

"You're not even looking," she said as if annoyed, but smiling back at him.

"This one's interesting," said Erold, noticing that one of the displays had dressed up clockwork automatons in a genesis scene from the tales of Fros. The machines silently watching the street, looked as if they were of Domiscus origin rather than the more modern porcelain faced feminine ones; they were ancient and rare to see some that had not been salvaged. He saw no poison darts like the one that had been pulled from Moon's shoulder, and the glass was thick.

"Ooh, a clothier. Let's go inside," Cherene said and pulled Erold in through the thick, wood door.

"Welcome to my shop," said the tailor inside, but when he noticed that it was King Erold. He raised his fist and Erold nodded, expressing that the man didn't need to sing the song too despite his attempts to begin at the refrain.

As Cherene and Arla began to look at prefabricated dresses and fabrics that stretched along the walls on large spools, Erold asked the man about the clockwork in the window.

"Ah, yes, they are from the days of Domiscus indeed. They had supposedly been rusted past the point of salvage, so I was able to get them for cheap. Then, I just buffed out the parts I could and removed the metal where it had rusted through."

"Fascinating. I would never have been able to tell."

"The clothes hide most of the wiring that would be visible," the merchant blushed. "A bit of a different use for them than for war."

"I'll say," said the king, thoughtfully.

"Of course, with all your men, it's not as if you need any clockwork ones," the merchant reddened further for some reason.

"Ah yes--"

"How much for this dress?" asked Cherene, interrupting them with a wide smile.

"That one is for a bespoke client of mine. She's very particular.

She'll be here today, or tomorrow, to try it on, hopefully for the final time. I would have to check my appointment book," the merchant said, touching his pockets as if looking for it, "If you would like your own of the same style, I'd be happy to. It would have to be full price, though. It's not on sale. I am no Elmore Quinn, but I try to keep up with the latest fashions in Akre, like the display."

"That's all right," said Cherene.

"I can get it for you, for Frostmas," said Erold, smiling.

"I thought you were going to get each other surprises for Frostmas like for kids."

"I can get both," said Erold, though one surprise that he was not happy with was how fast the remaining gold from his trip to the gulf was evaporating. It was not as if he could go back and get that job again. He would have to begin an enforcement of taxes, but it was not something that he wanted to do in the early days of his reign.

Cherene thought for a moment, "Oh, perhaps, we should focus on other dresses here, and buy some fabrics." She turned to the merchant, "We're doing a big donation in advance of the coming holidays."

"Please, take as much as you can carry," he smiled.

Erold nodded, though he was a touch more worried about splurging on many things rather than one dress, "Perhaps we will take a few of the dresses."

He purchased a few dresses, suits, and innumerous fabrics, many from Emiran rock sheep, that Cherene selected, and then they went back to continue their shopping. An attendant that Kutzbek had appointed to follow Erold, despite the king's assurance that he was fine, took the clothes and put them onto a pushcart that he had brought along.

They next bought toys for children and some dry goods that people could eat throughout the winter like wheat flour before completing the loop of stores at the church, where they gave many of their gifts, before they would ride further north, trying to ensure they could make it through the local towns before the day was done.

Erold was glad that wheat and other trade goods were still crossing the border to the Solgra, which neither side defended, but he knew that Akre had made public statements in the early days after his campaign, attempting to disavow his claims to his hereditary thrones.

* * *

The following morning of Solday, Cherene and Erold attended

church together as they had begun to do, and then he had spent the rest of the day reading through the history of Normany's various regions, which while Cherene understood, it had appeared to become more than a mere obsession.

Cherene and Arla then spent most of the rest of the day together while Cherene silently lamented that she could not be at the palace in Valgaard where she felt more useful. She still felt something for Erold, even more than she had before, but she was caught in a loop in Umfell, where she felt, especially now, she couldn't tell him who she truly was and she wasn't able to work on the affairs of her nation, which she had enjoyed doing for over ten years every day, whether snow or shine.

She looked around the large tent, which comfortably held two cots that she was lucky to have, but she had given up a bed, sheets cleaned or replaced almost daily, and too many pillows to count for one pillow she couldn't replace soon enough and sheets that she couldn't keep clean.

The men, most younger than her, had little better than blankets, and had slept in them on the ground, most without washing, for the better part of a year. At least Erold had his washed. She had seen him do it.

"I've been thinking Cherene," said Arla out of the silence and she leaned in closer before saying quietly just above a whisper, "If you're going to let him know you're the hmm, you'd better do it soon. It's almost winter."

"Things are good right now," said Cherene, "who am I to upset the balance?"

"Who's to say he doesn't already know," said Arla, "Besides, I can see when you look listlessly at this cot, and I feel the same way. I had a bed too."

"I can't just ask him, and what if he doesn't believe me, if I told him," said Cherene.

"You're just avoiding it even though you can't be completely happy with the way things are--"

They were cut short when they heard a louder argument in the makeshift command center beside their tent. Cherene and Arla put on another of layer of clothing to leave the coziness of the thick tent to find the source of the commotion.

Wermack and Kienber were arguing within the rickety building near its thin, wooden door. When Cherene and Arla entered, they could see Erold sitting and watching on the other side of the one room building, flanked by Elara Moon, who had just returned from the Ash Vale.

"What's going on?" asked Cherene, frustrated with herself for sounding like she was chastising children. Kienber looked at her as though he had won the argument by default with a smug grin, while Wermack's shoulders slackened.

When neither answered, Moon said, "They were debating whether to call a formal meeting of the generals."

"Why? What's happened?" asked Cherene.

"The civilian here believes that Akre plans to attack before the end of the year, and Kienber thought that since the king took it seriously, we should too. I think it's a silly waste of everyone's time," said Wermack.

"That civilian happens to be the former aide of Erolin Ardrada. If you need me to remind you, he was the king of Normany for over eighteen years, and she's spent the last ten years in the gulf with king Erold," Arla explained, so that Cherene didn't have to. Cherene had also long suspected that Moon was a member of the secret order of knights that had encircled the globe. They had even once been the precursors to the warlocks at Imor Valsen.

"My apologies," said Wermack, half-heartedly.

"And what does the king think?" asked Cherene, gazing into his blue eyes, deep in thought.

"Yes, let's call a meeting," said Erold, "Polesar has shown before that he'll attack during the holiday season to surprise his adversaries. With Frostmas just over a week away, attack is likely imminent."

"Even if a substantial portion of the army is still in Harupht?" asked Wermack.

"Rouse the generals," said Cherene. "Kienber and Wermack, the two of you go. Arla and I will stay."

"Yes, mam."

The two generals went off, leaving the four of them alone in the tent. Moon looked at her oddly.

"We had come in here to speak on the potential field of battle and catch up on the summer," said Erold, nodding to the map at the center of the room. "The two of them happened to be in here too."

"Don't let me stop you," said Cherene.

Erold nodded and glanced at Moon, "Your daughter, is she still in the Ash Vale?"

"Yes, with Mrs. Everett. And Mr. Everett," said Moon.

"I'm sorry you don't get to spend Frostmas with her, this year," said Erold.

"Polesar is mobilizing. It's time to act. If he's not sleeping on Frostmas Eve, neither are we."

"Understood," said Erold. Kutzbek entered the tent.

"Additional munitions, rifles, grenadier equipment, and one hundred pieces of artillery have been delivered to General Blaggard at Gulldalr," said Moon.

"Splendid," said Kutzbek. "I've heard the news. King Erold, I think we should retreat to Gulldalr immediately."

"We should discuss it as a group," said Plaski as he entered, along with Pasan and Eichlen.

"It's too risky to pursue a formal engagement here. There are too few routes to retreat in the case that he brings more men than we can defend against."

"There are risks to every move on the battlefield," said Eichlen. "We should not be rash."

"It would be rash to stay," said Kutzbek.

The rest of the generals entered quickly, and after formal discussion, whether skeptical of Moon's proclamation of battle or not, it came down to whether they believed they had better chances running for Gulldalr or defending Umfell.

Wermack insisted they could defend the city while Kutzbek insisted that they should combine forces at Gulldalr before committing to battle.

The argument was based on the information that without the return of the southern force to Akre from Harupht, they expected as many as one hundred thousand leaving Akre, which would put them at nine hundred thousand soldiers defending the city, the same as the number in southern Valgaard. There was no risk of a counterattack north, and they had a defendable position. At Umfell, they had entrenched positions and good access to water that could also be kept cold enough for the unicorns, who needed sustained access to ice, cold water.

If they stayed, they could ensure that they could use their cavalry in the near term at a healthy level and would be able to make up any additional deficiency in manpower through the strong cavalry.

Erold listened and in the end, put it to a silent vote by the generals, offering to have the deciding factor between the nine in the event that they were within one, be he and Cherene casting blind ballots as well.

As Arla withdrew the penned, anonymous paper, she tallied the votes.

Stay and defend Umfell.

Stay and defend Umfell.

Retreat to Gulldalr.

Stay and defend Umfell.

Retreat to Gulldalr.

Stay and defend Umfell.

Stay and defend Umfell.

Stay and defend Umfell.

Stay and defend Umfell.

By a vote of seven to two, they were to defend the city on the Evorul River. Perhaps making this the location of their final stand and ultimate victory for the throne of Normany.

1524 - Chapter 51

Graneuva sat down at his familiar, personal oak desk in the captain's quarters of the Santisma. He had gained numerous ranks over the years since the emperor had proclaimed him the "Hero of GoldArrow." Wherever he went, he was still known by that name, despite many accomplishments. Through all of it, his ship had remained the same.

He had the same desk, and many of the same officers had stayed on. The Santisma was still the largest military class airship built anywhere in the world. Albion, to his knowledge, had given up trying to figure out how to produce large enough brig class ships to match his, and instead was racing Imeria to keep up on battleships.

Graneuva had Imeria on pace to always be a step ahead, and the increasing bounty promised by the Westernlands supplied ever greater rewards, as colonies stretched further and further south into once blighted lands toward the mythical and exotic Bermulla.

In his younger days, his rage-filled days, before he had gotten rich, he had pined for his wife on these long trips, and now he missed her but not in the same way. Whenever he had left as a young man, it had always felt like it would or could be the last time he was to ever see her, but he had always come home, and he had grown further and further from the front lines as the focus shifted to maintaining a coordinated front in the Bacine and green seas where neither side pressed the attack.

He had sat down at his desk to write her a letter, because today of all days, she had captured his mind. Most elves of the modern world had similar lifespans to men, but she was as beautiful and youthful as the day he met her. He was on a particularly long engagement at sea and the desire had just come to him even though he hadn't sent her a letter since he was first an officer, on his very first assignment for the red and gold griffon of the Imerian states.

To my darling, beloved, if I was to have known when I first met you that there would ever be so sweet a flower as you, that when I picked it and took it home, that it would look as perennially beautiful as you do, I would have been too weak to approach you for fear of how beautiful you truly are. When I look at you, it is as if my heart skips the notion that anything else existed before that moment when I could gaze upon you. The curve of your face, the point of your ears, the depth of your eyes. These are the things that I hold dear as this, likely the last mission of my career plays out before me. I look forward to spending each day with you, and not the sea.

He lit a cigarette and looked over the letter, which he had written carefully with a fountain pen. There were none of the inkblots of quill, but he had stained his hand. He wiped the black ink away, but some faded bit remained on his palm. He planned to wash it later and set the letter aside.

* * *

Ivette lounged on a chaise in a sunny parlor in the rear of the Bowery Place estate. Ilrich, their son, and Dawn, King Stone's daughter were playing in the rear garden, which could be seen out the large, sunlit rear windows. The forest behind the house was filled with light.

The King and Prince Eduard were in one of the many rooms, discussing news from Valgaard and Akre. Onya had listened in and informed Ivette of what she could. After they had spoken at length of yet another bit of rising tension in the faraway east, Onya had gone to settle her own nerves by painting landscapes from a recent trip up the coast to the many bays and inlets of north Albion while Ivette watched the children play.

The palace was quiet enough that she could hear the men speaking from down the hall. They didn't seem particularly worried, but every day had felt like it might be the day everything truly started for quite some time. She was equally ambivalent to it as she was exhausted by the fear.

Ivette reclined her head back to look up at the ceiling and then caught a strange shadow passing over the checkered mural painted there. She turned over to look up at the grand entry across the ballroom floor of the foyer, where so many parties had been thrown over the years it had almost grown tiresome.

A cloud of dust was being kicked up by a four-horse carriage traveling down the long road between the central gardens to the house. Ivette stood up and rather than call a butler or valet went to the door herself. She had taken off her heels and when she hit the cold marble of the foyer decided to leave them beside the couch where they lay.

She hiked up her dress and hurried over the long foyer, sending an echoing patter through the hall as her feet practically froze on the icy stone, and the carriage stopped in front of the mansion.

Admiral Ferrara hopped out of the carriage, looking worried and dressed a bit relaxed as if she had been summoned at her city house. Her oversized boots and brown trousers made her look more like a pirate queen than head of Albion's maritime efforts in coordination with the Coltari. Ivette opened the door for her just as she burst through.

"Eduard? Where is he?"

"Jack. He's in the second office down the right in the south hall."

"Thank you," she said plainly and began to run although not gracefully across the slippery floor. Her boots screeching as they slipped slightly with each stride.

"He's heard the news of Akre!" Ivette yelled after her, but Ferrara waived her off. Ivette, similarly, waived off the house staff with a reassuring gesture and followed after. She grabbed a pair of sandals set to the side while checking to make sure Ferrara hadn't gotten too far ahead.

She got to the door just in time to catch the prince, her husband's initial reaction. At first, he looked dismayed and then a bit dejected, before a bit of courage flashed across his face and when he saw her, it grew that much stronger.

"We must make a decision on this at once," said the prince, and then he turned to Ivette, "The Santisma has been sighted off the southern coast again."

"Are we chasing it?"

Admiral Ferrara shook her head and seemed absorbed in the reality of her words, "That's only part of the news. We have reports that they've annexed the independent island of Pavol on the Green Seas. It must be the reason there have been decreased sightings off the coast. I'm glad I had scouts investigate."

"How could they do such a thing?"

"That's what we should find out," said the prince.

"You have suspicions?" asked the king.

The prince nodded, and the king gestured for him to share them.

"I believe it may be the staging grounds for an attack on the south coast. They had been testing our defenses for quite some time."

There was a moment of silence. No one wanted to be the first one to admit they weren't sure how dire that was until the prince fully explained it.

"They could attack the south coast as soon as tomorrow. We would never have a defense prepared in time."

"We would never be able to get aid here from Menetoris without at least a week notice either."

"That is, if we don't act first."

"What can we do?"

Ferrara cracked her knuckles and relaxed her neck, "A preemptive strike. A raid. We can take a single air schooner close enough to investigate and cause a commotion."

"If the reports are true, they may have as many as one thousand and one hundred ships or more there," said King Stone. "How would you get past?"

"Have you tried to see in the dark? Scratch that, of course you have. If we act as if we are just another one of the ships, they'll never know as long as we don't run up a clear flag. Then, we can get a good look and maybe start a few fires on the docking stations."

Ivette didn't say anything, but she thought about the test this would be for Menetoris's navy even if they could arrive in time to help. When the battle did finally occur, her nation would only send four hundred three-rams, and their highly trained mages would be tasked with taking on as many as three mages to one, or more.

"Do we have enough fire mages willing to pull this off?" asked the prince.

"One."

"One?"

"Trust me. We will only need the one," said Ferrara. Stone agreed, resting his hand on his son's shoulders.

"Well then, you have an air schooner in mind?"

"I had one made, yes."

"Fast enough to escape?" asked Ivette.

"Yes," Ferrara turned. "And small enough to not draw much attention up close or not.

"Then count me in," said Eduard.

The King tightened his grip on his son, "You can't go."

"He can," said Ivette. "I will go too."

"We must leave tonight," said Eduard.

"To get there by nightfall. We must leave now," said Ferrara with a mischievous grin.

* * *

The airship crossed through the lightning array, having given the signal that they would return in the dark to the tower crews just as darkness had engulfed the coast.

The ship was riding fast in the night--a dark black object, a single shadow, flying as high as the clouds, navigating to the largest island that split the two 'green' seas between the southern facing coast of Normany and the northern facing coast of the Imerian states.

Lightning raged in the distance, a dragon rolled through the clouds on its way to hunt in the ocean by night, and the crew pumped Orichalc into the furnace that churned out red flames and coughed red soot from the tiny air schooner. The steam engine whistled, and metal gears cried as hot water pushed them to their limits.

The ship ducked into the black-gray shadows of the wispy clouds and descended lower and lower, listening for the faintest of sound as they only heard the engines churn. Ivette grasped Eduard's hand.

Ferrara glanced at them and then to the mage graduate, top of her class, an orange-haired fire mage that had captured the stoic General Anglis's attention. No one said a word out loud as the ship pressed on.

The shovels shoveled more Orichalc into the flames from inside the belly of the ship, unaware of where they were going and not questioning it despite the fear that gripped their hearts until the sound of dragon's wings had disappeared.

Everyone had a feeling that this mission could be a one-way trip that was only settled by the fact that the prince and princess had come with them. Ivette's fingers tingled as she thought of what spells she might have to cast and at what scale. Perhaps, even a shield for the entire ship to protect it from cannon fire from all sides.

On the forward command deck, the bridge, the quartet, along with the senior crew members, saw the island approach and plans had to change. Silent swarms of black moved about hundreds upon hundreds of docked three-rams on tower after tower of airdocks, some blinking blue and others red lights in the night.

After brief discussion, they agreed to detach a three-ram in the cargo bay from the ship and send Eduard, Ivette, Ferrara, and the fire mage, Ti-Enna to the shore with two riflemen. They saw no sign of the Santisma or the Imerian battleships as the schooner closed in on the island.

The ship hovered over the quiet, rolling waves of the dark ocean as the three-ram detached and buzzed away with the shield mage readying and watching the beautiful fire mage ahead of her, rest against the forward bow, so self-assured, that it looked as if she would take on the whole Akrin navy.

They killed the engine and let it float the rest of the way on the air current as the long, thin island neared, and none of the buzzing ships on night watch above noticed the dark figure slip among them.

Ivette cast a simple spell of illusion as they passed deeper in, so that they could speak unheard, "Where do you think they took the Pavolians?"

"Shh."

"It's okay. She cast a spell. I don't know."

They passed through the quiet ranks of ships toward the center of the great network that had overtaken a quiet port town that appeared to have been looted and burned. Glass was shattered everywhere and the spaces, where the extra tall doors of the Pavolians would have been, were solemn, dark tunnels that looked like gaping black ghost mouths of the forlorn houses in the near complete darkness.

Ferrara guided the ship. The riflemen tensed. They had better guns than muskets, but surrounded by so many, there was no chance at survival if they had to fire a single shot against thousands. Ivette watched them, worried they might break.

Ti-Enna pointed Ferrara to the large central docking tower that looked like it might be fit for a battleship, "If you give me time, I can melt that."

"Melt that?" asked Ivette.

Ti-Enna nodded, "but, you have to get me close enough to touch it."

Ferrara eased the ship down to the point where they were hovering alongside the tall structure. There weren't as many three-rams docked against it as there could have been, but it was clear it had the most, circled around it like boats locked into a vertical dock, silently bobbing with the shifting of the wind. It began to drizzle lightly, and the riflemen covered the gunpowder and relaxed.

Ti-Enna pressed her hands against the dock. The buzzing patrol ships went by overhead, and the docked three-rams, lifted by their internal balloons, bumped together just as if they were floating in water.

For a time, nothing happened, and Ivette, her heart beginning to pound with each second as the patrols seemed to get closer and closer with each pass, began to doubt Ti-Enna until the surface turned red-orange and glow like lava. Once it started it began to spread quickly.

"Hey, you there!"

A rifle shot rang out, splitting the forehead of a patrol officer on one of the boats, and that alone would have been enough to trigger an alarm but then the entire airdock, like a giant spruce tree went up in flames that whipped upward in an unquenchable rage, swallowing many of the docked three-rams and sending the rest crashing toward the ground.

Ferrara guided them through the falling debris as the emergency alarms screamed amongst the Akrin men, crying out for fire. Ferrara twisted through the awakening and falling ships as Ti-Enna threw fireballs chaotically as quickly as she could. Ti-Enna readied a massive, growing flame ball, hissing steam with each drop of rain, to toss amongst a crowd of ships racing toward the chaotic fires.

Ferrara grabbed her and it hissed downward toward the ground, exploding on the beach. An Akrin three-ram got on their tail as they split out from the pack and began racing across the open ocean, and then a few more raced after them.

Ferrara moaned.

"Why'd you do that? How could you stop me?" asked Ti-Enna, but Ferrara was badly hurt.

"Sabotage, not blindly kill," Ferrara groaned. Ti-Enna's fury almost caused her to lash out again at Ferrara, but Ivette got in her way. Half of Ferrara's arm had been engulfed in flames and much of her side. She looked like she had been caught in a housefire.

Ivette sprang into action, healing the old woman while simultaneously casting a blue shield spell to repel what spells or bullets could fire at them in the increasing rain.

The fires behind them raged and more and more three-rams began to buzz in the dark night behind them like a hornet's nest had been upset in darkness.

Eduard fired one of the rifles back at the oncoming ships while one of the riflemen took over the wheel, directing the three-ram blindly in the general direction of the schooner.

Eduard's rifle jammed in the rain, but the other rifleman kept firing, and the line of three-rams chasing them seemed to only grow.

The schooner was nowhere in sight.

"Climb!" Eduard yelled over the buzz of the engine, burning Orichalc below and the moans of Ferrara while Ti-Enna had sat back in shock at the sight.

"What?"

"Climb!"

The ship climbed higher and higher as the enemy made chase upward on the night wind and into the drizzling rain that pelted their faces but did not quiet the raging fires that Ti-Enna could see far below with the shadows of ships encircling the red jet of flame, looking like little bits of ash around a distant campfire.

Higher and higher they climbed, and then the schooner burst out of the darkness to their left, firing a warning salvo that scattered the lead three-rams of the enemy. The docks opened underneath as the ship slowed to let the young man manning the air rudder to aim it expertly into the bay.

Bullets began pinging off of metal instead of the blue shield as the bay doors closed. The three-ram collapsed onto the floor of the docking bay with a crash, and the crew waited to take a breath until they could feel the ship begin to pick up steam and race off for the lightning line.

The long-range rear cannons began firing warning shots into the darkness, and the men feeding Orichalc to fire the engines could be heard down the small hull. The air schooner's unrivaled speed and size compared to the three-rams made pursuit unlikely, but no one relaxed until the sight of the Albion islands off the coast broke the sea ahead of them to the west, and they could cut back to the north, riding the northeast current until they passed the lightning array, stretching out along the coast like silent, metal lighthouses.

1524 - Chapter 52

Emperor Polesar Rolard kneeled in the pew of the cathedral of Saint Drosef with his head bowed low, dressed in the dark blue of Akre with gold and red trim, which were subtle references to the city's past. The empress, Aurelia, also in dark blue but a fantastic dress with a gold and ruby necklace, knelt beside him on his left. His sons were on either side of them. His eldest on his right.

Polesar placed a hand on his son's shoulder, and then began to speak silent words. Short was his prayer, but long were the threads that drifted through his head after he opened his eyes and looked up at the golden alter of Fros. It was the image of the man, burdened by fate and crushed by the weight of its evil as he held the key of the Otum in his hand up to the blue flames of Mount Aeron where their one mind connection was destroyed at last.

What could Polesar do but finish the path that he had started on like Fros before him? He thought to himself while he waited for the minister to speak, a guest from the supreme priest in Elessia, one of the Blue Jays, a reference to the eternal blue flame that the Otum had once worshipped until it became their talisman's doom. This Blue Jay had come at the perfect time to give guidance to the blue eagle of Akre that would soon fly alongside the red griffon of Imeria to crush the fledgling northern alliance.

The enemy had fallen into his trap. He had left Normany open to attack, and the Northern Alliance had taken the bait. It had been a surprise to learn that a pretender who claimed to be Erold Ardrada, son of Erolin, had taken lead of the rebel forces now stationed at Umfell, but it was a trivial matter. It was only fitting that the same valley where his father had perished ten years ago would be the usurper's tomb.

Polesar had sent numerous mages to the crash site, and they had diligently followed the paths of each survivor. No one had reported seeing any one of note, though it was also true that no one had truly seen Erolin's only son while he had been alive. His, Erolin's, adopted son had no royal blood and had been traced to Imor Valsen, where it was presumed that he died as well during the warlock trials.

It would be a fitting message to all those who thought they could challenge the authority of the Akrin eagle that he crush this usurper. He had feinted a move south to aid Harupht, hoping to hold his enemy in the Dalvalles hills.

The move had worked, and he believed that he had prepared

Harupht well to operate against the rebellion without his aid. He had a protégé, Danta, operating in his stead. After pulling the feint, his force had reunited with a portion that had moved west to distract the usurper by taking trains in the night and hiding among civilian housing. His main force was now ready to launch an attack through the Solgra and pin his enemy against the mountains.

The senate may have been beginning to doubt him, but under his leadership, the borders had increased substantially on every side but northwest. Losing the sliver of land at the edge of Normany that was the Silver Coast had been a blow to his reputation, but he had not been the one to orchestrate a failed coup. He believed the senate might have, but he did not press the subject.

Instead, he continued to act on his ambitions. In just four years, he had led armies in the east deeper than ever into Emira and after thwarting the Mondelvanian rebellion, he had positioned the empire further north than ever under the guise of anticipatory action.

These more than made up for the loss in total territory, and soon, they could push into the dwarven hills unchecked. Neither of those victories even came close to the success of his strategy in the Westernlands where the sparse wood elves had finally been subdued.

Aurelia turned to him, touching his waist gently and leaning her cheek against his. Her lavender scent drifted over him like he was standing in a field of flowers. She whispered something while the minister spoke that he could barely hear.

Polesar nodded. He knew that she didn't want him to leave, but it was his duty. The Northern Alliance had harried the empire on every front, and it was high time in more than just Polesar's opinion that he act.

When the minister finished his sermon, Polesar turned to her and simply smiled, whispering into her hear, "It will be a short campaign my love. Much shorter than Mondelvania or Emira. I will be back before Frostmas."

"You said that then, and you were gone for most of those four years."

"This will be short, I promise," he said. For a split second, he wanted to tell her that he planned to attack north, but he stopped himself. As much as he trusted his wife, they were in public, and he had begun to realize with the strange visit of Tanneran that he needed to invest in his own spies. The men he had trusted to get him here had suddenly revealed that not everything they knew made its way to him.

They, whoever it was in the senate, had made a shrewd, calculated move. Perhaps, they had made a number of such moves. He had no way of knowing the extent to which they dealt in shadow, and now that he knew that they did not fight with him in darkness, he had begun to question what they did in the light. While they, and he didn't know who they were beyond Tanneran, who was thankfully a friend enough to reveal the distasteful truth lurking in the senate.

In a game of shadows, he was alone. In the eyes of the realm, he was a hero. As such, he had prayed on it, and asked again today if what he was doing was right. If he were not throwing all his good will in the senate out if he made such a public display in their face.

They were worried about the coffers while lining their own pockets. He had seen the greed and corruption for thirty years, and he had courted power too long to let his mistress leave him in the night.

As he bowed his head and partook in communion with Fros as all good Frostians did, he turned ready to hear the last words of the Godspell on this Solday before exiting the church to where the papers and the press waited every time he returned to the city, but this time he had invited them with the tease of bigger news than ever.

While the senate had their secrets, he had his too. He knew the budgets. He knew by how much they ran a surplus. He also knew to whom he owed his true power. From when he took the reins of the south army at only fifteen and pushed them to save the city while his superiors waited to act, he had been supported by his soldiers above all else.

And while in that secret senate hearing not so many months ago, he had been reprimanded for not having taken any land back from Valgaard and been informed of the usurper while hearing of the concerns of the nation's debt, he had hatched a plan. When that night they had received an urgent telegram that this man had escaped to Peth in the morning, he knew it all came down to this coming fall in Normany.

As he said a grateful thank you to the father Blue Jay for administering a faithful service, he walked out, with his hat under his arm, into the open air and cold sunshine of Abrim plaza with the angelic statue turned north. He was met by the many notepads of a hundred extra men of the press.

"My lord!"

"My lord emperor."

"Emperor!"

"Polesar! Emperor--"

"My lord, what is--"

"You had something you wished to--"

"You invited us--"

The overlapping words of all the men with pens ready to put notes to paper began to quiet down as the emperor placed a hand in his pocket and bowed solemnly. It had the momentary grimness to illicit in the imagination that this grand man might step down while an usurper had attacked Normany. Sudden fear gripped many who had heard tales of the brutality of the north when they had sacked Akre.

The emperor then held up one hand, placed his hat back on his head and issued his planned address, "It has come to my attention that the state of the people of this nation is grave, very grave. The gravest it has been in many a decade. Our army is at its largest and our country is at its strongest. I wish to issue a heartfelt message of gratitude. I wish to show the world what power in the right hands can do. While our hills run rich with gold and our rivers thick with trade, our coffers filled and our milk plentiful..."

There were some laughs as the emperor placed an arm around the waist of his beloved wife.

"It has come to my attention that to be a citizen of this nation while a measure of pride may not mean that you have benefitted from the prosperity of this nation." He held a hand up to prevent questions. "So henceforth, it is my privilege to announce that from this day forward, to live or die in the service of the military, you will earn more than the average wage of a lifetime for a civilian of Akre."

The questions came and Polesar continued, feeling Aurelia embrace him tightly at his side. His sons, digging into each of his legs.

"No longer will a man have to fear for his wife or children if he is to die on the field at my command. Henceforth, his children will be put through the finest schools and be sent to university in the service of the nation, and his wife will be paid half his wage in perpetuity until she may perish or remarry. If a man is injured, he will be provided for at his same wage. And for the men in service, they will forever have the opportunity for an annual raise. In short, to repeat for those who didn't hear. To live or die in the service of the Akrin army, a man and his family will be better off than the average man of the empire!"

There was cheering. There was crying. There was an explosion of exclamations as men wept and went to tell the next man. Polesar knew that before noon on this Solday, the entire empire from one end to the other will have heard by telegram and even the smallest child would know the promise that had been made to the largest army ever assembled by either man or elf, the grand army.

He turned to kiss Aurelia, and then his royal guard, with Murdot at his side, helped him and his sons get through the crowd of weeping men.

* * *

Before the senate could respond and try to veto his maneuver and force him to retract his statement, he had ridden out of the city and taken the train to catch his men on the front. He knew that they had likely called a meeting for those who lined their pockets to stew in sudden hatred for him, but they had given him no choice but to solidify his support by touching the hearts of his political base.

His wife had been pleased at the response of the crowd as they began to chant his name louder and louder, and quickly those who had not yet heard the news, heard it. Aurelia had grown ever more charitable with each passing year toward the people of Akre, and in some ways, this political move had been so inspired.

Polesar and Murdot, still in their uniforms and straight from the church service, sat on red velvet oak chairs with gold embroidery looking out from the shining windows at the fast-passing golden countryside of the Solgra to each other. Murdot had an enormous smile, he couldn't contain, like a child about to burst into laughter. It was as if they were two kids that had gotten off with a schoolyard prank on a teacher and made off before they could be identified and not two gentleman officers embarking on a warpath.

A piano had been placed at one end of the cart, and a man played it alongside a soft violin. They were served refreshing lemonade along with tea and little baked sweets. Chocolate wrapped in dough and dough filled with caramel. These treats oozed sugar and decadence while exquisite paintings by the emperor's favorite painters hung throughout the cabin.

Soon, the vision on the plains shifted from the fields of golden wheat to tents and makeshift stockades. The new bivouac had appeared, and his men stood on the grass walls surrounding the campus that stretched for miles to hail the emperor with resounding cheers.

They were so loud that even on the train after a moment delay, he could hear them yell. When Murdot looked back from peering out the window, he found that the oft-stolid emperor had too been moved to tears like the men in the plaza. The violin and the piano kept playing.

Polesar took a quick drink and used a napkin to hide the tears, welling in his eyes. When he finally disembarked from the steam train, he found himself greeted by the remaining twenty-two of his senior officers, lead mages and all very accomplished, who stood around the platform backed by their adjutants, awaiting a moment to bow to him collectively.

He raised his hands to quiet them, but they only grew louder, and more than three hundred thousand men kneeled to him in a sea of blue jackets with dashes of red, gold, and white. He returned their gesture by taking off his hat, wiping his tears from his eyes, and bowing low.

He would describe his plans for a two-pronged attack by land with the force here on Normany, and by sea and air in coordination with Imeria on Albion, but that would wait. He would make a promise of certain victory, but they would have to quiet down first. He would let them know that victory here meant that a counterattack on Peth was inevitable. They had nearly the same number of troops in Akre as were known to be stationed in defense of Peth. In dealing a final fatal blow to the independence of these two states, the oldest of Old Galdir, the empire would be that much closer to being united across all of West Ahria.

By daybreak the next day, they would be three hundred fifty thousand strong. He looked at each of his lead mages one by one, meeting their eyes as they remained kneeled until they averted their gaze and looked down.

Davos, Naven, Tlous, Andhammer, Hilara, Tornes, Arnan, Genie, Ernadsier, Elzo, the young Geraldt who had impressed in Emira, Marandres, Bessarzo, Edron, Hurtberg, Ompa, Aftrin, Desi, Sonan, the Kederanian who refused to go by anything other than the Brown Mountain, and finally Groche and Junto, who would be from here on out, leaders of his royal guard.

His core army was well trained, and battle hardened. His enemy was not. Each of his lead mages commanded multiple squadrons of mages that were supported by at least fifteen thousand troops in a well-defined hierarchical structure. He doubted the enemy had ten mages who could compare.

For over ten years, Albion had been protected by its lightning defense array and the fog-filled forest of the Ash Vale. In conjunction with Menetoris, they had held out the vast Argal Ocean from the eastern powers.

The first steps to finally crushing the rebellious lord Stone of Albion and fracturing the frail alliance of nations that dared to stand against the Empire had already been taken. His most talented mages, and most experienced units would wait with him as royal guard, ready to deal a final blow if such a moment would present itself. As he looked at their joyful faces, ready to do battle, he hoped that many of those who stood before him now, although willing, would not have to leave the reserve. He wished only for the celebration to last with as many men as were here now.

1524 - Chapter 53

Summer's end was near at hand, and instead of focusing on Frostmas celebrations, the Normany army had begun preparations for the defense of Umfell by putting the troops into a state of movement, readying for positional placement and yet, still with no defined plan as word of the official specifics of the deployment had not yet reached the leadership.

Additional preparations were made immediately to empty the Erstber River valley, advocating strongly for its people to move for the fall or through the winter north to Gulldalr or even further to avoid being caught in the war and to choke the Akrin army's necessary food supply, which they could replenish through force if villagers and their food remained nearby. The people vacating the valley with their food and supplies would force the Akrin army to move north of the Evorul River into its well-fed farming region, where they'd be able to feed their horses and men during any length of engagement.

The people made the move, packing up and shipping out while it was debated whether the same should be done for the larger Evorul River valley, and especially for the nearby towns and cities, anxiously awaiting word from Umfell after hearing of the yellow army being on the move.

They were in another meeting, when Erold received word that the forces of Akre, once called legions, had not launched to a parade from the new monument built to honor the peace of the three Karles kings in Brandon's Square, they had snuck into the Solgra at night from many directions. It confirmed Erold's suspicion that the enemy planned to use the long holiday season of the fall against him, starting with a fast march over the Frostmas holiday, which if they hadn't already mobilized could have left them scrambling to begin.

His army could now focus on defensive plans and laying out the positions of their artillery to best defend the city. There was no word on the official size of the force, but the debate continued as Kutzbek adamantly advocated for retreat to Gulldalr. The risks of a south retreat were now obvious and despite his objections to fleeing northwest through the Evorul River valley and hitting the forests of eastern Gardnor, he advocated the same now. Anything to get west of the Práezwa River.

Erold watched as the old Field Marshall General, head of his armed forces, desperately attempted to avoid the conflict while the rest of his generals advocated to stay and fight from well-defended fortifications. The wall was high enough that it could avoid a ground attack and thick enough to support artillery. The keeps had a stunning view of the valley, and they could maneuver their cavalry across the flat ground, putting the enemy who had to come north of the river on the edge of the knife. They could defend the bridges as well and try to hem the enemy into the Erstber passes, forcing the Akrin army to either march extra days north around the Erstber, or fight their way to go north along the Evorul south bank or over the bridges.

If their forces were even closely matched, there was less risk in the defense than the retreat. To go straight west, would put them into the forest, where they wouldn't be able to feed their cavalry, whether horses or unicorns. It would be near impossible to move their artillery through and as a result they could not move quickly. Therefore, their only option at any point to escape was to march south through the hills, and while the men could be put on the move, they could be caught in the hills, out of position by the opposing army in a few days' time. They needed more time for a retreat, and they had put it to vote when they had the time.

"Our alternative options will run out just as fast," said Kutzbek before leaving in a huff.

Erold turned to Moon and said quietly, "How many men do we have in Gulldalr? Do you know?"

"Hard to say, because I didn't ask for specifics--I will make note to do so in the future--but I would say something close to the number of infantry units here, and definitely not anywhere near double the number."

"But combat ready, yes?"

"Not well trained yet, sir."

"How close to battle ready?"

"Hard to say without asking General Blaggard directly."

He searched his mind, because he still felt uneasy, "Do we have eyes on the opposing force yet? Do we know how many they have?"

"No, I have been trying. It has been hard to get accurate intelligence in the Solgra or Akre."

"I'm happy to have any intelligence at all. I won't ask you where it comes from," Erold bemused and looked thoughtfully at his generals who seemed calm. He had felt sure that Akre wouldn't empty its forces unless they had a considerable advantage over Valgaard in the north. It seemed like they had always had a ten percent advantage over the Valgaard green and gold. Something about the counterattack didn't seem right to him, and he was second guessing his decision to trust the majority.

The enemy had shown a willingness to use the timing of things against him, and while he had anticipated it, he didn't feel like it was a victory. He had emptied the Erstber under his own command to rid them of olives and eggplants, but what if the enemy prolonged an engagement in the Evorul valley?

He had begun to wonder even more about the posterity, and also if that was just a luxury of being able to make decisions rather than be mercy to them. If they fought one major battle, whether they won or lost, would the historians even call this a war?

And what would they name it? The victory or defeat of King Erold? No, there were far too many men involved for that. What if it became the death or rebirth of Normany? Could he live with being the last king of his ancestral nation when he didn't know what hinged on his survival in a murky prophecy. What would Louie say if he could read the runes now?

Likely, you must never use the orb, Erold. He looked over at Cherene. He wasn't supposed to join the fight, but what if she were at risk? Or Braddach? Would he want his last summer with his brother after ten years in the gulf to be one that he spent all his time without him?

He looked again from general to general. From Wermack to Plaski, to Gavo, Eichlen, Borgoron and then to Milton. The Doctor, Pasan, sat quietly just as he did. Kienber looked off toward nothing in a forlorn gaze. Who had been the second vote with Kutzbek to retreat?

* * *

Polesar had his army fast march to rush across the Solgra. He also made sure to use the iron trains, which ran all the way to Leidyn to bring key supplies and ammunition almost to the foot of Dalvalles's hills. The army regrouped near there while Frostmas celebrations neared. He was sure that if the enemy wasn't caught off guard by his movement that they would be pinned by the size of his force.

He had heard nothing of any enemy movement, and their window of escape had disappeared before they even realized they needed to retreat. With an army of over two hundred thousand and an additional one hundred fifty thousand in reserves, set to ship along the river from the east, his men would soon descend on their victims, outnumbering them five to one along with six hundred pieces of artillery.

He received an update from an adjutant that his men would be into the pass to the Erstber on Spirit Day, the easiest route into and through the hills.

Polesar and his main detachment would then cut across the Erstber after passing through Elklin in two days' time, where they would surely cheer him on in the streets. He couldn't risk being stuck on the rocky side of the Evorul, so he had to quickly push from the south to take the bridges that ran across the Evorul, northwest of the Erstber. He also wanted to loop men around through Graabern to cut off a northwestern retreat. While they intercepted any troop movement, his central detachment would win the Umfell bridges by force, if they were defended, and then the combination of his west, south, and east movements would have the Normany rebels completely pinned.

Supply chains were how wars were won. Once he was in the Evorul valley, he could spread out the enemy's defense by putting too many divisions than they could handle into the field and then bunch up his lines feeding his strongest mages and men through the enemy's weakest point to capture the bridges. After moving over the river, rather than fight directly at Umfell, he would be able to crush the enemy with artillery from across the Ilsa without ever having to deploy the infantry except in defense of his own position.

His force would arrive in the river valley no earlier or later than the twenty sixth of Ivanssun, a Disday. Then, he would deliver senate rule and the vote to the people of Normany for all of time, ending the antiquated line of kings whose days of tyranny had been banished to the past.

Polesar had to issue few orders after having determined the course the army would take. With the amount of advance work, he had done in building out his troops and chain of command, he merely spoke the determination, and they worked together cohesively to achieve it.

Because of this, they were ahead of schedule and the enemy had already lost. While they were asleep in their beds or dreaming of Frostmas gifts that had distracted them from achieving victory on the field of battle, he had won.

* * *

The Frostmas celebrations were muted and quiet throughout the camp of the Normany men. True, there had been few things planned, but not even a Frostmas song was sung. Instead, they watched the embers dwindle in the dying sun. Their effects were packed and readied to be moved behind the Umfell walls. They had all heard of that the battle for Normany had come. The future of their nation was finally in their hands.

"Psst, Patr, you in here?"

"Yeah, just a moment," Braddach said as he finished shaving and was putting away his kit, rinsing his face with a little water from his canteen before he would fill it up again in the evening after boiling water. Braddach turned around to see King Erold had entered his tent.

"I want to apologize for not speaking more over the summer, Patr," said Erold quietly, "Second, if you haven't heard directly, you likely heard indirectly that there is a fight coming." Erold crossed his hands and shrugged.

"Yes, I've heard." Braddach thought it looked strange that Erold didn't have a weapon on him after almost never seeing him without one in Cardane after they had been promoted to the Elite Guard. He watched as Erold seemed to sway nervously back and forth, "Are you coming for my advice?"

"Yes, something like that."

"What is it then?"

"I'm growing concerned that we should have retreated. I put it to a vote of the generals, and it was overwhelmingly in favor of direct engagement from Umfell. But, I would have voted for the retreat, and it still makes more sense to me. The argument is that this was a defensible position, but we have an additional force at Gulldalr that could make us stronger and there will be other defensible positions."

"Erold, I'm not going to pretend to be a master of the battlefield, but I will say this, if you believe that there is a road to take, whether battle or retreat, even if it is the unpopular decision, your men will follow you."

Braddach put his hand on his brother's shoulder, "Now, go spend your Frostmas with that lady friend of yours."

"Archmage Cherene?" asked Erold.

"Yes, that one."

"You think she's interested?"

"More than a little interested," said Braddach. "I've got my own group to attend to as well. Fros walks with you."

"And with you."

They hugged and parted ways with Erold leaving the tent first and heading back to his own. As Braddach left his tent, he saw Nido waiting for him.

"What was the king talking to you about?"

"Nothing," said Braddach, "Let's go eat. I heard one of the Stens bought fresh lamb."

"That he did," replied Nido as they found their squad already enjoying the lamb leg and ribs, flavored with salt and olive oil that had been brought in from the Erstber's valley over the previous week.

Braddach sliced off a bit of lamb leg and then held it over the fire stabbed through with a stick. Arne showed him how to get the salt on it by digging it in with his fingers. Braddach waived him off and touched it himself, joking he didn't know all the places that Arne had stuck his fingers. All the men laughed, because Arne laughed.

Frostmas was a time to spend with friends if not with family and as the quiet night passed, at least this squad was having fun, looking across the fire at each other.

Braddach told another story about being a mercenary. It was one of his proudest moments. He had led a small group of men through the forested lowlands of Verdas. Erold couldn't go that far west, so it was up to him to track the beasts that had lay waste to a village of five thousand souls in eastern Verdas.

He had hunted them across the forest, seeing marks on the trees and ash from fire pits. He found them after they had upended a small village, setting the heads of men, women, and children on stakes out front of the half-demolished wooden palisade like true heathens.

It was a group of ogres and trolls that had moved into Verdas, and they had set their sights on more. He and his men had gutted them like wild boars or domestic pigs that had eaten human babies in their cribs and had thrown their bodies into the ocean to feed the leviathans.

He remembered, too, so vividly the map that they had hand drawn of the places they had intended to hit, banking on the villages, even of five thousand, being too small to be the army's concern, and the police forces too weak to stop them from the account of being too powerful.

* * *

Erold returned to his tent to get the gift that he had bought for Cherene. He had been so wrapped up in the battle planning that he had forgotten to figure out how they would meet or where they would meet to exchange gifts.

He hoped that if she had forgotten that she wouldn't feel badly for not having gotten him anything. If the battle went poorly, bad gifts, good gifts, no gifts didn't matter to him. He had lived a good life.

Now, he was devoting the remainder to a better Normany and through that hopefully a better world. He understood, too, that this was core mission of hers. That's why despite the risk, she was here in Normany rather than safe in Valgaard.

When he was leaving his tent, there she stood with a twinkle in her blue eyes and her blonde hair, let loose, instead of pulled back over her forehead.

"Can I come inside?" she asked.

Erold invited her inside, where the only difference between his tent and any other man's that he had a little table and a chair to write at. He let her sit in the chair while he sat with his legs in front of him on the blankets.

They had been lucky and the day, either one of the last days of the summer or the first days of fall, depending on how the equinox fell, had been warm. During some of the summer, she had foregone the armor of the archmage and had worn, relaxed summer dresses that showed part of her legs and were not as tight or proper as formal evening wear. Tonight, was one of those nights, where she reminded him of a simple, country girl that didn't have battles or wars to tend to.

In that moment, watching her look up at him and back down, softly her teeth over her bottom lip, he didn't care what the 'Emperor' Polesar was doing or much of anyone else besides the two of them.

"I got you this," he said and held before her what had been in his hand, unwrapped. A still life painting of a unicorn that looked as if it was running into the hills. "I know how much like you unicorns."

"Thank you," she said, eyeing him with a slight look of confusion. She had never said anything like that. Not even when she was with him as the princess back in the ice palace. She took a moment, looking at the painting and then tears formed at the edges of her eyes. The absurdity of life that had brought them together and pulled them apart would do it again. She could already feel it whether they lived or died. War and peace, an ebb and flow, of stalling for time, trying to hold love before it left. So many of the men among them, good Frostians like her, young men, had never kissed or hugged their love.

She handed him the gift that she got him. Axe polish.

* * *

Wermack went to Cherene's tent to ask her if she wanted to spend the night together talking about anything at all. He had a little bit to drink, but he felt fine. It had been hard over the summer to get any time in with her, while she spent almost every minute with the king, but it was the holiday. They could dance like they danced together many times before at balls in the palace, but it would be here, under the moonlight as a full moon rose in the night.

When he arrived at her tent, she didn't respond at first, so he peaked inside. Arla was there sleeping alone and Cherene wasn't there. With the sliver of light in the night hitting her eyes, Arla's eyes shot open.

"What are you doing here?"

"Sorry, I was just--"

"I don't need to hear the excuse. Just don't let it happen again," Arla said. "I'm too tired to deal with you right now." She had her own feelings to sort through, and sleep was a wonderful healer.

Wermack meandered through the camp to the king's tent, where though there were sentries posted outside, he could get a glimpse through the flap. Glistening blonde hair in the barest hint of moonlight that bounced through, it was the princess. All of the meetings were not just planning ones after all. Wermack had known it all along, but he had volunteered to lead this cavalry just to get close to her. It seemed, in a way, she had done the same thing for someone else.

* * *

Moon returned to the camp the morning after the Frostmas celebrations, which she had avoided, with dire news about the enemy's troop. She had wished that it had come sooner, when this information would have been helpful for making previous decisions, but ultimately, she wasn't sure it would have made a difference whether they had retreated right away or waited. An immediate retreat could have just meant delaying defeat until Gulldalr. She saw the few men awake already had their packs readied, blankets rolled, and ammo packed as she walked between the tents--heavy weight they would carry wherever they went.

"King Erold," she said at the flap to his tent. He beckoned her inside. He was alone, dressed, and had shaven. His hair was still fairly short after it had been cut in Cardane.

"What is it?" he asked, smiling at first.

"The enemy troop's number is near three hundred and fifty

thousand. They are due to cross into Dalvalles today."

"Three hundred fifty thousand," he said, resting his hand on a chair to stop from falling down. "How did we not know of this sooner?"

"They ran effective cavalry screens making it appear as if the army was making movements south and shipped a force over the river. They are split into two, with one force acting as a main advance and a second unit acting as a reserve."

"We had committed to defending Umfell, and now we could be trapped," he voiced aloud. "The emperor is with them?"

She nodded.

"Three hundred fifty thousand?"

She nodded again.

"Call the generals. We must change the plan immediately to retreat."

"They are already in the hills. We would never escape in time."

"We have no option to fight and win. We must find a way to escape a battle where we could be outnumbered five to one."

"Yes sir," said Moon and left to help gather the force's leadership.

Erold tensed and relaxed. They had gotten stuck relying on faulty assumptions, and they had needed to adapt sooner. But, he was ready to step back on his previous decision and alter course, because there was no way he would commit to a losing battle. By deciding immediately that they were to retreat now, the army could focus on how to conduct the retreat rather than how to most successfully die in battle.

The generals, Cherene, and Arla were quickly dressed and organized around the map in the command center. Moon pointed out that the opposing army was likely forced to take the same path on the west side of the Erstber they had marched through earlier in the year. Erold looked over the field.

"We can still fight," said Eichlen. "We can force them away from the city with our cavalry and defend the walls from any advance that attempts to push close."

"We retreat," said Erold. "In a battle across rivers, we will lose to their artillery."

"Umfell has strong, wide walls and tall keeps."

"Mrs. Moon, how many artillery pieces, did you say that the enemy currently has?"

She stepped forward, "Up to six hundred."

"We retreat," said Erold. "It is now our mission to define how we can still make that happen."

"The army has ensnared us. There is no way we can escape without engagement," said Gavo.

"Looking at the circumstance," said Kutzbek, "I believe that that we must retreat directly west and form up with Blaggard, west of the Práezwa River. It is our only option."

"Most likely not," said Wermack.

"Why not?"

"If he's about to reach the Erstber River to our south, we could be trapped on the North side of Evorul as there are few bridges northwest of here that we didn't build ourselves, and we'd be running deeper into the Evorul mountain range rather than along the hills and plains of Sudryn to our south. Just as you said, we could get caught in the trees."

"Good point Wermack," said Kutzbek, "but, what if we go west and cut back through this pass south of Kaarmekello? We could defend Graabern on the pass and get to Hoenheim or one of the other valleys."

"The other valleys are no good. It's only Hoenheim that makes it all the way through the hills easily."

"We can't take the pass at Kaarmekello either," said Erold.

"Why not?" asked Kutzbek.

"I've walked it. Graabern can't be easily defended. Enemy artillery can easily make it through the pass and can fire on the city from above the walls. A defense of the city is impossible without also holding the pass, and the pass is too wide to risk the engagement."

"I see," said Kutzbek. "Indeed, a western retreat is too risky."

"I agree," said Erold. "We need a new plan." He looked at his generals. "We know these hills better than they do. We know the fastest pass through to the north is through Hoenheim. We've pulled resources out of the Erstber, forcing them to come to us. If we engage them, we are outnumbered by five to one. There is no way we can win a direct engagement without splitting their force."

"Then, it was my mistake to intend to stay and fight," said Wermack.

"It is no mistake unless it can't be corrected," said Erold, "As we expected, the emperor used the Ivanssun holidays to reach us when he thought we would have our guard down. They're at the foot of the hills, and now our plans need to change. We are ready to move, but we need to design an escape plan. Wermack, or anyone else, what are the ideas?"

After a tense pause, Wermack spoke, "the logistics of the field, are as such, he will have to come north of the Evorul, meaning he will put us between him and Akre, right? If we can't go west, is there a way that we can escape to the east side of the river?"

"I believe so," said Doctor Pasan, tentatively.

Erold nodded to him to continue.

"It's hilly terrain, and the river is not easy to cross. There are few bridges until Elklin, and the southbound pass is narrow, the shore heavily forested, and the route defensible. We are assuming he would cross the Erstber for the same reasons we did, and the same reasons he wouldn't expect us to attempt a retreat through the pass. He would have to avoid it naturally due to the size of his troop and the lack of supplies. When he comes north of the Evorul into the natural flood plain to feed troops and cavalry, we could move south."

"He'd be able to sweep through the city in a day," said Borgoron.

"Not necessarily," said Wermack. "If we act like we are defending these key bridges along the river in an effort to hold Umfell as we already appear to be, we could destroy the bridges along the Erstber that we've only partially built. We could force the emperor to meet us at Elklin."

Kutzbek smiled, "Yes, this would allow us to make directly south along the eastern side until the river cuts west as well. If we follow the river to Hoenheim, we could defend the pass through the valley, and if they tried to cut around us through the north or one of the other valleys, they would be delayed."

"How long would it take us to get to Gulldalr?" asked Erold.

"As many as three weeks," said Plaski.

"And for them?" asked Erold.

"We can assume that it would take them nearly as long, especially if their supply line is stretched. Looking at the map in detail, I believe that it would take them more than three weeks to go any route but through the Hoenheim. They may be forced to chase us through there," said Plaski. "The forest is too risky for them, and the other valleys protruding south from the Erstber do not stretch through to the sea. They'd be forced to climb through the hills, which with a pack would be almost impossible and with artillery and horses, would be completely impossible."

"The Gardnor forest will cover our retreat to the north. The hills will cover our retreat to the south. And they could never make it back around through the Solgra in enough time. It would take them more than two weeks to make it to the end of the Hoenheim valley from Umfell going through Godrland. As long as we can get to Hoenheim, we would have a head start in crossing central Gardnor, after which we can hold the bridges at Gulldalr after linking with Blaggard." said Kutzbek, tracing his finger along the map and pressing it firmly at the center of Normany's northern provinces.

"It's settled then," said Erold. "We effect an escape east of the Erstber River to Hoenheim, where they will be forced to pursue us. Therefore, we need a plan to buy time for the escape and we need another to defend the valley."

"I will draft it," said Wermack, glancing at Cherene who was absorbed in thought, "The cavalry will have to work as the rear guard as we can move faster than the infantry. The infantry will have to be the first to vacate Umfell."

"They can't all leave," said Kutzbek, "The emperor will be looking for them in defense of these bridges."

"Yes," said Pasan, "We need to convince him that we are still in Umfell or make him think that we are focusing all of our defense of the key bridges along the Evorul."

"Generals Wermack, Kutzbek, and Pasan."

"Yes, sir."

"The three of you will design the escape plan. We meet back here in an hour to go over what you come up with."

The hour passed tensely with most departing briefly to get water, coffee that had been reserved for the generals, or something to eat.

Before the hour was up, Wermack, Pasan, and Kutzbek had designed a plan of escape from Umfell. Wermack pushed Pasan, the architect of the escape to describe how they were to elude the much larger force and reach the Práezwa where they could link up with Blaggard before re-assessing the field.

"In essence, we've agreed to station rearguard positions with artillery along the retreat route, using the mixed units, operating within the cavalry as the rear guard." Pasan pointed to each of the towns starting at Elklin. "We believe that we will be able to outwit Emperor Polesar, who, as we've said, will have to move his troops north of the Evorul to resupply. To do so, he will have to access these four bridges. The two west of Donworsh and this one at Werentinn and this one at Günz. While appearing to defend these bridges, we will exit the city along the bridge east of the Erstber and south of Umfell. Once he has captured the north of the river, we will already be reinforcing positions at Elklin and throughout the Hoenheim valley. As we've described using the same reasons that we didn't retreat immediately along the Evorul, he will not be able to easily pursue us through the forest in southwest Gardnor."

"How can we be sure he'll take the bait?" asked Plaski.

"We know that he'll have to take his army north of the Evorul anyway. Logistically, the Akrin force will have to forage from the farms, and he can't do that on the south bank. If we present a force to engage him, he has to force his way to the north of the river. This will buy us time, because if we're defending Umfell, he'll expect resistance along the bridges. We can lure him into engagements and effect our retreat once he's committed to taking the northern side."

"And how will the rearguard positions be defended exactly?" asked Borgoron.

"Because, we'll be headed straight south along the Erstber tributary, we only have to make a move to the west once it runs out near the Sudryn's north hills. If we defend the key position at Elklin until it appears that he would have had the time to loop around through the Kaarmekello pass, we can use it as a choke point to prevent the emperor's troop from following us. Once the main rearguard has left Elklin, the cavalry will be the key to the defense of the Hoenheim valley. Because we have emptied the valley of supplies, we believe the enemy's cavalry will be our main opponent until the emperor has been able to fully resupply his forces near Umfell."

"Who will be leading these combined efforts? How many troops will be needed?" Erold asked.

"We believe that we could use five divisions of the infantry spread across the battlefield to create the false active positions for movements on day one and two when the retreat is initiated from Umfell, and we focus on forcing them into concentrated positions at the bridges," said Pasan.

"Then, once we begin the staggered retreat the cavalry will need at least four divisions supporting the infantry at first and then engaging the enemy while the infantry divisions retreat to Elklin," said Wermack and then he swallowed his throat, growing tight and looked at the princess, Cherene. "I plan to lead these detachments in the action."

"And who will lead the infantry?" asked Kutzbek.

"I will," said Kienber. "I will personally head the position at Donworsh, south of the river, on day one to make it look as if we are fully committed to the defense of the bridges. I believe this will help the dragon to chase the fish."

1524 - Chapter 54

On the night of the twenty fifth of Ivanssun, Emperor Polesar's troops reached the Evorul River valley, making camp south of the Evorul and west of the Erstber on the driest ground, with the intention of pursuing action in the morning of the twenty sixth. Erold and Moon spent the evening reviewing battle orders and logistics. The only two, other than Braddach, who knew it was the king's twenty seventh birthday.

The Normany leaders were not certain of how the enemy's attacks were to proceed, but it was clear that Polesar had taken the bait. They expected the attacks as early as the morning of the twenty sixth.

Kienber's men had been placed in Donworsh ahead of the night, and intended to pull west through the day, already covering the bridges and preventing a wide day one flanking maneuver, crossing the Evorul and then the Lechla tributary to encircle both Wermack's position at Werentinn and that of the mixed unit captain, Mael, who held the largest of the bridges, Günz to the east. Braddach waited with Captain Mael ready to hold the line.

Most of the yellow jackets of the men of Normany, along with the bulk of the cavalry, waited restlessly overnight under day one battle orders to pull out of Umfell and cross the Evorul in the east, rushing for Elklin with adequate supplies. Elklin lay empty, but a detachment of artillery and infantry units would later be stationed to await the rest of the retreating force that would pull out through Umfell on the second night.

As the morning broke on the twenty sixth, the emperor and his men began to survey the troop movement of the enemy, recognizing that fortifications had been dug in behind each of the four bridges crossing the Evorul. Polesar could also see that Donworsh, the city ahead of the bridges, held a considerable detachment of defenders as well.

It appeared as if Normany intended to defend the bridges with as many as fifty thousand men. Polesar had intelligence that the enemy had roughly seventy thousand men, whereas his central detachment was over one hundred thousand. Once he moved into the valley, he could attack or wait for his western and eastern pincer movements to arrive in the coming days, trapping the enemy's army at Umfell.

Polesar distributed orders, moving Naven with cavalry and

Ernadsier with infantry, totaling five thousand each, against the enemy's right flank. Once they secured the bridges, they could join the central attack on Donworsh by Davos and Tlous, who would take five thousand infantry each and attempt to take the city.

To prevent a retreat to the east and begin to take the two key bridges at the cities of Werentinn and Günz, Murdot and Tornes would each have a combined ten thousand men, in cavalry and infantry, respectively, to attack Werentinn. To prevent the risk of a cavalry flanking maneuver on the right-hand side, Marandres would take ten thousand in infantry and hold the right flank, watching the Günz bridge route. The emperor's remaining force would lie in wait to attack on the successive day or be sent in for a final blow if the enemy attempted to break out from Günz.

Shortly after noon, the Akrin motions were effected. Naven and Murdot's cavalries charged first. As the battle began, word was passed through to Umfell and the yellow army began to pull south along the bridge across the Evorul, east of the Erstber River, racing for Elklin with the cavalry at the rear.

Kienber watched the movements of the enemy troop and communicated with his officers. They were to engage the infantry from afar, using the vacated buildings as cover and then pull west toward the bridges, supporting the false positions west of the Lechla.

Kienber recognized Davos and Tlous, both summoners and once Akrin academy mates, leading the charge on him at Donworsh. The cavalries hit the right flank at the northwestern most bridge and pushed at the bridge in Werentinn at roughly the same time. Kienber could hear the guns of horse and infantry ring out through the cool air of early fall while he watched the line of men form up and begin their own rush on the city.

"First line, fire on my mark, and then disengage! Easy now, easy now," Kienber watched as the men began to run, led by mage's holding their swords forward, who began to fall slightly behind the line as faster runners pushed ahead.

Kienber had never revealed to Davos or Tlous what he fully could do, and he was sure they did not know that he had returned to his parents' homeland to fight for his people. He stood on the makeshift rampart and issued blasts of fire and lightning, casting echoing bolts from his fingertips shattering the air and pulverizing earth and men. The opposing mages scattered, readying their own bolts to send back.

"Fire!"

The first line fired, then retreated and reloaded. Kienber watched as some of the enemy mages fell while others struck back with their own furious spells, bolts of all kinds, colored green, red, yellow, blue, and white, striking at the walls of the buildings his men had vacated.

"Second line, fire!"

Despite the blasts ringing out as the enemy infantry began to near the city, Kienber issued forth another of his own vicious salvos, attacking the very ground on which they ran, sending shattered earth into the sky with fireballs. His second line retreated the third line readied.

"Third line! Fire and retreat!"

Blasts were issued forth from the mages, reaching windows and nooks while the third line, hidden by the clouds of smoke, attempted to take advantage of the break in defense and strike them down with muskets setting black powder ablaze in fury. As soon as the shots had been sent forth, the third line redoubled, crossing where the first line had regrouped and then the second, before settling at the edge of town for the first group to issue over the bridge.

Davos and Tlous reached the city limits as Normany's first line turned their backs, sending forth fully formed creatures to attack the escaping men. Kienber burst the figments with his own bolts and set a line of the ground on fire, hindering his old classmates' advance.

As his men retreated, he saw that his lieutenants that had held the bridge were engaged in a direct fight against Naven and Ernadsier. To cover the retreat of his two divisions, single divisions and his best men, had remained at the bridges to check any advance on the northwest.

Naven and the lieutenant traded blows until finally Naven pushed the lieutenant's fiery spell toward the frost and freeing a hand rung out a vicious mage's spear that split the young lieutenant in half. Now two on one, Ernadsier and Naven made quick work of the other lieutenant who could not equal the furious array of aura blasts that pecked at him until he was checkered with melted flesh.

As Ernadsier and Naven turned toward him, Kienber sent forth a simple illusion spell, making it appear as if time had stopped for his opponents. It was a spell that only worked on the unsuspecting and it was the last of his stamina, but it allowed Kienber to pull his men back to the bridge and reinforce the leaderless positions. When the spell wore off, the enemy infantry began to issue forth in waves, attempting to cross the stone bridge. Bodies of Ernadsier's infantry began to pile in fives and tens with each advance as the day waned on. Kienber promoted two mages and had them aid in the defense of the bridges while he rested, his fingertips, now gloved, marked black by his overuse of spells.

Before Davos and Tlous had ensured that Donworsh was secure, fighting had erupted in Werentinn. Murdot's cavalry had run into the heavy cavalry from Valgaard. Having never seen unicorn cavalry before, they were completely unprepared for Wermack fighting ahead of the bridge in a brutally effective countercharge.

Despite outnumbering the forest green Valgaardians at least two to one, the pressure of the heavy assault was as if a steel wall forty inches thick had been thrown forward across the field at him. Murdot was forced to regroup with Tornes's infantry before they could push Wermack's cavalry back to the bridge.

As Wermack pushed forward, Marandres made the odd move to push further toward the right flank and Günz. When Braddach saw this, he alerted Mael. If the enemy got too close to the Erstber, they would be able to see the retreating bulk of the yellow army streaming out of Umfell toward Elklin.

After a tense afternoon, only hearing the battle raging to their northwest, Braddach urged Mael to put the artillery ahead of the bridge south of Günz to attempt to scare off Marandres's advance. Mael agreed to the maneuver, and they pushed the howitzers forward, recognizing the push of the heavy cavalry's advance would ensure their right flank could not be immediately overrun. The artillery began to fire on Marandres's infantry, which pulled back into a defensive position as the day's light began to fade.

Wermack pulled north of the Evorul before Tlous could flank his cavalry unit, which had suffered almost no losses in the day one engagement. As he crossed the bridge and the enemy made one final advance at Werentinn, the infantry on the north side of the bridge issued forth musket fire. Before the enemy could push at Günz, Mael had his men pull back.

The yellow army had almost escaped, but they would need to walk through most of the night to almost reach Elklin. As the Akrin force began to pull back into a forward camp on the south side of the river and the waning moon rose, Kienber ordered his troops to burn fires to make it look like they were digging in, while in fact they were to move in the night, vacating the false fortifications, to the bridge over the Lechla, covering Werentinn's right flank and joining the contingents at Werentinn and Günz as reserves for day two fighting.

Wermack stood on the ramparts of Werentinn, watching the movement in the night, checking to see if the bath of moonlight that had lit the darkness in silver would alert the enemy to their troop movement. He also checked across the field, recognizing that the enemy would likely push from Donworsh to Werentinn in the early morning with the combined forces he had faced on day one, attacking again.

Before the morning of the second day broke, Wermack woke his men and had them line the fortifications placed north of the bridge. Kienber simultaneously switched out the night guard for men on little sleep, who would have to watch the Lechla River bridge. He sent an adjutant to Wermack to let him know of Davos and Tlous and that he could reinforce his position with as many as five thousand men, but Wermack held the adjutant.

With ten thousand men of his own, many who had only fired one round, he felt he could hold the bridge. He was also worried about Günz, where Mael only had two divisions. Despite being where they had their only artillery detachment, he felt that a concerted push on that flank would be devastating as it could cut off their only route of retreat.

As the morning light lit the field, turning the clouds of foggy white, yellow and red with a wash of color, the dark blue and white of the Akrin uniforms were already in motion. Naven and Ernadsier crossed the bridges, at first tentatively, and then at full steam, echoing cheers and rushing to hungrily raid the farms for food and supplies despite Naven and Ernadsier yelling orders and wanting them to hit the bridge over the Lechla.

This would prove fortuitous for the Normany yellow as the combined forces of Tlous, Davos, Tornes and Murdot attacked Werentinn in full. Wermack's men held the line for most of the morning as the oncoming infantry began to push bodies of fallen comrades over the bridge and into the water, but as the enemy added artillery to the onslaught, Wermack's own infantry had to pull further away from the river, allowing the enemy to begin pressing into the city as the battle shifted from standard lines to a firefight with knived muskets from door to door where battles in doorways were private struggles for life.

Sensing he was being overrun, Wermack ordered the adjutant to Kienber but too late. The adjutant was halved by a mage blast arched into the city by the attackers. Kienber recognizing that the fighting had neared to their rear at Werentinn moved his force of ten thousand into the city, abandoning the post on the Lechla River, which the enemy had disappeared from.

Wermack and his second in command led the resistance as mages on foot after he sent his cavalry to Günz on orders to retreat with the men there if he was not to return by dusk. As soon as an infantry position was established by the attackers over the bridge, Murdot's cavalry charged into the city, despite the shelling of their own men and the crossfire in the streets.

As Wermack watched his men die around him, pulled apart by mage's fire, struck down by shrapnel, or sniped indirectly by random musket fire in the street, he saw that the enemies lead mages had sought him out.

Murdot, Tlous, Davos, and Tornes, though he did not know their names, advanced on him through the central city, holding back musket fire and tearing through his men.

Wermack nodded to his second in command. Although a two on four battle would be difficult, he believed in the training of the Valgaardian academies.

They stepped out into the street, sending forth mage's spears at their adversaries. Murdot caught and broke them in the air while Tlous and Davos summoned dreaded giant beasts of the deep forests and Tornes sent mage's spears of his own.

Wermack and his second stopped the spears, but the raging beasts tore through their own spells and had he not stepped out of the way the snarling figment, it would have torn him to mere pieces. He looked over to see that his second was only a shred of clothing and a splatter of blood, leaving behind just his shoes and legs below the ankles.

Wermack hid in the door frame, screaming in frustration and recognizing that it was his time to die. He had volunteered for this mission just for this reason. He readied to enter the fray when Kienber's men arrived.

The force of ten thousand swung the field in the favor of Werentinn's four thousand and a few hundred remaining defenders, and Kienber's fire and lightning, a furious burst of a thousand strikes, forced the opposing mages back as their men too regrouped at the head of the bridge. Kienber picked Wermack up. He ordered the retreat on behalf of Wermack, and the men pulled out of Werentinn in the same staggered retreat as the day before, heading for Günz, where Braddach and Mael were also at risk of being overrun.

Mael unleashed a fury of white aura fire, but Marandres batted the spells away. The infantry had powered forward throughout the day, eventually taking the bridge despite heavy artillery bombardment, before Braddach had gone on an aggressive counter-offensive with the aid of the heavy cavalry from Werentinn, taking the wide, stone bridge back and forcing Marandres's men back to the south side of the river.

The Akrin force renewed the attack once more in the after noon hours, attacking Braddach harshly for over-extending away from his artillery cover. He had ordered a successful retreat, but now, the battle had become a mage's duel across the lines while four squads of eleven, two squads on each side engaged. The bloodthirsty Marandres and an Akrin lieutenant dueled both Braddach and Mael, sending their efforts back at them like ricochets while their ten men squads fought hard against the attackers, their spells bouncing into each other, preventing either side from gaining advantage until Marandres's third and fourth squads began to appear north of the bridge.

Nido sent forth a massive pile of city rubble, temporarily forcing their opponent's back, but the enemy mages appeared through the haze unphased. In a two on one fight across lines, Braddach believed he would have to be the difference. After the fight had developed, he felt that he was the only one who had any real command of spells. He threw down a warlock gate spell to seal off the enemy for a moment and buy them some time to regroup.

Braddach pulled his men together and began barking orders, drawing a map of the battlefield on his hand. As they went their separate routes, the retreating force led by Kienber and Wermack arrived. Kienber's power was undeniable as he sent blazing arcs of fire through the sky that snaked toward their prey like mini-dragons, consuming mages alive, leaving them husks of humans, smoldering into dust. Those who could protect themselves in time like Marandres retreated south of the bridge as the onslaught of Wermack's soul fire spears and Kienber's intense fire magic continued.

Dusk neared and the four leaders of the Normany forces met in the ruins of a home, the inside cratered out and black, the family having thankfully abandoned it to move north despite the coming frost of fall.

"They took the bridge twice today," said Mael, "We must hold out another day."

"We can't," said Wermack. "The rest of the army is away. We need to move tonight to Elklin. I have already ordered the cavalry to start their retreat as night falls."

As they spoke, the yellow army, having left a detachment of artillery at Elklin had already made it to Odinheim, just through the entrance to the Hoenheim Valley, and would have begun their march, considering the amount of food they had vacated from the Erstber River valley in advance of the fight. Now, they sent the people ahead of them to the north, knowing this would be the only way they could check the Akrin advance.

At the same time, Polesar met with his leaders, and discussed that the battles appeared won. Three cities in two days. He gleefully announced that the engagements were clearly decisive in their favor, having won the battles of Donworsh, Werentinn, and soon Günz bridge. They would have the opportunity to attack Umfell in the coming days. He would move his camp the following day north of the Evorul and west of the Lechla.

Wermack explained that Werentinn was completely overrun and under enemy control. Kienber explained that he had abandoned the Lechla in favor of defending Werentinn, but they were forced to retreat. In the morning, they would surely be surrounded by men on the north bank without being able to narrow their lines on the bridges.

"We've done all that we can. They went for the bait. We saw them move north of the Evorul, across from the Lechla River this morning," said Kienber, ignoring the pain in his hands. "We must move out as soon as night falls."

"The men will be tired," warned Mael, recognizing that the long day of fighting coupled with pushing and pulling their howitzers would leave them drained.

"It must be done," said Wermack, realizing that they had to push through exhaustion or die. They could shoot a gun tired, but they couldn't dead.

As the leaders dispersed to issue the orders, Wermack pulled Braddach aside, "Braddach, I lost most of my squad today. Will you join me as my second in command?"

"Gladly," Braddach said.

"Good, we can make it a formal promotion when we reach Gulldalr," said Wermack.

Kienber's men followed the cavalry to Elklin while Braddach and Wermack's infantry held the rear, pulling the howitzers by horse behind them, heading to Elklin, defeated but successful in having dodged total defeat. The waning gibbous of the moon hung in the air above them until the clouds rolled in and the retreat was covered in rain that as the night continued, turned to powdery snow, filtering down in thick, wet snowflakes the size of a child's palm.

As they went, the dull, yellow of the oil-lit lanterns appeared far in the distance, beckoning the weary men, on less than four hours of sleep over two days, to Elklin. Hand signals and calls were made in the dark and they were let into the city, where they could warm themselves in the empty houses left behind by fleeing civilians. Many slept despite their desire to not die in their sleep lest they be attacked.

Wermack told Kienber to move as soon as his men were able into the Hoenheim valley and begin laying any additional foundations for its defense. The captains, Mael, Etros, and Sefri would be setting up positions at the towns throughout the valley to help with same style of retreat that Kienber had already successfully deployed twice.

Wermack told him that if their rear guard could buy the larger army two more weeks, they could safely believe that they had made it to Gulldalr without issue. Kienber warned Wermack about Naven, who he didn't say that he recognized but he mentioned was a vicious killer who would not fight according to any preconceived rules of engagement.

It snowed on and off for the better part of four days while the men waited on the walls of Elklin for any sign of a force approaching along the bank. Wermack began to fear that they were being looped around, but on the first of Narsi-eld, the enemy finally appeared on horseback. A cavalry division appeared to be scouting for the Normany force along the bank when Wermack ordered the artillery upon them as soon as he noticed that they were doubling back. They had crossed within a comfortable range, but he had hoped to trap them in the city between the houses and annihilate the complete force. A move that he would never have risked or considered had he not suddenly felt as if he and his men were fighting against extermination.

Naven retreated his cavalry beyond the artillery line and then sent his men to attempt to light the city's front gate on fire. The muskets from the wall rang out against the advancing dragoon units who fired back and hopped off onto the rocky sides of the roads, trading fire back at the walls of the city while other members of the light cavalry rushed at the wall, attempting to permanently break the defensive hold. When they rounded the winding road, they found themselves checked by pickets that while they were easily removed, temporarily hampered their advance as shells continued to ring out from the artillery within the walls breaking against the stone road below, sending horses and men tumbling into the river or collapsing into heaps. Horses whinnied and men cried out in death.

Naven called a retreat and for the next day, there was no sign of enemy movement. On the following morning, Naven appeared with the cavalry again, supported by howitzers that rained fiery shells against the city's outer wall, demolishing it and setting its remains ablaze. Mages and horses attacked the wall, while Braddach and Wermack held them back, fighting off blast, bolt and bullet with the men at their side.

They may have had the higher ground, but the howitzers could easily exceed a forty-five-degree angle to fire from below along the high arc, while remaining out of range of Wermack's own artillery units that proved only able to check the advance of the enemy's fast-moving cavalry.

The wooden palisade burned, shells continued to rain upon them, and cavalry charged and sent blasts against the wall before slipping back toward the road and behind their lines. Wermack looked up at the sky, wondering how it was that they could win the war as he considered their next move.

"Braddach, we have to abandon the city tonight."

"They haven't been able to breach the walls," said Braddach sending fire down from a perch atop the rubble with his hands, beginning to feel the tingle and burn of over exertion on his fingertips, and wondering whether he'd be willing to force fire from them if he must. The realization of the desperation of fighting for an entire country of people, who had left their homes emptied rather than live another day under the empire, made him think carefully about what his own comfort meant.

"They will tomorrow, and it could be that they've sent another cavalry detachment around the Graabern pass. If it takes only three days hard ride from Umfell, then they would be at Hoenheim tomorrow cutting us off."

The two sides continued to fight through the early evening until the sun had set beyond the ability for either side to continue in the frigid cold that had begun to settle in as the frost of fall came to Normany. The enemy had left most of the wall an impassable pile of rubble, but the gate had stood firm and the Normany yellow and the

Valgaardian green, now well intermixed had pulled back to the inner fortifications that encircled the city's church, waiting while the artillery continued to hammer into the approaching darkness until they were sure that the enemy's advance on Elklin had halted.

Despite the partial success, the battle was lost. They abandoned Elklin in the night, setting fire to extra supplies and leaving the gates to the city barricaded, hoping to buy themselves time in the morning to have made it safely to Nordlind, where Captain Mael would have been installed with artillery and infantry, ready to cover their retreat by waiting for the enemy, engaging them where the valley thinned before retreating in the night passed the next line, just as they did now in Elklin.

In the morning, Naven threw aside the doors in a blast powered by frustration. He wanted the heads of the mages that had stymied him for three days, preventing him from being the first general to catch the next scent of the Normany army after they had disappeared without a trace from Umfell, their tracks hidden in the snow.

Naven got on his horse and raced after the retreating men like hounds following the barest scent of them on the soft morning wind. His horse neighed under him as if complaining, and his men followed suit, pushing hard across the ground, turned rock-like by frost, passed smoldering ruins beside many pristine buildings where all life had been emptied before them. Every one of them felt the eeriness of the ghost town and the desire to steal a peak at the hidden treasures left behind.

The thundering hooves could be heard by Wermack, Braddach, and their mixed unit as they turned into the Hoenheim valley and neared Odinheim. After that, it was even still a bit of a march to Nordlind and Mael on open ground. With the artillery and few men, they could be wiped out by the potential size of an Akrin charge. They had no time to build fortifications along the hills or to try to dig the artillery into defensive positions.

Braddach's heart raced. So far none of his mage squad had been injured, and his infantry unit had remained largely intact but being outnumbered by cavalry was a deadly proposition and no matter how lucky they had been that luck could run out. He looked to Nido and to Frof and counted the hours ticking away on his watch as they pressed onward, hoping to reach sight of Nordlind soon, having just passed Odinheim.

Wermack's perception of days had been accurate. Naven's cavalry would not have been able to catch them before they reached the narrowing pass at Nordlind, but it wasn't Naven's unit that rounded the entrance to the Hoenheim valley after the mixed unit of yellow, blue, and green. It was Murdot's, dressed in cleaned dark blue and white and appearing at the top of the hilly entrance to the valley, with the high sun shining down on them, ready to descend on the small, retreating troop, after having cut through the pass to Graabern.

Wermack thought through the numbers of his men. There was the infantry division and most of their reserve artillery units that were meant to defend the end of the pass at Snajrberg. He had two divisions of rear-guard cavalry with him, and the two other cavalry divisions had been split between the valley positions. Although they were close to Nordlind, he wasn't sure that even if they made it, they could hold back a charge by the force he could see just barely in the distance behind them.

The more he thought about it, the more he believed that the infantry and artillery could never make it to Nordlind unless he defended them. He ordered the cavalry to turn around and the infantry to continue.

"What are you doing?" asked Braddach.

"Buying you time."

"You'll never survive a direct charge against a larger force," said Braddach.

"We are the stronger cavalry," said Wermack banging on the metal of the unicorn's armor. However, even Braddach knew that the unicorns were tired and this was an act of desperation, not one of clear mind.

"We have to push for Nordlind," said Braddach as he continued to ride ahead, while Wermack slowly fell into the distance. He doubled back, still urging his men to continue. Nido fell into his place in the line, directing traffic.

"Captain Braddach, if I don't make it back, you're in charge of the rear guard," said Wermack.

"This is insane," said Braddach. "Don't do this."

Wermack looked off into the distance and bit back his nostalgia for home, "It's hard to watch the person you love the most in the world, love someone else, isn't it?"

He kicked off the unicorn's stride and the five thousand men rounded around him, ready to ride. Braddach directed the men forward, straining to not get caught watching the battle unfold himself. Soon, they were behind a rocky outcropping as the valley turned almost due west and Nordlind was in sight with a friendly, blank yellow flag raised over the town that blocked their path through the valley completely.

Five thousand unicorns charged against ten thousand horses, but this time Murdot was ready, and again he had the higher ground, using it differently for this battle to match his speed against their charge, hoping to offset the difference in size of the beasts. The two cavalries clashed in the snapping fire of pistol and rifle, in the silver clang and clash of sword, the swift thrust of pike through steel and bone, and the whistling cry of mage's spear and bolt.

Wermack and his men circled around, unsure of the damage done to the other side, but it was clear that he had lost a considerable number of men and beast. He signaled the retreat and began to ride forward intending to help defend his men as they worked to disengage.

Murdot noticed this, and he didn't want to let his quarry go easily. He reformed his lines and pursued, eventually falling a few atomic yards behind Wermack trading spells. Wermack shot each of his bolts out of the air, but Murdot saw clearly that he kept looking forward to check his distance between oncoming objects as they rounded the town of Odinheim, in whose fields the battle had been quickly fought.

Wermack looked forward catching Murdot's spell in the air with his own as if two swords clashing, but Murdot let his go and then threw it on again, dodging Wermack's defense and slicing him through the shoulder of his armor and watching the general slump and fall from his horse, his arm almost completely severed. Murdot saw the look of shock on Wermack's face, the last life of his dying breath disappearing.

As the rest of his men escaped to Nordlind, he cast a spell to light a fire of the valley. Murdot silenced him, watching the green and gold general die at his feet. The rider's unicorn came at him, and he killed it too, watching the pearly white beast crumple into the snow softened grass beside Wermack.

Braddach led the troops into Nordlind and awaited Wermack's return. When he didn't return with what was left of the cavalry, he ordered them to move through the city, and they departed through the deserted town. Braddach informed Captain Mael that he'd likely be attacked by cavalry soon.

As he walked through the valley, now void of life, he found flour that had been spilled over the ground and trodden on, grain that had been mixed with feces and anything else that could be used by Akrin that didn't easily burn, stained by piss.

Looking at the men of the rear guard, he saw somber faces and the dire sense of foreboding destruction hung over them more than the smells of decay. All he had to do was get to Snajrberg with the remnants of Wermack's corps, but he also knew that he had three more towns including Snajrberg to walk through that would have been left in shambles as the people of Dalvalles scorched the land behind them on their way north with the yellow army. He wished that he had something more to give them than just be passing through.

After the victory at Odinheim, Murdot and Naven regrouped together as the advance force. They rested a day in Odinheim, having trouble keeping the troops from trying to loot the abandoned houses. Neither could understand why the men of Normany would leave their towns and cities rather than welcome them as the heroes of the republic.

Murdot and Naven had both fought successive battles, but as Murdot had fought at Odinheim, Naven eagerly argued that he should be the one to attack the rear guard at Nordlind. The next day Naven's units attacked Nordlind as he had attacked Elklin, with a combination of artillery, mage power and his light cavalry, dismounting and mounting depending on where he was trying to assault.

Finally, he was able to break through the wall by focusing fire and digging through the rampart. Naven marched forward to engage the Captain, Mael, of the city's guard in a fierce mage duel. Whatever he threw at Mael, however, the captain defended and delivered back in full. Naven hoped that he would be able to outnumber the defenders in mages, but the narrowness of the pass prevented him from putting too many mages forward, allowing the defenders to pick off some of his best.

While mage's spears flew, Mael's guard had re-barricaded the hole in the wall. Musket blasts rained down on Naven's troop, and he was forced back away from the wall, relying again on his artillery to force off the defenders.

Muskets fired from the tops of the low makeshift walls and his men fired back, but the distances between them had become too great to cause any real damage. The walls were little more than mounds of packed dirt and clay, but they kept softening his artillery blasts and the defenders prevented successive mage's fire from taking them down.

As the day grew long, it became clear that the defenders had held the day and forced Naven to redouble his effort in the morning. When he returned after the sun had risen, the enemy had yet again left the town in the night, and though it was technically a victory, he felt the sting of defeat having lost more men than his opponent possibly could have and then finding the desolate town trashed as the enemy fled before him.

Braddach passed through Langholm, Brechtinn, and dug in at the hilltop that connected the Hoenheim valley to Snajrberg. A few days after he arrived, Captain Mael passed through with most of his men, heading for Gulldalr in the north. He left behind his few artillery pieces.

Having successfully defended Nordlind, his men were happy, and the captain believed they had surely put the Akrin army behind him. They'd be foolish to risk an attack further north into Normany after almost a month of fall would have passed before they could even have left Dalvalles.

Braddach listened, but he didn't agree. He had seen the zealous attack by the Akrin force, and he had a feeling, ice age or not, the enemy sought a complete victory before there was the risk Normany's new king could gain any more substantial support.

After another day of rest and the increasing difficulty in finding supplies to feed their horses had forced Murdot to temporarily double back and then send for help from the Evorul valley, where Polesar was still determining how best to move his forces through Dalvalles, Murdot attacked Langholm.

Langholm was a much wider town than Nordlind. Here, the buildings were built up into the rocky walls of the valley. This proved to be an advantage for the attackers despite their cavalry not being able to advance on the rocky hills of the town, because as infantry, they could spread the defenders' shots wide and then push a concentrated force through the middle.

Murdot's dismounted troops advanced along the walls of the valley toward the homes and barricades while his cavalry rushed the center attempting to envelope the defenders in pockets on either side of the central city.

Before they could be surrounded, the defender's captain announced a retreat and pulled a contingent from the fleeing line to block the advance of the cavalry in the street. With successful wizardry, the squadron of mages and infantry sent the infantry back, but they soon became in danger of being flanked while Murdot himself advanced down the middle of the field.

Captain Etros was flinging mage's spears through axes while his men were alternating fire lines on the enemy, encircling him when he saw Murdot. He sent his men away while his mage squadron defended his flanks. The captain took steps back as Murdot approached slowly.

Etros threw a spear. Murdot broke it in the air, shattering the oncoming bolt into pieces with the flick of his wrist. Murdot imagined that Etros was using these spells to conserve energy over time, but he would have a hard time defending against him if that was all that he had.

Etros ordered his mage squadron to retreat, and Murdot wondered for a moment if the captain was planning to surrender to him. When Murdot neared, Etros began to power up. Murdot sent a flurry of blasts at him, but Etros's pure energy field turned the balls to dust.

Etros unleashed a hailstorm all around him of blasts of the same yellow energy. Many of Murdot's men were caught in the tornado of death, but Murdot caught much of it in his own field of static force, obliterating the attack before it neared him, turning it into barely the whisper of the wind.

When Etros stopped his attack, he panted, tired, and fell to his knees. He looked up at Murdot, unscathed, surprised that he was still alive. Murdot placed a mage's spear through the man's heart and watched as life left his eyes.

Braddach watched from atop the high valley, unable to see what went on at Langholm, but knowing the battle likely raged across the valley. Each town had been quiet and abandoned with only enough food for his troop and cavalry left behind on Snajrberg hill.

By the condition, he worried that he might have been gaining on the main army, which might not have even made it to Gulldalr yet. If he could hold the enemy at Snajrberg for more than a day, he could almost certainly ensure that Normany would have been able to regroup in Gulldalr.

Despite the success of Nordlind, they couldn't have held out any longer, so it was up to Braddach and the design of his artillery placements and hillside defenses to buy the main army the rest of time it needed to combine into one force. As the retreating forces from Langholm had passed through Brechtinn and were on their way up the circuitous route to the top of the hill where Braddach watched over the field, the new captain noticed that Etros hadn't made it.

After another day of rest, the Akrin's advance guard, now led by Naven pushed forward through the valley, reaching Brechtinn on Narsi-eld, the tenth.

Naven was itching for the fight. Having already participated in most of the seven engagements that had occurred during Polesar's initial campaign to open the end of the war, he had yet to be awarded commendation for victory by the emperor.

When he neared Brechtinn, Naven recognized the enemy's strategy to draw them in and force an engagement that favored the defenders. Naven marched his cavalry forth, forcing the enemy to dislodge from their forward positions.

When the enemy regrouped throughout the town to try to engage the cavalry from covered positions, Naven did not pursue into the city to engage in close quarters. Instead, he secured the edge of the town and then pulled his mages to the high ground, defended by the infantry.

He would not lose again, so once his cavalry had vacated the entrance to the city, he and his men began to launch fireballs onto the wooden homes, ordering his men to do the same. The Akrin force threw blast after blast at the town until almost every building had been set ablaze.

Once they had pushed the infantry back, it was easy to reach the buildings with these arcing attacks, and the effect was devastating. Naven watched men run from the burning buildings and the tornadoes of fire, cascading through the town's streets caught them in flame, melting even the clothes that they wore.

Naven couldn't be certain how many had retreated, but in the morning, the entire town had been reduced to nothing but rubble and the path through to the end of the valley was clear.

Braddach saw the flames of Brechtinn in the distance after straining to hear musket fire ring out during the day. When the survivors--more than simply a retreating rear guard--came through, Sefri was not among them, and the men who did pass through, described the horrible bombardment that had lain waste to the village.

Many of the men had been in the town, but thankfully, most of the troop had started the retreat when the blasts had started to fall. None could imagine how many mages or how many blasts it had taken to reduce a town to unrecognizable rubble, and all were happy they and civilians weren't there.

Braddach waited on top of the hill above Snajrberg for two days and two nights, prepared for battle with Nido, Frof, the Stens, Sven, Patr D, Arne, Ivan, Avael, and Honter. They had barricaded the pass, prepared extra lines of magical defense and set up the artillery with a wide view of Hoenheim valley, spruce trees and cliff-like facades of the hill, blocking the top from direct attack from the valley below.

The enemy would have to climb up through the pass, winding through the forested edges of the valley, which itself ran close beside a rocky vertical façade on either side. One up and out of the valley and one, down into the valley, which had already had its fair share of blood spilled.

On day three, the morning of the thirteenth of Narsi-Eld, Murdot attacked with his cavalry. The artillery on the hill fired in response, and so did Braddach's mages. In two lines of five, they alternated throwing aura balls back at the enemy like the fire balls they'd heard were used on Brechtinn.

For the mages who did not have fire as a particular strength like Nido and Frof, they threw a different combination of spells down upon their foes. Nido chose lightning and Frof chose ice, while Patr D threw giant rock arrows pulled from the frost.

Murdot's men had trouble breaking for the hill, but when they did get closer, the remaining detachment of cavalry under Braddach, combined with his infantry, hidden by the pines and the shape of the hills, met them at the hill's base. Murdot's cavalry had gone from dodging fire to being thrust into the thick of battle just when they had felt they had escaped the onslaught from the hilltop.

Murdot tried to send spears up at the defenders on the hill, but Braddach knocked them away, sending some of his own back. He caught a number of the standard cavalry but failed to hit Murdot who retreated.

The next morning, on the fourteenth, Naven led his mixed unit of cavalry and artillery to attack Braddach's position. The defenders had banked on the steepness of the ascent and the relative shallowness of the valley below, helping to limit the damage of Naven's howitzers, which they had seen in action at Elklin.

The plan worked as the enemy's shot ricocheted into the edge of the façade, which the defenders' guns were able to fire over from far behind. The enemy's howitzers turned their guns to shoot then on the cavalry and infantry still stationed below, but before they could fire Braddach threw down a wide gate spell with all his might, sealing off his retreating men from the onslaught. The spirit gate stopped some of the shells and slowed others before it flickered out under the intense barrage of the howitzers.

Braddach's heavy cavalry passed through, leaving for the town of Snajrberg, while his infantry division hunkered down on the hill awaiting the enemy advance, hidden from the view of the valley by the trees. Naven's cavalry pushed forward more confidently as the mage's blasts from the hill slowed. Braddach could see that Naven himself, who he knew as the lead mage, had held back from the advance, avoiding the artillery.

When the cavalry broke through the line of fire from the artillery and mages on the hill, they began to make an unchecked charge up the hill. When a sufficiently large contingent had passed Braddach's men, the infantry began to fire their muskets on them toward the top of the hill in covered ambush, shocking the horses and riders, shredding them with bullets and sending the crazed beasts in mad dashes into and off the alternate facades. Some of the yellow jacketed men reloaded to fire again, while others charged at fallen riders, wearing dark blue, with knived muskets, finishing them off on the ground.

Seeing the confusion and not being able to see what caused it, Naven ordered an immediate retreat. Concurrently, Braddach sent word to the infantry to finish the ascent up the hill and rendezvous and alert the cavalry that they were heading for Gulldalr.

The cavalry would act as the rear guard with Braddach after he retreated following at least one more day if they could make it. The enemy had been unprepared for his battlefield maneuvers and had expected similar resistance to the previous valley towns, whereas Braddach, though he may have had less time to prepare, had a better position to check any enemy advance. Braddach checked the amount of shells that he had and believed that he had at least one more day of firing.

Before morning broke on the fifteenth, Murdot and Naven had already made the cavalry movements and were streaming up the hill as Braddach got the artillery to start firing and adjustments were made to where his mages would defend. Frof iced the floor of the path and the last of the infantry attached to the artillery awaited Naven and Murdot's cavalry.

When the cavalry saw the ice they peeled back their charge, but a pair of horses went down before the others retreated under a barrage from Braddach's infantry.

Braddach had his remaining infantry fire at will at the retreating force, while he waited to see what the enemy mages would do.

He ordered his lines of mages to fire on the advancing forward march in the valley of what looked like a substantial portion of Polesar's army. An infantry detachment and additional cavalry gushed toward the hill. Braddach's artillery continued to fire on them, but there were too few guns to make a significant impact.

The traffic at the bottom of the hill from the retreating cavalry gave the defenders a moment of time. Braddach threw out another gate spell, waiting for the infantry advance and the enemy's mages.

Braddach ordered one of his lines of five, including Nido and Frof, to form on him. The opposing mages tried to melt the ice but found that the gate had sealed them temporarily. The move alerted Braddach and the infantry to their presence, and muskets popped as bullets whizzed toward the seal as it faltered.

Frof, Nido, and Braddach worked together with efficiency to cast ground spells in defense, ice spells in attack, and mage's spears as well as the basic shield spell to prevent the enemy's strikes to land while Braddach's infantry continued to fire. Soon, night drew in, and Murdot and Naven pushed their men forward to attack again.

Braddach had the men count the bullets and shells, recognizing that they were running out of both. A mage's spear split one of Braddach's infantry men in half beside him.

When Murdot and Naven appeared, Braddach called Frof and Nido to him. The trio on the hill could only see Murdot and Naven due to the fires on the trees, and the spells that glowed on their hands.

Murdot threw a mage's spear. Braddach blocked it with the simple shield spell. Braddach threw his own mage's spear, but Naven knocked it out of the air with a lightning bolt.

The artillery and Braddach's mages continued to fire at whatever force could no longer be seen below.

Naven threw a flurry of white aura blasts, but Nido lifted frost rock in shards to block them and then sent the pieces forward at the opposing duo.

They each split the rock in half, sending the pieces careening in different directions. Just behind the rock were shards of ice hurtling from Frof's fingers. Both Naven and Murdot stopped the ice with fire spells that melted it to water washing harmlessly over them.

Braddach readied to try to respond to whatever they could throw at them, but Nido acted, sending a shockwave through the hill that became a rockslide from the high wall. The sliding mass of frost separated the two sets of fighters, and Braddach nodded to Nido. He threw a gate spell out to help buy them some time along with the new terrain.

He then ordered the last of his men on the hill, mages and a few of the infantry, to conduct a full retreat. He scuttled the howitzers with Honter by throwing fire. They would never make it away with the artillery now that the enemy was on them. The mages went with the last of the infantry to Snajrberg. When they joined the cavalry in the town below, they took off for Gulldalr, a few days ride over Gardnor, despite the darkness.

1524 - Chapter 55

When Braddach arrived at Gulldalr, he was immediately brought to King Erold, who had Kutzbek, Moon, and Kienber standing with him in the command center.

"Captain Braddach, I heard you were promoted multiple times by General Wermack. I also heard he's dead. Can you confirm this?"

"Yes, killed in action."

"Enemy fire? Artillery?"

"I believe a mage, sir" said Braddach, wondering why Erold seemed so annoyed with him.

"Likely Naven," said Kienber.

"Do you know Naven?"

"I didn't want to say as much," said Kienber, "but I'm a defector, I know most of them. Naven was the cruelest."

"I see," said Erold, "Cherene had made me aware you had fought for Akre."

"Yes, well, I didn't grow up in Normany. I knew Naven from our academy days. We were different classes, same school. He always had a reputation for violence."

"I appreciate the observation General Kienber. The last of the men have come in from the rear defense. We now have counted full battlefield losses on our side. Tell me, Braddach, why did you choose to completely abandon the artillery at Snajrberg?"

"The artillery had prevented our timely escape in Elklin. We were caught at Odinheim when General Wermack charged to buy us time. I wanted to ensure that we were not caught in the pursuit again, and I had noticed that during our retreat we had been gaining on the main force. If Naven, as the General calls him, had been able to get past us sooner, then perhaps they would have made it here sooner too. We fired everything we had at the advancing troops before retreating."

"Snajrberg was a tremendous success in that. He bought us another couple days in the retreat, and he lost few additional men," said Kutzbek, defending the younger officer.

"Understood, general, thank you. That is of course, besides, the additional cavalry engagements. Almost three thousand cavalry lost. The Akrin forces pursued you hard, Captain. Did you give them working guns, or did you at least burn the wagons?"

"They were not in working order. We scuttled them sire. They won't be in working order soon."

"Mrs. Moon, how many guns did we lose across the field, through each of the battles at Umfell?"

"Sixteen, total sir."

"And how many during the initial action versus Hoenheim valley?"

"We had marked twelve as in the direct care of the rear-guard across the valley, sir. Four were lost before this."

Erold thought for a moment, realizing the value of his artillery pieces for limiting the deployment of the opponent's mages into the field. He also had to recognize the importance of his own men, and the success of the escape from Umfell may have hinged on Braddach successfully holding the narrowing of the pass at Snajrberg. If the losses through the first nine engagements by the rear guard had been replicated across his troops, it would have ended the war and crippled Normany. He had also lost almost forty mages. If the loss numbers among mages had been as high as the infantry, it would have been equally devastating to the war effort. He believed they had been outnumbered by four to one in terms of number of mages, and he was sure that had gotten worse.

Kutzbek was the first to speak, "Sir, the value of our artillery is clear, but we still control over three hundred pieces. As you pointed out in the rear cavalry action at Hoenheim, we lost a considerable number of our heavy cavalry and also of our infantry." Kutzbek paused here.

"I'm ahead of you General Kutzbek. I know what the toll would have been if the rear guard had not held. It pains me to look at these numbers, knowing we could have retreated as soon as we learned the emperor had gone into the field. We lost as many as ten thousand men, and we couldn't have put many more than five thousand out of action on the other side. If results such as these continue--"

"The results of the war remain to be seen," said Kutzbek, defiantly. "For now, we need a replacement for Wermack at the head of the cavalry, and I nominate Captain Braddach."

"It will be Milton," said Erold.

"Braddach's action should be commended. His action to stay in the field firing those guns until the only course of action was abandoning the positions gave us more than enough time link up with Blaggard's troop at Gulldalr. We've been able to distribute the units among the generals and reorganize in anticipation of facing the next confrontation."

"Good point Kutzbek, Captain Braddach's action should be

viewed in a positive light. And that is how I view it. I'll be promoting Milton to lead the cavalry as I said, which I'm sure you'll agree is a wise choice in the long term, considering he was the second most senior officer of the Valgaardian unit."

"What about Captain Braddach?" Kutzbek.

"Captain Braddach, as Kutzbek has suggested, I'll promote you instead of reprimanding you, to First Major. You'll have a charge of additional cavalry support, a total of sixty-six guns, and a combined force of six divisions. May you prove your superior's faith in your methods in the coming days." A smile cracked over Erold's face, and he winked at Braddach when he appeared to have no other eyes on him.

"Mrs. Moon, should we call a meeting with the senior officers now that we have the final logistics to discuss? Or, should it just be us?" Erold looked around at Kutzbek, Kienber, Braddach and Moon.

"For now, I think this is fine," said Moon. "We can bring anything necessary to General Blaggard's attention after the discussion."

Erold thought of Cherene, "Let's bring everyone in now."

"As you wish," Moon said and called adjutants to gather the senior officers, who she sensed were tired of King Erold's meetings. When everyone had gathered, Moon began, "to repeat for Major Braddach, we've been able to integrate with General Blaggard's troop, here at the training ground in Gulldalr, while the rear-guard defenses fought battles in the hills. We've also been able to refresh supplies."

"Before we get into much more detail, I want to commend Major Braddach for his action in the rear-guard at Umfell. He will be with us going forward in our meetings," said the king. "Next, Milton I am promoting you to lead the Valgaardian heavy cavalry with Major Braddach acting as your second in command, taking lead of a larger mixed unit with the mobile artillery."

"Congratulations Major Braddach," rang out, and Braddach nodded at everyone.

"Thank you," said Braddach, unsure what else to say as he knew few of the people directly.

Erold continued, "The retreat from Umfell was a success, but we can't replicate those losses going forward. We'll catch up on the logistics and review our status after the recent battles. We need to figure out how we are going to manage the battlefield going forward."

Moon nodded, "with the addition of one hundred pieces of artillery from Albion and sixty-nine thousand five hundred troops raised by Braddach, we are now at three hundred and eighty-four guns and one hundred thirty-one thousand five hundred men."

"Is there any way we could get more artillery from Albion?" asked Blaggard.

"They are not willing to lend us any if that's what you're asking," said Moon, "At least not unless we join with them. They have three hundred pieces stationed with their units at the border with Normany in the Ash Vale."

"Now that we're larger, are we close enough nearby to join forces with them in Normany?" asked Kutzbek.

"At the moment, as far as I know, they still won't leave Albion, but even if we did, we'd still be outnumbered by as much as three to two."

"At least it's better than five to one," said Kienber, thinking about Wermack and regretting the way that the enemy had capitalized on their position to draw them into a false sense of security. It didn't feel real that his friend was dead, even though he had now heard it officially confirmed.

"If you still have a direct line of communication with them Mrs. Moon, please find out if we can get them to move further southeast. It might be our best chance in the long term," said Kutzbek.

"For now, they are likely concerned about an attack from Imeria," said Cherene.

"Yes," agreed Moon, "They are likely holding near enough to Rorik while Imeria is threatening off their coast."

"What is the likelihood of a southern attack?" asked Eichlen.

"My intelligence says that Imeria is collecting forces for an eventual mixed force attack on the Albion coast. Both Akre and Imeria have ramped up the production of airships as we speak," said Moon.

"If we keep retreating through Normany," began Plaski, "we will end up in the Ash Vale."

"Are you thinking it might be likely that they are planning a joint attack between Akre and Imeria, land and sea?" finished Pasan.

"We could have always just been the first step on Polesar's road to Rorik," nodded Plaski.

"In that case, it's our best option to link up with the Albion troop before engaging the emperor," said Erold, glancing at Cherene. "And Mrs. Moon, about mage assistance from Albion, how many mages can they divert?"

"They are not expecting to be able to divert any from the defense of Rorik."

There was silence in the meeting.

"They believe their academies have not been repaired for long enough, and its reputation is not what it once was, especially for a nation that doesn't have the lengthy history of battlemages such as Imeria or even Valgaard for them to have enough graduates to split their force between the navy in Rorik and the infantry in the Ash Vale."

"With the increased artillery, we can keep the mages at bay," said Gavo D.

"For now, yes, but we're running out of options. Do we have any news from Valgaard?" Erold asked Cherene.

"I have been informed that we will not commit any additional forces at this time," said Cherene.

"It's our war, the men who are already here and in Albion, to win or lose then," said Eichlen.

"Valgaard can't give us any additional mages or troops?" asked Erold, ignoring Eichlen's remark.

"We can speak about this in more detail later," said Cherene, smiling slightly.

"If we don't get more troops, no matter which way we turn, we may lose on numbers alone," said Erold.

"If Valgaard contributes any more troops, they would be attacked immediately. The only way to prevent the war from extending into more territories is to defeat the emperor here," said Cherene, quietly.

Kutzbek interrupted, "He's used to forming up large numbers of troops and bashing less sophisticated and often outnumbered units."

"What changes about that here?" asked Milton. "We remain outnumbered, and we are relying on fresh recruits to fight a desperate battle."

"Do not discount what the Valgaardian mages we have here are capable of," said Kienber, recognizing that while Milton wore the Valgaardian uniform, he was Normen.

Erold remained fixated on the fact they were outnumbered by more than four to one, but he held his tongue, "Do we really risk an engagement even if we numbered as many infantry, or artillery, with any mage discrepancy?"

"Yes, we are powerful," said Cherene.

Erold clutched at the orb, "Maybe if I was to fight." But then he caught himself and spoke into the silence of the tent, "I have heard the stories of your king, Hughgar, defeating twenty Akrin mages at once, from others and from him. Too many times. But we are not fighting a war that can be won with rage alone."

The silence of his senior staff continued.

"Retreating toward Albion seems like our only option. If we can get to the Kalopha River, they could fast march in a day or two out of Albion and reinforce our lines. Mrs. Moon, please ask them if that is possible."

"We would be staking everything on one final battle," said Blaggard. "With all due respect my lord, but we need to find an opportunity to strike. Small cuts over time equal large blows even for the largest armies. I have trained my men well, despite General Milton's skepticism."

"If we continue to march the townspeople ahead of us, and leave nothing behind, we worry his logistics. That may even the odds more than anything else we could do," said Kutzbek.

"It's not enough to wage war on these terms. They control the green seas and could resupply from there," said Moon.

"It worked in Dalvalles, but it may not work again," agreed Blaggard, "We must deal a blow."

People began to speak assent to Blaggard's comment. Erold didn't necessarily agree after the last sequence of battles. Only Kutzbek and Braddach didn't say anything. Neither did Cherene or Arla, and despite her share of intelligence details, Moon's face was as icy porcelain as she had ever been.

"And if he resupplies from the green seas, could he winter in Normany if the homes are empty?" asked Erold.

"Likely no," said Moon, "In that case I would agree with General Kutzbek."

"So, we either run away until the end of Vetfal makes staying in Normany impossible for him, when we might run out of places to go, or we find a way to whittle down his force, or we fight one, final decisive engagement," said Erold.

"Those are indeed our best options," said Moon.

Erold thought about it. He could be being cautious because of the disaster of the Umfell campaign, but he felt they needed a better window. As winter neared, running away would become more and more difficult, and his country was long and relatively thin. The closer he got to Albion, the closer he got to a decisive engagement. For the same reasons, he wasn't sure how he could initiate a death by small cut strategy in this case with few places left to run.

"Normally, I prefer retreat in all cases," said Kutzbek, "But, I believe linking up with Albion in Normany is our best option. A combination of strategies. We can't allow the emperor to dictate the terms of the engagement. Otherwise, we escaped the drake to find the dragon."

"I certainly believed that you preferred retreat in every case," said Erold. "We must choose our battles wisely. Mrs. Moon, do you have anything to add?"

"I will keep our eyes and ears open for opportunities my liege."

"Thank you, gentlemen and ladies, this discussion has been a pleasure. If anyone has anything to add, this would be the time," Erold stood up and nodded to Braddach to follow him.

"What is it, my king?" asked Braddach.

Erold laughed, "Please don't start that now too. It's enough for Elara to call me 'my liege' and 'sir' and 'my lord.' I'm glad you're alive. The losses are chilling. Forty-seven percent of the infantry."

"I wasn't aware it was that high," said Braddach. "It felt as if we won almost every battle."

"A lot of small cuts as Blaggard would say," said Erold, "now, Patr, how was your first senior officer's meeting?"

"Good."

"You didn't say a word," Erold laughed and slapped Braddach on the back.

"It's a lot to take in sih--Erold, but I agree with both lines of thought. We need to take the fight to the enemy before they close us into Albion, or we'll be outnumbered and have nowhere else to run. It also appears that the enemy has definitely determined to use this campaign as a springboard against the rest of the northern alliance with Albion next," said Braddach.

"Yes, it seems clear now. This campaign of Polesar's kills two dragons with one lightning bolt so to speak."

"The enemy would have gone directly to Albion after Umfell," said Braddach. "It was the right decision to retreat in the end Erold."

"Thank you, Patr, my friend. Let's speak again soon," Erold patted Braddach on the shoulder and retired to his tent.

* * *

More than a week had gone by after Braddach's arrival, and the advance of the Akrin army through the Dalvalles had been successfully checked by the strain on their resources. After the continuous failure to break cleanly through Hoenheim valley with the advance force, the emperor delayed movement from the Evorul valley where he resupplied and having already split his main force into two to attempt to catch his opponent in the valley, moved one half through Hoenheim to station at Ohrinsros with him at the head, and the other attempted to cut northwest through the Gardnor forest, which he underestimated. This maneuver bought the northern allies time at Gulldalr, but Kutzbek was convinced it was a ruse intended to force an engagement between the allies and one of the thirds of the emperor's force, where another third, closest to the fight such as the reserves on transport ships from the Solgra could join the fight.

Erold sat at his little table marking potential movements of the opposing force to Gulldalr or as near as they might get, knowing that with Halthi-eld nearing the likelihood of a battle would continue to decrease as temperatures began to consistently drop below freezing on the Odin scale. Depending on where the sea transport ships were, which could have made it to Marolno, the city nearest the mouth of the Práezwa River from Umfell through Akre and down the Atlan, in as few as five days, each of the opposing forces could be within as little as three hundred atomic miles from him, waiting for him to make any sort of mistake.

Cherene paced outside Erold's tent, but not close enough to it for anyone passing to recognize immediately that is what she was doing. They had barely talked to each other since Frostmas, and the death of Wermack, once so confident and talented, had shaken her more than she thought possible. To think that each of the people who had died on the battlefield may have had families or concerned parents, who hadn't wanted them to go to war, upset her.

Cherene wanted to speak with Erold, but she didn't want her feelings on loss to color the narrative. She wanted a sincere discussion, not to listen to him placate her. One of the reasons was because she worried that he was upset with Valgaard, because she, or they, couldn't offer more support. However, there were over one million troops now sitting in Akre, waiting on the results of the battles in Normany. If Polesar returned victorious, they would surely launch into Valgaard.

"Erold?" she tentatively pushed the tent flap aside, finding him still sitting at his desk with a ruler and a map.

"Yes, Cherene?" Erold didn't look up. He was calculating

possible results from different moves he might make.

"I wanted to speak with you," she said, but he appeared to be ignoring her. There was nowhere to sit. She felt like she needed a place to put her hands. She became a touch flustered, and then frustrated. "Are you going to listen?"

"You haven't said anything."

"You're not paying any attention."

"I'm in the middle of something."

"You're always in the middle of something lately," she could have almost screamed at him that none of it appeared to be anything more than a waste of time.

"If you haven't noticed Cherene, there's a war going on," he said calmly, putting down the ruler and looking up from the small table.

"The emperor's advanced has slowed. Not every day is a fight, and there are other things that are important," she stared at him, emphatically.

"Sorry, princess, but it's hard to think of anything else," he stopped.

Her mind raced, princess?

He sighed, watching her eyes, "When we're trapped, and there's nothing I can seem to do about it."

He stood up and offered the chair and as she sat, he whispered in her ear, "Yes, princess Valessa, I've always known that you had joined us, but I'm still not sure why you're here."

"You've kn..." her mouth felt dry, and she didn't want to say something silly.

Erold skipped past explaining how obvious it was, "Part of me feels, Cherene, that you're here only to keep me out of the fight, but I'd rather fight and die then send my men out to die before me."

She regained her composure, swallowing a bit of water from his canteen to wet her lips, "You may live like your people in this modest tent, but you are different--"

"I am, and I'm also not."

"For the sake of your nation, you must not fight. If you fight, you will die. Modern warfare is different. Mages are no longer invincible. It only takes one bullet, one shard of shrapnel in the right place. They move too fast to react to, unlike an arrow."

"All I have done, throughout my life, is fight to get here to this battlefield, to win back my nation. To give my people a better life. How am I supposed to that if we lose?"

"You think you can turn the tide, but you can't," she looked at him, suddenly looking at his eyes, she felt that she merely wanted him to kiss her. It was just a sudden craving and as soon as it crossed her mind, she couldn't get it out of her head.

"Our mages are outnumbered. If the enemy knew by how much, or maybe he does, he'd attack soon. He's trying to bait us out of Gulldalr. Unless we can deal a lasting blow, even if we lose, the northern alliance is lost."

"You think you can make up--,"

"The southern army returned to Akre sooner than we anticipated, and the emperor will surely attack before winter."

"--the difference? Of how many mages?" she looked up at him but found it hard to keep eye contact with what was in the back of her mind.

"Valgaard has given their support. Albion's options are limited. The Menetorian islands will likely pool their navy with Albion's. This is what we have available to us."

"How many mages are we outnumbered by? Do you know?"

He sighed, "as many as eight hundred."

She looked at him unable to form a coherent thought. He wanted to fight alongside his men outnumbered by eight hundred superhumans who could wield powers at a whim that could decimate villages, possibly destroy cities, or reduce creatures to nothingness in the blink of an eye.

The princess stood up and kissed him, her mouth wet with want and desire. Her tongue pressed against his. She looked into his surprised eyes and kissed him again, softly on the cheek, then she took her hand off his chest and quietly left the tent. She needed some time to think.

Moon overheard the archmage, Cherene, speaking with Erold about the battlefield, but not what happened next. When she saw Cherene leave, she entered Erold's tent without letting the blonde, distracted archmage see her.

Erold lived much more modestly as a king among his people than she had expected when they had lived such lavish lives in that far away capital in the east. He had always gone for the best of everything in Cardane, but that was a different time, and she wasn't sure how long he had been courting Zosin, a worthy adversary, to find a way to ensure his gold would be moved without suspicion.

After sleeping in a tent, just a touch larger than his own men, for the better part of a year and into the cold fall, she wondered how he'd adjust to a king's hall, or whether he'd avoid Seylil and its memories altogether. She had watched him limp and wince in pain from his various injuries without complaining or even showing a hint of being slowed down, but the signs that those recent bullet wounds continued to bother him were there.

"Elara," Erold nodded, "how much of that did you overhear?"

"I know that you want to fight, Erold. Unlike the gulf, you can't fight all these battles along, you need to trust your staff and your army. No matter the odds."

"I have to fight," he said, too weakly to convince her.

"And what about your injuries? The ones you suffered when you jumped unarmed from Zosin's tower?"

He wanted to be honest about the pressure weighing on his mind of the choice to use the orb or not. Whether it would make the difference, or it would be a waste. Making up the difference of eight hundred mages was surely impossible. He did not know the limits of the orb or himself. Without his axe and the dragonskin armor when jumping from that tower naked, he had indeed been reminded of his fragility.

Moon kept talking, but he couldn't hear everything she said as his head throbbed and he thought about Cherene kissing him and more battles coming.

"In Cardane, you did everything on your own, including planning the escape. You couldn't even be sure you'd get that opportunity to jump off that balcony. You need to let others help you," she finished.

After he had resisted the urge to sigh and rub his temples, he nodded and looked up at her from the small, wooden chair, "Is this all you came by for Elara? To scold me?"

"Can't I come by to see you when I want?"

"Lately or ever? Because lately, you're only here on official business, and while this sounds like a topic you've been planning to discuss with me, I don't think this was how you had planned to do it," said Erold.

"I'm here to call another war meeting to discuss key intelligence," said Moon.

"What is it?" asked Erold.

"We may have our best opportunity to attack a portion of the enemy force in a couple days."

"Call the generals," he said, "We'll discuss it further with them."

* * *

The generals gathered without Cherene and Arla. Moon opened

the discussion.

"To review and set the context again for this meeting, as we all know the enemy from recent meetings, has split into three to try to lure us into an engagement. However, as we've also discussed rather than retreat, we could look for an opportunity here to win a decisive interim engagement before pulling back further toward Albion. Recent movements by the reserve on transport ship suggest that the Akrin forces are likely to shift tactics to push hard north to try to put a decisive end to the war before the winter, which could be deadly for either of us to be spend wintering in place. The enemy's army also knows that they cannot sustain themselves on the supplies civilians have left behind."

"We all know this," said Kienber, "What's the point?"

"The reserve troop is set to arrive early, landing south of Gulldalr possibly as early as the morning after tomorrow, possibly to purposefully draw us into an engagement, but they'll be five days of forced march ahead of the force at Ohrinsros that has made no appearance of moving. The airships of Imeria have also left Pavol for the west, likely to reach their last staging grounds before attacking Albion. If we act fast, we could deal a blow to the reserve army just after they land."

"Why wait?" asked Braddach, "We could pin them against the coast if we move the cavalry to the beachhead now."

"Is such a risky move worth it?" voiced Kutzbek. "The fastest we could get the infantry there to reinforce the position would be that afternoon or evening."

"Most of the coast along here is marsh," said Braddach pointing at the coast across from Pavol, "I know it from academy summers. There are few places to land, the best of which is here, just south of Marolno. This north half is Notsen Hill. If we place artillery on the hill, we can push them against the marsh or back into the sea with consistent shelling and successful cavalry charges."

"I agree with the movement," said Milton, recognizing the area as well and realizing how he could utilize the slope of the hill to his superior cavalry's advantage, "I believe it is a good idea."

"It's at least eighty atomic miles," said Doctor Pasan, tracing the map between them. "You can't defend this artillery without any infantry, which can't make that trip."

"He's right," said Plaski. "Without artillery the plan can't have a chance of success. The opposing mages could assist their cavalry and only the cavalry and mobile artillery could ride there in as little as one day."

"We can transport troops with the mobile artillery, and if we leave now, we'd be able to make it there at the latest at the same time as they do."

"It remains a risky plan," said Kutzbek. "I'm not opposed to engaging them in two days' time, especially their reserves, which we outnumber, but I am not certain of the forward movement to the Marolno shores."

"If we can drive them back into the sea, then we can guarantee the right flank of any key positions that move into the north of us," said Braddach.

"If the main force moves into Marolno, the city, then we could force them to battle us for the only bridge large enough for an army to cross the Práezwa, south of Gulldalr," said Eichlen.

"I think the movement to Marolno is more than a necessity," said Milton. "We'll not only have the high ground, but solid ground from which to launch our attack, while they sink back into the sea."

"Do you know this area well General Milton?" asked Erold.

"Yes, I do. I grew up near Strilesa to the north of the Marolno area. There are few easy ways up those hills from the beach, and we could roll the artillery out along the top of the hill, firing upon the bay as they land."

"Can you initiate cavalry charges from the hill like Major Braddach suggests?" asked Erold.

"From the Notsen hill east of the Torrlawa river here, you could run an effective pincer movement into the beachhead, pushing any disembarking force against the lake here." Milton guided his hand along the map. "It's not on the map, but it's split from the sea and the river by the marshes just a little further to the southeast. Any troop landing at Marolno could be pinned into the marshes."

"General Milton, how many cavalry divisions would you suggest taking alongside the divisions currently under Major Braddach's command?" asked Erold.

"I would suggest at least another four cavalry divisions under my command could fit on the hill. The rest of the Valgaardian cavalry could be held in reserve for the following engagements depending on our success."

"Any objections to this movement?" asked Erold.

No one spoke. Even Kutzbek seemed impressed.

"It's a good plan. Major Braddach, you will lead the vanguard in this action. Officers, communicate directly with your men that we'll move our troops to the Torrlawa River while the major and General Milton, you rush your troop ahead of us to the hill. If we beat them to the beach, we'll march the larger combined force into the city while your forces protect the flank on the beach."

As the generals set out on the orders, leaving Moon and Erold alone in the tent, an adjutant entered, handing Moon a telegram from Rorik.

"Thank you, you're dismissed," said Moon. Once the adjutant had left, she read the telegram and handed it to Erold, who couldn't read the code. "In other good news, Erold, Albion has promised ground support and additional artillery if we can make it to the intersection of the two major roads at Pláedino on the Kalopha river. They'll begin movements there now. It seems they agree with our logic that if they don't join the fight, it will come to them."

1524 - Chapter 56

Milton rode his unicorn to meet Braddach at the top of Notsen hill as they could see the sliver of dawn begin to grow over the mountains in the east. The sails of the innumerous, wooden frigate transports dotted the horizon, stretching beyond the line of sight to the south.

It was a clear day despite a few wispy white clouds that hung shadowy in the air against the sky, beginning to turn bright blue, so the nearest Akrin ships were joined by the distant vision of dark green and stony gray of the shores of the island of Pavol that ran along this portion of the coast for nearly one hundred atomic miles to the northwest.

Braddach could see Milton's breath trail off into the air as he neared like white puffs instead of black from a musket. He imagined the marshes below would be frozen and crunch underfoot, and the small lake was likely frozen over. The hill gently sloped away from them down to the quiet white-sand beaches.

Their sixty-six guns had been placed to fire along the entire shore from the lake to the bluffs to their right, which blocked access to most of the Normendin province from much of the channel between Normany and Pavol.

Milton rode up and stayed silent for a moment as the enemy ships began to re-arrange in the distance after scoping the defense force on the hill. The lead ships appeared to be circling back toward the southeastern beaches. If the enemy decided to avoid engagement at the beach, then it would allow the main army to engage the reserves from the favorable position in the city of Marolno.

As Braddach thought this, he saw that several ships had tacked ahead of the line to draw up onto the beach first. A few more remained behind these. Winter birds that had not left the icy shores of Normany swooped through the air, looming as large as the ships, turning toward the beach in the distance.

"We'll fire on the landing ships and then see what's coming for us before we issue forth from the hill," said Braddach, grabbing a piece of bread from a satchel at his waist and handing some to Milton.

"I'm assuming it will be the cavalry," said Milton, grabbing his binoculars and looking despite being unable to see more than the nose of the enemy ship. He chewed for a moment, swallowed, and said, "They'll likely try to push us off the hill, or at least give their infantry enough time to disembark beyond the frozen marshes."

"Do you think they'll risk landing if we beat back the cavalry into the water or toward the lake?" asked Braddach. There was a small stream, called Goldchar brook, that ran through the center of the battlefield, separating the beach nearest to them from the far beach nearest to the lake. The Torrlawa River protected their right side, cutting through the gulch between Notsen Hill and the chalky, white coastal bluffs.

"The beach stretches too far away from the hill for us to give perfect cover to our own cavalry. I think even if we drive the cavalry off the beach, unless we can force their infantry back into the water, they'll be able to form up. If they know that the marshes are there, they won't land their whole force. Seeing that they are coming here in the first place, they must know about the marshes."

"So, you think if we can beat their first landing party of infantry back into the water, then they'll retreat rather than risk the rest of their force?"

"Yes," said Milton.

They sat in silence, Milton and Braddach on white, glistening unicorns, enjoying the cold. The ships, approaching as the sun slowly rose in the distance, were set to arrive just after the yellow ball of light had broken completely from the horizon.

Braddach checked his watch. It was just after half-past seven in the morning on the first of Halthi-eld. He was beginning to wonder if this battle was indeed worth the risk. Though, knowing that for the sake of the army's morale, they needed a victory, and that if they let the enemy land on this beach, the main force wouldn't be able to hold the town of Marolno, it felt as if pushing the enemy back from the Marolno beach was essential.

Because of the deepness of the bay, the ships were able to get close to the beach. Braddach was pleased to point out that only the escorts had cannons and that the troop transports that had pulled closest to the beach did not, for the sake of carrying the weight of the cavalry.

Milton and Braddach exchanged final salutations. The veteran cavalry commander had been right about the enemy dispatching cavalry first. They could see the horsemen lining the decks, readying to be sent off on landing ships.

The opposing frigates would likely fire on anything that tried to block the shore, but once their own cavalry was unloaded, Milton could sweep down onto the beach with his unicorns. If he drove the enemy cavalry toward the marshes, he could swoop back up the hill to the east to avoid the cannonade if he failed to drive them back into the infantry, who must have been the additional ships readying to land on the far beach. In the event, they landed, Braddach had placed four divisions of infantry in defense of the hill on that side.

As the enemy cavalry began to launch from the troop transports on shallow landing ships, Braddach yelled out to the artillery to prepare to fire. The landing craft released from the ships, floating through the bay, slowly in a line of hundreds, rowing forward. Braddach counted five deep, one hundred across, and then another series launched. He could see that they each had ten head of cavalry per craft. Therefore, each group was of five thousand horsemen. A third launched, a fourth launched, and then a fifth launched.

Twenty-five thousand cavalry were headed for the beach as he issued orders for his sixty-six guns to begin shelling the wooden ships that looked like flatter, squarer versions of the longboats they had rowed across the lakes.

Some shells splashed into the water, some hit their marks, causing a stir. Horses jumped into the water, swimming expertly for shore despite the cold water, while a few ships sunk, but hardly enough to dent the massive force approaching. Braddach only had twenty-four thousand men total.

The water assault vehicles began to let their cargo out in waves on the beach, beginning to find their footing on the sand and rush out of the water while shells rained on them from the hillside.

The enemy formed up on the beach in groups of near five thousand and then began to rush toward the hill. Milton had his unicorns rise in the sun, majestic beasts, shimmering like gold in the morning light. Some were black, some were white, and a few in between. Below them another five thousand of the Akrin cavalry had formed up on the beach.

Milton and the unicorns charged forward to meet the enemy's number, as another five thousand of the enemy horses disembarked.

The two waves of cavalry units clashed on the hill. The heavy unicorns cut apart the light cavalry, sending them off the hill like dark waves crashing against stone shores. The melee was brutal as riders clashed with sword, gun, and pike; and horses were speared through by unicorn horns. Milton's men had the upper hand from the start, as the line of brown and tan horses broke and folded. Its complete destruction hidden from sight as it was joined by the second assault group.

The horses raced up the hill, but they could not push the heavy, armored cavalry off their positions. The horses shattered their bones charging head long into heavy steel, and the Akrin, blue-coated riders tried desperately to avoid death as their swords failed to find weak points, and halberds and pistols, whatever was left in the green and gold unicorn riders' hands twisted into unguarded but hidden skin, unprepared to protect mortality against directed death.

The first line of horses was annihilated. The second line met and broken. The third line having briefly joined the fight was sent into retreat over the stream and the fourth and fifth landing parties had already shifted their route toward the far beach while Milton pursued the advance party.

The sound of shells firing from the frigates on their own men as well checked the general's advance. He turned the unicorn cavalry back, circling up the hill and reforming out of the range of the ships, watching the enemy begin to form into new lines and await the infantry that had just launched toward the far shore. Braddach could see the unicorn's horns and riders' weapons dripping dark, red blood onto the greenish hill pooling into little streams that formed puddles on the white beach below as if it had rained red.

Braddach wondered why Milton did not pursue, but he recognized that caution made sense. The infantry, too far away to accurately count, likely numbered a similar amount. Once the cavalries had fully disengaged, he ordered the artillery to reform and begin firing over Milton's heads and toward the far beach, where a contingent of fifteen thousand horses was reforming to counter charge at Milton's men.

This Braddach thought would be the decisive action on whether the infantry, just dark blue shadows against the light blue water, just beginning to float toward the shore would be able to land on the far beach.

The enemy cavalry, led now by a mage, named Sonan, charged forward in a pincer formation trying to wrap around Milton's cavalry to the left and right. Silently, he cast a spell, creating and improving the armor across his men that reached out in blue light and then disappeared. Milton, outnumbered, split his men into two to engage the force on either side while Braddach ordered the reserve cavalry to ready for action, and the artillery to begin shelling the enemy advance.

The two lines clashed, and this time the battle became far more even as the outnumbered unicorn cavalry was pushed back toward the line of artillery that had quieted behind them. Milton fought against Sonan, who was joined by two other mages, who used similar spirit magic, improving the fighting power of their men to nearly match the Valgaardian cavalry. They clashed spirit blades and shields against Milton, who used the more traditional forms of mage's spear and shield. Neither side yielded, and Milton easily matched his enemy's attacks while his cavalry equally matched the charge of the enemy.

Braddach noticed that the right flank maneuver was a disguise and the opposing cavalry had rushed through his infantry lines to attack the furthest forward guns. A pair of cannons exploded into fire.

The men, manning the artillery, were being slaughtered while Braddach's infantry scrambled to fire on the advancing troops as more horses raced up the hill toward them.

Braddach ordered the second cavalry forward, and four thousand more unicorns charged on the enemy horses that had broken the line.

They scattered before the mounted units, reforming below the hill where they clashed again like waves, but this time the unicorns did not break the line of the opposing cavalry as the fight raged.

The two cavalries disengaged and then re-engaged clashing on the beachhead again, on the foot of the hill, along the stream where bodies of horse, unicorn, and man began to pile, and where the hill flattened out near the lake.

Milton's men were being pushed back up the hill, and the infantry units of the enemy were beginning to land on the beach, while Normany's infantry waited tensely atop the hill, unsure when to fire. Their brothers in arms were still locked in an even duel with the enemy cavalry.

The charge of Braddach's reserve cavalry was repulsed, scattering back to their lines behind the artillery. He ordered his infantry to fan out to the left flank, worried about another attack on his artillery.

Instead of pursuing, the enemy cavalry disengaged once again across the field, forming up at the base of the hill while Milton moved his men to regroup with the rest of the cavalry, having failed to stop the enemy infantry from gaining access to the far beach.

Braddach ordered the remaining artillery units to begin firing again on the opposing cavalry, which had already endured almost four hours of direct shelling. He ordered the infantry to prepare for another charge, but it still did not come. The enemy infantry had begun to disembark into forward lines, and when Braddach looked through the binoculars at the opposing lines he recognized the new commander.

Disembarking among the infantry and taking the reins of one of the horses of the cavalry, it was Murdot from the battle of Snajrberg. Though he didn't know his opponent's name, Braddach recognized the cut of his well-tailored uniform, a bright white and red jacket with gold bars running across his chest with blue pants, and Braddach recognized, too, the curly black of his counterpart's hair, which unlike his own short curls, flowed in large waves down the length of Murdot's back. Murdot had joined the reserve unit as it had gone up the coast.

When Murdot had seen the detachments of the enemy on the beach head, he had discussed with Genie, the head of the reserve army, that he would lead the infantry on the beach himself while Genie could join the second landing once they had routed the enemy. After seeing the cavalry be broken upon on the beach while he was rowed forward, he determined to take control of a unit himself to rout the hillside position.

Milton rode from behind the forward lines to meet Braddach and discuss the next set of maneuvers, "Major Braddach, the enemy is readying for another charge. So far, we've avoided major losses, but I'm not sure how long we can hold. What do you think we should do?"

"You anticipated the battle well General Milton."

"Thank you."

As they spoke artillery from the hill still rained iron fire on the lighter cavalry of the Akrin troops that held formation to allow their infantry to disperse into their own lines on the beach in anticipation of another forward movement at the dug in position on the hill.

Braddach thought out loud, "So far, we've avoided major losses, but the opponent has prevented being caught against the marshes and has been able to land the infantry. They already took out some of the guns. We can't retreat now with their current positioning. They'd catch us. A successful charge by the cavalry could still force them against the sea, preventing the rest of the infantry from landing. Do you agree?"

"We could try their right flank, where they are massing now," pointed Milton. "Do you think the infantry can hold the center if they redouble the cavalry up the hill?"

"Should we split the cavalry?"

"I'll lead the two fresh divisions against their right flank, as they only are forming up two divisions of their own, and the men have been fighting since the morning. The rest of the cavalry will act as the reserve for the infantry lines, where it appears the opponent's next movement will attack as well."

The field of battle had shifted to in between the sea that glittered in the shining light of day, the frozen marshes between the lake and the sea, the large, shallow lake that was brown with the color of ice, which ran inland from past where the artillery sat on the hill to very near the ocean, and the stream that cut down the hill toward that same blue expanse.

The Akrin army's light cavalry held position still under fire along the stream, facing the hill, which rose high above the beachhead on the north side of the field and was steepest where the cavalry action had taken place in the morning. The infantry disembarked on the south side and angled to attempt a direct charge on the hill through the stream.

The artillery positions had been placed near the highest part of the hill, where it first evened out, but the Valgaardian green cavalry waited on the highest ring that plateaued further behind the artillery. The Normen yellow infantry had dug in, in front of the guns, facing almost the same direction where the Akrin force now planned to dispatch from.

On the west side of the field, the hill sunk toward sea level in a gradual flattening as it ran down toward the lake, making this a key portion of the field. If the dark blue and white of Akrin gained the ground, they could flank the infantry positions dug into the hill and easily encircle the allied artillery.

From the top of the hill, General Milton led the freshest of the green-uniformed Valgaardian cavalry, riding unicorns, dressed in blood and iron, in a wide arc to rush down this gentle hill. On the other side, Murdot did the same, taking the freshest two cavalry divisions against Milton to meet on the hill. The silent anthem of Sonan still worked its quiet magic upon the cavalry.

The rest of the light cavalry, still formed up at the stream, moved to try to hit the steep edge of the hill, while the remaining Valgaardian cavalry moved threateningly forward to check their anticipated advance. The enemy retreated, having lost plenty of their number for one day.

The infantry that had landed now distributed across the center where the artillery fire still actively rained down and began to press toward the Normany line and over the small blue stream, where blood of the fallen mixed in the near, stagnant, ice-cold water.

They marched through the water, splashing up the puddles of blue and red, coloring their uniforms in mud and blood, led by mage squads that the artillery aimed for. When the enemy infantry had come in range of the musket fire, blasts began to filter out from the top of the hill. At first in even lines of the first and then the second, but then the full assault of both sides became a heated exchange of volleys as the bodies of the dead were used for shields of their comrades who did not wish to test the hill. Across the field, mages dueled as four squadrons of eleven on each side, minus those that had been mowed down by Normany artillery, met with every kind of spell they could imagine. Ten of those were his own squad, leading one of the infantry divisions. Each line of mages summoned, threw spirit fire, and tore at the very fabric of the hill and space-time, only to be checked by their enemy's own guns and mages.

Murdot's line met Milton's as the two cavalries fired gun and clashed sword. Murdot sought Milton out, dueling him with mage's spear and shield, throwing them from his horseback, splitting the air with the wizard's bullet. Milton matched his every move, fighting off the blasts with his own spirit shield and spear.

These were low stamina moves for a wizard, originally designed for long engagements. A basic mage's shield could stop little more than other spirit blasts, but as Braddach watched from the hill, he worried for Milton's strength. Explosions nearby reminded him that he could not join the other general in that fight. Braddach threw his own combinations of spells to check at the advance of the infantry through the center of the field. Some had climbed to the shallow fortified line of the yellow infantry and had begun to brawl with knife and rifle.

Braddach saw what must have been the remaining Akrin infantry release from the ships. He saw Murdot's cavalry pull back to the far beach and be joined by the cavalry on Normany's right flank, and when Milton did not pursue, Braddach checked the general through his binoculars. The man had been injured when Braddach hadn't been watching. The rest of the Akrin infantry doubled back to the shore as well.

The day had been won, but the infantry had landed. Once again they could not hold the position. It looked like the opposition would soon be joined by at least another ten thousand soldiers. He wasn't sure of the numbers due to the inaccuracy of estimating losses, but if the enemy gained another ten thousand or more, they would have almost double the number of Braddach's men.

When Milton reached the summit, Braddach ordered the retreat while the enemy cavalry had been called back to the furthest stretch of the shoreline. First the infantry moved, then the horse-drawn artillery, and then the heavy cavalry. They would move north to the other side of Notsen Hill, where the bulk of the army was to make camp between Marolno and Strilesa. He would now become the rear guard and right flank while if Milton was capable, he would form up the full cavalry in the rear.

While not a complete failure, Braddach was still frustrated that they could not hold the beach head. It meant that the battle would shift away from Marolno in the morning, because they couldn't prevent the enemy from surrounding the bridges. There had been just too many of the opposing force, and he realized he should be glad that the hillside defense was not completely routed.

* * *

The main Normany army bivouacked on the fields just south of the Torrlawa River and near the city of Strilesa.

As soon as the king had gotten off Seaspirit, he met with Moon as the command center tent was still being pitched and set up by his men around them. For a moment it was just the two of them in the tent, so he dropped the formalities.

"Elara, status update. How did the engagement go today? Was there a decisive result?"

"As anticipated, the enemy, disembarked at the beaches this morning. Braddach, who had gotten there before daybreak was just in time to challenge them. He has since disengaged and is retreating to the north side of Notsen Hill. He will rendezvous with us tomorrow at the fork in the road at Strilesa where the coast road splits form the road that eventually meets the central road at Pláedino."

Erold grimaced, worried what the numbers could be, "Do we have estimated losses for both sides yet?"

"We lost roughly twenty-six hundred men and eight cannons, sir," Moon reported.

"Other than a forced retreat, was it a success, then?"

"Reinforcing his position tomorrow, will force the enemy to take the lake route, so they won't arrive in time to join any engagement tomorrow."

"That sounds promising. And how many men did they lose?"

"Spotters indicated nearly ten thousand in casualties."

"That sounds like our first major victory. Why not say that first? Did Patr get hurt?"

"No, you're just firing off questions, Ero--"

"Sir," Kutzbek cleared his throat and entered, "Do we have news of the battlefield?"

"I'm speaking to Mrs. Moon about it now. I believe we can form positions and engage the rest of the reserve in the field tomorrow as intended."

"We were able to deal losses to the enemy, but we lost the position," informed Moon.

"How did we lose the position?" asked Kutzbek.

"It appears that Braddach was outnumbered almost two to one at day's end."

"If we were not able to complete the main objective and force an engagement on the bridge, are we sure we should be engaging the opponent tomorrow in the field?" asked Kutzbek.

"That portion of the reserve won't be able to join the enemy for another day, so we should retain the numerical advantage," said Erold, "We may not get a better opportunity."

"That's true," reasoned Kutzbek. "Mrs. Moon, has Braddach returned?"

"He will likely make it near to the formation tonight."

"Good, if they've landed this early, we should assume that they have marched across the Práezwa and into Marolno or are near there. I would agree a battle tomorrow seems likely."

"I believe that they will be forming positions before night fall across the field."

"So, we should have some idea of how they see the field," said Kutzbek.

"There is other news as well," said Moon. "It appears that the emperor has ridden ahead with a contingent of cavalry. He will be across the field tomorrow."

"Once you have a vision of the field, Mrs. Moon, we should call the generals then," said Erold, "General Kutzbek, do you agree?"

"Yes, yes," said Kutzbek, suddenly rubbing his jaw and forehead above his bad eye furiously.

The dark, cold night of Halthi-eld quickly fell on the camp, but Moon brought the generals together in a small house on the outskirts of Strilesa with a fireplace to discuss the field. She had drawn up a map with the positions marked in blue and red blocks. Blue for Normany and red, a more traditional color than their blue uniforms, for Akre.

"We've all agreed it is time to engage the opponent to strike a blow, and now here we are, across that field. We must engage them or risk them fighting at our heels," said Erold.

Everyone stared at the map. No one spoke.

"We need a plan, and we need to think it through."

The doctor, Pasan, stood closer to bend over the map lain on the table in the Strilesa house. He traced his fingers above the two rivers, mumbling to himself.

"Their right flank is weak. We should attack there. If we can push them back along the Práezwa River line, we can prevent the remainder of the force from the beachhead from joining and then initiate a devastating cavalry charge from the south road through to Marolno."

"That sounds great to me. They only have a cursory detachment here." said Kienber. "If we can keep forty thousand troops from joining the fight, we will outnumber them for a change. Maybe by double?"

"It won't be that much," said Moon, "If we're lucky, by three to two."

"Does anyone disagree with the concept?"

Kutzbek coughed, and spoke in a clear voice, "If I may interject, Akrin split their force into thirds to tempt us into an engagement. They have succeeded. If we attack the right flank, it will put us in between two of their three armies. If we cannot disengage in time, we run the risk of being caught between two armies, in combination double our size."

"What are you saying?" asked Blaggard.

"Polesar likes to bunch up his lines, and we must assume he is joining the mission planning. It's likely that this open position is open on purpose. He tried to encircle us before and now he may be trying it again. If we abandon the hill that we are camped on, the battle will be lost."

"Mrs. Moon, how far away is the nearest reinforcement to the emperor's position?"

"Still at least five days forced march. They have not left Ohrinsros, and the other unit has just now left the forest of southeast Gardnor."

"King Erold, we can't risk defeat." Kutzbek said.

"General Kutzbek, we must seize victory if it is there for the taking. You see the same field as I do, they're outnumbered, and we have a chance to deal a crushing blow to a third of the emperor's army."

"I'm not suggesting we disengage. But, if even the two corps from yesterday's engagement form up and reinforce their line, then we'll be at nearly even strength. Engaging them here without a solid plan could lose us the war."

"True, we'll hold a significant portion of our troop and cannonade in reserve then and hold a strong line on the central hill as you suggest rather than attacking the flank."

"And what about mages?" asked Cherene quietly. "We have yet to, either of us, see the Akrin mages in the field, but from the numbers that Moon has presented here, they could field as many as four hundred mages tomorrow. That would outnumber ours by more than our total men outnumber them."

"What do you think, Mrs. Moon? We can't risk over committing our forces."

"Luckily, a significant portion of their divisions is still south of the field and will not join tomorrow. We expect that they will likely have sixty-two thousand men. Because only two thousand of these are cavalry, this likely means that they will only have two hundred sixty-four mages in the field, including any that may be held in reserve tomorrow. As far as cavalry officers are concerned, and the mages in the southern contingent, then it becomes more complex, but--"

"We have an opportunity here to fight an even fight. Perhaps, he's the one to have made the mistake," said Erold. "Doctor Pasan, General Kutzbek, you worked together on the escape, form up a battle plan to hold the central hill, Ontas. General Kienber, you will be in the reserve for this battle with me. Since you volunteered for the riskiest position in the first engagement, there will be no objections."

"You just said it yourself. We have a chance to defeat the emperor here. I should be on the front line."

"Despite your skill and your obvious desire to be in the action, we will need you if we don't succeed."

1524 - Chapter 57

In the early hours of the morning before dawn's light, the opposing armies moved unknowingly in concert like the circle of Yin, one dragon eating the other's tail. The yellow uniforms of Normany lined the Ontas hill and held a reserve in the rear of the main force, which Kutzbek took charge of, along with the bulk of their three hundred and eighteen guns, which lined the hill at its different grades. Most of the hill plateaued in a kidney bean shape around a central height, where additional artillery had been placed beside a church that looked east. This height rose very nearby the edge of the hill, echoing the meander of the Torrlawa river.

The Torrlawa itself curved around the field in a long 'S' shape. The sun had not risen yet on the field, but if it had, the men would have seen the many ponds breaking off from the Torrlawa River, hemming in the north of the field and forming frozen marshes between two separate streams of the river's sparkling blue.

The Torrlawa then snaked back to the south, cutting off direct movement to the west before, again heading west until it meandered in a large circle back to the Marolno beaches where the action had taken place the day before. It was between this central hill and the first curve of the river that Gavo held his infantry with Plaski's men, late as usual, still moving into position on the allied right flank.

To the east of the long Ontas hill was the same Goldchar brook that ran from north of the battlefield all the way to the beach, cutting a small ravine into the northern edge of Notsen Hill until the Notsen flattened near the Marolno lake. Notsen dominated the west side of the Goldchar Brook gulch and blocked off the south edge of this day's field, rising to over two hundred atomic yards in a near vertical slope after about fifty yards.

The only two routes around to the beaches were through the hillside road that met the main coastal road, that passed through Marolno, just west of its fork with the road that ran through Strilesa to the Kalopha river. The other road ran up from the beach along the right side of the ravine and beside Marolno's lake. The large hill cut off any direct movement from the east to west, south of the coastal road, which was wedged between the Notsen and the Ontas.

The small Goldchar ravine, extended north of Notsen, almost to Ontas, and was bridged at the coastal road by a sturdy series of stone arches supporting wood planks. Within this ravine was where the majority of the Akrin forces' blue and white had moved to in the night, hiding in fog that their mages rolled over the brook to obscure the soldiers from view.

A series of ponds and marshy ground on the east side of the field helped to hide the Akrin troop movement as even from the dominant heights of the Ontas Hill, it could appear at a glance that a large number of troops had camped between the six near ponds that filled most of the east of the battlefield. Directly east of Ontas were two of these ponds as well as the largest. The fog broke and rose along their edges and settled on the thin land bridge between them.

A small contingent of infantry moved along the ponds' eastern banks into the towns of Lett and Stilkol, hoping for a surprise cavalry reinforcement riding hard behind the emperor to reinforce them before the enemy could overtake them. Lett, a town of low houses and few roads, was situated in the small valley created by the Ontas hill and touched the large Venneck pond, south of Venneck town, that broke the Torrlawa in the north as well as the small Goldchar brook. Across the brook from the town was the northern edge of the large eastern pond, making the town almost the furthest point north where either army stood.

As the Akrin infantry reinforced this position, led by Naven, who had ridden alongside the emperor with a heavy guard of two thousand heavy horse cavalry, two columns of the Normany yellow, led by Pasan and Borgoron, slowly moved ahead of sixty-eight artillery pieces and forty-six hundred green mounted men, led by Eichlen.

First light had lit the day in a grayish hue, giving form to these shapes as the men had moved from line to line. The Normany yellow were frustrated by a late start, and the sun had broken the edge of the horizon near half past seven, revealing where the Akrin army had taken up defensive positions at Stilkol. The Normany columns could see a small battery had been placed on the single turret of the old, stone Stilkol castle, and muskets could be seen protruding from the ancient walls.

If any man had sniffed the air of the field, they would have remarked that it smelled like swamp gas, despite a swift and icy wind blowing southwest along the route of the river from the mountains. It might have reminded them of the death that still littered the beach, or they might have just mentally remarked that the ice had frozen the nostrils and made it almost hurt to touch the iron balls resting in their cartridges to be stuffed into muskets each time they reloaded.

At eight in the morning, almost directly as the hour changed, the battle commenced.

Bullets flew from the windows and behind the low stone wall like a farm's hedge stones around the southern edge of the town as the Akrin army struck first. Yellow coats, white pants, dripped blood, knees crumbling. The weight of the packs became too heavy as dying shoulders failed.

The next line stepped over the dead bodies and fired on the town as twenty thousand men in yellow converged on less than half of six in blue. Blue mages threw bolts of lightning and fire from cover aiming at breaking the line, but the mages moving ahead of the yellow line snuffed the fiery blasts out of the air, neutering their power as if it didn't exist.

The yellow mages responded by throwing explosive spears alongside the waves of musket fire as the line advanced, watching bodies fall across the town, stacked two high. They climbed the wall and fought with knived muskets as the blonde, brown and black hair of Normen fought against an enemy that looked almost exactly alike save some with tanner skin and fewer with blonde hair. Yet, they hated each other, slicing blades through chests and necks in pure rage as the melee routed the town's defense, pushing them into the brook, running for the Stilkol hill town.

It was then that salvation struck for the defenders rushing for the hill to the east, for appearing on the hill with the sun behind them were the riders of Davos's cavalry, which had rushed from Ohrinsros in its secret maneuver.

The yellow infantry formed upon the west side of the brook and within the town as artillery fire began to rain down upon them from the castle battery. The horses charged forth with the light behind them, hurting the eyes of the men who could not look directly up the hill.

The forward lines of eight thousand cavalry leapt the stream and into the town, breaking the thin, yellow line, fending off the mage's blasts and sending the men who had not yet entered the town of Lett into a short retreat along the stone wall. The Akrin infantry rushed down from the hill, supported by another round of the cannonade and met the Normany army at the brook with musket fire and knives, letting yet more blood into the current of the Goldchar brook that went out to sea at the beach.

Lett had been retaken, but Normany's infantry rolled up and pressed back against the cavalry and through sheer numbers forced them back to the brook where yellow coat brothers fought for their lives with any item, wood axe or rifle, that they could find. The bodies were strewn about the town and gulch of the brook. The cavalry, unable to maneuver in the small town, was pushed out to the north, and had to ride in a wide arc to re-form with the intention of attacking Lett again.

The green cavalry led by Eichlen appeared and though Akrin still outnumbered the Valgaardian cavalry, this movement warned them back. They rode to Stilkol and the blue jackets in the gulch retreated back up the hill as more of the yellow army fired muskets after them and their own survivors of the melee shook their wet hair and raised bloody wood axes and knived muskets into the air, cheering.

The celebration was checked by the artillery ringing out from the battery in Stilkol's castle and streets. The men took cover in Lett's buildings as stone, wood, and brick crumbled under the barrage.

Pasan ordered his own artillery detachment of sixty-eight pieces to fan out and begin firing on Stilkol. The howitzers filled the streets of Lett and lined its edges all along the colored blue water of the brook. Some were hit by the Stilkol fire, some of their gunners were too, but soon, they fired on the hill, bursting chunks of stone from the keep. Men caught by shrapnel fell dead off the side of the stone wall--never having had the chance to fire a bullet.

The mages in the town cast spells to shield themselves, if they wanted to risk the loss of stamina with further engagement drawing on, but few would dare risk an attempt to cast advanced magic that could shield more than just themselves. A simple, shield spell was one thing. Casting a forcefield large enough to stop the hundreds of balls of iron took a special magic, and even for those mages who cast such spells, took years to learn.

Naven and Davos met east of the castle town as it weathered the barrage to discuss strategy. They were outnumbered but had to hold the northern flank.

They decided to feign retreat to nullify the enemy's advantage in artillery and then pick the fight back up in the town when the enemy infantry reached the top of the hill. This would also help to delay the engagement of the enemy's cavalry.

When the blue jackets pulled away from the town's edge, fresh units of the yellow infantry cycled forward and tentatively rushed Stilkol. Musket fire rang out from the stone walls of the castle, and the infantry and mages below turned to unleash fire on the bastion.

Fire lit the rampart and musket balls checkered the sides of the wall. The defenders pulled away as another round of shelling carved deeper cracks in the stone.

When the men reached Stilkol, the opposing infantry doubled up and charged at the top of the hill. The yellow line fired at them, but many came unharmed to fight again in a raucous melee that more and more yellow jackets joined, pushing the infantry line back through Stilkol.

As soon as the infantry had finally been pushed back, carefully stepping backwards until breaking in a run, Davos and Naven ordered the cavalry around and raced at the town. Spells whizzed passed them as they rode hard, gradually increasing in speed, and the two master mages, two of Polesar's best, returned fire. Naven set houses ablaze and stone flying, and Davos summoned monsters as large as two houses that the opposing mages had to team up to take down.

The horse line crashed against the town's defenders and the dark blue infantry followed them, pushing what could survive of the yellow troop back to the hill. Muskets fired from each side, thousands of one on two battles played out across the field, and finally the yellow army retreated to the hill's edge.

Borgoron and Pasan checked Naven and Davos's advance with brilliant strikes of energy, coloring the daylight. As their men ran past to shelter in Lett, the two mages in yellow with more men behind them, stood at the top of the hill.

Two on two, the mages dueled, with Naven and Davos's infantry mages engaging Borgoron and Pasan's at the top of the hill. At first Davos tried summoning, but a single spear of Pasan's split his beast into cloud ash. Naven preferred energy fights and sent aura blasts stinging through the air, but Borgoron batted them away with one shield spell as if he was playing a sport. The quartet danced in an array of lightning-fast strikes colored golden yellow and shadowy blue, and Naven and Davos began to push their opponent's back. As if pulling from a larger reserve, their spirit strikes became quicker in succession, forcing Borgoron and Pasan to retreat shielded, draining their own power.

Eichlen saw this and rode his cavalry across the hill, breaking apart the battle and forcing an engagement between his heavy unicorns and Davos's lighter horses. The horses were quickly pushed back and deeper into the streets of Stilkol. When the pursuing unicorns entered the small town, they fought back the infantry that had taken up positions between the buildings. After vicious fighting, rather than risk further losses, Eichlen pulled his men back from Stilkol to Lett.

At quarter to nine, the emperor, who had also ridden ahead of Ohrinsros, received an update that the engagement had begun on the northern side of the field and that Davos had arrived in time as predicted.

Lett was just being retaken by the Akrin cavalry reinforcing the right flank, and the daylight had just shone the field. Polesar had hoped that the opponent would vacate the center, giving up the high ground in an effort to copy his own tactic of hammering a weak point with concentrated lines. However, the artillery lined the central hill and the infantry lines looked to be about twenty-five thousand strong.

His men awaited his command, but he was caught. He wondered if he should reconsider his attack on the center as he still wasn't certain of victory. He had even written to Tanneran and Alger that they weren't to let Empress Aurelia be informed of the battle. An Akrin defeat would be an embarrassment. He felt overwhelmingly confident that his men were better trained and had more ammunition. His opponent had only conscripted troops that summer and couldn't have put much process in place to acquire more bullets.

Polesar had over fifty thousand men poised to attack the center, plus better mages. He could trust Davos, who had thankfully arrived on time, and Naven to hold the northern flank. He had ordered a forced march from his other army groups across Gulldalr, so he had to force the enemy to stay engaged or to cripple and ensnare them. The only way to do this was to break through the center and force the army to retreat in halves. With a sharp enough blow, the war would be over.

At nine in the morning, while Lett was being counterattacked by Normany, Emperor Polesar ordered his men out of the fog of the gulch and onto the field, attacking the position that Kutzbek defended on the hill.

The first wave of men lifted from the gulch as if appearing from clouds of dust. In four divisions split into two columns, the men led by Andhammer began at first to slowly proceed toward the hill, knives affixed to the fronts of their muskets, ready to fire and then charge faster. The main batteries of the Akrin artillery pulled behind them led by Hurtberg, and the guns began to fire in support of the units pressing forward.

Kutzbek watched as the enemy filtered out of the fog, a walking wall of dark blue, and breathed calmly as they began to near, waiting to pick out the lead mage. Despite his bad eye, he had good sight, and he ordered the artillery barrage to hammer the charge, directing it to a specific section, well before it reached the gentle slope of the hill at the almost dead center of the battlefield.

Andhammer was torn to shreds by directed artillery fire and the wave of men fell around his body in succession as two hundred fifty guns unleashed fury and fire on the ten thousand charging men. Despite the shocking toll of the guns, the line rolled forward as if none had fallen.

Kutzbek called an adjutant to alert Plaski and Gavo to move to the right flank from behind the hill. He had not been sure of where the enemy would attack, but now he needed them to prevent the far flank from being circled by enemy troops who could use the southern half of the Ontas hill and its two miniature peaks as cover to get around his guns.

The first attack broke as if a wave on a shore, the line had neared the front and had fired upon it and been fired upon before the nerve of the men broke without their mage leader. They retreated faster than they had attacked, racing back to the safety of the gulch and past the artillery that hammered the hill. The first attack had been repulsed.

The emperor watched the charge recede and ordered Arnanne and Bessarzo to flank left with almost twenty thousand men. The move had the opportunity to flank the artillery without being directly fired upon and engage directly with the guns on the hill rather than fight through the ten divisions split into two lines that had dug into the front of the hill.

As the two generals departed the gulch and stretched their men along the road, Polesar ordered a second charge on the center to commence from behind the small eastern pond near Goldchar led by Hilara. The attack could use the shielding of the fog in the brook as well as a stream that ran from the center of Ontas as cover. Following those three thousand forward were another ten thousand men from Hurtberg's lines, leaving only Elzo's ten thousand out of the center.

The order from Kutzbek came late to Plaski to move out from behind the hill and therefore late to Gavo. They moved just over twenty thousand men between them around the west side of Ontas. When Plaski crested the hill's side, he saw that the enemy moved quickly along the road ahead.

Plaski pushed his men to race forward double time, running single file through frozen grape vines for ice wine that ran along the west half of the hill, which had been mostly covered in ten inches of snow. Gavo saw this and repeated the action, racing to get to the midpoint of the hill where the vineyard stopped before the enemy could circle them along the road. The snow crunched and packed beneath ten thousand feet, running forward, hoping not to trip or slip, thankful that knives had not yet been affixed to the front of their guns.

Arnanne and his men ahead of him, crossed over a second, smaller, stone bridge with one arch that covered an almost dried out stream bed. He saw the yellow coats on the snowy hilltop and alerted his men. They turned toward the northwest and rushed the hill meeting Plaski's unit at near even strength at the edge of the hill, firing between the snow-covered buildings of the old vineyard and using the steepness of the slope as cover to engage the yellow coats in a shootout.

Plaski's men took cover at the edge of the grapevines, and ran toward the buildings, muskets sending iron across the distributed line. Blood from both sides spilled into snow as plumes of black powder smoke hung in the air. Mages came forward from the blue line to attack the buildings, but they were fired upon instantly and Plaski's mages shot fire back from more sheltered positions.

Bessarzo's men ducked into the dried-out stream bed, filled with ice puddles, to attempt to hit Plaski's left flank, hoping to not draw the attention of the artillery on the northern half of the hill just to their right, still launching its cannonade on the second advance. General Hilara already lay dead in the ditch of the creek cutting off of Ontas. A few of the men of the second charge reached the forward line, engaging Normany at knife point while others still ran forward under the attacks from artillery, musket, and mage.

Plaski's men were successfully flanked by Bessarzo whose muskets hit a number of the men from the side, but as he rushed up the front of the gulch, Gavo's men joined the fray with a spray of musket fire warning Bessarzo back to the gulch and dropping his men.

The second wave on Ontas was repulsed despite men and mage still fighting forward with knives affixed and fire molten, attempting to break the lines alone. Polesar could see from his perch that he was not losing the battle of numbers.

His men's aim was true, and both of the first two waves had left the blood of yellow coats across the hill. The wind had pulled away much of the snow, but he could still read the color of red and fallen yellow like the falling leaves of summer's end, strewn across the brown grass of fall as if it were white.

Polesar would have ordered Hurtberg forward next, but his head had been taken off by a bouncing cannonball that had ripped through his over-confident, simple shield. Hilara had gone down during a mage's duel to a wayward shard of shrapnel. Andhammer had barely started to run.

Polesar sent his last ten thousand forward with Elzo and ordered the artillery to fire twice as fast, directing it himself, sending everything but brimstone and hail at the hill's defense and whomever their lead mage was.

The Normany right flank had been engaged in direct fire with the enemy for so many hours on the battlefield, despite neither side suffering the level of losses that its other portions had seen, that a few men had begun to find their cartridge packs empty at their waist, no iron balls waiting. Plaski noticed them slowly drop back toward the back of the line, looking for an ammo cart that hadn't been requisitioned and couldn't be.

Braddach arrived on the hill road that sloped steeply away from Ontas on the western side at about four in the after noon hours. Off to his right was a picket line pushed forward by Arnanne's men during the fire fight to cover their flank while the combination of Bessarzo and Arnanne's units had pushed Plaski and Gavo's men to the tops of the snowy peaks of the hill's southern half.

The clouds of black floating over the hills obscured how deep into the old vineyard the yellow coats had been pushed, but Braddach acted quickly. He ordered the Stens, Sven, Patr D, Honter, Arne, Ivan, and Avael to each lead a small infantry unit and an artillery piece around Ontas on the hill, while he brought the rest to bear from the road.

They could use their distance from the bulk of Akrin's force to protect their right flank on the tall hill while forcing Arnanne to disengage from the men in the vines. In turn, Bessarzo would be forced to retreat through the same gulch he had used to surprise his foes.

As soon as the firing from the south commenced on his men, they broke from behind Arnanne toward cover. Arnanne attempted to form them up to send a contingent at the small southern force on the hill, but when he saw the rest of Braddach's troop, including cavalry, he ordered a retreat to the nearest bridge.

When Arnanne and Bessarzo retreated, despite seeing that many of his men had engaged the enemy at the front of the line, Elzo pulled the rest back. He had gotten close enough to see the enemy general was Kutzbek and beginning to fear his mortality with three generals dead, called the retreat.

Kutzbek surveyed the field as the final wave receded taking the men attacking his right flank back with them. His men had suffered heavy losses, but he could see the bodies of blue distributed widely across the field. He could feel the cheers in the air like electricity before they came.

Polesar was disappointed in his general for retreating, but he saw the enemy cheering and imagined he would have a second opportunity to deal death with Murdot arriving from the southern battlefield, the following morning. They had split the cavalry off to help the infantry land on the south beach, which he would have been able to use to attempt to break the enemy's line today, but if they hadn't won the beach, they might have had to fight a grueling battle to get over Marolno's bridge.

Braddach signaled to his mages not to follow the opponent forward and had to ask Nido and Frof to round them up. With the attack on the right flank, repulsed, he didn't want to be engaged and then overwhelmed so far from the central line, despite having much of the cavalry at his side.

Kienber rode up to Erold where he had positioned with the reserves, north of the Torrlawa River, "My king, the enemy has been routed and has just started fleeing the field in the center and right flank. Please allow me to pursue with the remaining cavalry." When Erold didn't immediately comment he added, "We have an opportunity to cement the victory by chasing them into a full retreat."

Erold looked ahead calmly. He hadn't yet received the numbers, but he didn't share Kienber's enthusiasm. He had heard about ammunition shortages among Plaski's men and felt as if they had escaped a thorough loss with the arrival of Braddach's men from the south.

"My king, we should deploy the reserve," said Kienber, still enthusiastic though dampened in an attempt to sound less delirious with victory.

"We've already lost Stilkol and retreated to Lett. The battle for Stilkol still rages with the cavalry under Eichlen. Many have already died in the melee that followed the retreat--"

"But--"

"--from the town."

"--we can run them down when their backs are turned. From the right flank as we planned. They've over-extended in the center. A cavalry charge could be devastating if supported by Blaggard and his infantry and mages in the reserve forces."

"General Kienber," said Erold in a reprimanding tone, "If we did indeed emerge victorious, let's not turn a victory into a loss."

"Archmage Cherene, don't you agree with me?" Kienber looked at her, knowing that she had the ultimate rule over the Valgaardian cavalry, even if the King Erold didn't realize it.

"I will defer to King Erold on all matters where the lives of the men entrusted to his leadership are at stake," said the ice princess.

Erold thought about what both Valessa as Cherene, and Moon had told him. If something bad happened in the field, and they needed him to go into the fight, they would suddenly be risking everything on one battle when they had yet to combine forces with Albion at Pláedino. With the victory at Marolno and the enemy retreating from the center of the field, it would be easy to assume that this was similarly a victory.

Erold could hear the zeal in Kienber's voice. He believed that Kienber, though older than him, still believed that as a mage he could accomplish anything, but Erold understood the limitations of his power for he listened to the wisdom of Fros.

Or maybe Moon was wrong. Maybe, he was just afraid. The war and its battles were much larger in scope than his mercenary missions, even those missions when he mercilessly hunted the twenty-nine heroes of Malervna.

Here, Erold did feel over his head. He knew he couldn't take on the whole field at once without the orb. That made her right too, in a way, because it's only when things got desperate, like during the fight against the Brazgul, when the desire to use the orb came to him.

He didn't feel as if they could win the war here, and if they pursued the enemy, they risked further losses. If they could capture the emperor, it likely wouldn't even end the war. The senate could elect a new one while there were still two thirds of the enemy's attack force in Normany.

Normany had dealt the enemy a blow, but they had been dealt one too. If they retreated, they could reach reinforcements before the enemy's reinforcements could arrive here. It was beginning to seem more and more like the obvious choice.

If he did ever enter the fight, he would need to fight with his army and not in spite of them. Maybe running again was wrong, but no single member of his army would win alone. Erold believed that they couldn't risk it all just yet.

Erold looked at the blank yellow flag and the empty standards, with no creature adorning their tops, and the simple thought flashed to him that if he retreated now, he still had a chance to add a real symbol to those.

"If anything, we retreat. They're troop from the beach will soon be on the field. We weren't able to pin their right flank down. I see now that it was a trick, and it's possible another third of the Akrin army is closer than we suspected. We need to retreat again and hope to make it to the Kalopha river."

"We have a chance to score a decisive victory here."

"Mrs. Moon, how many mages does the enemy have if we include the numbers from the beach?"

"Again, it's hard to tell how many mages he has as this is the reserve unit, but we can safely assume that he has a full complement to his force. Eleven mages per division. They would outnumber us if reinforced from the beach."

"Without something to flip the numbers in our favor," said Kienber, "like a well-timed charge. If we strike now, we cut them off from the beach help and enclose their central force in with our own."

"They've already maneuvered a retreat of their own and could catch the whole of our flanking maneuver in effective crossfire, costing us everything. For now, we retreat. Mrs. Moon, distribute the order to retreat on the left. Hold the center. We can't lose the heights."

"Yes, sir."

"Kienber, if you want to get your horse going. Form up Braddach's unit in reserve of the right flank. If we need to, I'll move the guard in to support the center. We have numbers there, so we'll attempt to indicate that we're digging in for an engagement with the rest of their force tomorrow, while putting ourselves along the road through Strilesa."

"And then have the option to pull away along the road tonight?" asked Moon.

"Precisely. I have no doubt that they will try to prolong the engagement as long as possible, as it would give them the possibility of reversing the field and forcing it to be a final, decisive engagement."

* * *

"The troop from the left flank has successfully regrouped and joined the camp. We're holding the center line. And, it appears the enemy has moved the majority of their force into Marolno City."

"No doubt to get what fresh supplies they can."

"We've beaten them."

"Possibly to see if they can hold there until reinforcements arrive if we go on the attack."

"If? You mean, when!"

"Summary of result?" asked Erold.

"I'm tallying it now," said Moon.

Night hadn't quite fallen yet, when the commanders had checked in with orders of battle and having taken roll call, counted the number gone missing, to be presumed with certainty, dead. Moon tallied the numbers and having worked with the spotters, assumed estimates for the enemy as well.

It was hard to believe the numbers once they were right in front of the generals. Kienber was ashamed to have wanted to chase the enemy from the field. Kutzbek could not believe the numbers were truly real after repelling three separate advances on the center.

The generals' men had fought hard to a virtual stalemate across the field. They had once again held the lines, and the battlefield had not broken beneath them.

However, the gravity of the result stared back at them. It was a close loss, but it was a loss. It felt like a win, but more Normany men had died and not only that, of the men on the field, for they had the greater number of participants, they also had a higher casualty rate by over three percent.

Had they failed just slightly more on the battlefield that day, it could have completely wiped away the success that Braddach, who sat quietly digesting the numbers, and Milton, who had to be taken urgently to the healers, had at the beach.

Erold felt more than justified in his decision to have pulled the left flank behind center and to have focused on holding the road, but only in the sense that it meant they could disengage at night successfully without being pushed against the river and its marshes.

If the enemy's troop from the beach arrived in the morning, or one of the other army thirds arrived from Gardnor, they would have the opportunity to wipe Erold and his forces out like they had wiped out Sven. He had to retreat again, even though they had retreated in front of the enemy at every turn. It was possible that the next engagement could be the last.

"This result may be the best we could achieve," Erold looked at his men. They were no longer just his hired generals; they were his soldiers. "They attacked our center fiercely and had we not prepared for it, we may have lost additional troops or had to desperately commit our cavalry. We could have been pushed back into the river. Now, they know that we can't be pushed off a hill without them fighting that much harder." He looked at each in turn to press the point.

"We took out three generals as well," said Plaski, "Thanks to Kutzbek."

Kutzbek nodded, gravely.

"What about Milton?" asked Erold.

"He'll heal," said Moon.

"Good, we retreat to the Pláedino valley, where Albion has marked for us to join them. Everyone, make the orders to pull away in the night. We should put twenty atomic miles between us and Strilesa as soon as we can."

"Yes, sir," the generals spoke in unison, and dispersed, leaving Erold and Kutzbek alone.

"General Kutzbek, I'm glad you're here. No doubt you overheard the order and are likely satisfied."

"I'd be more satisfied if we had lost less men today," said the old man, rubbing the skin above his eye, and stretching, looking as if he could lay down and nap on the bare floor of the small house where they had planned the battle the day before.

"Right. Still, many of us owe you our lives, and the battle would have been a complete failure had I not taken your suggestion to reinforce our battle lines along the height."

"Thank you, sir."

"Our disengagement along the left was effective, because the enemy had retreated from the center of the field. From a quick recap of these movements as they've been drawn here, it's clear that you were outnumbered, but you defended the ground well, despite facing the enemy artillery."

"They used the fog to hide their positions as well, but given the success of Marolno, I still wish that we had been able to take the flank."

"I'd like you to be the chief general of the force into the next engagement."

"Thank you, sir. Aren't I already that, sir?"

"We've been running meetings by committee, but I've made the decisions. We've missed chances on the field and been too lucky. Doctor Pasan has an astute eye, but he's a civilian. With the addition of Blaggard's troop, we've been less formal. For this reason, I want you to be the one to draw up the positions and the defense of the field."

"Thank you, sir."

"Our battle plan seemed sound, but we failed to take their right flank, which allowed them to engage us along the length of the field. General Kutzbek, we were lucky that you suggested to hold the heights. I believe that attacking there had been their plan all along."

Erold pointed at the center of the map, and the old general watched him as the sun darkened outside and the oil lamps had not yet been turned on.

"We are fortunate that you listened, King Erold. Yes, even though it is disappointing to have not been able to strike a firmer blow, given the success at the beachhead, the men believed it was a victory on the field. Damn the numbers! This war will not just be won by mages in the end, but the actions of every member of the army!"

"Get what rest you can General, we can discuss this further after we've made a successful retreat to Pláedino," said Erold, placing his hand on Kutzbek's shoulder.

1524 - Chapter 58

The Albion army arrived at the intersection of the Semroeka and the Kalopha rivers ahead of Normany and began to dig out fortifications called redoubts and fleches. Kutzbek had communicated forward some suggested positions along the Semroeka River, which Albion agreed upon skeptically.

The northern half of the Normendin province was mostly the hills that ran from the southeastern portion of Dragnor to the cliffs south of Rorik in Albion. The anticipated field of the battle lay on a large hill that sloped gradually toward the river, taking up most of the east side of the field. The central road that passed through Gulldalr ran along the hill side, coming here by way of Borea, and the coastal road ran through Pláedino, running along the river until it crossed at the city's bridges. A series of ten much smaller hill tops peaked from the gradual descent.

The two rivers, the Kalopha and the Semroeka, ran together in confluence just east of Pláedino, which held two bridges that crossed the Kalopha on the northwest side of its intersection with the Semroeka. A third bridge was directly east of the intersection of the two rivers. The Semroeka meandered down the hillsides near due east and the Kalopha curved from the south to the west from where it met the smaller river.

Because of the ability to guard these two main bridges in the city as well as a key bridge over the Semroeka, most saw the hills between the two rivers on the northwest side of the confluence as central to the field. Kutzbek, on the other hand, saw value in fortifying the hilltops ahead of and behind the Semroeka River on the south and eastern sides of the field, whereas a cursory position had been planned to hold the middle bridge and the bridge on the hillside road. These bridges were smaller, and the river itself ran in sharp waterfalls down most of the sloping field from high in the hills to the east.

When the Normany army finally arrived, coming up the coastal road through Pláedino, two pickets had been lain ahead of each of these five bridges; five fleches had been dug in, three of which were on the southeastern side of the Semroeka; six smaller redoubts had been placed on the five northernmost hilltops; and two larger redoubts had been placed. One on the high hilltop just across the river from Pláedino city and the other ahead and due south of the western Semroeka bridge. Of the smaller redoubts, there was only one hill with two; on which, one covered the rear of a bridge over the Semroeka in the east and the other covered the rear of a bridge across the Kalopha.

The commanders believed that they could hold the two key roads to Albion just before they intersected in the hills, where the two rivers merged. South of the first and reserve lines of defense, there was a sixth bridge that the commanders assumed that Polesar would use to cross if he chose to attack the heavily guarded left flank.

It was unlikely that he would be able to go around and surprise them due to the lack of nearby bridges to the west. Many of the hills were too tall and mountainous for an attempt to flank to the east. The roads made the easiest routes to Albion, and Polesar had been looking for an engagement. Because of the concern that he may try to push across the river with makeshift bridges on the right flank, they placed three hundred artillery pieces facing across the river and to the southwest.

In all, within the vicinity of these roads, these rivers, and these hills where the fortifications had been placed, there were a total of ten quiet towns, ten sleepy hilltops, six humble bridges, two bustling cities, and one destination hot spring. In theory, the Akrin army was forced to have to cross at least one of the two rivers to engage the bulk of Normany's main force, interrupting the rhythm of each of the towns, cities, hilltops, and its myriad of wildlife creatures, attempting to prepare for winter.

From the low end of the field near the river, one could not fully appreciate the number of defended peaks that rose out of the snowy white field like snowcapped mountains rising above flattened clouds. From the top of the great redoubt at the center of the field, the allied leaders met for the first time, looking south over the city, that had begun to empty, and the confluence of the two rivers. The Normany artillery had been installed facing almost every inch of the radius of a semicircle that ran from due east to due west.

If one traced a line across this same axis, almost all of the defensive fortifications, except for the pickets southwest of the Kalopha and two fleches, rose to the north of it. The fleches and other fortifications created somewhat of a triangle with this central fixture, rising higher than any of the other points of the field, near the triangle's forward tip.

The crispness of the icy morning was not lost on the bundled men and women. Princess Valessa stood by Erold. Arla was behind her, tired of being cast in constant shadow, but enjoying the view and paying attention at the same time. Kutzbek spoke with the Albion general, Anglis. Moon listened.

Kutzbek pointed, "I'm worried these fleches may be too shallow. Was it the frozen ground that prevented them from being dug deeper?"

"We don't have long before the enemy will arrive, and I believe we are prepared," said Anglis, who flattened the folds of his red coat and stood at stiff attention.

Kutzbek wore yellow, his white shirt beneath his coat slightly unkempt, as he had dressed hastily to ensure making the meeting on time after the long movements across country. Erold had been dressed by attendants in his bright yellow coat that matched Kutzbek's. The princess wore the green archmage's armor, with its golden yellow detailing, a similar color to Arla's. Moon, almost casually, wore blue, similar to the color of the Akrin corps, but also the secondary color of historical Normany.

"This will be the largest engagement in the history of this world General Anglis. We can never be prepared enough," responded Kutzbek. "We should add more forward fleches ahead of the bridges if we can."

"'If we can' is right! Mrs. Moon, when did you say they will be here?"

"Either this evening or tomorrow."

"And how many men exactly? I have to hear it again to believe the figure."

"Confirmed numbers after casualties on either side are two hundred fifty-two thousand nine hundred and eight men for the Allies. Three hundred eighteen thousand eight hundred and twenty Akrin men for the emperor."

"It is staggering that you know this much about the enemy or us," said Anglis.

"Mrs. Moon's intelligence has been essential. Any other time of the world, and we would know almost nothing. The only thing we don't know is how many mages remain with the army after the successive battles," said Erold, "but we know it is somewhere above twice our number. Likely close to three."

"It is our only weak point," said Anglis.

"We will be ready," said Valessa.

"Despite our reinforcements, I fear it might not be enough," sighed Anglis, "We have only provided one mage per one thousand soldiers from the guilds."

"We will be ready," she repeated, defiantly. "We should focus more on making sure we limit the field of battle to force mage on mage confrontations that favor us."

Kutzbek looked out over the field, "We can't know where they will hit first."

"As you've suggested General, we have a double front, using the redoubts, fleches, and pickets ahead of the rivers, and we have this fallback line," Anglis pointed at the redoubts including the one they were on, which to Erold felt more like the forward line, despite the pickets ahead of the bridges in the city below them and twin fleches flanking the hill.

"Even if they outnumber us, they'd have to fight through hell to even take this point," Anglis continued.

"You forget not all our cannonade is placed in the same direction," said Kutzbek. "Despite the lay of the field, they could still attack us on our right flank, which we have to defend as it is our retreat, camp, and the road to Rorik, which, with you moving here..."

"Yes, it has no other defenses, beyond the navy, but there aren't many marines among them."

Erold pulled Moon aside while the generals switched their discussion to airships, and asked, "How many guns do we have again?"

"We have six hundred thirty-seven cannons and howitzers."

"And we could move them to point in the direction of the either advance?"

"Theoretically, yes. The majority are focused to the southeast with three hundred facing the west."

"How many mages do we actually have Elara?" he looked at her sincerely.

"Three hundred ninety-four, counting you and the archmage Cherene," she nodded at the princess, who listened closely.

"And them? Do you really not know, or are you sparing me the detail?"

Moon hesitated, but she could feel the pressure of the coming battle weighing on her as well--not only for their lives, but there was a lot at stake behind the scenes; even if she wasn't sure she could trust Valgaard, she knew the empire could not be allowed to extend--"They likely haven't replaced any losses, but even if they suffered similar losses to their mages as they have across the field at large, then they still have almost twelve hundred, including the seventy-two elite, royal guard."

Erold let the cold air of Vatna rush across his face and heard Anglis say, "If they take the line along the Semroeka River, we'll launch a decisive counterattack on the positions, which open up in the rear. The emperor will have no choice but to put his royal guard into the field, seeking rather to reverse the tide than deal a knock-out blow."

An adjutant appeared. Moon looked surprised. Erold turned around to see that it was Mr. William, Mr. Everett's only staff member, just arrived from the Ash Vale.

"It's been a long time, Sir Ardrada," bowed Mr. William, "If you'd care to speak with me and Mrs. Moon for a moment, in private, I am on urgent business from Mr. Everett."

The trio stepped away briefly. Valessa watched Erold go.

* * *

When they had found a private space that Moon had prepared ahead of time, she spoke, "Mr. William, I have told that old fussball, Theodore, that the orb is safe with Erold."

Erold was surprised that she had dropped the formalities when referring to Theodore, but he also understood that there was something less business-like to the relationship than she would ever admit to. He had never seen her visit during their time together in the Ash Vale, but when she went somewhere with her daughter, that was the first and only place she had spoken of and the mysterious Anifiel Coltari--Mrs. Everett now--whom Erold had not yet met.

"Yes, well, now that the king is this close; Mr. Everett wanted me to check on it. He can't come himself as a great naval battle is about to eclipse Angel Bay any day now."

Moon and Mr. William looked at Erold, who waited patiently to see what they might have to say.

"Well, Erold, do you have it?" asked Elara.

"Of course," he said and produced the orb. Dropping it into his palm from the faded, dark blue velvet bag he pulled from an inner pocket of his yellow coat.

"We've been worried at various times that we made a mistake letting it out of the manor, but we've gotten rare messages from Mrs. Moon alerting us to its safety."

It was as dull and yet as dangerous as ever, thought Erold as the three of them looked at it. He put it back in the small bag and hid it in the inner pocket, like a keep-sake stone or set of keys. It was hard to believe after all that had happened that he had only ever used it the one time against the dragon.

"If the battle goes poorly," said Mr. William. "I am to take you and Mrs. Moon to safety."

* * *

Braddach had just finished speaking with Nido and Frof about the enemy's movements southwest of the river when Erold entered his tent unannounced.

"Patr," he said.

"Yes?" asked Braddach, turning around to give his brother a hug. Despite meeting among the officer's planning sessions, they had spent little other time together since the fighting had gotten under way.

"I don't know when the fight will start, Patr, so I have a gift for you."

Erold picked up the axe case from behind him and handed it to Braddach, presenting it for him to take from him.

"You can't give me this," said Braddach.

"The battle, whenever it comes, will be bigger than any other battle that's ever been fought on Vatna, and there will be well over one thousand mages on the field. I am continuously reminded that I cannot fight and risk my life, so the axe that has been reforged has no better master."

Braddach opened the case and saw the twin blades of the axe catch the light of day filtering in through the tent, gleaming like a metal, black mirror. He touched it and felt the static power that the mage's staff wielded. He lifted it, and it was as if he could feel the flames of his own energy licking, hungrily, at his forearms.

He held it out. It was lighter than he remembered, and the power surged through his veins, as if his entire body had become a conduit for the energy of the frost. With it, he suddenly believed he could move mountains, end blights, and fly like he had seen Erold do so many times by extending a simple levitation spell that for Braddach lasted less than a minute. Wizards' staffs were often rare, expensive tools that you had to be given as an heirloom such as now rather than make or find.

"Wear your dragonskin armor on the field too," said Erold, reminding Braddach that the bullets and cannonades of the future could fly faster than a shield could be raised.

"I--"

"Promise me that you will," Erold said sincerely.

"I will," said Braddach. He put the axe down in its case and hugged his younger brother, who he'd seen grow up to be a messy teenager and now the king of their nation. Erold turned to go.

"Hey," said Braddach.

"What?"

"Remember that Fros will always walk with you."

"And also with you," said Erold and he left, leaving the tent flap slightly open, so the sun shined on the axe where it lay.

* * *

Valessa was pacing again, and Arla was becoming that much more bored and frustrated, waiting for the war to end. Arla missed feeling as if she impacted world events in the palace, and now she spent all her time, when Valessa even spoke, listening to the princess pine after a man that Arla didn't care for.

Arla didn't care much for any man at all. As far as King Erold was concerned, though, he didn't seem much different than any other, and had a past that Arla couldn't help but think of as a reason to avoid him when it came to romance. She cared for the princess but knew Valessa would never care for her in the same way.

"If there's something you want to say to Erold, by now you should probably have said it," said Arla, fighting off a sharp pain to her forehead.

"You think so?"

"You know my opinion on him by now. It's not going to change anything."

"Scandalous, distasteful, dishonest. Yes, I've heard you mention these things before."

"If none of those things have stopped you from being here, then I don't think anything else will."

Valessa looked at Arla and nodded. She had debated it, internally, long enough, but even if Arla wasn't quite aware of what went on in the princess's mind, Valessa knew what she was going to do.

* * *

A large package wrapped in brown paper was pulled by cart and manpower in front of the emperor, who was meeting with his generals in their fortified camp southwest of the Kalopha River. Akrin forces had been stationed here for a few days and rather than attack the opponent head on into their strong defenses, the emperor had a temporary fortress constructed, with tall and strong wood walls, in view of his opponent, just southwest of the southern bridge over the Kalopha and the town of Valenval. He preferred to wait and let the nearness of winter drive them from their small walls of packed earth and wood.

The men and generals looked at him, expectantly. His adjutant waited excitedly to remove the brown paper. Polesar nodded and the men tore through the wrapping, revealing Polesar's son, Drosef.

A bright blue-eyed, blonde boy like his mother. Almost a spitting image of her except for some similarities around the eyes and lips. Only ten years old and for some odd reason the people called him the 'Prince of Varince'--a city-state on the coast of Ithlin that once vied for the capital of that nation.

Polesar touched the curve of his son's face lightly. He missed so many moments, holding him as he grew, while the empire was attacked on all sides from invaders and splintering rebellions of miniscule proportion, likely funded by foreign nations. Now, he fought a war he did not understand. The enemy fought him back harder than ever before while he promised republic.

The emperor had thought he had his opponent surrounded, but they had slipped right past him as if mocking him. He had enticed them to battle at the Práezwa by sending his smallest force forward and they took the bait, but while he had won the field, the enemy had cheered as if in victory. The men of Akrin had been outnumbered but came away victorious, despite Polesar's concerns on the eve of battle.

Despite seeing the numbers and so few losses they had so far on the campaign, Polesar's faith in the mission of Akre, a republic for all where men voted for their kings had been shaken. The men in rag-tag yellow uniforms had retreated but not surrendered, and had they not desperately blocked the pass through Hoenheim, Polesar would have had a cavalry of sixty-five thousand race over the plains to harry the retreating foe.

He had thought he was liberating the people, bringing them into a larger network and giving them the currency of the empire, but still, they fought against him. If they didn't yield the field, here, hundreds of thousands of men, who would have been men of the empire less than a year ago, would die in defense of the nation that had founded it, breaking away.

"Are you okay, sir?" his adjutant asked.

"Yes, yes." The emperor blinked and he looked around. His generals stared. "General Elzo, you had just meant to say something about Normany's...?"

"General Kutzbek. I saw him at the head of the force at Strilesa. He is a non-mage; we can attack him with a mind spell of hypnosis, bewitching him, just when we engage the enemy."

"Yes, quite right. That is a good plan, and we will surely execute it. I can cast the spell myself. But, Kutzbek," the emperor paused, touching his chin lightly, "why does that name sound familiar?"

Bessarzo spoke, "He was one of the generals that fought against Ispiarda and in the Westernlands against the elves. He reported to Danta, sir. I can confirm that he is a non-mage, as I also fought alongside him."

A defector, fighting for the enemy. Polesar smiled at the adjutant, asked him to bring the painting to his tent, and bid farewell to his generals. He needed a moment to think, but before he could depart for solitude, the forward watch from Valenval had a report.

"The enemy, sirs, has moved into forward positions and is building new redoubts on the hills, with fleches between, just across the Valenval bridge in a third line."

"What are your orders? Should we attack?"

"We will issue the order to move in the morning," said Polesar, "Why interrupt them, now, when they are making a false movement? Let them move more of their force to the new, forward line before we take advantage and destroy the advance force while it's separated from their main lines."

* * *

Erold had just approved the movement recommended by Pasan and supported by Kutzbek to build new fleches and redoubts between the hot spring at Drodin and the intersection of the rivers, with one of the two redoubts in firing range of the bridge at Valenval and the second covering the rear of the first.

The Normany camp had suddenly come to life despite the dark and despite the cold. Everyone could suddenly sense that the battle may begin soon, despite no sign of movement across the river since the enemy had built their camp.

It was now the twelfth of Halthi-eld, almost Vetfal and soon the Great Day of Thanks for Normen. Erold wrote notes on a hand drawn map of the battlefield with pencil around the work of someone else in fountain pen. An oil lamp illuminated his private study as the sounds of the camp coming to life outside turned to blank noise.

His hands were cold from being exposed during the work as if he were outside. Lately, he would either be curled up amongst his blankets on the cleaned floor of the tent when years ago he may have been near a fire with his men, drinking beer. For the first time since he had left Cardane, he missed the heat, having not spent a fall so cold since his one year in Peth on the lake. He had spent many an evening beside the fire, speaking to Valessa then.

Valessa entered the tent. He knew it was her before turning around. It was her scent, the way that she walked. The liminal sound of her magical aura, teasing the boundaries of space-time like a true archmage.

Speak a dragon's name, and it appears, he thought, quietly to himself and put the pencil down, before lifting off the chair to turn to see her. She had been coming alone almost every night since they had made camp at Pláedino just to talk with him about nothing and everything.

Valessa stood there quietly, watching the way his eyes lit up, upon seeing her, dressed in not just plain clothes, but one of the dresses that he had bought for her in Umfell. It seemed so long ago that he barely remembered the moment he had said yes to the purchase.

Her long eyelashes, fluttered as she slacked onto one heel, her feet in simple flat sandals. How she did not freeze in the frigid air, Erold would never understand, but there she stood now, pale, bare ankles, her long arms, flattening her long icy, blue dress.

She looked at his long, messy blonde hair that he had let hang down rather than pull back in a warrior's bun. He had grown it out all year and his facial hair was now a blonde beard. His piercing blue eyes admired her as if she were more beautiful than gold.

"Come," she said, and the princess grabbed his hand and pulled him to the blankets where she pushed him down. She straddled him and then, for a moment rested her chest against his, tenderly warming him in the cold.

"Valessa," he breathed. Before he could say anything further, she kissed him. She was scared, but excited. She felt that she was more than ready for this moment. She had yet to be with anyone and now she was getting close to thirty. Time had flown, and all along, she had been deeply in love. Could she be completely naked with this man, she thought, as she silenced him with her warm tongue rather than her cold spells.

He was gentle at first and then began to kiss her back passionately. She undid his pants and began to fold up her dress while he looked up into her eyes.

"Are you sure you want to do this?"

"We have no idea what's going to happen. Even after all this is over," she whispered and recognized that he thought the same thing. Neither of them knew the future.

"I don't have a skin sheath."

"I know. I don't want one. I want to make love with you like the world's going to end tomorrow."

She tried to put him inside of her. It was difficult at first, because she was tighter than he could fit. Then, his girth slipped inside. At first it was a hot, quick pain and huge pressure as he entered her fully. As he began to thrust from beneath her, it was a little uncomfortable. He took her and put her on her back, and suddenly with her legs pushed back, just bent at the knee, with him above her, it was pure ecstasy as if nothing had ever been so pleasurable in her life.

She didn't know if they would survive. If they survived, she didn't know if they would stay together. But that night as they rolled together in the blankets for twelve hours, she wanted him more than anything to be her first and her only true love; no matter what came.

Her eyes rolled back in her head, she dug her hands into his shoulders, she curled her toes. Again and again, begging quietly for more as he joined her in bliss. Again and again. Again and again.

1524 - Chapter 59

Even if Erold didn't want the night to end. Even if he hated the thought of how many men might die as soon as the darkness turned to light. The daylight came and ended Valessa's sweet surrender.

It was a warm day, almost forty on the Odin scale. Warm enough that later in the afternoon, some of the snow might melt despite the frozen ground.

He didn't have to wait long for the first bullets to pierce the frozen chill of the Thorsday morning. As the first shots rang out, Erold wished that Kahron was there. His power would certainly have helped turn the tide, but he was about to begin a different battle far away.

There were three new fleches, half dug into the ground when the morning broke, looking much like half constructed doorways into a missing house above the snow. Between these were two hills where artillery had been moved in the night and redoubts hastily constructed of packed earth, with the guns sticking out above the walls, barely more than mud.

These forward positions fired upon the movement of the enemy from the redoubts and fleches as the Akrin force split into three cavalries and three infantries and began to distribute along the east bank of the river. The "Brown Mountain" and Tornes led the first cavalry corps of twenty-six hundred across Valenval's bridge, followed by Murdot and Sonan who led a second cavalry corps of the same number.

The first cavalry followed the road to circle the first redoubt and attack the second one from behind. Murdot followed Sonan as their men broke from the bridge to encircle the nearest redoubt.

The men on the hills fired cannon and musket viciously, but they were defending islands in a sea of multi-colored horses as Davos led the first infantry made up of multiple corps behind them, with Ompa at the lead.

Murdot could already see many of the yellow infantry in the distance crossing the central Semroeka bridge while the defenders valiantly fought from the encircled positions, stabbing out with knived muskets at anything that got close, while firing cannon and bullet.

When he saw his men round the first redoubt on the left, the realization hit him that there were far fewer men than they had expected on the field. Instead of fifty thousand, forming the line across the fleches, there were only men at these islands of chaos, being slaughtered despite the best efforts of their mages, who threw everything they had into a spirited defense.

The horses streamed so thickly that they ran out over the field toward the retreating line in the distance and circled back toward the woodwork strangely stacked at the rears of each of the positions.

The trap had been shut before the prey had realized it was a trap at all. From what would become known as the Kienber bridge, the bridge nearest to Pláedino city but over the Semroeka, the remaining Valgaardian heavy cavalry of just over twenty-five thousand had begun their own maneuver from between the hill where the central redoubt stood and the hill behind it, hidden perfectly by the darkness of the hill's shadow, opposite the rising sun.

The line of unicorns began to widen out and then with vicious speed turned to the east and into the rising sun shredding through the lines of the smaller horses, weak with malnutrition from lack of supplies and the cold of winter, which the unicorns thrived on, as beast to beast, they needed no rider to flatten thoroughbred or mustang.

Unlike the head on charges at Marolno, the chaos of the distribution encircling the hills made it impossible for the thousands of horses to redistribute and meet their foes, scrambling into each other, breaking legs, and crushing riders as they fell, all the while Milton's men charged forth, hitting the first redoubt and continuing east.

The massive hooves of the unicorns crushed skulls of horse and men like cracking pepper, breaking through the line like watching directed rocks of steel shred through waiting paper made of bronze. Though some few unicorns fell to shot or the few mages leading the horse cavalry, an observer on the highest height of the hill overlooking the road, would have seen the horses number dwindle rapidly as if catching an instant disease while the unicorn line appeared untouched.

Murdot pulled Sonan out of the Akrin forward movement, riding along the eastern road between two towns, toward the hot springs on the hill. Neither could imagine the true number of losses dealt on the field by the heavy cavalry, which continued forth passing the second fleche, leaving a field of tens of thousands of dead horses and men in their wake, littering the frozen, white field in clumps of brown, black, and white.

Blood flew into the air, still, as the Akrin first cavalry was caught, still attempting to turn on the gradually steepening rise of the hills, and then broken, shredded, decimated. The clash of swords and pike blocked the sounds of bullets and shells that let loose were from the defenders of the redoubt firing on Murdot and Sonan's men, or the first general of the infantry, Ompa, who crossed the bridge and took in the devastation of the field, which began to resemble a mass grave, sloped widely from the river to the hillside road.

The Normany men had begun to abandon the forward positions behind the advance of the unicorn cavalry, which had passed the second redoubt and after massacring the furthest forward of the Akrin horsemen, turned back along the hillside road and crossed the easternmost bridge.

Murdot and Sonan passed the redoubt themselves and caught Tornes rallying survivors near an orchard that stood on the road to Borea. Many were hiding among the trees, horses panting, some of their shirts drenched in the blood of the fallen beside them.

They all looked to Murdot, the most senior of officers for what to do, but he had no idea. Half of their number may have been decimated in one charge, which had done little damage to the other side.

The Akrin cavalry moved to threaten the yellow infantry and to possibly retreat to their lines, but from their position on the hill, they could see the three deployments of infantry begin to move into attack positions across the field.

The emperor had heard rather than seen the devastation and when he had stood on top of the fortification had felt the tension in the air. He had been tricked into engagement in the same way that he had tricked his adversary.

He had finished casting the spell and risen to hear more silence than expected. When he looked from the top of the wall now, he recognized in his men a sudden desire to slake their thirst for vengeance in enemy blood. He didn't so much as order the attack to advance across the field by his three army groups as voice the will of the crowd.

He raised his hand forward, and the crowd cheered too loud to hear any grand proclamation. They had already been issued hypothetical orders, and now they rushed forth, more an organized mob rather than a disciplined army. Genie took four generals to attack Pláedino city and capture the bridges. Davos would extend his morning orders to attack the central Semroeka bridge.

Naven led three generals and took control of the remaining

cavalry to attack the bridge from where the Valgaardian cavalry had issued forth. Pasan had attempted to avoid the remaining enemy cavalry and reach this bridge, but he was engaged by the forwardmost general under Davos, Ompa.

Pasan found himself locked in a mage duel while his infantry fired against the opposition, and Kienber ordered the men on the central redoubt to begin firing the cannons, crashing into Ompa's lines as the mages began to reform in the chaos, some struck down by musket fire.

Pasan went with simplicity, conjuring shield and spear of mage energy to combat Ompa's spiraling lightning. Each blast carved the air in circles like a snake winding around a tube.

Pasan sent forth spears in response, but Ompa knocked these away with his vicious lightning. Pasan felt a pressure wrap into his arm and the arm he'd used to conjure the shield fell. Ompa advanced.

Pasan threw a final spear. When Ompa lifted his hands, the magic didn't come and the spear thundered through his heart and until it blinked out, lit his back with purple.

Pasan ordered the retreat, but most of his men had already taken advantage of the enemy reforming and fled. Pasan couldn't feel his arm except for the pain, blood draining onto the white field of icy snow.

Most of his men were positioned with Kienber in defense of the central redoubt. Eichlen was defending the town and the small redoubt to their flank. Braddach and Borgoron held the central Semroeka bridge. Gavo and Plaski held positions along the river road on the far-right flank. The rest of the positions were held by Albion officers, but few of them were mages. Instead, their mages and men were interspersed among the lines, an array of yellow coats with dark blue hats, and red coats with dark blue decals about to fight a sea of dark blue still hundreds of thousands in number.

Forcing himself to stay in the fight, Pasan crossed the bridge passed the forward pickets, whose soldiers nervously checked their muskets and balls. One opposing general may have been dead, but Marandres had already moved into position to assault the bridge behind Pasan.

He bit back the agony. There were few natural healers in the world of magic and when it came to the first schools, most chose specialties designed to wreak havoc. He'd have to hope that like Milton, he'd heal. But Milton was wounded by mage, and iron had a way of turning poisonous if not removed quickly.

Marandres retreated to reform with Naven's generals, because the artillery from the hill had begun to rain down on them in chunks of fifty at a time. Casting spells to shoot them out of the air was a waste of stamina and watching Ompa die was a reminder to manage limited resources.

Naven commanded Bessarzo, Edron, and Tlous to attack the bridge with everything they had as fighting picked up in the city across the water from them. Marandres fell into step with Naven, holding the cavalry out of the fight as well, waiting for a moment when a charge may not be disastrous.

Kienber watched in awe as thousands of men descended across the field at Eichlen in the city. The mage blasts and muskets had begun to issue forth, but it appeared as if he was outnumbered by as many as four to one. The general waited until the last moment but abandoned the forward pickets.

Many of the men refused to go, entering a doomed melee at the rolled logs. Others were caught in the dirt street by the Akrin infantry. Muskets fired from between doors as most of the retreat successfully passed over the westernmost bridge, which Eichlen destroyed as he passed.

Kienber shook his head as he ordered men to take the fading Pasan to the back of the line. Two of the five bridges now led directly to him, and the forward pickets blocking the Semroeka were being bludgeoned brutally by mage fire and summoned creatures that paired with another mage's devastating telekinetic rock, making it look as if the horned creature had dug through the ground itself and emerged to swallow the entire position whole, sending rock, blood, and wood into the river and across the snow.

Kienber ordered his men to begin firing almost exclusively on the town, hoping to hold additional mages off his right flank. He was ready to go one on three. He pulled his gloves off, and now everyone could see the black marks of his force of will. Nothing, not even his deterioration, could stop him from fighting, even if it meant that he had to tear apart the fabric of his own body and soul to never surrender.

He jumped off the redoubt, spinning through the air and sending fire at the attackers from every direction. Fast fire, illusion, lightning. Those were his skills. Now, he faced beast, rock, and explosive area of effect spells as the enemy mages readied to match him just across the bridge.

Back came the drilling horned creature like a mastodon, but the color of iron. Kienber jumped ten atomic yards high, and sent thundering lightning through its face, leaving just the trace of a hole in the ground as the frost cratered. Kienber sent forth three bolts of lightning at his enemies.

They blocked them and returned moves of their own. The spirit of a giant snake with a mouth like a thousand teeth. Hurled ground the size of half a building. And a fireball, larger than any he could conjure. He sent three more bolts, crashing through each like tearing through water as he returned to the dirt below and the magic of his opponent's faded.

They began trading aura blasts, trying to weaken his defense and limit their own overuse, as he willed himself to continue by blowing each shot out of the sky with his own fire. He advanced on the trio, watching them sweat, feeling his finger's tingle, knowing that this might be his last day.

One spear through one face, Bessarzo couldn't react in time and dropped, skull cratered. Edron took a searing firebolt to the chest. Tlous tried in desperation to summon something like an eagle to carry him away, but Kienber snuffed the spell and the mage, watching body, clothes, and winged bird turn to ash as his spell glazed the general's skin.

Kienber returned to the redoubt and looked at his hands. He wasn't sure he would qualify the stubs of his fingers as fingertips as they too had been left as ash on the field. He wasn't sure how much more he could give, but he would give it. Even if it wasn't the country he grew up in, it was the country he wanted kids he would never have to believe in.

Naven and Marandres advanced across the bridge behind their men who fought through musket fire with superhuman acts of bravery to rush up against the redoubt as howitzer and cannon burst forth in iron and fire.

Genie had checked his advance out of the city after Arnanne had been hit by shrapnel, attempting to cross the bridge from the city to Kienber's redoubt. Partially out of fear, and partially due to Normany's Gavo and Plaski beginning to threaten his left flank from across the river.

This left only Marandres and Naven advancing behind the combined forces of the dead generals. The Akrin troops retreated and ran forward, swarming the fleches on either side of the redoubt, engaging in melees, and being brought down by all types of fire.

Their sheer numbers of mages and men overwhelmed the opposition and were reinforced by still more Akrin troops rushing forward despite the death before and behind them, bodies strewn across the field and piled high as if embracing their enemies in eternity.

Kienber fired blasts of arcing lightning at Marandres and Naven, recognizing them from behind the stone wall at the top of the redoubt, but Naven swatted them out of the air. He brought his own artillery forward from the rear, into range, and ordered them to begin firing on the redoubt as his men retreated from its crumbling walls. Genie did the same from the city while speaking with his generals about advancing on the redoubt that continued to burst black powder from hundreds of muskets within and on top, in addition to its firing artillery.

To the east on the field, Davos's third had turned north to face Braddach's redoubt, where he led the force combined with Borgoron defending a redoubt, similar in structure though not size to the one that Kienber defended, two fleches that flanked a road that split off the hillside road and ran to the bridge, and the two pickets ahead of the bridge.

They watched the sea of dark blue coats, heading toward them gradually over the white ground, almost like watching the water at the Marolno beaches. Braddach ordered the artillery to begin firing, and the charge began to pick up steam.

Aftrin, Davos, and Desi ordered their men to attack the defended positions, and they ran ahead, potentially hoping that the faster they ran, the less bullets could hit them, like running through rain. Musket fire went out and many dropped, but still more came, and many of the men on the charge stopped to fire muskets back at the walls and the fleches, leaving holes, riddling the wood and dirt.

Mages ran forward with shields, attempting to prevent bullet and shell, and sent fire and spear as soon as they closed in on the redoubt, attempting to light it ablaze, but the fires were snuffed out by Braddach's squad. Borgoron pointed out that the opposing mages were reforming.

Seeing the lack of success of their men, the generals coordinated to attack the redoubt. Aftrin and Desi suggested pooling shield spells as if they were advancing in a phalanx of old while Davos and other mages who did not specialize in this readied to hit the redoubt with whatever they had.

The line advanced at the redoubt that fired what it could, but while some of the fire broke through the shield wall, some of the howitzers' blasts surprisingly, bounced off. The mages at the redoubt prepared to fight two on three or more, across the stone wall of the fortification.

They readied fire, ice, water, energy, creature, or to conjure whatever it was that they could. As artillery continued to fire on the advancing mages, Braddach told them to aim instead for the opposing infantry in the distance. Muskets began trying to pick at the mages' defense. It still had no effect.

As they readied for the confrontation, Braddach noticed that many of the infantry had circled around to their left and attacked the fleches, desperately trying to take them from the defenders, while being fired upon by the muskets behind the walls. The small far redoubt tried to fire on the attackers as well, but they had already outflanked the guns and were locked in the confrontation with the forward positions.

One of the fleches they flanked from its right, and the other, was able to mow them down as they ran across the face of it before they looped back to try to take control of the road. Bodies littered the field and the cleared yellowish dirt of the road after them.

The mages were almost at the wall now as the artillery continued to fire on the infantry where it could. In the distance or near at hand. Many men's heads were so near to the barrels that there was nothing left of them when the smoke cleared.

Mage blasts issued forth from behind the advancing line, and Braddach called on his men to block the firebombs. Some made it through, starting gun and powder ablaze, while others were redirected out into the attackers on the field.

Braddach pointed the axe and sent spear after spear through the nearing defenders, cratering enemy mage's shields with the power of the staff.

The advance on the fleches was rebuffed and then continued as wave after wave fought through fire and fired back on the positions, riddling them with so many holes that new shots could find clear routes through the woodwork and into bodies that slumped in clumps behind the fortifications.

Braddach felt that unless they could completely break the mage line, the enemy would be able to use it to run their infantry almost unchecked behind it to attack the fleches. He suggested to Borgoron that they try to flank it to the right while portions of the redoubt burned around them, and their artillery continued to shell the enemy.

Guns had been brought forth now from Akre and had begun to hammer down on the redoubt, bouncing up and over the low wall or burying into the packed frost. Some others landed just beyond, catching bodies in their iron grip of death.

Braddach, Borgoron, and their twenty squad mages attacked the left flank of the Akrin line, sending it into a frenzy of rearrangement and defense. The redoubt was going up in flames and being crushed under barrages of fire and the sudden appearance of summoned monsters, but they would at least buy their men time to retreat to the reserve lines.

Shield, spear. It was an archaic duel of the most ancient technique as well as a mix of specialties as Frof, Nido, and company engaged in duels. Borgoron found the generals and Braddach followed him forward, engaging in battle against Davos, the summoner, Aftrin, a mage who attempted to steal and redirect spells out of the air, and Desi, a powerful shield mage who attempted to make himself impervious to damage.

Aftrin thwarted every spear Braddach tried to throw, and Borgoron engaged Davos, cratering each of his summoned creatures under barrages of molten rock. Braddach worried that Borgoron might be using up his stamina quickly and blocking the fire of both Aftrin and Desi, he felt like he needed to end things quickly. He threw as many aura blasts as he could at Desi, pinning him in place.

He blocked each attack by Aftrin, then faked a spear throw at Aftrin before tossing it instead at Desi, this time putting as much as he had into it and watching Aftrin whiff attempting to steal a spell that wasn't there. The smoke of Braddach's aura blasts cleared just as the spell appeared and Desi's mouth gaped open in surprise when the spell pierced his shield.

Davos called a retreat of the mages whose number had dwindled significantly in the risky tactic. Aftrin watched Braddach and Borgoron warily as they returned to the lines of their infantry that were redoubling for another attack on the fleches with the redoubt smoldering and cratered.

Murdot, Sonan, and Tornes rode up to survey the field just as the yellow mage squads crossed in front of the destroyed fortification. Bodies of the dead and dying were strewn about it as if set there as decorations. Murdot realized that one of the mages was not in yellow. He was in black and purple, wielding a black two headed axe. Had King Erold taken the field? Not even Polesar would dare such a thing, no matter his power.

When Braddach arrived at the fleches, seeing their disrepair and yet that the men, mage or not, had held, he cheered them on, man to man, tears welling in his eyes. He would not try to understand their private struggles, but they had battled through such malevolent death that it was a miracle that any lived through the hail of musket fire.

He counted his mages and found that Sten C, Sven, and Arne were dead and left behind. Braddach looked over the fleches as a cavalry appeared over the snow. He counted the number of men that were left and ordered a retreat. They would fall back to the reserve line of hills and the final redoubt as a cavalry charge rushed the position, unaware that its defenders fled past the pickets at the river bridge.

The first infantry led by Davos took the forward fleches and began moving artillery, past the husk of the redoubt, between and through the burst doorways of the fleches, to point them at the hill and begin shelling the small redoubts on the rear hill, while fighting raged ahead at the pickets on the bridge.

Murdot circled the far east redoubt on the southeast side of the field, forcing the position to retreat over the river at the easternmost bridge. Milton and the cavalry checked their advance across the water as the four smaller redoubts in the rear of the field that faced the Semroeka or the city fired artillery relentlessly forward, unassisted by the rest of the guns facing south over the Kalopha, where Gavo and Plaski formed up behind Eichlen's position at one of the smaller reserve redoubts to hem in the advance of the blue coats swarming Kienber's great redoubt that had become the prize of the field.

The whole of the forward line had been taken. The battle for the reserve line was on, and only one contested fleche of four remained under Normany control, while their retreating troops formed new lines on the hills on the north side of the Semroeka river.

The pickets at each of the river bridges had been abandoned, even the furthest east. Ernadsier and Geraldt's men had pressed over the remaining city bridge, forcing Normany's generals back to the west of the field, preventing the three mages from aiding Kienber in his redoubt.

The combination of Marandres and Naven were outdueling the talented mage, who tried to conserve his strength after fighting off countless squad mages thrown at him to die. The two leaders had finally pressed into the fight, while inching their artillery forward to fire on the reserve line behind Kienber.

Finally, Kienber, seeing the death around him, as another advance around the redoubt's eastern end, finished off the last of its defenders other than him, retreated, holding up his shield and backing away from the opposing generals who ushered the blue coats forward to prepare for counterattack. Kienber joined the men on the hill behind the redoubt, the widest of the ten hilltops, though not the tallest.

Many men fired their muskets at the abandoned positions. A few were Eichlen's men who had been separated from the general in the chaos and quickness of the city retreat. Most were either Pasan's men, as the general had not returned to the field, or Kienber's own, who had miraculously survived a battle that had dealt death at an astonishing rate.

Kienber reformed the lines on the hill, while the small redoubts still fired artillery at almost the entire field. Shots were returned by almost double the number of remaining guns as explosive bursts of the shelling, ripped stone and frost from the ground and thrust it into the air like child's toys.

Kienber could see from his position that the guns on the right flank were quiet. If they could be moved on the left, they would help to turn the tide as the opposing mages had advanced unchecked. He could see the line of the three Normany generals in yellow, blue, and red, developing below the hill where he stood to the right. He knew that the units of four opposing generals advanced on and into his redoubt.

He told the men nothing. He promised them nothing. He as well as they knew that a charge down the hill and up into the rear of the redoubt meant likely death for them all, but without it, all of the reserve positions, including those that sheltered Braddach and Borgoron to his east would be forfeit.

As he ran forward in a voiceless charge, the men followed suit, unleashing a hailstorm of musket and mage fire down upon the men of Marandres and Naven, who affixed knives to their muskets just as the Normany men had. Kienber threw lightning at the opposing generals, forcing them to abandon their unsheltered positions as bullets rained in ruthlessly, tearing apart cartons, bodies, and earth.

The Akrin men returned fire, but they were too few in number and the redoubt was retaken while the Normany generals moved to secure the right flank and begin pushing back the enemy from the center of the field.

* * *

Blaggard received the update that all of the forward positions had fallen with little reaction. Instead, he parsed through the detail with Erold, Moon, the archmage who he knew to be Valessa, Arla, Anglis, and the quiet Mr. William present with him in the command center.

Their camp was between three streams that formed a large shield-like shape just behind the hill where Kienber was reforming the positions to charge forward. Decisions had to be made whether or not they would somehow reverse the field, which appeared doubtful.

With the taking of the ground across the Semroeka, the enemy controlled most of the high ground, given the wide hillside of the east that extended over most of that side of the river, almost to the Kalopha. The three hilltops that the defenders still controlled, included the two lowest. Any charge that was issued forth from here on out would have to fight from the low ground.

"Where's Kutzbek?" asked Blaggard first.

No one knew.

"He should be here. I thought he was with the artillery on the right flank, but it hasn't been ordered in."

No one spoke, until Moon took charge, "I'll find him." She departed without another word, understanding that if she were to find him dead, she would order the three hundred guns to turn and direct fire across the Semroeka, herself.

Blaggard turned to the adjutants who had reported in from the reserve positions, "Send half of the infantry reserve to Braddach's position."

"Half, general?" asked Anglis. "We should be considering retreat."

"Braddach is a good general," said Blaggard, glancing at Erold knowing the king agreed. "If he can retake the forward positions then we will have the time to wheel around the guns on the two low hills to return fire on the opposition."

"I see the logic," said Anglis. "I will lead them myself, though I'm no mage." He departed with the adjutants.

"Arla, take the princess and depart for the Ash Vale now."

"General?" asked Valessa, annoyed, despite it only being five of them left in the command tent. She also knew that she was possibly the most powerful mage on the field. If anyone was needed to aid the final line of defense.

"Valessa, you must go," said Erold. "You know as well as I do that there are too many of the enemy mages. No matter how strong we are."

"What about you?"

"Mr. William and I will wait for Moon," said Erold, nodding at the expert driver. People of the future would remark on the talents of buggy whip makers, perfecting their craft, and they would forget the men who wielded them. But, men of Mr. William's caliber behind the reins were rarer than those who wielded magic powers.

Arla pulled at Valessa to get her to the wagon that they had ridden with their supplies in across Normany. Valessa looked at Blaggard and Mr. William, and then Erold, whom she kissed despite its publicity. Arla mentally sighed in frustration at Valessa's continual obsession while Erold kissed her back.

"Even if I'm not there, Fros will walk beside you," Valessa told him.

"He walks with you as well," said Erold, holding her hand as she departed, looking at him one last time.

"While we wait for Mrs. Moon," said Mr. William, "we should maybe consider getting our own transportation ready."

"We will wait here," said Erold.

1524 - Chapter 60

In an overwhelming reverse of GoldArrow, as the dusk settled with the bold yellow sun nearing the calm blue horizon of the Bacine Sea to the south on the twelfth of Halthi-eld, just over twelve hundred three-rams of Akre, having launched from Pavol alongside the five frigates, thirty three battleships and two brigs of Imeria, including the Santisma, began to grow out of the yellow-pink light of the sky, turning it black with the sheer number of airships that blotted out the final sliver of sun and swarmed toward the islands and the coastline, where the lightning arrays lay dormant.

For years, the blue crackle of static fire had doomed any Imerian ship that came too close, but as the wave of three-rams, neared the coast, they dipped low. Too low for the arcs to shoot at the approaching onslaught of ships. The posts were not abandoned, bolts of lightning still fired, even if these stray shots sizzled and crackled into the air before arcing wildly down to the sea, only hitting a ship by sheer accident, splitting them into exploding bits of erupting flame and steel.

Onward the shocking attack came, nearing the four major splintered islands that had protected the south coast of Albion where more lightning arrays had been placed along the bluffs that ran from where the Kalopha River met the sea all the way up the coastline to Rorik.

Bolts fired, arcing wildly in the shape of fishhooks into the soft waves of the deep blue sea. The buzz of the three-rams grew louder and louder like a million angry bees, homing in on the destructive towers, thirsting for vengeance.

As they neared, the shock troop mages, one to a ship began to let fly, taking the shapes of winged squirrels, speeding through the air at metal trees. The balls of lightning could be seen charging up and then firing off over the heads of the sweeping line of wizard men, who landed along the island beaches and began to hurl boulders, fire, ice, or call upon conjured spirits or animals to attack the towers.

The men in defense fired muskets back that were too far away to pierce the mages' thick armor. They battened down the doors, but many towers fell under the onslaught of magic. The steel collapsed upon the defenders as one by one the defense towers of Albion fell into the wispy grass and gray stone of the islands' hills and then into the sea, kicking up huge wafts of sand and water that rose as high as the three-rams that buzzed overhead, onward to the south coast, where more towers waited to be felled like rotted trees.

* * *

Early evening twilight had come to the Ash Vale as night was soon to descend in full. Theodore sat by the fire, alone, in his wheelchair, trying but failing to read a book. His mind was agitated with worry. The news of the Pavol launch point had reached him from Prince Eduard. He could not shake the feeling of doom.

There was a knock and a sound at the front door, then he heard a strange, familiar voice. Only strange because he had just been informed the battle at Pláedino had begun today. Mr. William unmistakably called to him loudly.

Theodore shook a bit. The hairs stood on his neck. He could only guess that a nighttime raid had forced him to flee with Erold, in which case, not hearing the king's voice, he had a moment of panic as to what might have befallen the orb.

"Yes, in here!" Theodore raised his voice and wheeled his chair over to the ajar door.

Mr. William frantically poked his head through and breathed a sudden sigh of relief, "Quickly, we must go. The battle has taken a turn for the worst."

"Mr. William, I did not expect you back so soon, but you very well know this is the safest pla--."

"No time to explain. Grab everything you can. Only the most important things. We must go to Ror--." Blood spurted from his butler's mouth, splashing across his face. Claws appeared from through the poor man's lungs and began shredding his body upward, until the man began to convulse, splashing red everywhere. His form flashed and turned pale gray, the murky color of...

"A shapeshifter. I could smell him for an atomic mile," said the Wolf Stone in a deep husky growl. There were some things that couldn't be changed. "You were right. They were coming for you."

"They've come for the orb. The Dark." He didn't have to say it out loud, but he did at the same time. It was the first time he was fully glad that he had let the object go. No matter how large Stone loomed now, he did not know what the dark would or even could throw at them now. He may have been at home, but the night was their territory.

Stone nodded, his wolf snout grinning, He had waited for this moment for a long time, and as he let his animal senses take control, he smelled them all around, nearing the house, only shadows bolting from point to point. They were merely whispers on the wind, but they smelled, reeked of blood. The fury that Stone felt at just the hint of their pheromones on the wind was enough to boil his own blood.

"Vampires. An elite strike unit. Perhaps forty or more." The wolf growled. They were approaching from all directions, covering each other's advances. They could move as silently as they liked, but it was like the smell of a burning cake to him. He was glad that Onya had helped him master his mind, and also glad that she wasn't there to hold him back.

Theodore hit a secret button on his wheelchair, "I've always wanted to use this." The chair morphed beneath him, turning into a bronze and dwarven metal exoskeleton. He cocked back the left arm, a four-barrel rifle he had loaded with nearly endless ammunition, always hidden beneath his seat. He revved up the lightning bolt glove on his right hand, super charged by the extra gear on the exoskeleton. "What do you say old friend? I just hope I'm fast enough."

"They know where--."

The glass of the massive windows lining the outer wall shattered and four vampires burst through.

Theodore turned and began unleashing rounds and lightning at the nearest two figures, watching their hulking forms be shredded by iron and light.

Stone curved around the exoskeleton's left and met the other two as they beamed for Theodore, readying to tear into his neck with their fangs.

Instead, the claws and teeth of a massive white, alpha werewolf tore into their brittle skin. His arms five times their size broke theirs easily, but they struggled against him like an elk being torn asunder by a grizzly. They had thought themselves masters of the night. Only to meet their doom.

Stone grabbed Theodore, lifting the exoskeleton off the ground and carried him through the house like a dog drags its pup in its mouth. He forced himself to run slower, on his hind legs, looking for the door to the Redbridge basement off to the side of the library.

Two figures burst at them from the hallway to his left, and he got between them and Theodore, who righted himself and fired over his friends back ripping the skull apart of one of the vampires, allowing Stone to wrestle the other until he had gained the upper hand and torn it in half.

Theodore could see that his friend was bleeding badly from bite marks and tears along his side, but the wounds began to heal slowly from his natural regeneration. Theodore back pedaled down the basement stairs as Stone shook off the shock of the wounds. Before he could get into the rock tunnel that led to the defensible basement bunker, another four vampires were upon him.

Stone wrestled one to the side as Theodore did his best to fire at them. One at a time, they took them apart, but while Stone wrestled the last, another two appeared in the wide stairwell, climbing on the ceiling.

Another two appeared, laughing on the ground as they rushed at Theodore, who fired wild bolts of lightning and bullets, luckily piercing the skull of the vampire to his left through the forehead, shattering its skull and then raking the vampire on the ceiling to the right with a bolt of lightning, shattering the creature and the stone it gripped onto.

The left arm of Theodore's suit was torn apart and all he could hear were the empty clicks. The lightning array petered out, and he wrestled against the strength of the vampire that tried to pin down his arm.

The other vampire, Theodore glanced left was being devoured by Stone, who then split the last in half and then pulled Theodore over his back, limping into the sealed basement, shutting the stone door behind them, as he directed Theodore to blast everything he could muster with his lightning glove through the slowly closing doorway.

Finally, the door closed and sealed by steel, the king wolf, Jack Stone began to feel his age in the werewolf form, resting against the cold stone. His own warm blood pooled beneath him, and he laughed at Theodore, whose paralyzed legs dangled lifeless, shaking in the air from the crippled exoskeleton. Only the central frame, enough of the legs, and part of the right arm remained. He had a few bloody scratches and surface level bruises, but Stone's mind painfully fought against the beast within to think that the enemy must have been intentionally keeping Theodore alive, but why?

The pair licked their wounds, and he pulled the scepter of Lyse from where it was tied to his leg and gripped it firmly into his palm. If rhodium was the secret to unlocking his power, and silver its antithesis, he was lucky again that Moon had delivered it to them. It would not be a full moon for another week.

The room shook. Whatever they were doing outside of the stone walls, they were trying furiously to break into Theodore's stronghold. Through the thick walls, the Wolf King could no longer smell where the enemy was coming from.

Theodore rushed around the room on his metallic legs. He imagined he might try to pinpoint a way to reinforce their breakpoint whenever they did breakthrough.

Another tremor. This one stronger.

Theo gathered up supplies from his work room while simultaneously refashioning a makeshift rifle on his left arm and connecting it to the last few rounds of ammo.

Another tremor, stronger still.

Theodore got the gun to work, playfully clicking at a wall, and finding a steel door, he motioned at Stone to lift. The old wolf didn't get a chance to move.

A tremor and then a sudden shaking feeling, cascaded through the pair, echoing through the room like sound waves bouncing in a cave. It felt as if the air had suffered an earthquake, and the bombardment stopped abruptly.

Theo went to the safety escape route at the back of the basement, walking in the exoskeleton, while Stone continued to rest at the entrance to the room, his wounds healing slowly. Theo looked down the tunnel through a small iron hatch, and briefly imagined that a creature of the night might hiss at him.

There was nothing.

Only the natural dark of the cave.

Something had drawn them off.

Theodore and Stone looked at each other. They were now prisoners of fate, waiting to hear what had happened on the battlefield in the east, where yellow, blue, green, and red jackets clashed one last time.

1524 - Chapter 61

Moon found Kutzbek frothing at the mouth, looking into space as if contemplating the edge of knowledge. His bad eye had welled up with water as if tears were being held in by the glass. The pupil of his lone, good eye was a black well, and the line of his dark, brown iris as thin as a mare's hair.

Moon knew the charm. She understood what happened. The enemy had attempted to destroy his mind, incapacitating it during the fight. A spell that could not work on most mages, but only the strength of Kutzbek's willpower still tethered him to the world.

Moon took a charmed necklace from the order of the Taivaan from around her neck and bestowed it upon Kutzbek, breaking the spell instantly.

"Mrs. Moon?"

"You've been paralyzed by mage treachery," said Moon. "We need the reserve artillery to fire on the left flank. Now! We are in danger of being overrun."

He had gotten up and ran ahead of her as she followed him, needing to retrieve her necklace before risking a fight against a mage.

She just hoped that they were not too late, and the battle had not already been lost.

* * *

Braddach and Borgoron received the reinforcements--all infantry, no mages left alive to spare--and yet, they led them forward, charging the bridge, betting the future of Normany on the men whose only superpower was bravery. Their remaining squad mages flanked them as they swarmed out from the hill and blasted the bridge with fire, ice, and spear. The enemy's mages countered the attacks where they could, but Braddach's blast had renewed zeal as his spears split through men and as the two lines met, his axe followed splitting limbs like lamb.

The counterattack laid waste to an entire division, meeting it at the near end of the bridge in melee, while the enemy artillery hammered the redoubts and hills, sending piles of frost, snow, and limb into the air.

The bridge retaken, the allied army stormed ahead of their lead mages, breaking against their own pickets, overtaking retreating foes, sending back musket fire as the two armies traded blow for blow.

Mages, men, and horses fell across the field and the Akrin

artillery gunners fought for their lives, sending forth shells at point blank through the charging line before being overtaken and snuffed like candlewicks.

The line of Normany yellow and Albion red thinned at the bridge and widened as it swarmed at the forward fleches that trapped their quarry in a mad scramble to escape the counter advance.

Not even horses could maneuver past the masses of bodies, stacked as high as one's head, as Murdot and his officers abandoned the cavalry. He saw the advance of the Normany king and knew he had to bide his time. If he could take out the usurper, the day would be Akre's. What horsemen could not retreat were left to fall to the frost as if they were spires of metal suddenly melting when touched by just the right heat.

War had never stained the frost so red with blood. Melees had never been so desperate in every facet as the private battles of a desire for life gripped the men, who silently battled without bullet, only to see another minute of life before another enemy advance would catch them again with knived muskets.

Braddach and Borgoron met at the fleches where Braddach retook the front, wielding the axe, sending back cannonball and mage's blast, directing his men to fire at all advancing parties as the thousands of Akrin troops and artillery still came, as far as the eye could see, regrouped and advanced again.

Musket fire bounced off his armor. Mage blast ricocheted off each spell he cast. He took out squad mages across the field, and only departed from the top of the wall when they had pushed back a second advance.

Patr D and Ivan had died, unceremoniously left for dead somewhere between the hill and the fleches. Whether on the bridge, in the river, or on the hills, he didn't know. Another advance of the enemy was coming, Braddach couldn't go back to look for the bodies of friends, no matter how great.

Kienber on the other side of the field had just retaken the great redoubt with the charge from the hill, but his allied generals had failed to secure the bridges, allowing yet another advance from Akrin to swarm the redoubt, which was little more than a blown-out husk surrounded by crumbled stone, with two routes in where the Akrin forces ran in headlong without fear.

The Normany men fired on them, dropping so many that it was as if the oncoming enemy had to climb over their own bodies to fight in the citadel of doom. Akrin mages burned some of the dead out of their way, putting a disgusting smell of charring remains into the air.

Artillery continued to rain over the redoubt, crashing into still more Normen men attempting to retake the reserve fleche that covered the left flank of the position. Naven led the mages at Kienber with Ernadsier, Geraldt, and Marandres. Kienber breathed heavily, exhausted, and suddenly realizing that if the generals were this far ahead of their men, the battle around the lone island of Normany control, might have been lost.

Kienber shot fire and lightning, defended against multiple blasts of spirit energy, fire, and ice shard. He had no idea who was throwing what, but he reacted on instinct, hoping to inspire his men who were being overwhelmed by the enemy general's squad mages.

Kienber, advanced on the enemy, cutting them into two groups and took out Ernadsier by shoving a mage's spear through his head at point blank.

He locked spells with Naven, watching his hands go up in flame before him. The fire surrounding him like a shield.

Geraldt sent ice shards into the swirling flame that somehow made it through, cutting into Kienber's lungs and dropping his defense. Naven cast the spirit blade that beheaded Kienber as he fell to his knees.

The Normany men fought for the body, but there were not enough mages to fight back the Akrin force. In the end, they retreated from the redoubt back to the hill behind it. Some crying for their leader who had saved them all at one point in the long battle.

The three Normany generals still fighting the westernmost fleche did not know what went on in the redoubt, but they willed their men to try to break the Akrin line and force them back while Naven moved to the east of the field to flank Braddach and Borgoron's advance and then take the bridge from behind, leaving the two generals ahead of the line to be crushed between a hammer and an anvil.

They had repelled a third advance when the enemy mages and artillery formed up in unison, advancing forward after each round of gun fire shelled the riddled fleches that were little more than stacked wood shards, being thrown up into the air again with each strike from a drumstick.

Braddach nodded to Borgoron that they had to retreat, covering for their men as they ran back to the river. Braddach saw that Akrin as moving quickly past the redoubt to the south covering the bridge behind them, and if they didn't make it back to the reserve line soon, they would be enveloped.

Braddach repelled mage fire and artillery, using every spell he knew whether warlock or offensive spell from Albion to strike the blasts out of the air or redirect them into the land. It was not enough. A blast of artillery cratered the ground beside him, and shrapnel shot into his leg, splitting through the dragonskin armor and taking him down while musket fire still pinged off of his shoulders and chest.

For a moment he looked around. His soldiers died around him, falling to artillery and musket fire in waves. Avael was struck by mage's spear through his chest as he failed to cast a shield spell in time. A spell that Braddach had once watched Erold master and expand upon. Honter was riddled by more than one shot of spirit fire before being hit by a musket shot in the chest and then as he fell, a cannonball burst into the ground where his body hit the dirt.

Braddach and Borgoron, and their last mages, were left alone ahead of the mostly successful retreat to the hills as the enemy mages advanced past the fleches ahead of them and from between the hills and the river to the right and behind them. They were surrounded quickly.

Naven speared Frof as he turned around to attempt to defend the rear, leaving only Sten S and an injured Nido from Braddach's squad. Braddach did not risk looking to see if Borgoron had any of his own squad left.

The duel began. Nido fought with ground and lightning against Tornes. Sten had only enough stamina left to throw aura blasts and shield himself, hoping it would be enough, as he fought against Sonan.

Braddach traded blasts with Murdot, who he had seen at Marolno beach leave Milton injured. Aftrin joined him, beginning to chip at Braddach's armor as Braddach's crippled leg rooted him in place. Quickly, Tornes brought Nido, still fighting, to his knees while Borgoron fought Davos.

Naven worked around behind the battle and then speared Borgoron, felling the gentle, friendly man like he was nothing more than animal.

Six mages on three now, Murdot and his men circled their prey, while Nido caught his breath on his knees and Sten charged aura blasts on his hands.

Murdot wanted to end this himself and began fighting with mage spear and shield. Trading blasts in the air with Braddach as if attempting to punch through his enemy and tear out his heart, blocking the swinging axe with just willpower.

Braddach could not hold on any longer. The blood loss from his leg turned the world to faded shapes. His well of stamina had been run dry. He fell to the ground and trying to get up, Murdot sent a spear through his stomach.

Murdot stood over him, wrestling the axe from his grasp and looking at him in disgust, not pity or understanding. The dying man was no king.

* * *

"Murdot has just sent word that they've held the line against the opponent's counterattack. He's requesting the royal guard be sent in to finish off the enemy."

"What are the losses at?" the emperor asked.

"It appears that in Davos's first infantry, where Murdot is requesting reinforcement, the losses are at almost fifty percent, but he says that the king has been fighting alongside his men in defense there, and the great redoubt at the center of the enemy's defense has been taken a second time."

"The king has been fighting alongside his men?" the emperor mused. In this day and age, when a bullet could kill even the most talented mage, was he out of his mind, thought the emperor, who had risen the ranks first within the mage's courts of Akrin's vast network.

"It is unconfirmed, but Murdot is adamant."

If Polesar committed his royal guard to the fray and they lost fifty percent of the force, it would be a devastating blow to morale, and being this far from Akre, almost impossible to replenish his lines, but if he didn't press the advantage with winter this close, the day would most certainly be a massive victory for Normany, potentially stalemating the war.

"What is your order, sir?"

"We have the potential to deal a decisive blow. Issue the order to Junto and Groche. Have them reinforce Murdot's position and break Normany once and for all."

* * *

They continued to receive the mixed reports from the front with Blaggard finally deciding to lead the last of the men to the reserve line himself.

Kienber and Braddach had both led successful counterattacks that had taken the positions and then held them, only for the constant advances of the Akrin corps to drive them into a retreat once again.

Kutzbek had yet to swing around the artillery, but the report was that he was back in the right mind. Everyone knew it was likely too late, despite not knowing the loss figures. Losing the battle of the mages meant that it was up to the men who fired the muskets and howitzers to seize the day.

Across all positions, the reserve line and beyond it were being threatened. If the men on the two near hills were overrun, the Normany camp would be threatened. They battled, there, at three small redoubts and as the Akrin army launched up the hill from Kienber's redoubt as the three positions still tried desperately to launch cannon fire onto the approaching Akrin army further afield.

Artillery had been pushed up to the river. Explosions had already begun to touch the tents as well as errant shot that had been aimed at these final Normen bastions. It remained to be seen if the three hundred guns, being pushed up to the hills from behind could somehow turn the tide in one final, desperate counterattack.

Mr. William had been taking it all in as the information had been relayed and watched Blaggard issue orders and ultimately decide to enter the fray. It had been hypnotizing. When he finally looked at the king, he realized that Erold had left.

Mr. William found Erold half-dressed in his dragon-skin armor, just finishing putting in on and just in time to stop him from entering the battle.

"If you're going to try to stop me, don't."

"You could die. The orb would be lost. If one battle is lost, it doesn't matter."

"I don't care about the battle. This isn't about the war anymore. Braddach is one of the only two family members that I have left, and if I don't get to the front lines now, he could be overrun."

"You can'--"

"He's my family!" Erold tightened his gloves and then in anger and frustration began to speak with passion. "Everyone else has died. I've always run. Now I'm powerful and I can do something about it. I have to go, instead of watching everyone die before me."

After a moment, Mr. William, thinking about what actually losing the battle could mean for Albion and the Northern Alliance that he'd heard so much about, made his own decision, "I'll drive you to the frontlines myself."

Erold looked up as Mr. William began barking orders to adjutants to get him a wagon with four horses. Erold picked up the old iron shield, wrapping it around his left arm, to hide the orb in his left hand from sight.

"We'll run an old Otum chariot maneuver," he said and then in a commanding tone he told the king. "When I turn at the edge of camp to stay behind the hill, you'll have to jump off and begin to run in the air at full speed or you'll break your legs. It will put you into the battle faster than a horse." Once also an old Olympic game written about in the battle tales of Elessia and Cardane, Erold mentally readied.

The team had been attached and waited outside. Seaspirit was at the front. The unicorns were all gone to battle, waiting in the east for a sign to re-enter the fray. They were about to get it, thought Erold.

Kienber was dead, along with so many others. Braddach could be dying. It was not time to issue orders from far off ivory towers. It was time to end the war for good. For that was the whole reason he had returned to Normany in the first place. To stave off war. And yet, it was here in all its gruesome evil. Played out by the people who were the victims of mad men playing with strings behind the scenes.

Mr. William was not lying when he said he would drive the makeshift chariot hard. He had it at top speed and Erold could see the guns being pushed up the hills about to reach the top, as Mr. William slapped the reins for the hard turn.

As if trying to round a giant boulder, he hit a sharp turn between the two hills where the battle raged. Erold was thrown off the side of the wagon and he began to run in the air, hitting the ground in full armor at top speed, not stopping and waiting to die like bullets and spears stopped flying.

The wagon rolled over itself as it hit the rear side of the hill, crashing into tents with the desperate cries of horses, trying to avoid a similar fate.

Erold ran between the hills, his men seeing him come in his black armor, wondering with his blonde hair flowing if he was out of his mind, attacking alone.

Erold saw Murdot jettison the spear through Braddach's stomach in the center of the bridge. There were six Akrin mages, easy to see in their dark blue and white, with red decals; and two of his own, in bright yellow, pinned on the bridge, dead bodies all around.

There was no hesitation no matter the risk. He knew the good outweighed the bad in the prophecy of old. He had no idea what was to come, but he held unlimited power in his hands. He was no judgment of good or evil, just the extension of fate to deal justice on one given day.

And he had fallen into the berserker rage of old, one with the decisive ability to end the war as if the gifts of angels, or of a higher power.

He threw white lightning as if it was not lightning, but thick and snaking through the air, calling the thunder and the rain, breaking through the barriers of Naven and leaving him in a seizure withering on the ground.

No match for the true speed of light.

What was Erold's power and what was the orbs? He could not know, but when they threw spears at him, he had conjured the blue forcefield around him like he had seen Kahron do. The blasts, artillery, musket, lightning, fire, water, beast, or ice, dinked off the blue shield like squeaking mice.

Erold's left hand gripped the orb, his right hand jettisoned another murderous white bolt of lightning, cutting through the air and splitting Davos in half.

Tornes launched himself forward to throw a spear as close to Erold as possible, hoping to dent the shield. Erold threw a mage's spear so hard as the mage came, that it split through his chest and blew up between an artillery battery across the river in the distance, as the fire of the three hundred guns followed him and Akrin men were cut down in droves.

With each lightning blast from Erold's hand, it was hard to tell what thunder was his and what was the thunder of guns that split through the air and cratered the Akrin army at the reserve fleches, in Kienber's redoubt, and at the edge of the river. Murdot blew the bridge and ran while Aftrin and Sonan ran with him, momentarily spared by Sonan's shielding spells.

Erold didn't need a bridge. He had been taught by Kahron to walk on water and he did so now, following the retreating men, seeing the man who carried the axe get on a horse and take off towards the fortifications in the west.

Erold looked for a moment at Braddach, near death, being carried to safety by Sten and Nido. If war had not come, Braddach would still be alive. If war had not come, his father would never have been killed. Nor his uncle. If war had not come, he would have been set to visit the ice palace and would have met Valessa in a world of peace. The Normen of the far ago ages were not all great men despite the tales, but if he was going to rewrite the tale of the future, he would start by not letting war come again to Normany.

Long ago, his life, his destiny was shaped by the decisions of men, doomed to death by the determination of senates and votes, vying for power, seeking things with desire. Now, he had been gifted an arbitrary tool of limitless energy and he did not seek or wish to use it. He had hoped that they could have wintered in Umfell and ended the war by treaty.

He stepped off the water and was met by three mages, who thought that his power must run out. He guided white lightning through them.

Then, came another three. Soon, he had killed twenty-seven mages in all, walking past the smoldering redoubt, as the men of Akrin ran from the battle and the men of Normany pressed forward to take back Kienber's redoubt, unable to follow the king across the river.

Milton led the cavalry out from the easternmost bridge as the sun disappeared beneath the horizon. The long day of battle was almost near at end, and they would end it as they started it charging across the field in the reverse direction, this time chasing down those running away.

Sonan and Aftrin turned around and attempted to battle Erold, using simple spear and shield. His blue forcefield flickered in and out, and he was surprised. Instead, he used the more powerful deflection spell of the islands to send spears away and then caught Sonan's horse in the chest, running through the rider as well, as the horse crashed into the smoldering forward redoubt.

Erold could see the battlefield covered in the dead and dying as far as the eye could see. Mainly horses and men in blue coats, suffering in personal agony if life still breathed in them. It was a horrendous act to have ventured forth from the Brandon gates, once built for peace. The yellow coats covered the hills across the whole of the field.

Erold didn't want to know the final toll. Not yet. Aftrin returned, and Erold sent a spear attempting to kill him just the same, but Aftrin deflected it back at Erold. Erold deflected that and sent yet another. Aftrin did it again, and Erold ricocheted it back, over and over it went until finally, Aftrin had nothing left and the spear caught him in the shoulder, and he slumped on the horse and then fell off.

Twenty-nine mages dead.

Erold remembered reading so long ago in the library at Peth that finding the spell was one of the trickiest things about being a mage. It wasn't always there when you needed it, and he thought too how so many resorted to the simplest spells as the fighting dwindled.

The unicorn cavalry circled around him, warning him that the royal guard of Akrin had taken up positions at the Valenval bridge ahead.

Erold did not care.

His brother lay dying behind him. Valessa had run away. He wouldn't.

He walked past all the blue coats, dead and dying, to the false forward fleches that they had built the night before where the horsemen of Akre had been brutally beaten.

Akrin forces had retreated from the redoubt and were attempting to hold the city, but Genie had reconsidered and ordered a full retreat that not everyone heard.

The shelling from the hill had increased as the guns of Normany doubled in number. Genie had the second bridge in Pláedino blown and many of the Akrin force began to pull away, abandoning the city, buildings falling under fire and bursting to flames as the retreat began.

Some of the Akrin army was caught against the river when the stone fell into the water, and they were gutted with the knives of the defenders who crossed the bridge over the Semroeka as Erold neared the Valenval bridge. Dying men and dead bodies kicked into the ice water to float in the evening twilight.

Erold arrived at the Valenval bridge where his men had captured the eastern end. None were eager to face the seventy-two mages that lined the other side of the river. They watched him approach, the high hill behind him, snow-capped and leafless trees covered the whole of it. His blonde hair singed from fire and fury. He held just a shield.

He walked forward to cross the long bridge.

Groche led, Junto behind him. All seventy other mages readied blue aura blasts in concert. Erold remembered what the King Hughgar had said about fighting many mages at once, combine their spells into one and deal with them at the same time. He had meant to lock spells against them, and looking at it now, without being able to call a forcefield, a well-timed deflection spell seemed useless. Erold had to search his mind for something or find a way to turn one deflection spell into seventy-two.

The storm came. Each mage throwing spells at him with two hands. Aura balls of white and blue and purple and yellow. The colors of spirit energy. Not the ones he had dodged when Kahron had thrown them, or the ones he had thrown. Not much more than a bruise if one of those hit you. These were designed to kill, coming in at hundreds of atomic miles per hour.

He put the shield up reflexively, casting as strong a shield spell as he could. None of his men could see him, the blasts decorated his body and shield in light. Tiny explosions puffed and the light built slowly around him.

The blasts continued to come and began to hit him, peppering his dragonskin armor through his shield spell. He had nowhere to run. If he moved, the spells would surely kill him. He felt as if the very ground beneath him sank as the pressure of the spells destroyed his spell and even his rare, steel shield, cutting into his skin.

Erold realized it. He would have to use the banishment spell that Kahron used, but not on the creatures of darkness for which it worked best, but on the spells themselves. All at once, holding the thousands of furious strikes at bay, he blinked them out of existence as one, following the attack with a stunning bolt of white lightning that separated Groche into two halves and screamed into the snow behind him, splattering blood.

The line of mages held strong but waited on Erold or Junto to make a move. The shield had been blown to nothing. The dragonskin armor was in shreds on the man's body. There was, theoretically in their minds, no object that a mage could not damage, hinder, or remove from existence. And yet, he remained, standing. Blood dripped down the black armor onto the stone at his feet from a myriad of cuts.

The legendary axe had been taken. Only the orb remained in Erold's hand, and the barest shred of the steel of the shield. The orb itself could not be reduced, for it offered a power that no one of this realm, even those who created it, truly understood and those who tried to destroy it before, failed to hide.

Erold began to strike out in fury at the mages. Bolt after bolt, calling forth the white light with his right hand. The vicious strikes moved before they could be comprehended, and the thunder roared through the air after the whip of light cracked the fabric of space-time.

The mages tried to block the spell to stop his fury. None succeeded, but Erold soon found that even the fury had deserted him. The lightning no longer came.

The blood splatters of seventy-one bodies littered the field ahead of the empty town. One mage remained. He surrendered and Erold spared him, passing on. Knowing that his true quarry waited ahead of him. The mage who had killed Braddach and held the black axe.

His men followed. Eichlen arrested the crying mage, praying thank you to Fros for mercy. The soldiers ran forth, bringing artillery along with them, ready to dismantle the fortification of the enemy down to the very brick, removing all trace of Akrin from the soil of Normendin.

At the fortification, Erold and his men found it defended with men on the walls and Murdot, standing before it held the axe. All Erold assumed that he could cast now was a simple shield and spear spell.

He knew that, but the enemy didn't. He wondered if he had overused the orb, but he hadn't. He had overused himself, and his own mind. He knew he could capture or defeat any physical creature, demon, or cloud, in the universe, but there was a limit to all worldly power. He had reached it now.

Erold just needed that much more to defeat Murdot. He prayed for it to be granted. Just that little bit more strength to fight his brother's killer. Even if he too had played that role in defense of the land.

Erold cast an ethereal spear, permanently affixing it to his hand, and tensed his shield arm, waiting to cast it. He dodged Murdot's strikes.

"What happened to all that power? Did you use it all up before you came to face me?"

Erold said nothing. He didn't need words or games to kill. He dodged a few more strikes, circling his foe as the men on the ramparts of the fortress watched. Snow decorated the ground, and Erold left trails like comets in the melt.

Murdot went for the kill with the axe blade. Erold stabbed the spear into the air, shooting it forward through Murdot's neck, watching the man fall. Eyes wide open. Erold took the black axe from the dying man's hands like a gift. He raised it to the men on the walls and decapitated Murdot.

A petty act that he regretted, but revenge had been his. The men on the wall jeered and booed, but then the fire of the artillery began to rain on them, and the wooden palisades burst into flames as the yellow coats of Normany and the green cavalry of Valgaard tore the bastion to the ground, laying waste to anyone who dared stay inside.

The bonfire could be seen for miles in every direction like the comet that had flown through the air earlier that year but was only seen in the islands, by mages of the stars, and in Roon Kalada. That day the sky in Normany had been overcast and rainy and no one had looked up to see it, coloring the heavy clouds a light white.

Erold let himself kneel, falling to the ground.

Erold watched his men counterattack, ruthlessly, annihilating their enemy. What great evil would come he did not know, but he wondered 'how could this be a great good.' He did not see a battlefield of dead orcs, trolls, ogres, elves, or dwarves, only a battlefield of dead men and the children of men. Of husbands, sons, and brothers.

He could see the face of Deronson in the eyes of the slack jawed dead men that were piled as high as hills. He could see Lynna's little brothers, and those of the merchant of Snajrberg, the gentlemen officers at the ball in Leidyn, the horse-keepers across the country, or that of the merchant from Umfell.

He did not feel relief as his forces poured forward from every hill, over every bridge, taking back every fortification and rushing the walls of the enemy's makeshift encampment. He felt only guilt, terror, and shame. How many will have died here today, so that others of other countries may live in peace?

He felt a hand on his shoulder, and he looked up to see Moon, and Valessa too. He stood and let the two women walk him back to the camp.

When he saw Braddach's mangled body. His brother, a Normen too, clinging to life, he was unable to speak. His black hair, his dark eyes. One of the only two people left on this icy Vatna, this frost, that he had known all his life.

He could not weep. He could not be angry. He could only kneel and pray that it would not happen yet again. He prayed that someone he loved would not be taken from this life.

1524 - Chapter 62

The Empire's airships refueled off the coast of Albion before turning northeast to strike at its heart, Rorik, the castle tower, and Angel Bay.

They followed the warm air current that crossed the Bacine Sea and aimed to cross the face of the city from over the thick forest of the green bluffs of cape Salgar to its south, bombarding it and crushing it from existence like Vilshala and Gangüt before it. There was to be no mercy as they ensured the resistance of the Northern Alliance would be permanently pacified after years of skirmishes over the seas.

After the fire of Pavol, despite limited casualties of ships or men, no one had reservations about unleashing destruction on the men and women of Albion.

On the ships of Albion, men waited to meet the larger opposing force in battle. They had heard of the stunning resounding victory on the fields at Pláedino, and they had to quiet each other from chanting a familiar cry, "Remember GoldArrow," and giving away their position.

Just like at the southern coast, when the defense array fell, the over twelve hundred Akrin three-rams jettisoned out ahead of the much larger ships from Imeria, which turned left to be parallel to the coast and cover the rear and left flanks of the smaller aircraft tasked with the bombardment of the city. They would then begin a backwards 'z-shaped' pathway across the city by taking another turn back to the right, aiming to force engagement with the enemy on their broadside where they held the advantage in sheer numerical superiority.

The allied navy launched its counteroffensive as the Akrin three-rams neared the bluffs on the cape of Salgar. The four hundred three-rams of Menetoris appeared to lift off the ground at the edge of the city and run, as the enemy three-rams rushed to engage them.

The Menetorian ships crossed into Angel Bay, and the Akrin ships pursued. As they crossed over the cape's bluffs and turned toward Angel Bay, something strange happened. It wasn't that the Albion battleships appeared. No, it was that the climate of the bay was different. The air was far more moist, and the change in weight dynamics caused the headlong ships to stall out, shake, fall, shimmy, swerve and run into each other by attempting to get out of the way, or by the force of the air current. The Menetorians had started on the other side of a natural wall in the air.

In the sudden confusion as more ships crowded into the shifting currents, flying higher or lower to avoid the crush, the Menetorians attacked back. The blasts of mages from both sides rang out as fire, lightning, and conjured mage spear became the rule of the day.

The Menetorian superiority due to the use of counter magic became clear quickly, and Graneuva heading the Santisma at the center of the rear line could only watch as the numerical advantage of the Akrin mages was wiped away by the sheer strength of the Menetorian island mages who, with only a fraction of the force could turn the fire of a thousand mages that swept across the sky into wisps of smoke barely visible in the distance. Akrin mages abandoned their ships and flew off with the same magic that they had used to dive at the towers, but they found themselves caught by hurtling shrapnel or sucked into air vortexes that sent them tumbling down or up until they were shredded by an islander's merciless phantom blades.

Out from the left came a familiar sight. Graneuva had seen the Thirdwind, an oversized battleship, and its captain, only a handful of times over the years but he knew it well. The opposing line had turned southeast, cutting Graneuva off from supporting the three-rams. He thought this might happen, but he hadn't anticipated them being caught in a crush in the air. He had also believed, having seen how powerful the Akrin university mages were compared to the Chancery mages of Imeria, that his force would be nigh unstoppable.

As the opposing Albion battleships closed off his view of the fray, he could see that the islander ships had encircled the Akrin three-rams, cutting off any attempt at retreat and forcing the ships into further frantic maneuvers, unable to find a clear pathway in the swirling wind of the bay.

Ferrara heading a schooner, cut off the front of the line and looped back to the northeast. Graneuva found it odd, but he ordered his men to ready to fire their broadsides when the opposing ships came into view.

If they all turned to follow the northeast line, he would have to chase them. He remained numerically superior with forty cruisers, which were mainly his formidable dwarven metal battleships. It took less than a minute to recognize that the opposition was banking on the three-rams not being able to catch them in between the two portions of the Empire's force. Even now, Graneuva could tell that the battle had begun to even out behind the opposing line as the light of fire and the rising smoke above the enemy lines grew.

The opposing ships turned. They made an arc, and it appeared that they recognized the risk. Even if they had slightly longer range to their guns, there was no way they could survive if the Akrin mages recovered and got the better of the Menetorian gunships that had ensnared them.

It was then that the forward ship pulled a move that Graneuva should have seen coming, but even if he did, he would have ordered the same from his men. The Thirdwind did not complete the turn to follow the faster schooner. Instead, it cut sharply, revved up its engines and led the line right at the middle of the Imerians. Graneuva recognized that from their slightly higher position in the air, the Albion ships had an additional advantage.

Across all of the Imerian airships, the order went up to fire at will at the forward vessel. If they could take it out first, it would be easy to take out a few more and dwindle the opposing forces before the two lines met.

Prince Eduard stood on the forward bridge, well aware that the Thirdwind was about to be opened up to the full fire of the enemy lines as the maneuver attempted to split the Imerians rear ships from the faster frigates and forward battleships, giving them time to engage the opponent when Albion outnumbered Imeria, and not the other way around.

The broadside cannon fire of the Imerian ships began. Each battleship unleashed with seventy-four guns. The Santisma fired all one hundred thirty-eight, slightly more than the other Imerian brig. It was well over twenty-five hundred cannons shot in total that aimed for the forward Albion ships. Blasts of red rang out from steel, and black powder filled the air. The true battle of Cape Salgar had begun.

Many of the cannonade found their mark. Most did not touch the Thirdwind, with the swirling fire instead hitting nothing and plunking the water below. Others blasted into the reinforced hull, or that of the second or third ship of the line.

Bits of the Thirdwind fell to the water and explosions ricocheted throughout, but it remained in the sky. It turned hard to port, cutting across the face of the line and ran toward the Santisma. Then, it started to drift downward, somewhere its inner balloon had been punctured.

Despite their lead ship slowly falling toward the sea, the Albion ships behind it followed suit as the sidewinding maneuver caught the rear half of the force and the bulk of its strength in a devastating pincer that waited, filing through until they outnumbered the forward half of the Imerian column two to one and surrounded the Santisma at the center. The opening salvo of Albion erupted from above, returning fire in crippling crossing blasts that shredded the decks of the battleships. One ship suddenly burst into flames, completely engulfed in fire and smoke and dropped like an iron ball into the sea. Through the sight of the devastation and chaotic bands of smoke all around the Santisma, Graneuva could see the dropping of the colors in surrender by the ships ahead, even as some of the Imerian men that somehow survived the salvo, among the many dead and wounded, fired muskets across the air at the Albion ships from the open top decks.

They had been circled quickly, and Graneuva ordered another round from the Santisma, but the shots that fired out in all directions couldn't turn upward to hit the closing Albion ships. The math played through his head. It was thirty-one enemy ships against his twenty-one, including the sinking of the Thirdwind and one of his own battleships.

He saw the emergency gliders of the downward drifting Thirdwind spit out from the lower bays and aim for his ship. He ordered his men to the decks to open musket fire. He looked out from the bridge to see that through the smoke, from each of the enemy battleships, the boarding crafts were launching, even to board the ships that had already hung the flag in defeat. The core of his navy was not just being overrun but captured. He had been a fool.

Graneuva looked around at the crew on deck, and began barking out orders, to turn the Santisma hard to port and signal to the rear ships just beginning to engage to follow suit. If they could turn the tide against the boarding parties here, he could rescue the Santisma and pull as many of the battleships out of the formation with him. Then, if the forward airships turned and joined him, they could enact a strong counterattack and still win the day. If they met the Akrin three-rams, still grappling with the Menetorians over Angel Bay through ice and flame, they could take the upper hand.

Prince Eduard was among the lead gliders, charging downward on the wind for the Santisma. They looked like hundreds of bronze doves, diving at a breaching whale. Boarding craft from two more battleships had launched with them and at full steam would soon crash into the sides of the massive brig.

Muskets fired from the decks while the cannons still could not turn upward high enough to hit them from how close they were. Bullets began to whizz past the prince and his men. The pellets of the shots struck against many of the metal gliders, sounding like heavy rain drops on the roof of a tin shack. Some found their mark on man, who fell spiraling to the ocean, their gliders drifting in strange motions, no longer guided, twirling toward the sea.

A bullet hit him in the shoulder, and he grimaced. He felt the pain, but he thrust his sword in its scabbard ahead of him and yelled for the men to press on for Albion, for GoldArrow. The Santisma was the prize. Ahead of them the boarding ships rammed into covered decks across the enemy's sides. From top to bottom, they would soon be assaulted from within by a heavily armed strike force, prepared and briefed on the mission to capitulate the enemy by capturing the banner flagship.

What was left of the hundreds of gliders that had launched from the doomed Thirdwind began to crash and latch onto the top deck of the Santisma, jettisoning the men they carried across the metal hull.

Pistols were drawn, muskets fired, and swords clashed as the bulk of the armed defense of the pride of the Imerian fleet and valiantly they fought back. Bodies were flung overboard, men collapsed around the prince, but onward he pushed, firing pistols into chests, slicing wrists with pistols poised, and locking arms against a man who tried to stab him with a knived musket, he dodged the oversized knife as they disengaged and delivered a quick thrust of this saber into the heart.

He looked around the upper deck, recognizing that the opposing force had committed their mages to the three-rams locked in the fight above the city. Imeria had done the same as he. He, his father, and General Anglis had gambled on the Menetorian marine mages being stronger than Imeria's. They had sent almost all of the Albion mages to aid on the eastern battlefield. Queen Onya was leading the people of Rorik to safety if they were to lose. Princess Ivette was meant to be with her, but instead was watching from a safe place on the cape below.

Albion had won the day on the upper deck, and he could hear the fighting below them, raging toward the forward bridge. He commanded the men to round up the enemy wounded and in groups of four to break the hunkered down defenses of the enemy throughout the ship.

He would attack the bridge. He rallied the troops again and

rushed downward, breaking the retreating lines of the Imerians and catching them exposed as they tried to stop the Albion boarding parties from the other end of the ship. Surrounded on deck after deck, the Imerians began to realize that the Santisma was being captured.

Prince Eduard blew the door to the bridge and his men rushed forward into an onslaught of gunfire. Many fell. The bridge was heavily defended, but his men pushed forward, engaging in guns and swords, shattering the glass above. Prince Eduard followed in with the third wave of soldiers yelling battle cries as they heard their friends and brothers meet steel with steel.

There he was, Admiral Pierico Graneuva. He had turned to look at the battle, watching as the forward line of battleships and frigates, cutoff by the Albion move had turned left and run. He could see that the Akrin three-rams had done the same. Even as they had begun to catch the wind and regain their unity of movement, they had jetted upward and like one cloud turned south together. He could not blame them as at this point in the battle, their Orichalc supply could be running low.

It was impossible to see how many had crashed into the bay, or how many mages had fallen with them. The core of his air navy was still being rounded and up and captured. The banner flag of Imeria and of the Empire had already been pulled down from his ship.

Graneuva knew deep in his heart that if the remaining Imerian ships could regroup and press the engagement, the day might still be won. The capture of almost all of his battleships was the largest blow as after today, the superiority of the Albion air navy would be unquestionable. The navies in reserve in Imeria would not challenge Albion, after this boon, for years. He had been outsmarted.

When Graneuva turned back to see the prince, he lifted the pistol in his hand and fired. Click. The chamber was empty. He hadn't loaded it. The prince holstered his own gun.

"Surrender Admiral Graneuva, you've been defeated," the prince turned his hands open, saber in his right, displaying the battle around them as the Imerian men defending the bridge were being slaughtered by the Albion attackers.

Graneuva lifted his sword, glinting in the light, before his face and kissed the air, "Grant me a warrior's death Prince Eduard, or none at all."

The prince stepped forward. Graneuva raised his sword, readying to fence to the death. A strike, a parry. The two found where their feet could stand on the thin strip in the middle of the bridge between crashed glass.

Graneuva dove forward with a strike, noticing as they clashed that the strain had forced the prince's shoulder wound to ooze blood that now soaked through his jacket.

The prince parried and swung in at Graneuva's hand, catching a bit more than just sleeve. They re-engaged; a saber cut at the side met with a dive backward. A strike at the neck, followed by inward parry, which was crossed away by the turn of a wrist. The duo tried tentative strikes again.

The prince began to push Graneuva back. His strength was amazing, even as a man. The prince had thought the wound in his shoulder would heal around the bullet, but the bullet was silver, and it left the wound open. He could feel himself weaken, but he had the advantage on Graneuva.

A bullet hit the prince in the back. Graneuva turned the prince's wrist over, and before he realized what had given him the advantage ran him through. The prince slumped forward into Graneuva's arms, shocked that his regeneration was not working, worried that Ivette who may have healed him too would never forgive herself for not being by his side just as she had been all these years.

She could have healed him too, or maybe not. He could feel the pain as his body began to fail. In the end, it was simply silver had brought him down.

A short man, stood on the deck, and yelled at Graneuva in rage as if to stand down or die. Yet, it was he, Graneuva could see the pistol in the short man's hand, who still held the smoking gun.

The Imerian Admiral kneeled and ordered what remained of his men to stand down.

1524 - Chapter 63

It had been a warm day, the day following the battle of Pláedino, almost fifty on the Odin scale and likely somewhat warmer in nearby Albion, where Erold had heard that a great battle of the sky, with almost two thousand airships, was actively raging, darkening the air above an entire city with black clouds of gunpowder and the shadows of steel ships.

For most of the previous night and morning, Erold had let the medicine mage heal his wounds, also made by mages, listening to the old man tell him that if he had been ten years older or hit by this much shrapnel or that many bullets instead of energy, he'd be dead. No matter how much he healed, his body would forever be decorated by the scars.

Valessa had spent the night with him, watching while the doctor tended to his wounds carefully. It was strange, because he wasn't dying, but they worried still at even the slightest change in him. Perhaps, it might be the amount of blood he might lose or had lost, but he relished being doted on by her and the soft, cold touch of her fingers.

When he was awake sometimes, he saw Moon appear at the tent and look in. Her face, as always, a mask of emotion, but he knew there was something troubling her. He wondered if she was disappointed that he had used the orb, which he had returned to the small blue velvet bag and held against his skin, checking for it each time he grasped consciousness.

In the evening, they finally let him stand. He acted as if there was no pain because it was welcome. He longed to feel it, the proof that he was still alive. Valessa helped him put on his yellow coat of Normany, and she walked with him.

Everything hurt. His stomach, his abdomen. His shins and thighs. His eyes. His neck, his arms. There was no part of him that didn't feel some ache even if minor, and more than anything his mind hurt, as if he had pulled too much out of it.

The back of it, not the front. Not a normal headache. The inside of his skull rang, but even before he had met with Moon, for that's where he was going, he had heard reports confirming that the Akrin army was fleeing Normany.

The battle of the sky would ironically determine sea superiority, but it would hopefully not factor into whether Erold could officially establish Normany as once again, its own nation, indivisible.

Erold walked upright as the yellow coated men raised their fists wherever he went, and even some of the red coats. They sang to him, and it felt as if he was in a fever dream like those first days, he had re-entered Normany.

Wherever he went, the somber mood lifted when he walked past, stiffly upright and masking his limp. The work of the day, cleaning up after the battle of the night, continued on. They would bury the dead while they still could, commemorating the field as a grand memorial graveyard.

Erold was glad for the hills around the camp, which hid the death that littered the fields across the Semroeka. He didn't want to see the field again as it was if he didn't have to. He had walked among the dead as they were.

Valessa's hand pressed lightly against his back, and he longed for the world to stay like it was at this moment. He entered the tent, where Moon had requisitioned more permanent seating and a table with a map, one of her and Valessa's favorite things. On top of this table was a strange, red sword.

"It's Kalsvebir. It's your family's ceremonial sword, and the symbol of war being ignited in Akre. It was captured in the counterattack against the Akrin camp after the battle. I wish it confirmed the end of things, but the Emperor Polesar and many of his men escaped, forgetting this in the rush."

Erold had no idea what he would do with it, but he glared at it, a touch angrily as it appeared to catch the flames of the sun and oil lamps in the tent and glow like it held the very embers of an infinite fire.

"How many men escaped?"

"Do you expect me to have that information already?" asked Moon, cheekily.

"It's not just that we're the ones that are here now. I want to know if the war is over," said Erold.

"They have already begun an unconditional retreat, likely to beat the coming winter and return to Akre before Vetfal," said Moon.

"That's not what I mean. If they regroup, can they attack us again?" Erold asked, touching Valessa's hand as it lay on his arm, remembering her race to conscript soldiers in Valgaard, and knowing that he would still need to do the same in Normany even as the ice began to form on the lakes.

"In that respect there is good news," said Moon.

"If Kutzbek has taught me one thing, it's that the loss of life is not good news. We may have prevented a greater catastrophe for now, but there may still be more storms to come."

Moon wondered if Erold was speaking of his using the orb or of potential future war. She wasn't sure, but she also couldn't read him through the mix of signals that his face gave. To her, he was in obvious pain.

"Do you want the figures, or to be philosophical?" asked Moon, glancing at Valessa.

"The figures if you have them."

Moon sighed, "At this battle alone, they lost one hundred sixty-five thousand one hundred twenty-nine men, wounded or killed, and almost seven hundred mages, bringing their total troop strength to an estimated one hundred eighty-four thousand and eight hundred seventy-one. For the first time in the short history of the Northern Alliance, the combined forces of the Northern armies outnumber the empire's. At the battle of Pláedino, we have achieved an outright victory of significant magnitude. The Akrin troop were driven back and apparently, leaderless, did not engage in peace talks."

"Apparently, leaderless?"

"It is unclear when Emperor Polesar retreated, but it appears he was rushed away by horse ahead of his men."

"Who led the defense of the fortifications?"

"It has been confirmed that the defense of the camp was initiated by the rearguard and was led by one of their lead mages and most successful generals over the recent years, Murdot. He was the one who defeated Braddach at the bridge and wounded him gravely."

"I know him," Erold thought, wondering if Moon knew he had taken Murdot's life.

"Hopefully Braddach's condition will improve," said Valessa, attempting to console Erold.

Erold nodded, knowing that his brother was likely to die any day. The shards of shrapnel were like poison that even one of the most talented healing mages in the world couldn't fix.

"Is there any additional information on the emperor?" asked Erold, "other than the sword." He nodded at the glistening, red object on the table.

"Nothing other than what I've told you. Do you want to know our total losses?" asked Moon.

Erold suddenly felt woozy and tired. Just thinking of the amount of lives that may have been spent in defense of a nation not yet born, with no governing documents or prospective mission other than being for its people and to their benefit rather than for its cities.

"Might as well, hear it out loud now. You say victory but it doesn't feel like victory with the bodies stacked as high as the buildings are tall."

"Allied losses were much less than Akrin's," said Moon.

"Each body is a person with a life and dreams," Erold said, wondering how many good Frostians had died who had never been kissed or held the woman of their dreams. There were certainly a few who were looking for men among them too, for which the reality was likely the same, where few people were willing to live their lives in front of everyone else.

"As you say," said Moon, thinking, as the inspector she always would be, of how many people had gone missing in Akre over the years and no one cared--and those who cared seldom did anything about it. If the number was duplicated in cities across the empire, the dead on the battlefield could be small in comparison. "We lost ninety-four thousand one hundred and forty-six men, across all of the allies. You would have to ask for the mage losses from Cherene."

Erold realized that Moon probably knew that it was Valessa from the start as well.

"It's amazing that you have so much information about everything that has occurred on the field," said Erold, wondering where her limits lay. Did she know what damage he had wrought on his own?

"We have a process in place to spot and check to make sure men report back to their commanders. There may be some changes for men who report late, or for enemies that show up, hiding in our own towns. However, it shouldn't be major changes. It may hopefully be some peace to you to know that we also have a larger army than the one that escaped at one hundred eighty-seven thousand three hundred and fifty-four."

Erold nodded, "Yes, you mentioned the Northern Alliance is now a larger combined force as well. I would imagine that this is the first time, since the days of Domiscus that Akre has not controlled the largest combined army in the world. Though it would take a scholar of the archives to know for sure."

"I would agree with that statement," said Moon, cryptically, as if she had been there or knew someone who had.

"Now we just need to hope that Albion and Menetoris can or have succeeded in the sky battle," Erold said and then he looked, cautiously, at the ceremonial sword on the table. "What we don't know yet is what that means. We can't know how the senate will react." He didn't verbalize it, because he understood that Moon did not want to speak on matters of clandestine business in front of Valessa; he worried what the red mark might do and whoever Theodore thought wanted the orb, if they were the same group and to what end.

"It likely depends on how many we outnumber them by," said Valessa, "but I would expect them to attempt to alter that number in their favor."

Moon didn't want to worry Erold about any future possibility of attack--no matter how distant--but if she counted the active armies of the shipping companies vying for control of trade across the oceans of the world, it was likely by one thousand or less in favor of the Northern Alliance. The two forces were so nearly identical that conflict felt inevitable.

"Mrs. Moon, any comment?" asked Valessa.

"No, I was just thinking."

"About?"

"I had wanted to ask for your permission to retire, sir. I had been thinking about it on the ship back to Peth, but I think that has officially changed now after recent developments," she referred as subtly as possible in front of Valessa to Erold's use of the orb.

"Permission? You never needed my permission if that is what you want to do," said Erold.

"Regardless, I believe it's off the table for now. I would like to stay at your side while I'm still capable," said Moon, forcefully, giving him no choice.

"I think we've established you're more than capable," said Valessa, "But, what about your daughter?"

"She'll understand, but I'll stay close."

"You could spend the Day of Thanks in the Ash Vale with her tomorrow," said Erold. "You'd be able to make it there by the evening tomorrow if you leave soon." It may not have been traditionally a celebration of the nations in the far west, but Moon had always celebrated it with him, and she had grown up in the 'east' in Newkassel.

"She's not at Redbridge, but I will, though I'd like to be here to communicate the results of the sky battle, whether it was won or lost, in Albion. I won't leave until we receive the communication either soon or later tonight."

"Mrs. Moon, a telegram from Mr. Everett." The adjutant handed her the sealed letter.

"Speak of a dragon by name," smiled Valessa, thinking of her father's love of that particular idiom. She longed to see him again soon.

Moon read through the battle report, "I won't waste your time with the details of the engagement over Cape Salgar. It appears it was a solid victory, though like here, the enemy retreated in time to maintain a strong enough threat to the coast, and the destruction of the coastal defense array may take years to repair."

"Control of the green seas remains in the hands of Imeria and Akre," bemused Erold. Moon nodded. Her lips turned down grimly despite the victory.

Valessa spoke after a moment of solace, "Why don't you head to the Ash Vale now then, Mrs. Moon? I can help to handle the rest of the administration and clean up with Arla."

Moon looked at Erold still with some hesitancy towards the archmage, especially with respect to the orb. She just hoped Erold knew what he was doing. There was a sudden pang in Erold's head as an old memory surfaced. He shuddered. Valessa held him tightly by his left arm. If Moon had been in the room with the elf elder, Louie, in Anpol, she might not have trusted him at all.

Erold forced a smile, looking up at her and her quiet strength, he regained his composure, "You're dismissed, Elara. Go get some rest. As my friend, mentor, protector, guide, and lately supreme intelligence officer, it seems you've never taken a day off. You have always been the closest thing to a mom I have ever had, and I know that Elenia needs that too. Since I was fifteen, we've been fighting together side by side every day. You've saved my neck well more than once, and I know no one more deserving of a break."

"I have heard the Ash Vale is lovely this time of year," said Valessa.

"Yes, it is," said Moon, glancing at Erold. She had spent many years there before and after he was born. "I've spent a few winters there by chance."

Erold thought for a moment, "Speaking of, were you ever going to tell me the rest of the story of your younger years, as an inspector, in Akre?"

Moon shot him a sideways glance, attempting to both indicate that it wasn't the time and that it was a topic that should not have been broached with the archmage there, "Another chapter, and perhaps soon I shall." She smiled at him.

"I'd love to know what Akre used to be like," said Valessa, "Have you ever been Erold?"

He shook his head, "No, and I'm not certain I'll ever want to go."

Valessa's mind wandered, "If only you could. The largest city in the world. Museums, theater, music. I've heard that they can get the best of everything."

"You forget that they also have murder, theft, arson. Just like anywhere else in the world," said Moon.

"You're not as dark as you pretend to be," said Valessa. The mystery of Moon intrigued her, likely more than it intrigued King Erold.

"Suffice to say, the past has already been written, and the story is too long when I must be leaving for Albion," Moon began to collect her things.

Erold hugged her as she passed by him on her way to her own tent and said, "I have a feeling that you'll have time to tell me many of these stories in the coming days."

"I have a feeling a few new stories await," she smiled, "Now, you have some other business to attend to tonight as do I." She glanced at Valessa and whispered, "Be careful and know that Fros walks with you."

"And with you too," said Erold as he followed her eyes to the waiting Valessa.

* * *

Moon borrowed Seaspirit and rode off into the setting sun without looking back. The next day as the sun rose on the day of Thanks, Erold found that Valessa had gone from his side. He was alone but for the guards Moon had personally assigned. He stood, finally feeling as if he had recovered enough to walk on his own and left the small tent.

An increasingly large guard followed him wherever he went, but the camp was quiet. The men were either sleeping or had been granted leave to return to the hills of Normendin, north Normany, and spend the Day of Thanks with family. There were likely many thousands left in the camp, but it felt eerily quiet as he, alone but for men sworn to protect him, would take in the cold day without Moon.

Mindlessly, he walked through the tents, unsure of where to go and yet also knowing. There was one family member left. His injuries were mortal, and Erold was unsure how much longer he would survive if he had even survived these two days, but if he could spend Braddach, his adopted brother's, last Day of Thanks at his side, he would.

He found the tent where Braddach lay, abandoned by all but one guard. He had done much for his adopted nation to be born again, but in the wake of such a terrible loss of life, the men of Normany were still reconciling with it themselves. The grim stench of death hung in the air, only muted by the hills. More than a hundred thousand had been buried the day before. Each man was tasked to bury one man on the fields where they lay before the tundra took hold and hardened ground to rock. The day after today, it would be one more.

Erold saw the broken form of Braddach lying in black, clinging to life, and kneeled immediately beside him. When he had once been overcome by anger, he now became filled with regret. Over two hundred fifty thousand men like him had lain strewn about the field, slain not for glory or the divine, but for freedom. And, each more than likely had a mother and a father to cry for them, to weep for them. Not Braddach. Braddach and he, Erold, had only truly had each other and Moon.

The guards in the tent watched on. Some recognized Braddach from the legends of the rear guard. Others knew him to be the brother of the king and whispered as much. They took their helmets off and stood in silent prayer. They did not imagine the many lines of thought that traced through the mind of the king, whose blonde hair draped to the shoulders of his yellow coat, hid his face.

Erold kneeled in private conversation with God, not hearing the answer, but asking him, why, quietly beseeching. He almost nodded to the Lord above that it was good that the ice princess, Valessa, would leave him now. For it was better she left alive than like Braddach did now.

Erold held the man's hand and looked at his eyes, still moving in their ungraceful slumber. There was an old, new nation to run, and despite the pain of his own injuries, though fainter now than the day before, he would have to grow stronger. Like Valessa always did what was right for Valgaard, whether in peace or war, at the expense of all around her, including love, he would have to begin to think on behalf of his people.

He loved her. He knew that. And for his nation reborn, her Valgaard was a necessary alliance, but many of his people had died for her peace as well as their own freedom.

Erold clasped Braddach's hands into his own and let the tears that had nearly overcome him subside. He held strong, unwilling to let the softness tug into him as a few stray tears ran down the sides of his cheeks.

* * *

Valessa and Arla walked between the tents on their way to what she hoped was the final war meeting before they moved to a nearby city for the army to winter.

"And we are going back to Valgaard in the spring?" asked Arla, confirming for what must have been the tenth time.

"Yes," said Valessa.

"You are certain?"

"Yes, why do you keep asking?"

"No reason," said Arla, but she wasn't sure she believed that Valessa would leave Erold behind in the end.

"The nation comes first, and I miss the palace. I miss my father," said the princess, but Arla could only think how it remained to be seen. There were many months to be spent, wintering south of the Evorul for once, and she would have to leave the side of the king of Normany.

Her thoughts of him were replaced by the sight as the pair entered the tent where the generals of the north stood or sat around the map that Moon had weighted down with rocks and stone pestle.

Erold looked up. Kutzbek's eyes remained closed as if he were sleeping. Milton nodded and bowed. Blaggard stood, bleary eyed and haggard, having taken up a forceful role in organizing the burial and distribution of soldiers on each side beneath white graves as far as the eye could see, north of the river.

"It's time to begin to plan and coordinate the spring movements," Blaggard said.

"Skipping the winter?" asked Pasan, uncomically.

"Yes. We'll have to winter in the towns surrounding us as we speak," Blaggard replied. He stood a bit taller and looked around at the remaining generals. Valessa watched as his eyes went from Pasan to Plaski, then to Gavo, then Eichlen, Milton, Kutzbek, and finally her, avoiding the inquisitive look of Erold. "The only true agenda item is do we keep a cursory force in Normany following the winter, or do we return to Valgaard?"

"We return to Valgaard," she said.

"Cavalry and mages?" asked Plaski.

"Yes," she replied. "We will move as soon as the ice thaws through Pili's Pass to Valgaard."

"Is that wise?" mused Eichlen.

"We are needed more there now than here," she said, adamantly, and Arla still wondered if it was true that she would indeed leave Erold behind.

"Is that true?" Blaggard finally turned to Erold, who nodded, and then went from staring at him to look at the map to which he pointed at various points.

"There are many points from which we will be able to prepare fortified positions in the coming years. As for mages, it will be my task to run our country's recruitment now, and I will see to that quickly. I thank you all for having served with us men of Normany. We will not forget your acts of valor."

"I'm not leaving," said Blaggard, standing straighter. "If you will have me."

"Nor will I," said Pasan.

There was some discussion. None of the men of Valgaard would stay.

"As will I," Kutzbek said finally after having remained quiet, "but I ask that you allow me to retire, my king, in the land of my fathers."

"You have earned it," Erold granted, placing a hand on the shoulder of the wise old man, who again closed his eyes as if it pained him to see before him even the map of the nation where war had raged.

"And what of the artillery?" asked Milton finally.

Valessa turned it over in her head. It would be fitting to organize it among the cavalry as it had been during much of the final campaign of the war, even just a few pieces, but it had been bought and paid for by Erold's mercenary years in Cardane, which felt so long ago.

"All that isn't Albion's will be used to fortify our positions," said Erold. "If it was purchased by Normany, it will stay in Normany."

* * *

After the meeting, Valessa cheekily ordered Erold to follow her, where they found a secret place, still guarded by Arla, where they could meet as one, tenderly. She kissed him passionately, and he returned each kiss, but his heart could feel a physical, painful tug as his mind flashed with the thought that she would leave on any given day.

She was tender, more tender than ever. It was as if the secrecy and knowing she would leave had changed her. She told him sweet things, but she also spoke bluntly. The words rang into his head, each time the thought returned, a headache followed.

"I cannot marry you Erold," she said, even as they made madly passionate love. "I must return to Valgaard."

She did not tell him that she could lose her hereditary first right to lead Valgaard if she stayed and married him. She was her father's only direct heir, but not the only royal with ties to the throne of Valgaard.

She did not need to explain. He never asked, but he could not understand her actions whether she was to leave or stay. She begged him for his seed but told him she would leave. The moral crisis in his mind of following the celibacy of Frost had long since gone, but each romantic liaison in the coming months of winter would make him wonder if he had made a mistake.

While she remained in Normany, they were together as one as each night, they grew closer in each other's arms but farther apart as the day she would finally leave, neared. Each night she begged for him to give her what she needed until one day she no longer begged, only smiled as if she had all she required of him.

1525 - Chapter 64

When they returned to the field in spring, the grass was green, and the river was high. The hills were peaked with snow and the mountains were gray in the far distance. A cold wind was in the morning air.

Hundreds of thousands of men crowded among the fallen to pay respects to the gravestone of Braddach. At the same time, they would pay their respects here for the fallen of Salgar, including Prince Eduard, whose body had been buried on the bluffs in the aftermath of the fight. He left behind the loving wife and princess of Menetoris, Ivette, who wore a dark veil and black garments along with their son, Ilrich, who followed her closely, sucking on his thumb. They were flanked by a massive Menetorian guardsman, named Fastian.

Grown men cried as they kneeled and flung themselves against the rectangular tomb of Braddach. The once unspoken hero of the war had become the symbol of Normen resilience. He may not have been blonde or blue eyed like so many of the men of the north, but his line had been just as pure if not more so. In death, he was even more a king among men than Erold, who while perhaps more powerful had not put his life on the line in so many key moments on behalf of them all. Each soldier could say they owed their life to Braddach, and perhaps their freedom to Erold if he remained a good king.

The celebrations of the first days of spring had already passed, and Erold had felt Valessa grow cold. The Festival Week of New Life had already happened, earlier in Áevonstar, to signal the coming end of winter. The golden days, celebration of Iodawn around the Vernal Equinox, had begun the six months of long sun, and the flowers had followed. Even men had picked the white dove flowers and curled them into laurel wreath rings to place on the many unmarked graves of the fallen.

The celebration of Fros and the Otum's Fall would be the day after tomorrow on the twenty fifth of Áevonstar. It felt only fitting to now commemorate the fallen, and their surrender to the Lord as the days turned longer and all the signs and symbols of renewal returned with the sun shining bright on the land of the northern tribes. Perhaps, their spirits would pass by the old lands of Asgard, Valhalla, Valheim, Starholm, Sovngrad, or the many others, now buried beneath the ice for an age, before transcending above.

Erold clutched the orb in his fist beneath his jacket. If he had used it sooner, more of these men might have been alive, and yet, how many future lives had he doomed by using it, at all? That moment of brilliance did not go unnoticed. His men feared him more than they loved him, for now. At the same time, using it to the fullest as he did, he had been spent. If he had used it a moment sooner, he may have died in their place, relinquishing the orb to the emperor while revealing its power.

His other hand clutched the hilt of Kalsvebir, the red blade, which hung at his side, gleaming in the light. Annually, the act of returning it to the stone in Akre had been the ultimate celebration of the Akrin peace for nearly a century, whereas before that pulling it from the stone in spring had symbolized an annual launch to war. Neither could take place on the day of Fros as here it would remain, in the hands of its ancestral wielder, perhaps no longer the last of the line of Arandil.

Erold had grown increasingly suspicious, but when he looked over at Valessa, who had spent most of the day speaking to the twins from Menetoris, Jasen and Muriel, there were signs. Even if she would not tell him, he believed she was pregnant with his child.

He knew now that they had recently slept together for the last time, but it still felt strange to look at her and not feel the visceral power of lust or love that he had once felt.

Erold looked from where he stood, behind a small stage and podium, out across the field of the dead. He was shaken by how far it stretched over the rolling hills where the fate of Normany and the Alliance had been decided.

His father, his brother, the many of the line of Arandil, like any, could have been one of those white stones with the dove flower rings. Even though his father wasn't there, Erolin's legacy would live on.

Erolin Ardrada had been a good king, even if he was defeated by the nuanced politics of his own ancestors' creation. He was a lot like Valessa. He was a master administrator, and his visions for Normany would not be forgotten. The work that he had begun to build the most efficient, modern, and economically powerful, independent nation that the world had ever seen would be continued by his son, Erold Ardrada, no longer the last of the line of Arandil.

Was he worthy to claim that name?

His father hadn't used the orb. His father had given it to him and protected him and charged him with protecting it. What if his father had used it? It's doubtful that he could have stopped the dragons or saved the ship if he even knew what he held. He had all the power in the world but no way to use it.

Perchance that was the way it should be? Erold had failed Fros, hadn't he? When he used the orb, was it for good? Or was he evil? Had he in fact doomed the world as the old elven seer had said many years ago. He was no chosen one and the words were stuck in his mind. How many millions would die, because of his choice of vengeance?

The field was proof that evil was still alive. He was no chosen one. He was an accidental handler of an object of pure power, who had merged with Brazgul. Was it true that power corrupted? He had failed his mission to keep it hidden, but could he yet keep it safe from the hands of evil?

The knowledge of this power could not be and for centuries had not been undone. Someone had been looking for it. There were those with a malicious intent to what end he did not yet know. And they too, a faceless enemy, he had connected with the red mark and confirmed with Moon, were unknown, lurking perhaps even here, locked in a shadow war with who?

The Taivaan Vartijat? Was that the order to which Moon belonged, and how many fought alongside her?

His choice to use the orb had ended only one war. Not them all. The war could have destroyed more of his nation, and he had protected the lives of his people, but what now? How many would pay the price for his vengeance? The future wars could destroy them all. A voice inside told him that Fros would never forsake him. He saw the good in all, even the unworthy that Fros knew to be corrupted.

Erold looked up at the faces of his friends, allies, soldiers, and brothers in blood and action, waiting for his speech. The world moved. The people shifted. Not just the wars of the past had brought about this future. Empty hills had been found and settled in days long gone. Forgotten valleys. Patient rivers. Untamed game fought in a death throw many ancient battles, still ongoing, between man and beast.

Beneath the eyes of Otum, Fros had once walked unseen by all but God who through him shared a lesson. A lesson of light that small things, miniature acts of good are what matter in the fight against ultimate evil.

That had been in a time when evil could be seen and named. It was different now. Even then, the only men who fought for the Otum owed debts or were slaves, eunuch armies of faceless, unnamed orphan soldiers. They had come out of the mountains of Elessia and had been destroyed there.

What could men do when the evil didn't just surround them? It was them. When they thought that they fought for good, but they only brought further evil upon the world like he worried he may have done? Did the small things matter that much more? What truly mattered at all?

Erold could only look to his ancestors, to the blood of his father and his father's father and so on. The mentality of the Normen tribes, who had merged into the faith of Fros. They were not all impartial defenders, but that was the spirit of his tribe, the Varanor, of Starholm and Valheim. That had always been their legacy.

It was defense of the family, not defense of the land that mattered. For they, all three tribes, had been driven from the old lands by the ice in Ragnarök. They had nowhere to go but people to go with, and wherever they had come, throughout the world, they had lived in the most barren, unloved lands and made them strong. They would defend these places when they must and retreat to new lives when they could not. That was the way of the men of Fros that had defeated the old evil. Defense of the hearth was the phrase. Not vengeance.

The old heart of the place was buried beneath the ice. The new heart, the people, surrounded him. And the new faces needed defending from the aggressors of the world, no matter the story of reclamation or vengeance that they had. From the enemies that hated him, now that he knew and those that he didn't yet know, who courted only power above all else, Erold would protect them, his people, from those enemies with swift justice.

Erold rose up the stairs to the small wooden stage slowly, readying mentally to speak in front of the leaders of the Northern Alliance, the generals who fought for him, his friends, and many of his soldiers. The black axe was strapped to his back, multiple pistols rested on his hip. Would there ever be a day when the men of the world could leave such weapons at home?

Members of the major papers from Rorik were in attendance with the modern fountain pen, only having begun manufacture in 1517, held above expertly bound identical notebooks. Each pen was a bit unique as if each scribe had gone to competing, local suppliers. There were correspondents from the press corps all around Normany too, though from where, he wasn't sure.

There were even men in the rear, preparing what he was told was called a photograph, only invented, modernized, and assembled for mass production on the exchange of capital in 1515. While he had been running for his life, someone, somewhere had lived a life dedicated to financial gain by invention.

Mentally, he returned to the moment. They were, on the other hand, dedicating an entire field to each buried body, from both sides of the most devastating war in the history of man, who gave their lives for more men of the future to have that freedom to pursue the pen or the photograph.

The wind picked up, pulling his long blonde hair across his face and twisting it in the air from the mountain. Some might say far away a dragon had flapped its wings. Not unlike the Taivaan Vartijat of old, whose old alabaster fortress of Ämelin stood partially ruined not so far away, these men, alive and no longer, helped to pacify a war machine like the sky watch had done with dragons of old. It would take constant vigilance, just the same, as that of the skyguard, to protect the new peace.

There were the leaders of Albion, King Jack Stone, his young wife, Onya, and their daughter, Dawn. There were the twins from Menetoris, Jasen and Muriel. Their sister, Ivette, sat upright and stony face hidden by black veil beside her son, Ilrich. Valessa sat near to them, with Arla beside her, no longer hiding who she was, and behind her were the surviving generals of the war, Kutzbek, Blaggard, Eichlen, Milton, Pasan, Plaski, and Gavo. Of course, there were also the leaders of Albion's navy and armed forces, Ferrara and Anglis. There, too, were Theodore and Anifiel as well as their daughter Charlotte and her son, Victor. Moon sat beside them with her daughter Elenia, cuddling against her.

"Four hundred and seventy years ago, our fathers, men of the north, joined, on this continent, in eternal union the history of New Galdir to hasten the fall of Domiscus, who conquered all other nations. This new and old nation, born yet again today, conceived in the pursuit of equal voice and dedicated to the right to be left to one's own life, unbothered by the rule of foreign or domestic law.'

'Now, we have been engaged in the greatest war of mankind's history, testing whether this nation, or any nation so conceived can halt the spread of those who champion violence. We meet now on the greatest battlefield of that war, celebrating peace and mourning loss. We were born as one nation meant for peace and so we held it for a time. Today, we are born again as that nation, may we heed its calling.'

'We have come to dedicate the whole of this field as resting place for those who gave their lives, whichever flag they fought for. It is altogether fitting and proper that we do this. It matters not whether they were our friends or enemies yesterday, judgment of their lives is left to the divine. It is not our right or place.'

'It is not for us to judge the outcomes of that fateful battle on this field, a day of judgment. It is far above our power to consecrate or hallow this ground. The world will little note, nor long remember, these words, or heed this warning, of what happened here. It perhaps will never care so much as I do now, speaking these words, for the lives lost for freedom's sake. That it may continue.'

'It is for us the living to carry forth the dream unfinished for which they who fought here dedicated their lives and so meaningfully progressed. The cause of Liberty. We do not honor the dead by continuing or beginning wars, but by ending them. We, the many, the voices, each a king's, all heard, all told, who stand together as one nation, indivisible under God, have been given a rebirth, a second chance, to extend our brotherhood of peace that this nation of its people and for its people shall keep the faith of the frost."

"The heroes of the First Alliance War, who others will speak about and many loved and knew, like General Patr Braddach, an excellent leader, and Prince Eduard Stone, a brave one, were good men above all else. Braddach was my brother and my friend. He taught me so much and was at my side from the moment we left Peth ten years ago until now. Every victory on the field can be traced back to him and not to me. No matter how much damage done to him, he did not surrender in the rear guard or the reserve fleches. He owes us nothing. We owe him, and all who stand with him in Heaven, everything."

Erold's speech was so quick that the photographer was not able to capture his visage on the podium, a place no one had expected him to be so concise. Others came and went speaking on the loss of those whose memories were commemorated, and after they were done, Erold stood to shake the hand of every man and woman of the allies that had come and stood to wait for their moment with the king.

As he stood there, shaking yet another hand and yet another hand, and returned many a fist thrown into the air, he looked at Valessa, and saw her still absorbed with the Menetorian twins, who were speaking as well to King Stone. Erold looked down, pondering how to not show what he felt, when he saw just the outline of a leg and a scent in the air. One he had not known for many a day but seemed intimately familiar.

"King Erold, sir, remember me?"

Erold looked up to see a ravishing beauty. Her long, strawberry blonde, red hair and dark blue eyes, seemed different and yet the same. He knew her and yet didn't remember from where at the same time.

"Ti-Enna Dashaine of Leidyn."

The Solgra flashed into his mind. The sea of yellow grass and rolling hills.

"I remember. I searched everywhere for you in the days after the Spirit Day ball."

"Well not everywhere, because you didn't find me. I found you."

"The battle," Erold said, forlornly, thinking of his uncle and Elksits.

"I enjoyed your speech," Ti-Enna said, breaking him from his momentary reverie.

"What have you been doing all these years?"

"After the events of Elksits, I went to study magic in Albion, luckily while it was still easy enough to get to."

"You're a mage now?"

"Fire," she said, "Can't you tell." She laughed as she tossed her hair into the light wind. What had once been the color of the Solgra did appear to have been touched by the color of fire. The roots were still blonde, but the tips were even more red than orange.

"You look different," he said, "and yet, the same." Her blue eyes too, had changed, and they stared back at him. Her pupils swelling as they stared into one another's souls.

Valessa looked over and saw Erold and Ti-Enna's chance meeting. She was speaking about visiting with King Mitas again in the coming summer months when airships could freely move about Valgaard. He didn't like to leave the islands, but she was doing her best, as always, to communicate that on behalf of Valgaard, she would go to him.

When she saw Erold talking with this younger woman, she froze, momentarily struck by how painful it was to see him smiling in that way with another woman. It was such a brief moment that neither of the twins noticed, and Stone had looked away. In a fraction of a second, she regained her composure, and her charming smile returned.

* * *

Captain Graneuva had watched the ceremony and was shaking. He had watched the first ceremony for Braddach, but it was not that had caused him to quake with fear. He looked down at his hand, to peak between the clenched fingers of his fist and see it again: the black spot.

It was not a simple blot like a bit of ink stained onto his hand by a feather quill. It was the magical mark of death that filled his palm like a growing abyss. It was a legendary marked curse of death and one of the oldest curses known to man. No matter what sorcery he tried, he knew it would not leave. As a sailor, he had heard the stories of its plague. He did not know from where they originated, but he knew he didn't have long now.

He didn't care much for the speech, but it was passable. He paid his respects to the tomb of Patr Braddach with a simple nod, while grown men flung themselves against it in tears. He had questioned why he had lived in the aftermath of the battle to walk the rest of his days in shame when he was to be eventually returned to Imeria on the promise of the King of Albion himself, but now that he was so marked, he only worried whether he could see his wife one last time.

He hastily fled the scene, shaking off Vintillo, who had been refusing to leave his side. He would get back to his place at the tavern in town under the watch of the guard and hope that he had at least one more day or could string a few together so he could see his short and thin, impish, elven wife one last time and embrace her.

He held his hand in a fist, checking over his shoulder, walking briskly. He saw no one but the guards standing along the walk and who followed him with their steadfast gaze. He nodded to the alert guards at the door to the tavern.

He climbed the stairs. He opened his room's door and breathed a sigh of relief. Vintillo would be along soon, but he needed a moment alone. All he wanted to do was go home, and to see his wife one last time.

Dist was sitting on the bed, sharpening his nails with his teeth. Graneuva recognized him immediately. His heart almost burst in fear, but not before the fangs of a vampire's death touch sunk into his neck.

Graneuva's body went limp in Dist's arms, and the vampire lay him down on the bed. He was going to cover up the marks on the man's neck when he heard someone in the hallway. In the next moment, he was doubling over.

His stomach revolted. It was too late. He had to hide what had happened.

He couldn't escape the room in time from the footsteps outside. He covered the wounds with a knife slice as the poison of elvish blood seeped through him.

Had he been more careful, a simple taste would have been enough to warn him of his own potential demise. How could he not have noticed that Graneuva was part elf, or have learned it, knowing of a danger of which countless wars had been waged, sending elves from country after country and if threats didn't work, by blight?

When Vintillo entered the room, he found a dead man lying against the wall, with his tongue swollen out of his mouth, who appeared to have been stabbed by a knife in the heart. Graneuva had collapsed on the bed, with his throat slit.

ABOUT THE BOOK

This action-packed epic fantasy follows Erold Ardrada, the exiled heir to the throne of an ice age world's largest empire as he forms a necessary alliance with the few nations that do not bow to the senate that commands the empire from the city of gold, Akre. After it seems the senate betrayed every other member of his family, the would-be king, Erold, could be the last hope to stop the senate's hunger for world domination.

While he attempts to resurrect a lost nation with the help of a former enemy threatened by the growing power of the empire's armies, the sinister ulterior motive of the hidden hands behind his family's betrayal has already been put into action across borders, and a secret, final gift of Erold's father puts him squarely in their sights as he unknowingly joins a centuries old conflict between good and evil.

Based off of the embellished magical histories of mostly forgotten earth kings, queens, and revolutionaries, relive the romanticized tales of the men and women who lead the ice age planet of Frost, a frozen mirror of earth, into the heart of the steam age. From each town, to each person, for each nation, all must decide what fates lie ahead as the battlefields of fantasy and frost will never be the same. For in this ice age world of fantasy where all myths are true and over ninety nations co-exist in false harmony, wars by light and shadow come for those who pursue peace, surrounded by the mythical creatures of land and sea, including dragons, demons, angels, elves, dwarves, werewolves, vampires, and more.

* * *

ABOUT THE AUTHOR

You can call me Aunt Claere. I'm your typical midwestern auntie who enjoys spending time with her family and has participated in her fair share of book clubs. I'm the voice of our trio. Over twenty years ago, my two friends C., C., and I decided to write a different kind of fantasy novel. One that regularly crosses oceans, isn't bound by them, while being full of towns and cities of all kinds; uses real physics, engineering, and technology, as much as possible; and keeps to the faith in God while transitioning fantasy mythos into a steampunk future with some of earth's most prominent, historical female leaders represented through their true actions as leaders. While we've worked on this novel and its preceding novels for almost twenty years as one combined story, I hope to share the rest of the abridged volumes of Frost's Steam Age before long.